Advance comments on "

"I must say you have had some incre[dible experiences looking?] at your story. Certainly nothing that eve[r?] comes anywhere close to this!"
Douglas Preston – Author of "Cities of Gold", "The Relic", and "Talking to the Ground."

"If it was any more authentic the reader would need a shot of penicillin when he finished the book."
Sergeant Bo Melin – French Foreign Legion, 2nd R.E.P.

"Khyber Knights accurately explains the Pukhtun culture, which few outsiders have been able to grasp. The story runs fast and tight, leaving the reader hungry for more. All in all it is a wonderful book!"
Dr. Amjad Hussain – Pakistani explorer and author of "Journey of a Native Son."

"After completing a 14,000 mile horse trip through the USA, I thought I'd seen it all when it came to equestrian travel. When I completed "Khyber Knights" I realized I hadn't scratched the surface."
Current long distance American riding champion, D. C. Vision.

"Asadullah Khan (CuChullaine O'Reilly) has revealed Pakistan's secrets, as well as her sorrows."
Professor G.M. Qureshi - Peshawar, Pakistan

"Your story was impossible to put down! It makes the things I've done on horseback look like kids' stuff."
American Equestrian Explorer Emeritus Marshal Ralph Hooker

"You are the only non-Pakistani I know who has got it right. I compliment you on your insight and intuition."
Khalid Hasan, Special Correspondent, Associated Press of Pakistan – Washington DC.

"You have written a masterpiece! This is the book that will top all other horse travel books."
Jeremy James – Author of "Saddletramp" and "Vagabond"

"If anybody asks, tell them I read this book straight through – TWICE!"
Dave Yamada – Adventurers Club of America

Khyber Knights

An account of perilous adventure and forbidden romance in the depths of mystic Asia

by

Asadullah Khan
a.k.a.
CuChullaine O'Reilly

All rights reserved. Copyright under Berne Copyright Convention, Universal Copyright Convention, and Pan-American Copyright Convention. No part of this book may be reproduced, stored in a retrieval system, or transmitted in any form, or by any means, electronic, mechanical, photocopying, recording, or otherwise, without the prior permission of the author, CuChullaine O'Reilly. This manuscript is registered with the Library of Congress # TXV917-424 and secured with the Writer's Guild of America under registration #132538.

ISBN: 1-59048-000-7

Maps and artwork by Dean Tolliver

Dedicated to Jake Dodds
the Chinese Bandit

There is no solace on earth for us – for such as we,
who search for the hidden beauties that eye may never see.
Only the road and the dawn, the sun, the wind, and the rain,
and the watch-fire under the stars, and sleep, and the road
again.

John Masefield

Author's Disclaimer

This is no cautionary tale of timid travels. No camera wielding water-boilers nor bleeding heart aid-wallahs inhabit these pages. If you are looking for a guide to the finer hotels of Pakistan go no further. Escape before the smells and sights and experiences of a totally foreign land assault your delicate senses.

I know what others have seen and written about Pakistan. But they write like they live, only on the surface of a complex and dangerous place which prides itself on hiding its secrets from the uninitiated.

This is instead a tale of travels that took me from palaces to prisons. I know Pakistan's heroes as intimately as her whores. Pakistan has molded me, at times almost destroyed me. It has shaped me into the man I am today and still holds the key to the secret parts of my heart.

Thus the following fictional account is based on a chronological sequence of actual events. Names have been changed in some cases to shield the innocent, as well as the guilty. Some incidental characters have been dropped for the sake of brevity and certain collateral events have been summarized. A few of the characters and incidents portrayed herein are composites based on people and places known to the author.

An in-depth explanation of highlighted words appears in the glossary.

Contents

Part One – The Jihad

Chapter 1 – City Under Siege 1
Chapter 2 – Kidnapped 11
Chapter 3 – Among the Pathans 23
Chapter 4 – Mode of Transportation – Horse 35
Chapter 5 – Something Wrong in Paradise 47
Chapter 6 – Ride or Die 57
Chapter 7 – Shavon's Fate 65

Part Two – The Prison

Chapter 8 – American Renegade 71
Chapter 9 – Flashman's Faded Glory 83
Chapter 10 – The Price of Torture 95
Chapter 11 – An Unexpected Accommodation 107
Chapter 12 – Little Man – Little Help 115
Chapter 13 – Pakistan's Bastille 121
Chapter 14 – Cell Nine – Block Four 137
Chapter 15 – Naeem 149
Chapter 16 – Even Sparrow's Milk 161
Chapter 17 – The Untouchables 169
Chapter 18 – When Smugglers Lament 181
Chapter 19 – A Flicker of Freedom 193
Chapter 20 – Raja's Secret 205
Chapter 21 – Stacked Deck 215
Chapter 22 – Truth Takes a Holiday 229
Chapter 23 – Judicial Murder 243
Chapter 24 – The Seed of Man 251

Part Three – The Journey

Chapter 25 – Kiss Me Deadly 261
Chapter 26 – Money, Guns and Horses 273
Chapter 27 – Sargohda's Secret 285
Chapter 28 – The Garden of Fire 295
Chapter 29 – Through Tribal Territory 305
Chapter 30 – Pukhtoon 317
Chapter 31 – Horseman's Horror 331

Chapter 32 – Dr. Ali Muhammad 341
Chapter 33 – Among the Centaurs 355
Chapter 34 – Religious Difficulties 367
Chapter 35 – Shakra the Killer 381
Chapter 36 – Gupis Pays in Blood 393
Chapter 37 – Where Horses Fear to Tread 407
Chapter 38 – Hunza Water 417
Chapter 39 – Pakistan's MacBeth 435
Chapter 40 – What Price Love? 447
Chapter 41 – Music of the Nomads 459
Chapter 42 – A Strong Dose of Sin 473
Chapter 43 – Pasha 487

Part Four – The Rescue

Chapter 44 – A Transitory Love 505
Chapter 45 – Uninvited Guest 517
Chapter 46 – Into the Lawless Land 527
Chapter 47 – A Friend Betrayed 543
Chapter 48 – Shaheen's Heart 557
Chapter 49 – The Death of Beau Fontaine 575
Chapter 50 – Maqbool's Revenge 587

Epilogue 601

Glossary 603

List of Illustrations

Facing page

Police Registration	2
Suffering Horse	40
Map of Pakistan	52
Shavon and Asadullah	62
Map of Peshawar	72
Ali Muhammad	78
Travel Documents	86
'Pindi Prison	122
Map of 'Pindi Prison	142
Babu	154
Baby Eater	184
Suliman	186
Godwin's Confession	196
Shaheen	268
Journey documents	280
Pakistani Weapons License	306
Pajaro and Raja	310
Map of Journey	320
Pasha and Asadullah	368
The Parri	414
Gilgit Documents	422
Maroof	454
The Burkha	534
Maqbool	552
Chopendoz	584

All illustrations and maps by Dean Tolliver

Part One
The Jihad

1

City Under Siege

When the bomb exploded the concussion punched me to the ground like a small child. My first thought was that **KHAD**, the Afghan communist secret police were trying to kill me again. I lay there on my back for several seconds as a tornado cloud of dust swirled up from the explosion and then rained down on me. I realized I was stunned and told myself that if in fact commie assassins were here to murder me, I had better manage to get up and make an effort to protect myself.

But my chest hurt as if my horse had kicked me hard across the ribs. My ears were ringing and my face, clothes and turban were covered in dirt caused when the tiny brick building fifty feet away had disintegrated into particles. Instead I lay there for a few seconds, too stunned to do anything except breathe. The first thing I managed to move was my tongue. It told me my mouth was full of filth from the road I was lying in and that my teeth were thankfully intact.

By the time it took me to rise up on one arm I knew instinctively that the bomb was another random act, meant to further frighten the already shaky inhabitants of Peshawar. No, I was moving too slowly to have gotten out of the way of danger, if it had been aimed specifically at me. When I managed to sit up I saw inert bodies lying on the road around me.

Already I could hear the screams of the wounded. The shrieks of pain told me the flying debris would claim a few more lives after the bombers escaped. People were starting to mill around in the dust filled street, running to bend over wounded victims or calling for help for the dying.

I sat up and blinking the dust out of my eyes saw the gaping hole where a few seconds ago a small restaurant had been serving lunch to now dead patrons. The thin two story brick building was sandwiched in between a tailor shop and a fish monger. Three brick walls had contained the blast, forcing it's terrific exit out the wooden front portion of the restaurant. The bearing walls were still intact. The roof and front wall had ceased to exist.

My first conscious thought was that they wouldn't find enough left of the diners to put in an envelope. I stood, wobbled slightly and shook my head gently. A policeman ran up to me, jabbering in Urdu, asking if I was hurt. When I shook my head "No" in reply, he rushed off, bending over a crumpled body close by. Sirens were starting to wail somewhere in the city in response to the emergency.

I slowly looked down at my body, feeling groggy but beginning to slip back into control. My ribs ached. Maybe something had hit me? There was no blood but already I could feel bruises swelling to the surface. I thought otherwise I was unhurt.

Khyber Knights

"Maybe that's a fire truck coming," I told myself. The neighborhood certainly needed one. A blaze had started in the rubble of the restaurant. Someone was screaming about a gas line. Shopkeepers were frantically shouting, waving their hands, searching for buckets and praying there was water in the city pipes today.

I hawked and spat a good deal of Pakistan out of my mouth. The fire was growing. More police were arriving. The crowd was swelling into a mob. Men were wailing now over dead relatives, cursing the Afghan terrorists that had laid their relatives low. Despair and anger were spreading like a communicable disease. Any concern I had about my physical condition was immediately shoved aside by a sharp new feeling of apprehension.

My Irish red hair was hidden from sight under my blue Afghan turban. My white skin and freckles were smothered under a liberal coating of brick dust. My baggy brown **shalwar-kameez** (pants-shirt) and knee high leather **buz khazi** boots shouted "**Kabuli**" (Afghan) to any one looking my way. To all outward appearances I was the only one in the crowd who even faintly resembled the perpetrators of this outrage.

I had seen enough blood mad Pakistani lynch mobs to know I was lingering in the wrong part of town. I would be lucky if I could explain I was an American Muslim, a journalist dressed in Afghan clothes. More likely these volatile citizens would ignore my entreaties and beat me into an unrecognizable pulp before throwing what was left of me into jail.

The age old Pakistani tradition of extending hospitality to strangers had been replaced by a new sense of self preservation when the bombing campaign started that year. A genocidal war in Afghanistan was barely twenty miles away, hidden behind the stony gates of the nearby Khyber Pass. The **mujahideen** (Muslim holy warriors) were caught in a five year battle there against not only the might of the Soviet army but its Afghan communist allies.

Initially the citizens of Peshawar had gladly welcomed the steady stream of Afghan freedom fighters and their families who came here looking for asylum after the Soviets invaded their country in December, 1979. There were stories of Peshawaris who had halved their homes in order to shelter these early refugees. Pakistan, one of the poorest countries in the world, had opened her borders and her heart to three million Afghan fugitives, as well as two million of their animals. Entire villages had crossed the border bringing with them goats, sheep, water buffalo, camels and horses.

A few months ago all that had changed.

Under Soviet direction, the Afghan communist secret police in Kabul dispatched saboteurs to disrupt Pakistani support for the refugees. The terror being spread by these unknown assassins had turned Peshawar into the new hunting ground of Southwest Asia.

The city's residents were now living with the suspense of being killed at any moment while going about the most mundane affairs of the day. We were a city under silent siege. Yesterday a truckload of explosives, aimed at killing a mujahideen leader as he drove by, was parked instead

Khyber Knights

"I would be lucky if I could explain I was an American Muslim, a journalist dressed in Afghan clothes. More likely these volatile citizens would ignore my entreaties and beat me into an unrecognizable pulp before throwing what was left of me into jail."

next to an elementary school. They were still pulling kids' body parts out of nearby fields. Scores of municipal buses and their unsuspecting passengers had recently gone up in smoke. Bombs were stuffed under seats in crowded cinemas, left in baskets in the busy vegetable bazaar, slipped into mosques and checked into hotels.

This was the second explosion so far today and it was still early. It was no wonder an ill-defined sense of civic paranoia had gripped Peshawar by the throat. Everyone's nerves were shot. Unlike incoming artillery, you couldn't even hear these mute messengers of death. One minute you were speaking to a friend over a cup of tea, the next moment you were both atomized.

Though they maintained a force of more than 125,000 men in Afghanistan, the Soviets only controlled a few key cities. More than 80% of the countryside was either lawless or in rebel hands.

This new Soviet strategy of attacking the exile's command post in Peshawar was working brilliantly.

Unable to pin down the resistance fighters in the mountains of Afghanistan, the Soviets directed KHAD to undermine the critical basis of civilian support in Pakistan instead. The various resistance groups openly maintained headquarters in Peshawar. No one gave this decision a moment's thought before the communist trained saboteurs started murdering Peshawar's citizens in revenge for their hospitality.

Everything was changing. Terror now overruled brotherhood.

Afghans, once seen as defenders of Islam, our mutual faith, proud warriors of the **Jihad** (holy war), were now viewed as trespassers, anarchists, suspects, interlopers, spies, the cause of grief and sorrow. No place in the city was safe now because of their foreign presence and the war they had unwittingly brought inside Peshawar's ancient walls. Tempers were raging and your life wasn't worth a **rupee** ((monetary unit) if you were found lingering around a bomb site dressed like an Afghan.

As the crowd swelled, I was shoved further back from what had once been the restaurant. Suddenly hostile Peshawari eyes were viewing me not as a potential victim but as a possible assassin. It was time to go.

What was there to stay for? The journalistic idealism and naive good intentions I had brought here many years ago had drowned in a sea of ugly reality. Peshawar was as bloody as Beirut, as full of spies as Berlin. The $400 million a year being poured into the resistance by the CIA had turned intrigue, propaganda and arms smuggling into cottage industries. Peshawar, once known as the Paris of the **Pathans** (tribesmen) was now reduced to eating her own young in response.

I started pushing my way through the crowd, avoiding eyes, ignoring curses, disregarding shoves, all the time making my way up the cobble stoned street and veering to the left as fast as my bruised body would allow. My thoughts were bitter as I fled towards my friend Ali Muhammad's house.

The restaurant had once existed in the wide **chowk** *(open space)* at the base of the old Cunningham clock tower. The bombers had deliberately picked this Y in the road because foot traffic and vehicles converged here from two different portions of the city. The road leading off uphill to the right was wide enough to allow **tongas** (horse carts) and **rickshaws** (tiny motor taxis) to pass through. It was now deadlocked, full of stoic horses standing in harness and sputtering rickshaws housing impatient passengers or greedy drivers. I chose the narrow lane leading off in the other direction. It was a bottleneck of curious men and boys, all adding their voices to the gurh burh (loud commotion).

The noise behind me was almost deafening. Police were pouring in, swinging **lathis** (clubs) and shouting at the crowd to stand aside. I didn't bother to look back. I kept sliding my lonely way between sweaty onlookers, twisted around a gap in the humanity and found myself in the relative tranquillity of a lane I knew well. Men were rushing my way. But each step took me and my telltale turban away from immediate danger and closer towards **Hasht Nagari**, the neighborhood I called home.

Peshawar was old before Christ was born. She had never been a stranger to violence. Her cramped age-encrusted streets had seen hordes of soldiers come and go over the ages. Until recently she had lain largely inviolate behind mighty walls and slept securely behind sixteen stout wooden gates that opened onto a violent countryside. The modern conveniences of electricity and telephones had made slow inroads into her bazaars. Alexander's armored Greeks, the bowlegged horsemen of Genghis Khan and the proud red-coated British had all washed her streets in the blood of innocents. Now those cruel conquerors were dust and she still remained, her fabled lanes a magnet for a new crop of warriors, the Afghan mujahideen and their new tale of trouble.

As I walked on I saw a ragged poster stuck to the leaning wall of an old brick building. I didn't have to read its tattered message or look at the faded photograph to know it was a hasty paper headstone pasted up in memory of a dead **mujahid** (freedom fighter).

In the first trusting years of the Jihad things had been different here. The streets were once awash with Afghans intent on re-conquering their country from those uninvited northern neighbors. If you showed the slightest interest in their activities, these sincere souls would pull out painfully hand-drawn maps showing secret mujahideen routes in and out of Afghanistan. Though often penniless, they quickly assured you that God was on their side and victory was certain.

Of course infiltration, assassination and political terrorism had ended all that.

The city's population had tripled to more than 700,000 people, 350,000 of which were refugees. Working under the supervision of their KGB overlords, KHAD agents had easily infiltrated a chaotic Pakistan, where they assassinated resistance leaders, infiltrated refugee camps, and stirred up trouble between the various mujahideen factions based in Peshawar.

That initial easy-going trust died when news of the deaths started rolling in.

City Under Siege

The slow-witted Afghans were the first to go, brave to the end but blown up by mines or ground into meat under Russian tanks. The bright ones died too, the former engineers, the student leaders who had escaped from Kabul University, the ex-Afghan army officers. They eventually went the same way as their illiterate cousins.

At first the resistance movement put up posters around the city, showing the faces of fallen comrades. The war, though geographically close, was still a long way off emotionally and Peshawar was glad to play host to a new army of men with at least a little money in their pockets. Besides, Peshawaris reasoned there were enough walls to host a few scraps of paper. Then the death toll increased.

Five years after the war started, posters showing dead men festooned the city like photographic weeds of death. It wasn't uncommon to meet people who had lost fourteen or more members of their family. One refugee camp sheltered women and orphans from the same village whose husbands and sons had all been killed. Eventually there wasn't enough room on the city walls to show every dead soul from the war-ravaged country next door.

But before dying the light hearted Afghans all came here, for one last cup of tea, one last walk in the old city's famous gardens, one last **gup shup** (gossip) with friends, one last meal with their displaced families before they willingly crossed the nearby mountains, bound for a war they knew would certainly destroy most of them.

Alexander the Great was dead these many centuries but Peshawar was still the Piccadilly Circus of Central Asia. Her streets remained an alluring mixture of the American wild west and a Bible epic. Bearded Pathan tribesmen with pistols on their hips shared the crowded by-ways with loaded camels just in from the deserts, horses bearing riders, water buffalo pulling carts, street vendors peddling their wares, women wrapped in **chadors** (light cloak), children running and playing, all shoving, shouting and all calling Peshawar home. The Afghans and I were just part of the recent picture.

As the summer of 1983 came to a scorching close, I could see the genocidal war being waged by the Soviet Union in nearby Afghanistan was taking its toll here too. The nightmare had crept in over the city walls, wiping out the innocence I once cherished in my adopted home town.

In all fairness, it was hard to blame the people of Peshawar. No other city would have taken in so many, would have suffered so long in silence. The miracle of local tolerance lasted until the city's children began to fall victim. Even the tradition of hospitality couldn't lay to rest the savage grief that had ripped through Peshawar those last few months.

More than three million Afghan refugees now called Pakistan home. Most of them survived in 250 enormous refugee camps running along the western borders of the country. These desperate tent cities, with their appalling child mortality rates, their disease and despair were mostly located there in the North West Frontier Province where I lived.

Khyber Knights

Peshawar, the provincial capital, was now suffering for supporting the enemies of the Soviet state. Her citizens, once happy to welcome their Afghan cousins, had lost their nerve when the war came to haunt their streets. Patience, like their dead children, were both casualties of the war.

Times had changed.

Many people now wanted the Afghans not just out of their city but out of their country. For the first time there were demands being voiced among the Pakistanis that a peace be brokered between the resistance fighters and the communists. The century old tradition of **melmastia** or hospitality which was always extended to strangers had now been put on hold.

Local laws were passed in Peshawar prohibiting unmarried Afghan men from residing within the city. Once inviting Peshawar now looked suspiciously on any Afghan seen loitering within her walls. They had better be shopping not gawking or trouble was sure to follow. Identity cards were always being demanded. Turbans were a cultural give away as to where your allegiances lay. The year 1983 had become one of the darkest periods of the Jihad and transformed Peshawar into a nightmare. Dozens of local citizens were already dead, with no end to the bombing campaign in sight.

There were endless promises out of Islamabad, Pakistan's capital, pledging to bring the elusive murderers to justice. But despite the soothing words, not a single person had been caught, much less convicted.

Peshawar was going to survive. She always did. But she had become a hot spot again, with her crowded streets running like a river full of daily intrigues, lurking spies, mad bombers, suppressed violence and tricky political currents. She would gobble up more victims and wait for time to ease away these pains.

Until then, I was convinced, it was time to go.

I kept walking, hurting all over from the shock of another damned bomb and hurting inside from watching this once-proud city descend into suspicion and hostility. I followed the street as it continued to twist and turn away from the butchery that lay behind me. After several years I knew my way through this city even on the darkest of nights. A few curious Peshawaris were rushing towards me, going to see what all the excitement was about. I turned left at the corner, passing the straw-floored tea house where I often ate, walking steadily until I veered right, onto an unnamed lane that twisted like a snake's back. It lead me by a shop selling medieval Qurans and then deposited me into the quiet safety of a narrow canyon of old three-story houses whose dark shadows cooled the grateful street. I followed my silent course until it finally came out onto what served as a wide boulevard in Peshawar.

This car-less ancient artery pointed due north, towards Hasht Nagari, towards the **Hindu Kush** mountains and towards my uncertain future. For today I was leaving this place I had long called home.

I made my way downhill. The street began to fill with people and animals as it gradually widened.

Horse-drawn, two-wheeled delivery wagons piled high with meat were stopped in front of little butcher shops. Hordes of flies and children lingered around the baker's goods. Shop keepers called to me, inviting me to stop in for a cup of tea. I waved and shouted that I was in a hurry. Peshawar is a city that delights in gossip. The comings and goings of cultural renegades such as my long time friend Ali Muhammad and me always kept the tongues in our neighborhood wagging. In Hasht Nagari they didn't just take notice of the size of your wallet or your political allegiances. They felt at ease discussing the morals of your grandmother and the failings of your ancestors. No scandal was ever laid to rest in Hasht Nagari and no secret was safe.

I was surprised I had been able to hide my own plans for so long.

Of course, looking straight ahead I could now make out the river of uncivilized traffic known as the **G.T. Road** passing by the end of this street a half mile or so away . It was the very proximity to this noisy ribbon of east-west traffic that made Hasht Nagari such an ideal place to live. The nearness of Pakistan's busiest highway brought strangers, travelers and saddle tramps into Hasht Nagari on a regular basis. Of course they seldom took up permanent residence like Ali and I had. The fact that I wore Afghan clothes, as well as my previous trips to that country, was a well-known fact around Hasht Nagari. Despite my turban I was a recognized oddity not a suspected bomber, just another piece of flotsam thrown up here by the latest war.

Many of Peshawar's educated citizens considered Hasht Nagari a lower class neighborhood, with its warren of blind corners, carved doors and legacy of Oriental secrecy. Its houses were hoary with age. Ornate gardens hid behind twelve-foot walls. Like all Peshawar, Hasht Nagari's streets were almost entirely occupied by men. The local women lived secluded lives, seldom venturing out except on socially acceptable occasions, and only then if they were shrouded in a *burkha* and accompanied by a suspicious male relative.

But even with all its gossip and noise, there was a palpable sense of belonging here, something I had never experienced in all my world-wide travels. It was dirty, sometimes dangerous, always intriguing and my soul's asylum. Plus, except for a few billion germs who also called Hasht Nagari home, I felt strangely safe there.

I turned right onto Sikunder Pura (Alexander the Great Street), passing the police station where a sentry stood drowsing outside the main gate, looking like he was going to fall forward and spike himself on his rifle's bayonet. A few more turns through walkways that had never been mapped and I came out into a brick cul-de-sac which had a few old houses grouped around it like suspicious maiden aunts. This was *Gari Syeddan*, known as the street of the descendants of the Prophet.

Ali Muhammad and Shavon were both waiting.

I couldn't say who I was happier to see.

Khyber Knights

"I heard the explosion. Thought I better come out and check on her," Ali Muhammad said, as he struggled to keep my horse steady by holding onto her reins. He had never been around horses except this mare of mine and they made him nervous. His open toed *chapplis* (sandals) were poor protection against her heavy hooves. He was almost tall, thin and surprisingly graceful for a man. A noble brown mustache graced a tanned face that looked world wise. His deep blue eyes twinkled, a warning to life that he refused to take her too seriously. Judging by his clothes you would could have passed him on the street and never suspected he was an American.

"It took out the little restaurant by the clock tower at *Ghanta Ghar* (clock street). The street's a wreck. I'm lucky to have gotten back," I told him as I took the reins to my horse.

"Anybody killed?"

"It'll take a week to find out."

Death was just another noisy neighbor around Hasht Nagari. Ali didn't even comment, just reached into his vest pocket, pulled out a round tin shaped like a Copenhagen can and took out a big pinch of *naswar* (snuff).

"God knows better," he said, then packed his lower lip with the bright green snuff. The bulge made his gaunt cheeks look even more hollow.

Shavon was glad to see me and turning her head gave me a gentle shove of recognition. A smile came to my face, the first of the day. The leanness of this palomino mare, the silkiness of her snow-white mane, the cleanness of her strong legs, the strength and width of her deep gold chest would have made any horseman smile. And before anything else I was always a horseman.

I stroked her head then turned to check the cinch. When I ran the buckles up I could feel her go tight with excitement. She was afire with vigor, my answer to today's madness, my ticket out of this town I loved.

"You ought to come in and wash up Asadullah. You look like most of the building landed on you," Ali said and he made a gesture towards the comforts of his nearby house.

The sun was well up. I was getting a late start. I was dirty as hell and the day was already full of snakes and scorpions. I was tempted.

Then Shavon stamped her left front foot impatiently and made up her mind for both of us. I threw the reins over her head and swung up onto the hurricane deck. That was still the best view in the world.

Ali Muhammad smiled. Not much that I did surprised him anymore. We had been friends for too long. During the course of our travels together we had embraced Islam, crossed cultural and physical deserts, shared adventures, explored little-known lands and seen men and countries die. We were ex-Americans. Hell, we were ex-everything.

My friend would be here when I got back.

If I got back.

"Did Pirgumber give you the map?" he asked.

I patted my shirt pocket in reply.

"Do you think he'll keep his promise?"

I shrugged my shoulders vaguely.

"You know Pirgumber," I said half-heartily.

"Yeah, I know Pirgumber," he said laughing, then spit a bright green stream of naswar in friendly derision. "Don't be surprised if he and those other tea-house mujahideen are still telling lies in Peshawar about the brave things they never did in Afghanistan, when you finally reach Chitral."

"Well I'm going anyway."

"*Pa makha day kha* (may you face good on your way) cowboy," he said and taking my out-stretched hand, shook it firmly as if all the things we weren't saying were pressed instead into this silent gesture.

"Adios," came to my lips as it always did, despite the country, despite the miles, despite the years that lay between me and my first horseback adventure.

I touched Shavon's neck with the reins and she wheeled to the left. A whisper from the spur and we clattered across the cobble stones, heading out of Peshawar, bound for an ambiguous kismet.

2
Kidnapped

It seemed like a good idea at the time.

Pirgumber Kul, **Turkoman**, horseman, mujahadeen commander and friend had explained it to me as we sat whispering over tea cups in the **Kabuli Jon** restaurant. He had a face like a rice bowl, all round curves and disappearing lines. Unlike most Afghans, his skin had a slight yellowish tinge to it, revealing the roots of his wandering Mongol ancestors. His eyes were jolly brown almond slits that slashed across his face. A wispy black mustache, more an embarrassment than a statement of strength, graced his lip. He had grown plump from staying too long in Peshawar, the lean fighting body unable to resist the many savory *pilaus* (rice) pushed on him by various hosts anxious to believe the tales of his fighting prowess.

He was an altogether likable rogue.

"There will more than a hundred of them. They'll be glad to take you along. An extra horse is always welcome," he said smiling and lifted his tea cup in a casual salute. "Dry cup," he said politely, draining it like a glutton to the dregs.

"I'm not interested in turning my horse into a pack animal. She's my mount," I said with a horseman's contempt, hoping to convey how much I detested walking.

He assured me it wouldn't be a problem. That was the thing about Pirgumber. If the Russians were pounding at the door, intent on our slitting our throats, this scamp would smile and still see the bright side of things. Being horsemen we had gravitated to each other, sharing tales of the saddle before life beached us both temporarily there in Peshawar. Born and bred on the plains of northern Afghanistan, Pirgumber had spent much of his life playing *buz-khazi*. When the Soviet invasion interrupted his equestrian lifestyle, it seemed natural to him to kill them when he could and loot them with no remorse.

A strong contingent of his fellow Turkoman tribesmen were now supposedly gathering in Chitral, having journeyed into our host country on one of the more than two hundred mountain passes used by the freedom fighters. Having come to Pakistan to pick up badly-needed arms and ammunition, these northern horsemen would soon be returning to the plains around Aqcha, Afghanistan, where they waged equestrian warfare against the enemies of Islam. With cold weather coming in a few months, they would undoubtedly be playing buz-khazi when they weren't raiding Russians. It sounded like my cup of tea and Pirgumber didn't hesitate to invite me to go and join them.

Khyber Knights

Of course talking about it in the shade of a tea house was a far cry from riding alone through three hundred miles of northern Pakistan to do it.

The palomino mare and I were off to a hell of a beginning. The weather was as hot as a blow torch as we made our way across the vast vale of Peshawar. It may have been the bread basket of the North West Frontier, but Shavon and I were only three days out and the heat was trying to kill us before the Russians did.

We seemed to be traveling on a treadmill, giving me the strange sensation we were passing the same blistered, fallow fields day after day. Our route was taking us due north through fertile but largely deserted farmland. The heat was so bad even the insects were hiding.

I could only guess at the temperature. I felt confident it was a 110 plus but didn't have a thermometer to confirm it. In fact, we were traveling light with not much more than a hoof pick for Shavon and a copy of "War and Peace" for me shoved in the saddle bags behind. The forged mujahadeen identity card complete with my picture, a letter of introduction to the Turkoman commander and a crude map were Pirgumber's last gifts to me. I had been returning with them when the bomb at the restaurant had almost canceled the trip. The documents were riding, along with my American passport and a wad of money, in a thin leather bag slung along the left side of my chest. Hidden under my billowing shirt and lying flat like it did I figured my secrets were safe.

The British Raj (empire) had once maintained sun-stroke huts along this route. They were built for English Tommies busy maintaining the unchallengeable Pax Britannica among the natives thereabouts. It had been a court martial offense for the soldiers to venture out in such heat without a hat. The glare brought about the unpleasant memories of last year when I dropped like a poled ox from sunstroke, going temporarily brain dead. Any sort of shanty, British or otherwise, would have been a welcome relief, but the builders and their huts were only a memory so we rode on.

Occasionally we would pass under the shade of a poplar tree planted outside a tiny house lying close to the road. Children splashing and playing in the cool waters of a roadside ditch would go silent as Shavon and I rode by, the noise of their little antics temporarily replaced by the road song of my creaking old British cavalry saddle.

I had pulled the tail of my turban across my face, which didn't help matters. It was a largely futile effort to protect my fair skin. After so many blistering miles on this unforgiving road, Shavon and I both kept out eyes downcast on the ground, trying to avoid the sun's unmerciful glare. But we must have looked more sinister than we felt, for the children always fell silent as we passed. It was an unintentional deception.

We were still passing through the flat plains that lay between Peshawar and the mountains up ahead. Twenty miles or so away, I could see what looked like a hazy, gray lump on the skyline. The steep foothills of the Malakand Pass were waiting for us with the promise of cooler weather.

Kidnapped

Once we entered the mountains our route would run due north on a road that was seldom open more than five months a year. It's terminus was Chitral, the only town of any size in north western Pakistan. Normally the Hindu Kush mountains cut the place off from the rest of the country like an afterthought of civilization. During the short warm season an occasional plane landed with supplies and visitors. When the inevitable winter closed in Chitral was a marooned island surrounded by frozen waves of snow-covered stone. But it lay close to several lesser-known passes that fed into Afghanistan and thus was the northern terminus of many mujahadeen activities.

I was thinking of many things as I rode, cold drinks, and an Irish woman and my mind had wandered a long way off from that molten excuse of a road. Motor traffic had grown heavier as we neared the foothills. Cars, buses and over-laden trucks were flying by within spitting distance of my mount. Their noxious exhaust fumes were assailing us. Trouble comes up on you like that in Pakistan, in unlooked-for places, at inconvenient times.

It felt like 1:30 p.m. and we both desperately needed a break. Parched and lonely, Shavon and I were looking for a spot to call home for a few hours, when we rode up to a nameless fly-blown village. It lay off to our left, a stone's throw away, a huddle of gray, one-story mud huts. A few listless Afghans could be seen near these temporary homes. It was a depressing refugee camp and I gave it only a quick glance. Even at this distance the place stank of despair.

What caught my eye was a shack sitting next to the road.

"A roach wouldn't live in that hovel," I thought.

Rough old boards pried from packing crates were nailed into three rudimentary walls. There was no fourth wall at all. The owner had been too lazy to put up any sort of door. Tree branches, complete with dead leaves, served as a reminder of a roof. The floor was barely five feet long by four feet wide. The entire mess was perched on short wooden stilts designed to keep the would-be-shopkeeper up out of the dust. Some nameless scrub tree threw a splattering of shade over the architectural exercise.

It wasn't just ugly. It was absurd.

The shack's one redeeming feature was a small enduring icebox, dilapidated but serviceable, sitting by the door in the dust. Long bereft of electricity, it was still clearly full of ice and cold soft drinks.

Shavon took me up to what served as the front door.

The shopkeeper was a seedy, middle-aged little weasel of a man who squatted in his shack, hogging the shade. He appeared to be a typical southeastern Afghan Pathan, with a nine meter **paunch** turban and a mouth full of naswar.

Sitting outside the shack on a **charpoy** (rope bed) were three crusty looking characters. Two of them appeared to be ordinary farmers displaced by a war not of their choosing.

I wasn't likely to forget the third man who was sitting closest to me. He was big. Dressed in a dirty, dark brown shalwar-kameez, his pants were too short, exposing thick hairy legs and callused ankles. His feet were smashed into sandals that were old when Moses was born. A grungy white turban was pushed partly back to reveal a shaved head. He had huge, hairy hands. What caught my eye was his face. It had been severely burned. His nose was the dividing line between grim-faced and ghastly. Half his face had a shiny brown texture like hard, melted plastic. His skin dripped down the left side, running towards his chin like warm, gooey brown wax. The cruel flames had blasted an eye as well, glazing it over, leaving a sickly yellowish film covering the iris. A dull, brown pupil squinted at the sunlight. To complete the insult, the left side of his lips were completely gone. Tiny, square teeth peeked out at me. These nasty little grinders and biters were covered in a brown film, built up from years of dipping naswar. He was as ugly as the wrath of God, an Afghan version of a Tyrannosaurus Rex.

"Russian napalm", I thought idly, then pointed at the icebox and asked the shopkeeper to hand me up a cold drink.

I didn't pay any attention to these rustics. I wasn't looking for gup-shup (gossip), just something cold. While a tired Shavon stood resting in the shade, I took the cold Fanta the shop keeper passed up to me. The questions started before I swallowed the first delicious draught of sweet orange cola.

The third man wasn't just ugly, he was nosy. He started drilling me before I had the bottle drained.

"Who are you?"
"Asadullah Khan, an American Muslim."
"Charta zee (where are you going)?"
"Chitral," I answered between drinks.
"Why?"
"I'm going to meet friends of mine there," I told him, trying to cut off the conversation. The last thing I wanted was for word to leak out about the papers I was carrying or the mission I was on.
"Why?"
"That's personal."

That's when things started to go wrong.

In defense of those unknown refugees, it wasn't such a bad idea to be suspicious of a white skinned stranger dressed like an Afghan. Things had grown too politically hot in the **NWFP**. Both the KGB and KHAD had paid informers in all the mujahadeen organizations. Spying was rampant. Assassinations were common, and every refugee camp had its snitch. Nobody trusted his neighbor, much less a foreigner on a horse.

Before I could defuse the situation my Irish roots almost got me killed.

Prior to leaving Peshawar, I had an artistic friend paint a large red hand on Shavon's golden right shoulder. This totem of Celtic defiance had represented O'Reillys riding into battle for centuries. I believed it appropriate considering the journey ahead of me. I never considered the idea that this idle bit of ancestor worship, this innocent token from faraway green Breifne, Ireland, could be interpreted as being anything

Kidnapped

but Gaelic. I rode out of Peshawar forgetting that many Afghans considered anything red communist confirmation.

I handed back the empty bottle. While I was working on a second, the guy with the bad complexion got up and casually walked around in front of Shavon, easing up close to her head. When he saw the Red Hand of **Cavan**, I saw him go stiff and my intuition told me it was time to ride on.

"Look at this," he told his friends and pointed triumphantly at the evidence he had discovered of my communist collusion.

Suddenly I didn't think the ancient sign of the O'Reillys was going to be bringing me much luck today.

"How much?' I asked quickly, handing down the empty bottle.

"Ten rupees."

This wasn't sophisticated Peshawar. I didn't argue about the steep price, just fished some rupees out of my shirt pocket and tossed them down to the shopkeeper.

"Get down," the ugly man ordered.

I glanced at the other Afghans. No help there, just suspicions.

"*Khuda hafez* (the peace of God go with you)," I replied politely and taking up Shavon's reins, started to head out.

"You're a Russian spy. Get down," he screamed and grabbing the reins just below the bit, tried to gain control of the mare.

I could stand a lot; the heat, this ignorant peasant, even his misplaced suspicions. But no one messed with my horse.

I snapped.

"You dog," I yelled at him, then slashed him across the face with my quirt before setting spurs to the horse and trampling him like a rag into the dust. The mare charged out of town. It didn't seem like the time or place to stick around and discuss the history of Irish resistance symbology.

We rode hard for fifteen minutes.

I thought we had escaped.

We hadn't.

The sun was a furnace. Shavon was black with sweat, her chest heaving. She would have run until we came to death or Chitral, which ever arrived first. But pity for her great heart told me to slow her to a walk. I patted her soaking neck and assured her I would be more careful in the future about where I bought our soft drinks. The Arabs always contended that mares endured hunger, thirst and fatigue better than stallions or geldings. From their bellies came treasures and their back was a seat of honor, they said. Shavon had proved she was all that and more.

I was thinking we were out of danger and was about to dismount and lead her. The motor traffic on the road was steady and I wasn't paying much attention until a large Toyota van sped by me, then came to a sliding stop sideways, blocking the road just in front of us. Before I realized it, the doors swung open and nine armed men, including my former burned-faced inquisitor came rushing at me.

They were all screaming.

Khyber Knights

"Get him."
"Stop him."
"Pull him down."
"*Kushad dushman mukhbir*, (kill the enemy spy)."

Then hands were reaching up, trying to drag me to the ground. I started whipping them with my quirt, trying to keep Shavon under control and stay in the saddle at the same time. But then time seemed to stop. I froze as my vision narrowed in on an old man striding towards me from the van. His face was full of fear and his gun hand was shaking. But the pistol he was holding was pointed at my heart. It seemed to be staring at me with its huge evil looking black hole. I waited for him to fire and told myself, "This is where I die."

Before the old man could take aim and shoot, I was swept off my horse by the crowd of angry, shouting men. But the wizened gunman made his way through the crowd and held his pistol pointed at me while various members of the mob started to beat me. I tried to cover my face with my arm. Luckily my turban took most of the impact of the blows aimed at my head.

There was no point in trying to talk. These fellows were clearly out for blood. Shavon's reins were ripped out of my hands. The old man shoved his pistol into my back and motioned for me to move away from my horse. I hesitated for a moment.

"*Ohdaghaim laywanay spay zoi* (fuck you, you crazy son of a bitch)" someone cursed and gave me a terrific shove in the back.

I had no choice. I started walking back reluctantly toward the refugee camp, encircled by my captors; Shavon a prisoner as well.

While this was occurring motor traffic was forced to a slow crawl in order to pass the mob and their van blocking one lane of the rural highway. I walked surrounded by my antagonists. But I could clearly see these motorists passing slowly, staring awkwardly at me, the guns and my angry captors.

When I noticed a shiny black car pull alongside, I discerned that the passenger in the back, a well-to-do looking Pakistani, was obviously being transported somewhere by his chauffeur. Instantly I decided to take a chance.

"Help. Stop your car. Stop your car. I'm being kidnapped," I shouted at the now alert passenger, while trying to break free from my captors.

Though my shouts brought a rain of blows on my back and head, my refugee captors were out of luck. I saw the Pakistani motion to his driver to pull over. He quickly got out and came walking back towards us.

The crowd parted to make way for the well dressed man. He took one look at my white skin and asked me, "What's going on here," in the British accented English of an educated, upper-class Pakistani.

I shook off the rough hands still holding me. Reaching under my shirt I unbuckled my leather bag and quickly slid out my American passport. Anxious to keep the documents Pirgumber had given me secret, I waved the little blue book for all to see and summed up the situation for this good Samaritan. In a few words he in turn told me he was a government official on his way down from Timargara, the district capital, heading back to Peshawar. More important, he was a Pathan.

"The bloody cheek of these refugees," he said in perfect English, when he heard my explanation. Then switching into Pushtu, he began verbally lashing the kidnappers with a torrent of abuse.

"You ignorant *khor ghods* (sister fuckers) I'll impale your sluttish mothers on spikes of fire. This is my country and this man is a guest here. You'll release him this instant our I'll have the army bulldoze those hovels you call homes and throw your squalling brats out on the roadside," he shouted as men began to lower their eyes in shame.

"We think he is a spy, your honor," the old man said from next to me, trying to sound sure of himself.

"*Chup shaw* (shut up) you old **marvasi** (child molester). Didn't he just tell you he is an American Muslim? Did the donkeys kick out your brains before you fled that miserable country of yours? Get back to your homes, all of you, before I have my driver radio for the **Levies** (national guardsmen)," he yelled.

Then turning back to the car, the tall thin man shouted to his driver, "Ghulam radio back to Dargai and tell them to send me a truck load of Levies instantly."

"No. No," men started shouting. Shavon's reins were thrust back into my hands and my captors began leaving as fast as they had arrived, all signs of pistols and revenge drying up in the face of this Pathan tribesman's wrath. The van had suddenly pulled up alongside, though the refugees were still making noises as if they had only been trying to do their civic duty.

I didn't wait to hear any more excuses but tucked my passport away, vaulted into the saddle, then turned to thank my rescuer.

He gave me a conspiratorial smile and waved away my sincere thanks.

"To tell you the truth, I was only bluffing about calling the Levies. I don't have a radio in the car. The ignorant fools will most likely leave you alone now. But I wouldn't chance it if I were you. I would leave at once, ride hard and not stop until you're far from here," he told me sincerely.

His encouragement was all I needed. I set spurs to the mare and we dashed away. I never looked back. I was so flooded with relief that it was several minutes before it dawned on me that I had never asked my rescuer's name.

Suddenly Shavon and I didn't care how hot it was. We alternated between a hard trot, a good canter and then a strong walk. The mare and I ate up the miles and nothing else. The sun started sinking off to our left but we pushed on anyway. By the time we reached the village of Dargai the palomino and I were both desperately tired. We had traveled several hours without any sign of trouble. But I was still edgy and wanted to hole up in some sort of relative safety.

It didn't matter what we wanted.

Dargai didn't even have a **chaikhana** (tea house). We had no choice but to travel on. At the outskirts of town we halted at a well. I hauled up on the rope. The old bucket was made of vulcanized tires. Moss clung to it like green fairy hair. That luke-warm water was our only dinner. I told Shavon we would ride out of town and bed down deep in a field, staying out of sight from the road. I figured we could find a safe spot where we could hide for the night. I didn't want my friend with the melted face looking us up after sunset.

Not knowing what was ahead we pushed on into the rapidly darkening countryside. We went mile after weary mile through desolate and unsuitable countryside. Well outside Dargai the road started climbing up into the mountains. By now I had dismounted. I simply followed the road and Shavon followed me. I was so tired I had forgotten about the mighty Malakand Pass. It wasn't until a bus roared by us in the dark, shooting its lights out over the edge of the road, that I saw how high we had climbed. That was when the despair began to really set in. I knew I could have fallen asleep almost anywhere. But that loyal animal couldn't stand there on a darkened Pakistani roadside. It was a miracle we hadn't been hit already.

Well after midnight and high up on the mountain we found a tree with enough level ground under it for the two of us to throw down our weary bones and rest. I unsaddled Shavon and brushed her down in the dark.

"Sorry old girl," I told her, as she nickered for her supper. "Double rations for tomorrow's breakfast. I promise," I said and meant it, though I had no way of knowing how I would provide it.

I made camp, such as it was. I leaned my saddle up close to the tree, wrapped myself in my *patou* (blanket) and lay down close to Shavon. The moon, that lamp of borrowed light, was starting to rise. The landscape around us was soon revealed to be a wilderness of rocks, some as small as hen's eggs, others the size of houses. It was a miracle we had found a flat spot to rest our heads.

The night held her breath. The distant white stars overhead were silent guards over our tiny encampment. The warm air was laced with a subtle perfume, good leather and warm horseflesh, wafting to me from the sturdy mare and trusty saddle. We were gypsies of the heart, Shavon and I. That night, even without the comforts of a fire, I was surprised to discover how happy I was. I was no longer a melancholy nomad trapped within the confines of four civilized walls. Out there I had to give no thought to the conventions, restrictions and horrors of the modern world. Even with its dangers, the open road offered me a sacrament unknown in any city, even a city as exciting as Peshawar.

The full moon rose, a brilliant glory, and my heart surged. I felt the stirrings of a thought I had kept hidden even from myself. Today's narrow escape had been the grain of sand that tonight brought on an avalanche of self-discovery.

Those Afghan refugees had been intent on kidnapping and most assuredly harming me. Oddly enough, I couldn't blame them. I understood all too well the colossal sufferings their people had undergone. My work as a journalist had shown me all the hideous secrets of a war seldom reported in the west; of writhing children burned alive in front of parents in an effort to force out information regarding the resistance, of women gang-raped in Russian helicopters hovering high over villages and then tossed out alive and wailing, of a line of bound mujahadeen captives laid down shoulder to shoulder in front of a merciless tank rumbling up to mash them into meat, of priceless buz khazi horses being chased and butchered by screaming MIG jets.

The mad dogs running the government in Kabul could have taught the Nazis a thing or two about the tactics of terror.

In my heart I still saw Afghanistan as the country I had once known, a place full of hospitable villages, dashing horsemen, mysterious mosques and turbaned warriors. Despite the war, despite the atrocities, despite the years, I still clung like a child to that dream I once knew. I had grown a suit of armor over this cherished memory. All the hardship and suffering and misery and killing I had encountered in my work .... all of that was part of a new Afghanistan, not the place that had captured my heart when I first rode like a hawk over her northern plains more than ten years ago.

Even the Jihad had not been able to dislodge my own version of the past. I equated what was happening with a sort of temporary madness running riot over the country. I silently reassured myself that some part of what I once loved there survived in some out-of-the-way village.

Earlier this year I realized I was ignoring growing proof that Afghanistan was forever different, that the Jihad was no longer a noble effort, that the war had torn the heart out of the people, that the hapless country wouldn't take years but generations to recover, that the ten million landmines polluting the countryside like hidden cancers would deny me the chance to ever ride reckless and carefree over the beloved plains of northern Afghanistan.

The refugees were no longer trusting and proud. They had grown silent, morose and jaded. Corruption was now an epidemic that sullied every portion of the Jihad. Refugees bribed Pakistani officials before they could get identity cards and permission to squat in squalid refugee camps. Saudi Arabia sent boat loads of donated dates to feed starving children. But before the fruit could reach hungry little mouths, it was sold in the street by the very people trusted to distribute the largesse. So many tons of arms and ammunition had been siphoned off from the CIA pipeline, Pakistan was now an armed camp from Karachi to Chitral.

The once vaunted heroes of the Jihad, commanders who had originally gone to war with only a few old Lee Enfield rifles, were now living like decadent warlords in Peshawar. There were whispers about opium harvests and heroin labs being guarded by Afghan mercenaries. Inside Afghanistan feuding rebel commanders assassinated political rivals and sold out foreign journalists to the Soviets for handsome rewards. Back in Peshawar these one-time heroes now drove through the city in extravagant imported cars, surrounded by squads of armed goons and yes-men, their humble beginnings just another casualty in a seldom-reported war. Many of them were no longer fighting for righteousness or in defense of truth. They had debased the self-sacrifice and deaths of thousands into a personal struggle for land, power and privilege. For such men the Jihad was no longer a struggle to free their country, it was merely an invitation to feast on violence.

Wagon loads, boat loads, and plane loads of money flowing in from the CIA and rich Arabs had turned the Jihad from a war of liberation into a scramble for loot. The seven émigré **tanzims** (resistance groups) waged silent urban warfare against each other in an effort to gain control of the wealth flowing to the resistance. Now it wasn't just the Russians and their communist lackeys killing mujahadeen, it was the holy warriors of Allah slashing and stabbing each other in a deadly but silent power struggle that roved the streets of Peshawar. Unity among the resistance leaders was a myth.

Yes, my Afghanistan was dead and to top it off there was the new Raj to contend with.

Aid wallahs and **water boilers** were huddled like an infestation of termites under the surface of an outlying Peshawar suburb known as University Town. They lived in fine houses behind tall walls and slept securely, knowing private **chowkidars** (night watchmen) were guarding their gates and their slumber. Few foreigners made any attempt at adopting native dress, a custom which requires practice but puts one in harmony with the surroundings. Unlike their Pakistani hosts, who were required by economic necessity to study foreign history, the two hundred odd water-boilers stayed largely ignorant of native affairs and customs. Most thought Islam a nightmare because they had no knowledge of it.

During the day the expatriates oversaw various foreign agencies guided by good principles but undermined by harsh reality. Sewing machines would be doled out to refugee women in the morning, whose husbands sold them in the bazaar that afternoon and then reported them stolen the next day. Running classrooms was another popular justification for living like stiff-lipped memsahibs. Few Occidental teachers realized the majority of their students saw learning English as a long term ticket to the west and a short term excuse to avoid being slaughtered in the Jihad.

Many of my fellow journalists spent their extra time working on books about the ongoing conflict. They recounted their expeditions into Afghanistan, recalling the horrors but seldom making any effort to understand the people. "*Se roz, yak kitab* (three days, one book)" my mujahadeen friends joked about such efforts.

At the conclusion of their busy days these various foreign elements retired to the comforts of the American Club. This sprawling white bungalow, with its guarded gates, tennis courts, aerobic classes, white linen table cloths, humble native servants and waves of liquor was the bulwark behind which the vast majority of foreigners hid. They went there to eat badly-disguised imitations of American cuisine, swig whiskey and maintain the arrogance of the racially self-righteous.

Their busy routine was only upset on Wednesday nights when the French threw open the doors of the **Bamboo Bar**. It was not a bar really, more of a liquid smorgasbord that met in a large conference room at one of the aid agencies. Pakistan policy prohibited it officially but winked at its existence. Outside the gate on the darkened dirt street would be gathered a host of expensive cars and idle native drivers.

Inside anything alcoholic was welcome and anything Islamic was damned. The air would be so thick with cigarette smoke it could choke a trooper. While the walls thumped to the music of the Rolling Stones or the Beach Boys, expatriates would whisper about conspiracies or shout for another drink. It had the feeling of an Al Capone speak-easy dropped into Peshawar by an errant tornado.

Here journalists, doctors, nurses, teachers, administrators and mercenaries met to discuss their individual efforts to win the war. The room would be loud with voices all abuzz with the catch phrase "inside." The latest hero to have returned from "inside" Afghanistan would regale his audience with tales of grueling hikes with steel hardened mujahadeen. If he was lucky he went to bed that night with a French nurse too homely to screw back home. "Inside" was the most over-used expression to hit the Indian sub-continent since the British invented "staying on" to describe stragglers who held out after 1947.

I had no ties to cut with that exile community.

I had seen what the Bamboo Bar had to offer. I was blacklisted from the American Club. My Muslim connections not only made me persona nongrata, I was officially banned from joining. I learned to live with it. I seldom saw any ferenghis (foreigners) anyway. They made occasional nervous shopping blitzkriegs into **Qissa Khani** bazaar (Peshawar neighborhood) while their native drivers hovered nearby. They never ventured into the dirt and danger that was an everyday part of my life in Hasht Nagari.

It was all just another layer of scab that separated my heart from the truth.

That day's developments had shown me the emptiness of my efforts. The Afghans I had come here to serve had wanted to kill me earlier today. That night was a turning point in my life, the sharpest turn.

My naive idealism, I finally realized, was as dead as my once cherished dreams. Peshawar was chock-a-block full of good intentions, offset by the weakness of human frailty. A misplaced sense of duty had kept me there at my self-appointed post for too long. Like many of my generation, I had mistakenly viewed the liberation of Kabul as the same sort of emotional mirage that lured young men to risk their lives defending Madrid against the fascists in 1936. The only thing separating me from the duped peasant boys of that earlier emotional jihad was the passage of time. The blind loyalty and the conniving statesmen were the same, only the name of the country had changed.

Gone were the days when Afghanistan could rightly be called "*Daulat-i-Khudadad*" (the God-given Kingdom). It was time to move on emotionally from a country that had been bombed into nothing more than a geographical expression.

Shavon and I were just two infinitesimal specks in the silver moonlight that night. We might disappear out there in those mountains without

Khyber Knights

leaving a trace of a struggle. But there was something clean and good about pushing your shoulders up against the brute strength of those mountains. The wilderness that lay ahead was no place for a man full of conflict and doubts and bad memories. You couldn't travel through the magnificent immensity of northern Pakistan and not trust in something more powerful than yourself. In the USA they had science and computers to run their world and trust in. On that shadowed mountain top there was only Shavon and Allah and no anesthetic for calamity except death.

I looked up at the honesty that was the darkened sky and told Allah I was resolved to turn in one direction or the other when I reached Chitral. Either I would go west into Afghanistan with the Turkomans to help the Afghan cause one last time, or I would turn east towards Gilgit and explore the seldom-seen mountain vastness that lay in that direction. Either way, karma had compelled me to be a writer. I traveled light and far and lived in lands other than my own. I had no roots in America, only felt at home among horsemen.

Shavon looked down on me with her kind eyes. I felt in my heart that I had stumbled onto a new path in the dark, the path of instinct, the path of inner exploration that one must travel alone. Every journey has a secret it waits to reveal to the patient traveler. The scales had tipped in a new direction at that nameless refugee village. I was hungry for the carefree life of the nomad with its strange places, its warm fires and open skies. I was tired of machiavellian intrigue and the slaughter of innocents. I knew where my duty lay but I longed now to escape, to make my living with my saddle, not my pen.

I fell asleep knowing I had pinned my decision on Allah's will.

3
Among the Pathans

My soul was dreaming and I was somewhere else far, far away when I heard the soft sounds of the mare somewhere above me. A whisper of a wind was cooling my face. I could feel a mist gliding over my sleeping eyes like a glimmer. I awoke to find the mountainside still slumbering, the suggestion of the sun slowly tugging off her blanket of white ground fog.

I lay there in my *patou* (blanket), comfortable on the warm earth beneath me, loath to get up. The silence there on the mountain was complete. I recalled yesterday's hardships and told myself I had the choice to push on or retreat back to Peshawar. Would it be foolhardiness or courage to continue after yesterday? When Shavon saw I was awake she started acting restless and hungry. I got up knowing I would not quit, that going back was not an option unless I was crippled or dying, a prophecy too soon to come true.

It took but a few minutes to break camp and leave. My clothes were crumpled. I had slept in my boots and turban. As soon as I buckled on my spurs, those thorns of misery, I was dressed. I brushed Shavon, then took the hoof pick to her hooves. I noted that her shoes had grown slick and worn thin. To saddle and mount took less time to do than it does to explain.

In the dawning I could see the top of the mountain not too far ahead. As we rode away, I looked back. The lonely tree, our silent hostess, looked like an afterthought of God.

We crested the Malakand Pass in about an hour, passing a well defended government fort hosting posted *Levy* (national guardsmen) sentries at the gate. It was still too early for traffic, which was lucky. There was a large prosperous village off to our left, running down the now widening hillside into a protected valley. There was no sign of a chaikhana and I was wondering if and when we would find some place to eat and rest. My immediate concern, though, was not my stomach.

Years of heavy traffic had smoothed the road. There wasn't a trace of traction. To make matters worse the fog had left the asphalt wet. It was as slick as a greasy blackboard. Shavon was treading cautiously, putting her front feet down like a ballerina tiptoeing on egg shells. I tried to urge the mare onto what passed as the shoulder. As we came around a rocky corner, Shavon lost her balance and came crashing down on her left side. I had sensed her fall and pulled free of the stirrups at the last second. As she went down I jumped off and landed on my feet beside her.

It was early. I was tired and hungry and still sleepy. I would have sold my saddle for a cup of tea. And now I had a horse down. I walked around to her head with the reins in my hands. She was just lying there, nothing hurt but her pride. She had her feet gathered under her comfortably as if she had decided there was no hurry in getting up. The disgusted look on her face told me plain enough, "After yesterday's rigors, I need a break."

Before I could urge Shavon to her feet, she got up on her own accord with a short heave. She shook herself hard, which set the saddle to jingling.

Suddenly a voice from behind startled me.

"Your horse looks tired," I heard.

I turned and found a dignified old Pathan looking us over with a skeptical eye. He could have been ninety but he still looked tough enough to whip Muhammad Ali, the world's most famous boxer. His face was framed by a snow-white beard. He lacked a mustache, preferring the local custom of keeping his top lip clean. Instead of a turban, he wore a small brimless round cap. His clothes, like his cap, were all spotlessly white. A lightweight cotton *patou* (blanket) hung around his shoulders like a matador's cape, lending him an air of dignity in stark contrast to the rough mountains surrounding us on all sides. He introduced himself as Hajii Shah Zaman, an elder of the nearby village of Piran. The old man told me he was waiting to board the bus heading north to Chakdara.

Shavon was catching her breath and I was too tired to start pulling her down the road just yet. When he asked me who I was, I felt for some reason I could trust him. The decision was helped by the fact that this regal patriarch looked like he talked to Allah every day on a first name basis. I told him everything, the ride, the reason, the refugees, the night on the mountain.

He never commented, just listened like a silent juniper tree. Standing out there on the roadside, he studied me for a few moments at the story's end, his eyes piercing me like an eagle. I felt ashamed, knowing I must look like a saddle tramp. He seemed to be studying something deeper than my clothes. Some sort of silent decision was made.

"Come on," he said in his blunt, old man way and pointed towards the village and the mysteries beyond. I was hungry and gritty but I had my pride. I might have turned him down if I had been on my own.

"Let's feed that horse," he added, my resistance collapsing when he recognized my weakness.

Leading Shavon, I followed the Hajii away from the road into a lane that skipped and wound it's way down the hill. As we walked he explained that this was earth trodden by his **Yusufzai** (Pathan tribe) ancestors for hundreds of years. Its hard-packed surface muffled our footsteps as we strode over this legendary land.

Sitting on the mountaintop at 5,000 feet, the village of Piran stayed remarkably cool. There wasn't a luxury to be seen, unless you counted the small white-washed mosque. But all the scattered houses were trim and tidy. The same families had lived here for generations, the old **Hajii** (pilgrim to Mecca) said. Knowing about the dangers of *badal* (blood feuds) among the Pathan tribes, I didn't make any jokes about good neighbors.

Among the Pathans

After a ten minute walk he led Shavon and me along a path that brought us to a sizable Pathan fort. The earthen walls were twenty feet high, capped by a turret in each corner. Twelve-foot steel gates painted a deep sky blue secured the place. As we drew near I had heard voices from inside. Someone had clearly been pulling guard duty and had watched us approach. A gate swung open before the old man had time to knock. I was surprised, though he seemed to be expecting such a sign of respect.

Inside the mud walls was a world unto itself, the architecture and amenities having been derived from the realities of revenge. Lying like arms on two sides of the fort were a series of rooms, sheltered by a deep verandah. Fruit trees ran along the other two sides. A grassy lawn served as a large patio. Roses were growing from ceramic pots. Two charpoys were standing close to a tree. An expensive **hookah** (water pipe) waited nearby. The secluded enclosure appeared altogether inviting.

Various men and teenage boys, comprised of the Hajii's sons, nephews and grandsons came up and introductions were passed all around. I was too tired to keep track of all their names. There were four generations of this patriarch's family living either in the fort or in the houses immediately outside its protective walls. As was customary, they maintained a strict **purdah** (female seclusion), keeping their wives and daughters out of sight from strangers.

I was told to tether Shavon under a large fruit tree. I managed to unsaddle her myself before Daud, Hajii Shah Zaman's youngest son, insisted that as a guest he would feed and brush her for me. I had been taught to never eat or rest until you've first seen to the welfare of your mount. But another son came and lead me to the charpoys, where the Hajii and two elder sons were already sitting. With a clear eye on Shavon, I sat down next to the elderly man and began cautiously to relax.

There wasn't a lot of talk. Proprieties had to be observed first. A son cleaned the hookah, filled it with coarse tobacco and Hajii Shah Zaman lit it. Walking through mountains all his life must have given him lungs like a draft horse because he soon had the old hookah billowing with smoke and bubbling so furiously it sounded like it was pleading for mercy.

He passed the stem my way and I got the water pipe to chatter mildly, not to the degree shown by the old man, but not an embarrassment either. One of the older sons on the charpoy next to me then took it over. The crowd of men and boys were now either sitting or squatting on their haunches in the grass in front of us. When Hajii Shah Zaman asked a question about my adventures things began to loosen up.

Several of the sons had traveled in other countries before coming home to live and marry in Piran. This wasn't unusual among younger Pathans who sought higher wages overseas, where they often took jobs in the military or construction. More than two million Pakistanis worked abroad, their low-paying local jobs snatched by desperate Afghan refugees.

Once content to live on loot, many Pathan tribesmen now left for four or five lonely years at a stretch. They toiled overseas in richer kingdoms, sending money back with unflinching loyalty to tiny villages like Piran. Eventually they returned, responding to that call of their hearts which brought them back to their spiritual center.

We who had traveled spoke of the merits of Mecca versus Medina. We all agreed Cairo was vastly overrated. They liked Dubai. I detested Frankfurt. When a young boy asked me what was the most beautiful place I had ever seen, I answered without hesitation, saying the Taj Mahal

"*Wah, wah* (bravo, bravo)," they all said loudly, revealing the Pathan's devotion to romance, and delighting in my choice of a Muslim monument to love versus some more industrialized structure in the west.

It was all pleasant and unexpected. Shavon was contentedly eating her way through a pile of freshly cut hay when Hajii Shah Zaman stood and motioned for me to follow him. A table and four chairs had been set up silently on the verandah behind us. Two elder sons, the Hajii and I sat down. They made do with cups of **chai** (sweet tea), while I was served six fried eggs liberally sprinkled with coarse salt, fresh bread still oily and hot off the griddle, and slabs of goat cheese. As custom dictated, no utensils were offered. I ate my meal using only my right hand, the left hand being considered ritually unclean. I would tear off a piece of bread and use it to scoop up portions of the hot eggs. I was so hungry I devoured it all and could have licked the grease off the plate to fill in the corners. They next plied me with countless cups of warm, sweet chai and within an hour I could feel myself nodding off in satiated contentment.

I was shown into a *hujra* (guest room) furnished with a charpoy and told I could rest for a while. Shavon was fed. The men were going to the fields. It was quiet and we were safe thanks to the **pukhtunwali** (Pathan code of honor) and its sacred observance of **melmastia** (hospitality). I thanked my hosts and laid down on the charpoy, having no intention of going to sleep. It proved to be a brief and fruitless argument with an overly tired body.

It was many hours later before I ventured out to the courtyard. I checked Shavon. A bucket of fresh water was nearby and she stood dozing in the shade. I busied myself with brushing her, making sure I kept my back to the house so as not to see any women by mistake. Shavon was frankly annoyed at the attention but I wanted to be heard and seen. Within a few moments Hajii Shah Zaman came out of an adjacent door and walked over. He watched silently as I brushed the mare. When I had finished he asked me to follow him.

We made our way across the courtyard, climbed a wooden staircase and found ourselves on the catwalk that ringed the top of fort. We stood looking out over the tall walls rimming this defensive perimeter. They were high enough to afford protection from either sniping government

Among the Pathans

troops or revenge-minded neighbors, both a distinct possibility in Pathan country.

The view from the guard's walk was fine. From up there the sky was suddenly revealed. It was late afternoon and the sun was thinking about setting. Pearl white clouds lingered like leftover petals on a rose red plate. The air had the beginnings of an alpine feel to it. Following the old man's gaze I saw Piran and her valley spread out before us, her houses, forts and the little mosque lying below. Trees shaded the brief lane leading down from the main road. Men were walking home from their fields. A band of goats was wandering among the houses searching for scraps and mischief. Far off I could hear children playing. Heat waves rippled off the rocks that dotted the mountain side. It was a desolate if peaceful sight.

No matter where I looked the world ran away from my eyes until they met the surrounding mountains. They were evident in all directions, rising up like Allah's stony battlements to protect this high mountain valley. Looking south I could see where we had ridden down the Malakand Pass. Its crest was still defiled by a string of abandoned British forts that once housed the soldiers of a hated army of occupation.

Hajii Shah Zaman may have looked like an Old Testament prophet but he had his wits about him. He questioned me about politics and other sensitive matters he had not wished to discuss in front of the family. He used the old fashioned Raj term "down country" to describe those people and developments occurring outside Piran and sought my feelings about many things. I told him the details as I understood them, mentioning the Jihad and how it affected the NWFP. I expressed my contempt for the politicians who had turned the war effort into a race for riches.

He laughed at my political naiveté and pointing to the crest of the pass said, "We know how to handle politicians in Piran. See over there. That is where we stoned Nehru."

Back in 1946 the famous Hindu politician, Pandit Nehru, already a legend in India before World War Two, wanted the Yusufzai Pathans to join a crusade the Congress Party was waging against British occupation.

"He came here in an open car with only a driver, convinced of his own importance. We listened for a few minutes before the crowd turned hostile, driving him off, wounded and humiliated. As much as we hated the British, we hated the Hindus more. And Nehru was never anything but a Hindu politician. He cared nothing for the Pathans and betrayed their needs," the old man said.

Ironically, when Britain was battling for its life during World War Two, Nehru boycotted that war effort. Though three million Indians eventually joined the English military machine, Muslims made up 65 percent of the largest volunteer army in the world's history.

Pandit Nehru went on to become the first prime minister of India. His descendants, including his daughter Indian Prime Minister Indira Gandhi, still had a choke-hold on the ruling Congress political party of that country. But Nehru was lucky to have escaped from the tiny village of Piran with his life.

This was bloody ground we looked upon. The British had fought their way up the Malakand Pass in 1885. I had ridden by the fort they erected on that crest after great loss. Queen Victoria's soldiers died in droves so that she might rule that rocky promontory and open the road I was following to Chitral in the north. Their sacrifice added another chunk to an empire five times as large as that of the Romans.

While the Raj immediately set about erecting a series of permanent forts stretching north from Malakand to Chitral, British political agents assured the Pathan natives the soldiers were only there temporarily. Local protests against the perfidy of Albion were dismissed out of hand. "Where there is not faith, there can be no breach of faith," one imperialist wrote.

But immediate conquest did not bring with it any long term guarantees of safety. The British officers, along with their Gurkha and Sikh mercenaries, were practically prisoners. They stayed locked inside their massive bunker at the top of the pass or in a series of high, inaccessible stone stockades running along the nearby mountain tops.

Entrance to these lofty towers could only be gained by raising and lowering a ladder. To gain admission, friends and foes alike had to climb up through a trap door in the stockade floor under the watchful gaze of many Enfield rifles. From their aeries the soldiers could train their rifles on Piran and the valley. Though they technically ruled the village, the conquerors exercised great caution. They had every reason to remain vigilant. Hajii Shah Zaman's father and friends were waiting patiently outside for an opportunity to slaughter them.

Even this uneasy armistice dissolved in the summer of 1897. A local religious leader called upon the Pathans to close the Chitral road and throw out the invaders.

War was imminent when a young Winston Churchill arrived in the area like a bird of ill-omen. Hajii Shah Zaman was kind enough not to mention that Churchill had also come to Piran on horseback, as a journalist writing for the London Daily Telegraph.

Unable to secure a posting in the invading army, but anxious to make a name for himself, the young subaltern had taken six weeks' leave from his Indian cavalry unit. His wealthy American mother had used her influence in London to secure Winston the posting as a highbrow war correspondent. The man who would later fight Hitler attached himself like a limpet to the commanding general and rode with the conquering army through Malakand and Piran, determined if not to make history, at least to record it.

Looking over the walls at this peaceful countryside it was hard to reconcile this place and these people with what Churchill had written about them. For while he gained no decorations for bravery during his journey among the Pathans, Winston made a critically important discovery. He could draw vast amounts of public attention to himself by filling the role of articulate imperialist intellectual. Convinced of the innate

Among the Pathans

superiority of the Anglo-Saxon, and their consequent right to rule as much of the world as they could grab, this clever propagandist for empire didn't have to wait long for a story.

Hajii Shah Zaman called the resulting conflict "The Pathan War of Independence." Churchill labeled it "The Pathan Revolt."

In a series of news reports, young Winston started by informing the British readers that his mere presence in these parts was a miracle of survival because "no white man would live to tell the tale," if they tried to befriend the Pathans of Piran.

Churchill despised the Pathans, calling them, "Stone-age savages whose only deeds are treachery and violence." He dismissed Islam as "a miserable superstition propagated by the sword," the founding principle of which was "an incentive to slaughter." The village mosque he deemed "a consecrated hovel." He hated the Pathan lifestyle, saying they lived in "fortified slums, amid dirt and ignorance, as degraded a race as any on the fringe of humanity; fierce as the tiger, but less cleanly." Even Pathan women came in for a journalistic beating from the future prime minister. "Their wives," he wrote, "have no position but that of animals. They are too filthy to handle and too noisome to approach."

Though critical of the Pathans, Churchill was quick to reassure the British public that the Gurkha mercenaries from Nepal recruited to suppress the rebellion were one of the Empire's best "subject races." In fact he described them in glowing terms saying they found more favor with British officers "than any other breed of nigger."

Young Winston believed war with the native populace of Piran was inevitable for several reasons. First, the Anglo-Indians who ruled the subcontinent believed they needed to control the extreme edges of their bastion of power in order to thwart their rival for conquest, the ever-expanding Eurasian empire of the Russian Czars.

In addition, the British made poor neighbors. They used any challenge or excuse to gobble up dozens of weaker kingdoms. Any sense of collective English guilt was dismissed by Queen Victoria who assured her eager overseas landlords the British race were not merely conquering the natives, they were bringing these backward and ungrateful people out of medieval darkness into the light of progress. Besides, she rationalized, it made no sense to go to war with the Pathans and then not rule their country. "Giving up what one has is a bad thing," she informed her ministers, sealing the fate of Piran and the Pathans.

Finally, Churchill wrote to his London readers that the British were forced to go to war with the Pathans because the 10,000 local patriots who had risen in defense of their "pestilential land" were "ignorant, depraved, squalid, athletic savages," who could not be negotiated with. "Extermination of the inhabitants," was a necessity because only by the use of brute military force would the Pathans realize, "the futility of resistance," against "the perpetual inheritance of our (English) race."

Churchill, the young paladin of imperial conquest, summed up his feelings for all things Pathan when he wrote, "Their name alone was an affliction. Truth is unknown among them." It mirrored his own beliefs and not my findings. His articles were unjust, his accusations slanderous, his racism poisonous, his one-sided legacy of greatness unsullied by his forgotten exploits in those rocky mountains.

Regardless, thousands of Pathans were killed, their bid for freedom suppressed in a colonial war exemplified by its resolution and ruthlessness. The mullah who lead the rebellion died. The revolt subsided. Antagonism remained. Young Winston and his ilk had colored the life of my host, old Hajii Shah Zaman, forever.

"I was a young man before I ever left Piran and went to Peshawar," the Hajii told me.

"My father was contemptuous of the Pathans who lived there. He warned me, saying, 'The English have turned them into women. They ride the train to Attock. It's only fifty miles but they've grown too weak to walk there from Peshawar.'

He paused as if remembering something. I watched as his eyes looked back on a world I had only read about. Peshawar in those days was even more dangerous for a European than now. Muslim conversions, the key to acceptance in that part of the world, were unknown. All *ferenghi* (foreigners) were considered contemptuous **Nazarenes** (Christians) and therefore not only suspect but ripe for the killing. The British maintained separate living quarters well outside the city walls in the "Cantonment." This military safety zone lay close to the gigantic fort overlooking the cities walls. Besides the train depot, the Cantonment housed numerous rambling bungalows complete with large gardens and well-kept lawns. Nearby, in what was termed "The New City," English businesses catered to foreign needs. The two races stayed apart, living under an uneasy truce. An English author of the time described Peshawar's Pathans as, "vicious, murderous fanatics."

There was evidence to support this contention. Soldiers patrolling the streets carried their Lee Enfield rifles chained to their belts in order to deter theft. There were several cases of Pathan servants going **ghazi** (insane) and suddenly killing their British employers, people who had often trusted and retained them for years. Some tiny factor turned the Pathans murderous, like enraged bull elephants suddenly gone insane with musth (rut). The situation degenerated into racial warfare disguised as political objectives.

In the spring of 1930 a British commissioner, Mr. Moxon, was holding open court when a young Pathan approached him

The commissioner asked him to state his complaint.

"That Pathan pulled out a knife and said, 'Here is my complaint.' And then began to stab him oh so many times like this, 'Yah, yah,'" Hajii Shah Zaman said, slashing the air with his fist.

An armed patrol came running but it was too late. The youthful commissioner lay dead.

"When he saw them running to arrest him, that Pathan shouted, 'Why are you running you fools? I am not fleeing from you. I am proud to have killed the *harami* (bastard).'"

Among the Pathans

The authorities hanged the assassin and then cremated his body, a grave insult designed to prohibit the family from providing a Muslim burial.

"When I arrived in Peshawar a week later the city was in an undeclared war against the British on all sides," Hajii Shah Zaman said. "A few days after I got there an open car drove through Qissa Khani bazaar. An Englishman was standing up in the back of the car. He was shouting, 'Free, free,' and throwing out packets of black tea to the people. The ferenghis had already encouraged the use of opium and now the mullahs told us that this was a new drug designed to keep us slaves to the English. The same Englishman put up signs around the city showing the people how to brew tea. Many people said to me, 'We will never go to this poison.'"

The fear of Anglicization and assimilation were everywhere.

"In those days no one wore trousers or tie. If you did people would beat you and say, 'Don't wear clothes of the *Angrez* (English). Don't go to their schools. It is home to their ideas.' There were two types of haircuts then, English or Pathan. We shaved our heads. If you had any hair they would say, 'Oh, you have hair like an Angrez. On Judgment Day you will be standing in line with them to enter Hell.'"

"After the commissioner was killed martial law was declared for three months. We were only allowed out of our houses for a few hours every day. People even had to lower the dead over the city walls at night. It was very terrible," he said in a soft voice.

Things snapped on April 23, 1930.

"A big crowd had gathered, hundreds of men shoving their way into Chowk Yadgar. I went marching with them towards Qissa Khani bazaar. We were all shouting, '*Todi batcha hai hai.*' That meant, 'You son of the British we pray you die.' When we got to the middle of Qissa Khani, a British officer met us with a company of Gurkha troops. He ordered us to go home. But we shouted for him to go home to England instead, that this was our city not his. Some men began to throw paving stones and the British officer told the Gurkha sergeant to order his men to fire. That Gurkha refused to fire on unarmed civilians. So the British officer told the Gurkhas to fall back. We were overjoyed. They later shot that Gurkha sergeant for insubordination," the Hajii told me.

Their joy was short lived. Within a few minutes two armored cars were brought up to contain the exuberant crowd.

"We were still shouting. Some people began to throw empty bottles and stones. That is when they opened fire. 'Ta, ta, ta,' is what the machine guns sounded like as they cut us down like wheat."

Hysteria gripped the crowd. The wounded were trampled. More than 100 men and boys were shot and slain. Peshawar's streets were once again decorated with blood. I didn't mention there was a small plaque on the spot commemorating the massacre. No one much notices it nowadays. We had a new war to worry about.

"I used to hate the British. My father and his friends had killed oh so many of them hereabouts. Father told me once we were free of the

Angrez we would rule ourselves and solve our problems. After what I saw in Qissa Khani I believed him of course," he said.

"Of course," I agreed.

He talked on, this old man who had seen more sunrises than I most likely ever will. He spoke in bitter terms of the disappointments that followed freedom and the failed dreams of so many Pakistanis. He recalled the heady day of liberation in August 1947, when the British left forever and the **Quaid-i-Azam** (Pakistan's founder Muhammad Ali Jinnah) briefly ruled the land with the wisdom of King Solomon.

Jinnah believed the only way to preserve Indian Muslims from complete economic and cultural subordination to the majority Hindu population was to create a separate Muslim state. He envisioned the new country as a utopia for Muslims, a place that would combine the principles of Islam with the benefits of socialism. The astute lawyer believed that a combination of the profound simplicity and piety of Islam with democratic values would bring about a Muslim homeland where there would be no exploitation of the poor and down trodden. Pakistan, in Jinnah's view, would be free from the ills of both feudalism and capitalism. After decades of struggle, his courage and implacable determination triumphed in 1947 at Pakistan's inception. The Quaid-i-Azam died soon after, thinking the country he had sacrificed to see born was free from the evils of feudal landlords, heartless capitalists, foreign overseers and local military dictators.

Yet that is precisely what had happened to Hajii Shah Zaman's homeland and Mr. Jinnah's dream.

Perhaps in His wisdom Allah had taken the Quaid-i-Azam before he lived long enough to see his dream degenerate into a paradise, not for the Muslim people, but the very forces he had spent his life combating. Jinnah succumbed to tuberculosis thirteen months after the founding of the country. Since then Pakistan had succumbed to civil war, sectarian strife and martial law in less than five decades. She had fought two wars with India, lost both, surrendering 93,000 officers and men in the last conflict. The current ruler, General Muhammad Zia-ul-Haq, Pakistan's Napoleon Bonaparte, had ruthlessly repudiated everything the Quaid-i-Azam had fought for. Zia had ruled the country since 1977 when he came to power in a military coup. He made no pretense at harboring the democratic ideals Jinnah had sacrificed his life for. A fascist masquerading as a Muslim, Zia proudly bore the title "Chief Martial Law Administrator." The diminutive general had banned all political activity, executed the former prime minister, imprisoned thousands of political rivals, censored all newspapers and imposed harsh "Islamic" punishments on his disheartened countrymen.

General Zia had also cleverly used the ongoing Afghan conflict to paint himself as the defender of the country in troubled times. Rampant spending had thrust his once sovereign nation critically in debt to overseas bankers. Record sums were spent to purchase F-16 jets, M-48 tanks, Harpoon naval missiles, as well as the development of a nuclear bomb. As the military grew, fundamental rights evaporated. Criticizing the brutal martial law regime was not just unpatriotic, it was deadly.

The Soviet invasion of Afghanistan had brought American influence in Pakistan to such a record level that the ambassador of that country was widely viewed as the unacknowledged viceroy of a new Raj. Victoria's England had been replaced by Reagan's America. Soviet tanks and American dollars now kept dictators on both sides of the Khyber Pass in power. Pakistan, the world's largest Islamic democracy, had been down graded from Muslim utopia to capitalism's hand-maiden. Her degraded role under General Zia was to carry out instructions from Washington DC. The vision of Mr. Jinnah had been slain on the altar of the army's interests. Public faith in the integrity and honesty of this hard-won government had evaporated, replaced by apathy and bitter disappointment.

"*Ya Allah* (oh God), my heart died with Mr. Jinnah. We have had only liars and thieves since his death in 1948. Too many soldiers have ruled us since then, saying it was for our own good. What a lie! Did we die in these hills fighting the English so that we could be ruled by rascals hiding inside a Pakistani army uniform? Now young men come here from down country with a new lie, saying they want to put Islam in our government. I know they are lying like Nehru. They don't want Islam. They want Islamabad (national capital)."

He looked disappointed, an old man suddenly bent by the years and the weight of knowing he would never live to see his country completely free. He turned and looked to the north, the direction I was soon to be heading, and pointed.

"In 1936 the British army pushed through here with an armored column. They even had planes fly over our heads. But soon after that they built a great irrigation tunnel through these mountains that brings water down to the plains. We are still using it. But after forty years our own government has never even built the Lowari tunnel which would allow our people to travel through the mountains during the winter. Instead they leave poor Chitral trapped for seven months of the year."

I didn't say anything, wondering if he knew the country was in trouble on so many levels. The country's 21% literacy rate was inflated to include those villagers who could barely scrawl their names. Many argued that despite the arrogance and exploitation, the British had also left a legacy that helped shape Pakistan's legal, political, educational and civil systems, as well as provide a model for their armed forces.

"Yes, I used to hate the British, " he said and looked back towards the Malakand Pass with it's abandoned stone stockades outlining the skyline, raping the horizon like the finger bones of long dead imperialists.

"Now I think they weren't all so bad. Many were honest men who served their government well. They brought us many blessings, though in those days we Pathans would have swallowed poison before we admitted it."

A look of cynicism played across his face.

Khyber Knights

"What ever became of that dream called Pakistan, the Land of the Pure? So many died that day in Qissa Khani so we could live free. We have taken their legacy and thrown it away on the wind. I no longer know what to think. My father taught me how to fight the British, not my own people," he said bitterly.

We stood there for a long time. The sun soon died altogether, taking with it the youthful dreams of old Hajii Shah Zaman.

4
Mode of Transportation - Horse

By noon of the next day we had reached the bridge at Chakdara.

Shavon and I were both well fed and rested after enjoying the hospitality of the gracious Pathans of Piran. The land had become cooler and greener as we continued north. We had not lingered at any of the numerous villages that dotted our route, pushing on instead to this historic and militarily important border fortress.

The two lane bridge spanning the Swat river marked an important crossing for us. Behind lay any reference to Peshawar and what I knew. Waiting ahead lay immense mountains that sliced across this land like a stony tidal wave. We would have to swim through those rocky currents on thin trails and treacherous passes, living off the land until we located the Turkomans in Chitral.

As I approached the bridge I saw a large hill facing me from across the broad river. At the hill's base sat the main fort, now conscripted into the Pakistani defense effort. Higher up I could make out a smaller, older outpost. Both had been manned in the war of 1897 by a force of 1,000 British officers and native soldiers. They withstood a siege by a vastly superior force of Pathans, repelling waves of attackers during 96 hours of continuous fighting.

Two vastly different accounts were recorded of the deeds that occurred there.

Rudyard Kipling, the laureate of British empire, had chosen to record the noble actions of the Indian water carrier Gunga Din. The diminutive man died caring for thirsty soldiers loyal to Queen Victoria, hauling water up that hill under the gun sights of the furious Pathan tribesmen. Kipling immortalized the individual courage of the low caste noncombatant who sacrificed his life serving a foreign monarch. Ironically all trace of Gunga Din and the other natives who had fought on both sides here were now forgotten and erased. Etched on the mountainside in large white letters were stones spelling out the name "Churchill."

The irony of this decision was not lost on me.

Upon his return to England, Winston Churchill had used his newspaper accounts as the basis of his first book. Now largely forgotten, "The Story of the Malakand Field Force" read like a "Mein Kampf" of British imperialism. It depicted a distorted version of events, comparable to General Custer's account of the Battle of the Little Big Horn.

Winston viewed the British as heirs to the Roman empire he so admired, clearly viewing anyone who resisted the British encroachment as barbarians.

He used words like "plucky, dashing, courageous, gallant, charming, brave, and zealous," to describe the handful of British officers who held

Khyber Knights

the forts at Chakdara until reinforcements could arrive. The overwhelming Pathan forces arrayed against them were collectively referred to as "mad dogs, superstitious, fanatics, and depraved savages."

I brought Shavon to a halt and looked at the forts across the river.

Considering the fact that the British were outnumbered ten to one, it would appear as if Churchill could be forgiven for crowing about the brave deeds of a handful of defenders. What he underplayed was the fact that few of the natives even had guns. They attacked the forts with "bold sword charges", stones, burning straw, and even their bare hands.

Waiting above them on the heights were native mercenaries, "trusting the young white men who lead them," and more importantly armed with Lee Enfield rifles firing "Dum-dum" bullets. Recently invented by the British in India, the ammunition was so devastating many European nations had urged its total ban from the field of war. Churchill, however, lauded its effects.

"It is a beautiful machine, causing wounds in the body which must generally be mortal or force the amputation of any limb," he wrote.

Rounding out the defense of Chakdara was a Maxim machine gun.

"The terrible weapon stopped every rush. Nothing could live in front of such a fire," Churchill wrote. Yet the Pathans charged into the mouths of the guns repeatedly, causing "losses that were enormous."

The British butcher's bill was paid by buckets of Pathan blood.

"All were swept away, not once, but twelve times in six hours."

When reinforcements finally arrived, the defenders had fired off more than 22,000 bullets but lost only 20 men. Animated by a longing for liberty and bound by the principles of freedom, 2,000 Pathans lay dead on the ground outside the fort.

The legendary Bengal Lancers who helped rescue their fellow soldiers in the fort then started slaughtering any native survivors unlucky enough not to have escaped the initial carnage.

"No quarter was asked or given. Every tribesman caught was cut down at once. Their bodies, speared in every direction, lay thickly strewn about the fields as a terrible lesson," Churchill gloated.

He bragged to his London readers how he had laid aside his pen, taken up a gun and helped the troops "because we do not hesitate to finish their wounded off."

Once Chakdara fort was relieved, the British forces spread out and began destroying adjacent villages. In Batkhela, the first hamlet I rode through that morning, eighty civilians were bayoneted. All this bloodshed had been necessary because Churchill wrote, "that such an outrage as the deliberate violation of British territory by these savages should remain unpunished was of course impossible."

In the end Churchill reported to his readers that he and his fellow officers had rewarded their martial efforts with vermouth, cigarettes and pleasant conversation. He and his clique unknowingly stood at the apex of their empire, intoxicated with the pride of race, an exclusive people whose interpretation of God was so narrow they proudly boasted that

"God is an Englishman." Upon asking a native the name of one of the nearby destroyed villages, Churchill boasted, "One unpronounceable name is as good as another and the village will go down in official history christened at the caprice of a peasant."

The future prime minister and his brother officers were content to justify their campaign of terror by believing Islam must be a barbaric religion because it was connected to a subject population. By first degrading the religion it was an easy step to believing that Muslim Pathans were a lesser breed of human being, ones devoid of the same kind of feelings as Christians. Hence any Muslim religious beliefs could be despised without guilt or moral consequences. It was hard for such racially arrogant men to believe that the Pathans who fought and died at Chakdara could possess anything of value, even spiritually, when they were so materially backward. Churchill thus avoided his own soul. Back home in England he discovered it was easier to evade the sight of the London slums by turning his attention to the sorrows of a distant country.

As I sat there looking on this scene of former carnage I realized time had tamed the Pathans like Churchill never could. Hajii Shah Zaman's father, and the men who had charged the Maxim machine gun with bare hands, belonged to a fiercer, more violent age.

No one in Pakistan now recalled Churchill's poisonous account of events or his contempt for the native patriots who died trying to liberate the fort. No one in Piran had read the racial and religious slurs thrown on her people. No one in Chakdara recalled the arrogant and bigoted nature of this man. Like infants or idiots, the grandsons of those blood-thirsty freedom fighters had innocently commemorated the very man who epitomized everything their forefathers had fought against.

Churchill must have known I would sit my horse one day and stare at this scene of his first triumph. He closed his book by reminding his readers that, "In some future age unborn arbiters will judge our efforts." Those witnesses would discover the British had proved that "rationalism and machine guns" had finally taught the Pathans "the happiness, learning and liberties of mankind," while proving that "the higher destines of the English race had been achieved."

Heading Shavon towards the bridge I pondered how out of harmony the Englishman's name was. The gaudy white letters lay splashed across the mountain like a nostalgic spiritual pollution. To delegate a memorial, however humble to a man who so vehemently scorned your people was like stumbling onto a monument in America dedicated to Charles Cornwallis, the British general who fought to destroy the United States in its infancy. In America they honored George Washington the hero of the Revolutionary War for Independence. In Chakdara they erected a marker in naive innocence to a man who symbolized English oppression.

Once across the bridge I was required to sign a register maintained by the army which charts the comings and goings of any foreigners venturing further north. Under the heading "Mode of transportation," I wrote, "Horse."

Khyber Knights

The irony was not lost on me that riding on horseback, once so much a part of the Indian sub-continent, had even here become a thing of the past. India under the British Raj had often been called "The Kingdom of the Horse." Equines not only helped the British hold onto their conquests, they helped them enjoy them. English soldiers mastered polo soon after seeing it played in the northern city of Gilgit, then promptly exported it home to Britain. The exclusive Peshawar Vale Club maintained a fox hunt, complete with imported hounds, until after Pakistani independence in 1947. Cross-country racing, pig sticking and other equestrian events were once immensely popular forms of recreation.

Sadly, the horse had faded from view in most of Pakistan. Thoroughbred racing was a thing of the past, outlawed by the current military dictator. A few army and police officers maintained polo ponies. However, the majority of the country's horses had now descended into the humble ranks of either tonga or cart horses. These hard working and often mistreated animals showed the long-term damages inflicted by a reliance on isolated local blood lines. Most Pakistani horses are descended from either a local Indian breed or horses imported from Australia.

The Indian Kathiawari descended from tough native ponies crossed with Arab horses that swam ashore from a cargo ship wrecked off the west coast of India. The Arab influence improved the appearance, without detracting from the ponies hardiness.

Australia's donation to Pakistan's equestrian culture was the "Walers." These tall thoroughbreds were imported to India by the Raj army in the 19th century from the colony of New South Wales, Australia. Through the years many of the once fine features of both breeds had degenerated, until today most of the best horses in Pakistan are tall, long legged animals with extremely high withers and narrow pinched chests. Their most amazing feature is that the tips of their ears often curl over and touch each other. This exaggerated deformity, inherited from their Kathiawar forefathers, has assumed a level of outlandish regional importance based on superstition and groundless fashion.

Shavon had none of these faults. She was, in fact, by local standards a miracle.

I had searched through Peshawar for weeks for a suitable mount. Teamsters had brought me cart horses so crippled it would have been a mercy if I had shot them on the spot. I saw tonga horses, thin and dejected, who wore the signs of their master's vanity all over their hides, victims of a common practice on the Indian sub-continent to slice off thin layers of the horses skin, leaving scabs and scars in geometric patterns. I saw giant sun bursts spreading pain across horses' haunches. I saw zigzag scars encircling enflamed legs. I saw scars shaped like star bursts deforming weeping eyes. I saw a horse with knees swollen as big as cantaloupes hopping in agony as he pulled a wagon load of bricks. I saw a horse lying dead in it's traces, free at last of the bully who stood over him in death still beating him with a cudgel. I saw things no horseman should ever see or will ever forget. I saw pain and suffering

Mode of Transportation - Horse

and hopelessness and hunger and Hell on Earth for horses there in the streets of Peshawar.

Though the Prophet Mohammad (**PBUH**) had warned Muslims never to abide cruelty to animals, Asia is often a heartless place for horses who are often viewed merely as breathing commodities placed on this planet to be used by men, however cruel. I had chosen to live there. Yet nothing separated me from the local population, not language, not religion, not food or water or sun or moon, like the difference of opinion we had regarding the treatment of horses.

There were unconfirmed rumors that the Pakistani army had beautiful horses secreted away somewhere in the **Punjab** province, but I had never been able to confirm that information. So, I was skeptical but intrigued when a shopkeeper friend of mine said he knew a man who had a beautiful horse. I was running out of time and places to look in Peshawar, so agreed to come back the next day.

Thank God I did.

Shavon stood there like a beam of bright yellow sunlight that had solidified on a cloudless day. Her thick flaxen tail looked like a bridal veil. She had strong, straight legs that could make a horseman cry at the sight of their perfection. Her back was strong, her chest broad, her shoulders sloped with the grace of a poem. Amazingly enough the closest thing she resembled was a full-blooded American quarter horse, all muscle and width and perfection. She was magnificent and her owner hated her.

"She is Jew yellow," Razzaq, the mare's owner told me, as if to test my knowledge of local matters.

"I can see that," I told him. I stayed seated in the shop, drinking my tea, studying the horse from a distance, keeping any trace of my excitement well hidden. I had played horse poker often enough to know not to reveal any signs of premature interest.

"But she is still young and very strong," he added, alarmed at my recognition of the disparaging equestrian term he had mentioned.

Though horses were slowly being replaced by engines even there in Pakistan, the traditions of Islam still largely dictated local concepts of what made a suitable mount. The Prophet Muhammad (PBUH) had taught the first Muslims the critical importance of horses. Anyone in Peshawar could have recited the ayat (verse in the **Qu'ran**) that expounded on the grace and beauty of the horse Allah created for mankind as a sign of his love.

"I will make you from the wind. You shall fly without wings and be preferred above all the other animals and all the blessings of the world shall rest between your eyes," the Almighty had said of the first horse.

During the early days of Islam when religious strife threatened to destroy the ancient world, the horse was viewed as a valuable weapon of war, a secret of state to be kept out of the hands of the theological enemy at all costs.

Early Muslim rulers kept in mind the Qu'ranic injunction to "Put none on his back but men who know and adore Me."

The chieftains used this as a precedent for prohibiting in God's name, under penalty of sin and damnation, the sale of horses to anyone but Muslims. Men were often put to death for selling horses to unapproved buyers. Many Muslim countries made it illegal for Jews or Christians even to ride horses, reserving for their use only ignoble mules and donkeys. The only equine exception to this hard and fast rule was the palomino horse. Most horsemen believed the color of a horse's coat was the quickest indication of its good qualities. The bay was considered the hardiest, the chestnut the swiftest, and the black brought good luck.

Conversely the palomino was thought to be the mount of misfortune.

"That color brings on calamity," they used to say.

Only the pinto was considered more ignoble.

"Fly from the spotted horse like the plague. He is the brother of the cow," ran an ancient Arab axiom.

These folk tales regarding lucky and unlucky colors kept traveling long after the last Crusader died. Muslim invaders left these myths behind in Spain. Cortez and his conquistadors carried them like an unseen pest to Mexico. Hundreds of years later the vaqueros rode north and whispered the same prejudices to the cowboy, who repeated it as gospel to Yankee greenhorns well into the late 19th century.

None of these latter-day horsemen knew the oft-repeated ancestral prejudices swirling around equine colors originated as a Muslim invention. They simply repeated the dogma that said bays worked harder, chestnuts ran faster, palominos brought bad luck and white horses were better swimmers. It was just more proof that there was no isolation of ideas or myths in the world of the horseman.

Lucky for me I had grown up with Roy Rogers and Paladin. At the age of six, Trigger had always looked just fine to me as I sat glued in front of a black and white television set. So I paid too much for Shavon without hesitation, this mount of misfortune who was now carrying me so steadfastly. Shavon was seven when I discovered her pulling a wagon load of vegetables for a living. That didn't seem fair. She was kind, steady, dependable and vigilant. I had been around a host of horses and seldom felt so good about one. In the United States she would have been a jewel. Here she was just a bane of bad luck.

Night found us in a nameless village, a bucket of blood hole inhabited by villagers so grimy it looked like they slept with their sheep during the winter. What passed for gutters were filled with offal. A pack of barefoot urchins, most half naked, sported a host of runny noses. The local chaikhana was too dirty to be burned. Even at a distance it reeked of sweat, bedbugs and vermin. A group of seedy characters were gathered inside nevertheless. They looked like they would slit a priest's throat on Palm Sunday for a penny. A cringing blob of a man wrapped in grease-ridden rags not fit to be called clothes came out and offered us the hospitality of this road house.

I sat my horse, looked at my potential roommates and then hawked and spat.

"Bring me a charpoy. Put it next to this horse. I sleep outside tonight."

Khyber Knights

"I saw tonga horses, thin and dejected, who wore the signs of their master's vanity all over their hides. I observed a horse with knees swollen as big as cantaloupes hopping in agony as he pulled a wagon load of bricks. I saw a horse lying dead in it's traces, free at last of the bully who stood over him in death still beating him with a cudgel. I saw things no horseman should ever see or will ever forget. I saw pain and suffering and hopelessness and hunger and Hell on Earth for horses there in the streets of Peshawar."

Mode of Transportation - Horse

When I climbed down I was stiff from so many miles. I was sure even the water hereabouts must be filthy. However I managed to find enough to wash the dust of the road off my face and hands.

A journey that fatigues you also teaches you many things. Water is sweeter than wine. Food, however meager, tastes delicious. The coolness of a shadow is a blessing after the heat of the sun. The pleasures of a deep sleep are almost as satisfying as a sexual encounter.

Despite this pilgrim philosophy Shavon and I suffered.

They brought her two arm-loads of bhang (marijuana) for dinner and tried to feed me a bowl of swill so foul even I couldn't choke it down. We refused both, slept with one eye opened and pushed on before the sun did.

When we entered Dir several days later, I found the town squatting on the road like a malignant toad. I couldn't go around. The trail to the Lowari Pass lay a few miles further on. You had to ride through if you wanted to reach the promises that lay up ahead.

Shavon had brought me past the last of the foothills on our way up here. This was already beautiful mountain country with cedar trees, delicious air and a slower pace. Dir should have been an alpine paradise. Instead the small capital felt mean and hostile, a sad, furtive little principality fallen on hard times.

The beauties of the mountains fell mute when we came riding down the main street. It was like riding into Tombstone. The place had that feeling of sullen anticipation. Hard eyed Kohistanis stared suspiciously. There was no sign of police protection. You knew you weren't wanted, just tolerated. One false move and you became another statistic.

The mountains themselves seemed to want to reach down and smother this vile manmade intrusion. They rose straight up on either side, forming a narrow chute with the town in it's center. A noisy river ran close by, its roar a constant grind in the back of your ears.

The traveler had two choices of accommodation, an old hotel in town or the Nawab's guest house hidden further up in the mountains. I chose the former, tied Shavon and went looking for food and supplies.

A single main street, stretching several hundred feet, boasted a few small shops selling the usual stock of soap, combs, paper, kerosene, dried fruit, cheap pens and naswar. The shopkeepers seemed indifferent to my purchases, acting as if they wanted me to keep my money and ride on.

A few days prior to my arrival the town's school teacher had failed a student. The brat's father had promptly murdered the teacher for shaming the family. No one had been arrested. The town's sense of moral decay was palpable.

Though I had long grown used to seeing all types of guns being carried in Pakistan, the men in Dir gripped their weapons like they had every intention of using them. This wasn't the attitude down country where Pathans carried guns like over-sized jewelry. As I strode the streets of Dir I saw 14-year-old pimply faced boys sporting the latest **AK-**

Khyber Knights

47 machine guns. I counted more guns in one block than I had seen since I left Peshawar.

The place was tense. I wasn't sure if it was only because of the recent homicide. For the first time I wished I had ignored Pirgumber's advice. He had assured me the Turkoman mujahadeen would arm me in Chitral. Yet I now suspected I should have at least bought a pistol before leaving Peshawar.

The men in these streets lived hard and bitter lives in nearby fortified villages. Savage blood feuds killed many before they were forty. They called themselves Pathans but their history contradicted this. Only in this part of the frontier could you find petty kings ruling over men who claimed to be freedom-loving patriots. Even the suggestion of such sturdy individuals swearing allegiance to a tyrant would have brought on a detestable curse in any other part of **Pukhtunistan**.

The **Nawab** (king) of Dir had been forcibly removed from office in 1972 when the prime minister of Pakistan had deposed the former princely rulers of numerous small states. Nearby Swat had lost it's Wali, Chitral her Mehtar, Hunza her Mir and Dir her Nawab. All of the positions were hereditary and initially depended on keeping the local English political agent happy. Except for political allegiance to London, there had been few restrictions placed on these petty Oriental despots. The people lived or died at their pleasure. None suffered a worse reputation than the Nawab of Dir. The only hospital in town had been maintained for the convenience of his beloved pet dogs. Dir's citizens were forbidden to wear certain color clothes, own guns or build two-story houses lest they peek inside his walled fortress.

Yet when a Pakistani army helicopter flew in and swooped the Nawab up in an unannounced commando raid, many locals, consumed with grief, committed suicide by throwing themselves into the river.

I bought a few things and loaded the saddlebags that night. Early the next morning I rode out of the festering sore of a town, bound for the Lowari Pass.

A few miles later the asphalt faded in the bright sunlight, leaving me to ride on a smooth, wide dirt road. It seemed refreshingly honest compared to Dir and her tattered remnants of civilization. The mountains seemed to forgive me for my choice of lodging, throwing out their arms in welcome, revealing an unsuspected breadth and beauty never hinted at in the town below. Large well-built log houses lay resting like doves on the mountain side, their cedar logs shining in the clean sun. The air itself was glad to be alive, full of the fragrance of pine and freedom. Though the trail led ever upward, it was a gradual ascent that posed no great obstacle to the sturdy palomino mare.

After many hours of climbing it was totally quiet. No bird song swayed the silent forest. Only the gentle click-clack of Shavon's hooves on the stony road broke the air. The houses had thinned and I thought any trace of humanity lay far behind us. I was surprised to turn a corner and discover the village of Lowari. It was so near the mountain's crest, I could make out the top from where I sat on my horse. Small sturdy log houses

Mode of Transportation - Horse

sat on both sides of the road. I saw no one about and rode on. I could not help but wonder what manner of people could survive in so frigid and inhospitable a place. Though trees grew around it and the sun poured down, the wind must have relished the chance to try and blow these puny invaders off the mountain during the forbidding winters that ruled this land.

As if to justify my amazement, a mile or so further on I came across men from the village. They were perched on top of a glacier whose glistening walls lay pierced by the road like an arrow. My course lay along a graveled thread running between matching twin slabs rising thirty feet high. A small Toyota pickup was parked at the base of this dividing line of living ice. The driver waited patiently inside while the men of Lowari chopped off huge chunks of ice, skidding them to the truck below. The ice would be delivered to the still blistering city of Peshawar. The Lowari men were selling their only natural resource, hacking away vigorously with old axes, all the while standing and working on the ice barefoot.

Just shy of the crest a wide alpine pasture lay covered in delicate blue flowers. After seven hours in the saddle I dismounted, letting Shavon graze and rest, then we pushed on to what I could clearly see was the Lowari Top, as it is called thereabouts. A small stone guard hut stood on this side of the crest. Four armed Kohistanis came out to investigate my passage, took one look at my turban and went back inside, fleeing before the cold that permanently resides there. With anticipating heart Shavon took me on to the top.

We stood 10,528 feet above sea level, two wingless eagles looking at all the world below us. I, who have seen many things and many mountains, was taken aback by the grandeur and majestic sweep of what lay revealed before me. At that moment my eyes told me what my heart already knew, here was a new country the likes of which I had never envisioned.

The wind was howling up there, sweeping away all my human cobwebs, a fierce and unbridled beast determined to blow us off this secret place he protected. Mountains lay before me, deep with distance, a sea of unbroken waves. Far ahead I caught a glimpse of Tirich Mir, the highest peak in the bastion of the Hindu Kush mountains. To the west I could see Afghanistan, to the east lay **Yaghistan** the land of murder, behind me lay heartache, ahead lay Chitral.

I did not see just the skyline of the mountains but sensed a crest in my own life as well. Some of us are made that way, to take delight in the wilder, harder portions of the world, while the majority of our brothers prefer the softer charms of richer country fragrant with flowers and rippling brooks.

I have always had an opposite taste, thinking the dreaminess of slow rivers and drowsy hamlets drains away our courage. I prefer the hard road that leads through deep valleys and finally up onto sunlit peaks, a road that can only be reached by high endeavor, a road that demands faith in oneself if one is to reach the mountain top and not stay drifting among the luxuries of the lower levels. This was such a road, these were such gold-splashed peaks.

No man knows his time. I drank in the wind for long and silent minutes, carving that stony scene into the secret parts of my heart, knowing I might not be there again for years. Or ever. For even the fairest sights on earth will one day become as dust.

Waiting below was a mountainside utterly different than that which we had just climbed. Where as that had been gradual, this was a hair-raising apology of a track. It was barely wide enough to accommodate one vehicle and ran back and forth in zigzags so deep I could only guess at their ending. Deodars and pines clothed the steep slopes. The road lay daring so on we went.

Down and down we dropped. Here on this hidden slope the mountain was pitiless and untamed. Treacherous potential landslides hovered above us. Chasms were revealed. We came to understand that nothing we had seen matched the hard impersonal cruelty of these dangerous mountains. I sat my saddle, prayed to Allah and gave the mare her head, listening to the sickening sound of her hooves sliding on loose rocks. A slip here, a body out of true and death lay waiting with it's open, bottomless maw. If they thought to think us missing, I doubt they could have found us.

That night, safe on level ground, I berthed in a tent with a group of Pakistani soldiers sent to clean landslides off the mountainside. The next morning they urged me to turn back, believing in confidence that Shavon would be eaten by snow leopards if we continued. I thanked them for the advice, as well as the tea and bread breakfast, then rode on.

Days and nights and village after village passed. I grew closer to my goal of reaching Chitral and the Turkoman freedom fighters. But the weary miles had taken their toll on both the mare and me. She was thin and tired, her steel shoes worn to ribbons. I felt exhausted, longed to rest, but worried about missing the mujahadeen if I didn't press on.

Yet I had an option.

Before arriving in Chitral, I could turn off for a brief recovery in the side valleys of **Kafiristan**, riding at anchor among a group of indigenous natives who were the last living relics of a former pagan empire. Supposedly descended from soldiers left behind by Alexander the Great, these natives known as the Kalash had a poor reputation among Pakistan's Muslims. Reputed by legend to be devout pagans who worshipped idols and practiced unspeakable acts of sexual shamelessness, the Kalash were a historical enigma and a mullah's worst nightmare.

But I was not on any mercy mission. I aimed to take my horse into the wilds of Afghanistan. True the Kalash had grass, lots of it. Yet when I came to the canyon that led west, towards grass, towards rest, towards Kafiristan, I admit I hesitated, unsure about my course.

Then I remembered what a companion of the Prophet had said, "For the love of God, do not be negligent of your horse, for you will regret it in

Mode of Transportation - Horse

this life and in the next. Each grain of barley, each blade of grass you give to a horse is inscribed by God in the ledger of good works."

Shavon was my lifeline. I headed her away from my Muslim brothers in Chitral and on towards her well earned respite, pagan or not.

5
Something Wrong in Paradise

They say in Pakistan that Allah knows better about all things. Perhaps that is why before He tested us so severely He allowed Shavon and me to discover and rest in such a beautiful Arcadia.

Finding a seldom used bridge we crossed the Chitral river and made our way through a landscape barren not just of people but of any blade of grass, any shade of tree, any trace of human hospitality. We traveled like this for many miles, hugging the mountain we were rounding on our left, and staying away from the river running on our right. The bleak road was deserted except for an abundance of sunlight which burdened me with a blinding headache and threw Shavon into a black sweat.

At last we came to the small village of Ayun. This in fact was barely the beginning of our journey, for the place we sought, Kafiristan, was still many miles away, hidden deep within the mountains. We drank long and deep from a well and then began to wend our way back inside the canyon that beckoned. At this junction we left behind Pakistan and the modern world.

The valley never widened. It seemed to be a rocky definition of the word narrow, some times thin to the point of absurdity, at others broad enough to breathe comfortably. The road was a jeep track, much used, thick with dust, hot as a griddle and devoid of so much as an errant goat. The silence in this mountain valley was total. There wasn't a bird in the sky. Even the saddle had lost his voice, forgetting to creak in the scorching heat.

Several times I thought our journey was going to be blocked by landslides. The mountains were loose gray rock. Riding along I would look ahead at what appeared to be a wall of stone, only to be surprised when we reached it to discover the road curling around an invisible twist, revealing another fold lying in wait at a new angle. Though used to degraded roads in all conditions, this was the first one I had encountered which took the rider through the living stone itself. Not a tunnel per se, our route ran under rock walls that came straight up and then swooped over our heads, rolling part way down past my right shoulder like gray icing. The roof of these rock walls under which Shavon took me was not much taller than I was sitting in the saddle.

I was glad to be heading to what I hoped would be a brief rest. The last few days seemed to have taxed me more than they should have. I blamed my headache and aching bones on too much sun and too many days in the saddle.

Winding through the silent, twisting canyon gave me the opportunity to contemplate how slowly one travels on horseback. The saddle taught me that every contour on the horizon was a long time coming. There was

Khyber Knights

no element of magic involved, no boarding an air machine that flies you in comfort to another country without delay or denial. Out there you watched as a landmark hove slowly into view, and then just as slowly, fell silently behind a long, long, long time later. Shavon and I weren't just traveling through Pakistan, we were crawling over it's surface at whatever speed the golden mare could manage.

After several hours the valley suddenly opened up like a birthday surprise. The stony walls fell far back revealing a hitherto unimagined glen, broad, fertile, green and thick with aged, regal trees. It was an oasis both discovered and confined beyond desolation.

After years of persecution, the **Kalash** natives were now restricted to three valleys running parallel to each other, their four thousand strong population hidden in this geographically small location. I guided Shavon off to one side, aiming for the little village of Rambur.

As if to ease our toils, the road soon brought us under the shade of magnificent mulberry trees that were old before Columbus sailed. Our hearts started to ease. Tidy stone walls ran along the roadside, fencing in fields of waving corn. Wheat swayed golden in a wind blowing gently down off the mountain. A broad stream of rushing fresh water ran through the middle of the grassy valley. Off to the right I heard the crisp rippling of water running along a series of small irrigation channels.

Situated higher on the slopes, so as not to encroach on the cultivated land below, were many large log houses. Their flat earthen roofs served as the front porch of the neighbor's house, sitting directly above and behind them. They were grouped together like swallows nests riding up the hillside. Notched walnut logs served as crude ladders leading up and down between neighbors. Children and dogs peeked out their doors, watching in excitement as Shavon and I rode by. Kalashi men were working their fields, guiding small oxen pulling stout wooden plows. The local women were plainly visible too, something I had been warned about but was still shocked to see.

Despite my American upbringing the morals and customs of my Pakistani hosts had long since silently and slowly infiltrated my field of experience. Being a bachelor I was not allowed to converse with the wives of any of my Muslim friends in Peshawar, a social taboo of unbelievably dangerous proportions. I seldom interacted with western women. Having become a reluctant sadhu of the saddle, confining myself these last few years to a mantra of horses and adventure, I had not found much time to search for a full time female companion.

I was surprised and embarrassed then when an attractive young Kalashi woman coming directly at me on the road held up her hand and said, "Ishpata bahyah (hello friend)," in a casual but candid tone of voice. Her greeting and manner betrayed no hint of subservience, coming as easily as two chums passing on opposing escalators.

The shock must have shown on my face. I blushed and started to say, **"Assalaam alaikum** (Peace be upon you) in return, thought better of it and stammered out "Hello there" instead, the English tasting strange and foreign on my tongue. She smiled, then broke out in giggles at my

Something Wrong in Paradise

tongue-tied idiocy, pleased it seemed at being greeted in anything besides an Islamic manner.

As she came nearer I was able to get a close look at her clothing, which if anything, was even more remarkable than her forthright behavior.

She wore a one piece black dress made of home spun cloth that reached to her small brown ankles. Its long sleeves were loose and swinging free. The upper portion, serving as a billowing blouse, was lightly embroidered in yellow geometric designs around the neck. Gathered around her slim waist was a brown sash, eight inches wide, whose long ends swished freely as she walked. The dress fell beneath that sash like an obedient servant, lying in long silent black pleats awaiting their mistress' bidding.

Gathered around her neck were what looked like a hundred strands of small red and white bead necklaces. They rested on her with no apparent order, as wild as their owner.

Her thick black hair was braided into a host of glistening plaits, pulled back and reaching nearly to her sash. Gracing the top of her hair was a kopa, a flat headdress shaped like a keyhole. Its thick black material was covered with perfect rows of white cowry shells, sewn in place with red thread. It covered the top of her head like a large flat cap and then came down at the back as low as her shoulders. It framed an oval face with mischievous gray eyes. She looked nineteen. Her skin was remarkably light.

That wild creature wore no sign of any veil. No burkha had ever hidden her face from the sun. Instead silver bracelets tinkled insolently around her wrists. She walked as barefoot in the dust as Eve. She was graceful and sassy, the most untamed woman I had ever seen in my life. She didn't belong in Pakistan. She didn't even belong in the same century.

As she passed right next to me I could smell her. She carried a perfume of wood smoke and long black hair warmed by the sun, of easy days and moonlit nights, of animals and tree bark and dusky mysteries of the earth my people had long ago lost. The smell of her wafted up to me in one heartbreaking moment.. For a split second my life narrowed down into conflicting desires, to sweep her up onto the saddle and carry her away, or dismount forever to learn her secrets and her name.

She was so close I could have reached down and stroked her face with my fingertips. Instead, I tried to hide my embarrassment at the sight of this lovely Artemis by sitting up straighter in the saddle. Like a fool I kept silent and rode on.

Shavon was glad I did.

She was hungry and had no patience for beautiful women, unwashed or otherwise.

I found lodging in a small hotel-cum-chaikhana. It was owned by a Kalashi sheik, one of the many converts to Islam who were slowly swinging the cultural tide in the three valleys. Saddiq was a talkative cheerful fellow, only saddened by one misfortune in life. When I asked him the size of his family he sighed and said, "My wife is barren. I have three daughters and no children."

Knowing how highly esteemed Pakistan held her sons, Saddiq's patriarchal attitudes to his lovely daughters came as no surprise.

Before the sun set, Shavon was happy to find herself up to her belly in the pasture of succulent grass I had bought. After rolling several times, she settled down to try and eat the entire field. I left her to enjoy her well-earned reward.

Kafiristan was unlike anything I had ever encountered in Pakistan. I had read so many conflicting accounts, heard so many legends, that I had arrived prepared to be skeptical. It felt good to be wrong. It was absurdly beautiful and I was so thankful to see it. What had Marco Polo been thinking when he wrote those terrible things about this lost Eden.

While Shavon grazed I set out on foot through the gloaming in search of answers, a rare occurrence for a man who detests walking, believing anything further than the bedroll to the saddle requires a horse.

The Kalash do not fit into the puzzle of **Dardistan**. Like the Bushmen of Australia you have to travel back not just years but ages to get a hazy glimpse at their beginnings. Scholars believe the first aboriginal inhabitants of these mountains lived in isolation from the tide of warfare and civilization that was pushing into Peshawar and across the Indian subcontinent in the Bronze Age.

Sikander, known to the west as Alexander the Great, was traveling east, conquering anyone foolish enough to oppose him. After years of battle, conquest and looting, Alexander stopped his mighty army at the banks of the Indus river in the year 326 BC. His legions of soldiers were now thousands of miles from their Macedonian homeland. Weary of battle, the troops demanded Alexander lead them back to Greece. The known world lay behind Alexander, they reasoned, a vassal waiting for its master's return.

They say Sikander wanted to press on, to vanquish India, to grind China under his Grecian sandal, to stop at nothing except the sea. They say his men threatened to mutiny at the idea of crossing the Indus river and fighting on into India. They say Sikander only turned aside with reluctance. They say he never reached China because his men had grown too exhausted to continue.

I say they are wrong.

His mighty war horse, Bucephalus, friend of his youth, a kingly and constant companion through every dangerous campaign, lay dead on the banks of the Indus river, slain by some petty foot-slogger's arrow. An ignoble end for so great and glorious a comrade. The eminent equine had lead a charmed life until reaching that unimportant town lying like a horseman's curse by the mighty river. There, a thin arrow tipped with a sliver of barbed stone had slain the world's first great horse. His master's grief was mighty and he spared no one. Men, women, and children were all slaughtered to appease Sikander's grief.

He ordered the black horse buried with honors and left behind a strong garrison to defend this, the last outpost of his empire. That city he

Something Wrong in Paradise

named Bucephalus to glorify his companion of the saddle. Only then did Sikander agree to turn aside with a heavy heart, sailing down the Indus with his army, before heading back towards Babylon and his untimely death.

Lying behind in the wake of Alexander like seeds of the Grecian civilization were outposts of Greek soldiers, diplomats, colonists and merchants stretching from the Aegean Sea to the Indus river. The world changed. Alexander became a myth. Christianity arose. By 900 AD Islam was beginning to push across what is today Pakistan, rushing northward like an inexorable wave towards the descendants of Alexander's outposts. Eventually Islamic fervor met Greek resistance. Rather than submit to a foreign doctrine, some descendants, with their Greek blood and ideas, fled before the storm, leaving behind their rich settlements in the plains, seeking refuge in the high remote mountain valleys of what is today Kafiristan.

Here they encountered a primitive aboriginal people wearing goatskins, worshipping spirits, hunting with stone axes or bows and arrows. These people had been bypassed by every religious and cultural development in the last 1,000 years. Here in these hidden valleys the handful of Greeks sought refuge. They intermarried and imposed their authority on the original inhabitants, their common descendants staying hidden for nine hundred more years. Over the course of the following centuries they produced the Kafir (pagan) population with its European features consisting of light skin, blue eyes and fair hair. They gave them one more legacy, a deep and total hatred for all Muslims.

Marco Polo spoke of these people when he rode through the Pamir mountains in the late1200s on his way to China, calling their country "Balor."

"They are idolaters and utter savages living entirely by the chase and dressed in the skins of beasts," he told his European readers. But no one from that continent would see the Kafirs or learn their secrets for another six hundred long years.

By the 19th century the Kafir pagans and Muslims were waging a brutal race war against each other. The Muslims vastly outnumbered the Kafirs. Several times they tried a full scale invasion of Kafiristan, only to be repelled back from the stony heights.

The enemies of Islam waged a different type of warfare. Their success lay in their Apache-like methods. Kafir warriors would slip down from the mountains, silently surround a home and lie in wait, watching the doomed Muslim inhabitants. Their common practice was to break into the home after nightfall, killing the residents, man, woman and child. Instead of scalps they often cut off ears as grisly prizes, before retreating like ghosts back to their inaccessible mountain valleys. Both races hated and cursed the other as ruthless fiends.

At the end of the 19th century the Kafir kingdom was living on borrowed time. A loose confederation of pagan people, Kafiristan extended for hundreds of miles, a far larger area than what I was walking through that night. The remaining three little valleys were but a scrap of the once powerful pagan empire that stretched down into Afghanistan and took up part of Pakistan. The Bashgalis, or Red Kafirs, were the dominant, larger group. They numbered about 70,000 souls, residing in the upper north east portion of Afghanistan. In the area now known as Pakistan lived a smaller servile pagan tribe, the Kalash or Black Kafirs.

Partly isolated from their more powerful cousins, the black clothed Kalash had fallen under the political power of the Mehtar of Chitral in the 14th century. Legend says this occurred because of the wicked deeds of King Rajawal, the last Kalashi ruler. He slept with his daughter and enslaved other Kalashi girls, forcing them to dance before him naked. His despicable behavior brought on the curse of a powerful *dehar* (pagan priest). The wicked king died as a result of the curse. Soon after the Black Kafirs, the Kalash, became political vassals of Chitral's ruler.

This apparent misfortune was later to save them from the total extinction that was the fate of their more powerful cousins, the red clothed Bashgalis living across the mountains in Afghanistan.

By the late 1880s the powerful British Raj had pushed its way into Chitral, coming in over the mountains from Gilgit, faraway to the east. In 1889 Major George Robertson went into the mountains alone, determined to discover the truth behind the legend of Marco Polo's lost Balor.

The stage was set. The players were in position. The stubbornly independent pagan empire was about to be driven into extinction.

In his notes Robertson recorded how Kafir guides brought him to their village, which he described as , "Ultima Thule, the end of the known world."

Hidden there deep in the mountains, Robertson was surprised to discover tall, fair skinned Kafir men who resembled Europeans with "the heads of philosophers and statesmen," who spoke a language made up of elements of "Greek, Persian and Sanskrit." Though they possessed splendid courage and an overpowering love of freedom, he believed their original civilization had become, "as degraded as possible."

Robertson's greatest shock came when he learned the Kafirs looked upon him not as an enemy scout but rather as a herald of their long lost brethren, the British. The Kafirs believed the lone Englishman signaled the rejoining of different branches of the same tribe. As a white warrior like themselves, the Kafirs thought Robertson must also be an enemy of the dark skinned Muslims. The pagan people viewed Robertson's arrival as the glorious fulfillment of an ancient legacy. They believed their star had at last arisen.

Thus they held nothing back from him.

They reveled in his arrival, took him into their hearts, hid no secrets.

In confidence they showed Robertson where they buried their dead, explaining how they placed the deceased above ground in intricately carved wooden caskets. The graves were protected by life-sized idols of men on horseback, an odd custom for a pedestrian people who never owned horses. Robertson was invited to watch as their shamans sacrificed goats in his honor in the darkened, blood stained temple of

Khyber Knights

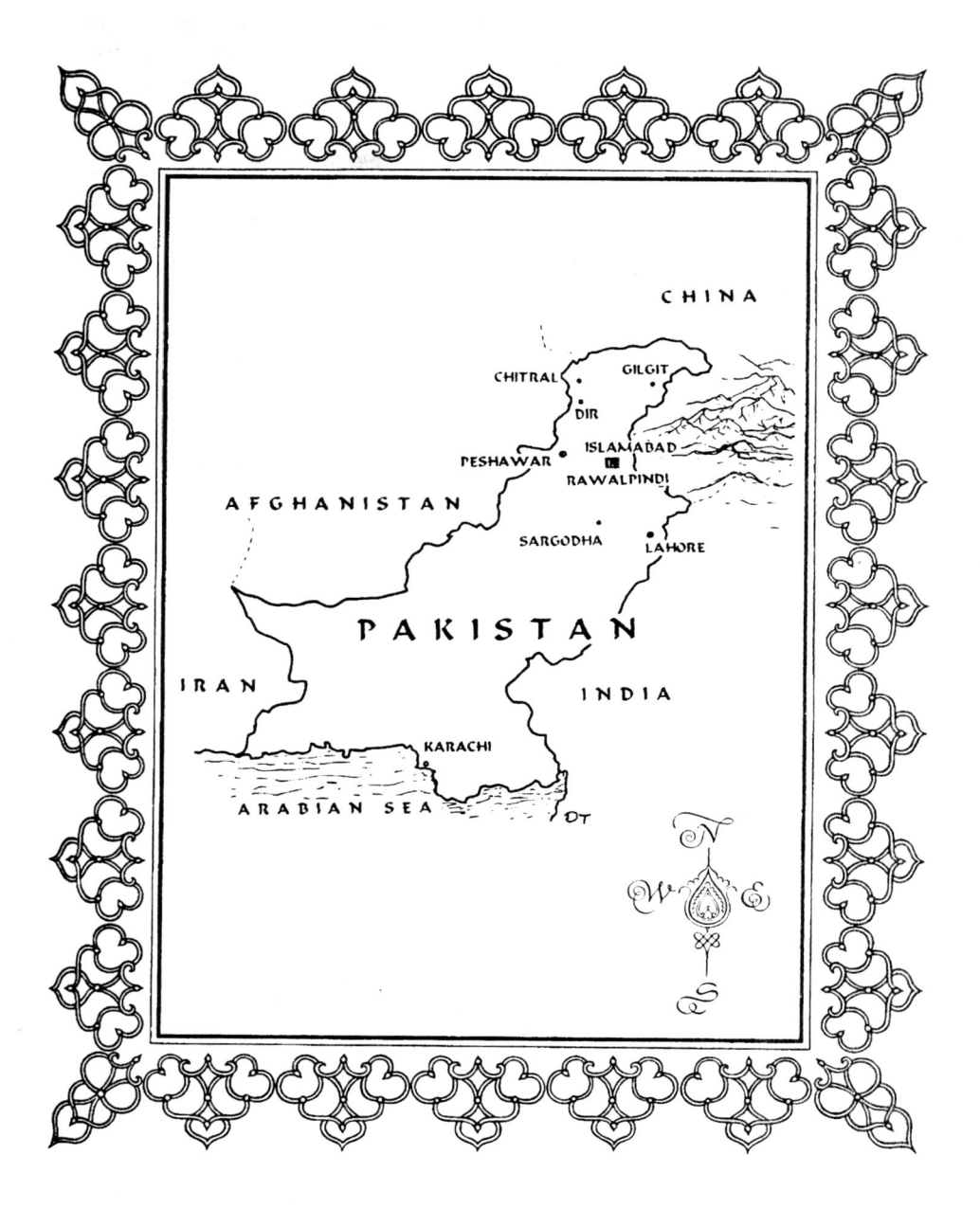

Something Wrong in Paradise

Imra, one of their many gods. The Kafirs warned him of the *deo-log*, the invisible impish fairies residing in their valleys. Earthquakes, they told him solemnly, occurred when a fly irritated the bull on whose two horns the earth is resting. Foul weather occurred when women or hens approached a sacred place. Thunder was a result of fairies fighting on horseback in the sky, the lightning coming from their striking spears.

Finally they told him in whispers of their festivals, Jyoshi to celebrate the spring and Phoo the fall.

Robertson condemned this last festival as, "an orgy of unspeakable obscenity."

At harvest time in early autumn, while the drums pounded, the people danced under the starlight to express their thanks for their crops and blessings. As the dancing and singing proceed, the strongest young shepherd was chosen as an embodiment of the gods. For a single night he was allowed to enjoy sexual relations with as many women as he could manage. It made no difference if they be widowed, married, single or virgin, their sexual compliance brought honor not just to them, but their fathers and husbands as well.

It was this lewd custom, as well as the idols, the blood sacrifices, and the murderous insistence on freedom that made the pagans so despicable in Muslim eyes.

The Kafirs were loath to let Robertson leave. When he refused the friendly offer of some going-away sex with a young Kalashi woman, the pagans seized on a new way of sealing their friendship with the British explorer. A young man, Gumara, was selected to become Robertson's adopted son. A goat was killed by the shaman. It's kidneys were cut out, warmed in a flame and then presented to the two men on knife point. Each was required to chew off a piece of the warm organ.

At this point, Robertson writes, "Gumara tore open my shirt and sucked on my left nipple like a vampire. Thus were the children of Gish, the great war god who was supposed to have fled Kafiristan for London, reconciled with their lost brethren, the children of Imbra."

Robertson's trip among the Kafir had unexpected results. Their very hospitality betrayed them. The Kafirs thought they were hosting a long-lost brother. They never dreamed he was employed by one of the world's most perfidious empires. In London, the men in power had never heard of any ridiculous war god called Gish. But they knew and feared the Russian bear lurking to the north of their Indian empire. The British politicians reasoned that if the ignorant Kafir savages welcomed a white skinned English man today, they might welcome a white skinned Russian tomorrow. Political realities outweighed any romantic gimmick.

Fearing Russian invasion into India via Kafiristan, the English Raj signed a treaty with the Czar. The Emir of Afghanistan would provide a long, narrow strip of land to be called the Wakhan Corridor. This would act as a buffer between the two European rivals. Unknown to them, the Kafirs were now surrounded on all sides by antagonists. Lying like a ripe plum surrounded by three bandit chiefs, lay the centuries-old kingdom of Kafiristan. Her crime was that she did not belong to the modern 19th century. Her people were backward. Her very freedom was perceived as a threat. Her denial of an invading religion was not to be tolerated. The vote was cast between Moscow, London and Kabul.

Kafiristan must die.

For centuries the pagans had successfully resisted all attempts at conquest by outside enemies. All previous Muslim armies had dashed themselves uselessly against her mountain walls. The triumphant Tamerlane had even been defeated when he tried to conquer the Kafirs. He was forced to retreat from Kafiristan, lowed down a cliff in a basket like a head of cabbage. Tamerlane's spiritual heirs, the Muslims of Afghanistan, thus hated the Kafirs. For centuries they had longed to crush this last outpost of independent spirits.

In exchange for his help in creating the Wakhan Corridor separating British and Russian geographic interests, the Emir of Afghanistan demanded a steep price. He got it. The British crown modernized his army, supplying it with high caliber Lee Enfield rifles. Armed with this superior fire power, the Afghan Muslims promptly invaded Kafiristan, murdering or enslaving the Bashgali population. The few stunned survivors were forced to convert to Islam. Their country was seized and incorporated into Afghanistan. Every known trace of the pagan culture was wiped clean. The once mighty empire of the pagans, the sons of Alexander the Great, were gone. Kafiristan ceased to exist, replaced by a new political state named Nuristan, the land of light.

Only in the three little valleys of the black clad Kalash did any remnants of the Greeks survive. As I walked through the dark I recalled an Afghan friend who had once casually told me how his grandfather had owned many Kafir slaves. He assured me they were little better than dogs and nearly as dirty. As I made my way through the dark that night I couldn't help but wonder how long that last remnant of the pagan empire could survive.

Following the directions given me by my host, Siddiq, I came across a small trail that lead away from the village. Like most people in Pakistan his definition of a short walk was far different from mine. Already I had trudged much further than I had anticipated. The stars were up before I heard the music I sought. Even without directions a blind man could have found the appointed place. The sound of drum music was so loud it must have carried even back to the village. I made my way into Stygian darkness, walking under tall walnut trees, until I came across what the ancient Greeks would have recognized as an agora. The Kalash called it a gromma. It served the same purpose in either culture, being a large level gathering place reserved for ceremonies. This one was flattened from hundreds of years of use.

As I emerged into the clearing I saw a sight that had no touch stone in the modern age. The clearing was lit by bright starlight. The moon was slowly rising, peeking over the mountains that hid this valley, these people, this ceremony from the modern world. I was sure that the spirits of Imra, their creator, and Gish, their war god, were watching from the shadows as the last pagans of Kafiristan celebrated in their honor.

Something Wrong in Paradise

Standing around the edge of the trees in a large circle were a number of Kalashi men and children. Like me, they stood silently as an unearthly music filled the air.

Two men were providing a loud rhythm with a set of large skin clad drums. "Thunka-thunk, thunka-thunk, thunka-thunka-thunk," went the drums, thumping and booming and filling the night air with the music of long ago. But hovering over that primitive cadence like a bird song was the sweet song of the women of Kalash.

For as the moon arose she threw down her white beams on the Kalashi women as they sang and danced. They were standing close together in a long straight line, their arms raised and resting on the shoulders of the women on either side. It was hard to see exactly but there seemed to be ten or more of the women in the line. As the round drums throbbed out a beat, the women swirled their bodies in unison under the moonlight, providing a choreography as old as the mountains that watched. As the line swung around towards me their voices rang out into the dark.

"Oooooooooooooo," they sang as they swirled one way. The line came to a slow stop. They then reversed their gliding dance and swung in the opposite direction, their long black dresses swinging around them, throwing a mosaic of shadows.

This time their voices sang, "Ahhhhhhhhhhh," as they swirled their bodies like black clad flowers swaying in this macabre scene. It was a dance that was old when man was new, a dance that washed away time.

"Oooooooooooo, aaaaaaaaaaa," filled the clearing in their eerie cadence, their voices rising and falling together in an undirected symphony of prehistoric sound. Their faces were masked in anonymity, but their voices were ringing out to the mountaintops.

Someone lit a bonfire. Orange flames licked the velvet black sky. The smell of burning cedar wood filled the air. For a few seconds the only sound was the crackling of the great logs.

Then an old man began to sing in a reedy voice, his song a testament to blood-stained gods of long ago. Men now jumped in, beginning to twirl in abandon. Their capering in the flickering light helped to bring on a sense of intoxication that filled the little glade. Children were chattering. More Kalashi were coming up out of the darkness, hallooing the crowd. The pleasant smell of wood smoke filled the air. Overhead the Milky Way lay strewn across the sky, its trail of white dust evidence left behind of a race between a magic cow and horse who ran across the sky. Or so the Kalash told me.

It seemed strange to think this-once savage people, fierce legendary killers of Muslims, had reacted to my own presence so courteously. I had sensed no hostility, found no murderers here. They simply wanted to be left alone to live and worship in their own manner. Any antagonism against Muslims was gone. Their primary desire was to survive.

The Muslims down country denounced this remnant of another age. They were anxious to come there and wave the flag of social and religious improvement. I had been told the Kalash were dirty, their women unchaste. Critics said progress was held at bay, civilization rejected, Islamic values unwanted there.

The Emir of Afghanistan probably once voiced the same arguments saying, "Don't worry men, we're killing and converting them for their own good."

My friends in Peshawar would have been shocked to learn I had been to Kafiristan and not enjoyed the charms of the local women, nor witnessed any debauchery, nor been murdered in my sleep. They would be disappointed when I told them I had seen nothing more exciting than black clad pixies dancing in the moonlight, that I had discovered nothing in Kafiristan except the slowly dying ashes of a once vigorous race.

I walked back towards Shavon alone with my discoveries and my feelings. I pondered over the everlasting mercy of God and the short-lived mercy of men. I was glad I had journeyed up into the tiny valley, thinking I had made the right decision, thinking things were going to work out, thinking Shavon and I were safe.

Nothing could have been further from the truth.

6
Ride or Die

I awoke with a blinding headache.

The sun was well up. Outside the tiny room I could hear voices, rushing water, birds, the gentle singsong of Kafiristan's natural hymn. I pulled on my riding boots, feeling strangely listless. I attributed the headache to the homemade Kalashi wine I had imbibed at last night's celebration. The fatigue, I reassured myself, was only the result of a weary body denied its daily dose of adrenaline.

Shavon was glad to see me. I led her to the stream running a few hundred feet from the chaikhana. While she drank I was overcome by the urge to rest. I sat down beside her, telling myself I was only taking in the beauty that lay before me. The sun was shining. The trees were green and the grass was fair. Faraway in the fields I could see men and women working. I was merely letting my soul pause, I tried to convince myself.

The mare lifted her muzzle, dripping water and snorted, wetting me all over.

"So that's my thanks," I said, laughing at Shavon's joke, then led her back to the pasture.

I ate a hearty breakfast, fried eggs, delicious coarse bread, many cups of sweet black chai, and promptly threw it up in the woods behind the chaikhana. As I made my way back slowly to a chair that sat in front of my bedroom door, I told myself there was nothing to be alarmed at. It was probably nothing more serious than another case of amebic dysentery. I suffered from it off and on all the time. On my first trip to Afghanistan I had been so stricken with this particular lament, they had taken me down to Kabul stretched unconscious in the back of a truck. A friend in the city had scrounged up some tins of Campbell's soup and I had recovered. Since then I had survived typhus, sunstroke and malaria, had long ago grown used to being mildly diseased, knowing I was carrying every germ known to that part of Asia around in my system. The little parasites were stowaways that made themselves known once in a while. It was one of the secret taxes you paid for living free in the Frontier.

I settled back in the chair to sit in the sun. Shavon was nearby in her grass. The stream was close enough to hear. It was peaceful. I would be fine.

By late afternoon I was feverish.

Saddiq tried to serve me lunch but I had no appetite. This didn't surprise me. Dysentery left you weak. Even the word "food" was unappealing. But unlike any other case of dysentery I had suffered through, this time I wasn't running to the toilet. In fact my guts seemed to have dried up. I was instead thirsty.

When Saddiq came in the early afternoon with another offer of lunch, he found me asleep in the chair. I told him, and myself, I was just resting, then ordered some chai to make him feel better and to put my thirst to rest.

While he was gone I went in and got my patou, wrapping myself in it, though it was warm in the sunshine. The chai was a long time coming. It works like that when you have to chop wood, start a fire and brew up a pot. I took the opportunity to visit with Shavon.

I'll never forget how she looked. She was standing there surrounded by tall grass, contentment painted on her pale gold face. I walked up to her and she didn't even move, happy to be close to me. When I ran my hand down her side I felt her flanks had grown warm in the sun. She was full and happy and resting. For the first time in her life she could just stand at ease in a good, safe place. Oh to God that she could have stayed like that.

Walking back the short distance to the chaikhana I began feeling woozy, could barely make it back from the pasture. I staggered to my chair. Saddiq brought me the chai. I drank it down and again was violently ill.

That night I lay in a shroud of sweat. My dreams were awful, full of Afghanistan and things too horrible to recount. I woke up the next morning trembling. My clothes were damp and stuck to my body. My eyes hurt so bad I thought I was going blind. I knew I had to take Shavon to water but I was almost too weak to sit up.

I was starting to get concerned. I had reason to. It only got worse.

I was so lethargic, it took all my strength to walk outside. I made it as far as the chair and collapsed. Siddiq had heard me and come out of the cook shack that sat apart from the three room chaikhana.

"Please bring me some water," I asked him wearily.

When he saw me his face took on a look of alarm.

"I must look bad," I thought and tried to raise a smile to reassure him I was all right.

He brought me a tin cup full of cold stream water. I took it in a feeble hand, the cold water feeling good through the metal. I took a long draught and my stomach went into convulsions. I fell to the floor retching violently. Now I was beginning to worry.

Siddiq helped me get up. I staggered back to my room, hit the charpoy and passed out.

The following day I opened my eyes. Nothing else worked. I lay on the bed shaking with chills but soaked in sweat. I could hear Shavon neighing frantically. I wondered what time it was. I told myself I had better get up and get on the road again. I had lingered too long in Kafiristan. Shavon was well fed so there was no reason to delay now. I could hear her outside neighing.

"She must be thirsty," I thought and tried to sit up. I couldn't. In fact I was so weak I couldn't move a muscle. During the night I had crossed

Ride or Die

into some invisible place where nothing worked. My body had grown so still I could hear my heart beating. The breath in my lungs was a trickle, running on automatic. Only my mind was still alive.

As I lay there I drifted in and out of a delirious state of consciousness. The day passed. I would awaken and lay there paralyzed. As the day wore on I would wake, try to move and then pass out. This happened repeatedly. Finally I opened my eyes. Something told me it was late afternoon. I knew I had to force myself to get up, that I was acting cowardly, nothing more. Slowly my vision narrowed in on my right hand, which was lying close to my head, with my fingers open

"Move your fingers. Move them," I ordered myself silently. "Just do this one thing damn it!"

"Come on, close your fingers," I thought, not believing I could not summon the strength to accomplish this.

It was impossible. I couldn't find the energy to perform this simple task. At first I was angry. My body had betrayed me. Then I heard Siddiq passing by my closed door, but I was too weak to call out for help.

That is when the fear set in. If I had been lying in a pool of my own blood I couldn't have shouted for assistance. I wept silently, the tears running down a face as still as stone. Once again I passed out and drifted down into a black hole of sickness.

Later, well after dark, Siddiq gently shook me awake.

"Your horse was crying. But don't worry, I watered her."

"Help me," I whispered.

He put a cool hand on my forehead.

"You're very sick. I will bring a doctor in the morning."

I opened my eyes at first light and listened to the soft sounds of Kafiristan awakening outside my open window. I could hear Shavon stamping close by in the pasture. Children were playing. People were talking. It all made for a perpetual undercurrent of muted sound, animal for one part, human for the rest. My head was resting in the hollow of my saddle, that noble object. That day its soft texture and warm leather smell helped me not at all. I felt too weak to rise. My mind was alert and I could converse silently with myself but lacked the strength to speak out loud. I had not eaten in three days.

Siddiq soon came with another man, a middle aged Chitrali teacher who also served as the village medic. The amateur physician sat on a chair next to my bed and looked me over cautiously. He was well-meaning if slightly ill-equipped to handle my particular illness. But that didn't stop this man of letters from coming to a brilliant diagnosis. He didn't take my pulse. He didn't look at my tongue or feel my forehead. He had never seen a stethoscope. He had been voted doctor because he could read the words on the bottles. That skill served as a medical degree in those parts.

He sat staring at me intently for quite a while, moving his head slowly from right to left as if he was studying the germs that were slaying me. After a few minutes he wagged his head up and down at some decision.

Khyber Knights

Looking satisfied, he turned towards Siddiq and informed the chai-wallah of his prognosis.

"Well its obvious he is suffering from general weakness," he told Saddiq.

"Must be fact," the hotel owner said, concurring with his learned colleague.

I wasn't asked my opinion.

The self-taught medico told me the cure for this malady was an intravenous drip of glucose water. They left in order to round up my rescue.

It took a while to bring back the supplies. The teacher didn't bother to wipe down my arm with any alcohol, probably didn't have any. He had brought a large, clear plastic bag filled with glucose water. A long tube ran from the bottom of the bag. He shoved a needle into the tube, got the bag to drip, and lanced the works into a vein in my left arm. He very kindly sat on the chair next to the bed and held the contraption above my head as a courtesy. I'm sure if I hadn't been a foreigner I would have had to hold it up myself.

I never asked where they got the needle. I smiled to myself, thinking they most likely used it last time to treat a goat. Well, a goat was more important than a sick Muslim foreigner in those parts. Besides I was too weak to care about medical niceties. I figured if the unknown illness didn't kill me, this treatment might. But I didn't say that. They were both well-meaning and doing everything they could. I was just glad Robertson's adopted son Gumara hadn't dropped in to suck my nipple in an effort to heal me.

As the sugar water slowly coursed into my veins I knew I was dying, knew for certain something was killing me by slow degrees. If I stayed in that backwards village I'd end up being buried above ground in some carved box by my pagan attendants. I didn't fancy my bones moldering for eternity, surrounded by the Kalash of Kafiristan. My greatest worry had always been dying in some forgotten corner of the world and getting dumped into a nameless hole. The nearest real doctor was in Chitral, at least thirty miles and a hard day's ride away through a sandy, mountainous no-man's land. I didn't have a choice. I knew what I had to do. I had to get to Chitral or die in Kafiristan.

When the drip finished I felt surprisingly better. The sugar water seemed to have temporarily rejuvenated me. Even my headache was gone. The doctor was optimistic and assured me I was going to be fine. With their help I sat up. I took a deep breath and pulled on my boots. By the time I wrapped my turban I was tiring. I ordered myself to ignore any desire to lie back down. I had to go now or I would never manage to leave. I asked Saddiq to bring Shavon around and saddle her. While he threw my saddlebags on her back, I walked out on my own. As the doctor helped me mount, Saddiq came rushing back from the cook shack. He had filled my small canteen with creek water, which he hung on the pommel of the saddle. With a look of genuine concern, the little

Ride or Die

hotel wallah opened my right hand and gave me two aspirins as a going away present.

It must have been the glucose. I was light headed but coherent for the first time in days. My course lay before me. I told myself I could handle this challenge. I waved goodbye and headed down the Shangri-La valley towards help. I never saw that beautiful Kalashi girl again.

My condition didn't take long to catch up to me.

The glucose gave me strength. It didn't take long to lose it.

I had left behind the village, and was soon making my way down the narrow canyon road leading back to Ayun. With all the trees gone, it was so hot. As I rode I could feel the effects of the sugar water evaporating in the blazing sun. Within a couple of hours I was racked with a blinding headache and very thirsty. I stopped Shavon and swallowed the aspirins with a slug of warm canteen water.

Wrong !!!

I felt like I had been poisoned. My stomach revolted and threw it back up. I slumped in the saddle, heaving, my fingers locked around the pommel to keep me from falling off. Humiliated, I wiped the spittle off my face. After that I just settled in and kept going. I was ill but felt like I was still in control.

It was early afternoon when we hit the main road. We soon passed Ayun. The villagers stared.

"Must be the turban," I thought.

I headed the mare due north towards Chitral and safety. We passed into a isolated, uninhabited, desert country, all gray rock, gray dust and the gray water of the Chitral river. The world was all gray now except the sun. It was white hot and hammering me mercilessly. The river lay far down a steep slanting cliff face, well below the road. I could hear it's roar, could see it so close. I was very thirsty and was sure the water must be cool. I told myself not to be a fool. If I managed to get down there, I wouldn't have the strength to climb back up. At that instant some strong instinct warned me that I had to stay in the saddle at all costs, that my survival was dependent on remaining with my horse.

Shavon took me on, the two of us traveling through an uninhabited land of heat and heartbreak. The silence was deafening. There was the roar of the river, the soft plodding of the mare's hooves in the thick muffling dust. But those sounds seemed to lie outside the world I was traveling in. Somewhere I heard a soft little song floating high off. Shavon was by now directing her own course. I was holding the reins but they lay limp in my fingers. I had given up all conscious thought of being in charge of the mare. The sun had reduced me to a lump of warm baggage. All I could concentrate on was the soft song I could hear coming from far away. The sun was so bright and my eyes hurt so badly. I wanted to close them for just a brief second. That little song kept nagging me. I had heard it somewhere before.

"Oh, it is the saddle creaking," I realized, and smiled at my foolishness.

Khyber Knights

That is the last thought I remembered clearly. Then the bad times started. I began to slide in and out of consciousness, delirious one moment, weak but cognizant the next. I could feel myself starting to sway in the saddle. The sunlight pounded inside my head, causing a fire-flecked pain to blind me. I simply had to close my eyes.

The next thing I experienced was the taste of dry, thick dust in my mouth. I could feel my breath coming very slowly. I realized I was lying face down on my stomach. I could feel the hot, sun-baked dirt of the road under my palms. I opened my eyes. I had fainted, slipped from the saddle and fallen to the ground. I groaned, managed to sit up and saw Shavon standing patiently over me. Her reins were trailing in the dust as she partly shielded me from the sun.

To this day I have no idea how long I had been lying in that road. It could have been seconds or hours. It did not matter to the mare. Her rider lay motionless. This was a difficulty she could not resolve alone. So she stood over me waiting for guidance, wanting her horseman to make a decision for us both. If she had left me while I was unconscious I would have died. It's that simple. It's that true.

I'll never know how I got back in the saddle. When I looked up at Shavon I saw an unbearable look in her eye, an almost human expression of anxious concern. That look helped. I knew I only had enough strength for one supreme effort.

I grasped the stirrup iron and pulled. I rose so slowly I wasn't sure I could make it. Shavon stood there like a patient cowpony, her legs spread, her head up, an immovable rock of support. I struggled up, got to my feet, stood there swaying, a filthy, dusty mess of a man. I leaned against her warm, moist hide, grabbed the saddle and then heaved myself up onto the hurricane deck with no pretense at grace.

I felt naked and alone up there, totally vulnerable to fate, betrayed by my own dreams. The need for sleep was wringing my entrails. Something told me I only had a few moments of clarity. I pulled off my turban, wrapped it around myself several times and tied it to the pommel. Revealing myself to the sun was a last desperate measure. The white hot star was now threatening to burn out my brain where I sat. I could feel myself going dizzy. I started weaving again. I tried to focus. I tied the reins together, then laid them on the mare's neck.

"There," I said, "I can do no more than that."

I clicked to Shavon and she began to walk, slowly, as if to assure me she would not throw me off.

I told myself to stay awake, but the motion, the unknown illness, the sun, the thirst, the weakness, all conspired to destroy me. Within minutes I was unconscious again, slumped in the saddle like a corpse.

From that moment on Shavon was in total command. She could have stopped in her tracks or wandered off in search of grazing. Instead she faithfully took me on a journey through a land of dreams where it was hot and shadowy. We traveled on and on forever, until somewhere in the distant future I could feel the air growing cooler. The darkness became complete but Shavon kept walking, insisting on taking me to some

Khyber Knights

"Within minutes I was unconscious again, slumped in the saddle like a corpse. From that moment on Shavon was in total control."

destination whose importance I could no longer remember. It grew cold in my dream and utterly black.

Eventually I felt her stop and I heard voices from far away.

I wanted to open my eyes but couldn't. I wanted to speak but couldn't.

As unseen hands pulled me down from the saddle I remember hearing, "*Allah Shokur*, thank God he is alive."

And that is all I knew.

7
Shavon's Fate

The driver helped me out of the battered little Suzuki truck. Opening the passenger door he took my arm and assisted me up to the clinic. I walked like an old man carrying the burden of many years. It was only thirty feet. I thought the effort would kill me.

"Wait here," he said, showing me to a crude bench outside the small building's front door. "I'll tell the doctor you are outside."

"Thank you," I managed to whisper, then leaned back against the mud wall, completely done in. An old man, his beard white with age, a **pakul** (wool cap) on his head at a jaunty angle, was sitting on the other end of the bench. Three women, chadors (veils) draped around their heads, were squatting in the dust next to the road. Two of them were trying to control a couple of squirming infants intent on escaping from their mothers' grasp. It was the Chitrali version of the doctor's waiting room.

I had been in town for two days and this was the first time I had been out of bed. Shavon had brought me in some time after dark. Locals had found me and taken me to a decent hotel. Despite my weakened condition, no one had treated me with anything but kindness. My little leather bag had more money in it than most men made in a year. Yet I hadn't been robbed in my sleep. Additionally, while I was being cared for, Shavon was unsaddled and staked out in a rough field next to my lodgings.

Pakistan was like that, one minute trying to kill you, the next pretending she didn't mean it.

When I awoke the day after arriving a man came to say the doctor was away for a couple of days. Could they do anything for me?

"Bring me glucose," I told them.

By now I knew in my heart I didn't have a simple case of dysentery. I wondered if I wasn't suffering from cerebral edema, a form of altitude sickness. I knew its symptoms were similar to mine, extreme tiredness, vomiting, severe headache, drowsiness and coma. Kafiristan was high enough in the mountains to have brought on some of these symptoms. I didn't know what was wrong with me. But I knew in my heart that the self-taught doctor back in the village had saved my life with his dirty needle and his glucose drip. I reasoned more of the same couldn't hurt.

A runner was sent to the bazaar and soon returned with a large box of powdered glucose. Mixed in cold water it tasted delicious. I could literally feel its power coursing through my veins. With help I could sit up by late afternoon. I was too weak to visit Shavon. They reassured me, saying she was fine.

I rested, slept, awoke, drank more glucose, worried about Shavon and considered how to send word to the Turkoman mujahadeen commander. The last thing I wanted to do was draw official attention, or worse yet get tossed in jail on some flimsy charge of border violation. I was feeling weak and sick, two conditions guaranteed to put me in a foul humor. I thought it best not to run the risk of meeting the police under those circumstances. I decided to keep my plans secret and wait until I was better before contacting the freedom fighters myself.

The driver came back to tell me the doctor would see me.

"He says to come in. Do you need any more help?"

"No I can make it," I said and gave him money.

"This is too much."

"Take it. I am very grateful."

"You are our guest. It wouldn't be right," he said and gave me back half the rupees.

I'm glad I wasn't expecting a state of the art medical facility. I would have been mildly disappointed. Instead I walked into a small room crammed full of every kind of bottle, bandage, book and bedpan one can imagine. There wasn't a spare two inches of uncluttered space in the entire room. Even the shelves on the wall, piled with old ledger books full of medical records, were groaning under their burden. A large table sat in the middle of the room. It too was stacked with the debris of the healing arts. There was no electricity; a single large window facing south provided the sole illumination. The sun was pouring in on a workbench placed in front of that window. The room's only occupant was sitting on a stool there. He was in his early forties, dark hair a mess, his shalwar-kameez expensive. He was bent over a microscope, studying a slide while the light lasted.

"What's wrong with you?" he asked without looking up.

"I'm sick."

"You wouldn't be here if you weren't. What happened?" he asked and kept peering at his work.

"You have a poor bedside manner," I told him, my voice betraying my irritation.

He stopped, then looked up for the first time. A good twenty feet, and a table full of medical refuse lay between us. Yet this sawbones didn't have to make a house call to pronounce judgment. He just glanced at me for a moment and said, "You have hepatitis," then turned back to his work.

I don't know what upset me more, this medical buffoon or his hands-free diagnosis.

"How can you tell? Don't you have to give me a test or something?" I said angrily.

He looked up again.

'Have you seen yourself lately?'

I admitted I had not. He pointed at the wall behind me. When I turned I saw a small mirror tacked up shoulder high on the wall. I walked over and beheld myself for the first time since I had left Peshawar many weeks ago.

The sight of my own face shocked me. I didn't recognize myself. Staring at me was a man with sunken cheeks. The eyes were urine yellow. They looked back at me like a stranger, bloodshot, feverish and half mad. My skin was sallow, a sickly jaundiced color that screamed "disease" to anyone glancing my way. I was unshaven, my whiskers a scraggly mess, my long red mustache lying limp and exhausted across my lip. My head swayed from the effort of looking in the mirror. No wonder they had stared at me as I passed through Ayun. I looked like a ghoul wearing a blue turban.

Being the obstinate fool I am, I turned back unconvinced.

"How can you be sure? Don't you need to give me a test?"

The doctor let out a sign of exasperation, looked up from the microscope, paused for a moment, then decided to humor me.

"Sure," he said. Then reaching over to the bench he picked up a dirty test tube and held it out towards me.

"Here, go piss in this."

"Where?"

"Hell, anywhere. Go behind the building. Then bring it back."

I did as I was told, trying to walk past the old man and the women as casually as circumstances allowed. Behind the building but in full view of the road I untied my pants and squatted. It is common for men in Pakistan and Afghanistan to urinate publicly so long as they kneel and keep their back to passing pedestrians. But this was ridiculous. It reminded me of that carnival game where you shot the water pistol into the clown's mouth. The stream of water filled a balloon on the clown's head. The first one to pop the balloon got a prize. I shuddered to think what stories my friend Ali Muhammad would tell at my expense if he learned about this episode.

"Did I ever tell you about the time Asadullah had to clutch his long shirt tail in his teeth, then hold up his pants, grip his tool and piss into a test tube on the side of a road in Chitral?" he would inform every loafer in Peshawar who bought him a cup of chai. I could hear the laughter now.

Yes, I thought, as I aimed at the tiny opening, this situation could lead to extreme embarrassment, perhaps loss of respect, certainly a wet mess unless I operated with maximum caution. My mission completed, I didn't pause to look at the results, just tied up my pants, and holding the guilty tube walked back inside with as much haste as my weakened state would allow. I handed the warm test tube back to the doctor. He held it up at arm's length in the strong sunlight. I was shocked to see the warm urine looked as dark as Coca-Cola. It was impossible to believe that murky substance had come out of my body.

The doctor held it up to the bright sunlight, swished it around, took a quick look, then turned to me and said, "Yep, hepatitis."

He then dumped the test tube and my dreams into the sink next to him.

"Well can't you give me something for it?'

"No."

"Nothing?"

"Look, we don't have many medicines in Chitral. Nothing for what you've got. I can prescribe some cough syrup with honey in it. You say you're drinking glucose in water? Fine, continue that. Eat plenty of fresh vegetables, avoid all grease and meat, get plenty of rest. That's all I can tell you."

"Isn't there more than one kind of hepatitis? How do you know what type I have?"

By now he had grown weary of my questions. An expression of finality crossed his face as he turned to look at me.

"I don't have any way of knowing what kind you have. I don't think anyone in Pakistan has access to the medical equipment capable of telling you that. I suggest you consult your doctor at home," he said in an obvious dig at my foreign roots.

I felt a sense of panic rising in my throat. A host of questions and problems suddenly presented themselves, none of which I dared examine, much less answer.

"I've got a horse. I'm supposed to be going on," I said. I didn't need to mention my travel plans. Dressed like I was it was obvious to anybody except a blind man I probably had connections to the mujahadeen.

He had returned to his work, peering back into the microscope. When he heard this new information he didn't even bother to look up.

"Go ahead. Your liver's shot. If you leave here on that horse you'll be dead in two days. I guarantee it," he told me in a voice laced with impatience, dismissing me like a bug.

I walked outside slowly and slumped down on the bench. I didn't know where to go, nor just yet what to do. I sat in shock, my mind blank. I stared ahead and saw nothing. If the sun shone, I did not feel it. If the earth still spun, it went on without me. For at that moment in my life all my being had narrowed down into one truth. I was a horseman and I knew in my heart what had to be done. I knew the doctor's words had not meant my death but Shavon's.

I sat there for a long time. Finally I heard a voice. The old man sitting on the bench had said something to me.

"What?" I asked.

"I said you look like a *malik* (tribal leader)."

"Well I feel like Hell," I told him truthfully.

"You rode here, didn't you?"

I answered truthfully, saying I had, though at the moment it gave me nothing but grief to think of it.

"No one's ridden up here from Peshawar on horseback since 1937. That's the year the last mounted British patrol rode down out of Chitral. The Raj had cut a road through from Chakdara the year before. When the soldiers returned it was in armored cars," he said and smiled at some ancient memory.

I turned to look at this old fellow. He had a strong lived-in face and gentle eyes. His white beard was neatly trimmed, ending in a sharp

Shavon's Fate

point. The pakul he wore had a small flower stuck in the brim. I would have guessed his age at about 70. He looked wise. I wasn't expecting to meet anyone of his caliber on the village bench.

"It was a hard ride," I said and choked back the emotions I was feeling. "I fear now I will not finish it. I had thought to go on."

"A good horse?"

"A fine horse!"

"Many miles?"

"Certainly many miles and a good companion," I admitted and the air hung heavy with what wasn't said.

"You know horses then?" I asked him.

"I was a Chitral Scout for thirty years."

"Ah, a fine outfit. I have heard of them many times."

"There is your problem," he said softly and pointed at a mountain that blocked the horizon, a snow-covered peak that dwarfed her lesser sisters.

I followed the direction he was pointing but saw nothing, just mountains I had meant to cross on a horse I knew I was about to betray.

"In Chitral we say that when clouds hang heavy on Tirich Mir it will bring sorrow on a man. I fear you must be that man."

I didn't argue.

Grief never takes a vacation in Pakistan.

I stood to go.

"Thank you."

"You can still see those places you spoke of," he told me.

I told him what the doctor had said, told him I was beaten and knew it, told him I would never ride into the crow's nest of mountains lying so tantalizingly close.

"I would see those things."

"Then this time you will die. Better to return."

"And my mare," I asked, knowing what the answer was going to be.

"Animals have no souls," he said, then added, "but I too have lost companions of the saddle. I am only an old man but I remember that particular pain."

I told him goodbye and walked with great difficulty down the hill to the main road. I was so weak I sat there in the dust until much later, when I finally managed to flag down a ride. I returned to the hotel and sent for the manager, gave directions, sent messages, awaited results.

The next morning a boy came and picked up my saddle bags and my saddle.

"The jeep is waiting."

The glucose I just drank gave me the strength to walk out on my own. I found the fat rug merchant waiting for me by Shavon. The beautiful palomino mare nickered, like she always did, and I rubbed her head, like I always did, for the last time. I got in the jeep and she started to get impatient, whinnying when she saw me leaving her behind. In answer, the man who now owned her snapped her rope hard and hurt her. In that moment of sorrow Shavon recognized my betrayal, knew she was enslaved again in cruel Asia where the divine spark residing in her loving, loyal heart was forever denied.

They had to help me walk up the steps that led to the airplane flying back to Peshawar. I was weak from the illness but dying from the heartache that came from knowing Shavon's life was once again a painful one, that the hard miles we shared had ultimately not been enough to save her, that all my good intentions were fairy tales and she was lost forever.

I never looked back as the plane flew away. I retreated instead like Alexander the Great, fleeing down the Indus river from the heartbreaking loss of a beloved horse. I told myself to be strong. I reminded myself that this was Pakistan, not America, that there was no place in my adopted world for sentiment, that this was a hard land ruled by hard men making hard choices, that there were no such things as horse trailers to carry her back to Peshawar in, and that I had no place and no one to take her back to. So I had accepted the merchant's offer, that transparent lie which told me what I longed to hear, that Shavon would be used as a polo pony.

But as the prop plane leveled off I knew that was the second fabrication I had encountered on this trip. The Turkoman mujahadeen Shavon had struggled so hard to carry me to, the gallant freedom fighters that were to take me into Afghanistan?

They were nowhere to be found.

I was going back to settle things in Peshawar.

Part Two
The Prison

8
American Renegade

Peshawar seemed to have relaxed with the demise of summer and the death of so many innocents. The end of September had brought on cooler weather during my absence, a small blessing for a man in my condition.

I had been back in the city for several weeks, arriving in such impoverished health the rickshaw driver dragged me up the stairs to the third floor of the Amin hotel. Having previously lodged there for years, I was welcomed home by Suliman the owner and his staff. Thereafter room 301-A became my sanctuary, hospital and prison.

The busy three-story Amin was the native equivalent of a Hilton hotel gone to seed. The majority of her patrons were legitimate middle-class Pakistani travelers. It was an open secret, though, that the multi-roomed residence also played discreet hostess to a United Nations of interesting, albeit shady characters. Registering under your proper name was always optional. Opium growers up from Landi Kotal, money smugglers in from Dubai, gun runners down from Kabul and recuperating equestrian explorers staggering back from Chitral were all welcome under one condition. Privacy and protection were guaranteed only as long as your money held out.

A decent restaurant was situated on the ground floor. The full sized rooms all had hot water and a real bed. Plus agreeable hotel servants ran down the stairs, or across the town, gladly serving your needs. A large courtyard allowed discreet patrons to enter cars driven in from the street. During times of urban conflict an armed guard protected that entrance. A stone's throw across the bustling noisy traffic of the G.T. road lay the Hasht Nagari neighborhood and my friend Ali Muhammad's house. The Amin Hotel was comfortable, convenient, helpful, interesting, discreet and in my weakened condition the best wife, friend and doctor I could have wanted.

Not that Peshawar cared if I lived or died.

While she was many things, the ancient city had little tolerance for the weak.

The state of local medical care reflected that philosophy. The old British-built Lady Reading Hospital was so overcrowded patients shared beds. One man's feet would be placed next to the other fellow's head. The sick ate food brought from home. Medicine had to be purchased in the bazaar and returned to the hospital by a family member. Wives and children, acting as attendants, slept on the floor nearby. More often than not the doctors were on strike. It was a jolly, germ-ridden, bedlam sort of a place. If you didn't die getting there, you could praise Allah if you came out alive.

Consequently, I decided to forego the miracles of modern medicine, opting instead to place my health in the capable hands of Hajii Mahboob. While technically only a pharmacist, the good Hajii practiced one important remedy that legitimate doctors neglected. Before administering any remedy the pilgrim turned physician always prayed over that medication. Call me superstitious, but Hajii Mahboob, healer and holy man, along with his mixture of tonics, elixirs, pills and prayers had never failed to cure me.

Having agreed with the diagnosis of hepatitis, Hajii Mahboob had regularly brought me glucose which he first praised with pray. Those blessings of Allah, fresh vegetables and three weeks of enforced rest had finally given me enough strength to leave the sanatorium known as Room 301-A.

Walking Peshawar's streets for the first time since my return, I felt like an enfeebled old man. My steps were slow and deliberate. My eyes roved to a place long before I got there. I seemed to be crawling through the city, not striding her streets, as I went to meet Ali Muhammad. I still tired easily, but I knew the worst lay behind me. My strength, though severely eroded, was on the mend.

Nothing could have been more therapeutic than to be in that city again. I hungered for it when I was away, missed its exhilaration, its winding pathways, its tangible history. Its very turbulence was a subtle addiction. Every city has an ambiance and mystique. In Peshawar one never felt alone. You walked in the present, felt the past pressing close behind, caught a glimpse of the future peeking around the corner. It was a mosaic of people, actions, and experiences so captivating my senses begged me for relief.

Passing through Peshawar you could feel a throbbing, boisterous vitality. Its everyday noise gave it a carnival atmosphere of thunderous pandemonium. Tinkling bicycle bells, donkeys clip clopping, radios blaring love songs, squatting street-side peddlers shouting about services ranging from tooth pulling to ear cleaning to foolproof aphrodisiacs, braying of sheep going to market, open-fronted restaurants with screaming waiters and clanking dishes, shopkeepers yelling gossip to one another across the street, rickshaws puttering. The symphony came in so fast your ears struggled to decipher the exotic cacophony.

At every turn in the crowded streets you became aware of a keen new smell. There were no noxious odors, no human excrement to foul the air. Instead the breeze was alive with a potpourri of perfumes. Sizzling kebobs cooking over charcoal fires, jasmine garlands hanging at the flower vendors, traces of sandalwood incense, frying fish dipped in

Khyber Knights

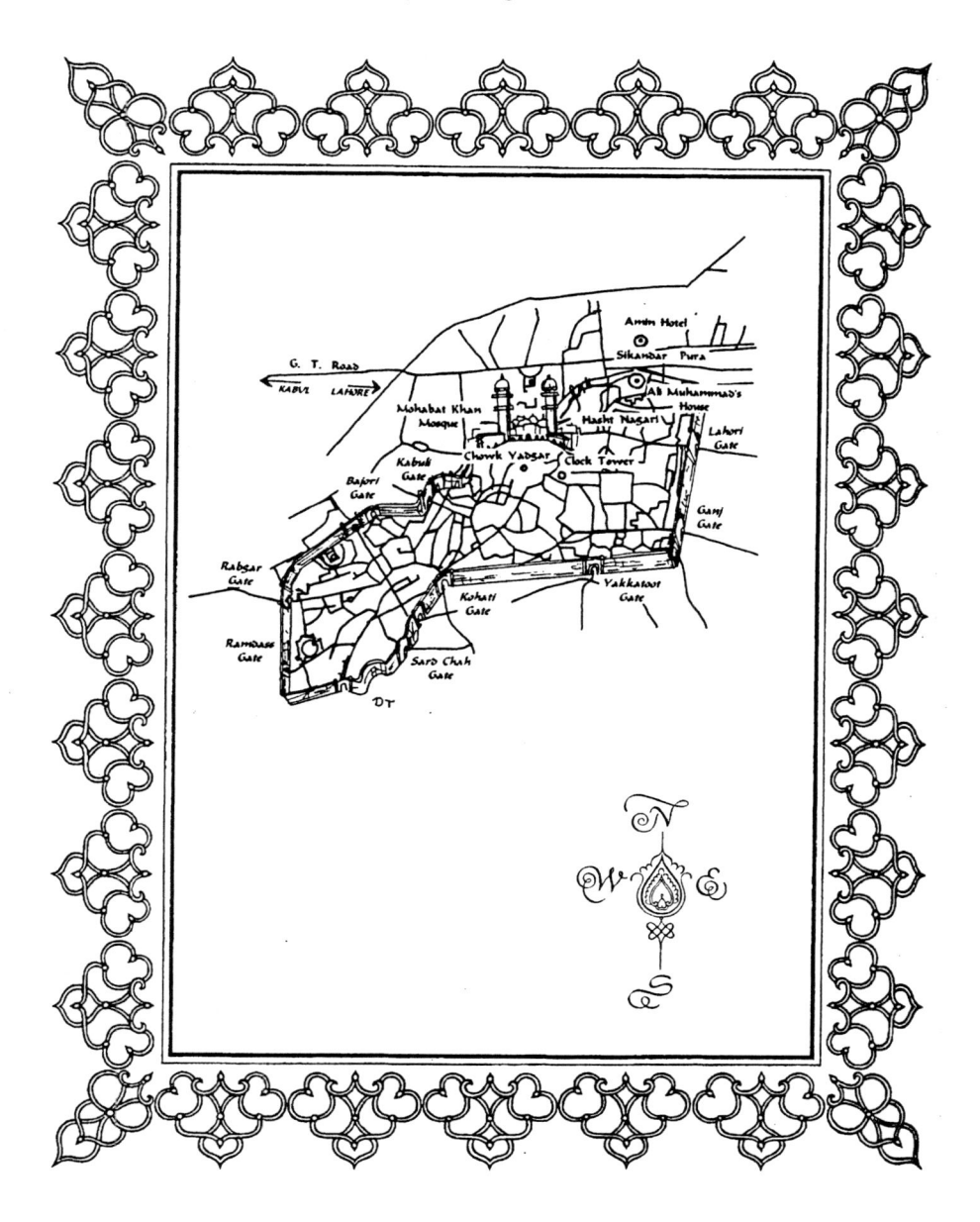

Peshawar

peppered spice, crates of strong black tea, sticky sweet pastries, ripe mangos were all waiting to be appreciated.

Everywhere humans shared the little cobbled streets with animals. Horses trotted by gaily with tongas in tow. Lumbering water buffalo, skin glistening black, horns weaving like broad swords, dragged heavy, creaking two-wheeled wagons down the roads like living tractors. Baskets full of complaining chickens sat waiting to be chosen for dinner, the owner kindly cutting the neck if you wished to keep your hands clean. Cats roamed the streets looking for tidbits. Above my head I could hear the soft whirring of beating wings, as acrobatic pigeons and regal hawks shared the air. Few streets

were wide enough to tolerate anything larger than a rickshaw. A modern car appeared extravagant and absurd in such a medieval metropolis.

It was a city designed for the pleasures of pedestrians, even a weakened one such as myself.

As I walked along I sliced through conversations in the city's many tongues. **Hindko, Urdu, Punjabi, Pushtu, Farsi**, and English, were all common in this polyglot town. Unlike India there were no whining beggars lurking about. This was a city of proud, happy, tolerant, polite, industrious, intelligent people. Even the paupers had an air of distinction. When the British took the first census in 1868, they counted 473 merchants, 145 policemen, 121 prostitutes, 86 beggars and 7 Americans. It was a good place for adventurers, a portal to another world, even then. Peshawar remained the crossroads where Central Asia met Central India, a place where poverty and wealth resided side by side. For the past five years it had been home.

The sun-dappled streets played host to a variety of Oriental demands and dreams. Each lane I passed was a compliment to commerce, every one devoted to a different merchandise or talent. Thus in accordance with ancient custom all the merchants of one type were grouped together. This not only helped funnel rich rustics in the direction of cunning merchants, it made prices murderously competitive, competition fierce, and haggling routine.

There were truck parts, leather holsters, plastic goods, shoes, blankets, clothes, books, medicines, printers, fortune tellers, cassette tapes, pet birds, turbans, guns, musicians, fish mongers, cinemas, bakers, jewelers and money changers to choose from.

One avenue displayed tobacco in rows of baskets, the leaves all shades of brown, green and gold. Gathered on another street were small mountains of spices, bright red pepper, brilliant yellow saffron, brown nutmeg, all perfuming the air. Here shopkeepers sat behind glistening produce just arrived from the countryside. Laid on the ground across lengths of canvas were heaps of dried apricots, fresh spinach, sweet corn, roma tomatoes, succulent oranges, turnips, red onions, potatoes and watermelons. There coppersmiths beat out their wares with noisy abandon. The Meena, or beauty bazaar, lured in women shoppers with cosmetics and luxuries imported from the Occident.

The treasures of Pakistan were all available on that mild fall afternoon.

As I made my way through this maze of twisting streets, I was surrounded on all sides by the currents of an honored tradition. The Peshawaris were mad for tea and talk.

Every shop was within shouting range of a small chai-khana. Time was a stranger. There was no such thing as hurry. A successful shop keeper must first be a host to his customers. No deal was closed with out chai being served.

"*Wa allakah* (O' boy)," could be heard from dawn till dusk. Young servant boys acting as waiters would dash from the neighborhood chaikhana's blazing brass samovar, racing down the street to a nearby shop of impatient, thirsty patrons. Tallies were kept. Chits were signed. Petite yellow enamel tea pots full of the scalding liquid were placed down next to delicately thin china cups. Dirty cups from the previous transaction would be taken back on a tin tray, hurriedly rinsed off under a city tap, before being sent out again. Sweet green tea from China, called kehva, or black tea brewed with milk and sugar, called chai, were the social seal passed on any agreement.

It took me longer than usual to walk across the small city and left me weaker than I had expected. When I neared the white marble minarets of the Mahabat Khan mosque I knew I was drawing close to where Ali Muhammad awaited me. As I walked beneath the shadows of these two ancient minars, history hung over my head in more ways than one. In 1823 Peshawar had been conquered by the ruthless Sikh king Ranjit Singh, ostensibly because her Muslim governor refused to surrender a prized horse. Loathing her conquerors, the city's Pathan population simmered. Rebellion seemed imminent. Fearing he would lose the valuable asset, the wily Sikh king sent a trusted Italian mercenary, General Avitabile, to strangle Peshawar with an iron hand. The proud city leaders were amused when they received an ominous message from this newly appointed military governor. Already enroute from the Punjab, the mercenary sent an ominous message on ahead.

"Obey my master or I will conquer your miserable town with a length of rope," the letter read.

The scornful sound of Peshawari laughter could be heard all the way back to Ranjit Singh's palace in Lahore.

Upon entering the city the Italian ordered his army to seize 20 leading citizens. Sitting his horse, he looked down with contempt at the formally arrogant Peshawaris now cringing before him. There on the ground lay a large coil of rope. While the city fathers watched in mystified silence, Avitabile's soldiers cut it into long lengths. They were then horrified to learn the answer to the Italian riddle. Without a moment's warning the terrified patriots were seized and lynched, hung from the minarets of the beautiful white mosque like twitching, turbaned ornaments. Peshawar kept a civil tongue in her head until the British took over a few years later. By then half the population was dead anyway, killed by the Sikhs and their foreign mercenaries.

The city remained in foreign hands until 1948. Through the decades of capture and degradation her enemies retained only physical control of Peshawar's ageless streets. Even in chains her wild heart could not be confined. Dwelling unconquered in the nearby hills were her true owners, the liberty loving Pathans. The tribesmen might shop in the streets one day and loot the bazaar the next. She was their dusty monument to freedom and free men, a gun-toting place where the bloody past met the furious future.

Peshawar thus rested on the edge of vast possibilities, in a man, in his life and across the land. Lying unseen in the gaunt mountains nearby was the Khyber Pass. Its very existence brought on a quickening in a man's blood. That rocky portal was the gateway to Kabul, Samarkand and Khiva. History had been made on the blood-soaked ground thereabouts before and would be again. My adopted home rested between disasters, taking advantage of a reprieve as brief as the halting of a camel caravan. Thus the nearness of the fabled Khyber Pass reinforced an unspoken feeling prevalent in Peshawar. Her citizens were animated by the fact that they knew they were living on borrowed time, aware that the quickening of their blood came from the knowledge that the pervasive unseen presence of Allah and the Angel of Death were closer here than in other cities. For nowhere was it more true than in Peshawar that this dream called life lasted but an hour.

Five years is a big slice out of a young man's life. I had arrived in Peshawar from the United States with a desire to cover the Afghan jihad for the western press. Behind me lay only regrets, a tramp for a wife, an embittered divorce, no children, friends whose lives had taken traditional routes. The wanderlust that characterized my Celtic roots had eventually shoved me out the door and down the road. My emptiness pulled me like a magnet from one country to another, never happy, never staying for long. No home, no land and no endearments held me. A wind blown American, I washed up at last in those cobbled streets with no preconceptions. Peshawar was waiting like an unremembered lover from another age.

Cautiously venturing into her streets for the first time I discovered a world I never knew existed. None of the things that either bored or disturbed me in America were evident there. The urban blight that had compressed my life in the United States into a routine of traffic, anxieties, endless bills, placebo television and treadmill consumerism belonged to a place and a state of mind I had left behind. Much of the ugliness of the late 20th century was held at bay. In Peshawar men walked with straight backs. They had not lost their virtue or vigor. They lived by their word and expressed themselves in action. They were what Americans had once been and were now no more. Men there were not reduced by their jobs to become flesh and bone servants of the machines that once served them. They were not slaves to credit, did not sell their souls to survive. Even poverty was nothing to be ashamed of there. Peshawar's people lived a communal life. They depended on each other. They were more than mere neighbors, they were friends.

On the first night I was brave enough to venture into her streets alone I expected to be murdered. Instead I saw only a canopy of stars above my head, the shops warmed by the glow of lanterns and generous, friendly people glad to see me. I discovered no assassins, only equality and fraternity. After 37 countries, countless airports, meaningless miles and enough loneliness to break your bones I knew I could rest.

Pakistan and Peshawar had their problems. This was no "Gilligan's Island," without dangers or social repercussions. Yet there I resided in a daylight dream of my own making. I learned the rules, covered the war, and by local standards got rich from selling my stories. Those were the external factors of my new existence. What occurred to me internally, outside my professional life, had been so poignant it set me apart forever from the country of my birth and the life I previously lived. An old woman had once told me I was a tree without fruit. Maybe. I still had a gypsy's soul. I often left the city because of my work, drawn away for a time to wander. Eventually I would remember Peshawar and then my heart would beat with anxiety and expectation, for she had long ago thrown a net over my soul. Yes, I often departed but I would never call another place home as long as I lived. Though I might leave her cobbled streets, it was here my spirit lay at rest.

I was relieved when I reached the Libya restaurant near Chowk Yadgar. It passed for a fancy cafe in Peshawar, meaning it was an enclosed room with tables and chairs and a door. You didn't have to squat on a stool along the side of the street, eating your kebobs over a charcoal pit, while every carter in town went by splashing dust on your meal and watching you chew.

Ali Muhammad was sitting by a table overlooking the street. His thin, languid body looked as undernourished as ever. The expensive shalwar kameez hung on him gracefully. It was pale green, almost white, what the Peshawaris called Nile green. Not a suitable color for the Jihad but totally in keeping with Ali's reputation as a dandy. He wore a long waistcoat made of the finest snow-white linen. In a city full of dust and din, his clothes were exquisitely spotless. He had long ago given up the Afghan turban, thinking it rustic. He favored the brimless white Peshawari cap, under which you could plainly see his neatly cut dark brown hair He had long musician's fingers adorning smooth white hands never torn by manual labor. His wide sensuous mouth was topped by a thick, dashing

Hussar's mustache. A generous nose, a broad forehead, a strong chin and the kindest blue eyes I had ever known made up his face. Now close to forty, the tiny lines forming around his eyes were the only whispers of his age.

"What will you have, black or green tea?" he asked as I walked up to the table.

"Just your sweet face," I answered in the traditional Peshawari manner, before sitting down feeling all done in.

"Then green," he said and barked out an order to the boy standing across the room.

It was early for dinner and we had the place to ourselves, the other ten or so tables still being empty. The cooking was done outside on the street next to the front door. A metal trough three feet long and a foot wide stood waist-high to the cook. Red-hot charcoals stacked eight inches deep provided the heat to roast the entrees. Over this aromatic fire local gourmet delights were roasted or fried. The diner had robust, if carnivorous choices. He could sample keema, minced lamb fried in a skillet with potatoes, peas, pomegranate seeds and spices. Chapali kebob is a local hamburger distinctively flavored with coriander and onion. Seekh kebob is minced meat shaped into a sausage shape and fried on a skewer. Ali's favorite was tikka kebob, small chunks of lamb meat plunged into a spicy red yogurt paste, then grilled over the glowing coals.

With my tea came my friend's kebobs. I assured him I was not hungry. He didn't stand on ceremony and dug in. The wheat **nan** (bread) served with his meal was hot from the oven. Following local tradition, Ali tore off pieces of the bread, then used them to pull a portion of the hot meat off a metal skewer. The result was a bite sized morsel which he popped into his mouth with great gusto.

"Sure you won't eat?"

"No. Hajii Mahboob has told me to stay away from grease and meat. Though I must say, for the first time in a month it smells good."

The comfortable silence of close friends fell between us. I looked out the window at the mix of old world and new marching past, while Ali effortlessly polished off eight skewers of kebob. Though thin as a fence rail, he ate enough for two men. The waiter had brought Ali his after-dinner tea before I broached the reason for my visit.

"I'm going to Dublin for a month. Thought I better have a real doctor look me over," I said casually.

"Oh," was all he said as he sipped his tea. Be it Dublin or Denver, neither intrigued him. In fact only Peshawar interested Ali Muhammad and therein lay my problem.

"Are you up to that kind of traveling?" he asked, genuinely concerned.

"I'm still feeling pretty weak. I thought I was going to have to rest just walking over here. But I need a break. Think it's time for me to catch a

Khyber Knights

movie, take a hot bath, listen to Mozart and eat Mexican food. I want to visit Kathleen the lady pirate. She's always helpful."

"I bet," he said laughing. "Any news on Pirgumber Kul?"

The name of the mujahadeen commander brought with it memories of Shavon and the bitter price the mare and I had paid for his misleading information. I swallowed my gall and told Ali Muhammad the news, that Pirgumber was nowhere to be found. He could be anywhere from Multan to Maimaina. I hoped a change of scenery would help ease the disappointment of losing the palomino and not squeezing Pirgumber's pudgy neck.

"I was wondering if you would mind going with me down to Rawalpindi. I don't think I'm up to carrying my bag, shoving my way through the crowd at the bus station, getting a hotel room and all that. Thought maybe you could help me get out to the airport the next morning," I said, hoping I hadn't asked too much.

"Well ....," Ali Muhammad said and trailed off, the reluctance in his voice clearly audible. He then started to weave a litany of excuses, how busy he was at his recording studio, all the appointments he had with local musicians, all the things I had expected him to say and not one of the them the real truth.

My friend just didn't like to leave Peshawar. Period.

He would rather live there than anywhere else in the world, and like me he had seen plenty of it. The experiences which had brought him to that stage in his life were hidden beneath his easy-going exterior.

They probably still called him Beau Fontaine back in New Orleans, though no one in Peshawar associated him with that name. His family had resided in the Mississippi river port since 1809, when his French ancestors had fled the slave revolt in Haiti. Those early Fontaines made a fortune in cotton, visited Paris and lived in an elegant Greek revival mansion on Esplanade Avenue. During the first part of the nineteenth century the extended family spent languid afternoons in the house with its high ceiling rooms and filigreed verandah. Evenings brought cool breezes up from the bayou. It was a refined, steamy, sensual life that Beau's ancestors enjoyed.

The city and the family found themselves reeling after the Civil War. The prominent Fontaines splintered from within, jealousy, scandal, abandonment, divorce and fraternal murder taking their toil. Beau's Papa had been the last of a tragic line of Fontaine gentlemen. Obsessed with his noble family lineage, Ali's father was a courtier without a calling. A leftover from another age, Papa had been too proud to work. Dignified, if always broke, the Fontaine patriarch was a gambler famous for always betting on the fourth horse in the race of life. He never could win, place or show on anything of financial importance. But surviving with style was never a problem in the generous southern city who proudly called herself "The Big Easy."

"They probably still called him Beau Fontaine back in New Orleans, though no-one in Peshawar associated him with that name. He lived on a quiet lane called Gari Syeddan, where he delved into the lives of the people, played his music, and was thankful that America had forgotten him."

Papa's family never approved of Beau's mother, a pretty Creole girl from a sugar cane plantation outside the nearby village of Vacherie. Some said Papa only married her because she had a little money. Spiteful cousins whispered Mama married Papa quick because of the growing bulge in her dress.

Like New Orleans, little Beau grew up a Gemini, existing in the fierce glare of the Louisiana daylight, but only really coming alive when the moody gas lights flared up at night. The boy roamed the city, sometimes in search of Papa, sometimes on his own. He was a well mannered, richly dressed pauper, a Fontaine, at once welcome in the whore houses, quadroon balls, raucous jazz clubs or stately cathedrals that had known and honored his family name for more than one hundred years.

By the late sixties everything was gone and Papa was dead, a willing sacrifice on the altar of alcohol. The old nobleman had celebrated life to the end and left Beau nothing except the parting advice that a true gentleman never held a lady to blame for anything. Mama never talked much, either before or after her husband's death. Early on she had taught Beau that worth was within you. But if that truth sank into her son, the silent woman never knew it. It seemed a natural step when Beau became a musician and drifted away. All those nights he spent growing up listening to brass band jazz in the clubs off Congo Square had their effect. His amazing talent with the guitar, like his ability to absorb languages, was the last gift Beau got from his talented gene pool.

He moved on the wave of his music, always further and further east. Atlanta, New York, London, Paris, Madrid, Tangier, and Cairo all held him for a while. His intrigue with the Orient eventually landed him in Delhi, where he studied the sitar with Ravi Shankar. In his thirties rootless chance brought Beau Fontaine up to Afghanistan. He played the dutar in Herat and mastered the rebob in Kabul. Enchanted by that country's customs and people, he had returned to New Orleans and opened an Afghan import shop. It didn't last. The Creole capital in the late 1970s had changed, grown seedy, was ashamed of her voodoo past. Beau reacted by embracing Islam, quietly changing his name and his creed. Every year his buying trips to Afghanistan became longer. His disaffection with the United States grew more intense. He returned to New Orleans reluctantly and less often.

He was in the Afghan capital when it fell to the communists in the spring of 1978. The Red killers didn't know what to make of him. He was too charming to be a spy. They put him on an airplane bound for Peshawar and laughingly told him not to return. He hadn't, not to Kabul, not to America, not to New Orleans. Once he discovered the charms of Peshawar you couldn't get him to leave.

The courteous musician had stumbled upon the unspoiled sister city of his boyhood home. When he strolled through the narrow streets of Peshawar instead of baking French bread, he smelled hot nan. Fragrant gumbo gave way there to spicy curry. Overhead he no longer enjoyed the shade of ancient live oaks but rested under the purple flowers hanging off the jacaranda trees. Both cities boasted sheltered balconies, hidden courtyards, dark mysteries and secret sagas. Peshawar, Ali decided, was as close as he was ever going to get to the mysterious, enchanting, exotic New Orleans of Papa's storied boyhood.

I knew that no one in New Orleans would recognize the exotically dressed man sitting before me in the restaurant. "Beau Fontaine" was now only the name of a ghost listed on Ali Muhammad's passport. Mama was still alive back in New Orleans or he would have even dropped that last official link with his French-American past. Like his ancestors from Haiti, my friend had moved on.

Ostensibly Ali Muhammad ran a recording studio, where he and a host of local Pushtu musicians created cassette tapes full of love songs and ballads of rebellion. He made a comfortable living. More importantly he lived.

The former Beau Fontaine completely and purposefully disregarded the expatriate community, devoting his time to discovering the intimate secrets of Peshawar. He dwelled in the quiet backwaters of a lane called Gari Syeddan (street of the descendants of the Prophet Muhammad). Here he delved into the lives of the people, played his music and was thankful that America had forgotten him. For he had long ago learned that the people of his Hasht Nagari neighborhood had solved the enigma of modern life. For them there was no riddle about how to find happiness, for they were unburdened by the paraphernalia and troubles of modern western society. Ali Muhammad learned to disavow political anxieties, social messages and the restless aspirations of youth. Even with its streets crowded with turbaned refugees and animals, he preferred Peshawar's physical pollution to the cultural pollution he had left behind in the west.

Sitting there in the restaurant before me his face displayed the contentment you sometimes find in men who inhabit unfrequented places. There was a look in his eyes that turned inward. Though he seldom lost his smile, his manner was always slightly aloof, revealing in flashes the hidden life he so highly cherished. Charming if met by chance, he loathed all things foreign and hated to venture outside the old city. He spoke several local languages with a slow southern accent and was universally respected by the Peshawaris, who felt happy and honored that he chose to live among them. I had never heard a single soul speak badly of him. He was that rare breed of man who had come home to a foreign land. In Hasht Nagari he was considered their malang, a Muslim who worships God through the music he plays. And when he strummed the rebob, that sweet voiced local instrument, you believed the tales told of him.

I played my last card.

"I'll get us a good room at the Flashman's Hotel."

Ali Muhammad snorted in derision. Under the British Raj the well-known inn had once been the pride of Pakistan. It had long since fallen on hard times. Businessmen and tourists staying in Rawalpindi preferred the modern air conditioned luxury of the Intercontinetal Hotel. Flashman's was a part of Pakistan's disregarded past.

"I need the help or I wouldn't ask," I told my friend honestly.

A pained look crossed Ali's face.

"Have you made the reservations?" he asked.

"I've got an open ended plane ticket."

"I meant at Flashman's Hotel."

"No, I was hoping you would call them from the public call office and see to that," I said and winced.

It was a lot to ask. The public call office was located in Saddar Bazaar, across town in the new part of Peshawar. You went in, told the operator on duty who you wanted to call, then waited while the operator and his mates drank tea, and waited while one of them made an attempt to get a clear phone line, and waited if the trunk line was busy, and waited while the phone wallahs gossiped between efforts, and waited while they tried again, and maybe again and yet again, until with any luck an hour or so later they screamed at you to hurry into the little wooden phone booth there in the office. Then the waiting was over and the sweating began.

The heavy glass door sealed you in a clear tomb. You started perspiring the moment you closed the door to the narrow airless booth, which of course you had to do in order to be heard. Pakistan's phone lines were notoriously fickle. You held the old fashioned, heavy black receiver to your ear and listened to the line crackling with static. It was as if you were listening back through time. With luck you eventually heard someone hundreds of miles away shouting, "Hallo, hallo. Is anybody there?," in a metallic, disembodied voice. You started to shout in return and prayed that "atmospherics" didn't prohibit them from hearing you.

There was no way of knowing who was listening to your conversation, privacy being an unknown delicacy along the public phone line. Your business was Pakistan's business. No secret was safe, so no secrets were discussed. The public phone was used to announce the birth of sons, the death of fathers, the arrival of trains or the departure of tired horsemen going to Dublin for a bath and a girlfriend. It was a colossal pain.

Ali Muhammad groaned, reluctant to leave his comfortable surroundings and his wide circle of native friends. Then he agreed to help like I knew he would. We lived largely alone, without foreign influence, orbiting around Peshawar like two complimentary stars, relying on each other to hold onto memories only we two could appreciate.

As we walked back through the city we neared the Hasht Nagari mosque. Sitting on its steps was a local beggar, a blind man dressed in haphazard clothes. He was bearded, white haired, looked about sixty. I often saw him in our mosque, where he enjoyed a reputation for piety. I told my friend to go ahead, assuring him I would catch up at his house. Then crossing the street, I greeted the blind man quietly without revealing my identity. Taking his dirt-caked hands I placed them securely around a large bundle of rupees, the same money I had received from the Chitrali rug merchant for the sale of Shavon.

"*Allah akbar* (God is great)," I told him softly, then walked away quickly.

A friend of the Prophet once said, "Money spent on horses is in the eyes of Allah like giving alms." Muslims strongly believed all gain should be honest and honorable. I only hoped that by giving away what I believed was tainted money I had brought the palomino mare good luck.

9
Flashman's Faded Glory

It was a nice hotel for such a lousy part of Asia.

A three-hour trip eastbound on the Grand Trunk Road had brought Ali Muhammad and me to the sprawling city of Rawalpindi. Early that morning we had arrived at the Peshawar bus station, though any need to hurry had long since expired. My friend had delayed our departure for three days. He possessed a lot of talents but punctuality wasn't one of them. I didn't mind. I felt lean and rested, was thinking about calling the whole thing off, when after several days of procrastination Ali finally got around to calling the Flashman's Hotel. A room was reserved. I was thus committed quite by accident to a trip not to Dublin but to Hell.

As Ali and I trundled halfway across the country in the Flying Coach, I assured myself a few weeks away from Peshawar would do me good. Allah must have been laughing when he granted me that wish.

Our drive down the treacherous G.T. Road had been anything but boring. As custom dictated the bus driver leaned on the accelerator so hard it felt like we were on a low level plane flight. We went screaming down a pot-holed two lane road with no center divider, no shoulder, and no laws. Screeching Pushtu music was blaring over a loud speaker, providing a sound track as the bus dodged between a plethora of people, animals, carts, bicycles, children, derelict taxis and overloaded trucks. Risking your life was the price of admission to that road of death, getting to your destination alive was the prize.

I largely ignored the deadly drive, having long since grown accustomed to its bone-shaking demands. Instead, I passed the time picturing the pleasures of Dublin, or slipping into reverie about that night's upcoming accommodation. I had heard of the Flashman's Hotel for years. During the days of the British Raj, the gracious colonial baroque had hosted the British governor-general and his retinue of servants in style more than once. But the Empire was dead and her buildings were following her. A Rawalpindi taxi had delivered Ali and me from the crowded bus station to the old hotel in under ten minutes. When we arrived I was surprised to discover that the famous Flashman's complex looked shabby in the bright morning sunlight.

While Ali Muhammad signed us into the register at the main desk, I rested there in the lobby, content to sit in a comfortable chair and look outside. The hotel was a sprawling private compound barely visible from the adjacent street. Four foot walls protected a series of small bungalows, their white adobe walls and red tile roofs looking more Mediterranean than Pakistani. A well maintained gravel driveway swung in off the main road. It made a lazy loop past a series of dignified shrubs, then disappeared out one of the two gates protecting Flashman's fading glory. The lobby was in the largest bungalow situated there next to the driveway.

Until 1947 Rawalpindi had been one of the critically important links in a chain of British garrison towns. The hotel was located in what had once been that city's most prestigious neighborhood. Despising the crowded, noisy bazaars and narrow alleys of the old city, Queen Victoria's imported citizenry had created a green haven from which they governed and into which they retreated. While the natives dwelt in noisy squalor all around them, the British invested their ant-like energies into building an English town on the hot Indian plain that would suit their needs. The Mall, as the official portion of Rawalpindi was called, was a monument to British empirical ambition, architecture and philosophy. With the garrison at its hub, the new town was laid out with broad tree-lined avenues, parks and colonial baroque structures. It was an island of greenery and English values surrounded by an alien culture. Flashman's had been the hostel of choice in those heady days of empire.

Rawalpindi's privileged foreign inhabitants represented less than 10 percent of the country's population and held 90 percent of it's power. Brave cavalry men from the Queen's Own Corp of Guides rode the Mall's streets in resplendent khaki uniforms. Imposing memsahibs dressed in posh European fashions took the air from carriages driving along the wide avenues. Solemn business tycoons with solar topees atop their heads passed down the sidewalks on their way to nearby offices. Foreign service civilians tended to the tiniest details of their empire in imposing administration buildings, while army officers oversaw military operations in their nearby headquarters.

The British living in India were a small military, administrative, and trading caste superimposed on a huge native population. Calling themselves "Anglo-Indian," their slice of the world's largest empire was a complex, and protocol ridden society, though its members agreed on the grandiosity of their collective purpose. The imperialists believed the very superiority of the way of life they carried into the less materially advanced parts of the world was a guarantee of its eventual acceptance. Like their close cousins, the nineteenth century evangelical missionaries, they believed they could convert the natives they ruled into accepting their political world view. Their day-to-day mission was to keep their excitable subjects out of trouble and socialize with them only on official occasions.

After so much daily effort, these white-skinned male conquerors stopped work in the early afternoon, retiring nearby to the prestigious Rawalpindi Club. There white-coated native waiters brought them a chota peg or a cool "sundowner" to drink. Life in India was a good deal more spacious and amusing than which these men had left at home in England.

Flashman's Faded Glory

It helped that they only worked four days a week. Thursday was a holiday in the Indian Army because Queen Victoria had proclaimed herself Empress of India on a Thursday. Only Monday, Tuesday, Wednesday and Friday were full working days.

Close by were a host of tidy bungalows where wives, children and an army of fawning native servants awaited the sahibs' return from work. The word bungalow means, "Bengal style house." They incorporate what is today known as Anglo-Indian architecture. Surrounded by verdant gardens, each house was built with windows set high in the exterior walls, broad shady verandahs and high-ceiled interiors. Years before the advent of air conditioning, the bungalow was designed as a pragmatic defense against Rawalpindi's sweltering summers, which often hit 112 degrees Fahrenheit. The cottages at Flashman's were remnants of such architecture.

It was a busy and undoubtedly fulfilling life for the men and women who worked and resided around the important hotel. Not only did these people have an empire to run, there were grand balls to attend, cricket to play, museums to visit, outdoor concerts to enjoy. They led a gracious existence, all the while trying to ignore the isolation and the thousands of miles that cut them off from a sea-swept homeland many would never live to see again.

Overlooking all this luxury and effort was the Gothic-style Christ Church, which I could see from the hotel lobby. Built in 1854, it's towering white washed walls hid lofty vaults and dark beams. The walls were adorned with plaque after plaque honoring Queen Victoria's dead. These included the thousands of enlisted men, known as BORs, British Other Ranks, who guarded the city's arsenal and resided in barracks close by. Outside in the church graveyard rested the legions of unremembered and untended mortal remains of those soldiers. Lying in eternal silence among them were their neighbors; the officers, businessmen, women and children who now all slept in that forgotten corner of their once-mighty empire. From where I sat I could almost hear them whispering, "All our pomp and yesterday is one with Nineveh and Tyre."

They were energetic. They were elegant. They were gone.

Only their legends and their crumbling buildings remained in Rawalpindi.

In an unmarked grave lying near them was the last fatality of that regime, their religion. If you needed unassailable evidence that the Raj was dead forever this was it. As soon as the British pulled out in 1947 their foreign faith collapsed. "Christianity came to India riding on a bullet. It went back to England with the bayonets," was what they said in the bazaars of Peshawar. The Christ Church was a forlorn empty reminder of another age.

A glance at the busy road outside the main gate brought me back to reality. The four lane thoroughfare was crowded with old buses, donkey carts and dilapidated Morris Minor taxis left by the departing British. The road was packed bumper to tail. It looked like half of Pakistan was going past Flashman's Hotel on its way to lunch.

I told myself I had been foolishly sentimental by coming to the decaying hotel, but its legacy of nostalgic Anglo-Saxon ambiance had lured me. More importantly it had a reputation for being clean. Yet as Ali Muhammad walked over from the front desk I remember feeling happy about my choice. The last thing I wanted was to drag Pakistani fleas into Kathleen's bed.

"All set," my friend said, waving a key as proof. "Room 21."

"Three sevens, must be my lucky number," I told him.

A porter took up my duffel bag and Ali Muhammad's small overnight suitcase. We followed him outside, turning right and going directly to the first bungalow. Ali could have left the key at the desk. The door was already wide open. The petite white house was very pretty if you didn't look too closely. The white paint was peeling but an immense bougainvillea framed the door in red flowers. It looked cheery, if a little down and out and I smiled when I saw it.

The glamour stopped at the door. As soon as we stepped inside the main room I wrinkled my nose in disgust. The place stank like some unholy mixture of piss and Pinesol.

"Whew, I thought I was familiar with all the bad smells in Asia but this is a new one," I exclaimed.

While Ali tipped the porter I glanced around. The room was painted that off-white color the British had been so fond of splashing everywhere. Otherwise the walls were bare. Two ancient twin beds, looking like occidental orphans lost deep and left behind, sat with their heads shoved against the back wall. They looked like they had been in this room since Lord Mountbatten fled. I walked over and sat down on the bed closest to the door. The old mattress sagged. But in Pakistan any mattress was a luxury. I stretched out full length and sighed. Except for the smell I rather liked the room.

The luggage had been tossed at the foot of Ali Muhammad's bed. While I relaxed he started talking about lunch. It was 11:30 and I had an appetite for once. The room had a small table and two chairs. He sat down and rang up the kitchen from a 1940's style telephone sitting on the table. He was soon busy ordering us two baked chickens, with French fries and sliced tomatoes. I wasn't listening closely, having become preoccupied instead with the scene I was watching unfold outside.

Our bungalow sat at right angles to the hotel lobby, separated by a distance of about one hundred feet. Lying on my bed I had an unobstructed view of the lobby's front door as well as a portion of the adjacent gravel drive. Two large American cars had pulled up while Ali Muhammad was discussing the culinary delights Flashman's had to offer. Both cars were white and each disgorged a number of men. I watched

Khyber Knights

"It was a nice hotel for such a lousy part of Asia. But the glamour stopped at the door. As soon as we stepped into the room I wrinkled my nose in disgust. The place stank of some unholy mixture of piss and Pinesol."

one of the strangers step into the lobby. He returned outside almost immediately accompanied by the hotel manager.

"Probably a bunch of minor Pakistani bureaucrats come to pick up a foreign visitor," I thought silently.

Then things slammed into high speed. I saw the manager talking to the Pakistani who had brought him outside. That unexplained stranger was wearing sunglasses and had on a suit and tie. The men from the cars were all milling about so it was hard to get a head count. I did notice that the four fellows who had got out of the car nearest to me wore shalwar kameez. Oddly enough however the two men riding in the front car were also dressed in western style pants and shirts. Before I had time to consider how strange that was, I saw the manager point in the direction of our room. The man with sunglasses said something to the others, and with the manager in tow, the group started walking rapidly towards our bungalow as if they had urgent business in mind. As they spread out I counted eight of them, including the manager. Must be coming to meet someone important, I thought again.

OK, lunch should be here shortly," Ali said as he hung up the phone, then leaned back in his chair with a look of anticipation on his face. He was looking very dapper that day in a rich blue shalwar kameez.

"What time does your plane leave tomorrow?" he inquired nonchalantly.

I never answered that question.

"Are you sure we're in the right room?" I asked him instead, but never got a reply.

The men were suddenly rushing towards our door. The one closest to me was one of the two in slacks. He had a fat face, looked short but solid. As he got closer I saw he was wearing a dark pumpkin orange sweater over a white dress shirt.

"What odd clothes to be wearing here," I thought to myself. When he saw me staring at their approach a look of anxiety crossed his face.

"We're the hotel electricians," he said loudly in answer to my silent question and kept on coming.

I glanced up at the overhead light bulb which was burning brightly. Things were happening so fast I didn't have to raise myself up off the bed or warn Ali Muhammad. All I managed to do was say, "The lights work," and then they were in the room, and the beatings began, and everything we knew, and everything we expected, was invalidated by the brutality of fate.

"Stand up, stand up, stand up," the men were screaming as they came running into our room. I saw Ali jump to his feet startled by the appearance of this crowd of maniacs. The man claiming to be an electrician, as well as two of the men in shalwar kameez ran over, dragged me to my feet and slammed me into the wall so quickly that I had no chance to resist. I was too shocked to speak.

"What the hell is going on," Ali Muhammad shouted. As he said this he stood up and turned towards our uninvited guests. The other man in slacks and shirt was a bruiser. He stood about 6'3" and weighed about 240 pounds. His broad face sported a gigantic drooping black walrus mustache. The moment Ali spoke this man rushed over and instantly smashed him in the mouth. The blow took both of us by surprise. I saw Ali fall over the chair backwards and hit the floor hard. He managed to roll over onto his stomach, but before he could sit up, the big man walked over and deliberately stood on both of his wrists. One of the native dressed fellows started kicking my friend in the ribs. Then I saw him kick Ali Muhammad in the right side of the head so hard I thought he had killed him.

"Stop it," I screamed.

My request was denied.

"Shut up," came the reply from the "electrician" in front of me. While his two friends held my arms tightly spread-eagled against the wall, he frisked me thoroughly.

"This one's unarmed," he shouted over his shoulder.

"So's this one," I heard, and an invisible tension seemed to ease off.

The man wearing sunglasses was obviously in charge. He was still standing with the manager at the doorway.

"Get them against the back wall," he ordered.

Ali Muhammad was hauled to his feet. He looked stunned, in pain, but alive. The two of us were pushed across the room, told to face the wall furthest from the door and ordered to put our hands behind our backs. When we complied, I felt the metallic bite of handcuffs for the first time in my life. Behind me I could hear the sound of the men tearing the room apart. Out of the corner of my eye I saw them dumping out the duffel bag and suitcase onto Ali's bed, obviously searching in great haste for something. The mystery eluded me, but I had been in Asia long enough to know we had wandered into trouble. We stood there for a few moments without saying a word. A quick glance showed me Ali Muhammad looking sick with apprehension.

"Are you all right?" I asked him quietly.

Before Ali could reply, the same brute with the drooping mustache that had worked him over, punched me hard in the kidneys. I started to sink toward the floor but the big man caught me and shoved me back hard against the wall.

"You two shut up and stand there."

His breath stank.

I took it quietly, disoriented by the sudden pain. It took all my effort just to breathe. I was done talking for a while.

There was another door in our room. Knowing Pakistan, I had assumed it lead to the toilet, but we had been in the room too briefly for either of us to venture in there. Now I saw this door opened. It surprised

Flashman's Faded Glory

me to see first a small room, then another door that lead into the toilet beyond. I couldn't understand why this bungalow had a hallway into the toilet. Two of the men searched in these adjoining areas only a short time before we heard one of them shout, "I've found something."

While the bully who had hit me stood guard, the rest of the crew pushed into the small doorway, peering at something out of my line of sight. Finally I heard the man in the sunglasses say, "Bring one of them in here."

As I was closest to the door the bully grabbed me.

"Let's go," he said and shoved me through a gauntlet of dark smirking faces before I had time to object.

The hallway turned out instead to be an old-fashioned ladies boudoir. Just to the right of the door was a large, dark, wooden armoire. Situated mid way in the small room was a small bench and a dressing table. A very old mirror was affixed to the wall just above it. I doubted if the antique looking glass had ever reflected a barbaric scene like the one I found myself thrust into. The little dressing room was a relic of a more civilized and refined age. Its very air felt assaulted.

Leaning into the open armoire was the fraudulent electrician. As I walked in I saw him bring a cheap, green canvas suitcase out of its interior. He turned and placed it on the dressing table.

"Whose suitcase is this?" he asked me, clearly excited.

"Neither of us know anything about that bag. I swear it. We only got here a few minutes ago."

I could tell by the look on his face he didn't believe me.

The bag was devoid of any outside identification. As he unzipped the suitcase, I was as curious as the men crowding around me to discover its contents. Inside he uncovered a large brown towel, which he placed on the dressing table, a pair of old but serviceable jeans, a decent 35 millimeter camera, film, some cheap dark socks, worn white boxer underwear, two garish Hawaiian shirts, a Pakistani guide book and a pair of tennis shoes. Then he grunted in surprise and lifted out a large clear plastic bag from the bottom of the bag. It's brick-shaped light brown contents appeared to be quite heavy. As he lifted the bag with loving concern his assorted comrades let out a sigh of pleasure, saying "Ah" in unison as if they were watching a small child blow out the birthday candles.

The man with the sunglasses was standing across the room to my left, partly obscured by his followers. At the sight of the bag I saw a smile cross his face. He walked over to the dressing table, cautiously pinched a small hole in the bag, then wet his little finger before tucking it into the contents. When he pulled it back out, his finger was covered in a fine brown powder. He touched the end of his finger to his tongue to sample the taste.

Satisfied he turned to me and said, "What is this?"

Khyber Knights

I was too stunned to answer because it was such a Pakistani moment. The man was very dark skinned and had a handsome face adorned by an immaculate black mustache. His clothes however were out of the past. They looked like something he had pulled off a discount rack when disco was king. He was wearing a cranberry colored sports coat made from cheap synthetic material. An extremely wide red-wine tie graced the top of a cheap white shirt. His bell bottom slacks were gray. His loafers were black. Even by Pakistani standards it was an absurd attempt to look cool. Instead he looked like a bit-part actor who had wandered off the set of a 1970s television detective series by mistake, a thug suffering from amnesia who woke up in Rawalpindi.

The clothes amused me. The sunglasses closed the case. They were an expensive aviator type complete with yellow lenses. They were perfect except for one minor detail. In order to show off their foreign origin, their owner had deliberately left the small sticker reading, "Rayban" glued to the upper left hand corner of the left lens.

I closed my eyes and sighed, all doubt now gone from my mind. Only cops dressed this badly in Pakistan. I opened my eyes thinking I would berate this group of buffoons for breaking into my room and was startled to see the man in charge had removed his glasses. He must have picked up on some subtle psychic message I had sent off. Instead of the ridiculous sunglasses I was staring into two coal black eyes that had never known the warmth of kindness. His eyes pierced my flesh, laid bare my weaknesses, and dared me to test his strength of purpose.

I knew I was in trouble.

"I said what is this?" he asked again in American. Having studied in London I appreciated the difference.

It was one of the few times in Pakistan I ever felt I was really in over my head. I looked at the bag, remembered he had brought out some kind of powder, thought hard and then remembered Shavon.

"*Atta* (flour)," I ventured, remembering how I had once fed her damp straw mixed with brown flour. It was an old peasant trick when you ran out of decent fodder.

They laughed uproariously. The electrician thought the joke so funny he slapped me on the back. Even the hard eyed man smiled weakly.

"*Atta*," some one yelled out to the men waiting in the other room, and I could hear their laughter rolling in as an answer. I smiled, thinking somehow this was some sort of honest mistake after all.

I was wrong.

"It's heroin," he told me and I sucked in my breath in fear.

Before I had time to consider what to do next, I was grabbed and shoved back outside into the bedroom. It was obvious to me by now that these men were all cops, though they had never bothered to identify themselves as such. Within seconds I was once again facing the wall next to my friend Ali Muhammad. I had only been there a minute when I heard

Flashman's Faded Glory

someone behind me shout, "Hey who's hungry?" The question was followed by the sound of more laughter.

When I glanced over my left shoulder I saw an obviously fearful waiter standing at our front door. He was holding a large tray adorned with the lunch Ali Muhammad had ordered. The bully who had stood on my friend's wrists took the tray and told the waiter to get lost. The frightened servant disappeared as fast as my travel plans. The tray was put on the table. Because there were only two chairs, as soon as the beds were pulled into service, the men began to tear into the chickens and French fries. The man who had interrogated me remained aloof, standing by the front door talking to the hotel manager.

"You want to eat?" one of our captors asked us.

To beat us, then invite us to temporarily forget our differences over a meal, both with equal sincerity, was typical of Pakistani emotions.

Ali Muhammad looked their way and told them "No" in an icy voice. You don't break bread with your enemies in Pakistan. He didn't have to be told the details to know we were dealing with either cops or crooks. I thought I better tell him.

"We're in trouble," I told Ali softly.

"No kidding," he whispered back.

"They found someone else's suitcase in there. It had a big bag of heroin inside."

"We're in trouble," he agreed.

There was both an unwritten and a written law in Pakistan.

Written law said any Muslim caught drinking alcoholic drinks could be publicly flogged. It never happened for several reasons. First, the majority of Pakistan's citizens looked down on drinking, thinking the only thing worse was eating pig meat. Second, you couldn't get a drink if you wanted one. It was a dry country. A couple of high class hotels had a few bottles stashed away for the consumption of foreign guests in the privacy of their rooms. The average Pakistani national could never have walked in to such an establishment and been served a drink anyway. You had to show proof of foreign citizenship to earn that dubious privilege.

The unwritten law in Pakistan, however, was that a lot of people smoked hashish. It had been around for centuries and no amount of foreign or domestic legislation had ever eradicated its use. Many Pakistanis smoked small bits of it rolled together with tobacco inside regular cigarettes. While the law officially condemned its use, society at large took the attitude of Americans during Prohibition. Most people either looked the other way or occasionally imbibed. Even Pakistani police officers smoked it with no more social repercussions or ostracism than an Irish cop sneaking a drink back in Chicago circa 1926.

Heroin fell outside the law, written and otherwise.

It was a social evil which had appeared in Pakistan soon after the start of the Afghan Jihad. Shortly after the neighboring country fell prey to it's long-standing war, all effective anti-narcotic border control ceased to exist. The Soviet army's main concern was to locate and destroy the mujahadeen freedom fighters hiding in the mountains. The Reds spent the majority of their time searching the towns and patrolling the roads for their enemies. So long as there was no reported military activity, what happened in the quiet corners of the mountains bordering Pakistan seldom interested them.

Taking advantage of this diplomatic void, renegade Pathan drug dealers set up a string of clandestine labs. Raw opium was easily obtainable from local farmers. Whereas wheat and other crops were labor intensive, the hardy poppy flowers flourished on scrub land with almost no cultivation. More importantly they provided an immense amount of profit in comparison to grain harvests, etc. In a country racked and ravaged by more than five years of savage warfare, the opium poppy seemed like a gift from God to many struggling Afghan farmers. They knew it was being made into heroin. Yet they explained away their behavior by telling themselves it was being smuggled to the West for use by decadent citizens of other far away countries. Muslims didn't use hard drugs, they rationalized.

A lot had changed in the heroin business. In less than a decade Pakistan, once just a conduit, was now addicted.

Originally the dope was grown, processed and smuggled overseas. Then in the early 1980s some innovative local dope smoker cut a little off the top of an outgoing shipment and sprinkled heroin into a cigarette. The smack was almost 90 percent pure. He got the rush of his life. He got hooked. By now he was dead.

Reports of this new Kabul cocktail soon leaked out. What started as an experiment developed into an unacknowledged social epidemic. From Karachi to Kashmir Pakistanis were lighting up and getting hooked. Mainlining the smack American style was never popular because of the difficulty in obtaining needles. Besides, you could buy one cigarette at a time from any shop in town. "Powder" as it was called could also be found in every city. The country had a great many unemployed, frustrated young men. Getting high on heroin-laced cigarettes was their cheap ticket out of reality.

The Afghans had only been partly right. Heroin remained a major export and most of it was still consumed overseas. There was so much powder coming down out of the North West Frontier Province, Pakistan now rivaled the legendary Golden Triangle of Burma and Thailand in yearly output.

Yet the "black money" realized from the sale and manufacturing of powder was seeping into all levels of local society. Officials at the government-owned Pakistan International Airline were often implicated for smuggling. A son of the former governor of the North West Frontier Province had been busted for smuggling smack into New York City in a diplomatic pouch. Drug lords lived openly in unassailable fortresses deep in tribal territory. In a country where the average yearly income was under $500 a year, it was an easy enticement and was turning everyone from cops to Hajii's into crooks. You heard stories of it everywhere.

I had never seen it before today.

"Which one of you is Asadullah Khan?," I heard someone ask.

I turned in response.

Lunch was over. The chickens were picked clean. Greasy fingers were being wiped on paper napkins. Some of the men were already standing up. The hard-eyed man in charge was still standing with the manager by the front door.

"He says you owe him 350 rupees for the room," this fellow told me, indicating the manager.

The six men with our lunch under their belts were ready to leave. The electrician came over, unlocked the handcuffs, told us to put our hands in front, then locked us up again. Two of the men grabbed our luggage. The big man who had beaten up Ali Muhammad and me carried the green suitcase out of the dressing room.

"Let's go," the electrician said and pointed me towards the door.

"Where to?"

"Shut up."

"I told you that bag doesn't belong to us. This is a mistake," I said frantically and started to struggle.

"And I said shut up," he repeatedly impatiently, then grabbed me by my left arm and started hauling me towards the door. Ali Muhammad followed quietly on his own.

The electrician stopped me before the hotel manager. Suddenly I wanted to dig my nails into the floor if it meant staying in this room

"Help us," I said silently, pleading with my eyes.

But the manager's face was a portrayal in contempt. We could have been bleeding to death and he wouldn't have tossed us a band aid. He stood there like a vampire waiting for his money. I knew we were utterly alone. I almost groaned in despair.

"My money's in a bag under my shirt. I can't get to it with my hands locked," I said in a dull voice.

The electrician got a nod of approval, then unlocked the right handcuff. I reached under my shirt, opened the bag and pulled out my money. I counted out 350 rupees and handed it to the manager. He looked like he had taken money from a diseased hand.

"The lunch is 100 rupees more," he told me.

I didn't protest, just handed over the extra bit of extortion. This time it was my turn to act like my hand had touched something unclean. I was surprised they let me put the rest of my money back in the bag. My captor immediately locked me up again.

Ali picked that moment to shock me.

"I want to call the American Embassy," he said in a firm voice.

My eyes must have widened. Now I knew with absolute conviction we were in trouble. We never had anything to do with the embassy types. They didn't even hold our mail for us. Back home in Peshawar official policy urged American citizens to avoid any prolonged stay in the old city. Consequently Ali and I weren't considered in left field, we weren't even in the same ball game. We had always prided ourselves on our ability to play it alone.

Until now.

"I demand to call the American Embassy right now," Ali Muhammad repeated, the desperation in his voice apparent.

The man in charge just smirked. We had never been shown a search warrant, a badge, any sign of official authority. Everyone in the room knew Pakistan didn't require such domestic trivialities. In such circumstances my friend's bluff didn't rate any serious consideration.

"Plenty of time for that," the hard-eyed man said in a voice without pity, then turned and left.

"Let's go," the electrician said from behind us and shoved me out the door.

10
The Price of Torture

It was their bragging that tipped us off. Their chief had taken off in the first car with three of the men dressed in shalwar kameez. The fourth man in native dress took the driver's seat of the second automobile, a late model Jeep Cherokee. He slid behind the wheel, then fired up the engine. Our luggage and the mystery bag were tossed in the back by the bully, who sat up front next to the driver. The electrician opened the passenger door on the right side.

"Get in," he ordered and I obeyed. Ali Muhammad slid in beside me. The electrician came in last, then pulled the door shut, crowding the three of us together in the back seat. The windows were all up I noticed, then glancing around I observed that the door handles had been removed. A shudder of involuntary apprehension ran through me. I started to sweat, from fear or sickness I couldn't tell

Desperate, I looked outside the car window. There was no one to mark our departure from the Flashman's Hotel, no hotel staff, no fellow lodgers, no passing Good Samaritans. This time I couldn't shout, "Help, I'm being kidnapped," and ride off to the mountains on Shavon. Instead, as the anonymous white car pulled out into traffic, Ali Muhammad and I officially disappeared.

When I looked down at my hands, I noticed for the first time that the handcuffs I was wearing bore the inscription, "Made in the USA." I didn't have any clever insight. I wasn't Sherlock Holmes. I just got lucky when I asked, "Who are you guys? How come you've got these cuffs from America?"

The bully turned around in the front seat and smiled. His big black mustache drew back, revealing a row of beautiful white teeth that twinkled like stars in a carnivore's mouth. I was right, the thundering brute was carrying about 240 pounds and not an ounce of fat on him. But he was a mindless braggart and that gave us our first break.

His name was Ashgar Ali. The electrician was called Niazi. I had been correct about the man in the sunglasses. He was their boss, Inspector Gilani Khan. Our driver and the other three men in shalwar kameez were drones. The whole crew worked for the Narcotics Control Board, a loosely run, shadowy police outfit whose official function was to curtail the burgeoning heroin trade. Though officially Pakistani in origin, it was an ugly stepchild of the American Drug Enforcement Agency.

Niazi gave him a look as if to warn his big partner to be quiet but Ashgar was clearly not intimidated by the smaller man. I was glad to hear him talk. He revealed how he, Niazi and Gilani had recently returned from the United States where they had been trained by the Americans. Ashgar Ali bragged about drinking in bars in Houston, threw out broad hints about his sexual exploits with American women in Nevada, recalled a baseball game, in short he reveled in his memories.

As he talked his face was alight with excitement and nostalgia. He couldn't hide his hunger for all things American. It was an unconcealed addiction. Ashgar was living proof of the old saying that the visa to the United States was the passport to Paradise. He would have sold his mother's soul to go back.

But he was stuck with us in a car in Rawalpindi and oddly enough he didn't seem to mind. He was glad to have arrested us, if only so he could chat up some Americans. He saw nothing wrong or obscene about his boasting behavior.

I had seen his type a hundred times around Peshawar. Desperate, poor, intelligent men who latched onto some foreign aid agency like emotional limpets. They became drivers, office wallahs, chowkidars or hit the jackpot and got a field supervisor's job. Regardless of what country hired them men like this shared one thing in common. They weren't seeking a wage. They were seeking escape and they reeked of unhappiness. They hated their country, their origins and usually themselves. They were cultural Quislings with hungry souls, aping anything foreign, despising anything native, willing to do anything to escape from Afghanistan, Pakistan, India, Nigeria, wherever life had trapped them at birth. The man leering back at me from the front seat could have been their poster boy. The only difference was that Ashgar Ali was a monster.

Until that moment I was convinced our arrest was some local mistake, wrong room, wrong identity or something of that order. When I heard of the DEA connection I knew things were getting complicated. This at least explained why our captors were wearing American clothes . But I still hoped that a few phone calls would reveal our innocence. I could catch tomorrow's flight. This would turn out to be nothing serious, an amusing story to tell the beautiful Kathleen over an Irish dinner, just another private joke to be shared later between Ali Muhammad and me.

In my innocence I still had not discovered how zealous our captors were.

My first clue came when they didn't take us to a police station.

The driver drove us for more than half an hour, winding in and out of the city until eventually we arrived in a nondescript suburban neighborhood. I had been all over Rawalpindi but hadn't a clue where we now were. We had left the old city and any place I might have recognized. This unfamiliar area consisted of expensive homes modeled along western lines. It was a part of the city most of Rawalpindi's poverty-stricken citizens never visited.

The Price of Torture

When I looked down the street all I saw were a series of walls and closed gates. By now it was about 2:30 in the afternoon, but unlike the crowded old city we had left, here there wasn't a soul in sight. The modern American style homes lining both sides of the avenue sat sullen and secure behind their mortar walls and steel gates, resistant to tradition, disdainful of visitors.

The Jeep stopped in front of a set of green double gates. The driver honked twice. While we waited I noticed that the street numbers had been removed from the gate post. In their place were little black nail holes looking back at me like lies. A chowkidar swung open the gates and we drove in.

The concrete drive went straight ahead for thirty feet, then stopped next to a sprawling one-story home. It was painted pink and in obvious disrepair. It had a badly tended front lawn. An eight foot hedge lined the inside of the walls. The place had a secretive air. I got the ominous impression the house had been chosen because it was so quietly average that it was able to blend in and hide its real purpose.

As if to confirm my worries Ali Muhammad whispered, "I have a bad feeling about this."

"Shut up," Niazi said and jabbed him with an elbow.

Ashgar Ali opened the door on Niazi's side and we were ordered to get out quickly. Before we could even consider looking around and orienting ourselves, the two narcs grabbed each of us by an arm and pulled us through the wooden front door.

We found ourselves inside what had once been a large living room. The concrete floors were devoid of carpet or rugs. The dirty white walls were so bare they didn't have memories. A couple of cheap light fixtures hung from the ceiling giving the room an ugly glare. Two doors led off, right and left, in either direction. Any trace of family warmth had been surgically removed.

In the far corner away from the door stood an ancient wooden filing cabinet. It had four drawers and was scratched and scarred all over. There were six sturdy wooden office chairs scattered around the place. The center of the room was dominated by a very large, very old, wooden teacher's desk. As we were lead towards it I could see the desk was chewed up, its corners rounded from age and abuse. A straight-backed wooden armchair was placed behind it. All of this traumatized public school furniture was collectively reminiscent of the Eisenhower era.

Inspector Gilani Khan was sitting there waiting for us. There wasn't an apple on his desk and he didn't look like a kindly first grade teacher. All seven of the men who invaded our hotel room were gathered together, only now there was a palpable feeling of excitement. Gilani ignored us when we entered, continuing to work on some papers placed in front of him on the desk. Ashgar Ali walked me past his boss, bringing me up in front of a wooden chair placed on Gilani Khan's right, furthest from the door. Before I could protest Ashgar reached under my shirt, unbuckled my leather bag and took out my wallet, money, air plane ticket and passport. He threw these on the desk and then motioned for me to sit down. Niazi directed my friend to sit in a chair across from me on the other side of the desk. Like me, Ali Muhammad's official paper life lay tossed out waiting for inspection. Without those slips of paper we were stateless citizens.

The driver had carried in my duffel bag and Ali's little suitcase. Niazi crossed the room, sat in one of the chairs and watched as two of the cops dressed in shalwar kameez tore our bags apart. They began making an inventory of our possessions. But more importantly, there was no sign of the mysterious green canvas suitcase, which we never saw again.

Despite the seriousness of the situation I was growing impatient with this game of mistaken identity. The handcuffs were snapped so tight they hurt like hell. I wanted to leave this dumpy house and its slum-ridden country, was anxious to take a break from a nation that could rip you out of bed, kick you in the head and drag you across town to a forbiddingly ugly pink house.

The clothes of Inspector Gilani Khan and his two primary henchmen, like the battered furniture, were so blatantly American I lost my ambiguous feelings and began getting angry. I had always been intolerant of authority figures. Suddenly I had the feeling I had been hauled in again before Mr. Rupp, the Boys' Vice Principal back in William J. Mulholland Junior High School. I looked across the desk at my pal Ali Muhammad, shook my head to signal my disgust and smiled at him as if to say, "OK I've had enough. Can you believe this !" The look of bemused tolerance on his face told me my fellow expatriate hadn't given up hope that the situation was merely a mix-up.

It didn't matter what we thought of the furniture or his clothes, the narcotics inspector had a job to do. Despite his odd apparel, I could see Gilani Khan had the body of an athlete, all bone and muscle. He had gray reptilian eyes. His skin was very dark. His hair was cut short. His black mustache was perfect. He looked like a Pakistani Prussian. Though Ashgar Ali was much bigger than his boss, he was only a lackey obeying Gilani's orders. This man sitting before me was a leopard, and like that big cat, I learned he tortured his prey.

Before I could protest the narcotics commander turned and asked me, "Father's name?"

He had a stack of typed forms laid out neatly in front of him. In between the forms were placed several old fashioned sheets of carbon paper. Gilani gave me a hard look, his imported ball point pen poised to record my information.

"Look I don't know what this all about but I know we've got a right to call our embassy. I want to call them right now. You can't hold us. We haven't done anything."

The Price of Torture

"Father's name?" was the answer I got from Gilani in that flat, emotionless, aggravating voice of his.

"Let's go, Ali," I said and stood up as if to signal our departure.

My bluff lasted less than a second. Before I could move away from the desk Ashgar Ali came up from behind and slammed me back down into my chair.

"Father's name?" Ashgar's boss asked again.

A heavy silence fell between us. I looked into his eyes. He must have seen the contempt I felt. He matched it, looking at me like I was some lower form of life. At that exact instant Gilani Khan and I became sworn enemies for life. Ashgar came later.

I took a deep breath, looked at Ali Muhammad for emotional support and saw his eyes give me a silent approval. He seemed to be telling me that maybe if we cooperated we could still walk out of this charade. I answered Gilani Khan's questions. The words burned my tongue. Speaking of my family and my past in front of those bullies shamed me and I told myself someone would pay for the insults.

Gilani grilled Ali Muhammad next. Parents, date and place of birth, occupation, military service, university degrees, professional experience, everything except the obvious was asked and noted. While the cop was writing down the last of these answers, Ali Muhammad brought up an important but over looked fact.

"We're fellow Muslims. We wouldn't have anything to do with heroin," he told the inspector without being asked. The sincerity in his voice was transparent. He was clearly a good man, scared and out of his element. At that moment in our camaraderie my heart went out in pity and protection to my faithful friend. Even if I could have foreseen the horror that was coming I would have let Ali go and stayed in his place.

It didn't matter what my friend said. America had killed Gilani Khan's religion. He wasn't a Muslim anymore. He was a narc and a heretic.

"Every dope smuggler in Pakistan is a Muslim. What makes you two any different?" the inspector asked Ali Muhammad, then started shuffling a different set of forms together.

In a moment Gilani had these new papers in order. He turned to Ali, who I suspect he thought was more reasonable.

"Who did you buy the heroin from?"

"I told you we don't know anything about any heroin. My friend is flying to Dublin because he is sick with hepatitis I only came down from Peshawar to help him get a room and get on the plane tomorrow," Ali Muhammad pleaded. "Anyone in Peshawar will vouch for us."

The musician went on to explain about our work and friends and long ties to Pakistan.

"Clever," Gilani said in open contempt, dismissing our lives with a word. "Who did you get the heroin from?" he asked again.

Khyber Knights

While this cat and mouse game was being played, Ashgar Ali walked over to the old filing cabinet behind me. I heard him open the top drawer, withdraw something and come back. He pulled up one of the old chairs and sat down next to my corner of the desk. In his left hand he had a big ball peen hammer. He held it out for me to inspect. That beautiful killer smile of his was spread all over his face. I took the proffered tool. It was heavy. I let it swing in my right hand a little, then tossed it on the desk as if to say, "So what." The hammer clattered when it landed. The noise was loud but Gilani ignored the disruption and continued to grill Ali Muhammad. He was getting nowhere but at the same time he was obviously granting his lieutenant silent approval to conduct this second interview.

Ashgar Ali laid his left hand flat on the desk, spread his fingers wide, then lifting the hammer, he pantomimed crushing them one by one.

"You better talk," Ashgar said to me. Having my fingers atomized was obviously going to be the penalty for any continued refusal to cooperate. Ashgar Ali was enjoying every minute of this little interchange. I wasn't amused, however, and stared back in silence.

"Talk," he said again in a whisper, only this time Ashgar took the hammer and reaching over, quickly cracked me on the right kneecap. It wasn't hard enough to permanently injure me, just enough to hurt sharply. I gritted my teeth and winced. Ashgar lifted an eyebrow as if to ask me if I wanted more. It was obvious to both of us Gilani's lack of interference was upping the ante at persecution poker.

Suddenly I had had enough. This was Asia and bad things occasionally occurred there. Until that moment I had remained patient and philosophical. I thought it was going to be late plane flight and apologies all around. When that hammer touched me my blood turned to ice water. I knew there was some hidden agenda here, that these men either knew the truth or didn't care about finding it. I now understood we weren't going to convince them the suitcase wasn't ours. They knew that already or refused to believe otherwise. All doubt drained from my body as it dawned on me who and what I was dealing with. I wasn't dealing with Pakistanis or fellow Muslims. I was dealing with American thugs.

My face became steel. I glared at Ashgar Ali and snarled, "Go piss yourself *behnchowd* (sister fucker)," in a voice loud enough for the other men in the room to hear, making sure I emphasized the vile last word.

The big cop came at me like a tornado, knocking me out of the chair onto the floor. Before I could raise my handcuffed hands to protect myself Ashgar started kicking me. I saw him raise the hammer over his head and thought he was going to kill me.

Gilani Khan saved my life, if not my ribs, pulling the brute off me before he could do much damage. I saw him grab Ashgar and pull him back.

The Price of Torture

"Stop it," he shouted. "Leave him alone. We'll deal with him in a few minutes."

Niazi and another cop had rushed over. I rolled up on my left elbow. Niazi pulled me to my feet and slammed me into the chair the other cop had righted. Ashgar reluctantly walked away, his face a murderous mask of unconcealed hate.

The narcotics inspector was plainly furious. He shoved the new set of papers towards me without explanation.

"Sign it," Gilani ordered me.

"What's this?"

"It's a confession saying the heroin we found is yours. Sign this and I'll only charge you with possession."

"Go to hell *munafiq* (heretic)," I told him.

The infuriated cop turned to Ali Muhammad, offering him the same set of papers.

"You look like you're smarter. Tell me it was his idea and I'll let you go free right now."

I saw my friend swallow hard, digging deep for his courage.

"You heard him. Go to hell," Ali told our tormentor in a wavering voice.

Gilani Khan stood up, the interview obviously at an end. He motioned to the cops lurking nearby to come and get Ali Muhammad. Two of the underlings each grabbed an arm and scooped my pal up out of the chair.

"You can't hold us like this," Ali shouted in a desperate attempt to restore sanity to our situation.

The inspector paused for a moment to look at him.

"Yes I can and yes I will, unless you decide to sign this paper."

Ali Muhammad's silence was his answer.

"Bring this one with me," the inspector said, indicating the mild mannered musician, then turned and walked toward the closest of the two doors that lead into nearby rooms. The two cops dragged Ali Muhammad off behind Gilani Khan. Meanwhile Niazi had come over, grabbed me by the right arm and was leading me toward the door on the opposite side of the room. Out of the corner of my eye I saw Ashgar reaching into the filing cabinet again. Before I had a chance to turn my head fully and see what Ashgar was doing, Niazi had opened the door and pulled me into a small adjacent room.

It must have been a bedroom at one time. Why anyone would have painted it pea green was beyond me. In comparison the room I had just left was luxurious. The only furnishings were two of the old fashioned wooden desk chairs. Only neither of these had arms. They were sturdy, straight backed, dark wood, utilitarian objects from a slightly earlier age.

Niazi knew what he was about. He walked me straight to the first chair, directing me to face it, not sit down. He unsnapped the left side of the handcuffs. Before I could consider hitting him and escaping, he pulled me down toward the back of the chair. I didn't have a clue what he was doing. He took the unlocked portion of the handcuffs, passed the short handcuff chain under the support that ran between the back legs of the chair, brought up the cuff and snapped it onto my left wrist again.

I now found myself drawn over the chair, with my armpits resting on the top of the chair back, my knees pulled against the front of the chair seat, and my body bent in an arc. I was stretched so tight I was almost on my tiptoes.

Niazi left without a word, shutting the door behind him. A single naked light bulb hung from the ceiling. My position was painful. When I tried to shift my body I discovered the chair was bolted to the floor. The handcuffs were hurting my wrists and the chair was digging into my armpits. But try as I might, I couldn't budge the chair and could barely twist my body right or left.

I was in discomfort but strangely enough I wasn't afraid. This came from a lack of experience. The only run-in I had ever had with Pakistani police was when someone stole my bicycle back in Hasht Nagari. It was never found but I drank countless cups of tea at the neighborhood station and heard a host of apologies from the chief down to the patrol men. I had never looked at a native policeman with anything other than respect. They were underpaid, sometimes a little corrupt, but always friendly.

"OK," I told myself. "No need to panic. They're going to question us separately to try and trip us up. We've got nothing to hide, so we've got nothing to worry about. Thank God I watched 'Hawaii Five-O' as a kid. Book'em Dano. Heroin One."

I was wondering when they would let us call the embassy and thinking what trouble I was going to cause for these guys, when I heard the sound of a terrific blow followed by Ali's scream. A cold chill ran down the left side of my spine. I could feel the hair standing up on the back of my neck.

Thud. Scream.

I felt my heart beat fast three times running.

Thud. Scream.

My eyes grew wide with disbelief and fear.

Thud. And a scream of anguish came wailing in from the far side of the house.

Thud. Scream.

Thud. Scream.

And then a long dreadful silence which whispered to me of anticipation and the forthcoming arrival of agony. The whole world was holding its breath with me now. Suddenly my courage was fleeing. I just wanted to grab Ali Muhammad and get away from that posse of lunatics. But I didn't have time to consider any daring plans for escape. The door was snatched open. My mouth went dry.

I saw Ashgar Ali holding it open politely for his boss. Inspector Gilani Khan walked in and went straight towards the chair behind me. Then I saw Ashgar Ali enter. He closed the door behind him, then walked over

The Price of Torture

and stood off to my right. The big thug was holding a *chittar*, a Pakistani torture instrument whose infamous existence was officially denied. It resembled a child's cricket bat. Like all wooden cricket bats, this one was extremely thick and very heavy. One side was six inches wide and cut perfectly flat to hit the prisoner. The other side was curved to give it weight and balance. It had such a long handle Ashgar's big pig trotter hands had room to spare. What made this bat different was that the end had been lopped off, leaving the nasty looking remnant only two feet long. The handle had been wrapped in black tape to afford a better grip. The striking surface was covered in tight black leather. The once innocent plaything had been twisted into a child's toy from Hell.

Ashgar stood there with the flat side of the bat pointed at me. He looked slightly out of breath. I wondered how bad off Ali was. Suddenly I knew I could expect no mercy. No matter. My pride made me silently resolve I would rather die than give Ashgar Ali the satisfaction of hearing me cry out as well. Ignorant fool that I was, I told myself I was made of sterner stuff.

I had heard Gilani Khan getting comfortable in the chair behind me to my left. I had to twist my head in that direction as far as I could in order to see him. This swung my back towards Ashgar Ali, leaving me exposed and blind in that direction.

Gilani Khan appeared relaxed and slightly bored.

"Mr. Beau Fontaine told us everything," he said.

I could see the deception written on his face.

"You're lying," I told him with disdain.

He sighed.

"Why don't you just save us both a lot of trouble and tell me what I want to know?" he urged me.

"I've already told you. I don't know anything about that bag. It's not ours. I never saw it before today."

"Why don't you stop lying?"

"I'm not lying."

"This is such an awkward moment for you to say that."

He looked at me, visibly weighing me like a clinical specimen. I saw the look in his eye and knew he had made some silent decision. I stared back hard in return.

"Things could be worse," I told him, my defiance flying in the face of reason.

"They will be," he assured me.

Before I grasped his warning Gilani said, "*Theek hai* (OK)."

The words hadn't registered before I felt the cricket bat smash into my back directly over my kidneys. The impact felt like my internal organs had been driven out the front of my body. I didn't scream. The wave of agony that instantly enveloped me wouldn't permit that. I had been dipped alive into a vat of pain so intense I was mute from the shock of it.

My arms and legs shook uncontrollably. I ground my teeth together and breathed hard and fast through my nose. The pain slowly ebbed and only then did I manage to take a deep breath through my mouth. The handcuffs had sliced into my wrists. I could feel blood trickling down onto my hands. I looked over my right shoulder at Ashgar Ali, trying not to pant audibly or reveal how much he had hurt me.

"You son of a whore," I told him.

"My father was an imam," he warned me with death lurking in his eyes.

"You son of an imam's whore."

Ashgar spat a great gob into my face.

"I'll beat you till your bones drop out for that remark," the policeman promised me, then tightened his grip on the cricket bat so hard I could see his big knuckles go white.

Before he could follow through on his threat Gilani Khan interrupted.

"Maybe now you want to tell me who you bought the heroin from?"

I looked over at the inspector.

"That bag belongs to someone else. I swear it."

"*Theek hai.*"

Before I could scream "No" it was too late.

The next one caught me directly over the spine at shoulder level. The impact buckled my knees and drove me into the back of the chair. It felt like someone had stripped the meat off my bones. I thought the pain of it was going to stop my heart and snap the soul right out of my body.

"I want you to understand that the choice to continue is yours. Just tell me the bag belonged to your friend Ali Muhammad and I'll let you go."

Nothing passed my lips, nothing could. My eyes had rolled back into my head. The room was tilting. I was sure Ashgar Ali had crippled me. I couldn't take a breath, much less implicate my pal.

Gilani Khan waited patiently. The room was trying to spin. I braced my feet on the floor and stared straight ahead at that ugly green wall, trying to regain control.

"God damn your souls," I finally answered in a horse whisper.

"*Theek hai,*" Gilani said in a bland voice dripping with resignation.

The back of my buttocks exploded so hard I almost pissed myself.

"You bastards," I screamed and tried to rear up from the chair to pull free and kill Ashgar Ali. But I was no better than a chained animal. My curse turned into a roar. My fingers opened and closed as I was brought up short by the handcuffs stripping the skin off my wrists. Yet as I turned I saw Ashgar and through the red haze of my hatred I tried to get my hands on him so I could destroy him.

Grabbing me by my hair with his right hand, my captor slammed my forehead into the top of the chair, stunning me and bringing my revolt to a halt. Then, not waiting for the command he swung the bat against the back of my legs.

The Price of Torture

I wilted.

I died.

All resolve left me. I swam in a sea of pain so bright I knew I would never live to see the far shore, and in that instant I knew I would tell them anything, anything, anything, anything they asked me, that all the heroin ever made was mine, that Ali Muhammad did it, that I would beg on my knees for my life if they would only stop beating me. But at that moment, when my courage fled, Ashgar Ali made the mistake of letting his anger run wild. He attacked me without mercy. From my shoulders to my knees the bat fell on me like Satan's whip from Hell. I understood then that Gilani Khan had finally unleashed his henchman and that the big cop at last had his boss's permission to beat me to death. As I fell down through an abyss of pain I could never have known existed, something in me latched onto a tiny rock of resistance in this sea of brutality.

And then I screamed, like a man on fire, like a man who knows he is dying. A woeful howl went up in protest to the God who had abandoned me and let me slide into that torturous pit. The pain was so unbearable I longed for death. I slobbered and pitched and screamed and fought against the chain, trying to pull the chair out of the ground. My only thought now was to reach Ashgar Ali and rip out his throat with my teeth.

But the beating continued until the brute literally drove me down, until all resistance crumpled and the force of the blows threw me up against the chair's back. Somewhere in the far distance I heard the savage policeman starting to breathe heavy and the blows, though still hard, began to lose some of their ferocity, falling mainly on my legs and then eventually stopping all together.

I lay there like a bent bow, with my head hanging over the chair back, and my knees pulled up tight against the front of the chair. The only thing holding me up was the unrelenting grip of the handcuffs.

I heard Gilani Khan and Ashgar Ali talking but I no longer understood language. I was gone. My eyes were closed. I felt the saliva drooling out of my open mouth onto the floor below. There were now two parts of my body, the front half which counseled me that I was a human, and the back half that said I was dead. I felt my heart refusing to believe it beat in that battered body. Life flickered in me like an ember.

The chair behind me scraped as Gilani Khan stood up. From far, far away I dimly heard him say, "I didn't think he'd talk. This one's got a length of tiger's blood in him."

Then I heard the door open and close. Fear gripped my throat. Even then, in what was left of my unreasoning brain, I knew if Ashgar Ali stayed behind he would murder what little was left of me. But through the slits that I called eyes I saw they had both departed. A deep groan passed out of me and I was sucked into a deep blackness that shut down my mind completely.

11
An Unexpected Accommodation

It was the sound of Ali Muhammad's voice that brought me back to reality. I hung there over the chair, a coma with a name, head down, mouth open, brain blank. His soft melodic southern voice floated down to me like the promise of a previous life.

"Ali," was my first conscious thought.

Men were talking in the other room. I could not understand what they were saying but occasionally the cadence of my friend's voice filtered in soft and reassuring. I swam to the surface of consciousness in search of it.

As I opened my eyes and shut my mouth I heard Gilani Khan once again and remembered fear. I pulled my head up, blinked several times, told my soul to take its place and tried to regain control of my body. It wasn't easy.

The handcuffs had scraped the meat off my wrists. They were on fire. My shirt was sticking to my back, from blood or sweat I couldn't tell. If I moved anything except my eyelids I was plunged into agony. I momentarily decided to postpone any effort to escape.

I had no idea how long I had already hung there or how long I waited afterwards. When Niazi finally opened the door I pulled back like a whipped dog. He strode over like he was in a hurry. If he had looked me in the eye I would have started shaking. If he had grabbed me I would have howled like a fear-crazed animal. The way he studiously ignored me was proof Niazi had seen men in my condition before.

Reaching to the bottom of the chair he repeated the procedure that had originally imprisoned me in this room a hundred years ago. The portly cop unlocked the left handcuff, pulled it from underneath the support running between the rear chair legs, then grabbed the left handcuff and snapped it back around my wrist.

When he pulled me erect I screamed.

The flesh of my body had become a primer in persecution. I was living grief from my neck to my knees. Niazi didn't have time for such low priorities. He snatched the short chain running between the handcuffs and lead me like a dazed beast back into the company of men.

Walking was difficult. Sitting in the chair he shoved me into was so painful I wanted to weep. Everything was the same. Nothing ever would be again.

Ali Muhammad, his face a battered mess, was once again sitting across from me on the other side of the desk. He looked terrible but he managed to smile at me, as if to give me courage and reassure me that we were going to pull through this. Inspector Gilani Khan had taken up his place in the wooden armchair behind the desk. Niazi, Ashgar Ali and the other narcs were walking about and talking.

The only new addition was a balding little Pakistani man in his late fifties. He was dressed in a crumpled brown suit that looked like he had slept in it for years. He was smoking a foul smelling cigarette and setting up an old fashioned camera on a tripod. He went about his work with a sense of curious detachment. When the unwieldy photographic contraption was assembled on its spindly legs he turned to the inspector.

"Ready," he said and then motioned for Ali and me to take our place in front of his camera.

We were told to stand shoulder to shoulder and face the camera. My friend asked if the picture was to be used as a mug shot. No, it was to accompany a story in tomorrow's Urdu newspaper about two American heroin smugglers. The flash bulb exploded and our images were locked away with our innocence.

"You'll be famous tomorrow," someone said laughing.

The photo was the second biggest mistake they had made that day.

"Let's go," Niazi said, pointing towards the now open front door. Ali Muhammad started walking in that direction without being told. I shuffled slowly behind him, every step an injurious exercise. "Come on," Niazi said impatiently. He took my arm like he was dealing with the village idiot, hurrying me along.

Outside it was pitch black.

"Must be late," I thought, surprised to discover I could still think straight. The big white Jeep was waiting. The right side rear door was open and waiting. I climbed in slowly. The door was slammed shut behind me, then Niazi jumped up front in the passenger seat. I found Ali Muhammad sitting next to me.

"Feeling better?" I heard and looked up to see a smiling Ashgar Ali sitting behind the wheel.

I was too tired and sore to want to kill him anymore, was dimly aware I was in some sort of shock. I just wanted to be left alone either to heal or die. The bully drove us through the darkened city. If the door had flung open on its own volition and I had rolled out of the car to freedom, I would have been too weak to get up and run away. Instead I remained huddled deep inside my silence. I sat. I breathed. I ached. I lived, barely. That was all.

Plus I had to listen to Ashgar Ali shoot off his mouth. He was feeling chipper and bragged, "Don't worry, I'll be back in America before you will," laughing uproariously at his own joke.

Eventually the Jeep brought us all to a very poor section of Rawalpindi. We passed down a shadowy street and turned into the gate of what could only be an old Pakistani jail. The two uniformed cops

An Unexpected Accommodation

lounging at the gate with rifles were a dead giveaway. The walled compound was completely darkened. Ashgar stopped the Jeep in front of a small brick building. The warm yellow light of a dim bulb shone through the open door. The narcs left us on the back seat like two unimportant bundles, then went inside.

It was the first private moment we had enjoyed since the cops burst into our hotel room. "God, was that only this morning," I thought. Ali Muhammad, man of many travels, philosopher, student of cultural diversity, wisely used the chance to put the situation in perspective.

"I think you're going to miss that flight," he drawled.

When I looked at him I saw a man bruised but not beaten. I returned his smile. At least that didn't hurt.

"Last time I let you make the hotel reservations, buddy," I replied.

Ali's door shot open. Niazi was standing outside.

"Let's go," he ordered, directing us toward the small office.

We walked a few steps through the dark, arriving at a brick building barely big enough to hold a desk, the police sergeant sitting behind it and Ashgar Ali. The room was so little we slid inside the door and stood there in respectful silence. While the other two men argued, Niazi unlocked our handcuffs.

"And I tell you Inspector Gilani Khan says you're to keep them tonight. He'll press the formal charges when he sends you the F.I.R. (First Investigation Report) tomorrow," Ashgar Ali was saying in a loud, angry voice. The policeman looked like he couldn't care less. It was obvious there was no love lost between these two branches of Pakistani law enforcement.

The sergeant sat ramrod straight.

Nothing about the man looked soft, complacent, or most importantly, corrupt.

He appeared to be about fifty years old. His skin was nut brown. His nose was a straight-edged necessity, not an ornament. He was as skinny as a rawhide string and looked just as tough. The David Niven style mustache was his only concession to vanity. I was sure when he wasn't fasting, he lived on ground glass and starch.

Ashgar Ali had almost a hundred pounds on the sergeant but I had no doubt this tough old bird could have done a lot of damage to the big bully. The short sleeved uniform shirt the policeman wore was steel gray. You could have sliced bread on its sharp creases. Several service ribbons were pinned above his left pocket. A small black nameplate rested above the opposite pocket. White letters spelled out the name "Hiyat Mohammad." Unlike our two civilian dressed captors, the word "Police" was proudly spelt out in silver letters on his shirt's epaulets. Three big bold red stripes denoting his rank were proudly displayed on the sergeant's left sleeve.

Even here in the office he wore a blue beret over his salt and pepper hair. On the cap's left side was a square red patch. The silver metal wreath adorning the middle of the patch prominently displayed the words "Police" once again. From where I stood I could see he was wearing khaki service trousers. A large black belt with a silver buckle, decorated by the same police wreath, encircled his thin waist.

Sergeant Hiyat Mohammad and Narcotics Officer Ashgar Ali were two opposing forces of nature. They served different masters, their clothes symbolizing their cultural allegiances and the conflict running beneath the surface of the Pakistani nation. Something was about to snap when Niazi grabbed Ashgar by the arm and urged him to leave. I heard them go outside and start the car. It wasn't until the narcs drove away that I realized our tormentors had finally left us alone.

That old policeman had seen a lot of bad men. He scrutinized us both without so much as a blink. His eyes were two black flints looking for lies. If this man had glanced at my pockets, my face would have told him how much change I had hidden. Besides I was too far gone to try and look tough. I just tried to look unimportant and polite.

"You're both in big trouble. Sit down," he finally said. His voice surprised me. It was professional but seemed to contain a note of sympathy within it. On the left side of the policeman's desk, next to the room's brick wall, was a wooden bench. It only took Ali three steps to reach it and sit down. I followed suit. Yet when I bent my body and gingerly sat on the bench I felt like I was on fire. Hiyat Mohammad saw me wince. My wounds were invisible underneath my shalwar kameez. Ali's face however was clearly red from where he had been slapped around in my absence. Therefore Hiyat Mohammad asked him, "What happened?"

Ali Muhammad told him our story, not missing a detail. The policeman listened carefully. I couldn't tell if he was making mental notes or getting bored and ready to whip us himself. When my traveling companion finished Hiyat looked as us both again and asked a single question.

"You say you're Muslim."

"Yes, Muslims," I croaked out. "I've been to Mecca, and we didn't do anything, and they beat us and tried to force us to sign a confession," I hastened to add.

Whatever initial determination the tough old cop had been weighing came to an abrupt termination.

"You look like you could use a cup of tea. *O Larhke*," he summoned in an authoritarian tone. An elderly servant came in, took the policeman's order and just as quickly disappeared again.

This time the sergeant asked the questions. Who could have overheard Ali Muhammad make the reservations at the public phone office in Peshawar? Did we meet anyone suspicious on the bus? Had anyone asked us to carry any packages? Had we ever met the taxi driver

An Unexpected Accommodation

before? When we arrived at our hotel room did the porter act surprised when we discovered the door open? Did the beds look unmade or was there any evidence someone had recently left? Did either of us go into the dressing room or look inside the armoire? How long were we in the room before the narcotics police arrived and how hard was it for them to find the other suitcase? Why didn't they show the heroin and the unidentified clothes to Ali Muhammad instead of just taking my word that none of the things in the green suitcase belonged to us? Had Inspector Gilani Khan suggested any names or places to us in connection to the heroin's origin? Did either of us have enemies in Peshawar who would falsely implicate us in order to extract revenge?

We both answered honestly and politely. Ali recalled that when he made the reservations over the phone he mentioned I was sick and walking tired me. The man who spoke to him said he would reserve Room 23 for us. Instead we were given Room 21. I hadn't been privy to this detail and Ali had thought it unimportant when we checked in.

The tea came. The cup was hot in my hand but the warm sweet liquid helped restore me to life. While we drank it the sergeant continued his questions. What time had we arrived at the hotel that morning? Did the narcotics police tell us we were under arrest or inform us where we were being taken? Where was the pink house located? Had we seen the address? How long did they hold us there? Did Gilani Khan order his lieutenant Ashgar Ali to strike me with the hammer? Which man beat us? Who gave that order? Did they ever let us call our embassy?

The tea and questions ran out at the same time. I was beginning to think Hiyat believed us, would call the whole thing a mistake and let us leave. Then he sat down his cup, informed us we were prisoners, and crushed out the last remnants of our pathetic hopes.

"I don't believe you are lying, nevertheless I'm afraid you will have to remain here tonight."

Ali Muhammad must have been reading my mind.

"Can't we just overlook the whole thing? I know they beat us but we're ready to forget it if you can just let us go," he asked, though he didn't look any more hopeful than he sounded.

"Sorry! The narcotics inspector is going to file a complaint against you tomorrow. If you go free I'll be arrested myself."

Hiyat Mohammad stood up, went to the door and called in another policeman. The sergeant asked him to bring in our bags. Before leaving, Niazi had tossed them outside the office door. Within moments our two weary looking pieces of luggage were once more sitting in front of us.

"Did they steal anything from you," the sergeant asked.

Coming from a policeman the question startled me.

"I don't think so," Ali Muhammad answered cautiously.

"They're not good Muslims," the sergeant said offhandedly.

The two policemen then made an exact inventory of our possessions. Our passports, foreign registration papers, cash, travelers checks, my plane ticket, all the effects of our official lives were placed in a neat pile on top of the sergeant's desk. Last of all he asked us to surrender our personalities. Within a few seconds my thick, antique silver bracelet and gold encrusted emerald ring were locked away with our other valuables in his desk drawer. I felt naked, stripped of any last remnants of my previous ego.

Finally Hiyat had us each sign the inventory listing our personal belongings. The long handwritten document had a Pakistani flag stenciled on top of the stationary. It was the first time I had ever felt sad to see the star and crescent of that proud banner.

"I will give these documents to the magistrate in the morning. His signature will authorize me to keep your things safe here in police lockup until your case is decided."

He stood up, a note of finality was written on his face.

"You will come to lockup now."

It was a simple fact, an order, a promise. Hiyat Mohammad walked out the door. I went next. I didn't wait to see if Ali Muhammad followed. I knew he was like me, more afraid of being left behind than marching straight ahead.

"This way," the sergeant said and lead us off into the jet black night. First we turned the corner of the building, then walked a hundred feet across the compound to another small building. A policeman with a rifle emerged from the shadows of this buildings porch. He and Hiyat Mohammad spoke softly. The sergeant disappeared into the darkness surrounding the structure. Then I heard a sound I had never heard before but was going to learn all too well. It was the rattle of an enormous key being turned inside the lock of a Pakistani prison. This was followed by the noise of a large door moaning as its hinges were awakened.

Hiyat Mohammad's voice came to us from some where in the inky distance up ahead.

"Inside please."

I walked forward carefully. It was so black I could barely see where to put my feet. When I was right on top of him, I discovered the sergeant standing next to an opened, metal barred cell door. It was pitch black out there in the Pakistani night but it seemed like noon compared to the Stygian gloom awaiting me on the other side of that portal. It seemed to be alive, this hole, holding its breath in anticipation of swallowing us. I put my hands out like a blind man and walked in cautiously. If there had been a cliff at my feet I would have stepped over the edge without seeing it.

Ali Muhammad came in and like me turned to face the door. We didn't say a word, just stood there like two mutes and watched as the policeman locked us down for the first time in our lives. The door first groaned on its rusty hinges then clanged shut. The key turned. The lock rattled. Hiyat

An Unexpected Accommodation

Mohammad left. We would not walk outside in Pakistani sunlight without wearing chains for a long time. It seemed the world had ended.

We stood there in the darkness, all hope gone. At first I couldn't even make out Ali Muhammad, even thought he was standing next to me. Eventually our eyes became adjusted to such a degree that we could see the walls of the small cell we were in. Looking around, the first thing I noticed was a body sized lump lying on the floor against the far right wall. It was impossible to tell if it was dead or alive. I pointed it out to my companion and motioned for us to silently go to the opposite corner.

The pain of my beating had been temporarily held at bay by the fear of entering this black pit. But after several heartbeats my eyes could see it was only a dirt floored jail cell. I knew I had to sit down before I collapsed. I made my way to the left corner, turned gingerly and slid down gently. The pain almost killed me. It was an effort to breathe. I could feel straw under my hands on the floor. Ali Muhammad sat down beside me. After a few moments he leaned over close.

"I heard them beating you," he whispered. "It sounded pretty bad."

"It was."

"They tied me across a bed. Said if I'd blame you they'd let me go."

He paused for a moment, remembering what had happened.

"That big guy Ashgar beat me really hard when I wouldn't talk."

"Yeah I think I'll have to kill him when this is all over," I said with more bravado than I felt.

We sat there together wrapped in our memories and nothing else. No one knew we were missing. No one knew where we were. No one knew we were buried alive. No one knew things were bad and going to get worse. Ali summed up our situation with his wry Cajun wit.

"I guess this means we're in trouble, mon ami," he said softly.

"I wondered when you would come to that conclusion," I answered and managed to smile even in that pit.

"Do you think they're going to come back tonight?" he asked me.

"Oh God I hope not. I couldn't survive another beating like that one, Ali."

Paranoia started to grip me at the mere suggestion. I could feel my heart racing as I imagined Ashgar Ali looking at me through the cell door.

"If they come back I'm going to fight them with my bare hands before they have a chance to handcuff me again," I told him emphatically. "I think we should take turns keeping watch. I'll go first. I hurt so bad I can't sleep anyway."

"OK," my friend agreed. "But wake me in a little while."

He rolled over on his right side and was asleep within moments. I tried to stay awake. I ached, could feel the pain rolling through me in waves, thought I would vomit from the agony. It became so distressing to sit on my damaged buttocks that I lay down on the straw instead. But every part of my back was on fire as well. I turned on my stomach. I warned myself not to fall asleep on my watch. Then I was overcome by weariness and the next thing I knew the American from the embassy was at the cell door.

12
Little Man – Little Help

The stench awoke me. My eyes snapped open and stared straight ahead at a sight I did not comprehend. The early morning light was sliding through the iron bars. Next to the cell door was a man sitting on a coal bucket defecating. His pants were at his feet. He was calmly smoking a cigarette and staring at the wall in front of him. The smell was overpowering.

I lay there a moment, not quite awake, but knowing exactly where I was. Waking up in jail in Rawalpindi was a singular experience. It had nothing in common with a European hotel where you greeted the day slowly, awaking befuddled and trying to recall if you were in Lisbon or Venice.

The man must have felt my eyes on him.

"*Assalaam alaikum* (Peace be upon you)," he said, lifting a hand in greeting, then farted and smiled.

"*Walaikum assalaam* (Upon you be peace)," I replied.

Our cell mate reached for the *lota* (metal jug full of water) and I turned away to afford him some hint of privacy. It is common practice in the Indian subcontinent to clean yourself with water after defecating. The western tradition of using toilet paper is considered a filthy habit in that it only wipes the surface of the anus. The small water jug reserved for this purpose was kept next to the toilet. It has a spout but no handle. You grab it by the neck with your right hand, pour water on your cupped left hand and quickly bring it up to wash your posterior. Splashing ice cold water on your butt first thing in the morning is a convincing argument that you are a long way from home.

When our cell mate finished using the lota he pulled up his pants, tied off his pants string, then walked back to his corner of the room. The residual odor lingered on our end. The smell was unbearable, simply blinding. Suddenly I was feeling crabby, hungry, tired and sore all over. Misery loves company so I shook Ali Muhammad hard.

"Wake up, it's time for breakfast."

When he opened his eyes he looked like a sleepy owl. There was straw in his dark brown hair. His normally immaculate shalwar kameez looked as lethargic as its master. He slowly raised himself up on one elbow, neither the hard floor nor the early morning hour being to his liking.

"That's not *samosas* (pastries) I smell," he said with a perplexed look on his face.

"The chef just left," I assured him.

He glanced around, took it all in a glance, said "Oh God," and sank back down on the stone floor.

We stayed that way, very hungry and depressed for a few hours. Outside the cell door a different policeman with yet another ugly rifle paced back and forth. There was no sign of Sergeant Hiyat Mohammad. Eventually the old servant from last night appeared. He brought us three prisoners small pots of chi and three cups. Neither Ali or I had eaten since leaving Peshawar, unless you counted the metaphorical fruit of the Zaqqum tree we had sampled at the narc's headquarters. That legendary "Tree of Hell" grew in the deepest depths of Hades, where it gave sinners only bitter, pungent fruit. By early morning I was starving. I told myself that my hunger was an encouraging sign the hepatitis had almost run its course.

The embassy wallah showed up about nine a.m.

"Are you the Americans who were arrested last night?" the little man said from outside our cage. Ali Muhammad sprang up and rushed to meet him. I followed with all the haste I could muster.

"Yes, we're Americans. Are you from the embassy?"

It was a rhetorical question.

Standing before us was a man who looked like he belonged in Wall Street not Pakistan. He was short for an American, about five foot six. He looked like he was in his mid-forties and trying hard to hide it. He sported a closely cropped beard and mustache. Like his finely trimmed hair, it was an odd dark shade of brown. When I got close I was almost sure his hair and beard were dyed. His most prominent facial feature was a broad nose that had a hint of an overhang.

You didn't have to be a mind reader to see that everything about this manicured little man said "Ivy League." He made Ali Muhammad look like a cheap dresser. He wasn't clothed, he was adorned in an expensive blue pin-striped suit, a red necktie, a pair of round tortoise rim glasses and shiny black oxfords. In his right hand he was gripping a black Samsonite briefcase tightly. It seemed to represent his ticket out of there.

"My name is Eugene Crouch. I'm the vice-consul at our embassy here in Islamabad," he said and cautiously stepped a little closer to the door. His thick New York accent made him sound like he had just disembarked and driven straight from the airport to visit us.

I had seldom seen a person more out of place.

Our situation called for Teddy Roosevelt. Unfortunately, standing before us was Calvin Coolidge.

It took only a second to realize he was looking at us like we were two strange animals. He was trying hard to disguise the fact he was shocked to see two fellow Americans dressed like Pakistanis. It obviously offended his sense of western priority to discover his countrymen had gone native.

"It's great to see you. They wouldn't let us call you last night," my friend said anxiously.

Little Man – Little Help

"No one called me. One of my house servants read about your arrest in the local Urdu newspaper this morning. He told me about it while I was having breakfast. All I knew from his version of events was that two Americans had been arrested for drug smuggling. The story never said where you were being held, so it took me a little while to find you guys," he told us in his nasal New York accent.

"You mean, no one notified you of what's happened to us?" I asked incredulously.

"No, I called around until I discovered who was holding you. I canceled my morning appointments so I could come over here."

"That's swell," I said sincerely through the bars. "We really appreciate it. To tell you the truth we were getting a little worried. How soon before you can get us out?"

"I can't get you out," he answered bluntly.

The little man's face was suddenly a stone wall. It told me nothing. I tried not to react to the fear that was balling up inside my stomach.

"Sorry to have to tell you this," he said, "but the embassy can't interfere with the normal course of Pakistani justice."

"What justice? What the hell are you talking about? We got kidnapped and almost beaten to death by guys who were trained in the US. Come on, you know how Pakistan works. It's all about who you know and how much influence you can muster. This has got nothing to do with justice. A phone call from you will set us free before lunch," I said, my voice rising in anger, frustration and fear.

The diplomat was obstinate. He ignored my plea for help.

"Were you beaten?" he asked, clearly hinting he didn't believe me.

"To put it mildly," I told him. I then turned around away from the door and pulled my shirt up past my shoulders

"Oh my God," I heard Crouch say.

I hurt all over but I wasn't expecting that response. I looked to the right at Ali Muhammad who had a clear view at my back.

"Is it bad?" I asked naively.

The look of shock on Ali's face would have been answer enough but he said, "It's real bad."

Ali Muhammad went on to describe to me how I was a solid mass of black and green bruises. I dropped my shirt and turned back to Crouch, believing such massive evidence of brutality would give him the courage to overcome his cowardice.

"Listen, we're old Asian hands. We understand things sometimes get a little crazy out here. All we want is to get out of this stinking hole. No hard feelings," I said, even though I knew I was lying about the last part.

The vice-consul tried to look concerned. I guess in his own way he was, but he was a weak man at heart. He started explaining how the United States only had prison to prison agreements with six other countries. Pakistan wasn't one of them. Additionally the State Department

Khyber Knights

handled 190,000 pleas for help a year from distressed Americans. More than 6,000 Americans were arrested every year, half of those on drugs. Three hundred ended up in prison worldwide annually.

Eugene Crouch let us know he wasn't going to step outside normal channels to help to us. No phone call, no official outrage, nothing. He was a play-it-by-the-book kind of fellow. He tried to cheer us up by telling us things could have been worse.

"The cops in Peru would have broken your arms when you didn't cooperate."

Everything about this mole of a man was proof of his own self interest. He belonged to an insulated sub-culture, the State Department, that was obsessed with the more important issues of pecking order and social prestige. These people weren't hired to be commandos but compliant paper-pushers. Eugene Crouch's career goals included getting posted to London or Paris, not helping two suspected drug smugglers. In his estimation we were guilty until proven innocent.

Plus this was Pakistan where things were never as they appeared to be. With the large scale war going on next door in Afghanistan, America had a lot of irons in the Pakistani fire. In return for fighting the heroin trade and aiding the mujahadeen, the country's military dictator, General Zia, was paid more than $280 million a year by the US government. Some called it foreign aid, others labeled it a bribe. Such a Faustian deal was bound to have strings attached, as well as men lurking about who manipulated those strings. Anyone who rated a new car and a driver, like Eugene Crouch did, was just as likely to be monitoring Russian military activity as he was attending to routine diplomatic affairs. We were a small concern to a man riddled with other priorities.

My work and travels should have prepared me to not have expected help from my government. The previous year an American grandmother on a cruise ship had gone into Istanbul, Turkey on an sanctioned shopping trip. Returning with her purchases in the company of other elderly friends, she was arrested on suspicion of smuggling antiquities. She languished forgotten in a jail for more than a year. One of my own friends had been involved in a minor traffic accident in Morocco. Local cops threw him into a dungeon so crowded the prisoners had to sleep standing up. Regardless of the country, many Americans discovered the hard way how little the Eugene Crouchs of the world would do for them.

I thought of Ali Muhammad and me as being a lot wiser than most travelers. During my years as a journalist I had heard dozens of similar horror stories. The difference was I hadn't found myself involved in one before that morning.

Too often United States citizens left home fearing that nothing more serious than a mild case of Montezuma's revenge lay in wait for them. They packed a bottle of Pepto-Bismol next to their phrase book and willingly walked away from the country which guaranteed them civic rights and legal privileges. But as Ali Muhammad and I were to discover it was a dangerous thing walking through your front door. Outside lay a road that could lead you unawares to mystery, danger and death. There were few rules waiting to protect such unsuspecting American travelers. No little pink bottle was going to heal their stomach ache and no little man from the embassy was going to fight for their freedom. On the contrary, in Pakistan there was no guarantee that when you walked through your door you would not lose your health, your freedom, or your life.

"I'm sorry. The Pakistanis are under a lot of pressure from Washington right now, so they're sensitive on the subject of drugs. All I can do is make sure you're well treated by the authorities and that you're provided legal counsel in court," Crouch said in a voice that mirrored his defensive body language.

As if to emphasize his point he reached into his coat and brought out a typed sheet which listed the names of several local lawyers.

"Who do you recommend," Ali Muhammad asked hopefully.

"I can't recommend any of them, not allowed. They're all qualified advocates. Take your pick."

"God damn it. You're a lot of help," I said angrily. I wanted to reach through the bars and squeeze his skinny New York neck.

The tidy diplomat didn't respond, only looked at me like I was already convicted in his mind of smuggling heroin. I jabbed my finger at the paper. "Number seven, my lucky number. We'll take number seven."

"Naeem. Kwajher Naeem. I hear he's pretty good. I'll have him contact you," the embassy man said.

"Thanks," I replied sarcastically.

The bureaucrat concluded by assuring us he was going to file an official protest with the government of Pakistan about the beating we received. When Crouch left he had a satisfied look on his face that told us he believed he had just done an honest day's work.

Ali Muhammad watched him leave, then turned to me and said, "We're on our own."

We didn't have time to brood over it.

Sergeant Hiyat Mohammad arrived soon after lunch. We had been given two pieces of roti (bread) and two pots of chai. That banquet was barely finished when the stern policeman unlocked the cell door and ordered us out. We followed him to his office where a handsome middle aged Pakistani was waiting for us.

Doctor Mohammad Ashraf could have passed as a soap opera star. He was ridiculously handsome, swarthy, and tall. He seemed oblivious to his good looks. He was just a busy man who had taken a few moments leave from the local hospital in response to a police sergeant's request for medical advice. The doctor examined each of us with our shirts off. He gently pushed and probed the mass of bruises we each showed him.

When the doctor finished he turned to Hiyat Mohammad and explained his conclusions.

"They've obviously been beaten by hostile hands."

"Beaten by what please?"

"A blunt instrument. From the size and nature of these contusions I'd say it occurred within the last 24 hours," Ashraf told the sergeant. "Will there be anything else?"

Hiyat Mohammad thanked him for his help. After the doctor was gone the policeman motioned for us to take a seat on the small bench next to his desk. He opened the top drawer of his desk and pulled out an ink pad and two small cards.

"I have to fingerprint you," he said matter of factly.

It was another one of those situations where the American television culture of the early 1960's failed me. When I wasn't watching celluloid cowboys as a kid, I was glued to the tube watching "Dragnet." I had seen Joe Friday fingerprint a hundred guys. I knew the routine. Of course Joe never fingerprinted good guys like me and Ali Muhammad and he didn't use a dried up ink pad older than honest Abe Lincoln. Hiyat Mohammad made us rub our fingers frantically on the ink pad trying to get them black. Even that didn't impress the dusty relic. Frustrated, Hiyat spat on the pad several times and made me grind the saliva in vigorously.

Finally satisfied that I was sufficiently inky, the old cop took my forefinger and placed it on the card. Unlike Sergeant Joe Friday, Sergeant Hiyat Mohammad didn't roll my digit lightly across the paper. He jammed the long fingernail of his left forefinger under my own fingernail, cutting into the quick and making me wince.

"Push hard," he ordered. Before I had a chance to say, "Yes or No," he shoved down on my finger with his free hand, while rolling his left hand in the direction he wanted me to go. His long fingernail was dug so deep into my own digit, it followed willingly. He thus shoved his razor sharp nail into me ten times before he was satisfied with the results.

When Ali's experiment in finger painting was done, Hiyat Mohammad allowed us a chance to wash our hands outside using water from a lota. Neither of us had a clue what to expect next. I thought we would be spending the night in the jail cell again.

While we had been cleaning our hands Hiyat Mohammad had directed a policeman to bring him a pair of handcuffs. He now snapped these on us, attaching me by my right wrist to Ali Muhammad's left.

What he told us next stunned me.

Less than thirty six hours had passed since I walked out of my hotel in Peshawar, at which time I had naively and willingly stepped onto a road that lead I knew not where. Yes, less than thirty six hours had passed and already Sergeant Hiyat Mohammad was taking us to prison.

13

Pakistan's Bastille

My vanity told me I was a man of the world. As a free-lance journalist I had seen the ravages of war as well as the beauties of exotic places. I had known soft arms and rugged hardship. I counted among my friends revolutionaries, brigands, poets and patriots. Despite my recent illness I was young, strong and unafraid of physical adversity. I was at the apex of my life and more capable than I would ever be again to face what lay ahead.

Ah, but if youth only knew.

None of what I had seen mattered. Nothing could have prepared me for the horror that was Pindi Prison. When others died in the days ahead I lived on, surviving only by luck and the will of Allah.

In typical Pakistani fashion we three, the sergeant, Ali Muhammad and I arrived at our destination in a small Morris Minor taxi after a short drive from the police station. The driver refused to even stop in front of Pindi Prison, preferring to pull up across the street on a side road. Sergeant Hiyat Mohammad had allowed each of us to retain a few rupees in our pockets. He hadn't explained why. The poorly paid policeman now informed me that I should reimburse the driver. It was the first time I ever paid to drive myself to prison.

I gave the driver my last twenty rupees. Ali Muhammad then opened the back door and the two of us slid out, handcuffed at the wrist. The driver didn't linger.

"Out, out," he yelled at me, as I struggled to pull myself, last of all, from the tiny taxi. Before I could reach around and shut the door, he drove away. My friend and I stood there in the street, silent and uncertain. A hundred yards away across a busy boulevard stood a massive citadel, a monument to man's inhumanity to man.

Winston Churchill had once written with uncanny accuracy about the emotions I experienced when I first saw Pindi Prison. He predicted that if the mighty Raj were to fade away the traveler would still find himself staring at "those few scraps of stone and iron which indicate the British occupation of India," mighty buildings which the English built "for immediate use and not future ostentation." The reminders of such an empire would never be "obliterated by time."

Pindi Prison was a living relic of that colonial past. She was a stone and iron ghost ship still fulfilling her mission though her European masters had long since turned to dust. I could feel the presence of the place from where I stood. Her walls emanated a sense of old evil. I could see men walking by her on the street shunning her, averting their eyes from the stone cancer growing on the face of that otherwise beautiful city. As I studied her mighty walls I saw her patiently waiting there in the fading sunlight like a sinister old woman. She was anxious for Ali and me to cross the road so she could draw us to her withered bosom.

There was no sign informing the passing tourist that this colossal structure was a prison. Its mission was disguised from the casual eye. The portal into its hidden world was constructed to resist a siege, not attract the idle curious. A forty foot high battlement faced the boulevard. It was constructed of massive stones and topped by a series of loop holes designed for snipers. Three broad, barred windows were spaced evenly across the top of its front wall. Like the loopholes, they existed for defensive purposes, not decoration.

Standing in the middle of this rampart were a pair of colossal, twelve foot high, solid steel doors. It would have taken a Panzer tank to dislodge them. Arched across their top were thick, five foot high bars that allowed light to infiltrate in from outside.

Glancing right and left I saw twenty foot high walls running off for a block in either direction, before taking a sharp ninety degree turn and disappearing. That was my first clue to how immense an area the prison actually encompassed.

To top it all off she was ugly. Her walls were painted a faded, jaundice yellow. The putrid color only succeeded in giving the place the look of a sprawling sore. The doors were a smoky steel blue. Flying over the top of it all was a once proud Pakistani flag. The original colors had been burned by the tropical sun for so long that they were no longer recognizable. The green portion was now flat black, while the white had withered into a dull gray. The banner hung over the gate, a limp symbol of life faded to death.

Clearly, once you entered this stepchild of Churchill's empire you didn't leave as easily.

Hiyat Mohammad had seen it all before.

"Prison," he said matter of factly, then pointed towards the main gate and directed Ali and me to walk in front of him across the street. He was unarmed but handcuffed as we were together it never crossed our minds to make a run for it.

My friend and I crossed the wide boulevard, walking fast as traffic hurried our way. As we drew near, the first thing I noticed was that three strands of rusty barbed wire ran around the perimeters of the walls. As our steps took us towards the blue gates we discovered a small, previously overlooked wall to our left. It was painted the same yellow color and from across the street had faded into the main wall above it. Yet gathered in the undisclosed space between this main wall and the smaller one was a group of civilians; men, women and even small children. They were standing in front of thick steel screens reaching six foot high,

Khyber Knights

"Pindi prison was a living relic of the colonial past, a stone and iron ghost ship still fulfilling her mission though her European masters had long since turned to dust. I could feel the presence of the place from where I stood, her walls emanating a sense of old evil."

running fifteen long. The noise emanating from this mixed crowd was ear splitting. They were all screaming and shouting, pushing and shoving, trying for some undisclosed reason to get close to the screens. I had no clue what this macabre little theater represented.

There were four prison guards standing at the front gate. Their uniforms were different from the police sergeant's, a darker gray and not nearly as well kept. Each man was armed with a antiquated bolt-action rifle topped with a bayonet. They saluted Hiyat sharply when we approached.

"Open up," the one nearest to the door shouted to his unseen colleagues inside.

A crack appeared in the massive steel door, then a Judas gate swung inwards, revealing a tiny black hole barely big enough for a man to stoop through and enter. It was only a minor humiliation, but Pindi Prison did not allow her inmates to enter her secret domain with their chins up and heads held high.

The guard with the rifle gave us a hard look as well as a silent order. The air hung heavy with the threat of violence if we did not obey. Regardless, Ali Muhammad and I both hesitated at the thought of entering such an ill-omened place.

"Inside," Hiyat Mohammad ordered.

I was too numb to be scared. Maybe as a boy my friend had visited some chain gang ridden Louisiana prison farm with his roving father. If so he never told me. But from some secret reserve Ali Muhammad found the courage to go first, stepping into the blackness awaiting us on the other side. The handcuff immediately pulled me after him like a man being dragged down into deep water. I bent my head and plunged in.

When I stood up inside I discovered we were in the bowels of the prison. An immense room as high as the gates and thirty feet wide enveloped us. On the opposite side sat a silent sister to the main gate, only this other one guarded the inner secrets of the prison beyond. The chamber I found myself in was cool and dimly lit. Despite the reassuring temperature anyone with half an eye could have seen we had stumbled into the foyer of Hell.

Running off to my left was a long corridor. On the right side of that hall, facing away from the prison, were a series of three office doors. On the corresponding left side of the hall were the tall metal screens I had just observed from the exterior.

The mystery of the civilian's noisy behavior was now revealed. Eight or nine prisoners were sitting in front of the screens on thick stone benches. This small zone served as the prison visiting area. The prisoners were talking through the thick mesh to family and lawyers gathered together outside. Though the screens were securely bolted in place a few small holes had been cut through the metal veil. Relatives were busy pushing fruit, small packets of tea and rupees (Pakistani currency) to the prisoners inside. We soon learned the guards turned a blind eye to this practice as they searched the returning prisoners before allowing them back inside the prison, confiscating what booty they wanted.

It was easy to see that there were far more visitors than prisoners. They shoved and pushed their up way to the screens, screaming and yelling the names of men lost in the depths of Pindi Prison, or pleading for the prisoners on my side to take messages back to their loved ones. One woman, clutching a small child, was smashed up against the unforgiving wire wall. Realizing she would not see her man today, or maybe any other day, she hung on the wire screaming out his name over and over. In between screams, she sobbed and wept pathetically. She was the Madonna in a scene of complete despair, grief driven to madness, held at bay by a slip of wire mesh.

Everyone ignored her.

There were five guards on duty inside the area between the two gates. One guarded the Judas gate we had just entered. One kept an eye on the visitor's area. One frisked prisoners about to reenter the prison for contraband. Another operated the gate on the opposite side. The fifth man ran the show. As soon as Sergeant Hiyat Mohammad entered he walked straight to this guard.

These two held a rapid, muted conversation while Ali and I stood near the gate, trying to orient ourselves. Several times the chief guard looked our way as if he were surprised. Once I overheard Hiyat Mohammad use the word "Muslims." After a few moments the guard walked over to the first door, knocked timidly, waited patiently, then disappeared inside. After a few moments absence he popped his head outside the door and motioned to Hiyat Mohammad.

"This way," the sergeant said in a voice loud enough to be heard over the turmoil of the visitors area. We didn't have to be told twice. We followed him, our only lifeline back to reality, towards the door and the unknown room that lay beyond. The first thing I saw when I entered was a desk as big as an ocean. A burly man stood behind it like the captain of some great mahogany ship. The police sergeant snapped to attention and saluted the other man smartly. He then handed over a document he was carrying and began explaining who we were.

The big man confronting us was about 50 and stood a little more than six feet tall. His dark gray prison uniform was very spruce. On the epaulets of his shirt were silver pips denoting the rank of major. His once powerful body was now soft and fleshy. He had a ponderous head. Dense eyebrows rested on top of dark eyes. His black mustache, though still thick, was now heavily laced with gray. It was cut in a straight line across a wide sensuous mouth. I suspected the desk and uniform were used to intimidate or impress prisoners. Up close the fellow just looked greasy. The costume shop uniform and the big desk gave him the unintentional look of a "B" movie heavy.

"*Bally* (yes) sergeant, *bally* (yes), *bally* (yes)," the prison official kept saying politely, nodding his big head as Hiyat Mohammad explained when and how we had come into his custody. The man gave Ali Muhammad and me a smile that left me uneasy. When the policeman finished his report the official looked at us and said, "I'm the DSP."

Obviously that statement was meant to impart a great deal to us. We stood there mystified for a moment until he explained.

"Deputy Superintendent of Prisons."

The new look of understanding on our faces seemed to please him.

"I've been expecting you since I read about your arrest in yesterday's newspaper. Heroin smugglers are a very bad lot. You shouldn't have got mixed up with them."

Neither Ali Muhammad nor I volunteered to correct his mistake or explain our situation. The man looked too jaded to believe the Pope was catholic. He turned his attention briefly back to the policeman who had delivered us.

"Take off their handcuffs, sergeant," he ordered.

"You're inmates of Rawalpindi Prison now. You'll remain here until the court hears your case or sets your bail," the DSP told us, as if to confirm our official status.

While the handcuffs were being unlocked the DSP signed a form accepting custody from the tough old cop. Watching how easily it was done unnerved me. Neither of the two men gave us any notice. They simply transferred us as if we were human commodities, two slabs of foreign born meat whose past was of no importance and whose future was undecided.

The burly jailer had barely lifted the pen from the document when the phone on his big desk rang. He picked it up and spoke briefly. After a few moments, he covered the end of the receiver with his left hand and turned his eyes back to Hiyat Mohammad.

"Tell the guard to put them into Char Chuki (Barrack Four)," the DSP said, then turning his attention back to the phone conversation, sat down. Like the police sergeant, Ali Muhammad and I were obviously dismissed.

"Ah cha, yar (OK, friend)," was the last thing we heard as we quietly left our new master's office.

Our former jailer lead us back into the hallway, past the moaning mob and close by the main gate leading back out to freedom. He directed us to walk to the far gate that lead into the heart of the prison instead. An old guard standing guard at that gate began to carefully search us. He was bitter faced man and sported a long beard dyed a brilliant orange by a liberal coating of henna. As one of the deorhi (main entrance staff) it was his job to conduct our jharti (body search).

"Assalaam alaikum," I said to him politely as he patted me down. The guard was obviously not keen on exchanging Islamic pleasantries with prisoners. He gave me a sour look as if to tell me to keep my tongue in my head. As he began to search me, poking and prodding, searching and feeling for contraband, the guard kept quietly repeating the word "No," quietly to himself. He looked in my clothes, even running his fingers down the seams, carefully checked my boots and finished by tearing my turban apart. All the while whispering, "No, no, no," again and again as he continually found nothing of interest.

When my search was finished he turned his attention to Ali Muhammad. While the search went on Sergeant Hiyat Mohammad stood nearby watching in taciturn silence. The stern cop wasn't saying anything but I was getting used to that.

"No," the guard said again as he began patting Ali Muhammad down.

"No, no, no," he kept softly repeating as he searched my friend thoroughly.

"Ah yes," he finally uttered.

The guard had found the 10 rupee note the police sergeant had allowed my friend to keep. The green colored currency had been shoved into the bottom of Ali Muhammad's shirt pocket. I couldn't help but feel Hiyat Mohammad had anticipated such a search. The gruff guard made no attempt to hide his delight at the discovery. He stuffed the money into his own pocket, smiled and said, "Money not allowed."

His job done, the searcher motioned us to move to the other gate prior to entering the prison. We marched to where we were told. The bored young guard waiting on duty there opened a second Judas gate. A bright shaft of late afternoon sunlight came tumbling into the dim room through that small door. Its jolly light looked woefully out of place.

"*Chello sahib* (hurry up mister) ," the young guard at the gate said, and motioned for Ali Muhammad and me to step through the Judas gate into the prison beyond.

Suddenly my traveling companion and I both realized we were only seconds away from losing the partially reassuring presence of the dour Hiyat Mohammad. Anxious to delay our departure into the depths of the prison by even a few moments, Ali Muhammad and I both turned to bide the sergeant adieu.

"Goodbye," Hiyat Mohammad told us. "I will study your case. If you are innocent Allah will help you."

"Thank you. You are a good Muslim brother," Ali Muhammad said sincerely.

As I in turn shook the policeman's rough hand goodbye I tried to say with my eyes what I was feeling. When Hiyat Mohammad released my grip I felt alone, adrift and unprotected at the imminent loss of this old Spartan's attendance. I started to walk through the Judas gate then lost

Pakistan's Bastille

my nerve. I turned back towards the sergeant in desperation but his tough old face shamed me into silence.

"Goodbye," I said, pretending it was an afterthought, not the taste of fear that had made me linger.

Then, choking down my anxieties, I bent down and stepped through the small gate like a stiff zombie. Ali Muhammad was the next to emerge into that wretched other world, followed by the young guard who slammed the little door shut behind us.

Pindi Prison had me.

I found myself standing on a long, narrow road that ran like a knife straight to her secret heart. On our immediate right was a small building built to hold female convicts. A similar building on our left was the prison kitchen. The road running straight ahead was deliberately placed between two twenty foot high walls paralleling its length. This not only forced prisoners to stay in sight of their captors at all times, it also gave them only two possible destinations, either the Judas gate behind me or the guard tower located far ahead at the center of the prison.

Originally built in 1869, Pindi Prison had been designed to hold 990 men. Things had gotten a lot more crowded since Churchill's day. There were almost two thousand souls unwillingly residing in the cross bar hotel. As Ali Muhammad and I began walking down the dirt road behind the guard, we were prisoners number 1888 and 1889 respectively.

Pakistan's most infamous prison was laid out like a sliced pie placed within a box. The high walls facing the outside world made up the box. Seven different slices of prison life made up the penal pie. To lessen the danger of riots each section of the prison was independent of the others. Twelve foot interior walls enclosed several buildings within each of these sections. Four segments of the prison were devoted to housing prisoners, both convicted and "under trials" like Ali and me. The hospital sat in its own thin slice of this prison pastry. The administration building, kitchen and the women's quarters behind us made up the other three sections.

Walking the length of the prison road took about three minutes as it was more than a city block long. The lane was fifteen feet wide. If dirt could be clean the dirt on that road was. The two walls hemming us in were originally whitewashed. The bright Pakistani sunlight had faded them to a sickly yellow corresponding to the outside of the prison. Our little journey was devoid of decoration unless you counted the whitewashed rocks placed every so often on both sides. Walking down the silent road gave me the impression we were being lead deeper and deeper into a funnel, wide at the mouth, narrow at the end, impossible to back out of. Neither Ali Muhammad nor I said a word, we just followed the guard like two displaced refugees.

The conclusion of our walk brought us out into the center of a parade ground. Here I saw a watch tower posed in the dying sunlight. It was circular, about eighteen feet high, painted bright white and topped in red tiles. A single guard paced back and forth in the open aired aerie. Four red buckets filled with sand, the massive prison's only defense against fire, hung on the side of this building. The five largest pie shaped sections of the prison all opened out onto this parade ground. The narrowest portion of each segment had a single iron barred gate that faced out onto the parade ground. Each of these gates was kept under constant guard, not only by trusties on the inside but the ever vigilant tower guard on the outside. The wider back end of each segment butted up against one of the outer prison walls. These walls presented little security threat however because the prisoners were never allowed to move within twenty feet of those high defenses.

Close to the watch tower was the "Warden's Tree," a large banyan tree which shared its life-giving shade with the prison personnel. The four wardens responsible for overseeing the four main *chukis* (barracks) often gathered at this spot to sit on straight backed chairs and gossip. Their immediate boss, the Chief Chakkar, reported directly back to the DSP. Our young guard ordered us to halt a few steps away from the tree. He then walked over and held a brief conversation with one of the uniformed men sitting there.

The minute the guard turned his back I hurriedly looked around. Despite my own mountain of troubles I couldn't contain my reporter's instincts. I realized I was standing at the center of a site where one of Pakistan's most celebrated misdeeds had occurred, the judicially approved assassination of the country's former prime minister. Everyone in Pakistan heard whispered rumors about Pindi Prison and the role it played in helping bring about the country's most infamous tragedy. During our guard's absence I looked around frantically, trying to place the details of the place with that previous event. For like the infamous Dallas School Book Depository, I realized I was suddenly standing at Pakistan's ground zero. This was the same stretch of barren dirt that former Prime Minister Zulfiqar Ali Bhutto had crossed on his way to the gallows, a sentence passed by his trusted military chief, the current dictator General Zia.

Trouble hadn't waited long to appear in the new country after the untimely death of her founder, Muhammad Ali Jinnah, in 1948. Pakistan's next prime minister, Liaquat Ali Khan, fell to an assassin's bullet in 1951. Two years later a puritanically orthodox Muslim minority demanded the government outlaw a non-conforming sect known as the Ahmadiyahs from the Islamic community. When the new prime minister temporized over the harsh decision, rioting enveloped Lahore and other Punjab cities. Martial law was declared for the first time before order was finally restored. As the decade progressed the country's twin pillars of power began to bicker. When Pakistan had won her independence from Britain the new nation's geographic solidarity had been split down the middle. East Pakistan, known today as Bangladesh, could only be reached by crossing Pakistan's hated rival, India. The millions of Muslim citizens residing in Bangladesh saw themselves as geographic and political orphans, isolated from the power-brokers residing in West Pakistan. The political situation between the two culturally diverse sections of the country continued to deteriorate until 1958, when the country's elected leader, Iskander Mirza, announced that political parties were abolished, the constitution abrogated and the country again placed temporarily under martial law.

In a sense of misplaced trust Mirza voluntarily handed over power to General Mohammad Ayub Khan. The president believed the military would shield him as he consolidated his civilian control. Instead General Ayub seized control, exiled former leader Mirza to London and placed trusted generals in vital civil-service posts. In 1965 India defeated Pakistan in a war over the boundaries of the province of Kashmir, a section of the Himalayan mountains claimed by both countries. By this point General Ayub had ceased making any effort to disguise his choke hold on power. Fatima Jinnah, sister of the country's dead founder, tried to rally the dispirited people but failed. Ayub withdrew behind a curtain of dictatorship, becoming a remote figure rarely observed except in a bulletproof limousine.

Things only got worse.

Protests and strikes against Pakistan's first military dictator flared up everywhere, becoming especially militant in Bengal. Sensing the country was about to implode, General Ayub finally resigned, relinquishing power to a military crony, General Yahya Khan. By 1971 the people of East Pakistan were calling for total independence from their Muslim overlords in West Pakistan. When Bengal political leaders were denounced as traitors, rioting broke out in their provincial capital of Dacca. General Yahya quickly launched his country into a civil war, sending in West Pakistani troops to reoccupy the rebellious province. The resultant blood bath was catastrophic. Millions of Bengali refugees crossed the border into neighboring India, whose leaders were clearly delighted at the political chaos. In December 1971 Indian Prime Minister Indira Gandhi ordered her troops to invade East Pakistan. The Pakistani army was quickly surrounded and shortly surrendered almost 100,000 officers and men to the victorious Indian forces. Bangladesh was established as an independent nation in 1972.

Accepting responsibility for his army's humiliating defeat, as well as the breakup of the country, General Yahya resigned. Into the power vacuum stepped a dynamic lawyer named Zulfiqar Ali Bhutto. The Oxford educated barrister was undeniably popular. Despite his privileged feudal background Bhutto preached a doctrine of democratic socialism. The war-weary people of Pakistan eagerly followed his promises of "*roti, kapra, aur makan* (food, clothes and a house)." A brilliant demagogue, Bhutto instituted land reforms and nationalized industries, all the while alienating the powerful troika of feudal landlords, conservative mullahs and the military, who saw his socialism as a threat.

A new constitution was adopted in 1973 and for a time it appeared that newly elected Prime Minister Bhutto was going to lead his country back in the direction of Ali Jinnah's democratically inspired Islamic republic. Unfortunately by 1976 the power-hungry Bhutto had become increasingly autocratic, suppressing criticism, jailing opponents, creating a personal secret police force and employing brutal militant methods against the restive Pathans of the North West Frontier. When elections were announced in January, 1977 a hasty consortium of political forces banded together against the prime minister and launched a demand for a return of Islamic values. The campaign was violent and the election results patently fraudulent. Though he lost in three out of the four provinces, when the votes were counted Bhutto had miraculously retained a vast majority. The country was already on the point of anarchy when religious leaders declared the prime minister an illegal ruler whom it was no crime to kill.

Into this tumultuous maelstrom stepped General Zia.

He and Bhutto were poles apart, politically, socially and religiously. Bhutto favored beautiful women, fine whiskey and tailored suits, whereas Zia was the son of a poor army mullah. The tall, fair skinned, aristocratic Bhutto was Pakistan's version of the imperious Louis XIV, a Sun King from the province of Sind. His rival to power, the small, dark skinned, dour, puritanical General Zia, could have been the religiously zealous Oliver Cromwell reborn.

General Mohammad Zia-ul-Haq had come to the attention of Prime Minister Zulfiqar Ali Bhutto on the advice of King Hussein of Jordan. In 1969 the rigorous Pakistani religionist had been temporarily seconded as a military advisor to Jordan's royal army. While the catastrophic civil war with Bengal was brewing back home in Pakistan, Zia was busy making himself useful to Jordan's monarch. In 1970 when the Palestinian Liberation Army, operating under the command of Yasser Arafat, rebelled against King Hussein, Zia took part in a massacre of the Palestinians. Remembered as "Black September", the Jordanian troops routed Arafat's PLO, driving them into exile in neighboring Lebanon. A grateful King Hussein returned the favor to the brutal Pakistani who had violated his charter of duties as an officer. Bhutto was informed that Zia was dull, dedicated, loyal, and most importantly, controllable.

The prime minister called Zia his "monkey general" but elevated him above six senior ranking generals to the position of chief of staff of the armed forces. After the 1977 election fraud Bhutto believed he could rely on Zia to maintain control of the increasingly restless army. Yet outrage at the scale of Bhutto's political shenanigans prompted Pakistan's citizens to riot for six weeks. Business was at a standstill and once again it appeared that Muhammad Ali Jinnah's Islamic homeland was about to destroy herself. On July 5, 1977 General Zia lead a military coup known as "Operation Fair Play." He announced that new elections would be held in ninety days and placed Zulfiqar Ali Bhutto under house arrest to prove it. Very little was known about this Bhutto military appointee who had once again declared martial law. Many people at home and abroad believed Zia was only a spokesman for the group of generals who had taken over the country. Pakistan, like Prime Minister Bhutto, was about to learn how high a price they had to pay when they underestimated the little general.

The moment he came to power Zia began using the military's discipline, communications system and organizational skills to consolidate his position. He put the army's transportation network to work maintaining efficient distribution of the necessities of life, including tea, cooking oil, wheat and sugar, to the disaffected masses. His military rivals to power were quickly sent overseas, posted into lucrative ambassadorships in comfortable western countries. Zia then promptly arrested the deposed prime minister. The imperial Bhutto, who had enjoyed the perks of power for six years, suddenly found himself locked up in Pindi Prison, charged with attempted murder and facing possible execution. With Zia's guns turned on the people and their former leader imprisoned, the country realized that the army who had lost every war had suddenly conquered the nation without firing a shot.

Democracy was the first victim. Bhutto the next. Ali Muhammad and I were on the list.

While we waited for the guard to return I took in the scene of Pakistan's final political degradation. When she won her independence from Britain in 1947 the new country inherited not only the buildings constituting Pindi Prison but the rigid class structures of her former English masters as well. There were even social distinctions drawn in prison. Ali and I were to be incarcerated in "C Class" with the other common criminals. The largest category of inmates, C Class had been founded for the illiterate masses, its earliest recruits being those Muslims who had mutinied against the East India Company Army in 1857.

"B Class," reserved for political prisoners, was seldom used. When it was, those prisoners were confined by themselves inside the tiny hospital located at the back of the prison. Looking straight ahead past the guard tower I could clearly make out that medical portion of the Pakistani gulag. It was there that the once powerful Prime Minister Bhutto had been imprisoned. Like that famous former prisoner, I was to soon learn that my rights as a human being were non-existent in Pindi Prison. Privacy was a vanished western concept, hygiene was an unknown luxury, and disease was rampant behind the walls of General Zia's private prison camp.

After a few minutes our guard returned from reporting to the uniformed men resting beneath the "Warden's Tree". Our previous captor walked past us on his way back to his duty station at the prison's main gate. A well built, handsome man in his late forties returned to take charge of us instead. His gray shirt boasted sergeant's stripes. Like his khaki pants, it was stiff with starch. He wore a dark gray beret at a jaunty angle. His short hair and his big handlebar mustache were both going gray. He had a square head, big ears, strong jaw and eyes that had a "take no prisoners" kind of look. Though middle aged he appeared remarkably fit. His short sleeved shirt revealed muscles in his arms that resembled thick cords.

Tucked under his right arm like a riding crop was a four foot long lathi. The heavy wooden cudgel had been broadened and weighted on the top. A silver metal cap rested on that end. I had seen enough riot control in Pakistan to know the lathi, part blackjack, part stave, was a brutally effective weapon against unarmed men at close range.

"I'm Sergeant Shafi. I run Char Chuki and I don't tolerate trouble," he told us in a voice laced with warning. His blunt statement of facts left no room for debate. We were looking at the big dog, the muqaddam (warden) of our personal portion of Hell.

I shook my head in agreement for both of us.

"No trouble from us sergeant."

"Good. I have another European. Do you want to be placed in his cell?"

"Yes, we want to see him," I said eagerly. I had seen enough Jimmy Cagney prison movies to know we needed to learn the score as fast as possible. The quickest education we could get would come from someone who already knew the ropes.

Shafi told us to follow him and started walking across the parade ground towards his section of prison fief. The sun was low, almost ready to set and many of the prisoners in the other three chukis were lounging near the gates adjoining the parade ground. Knowing they were spending the last free minutes of their day before being locked into their cells for the night, the bored prisoners were passing the idle time by looking through the gates at the wardens. When they saw Ali Muhammad and me walking towards Char Chuki a great commotion arose. Despite our native clothes, they could tell we were Caucasian foreigners. Men started to yell to their comrades to come look at the new prisoners. Within moments someone yelled, "Hello Angrez hello."

It sounded like a genuinely warm greeting so Ali Muhammad waved in return. They began cheering and shouting. Many were laughing. A few waved back.

Sergeant Shafi, unimpressed at the horseplay, halted before the gate of Char Chuki.

Ali took that moment to inform me, "Either they're bored or they like us already."

I didn't answer, concentrating instead on the men who had met the sergeant at the gate. There were about thirty curious prisoners crowded inside the gate, waiting to witness our arrival. The difference between their clothes was unmistakable. Some men were dressed in spotlessly clean shalwar kameez. Others were clothed in the most shocking rags I had ever seen draped over a Pakistani body. Two men inside the gate wore a basic uniform, consisting of a well worn white shalwar kameez and a bright red beret. They were obviously trusties.

The warden of Char Chuki took a large key hanging by a chain to his belt and unlocked the gate. The older of the men in white uniform who stepped forward to meet the sergeant was in his late fifties, tall, narrow faced and as evil a looking man as I ever had the misfortune to meet. He did not salute Shafi. Yet some invisible signal passed quickly between them.

"Babu, put them in with the Dutchman in Cell Nine," the sergeant told the old man.

"Yes sir," the trusty answered.

The gate was opened. Ali Muhammad and I stepped in. The gate was closed, leaving Shafi outside. The funnel was getting smaller by the minute.

"Follow me," the tall trusty told us, then began pushing his way through the crowd of curious prisoners.

The other trusty, who was smaller and much younger, started yelling at the prisoners milling around, ordering them to get back to their cells, that lock up was imminent. I suddenly found myself in a world of images I did not have the time or the information to comprehend. As Ali and I followed the old trusty I saw one bearded man walk by screaming and jabbering to himself. He was not only clearly mad, he was the filthiest man I had ever seen in Pakistan. Several men were wearing medieval leg irons. An older obese man strolled by holding a young boy's hand possessively. There appeared to be representatives of every section of Pakistani society, killers, saints, patriots, black sheep, scoundrels, madmen and sinners tumbled together into the snare known as Char Chuki. Regardless of their previous lives or loves, in Pindi Prison they were all the shipwrecked of Allah.

Directly in front of us was an immense barrack. The front of this building was guarded by a cell door made from thick iron bars. Glancing through that opening I saw a mob of men tightly jammed into that room. They were crammed together, standing and lying on the bare dirt floor beyond. The old trusty gave us no opportunity to linger. We followed him to the front of the barracks building and turned right. Close to that corner of the building was a water faucet. Sitting in front of the tap was a shallow concrete trough where prisoners could wash or get water. A small dark haired man was squatting by the trough splashing water onto a pile of clothes he was washing. As the trusty turned the corner of the building we had to walk directly in front of this soaking wet little laundryman. When he looked up and saw we were foreigners he began shouting, "Nixon, Nixon,

Nixon," at the top of his lungs. I was sure we were going to meet the Mad Hatter and a large white rabbit next.

The trusty lead us down a brick sidewalk that passed down the right side of the barracks. On our left we passed a series of small cells that were built up against the side wall of the main barracks building. Each of these small cells was located well back from the sidewalk, intentionally placed at the rear of a tiny courtyard. We went by one, two, three of these cells, each filled with men, each affording me a peek at things I could not yet understand. I thought I saw the flicker of a cooking fire, perhaps in some sort of stove. I couldn't be sure. None of it made sense.

The old man turned into the fourth courtyard. We followed obediently. The enclosed area of this small courtyard was ten feet long and six feet wide. It was separated from its identical neighbors on either side by two seven foot tall stone walls. Directly at the back of the courtyard I could see an open cell door awaiting our arrival. The trusty stopped at the side of this steel barred cell door and ordered us to enter.

At least it wasn't dark. In fact as I came up to the door I could see that the cell beyond was brightly lit. A single exposed bulb hung from the ten foot ceiling by a withered wire. When I stepped in I discovered I was in a room that was eight feet long but barely six feet wide. High up on the back wall was a small barred window. The noise of voices pouring through the little opening told me I was hearing men lodged in the main holding cell beyond. Judging from the depth of the window, the walls of the cell appeared to be two foot thick. They were clammy and covered with white washed stucco. Just inside the cell, to the right of the door, was a large ten gallon earthen water pot and a small lota. There was literally nothing else to look at unless you counted the two men sitting on the dirt floor staring up at us.

One was obviously the Dutchman. The other fellow was a young Pakistani.

Except for these two forlorn specks of humanity the tiny room was utterly devoid of any element of civilization. There were no beds, no chairs, no water tap, no toilet. Nothing. It wasn't a cell for men. It was a dirt floored cage not fit for animals.

It was Cell Nine-Block Four and it was to be my home for a long time.

Ali Muhammad and I had barely manage to step in when the trusty locked the cell door behind us. The air was suddenly filled with the sound of iron doors slamming and locks clanking all around Char Chuki. Over the noise of the voices coming into my cell from the central barracks I could also hear an old man's voice crying in despair.

"Mercy, mercy," said the invisible old voice and the hair on my neck rose.

Then I heard the words, "Chup shaw (shut up)," followed almost immediately by the sound of blows. The unidentified old man began softly weeping.

The shock must have registered on our faces. The Dutchman looked up at us and smiled.

"Welcome to the Rawalpindi Hilton," he said in a gravelly voice.

Khyber Knights

14
Cell Nine – Block Four

That first night we slept like animals, huddled under burlap blankets I wouldn't have thrown over a bad horse on a wet night. Whimpering from the old man in the central cell was the last thing I heard before sleep thankfully rescued me.

Hans von Dueker, the Dutch smuggler, served as my alarm clock. Despite the early hour he was standing at the cell door shaking the bars furiously.

"Come on Babu, come on," he yelled at the top of his lungs.

I could hear other men calling just as desperately, followed by the sound of cell doors being unlocked.

I stood up, all traces of sleep by now vanished. My need to urinate was urgent.

"Where does one commit nuisance around here," I asked him.

Before my cellmate could answer, the old trusty strolled into the small courtyard outside our cell. Babu was clearly in no hurry, delighting in making Hans suffer in this minor manner. He unlocked the door, then walked away without giving us another look.

"Follow me," Hans said desperately. He had the cell's lota in his hand.

The implication we were going to the toilet was clear so I followed him. As soon as I stepped outside Cell Nine I felt the cool morning sky pour down to greet me. I wanted to linger at the feel of free air but Hans was in a such a hurry he was almost running.

I walked quickly behind him. We went to the end of our courtyard and turned left. I saw there was one more cage, Cell Ten, remaining on our side of the building. We passed it, the Dutchman walking briskly and turned left again at the end of the cell block. Sitting off by itself behind Char Chuki (Barracks Four) was a previously undetected building. This smaller adobe structure was modeled on its larger sibling up front. However a cursory glance revealed it was even more run down than Char Chuki. A six foot high wall masked its perimeter. The single hole in the wall which served as the gate only managed to give the building a secretive, off-limits look. Behind this barricade I could see cell doors running down the side of the building. Hans didn't give me time for more than a hurried look. He led me across the widest portion of our pie-shaped segment of the prison, all the while making his way towards a little building set off by itself.

Defecating and urinating are very private matters in the Muslim world. A public restroom such as one finds in a western sports stadium, where male strangers stand urinating shoulder to shoulder, is unheard of. In addition the local toilet fixtures are themselves unique to the Indian subcontinent. While Americans sit upright on toilets, Pakistanis squat over ceramic bowls fitted flat into concrete bathroom floors. A traveler was as likely to find a western style toilet in Rawalpindi, Pakistan as a French bidet in White Fish, Montana.

Some said this habit of squatting was derived from the age old teachings of Yogis who believed it was more beneficial for the body to evacuate waste in this manner. Cynics said it was because early Indian households couldn't afford the more expensive western-style toilet.

Regardless of the reason, custom among Muslims therefore decreed that people squatted on their haunches to attend to their business. Because urine is considered a spiritual pollutant, and Islam requires five prayers a day, Muslim men were thus extremely careful to keep it off their clothes. Wearing baggy pants and a shirt that reached to your knees made such an daily operation a tricky one under ideal conditions. What I found in the prison toilet were not ideal conditions.

If I had been stone blind my nose could have guided me to this stinking abscess. Hans hotfooted it into the small structure, passing through what had once been a doorway and was now only a gaping hole. I stopped in my tracks. A fetid miasma greeted me. The smell of corruption was so strong it required a real effort of will to go inside.

Dante had never been to Pakistan or he wouldn't have overlooked this section of Hades. The room was twelve feet long and eight feet wide. There were no windows. The door served as the only source of ventilation. What natural light managed to penetrate the gloom was extremely poor but sufficed to show me as degraded a place as I had ever encountered. A two foot high brick wall split the room into two sections. Five tiny stalls were on each side of the room, shielded from their neighbor by another section of low brick wall.

The effluvium increased in strength as I moved inside. A single stall on the far side was unoccupied so I made my way there. The other nine men inside were staring at the walls or at the ground in an effort to retain their dignity. It was a futile exercise. They were separated by less than twelve inches.

Every stall had two concrete blocks standing ten inches high and twelve inches long. The space in between was filled with decomposing excreta. It had been so long since anyone cleaned out the putridity, it now threatened to reach the top of the blocks. Urine leaked out of each stall into a small two-inch wide trench that ran in front of the stalls. Because the men used water on their left hand, and not toilet paper to clean themselves, the floor was awash in an ugly wet mixture. Previous users had possessed a poor sense of direction. The short walls on both sides were not only stained, they were marked with brown streaks left by desperate hands. I stepped gingerly on top of the blocks, carefully

Cell Nine – Block Four

loosened my pants, took care to make sure my shirt tail was not dragging behind me and bent down.

I was almost overcome by the noxious, sickly vapors. It was an effort not to gag and retch. I urinated quickly, stood up with care, tied off my pants and started for the door.

As I emerged from this malodorous experience I discovered a host of men anxious to take my place. Like me they were driven inside by a force of nature, the vile hovel serving as the single toilet for more than one hundred men living in Char Chuki. I had overlooked a open cesspool nearby which was full of decomposing excreta. Once every few months some unfortunate prisoners were chosen to perform *laipa*, cleaning out the filthy toilet stalls and shoveling their ordure into the pit.

Hans was waiting for me. I was stunned by the gloom I had just observed. The Dutchman seemed unconcerned and philosophical about our early morning experience. Before long I too stopped being so fastidious, learning like Hans that the horrific, foul smelling, and unnatural conditions were a part of normal life in Pindi Prison.

On our way back to the cell we met Ali Muhammad heading to our previous destination. He gave me a quizzical look.

"Its a little rough in there," I warned my genteel Creole friend.

While I waited for Ali's return my two cell mates and I sat on our burlap blankets and leaned against the wall. They took the opportunity to answer my questions. Only chance could have thrown two such dissimilar men together.

I had been right about the Dutchman. He knew the ropes, but I was glad Raja Bahadur Khan, our other cell mate, was along for the ride. If I felt out of place, this young man looked it.

Raja was tall for a Pakistani and as lithe as a cat. The slim youth was blessed with clean good looks. Dark wavy hair crowned his head. His skin was lightly tanned. His enormous dark eyes made him look even younger than his nineteen years. Since our arrival last night I had learned almost nothing about him, not even the crime that brought him inside Pindi Prison. But while Raja was reticent about his past, his face couldn't hide an unaffected boyish charm or his natural intelligence. He appeared to be trusting, warm hearted and quick witted. His English was excellent, revealing a capacity for hard work.

Where Raja carried some secret shame, Hans was an open book.

The Dutchman wore the remnants of European clothes. His striped green and gold tee shirt was riddled with holes. His dirty brown pants looked like something he had begged off a rag man. Even though he was short, Hans's old frayed pants still hung above his bony ankles. He had never heard of socks. His dirty bare feet were shoved into cheap plastic flip flop thongs. He had thin brown shoulder-length hair. Completing his dapper appearance was a wispy mustache and a scraggly goatee. He was never without some sort of cigarette, smoking being almost a sacred sacrament for him. His fingers were tobacco stained. His teeth were brown and crooked. The smoking made him growl out his English like a macho Marlene Dietrich. He was twenty eight and looked forty.

Regardless, he was an unrepentant dirty little scamp who wore his rags like an emperor down on his luck. He was utterly unimpressed by authority, and there in lay the major difference between our two cell mates. Though Raja was stronger physically, he lacked Hans's emotional depth. The Pakistani was soft spoken, well mannered, and reverent. The Dutchman was stoic and felt no remorse or self pity. In fact he took a perverse delight in having landed in Pindi Prison. He was determined to beat it.

At first I thought Hans was kidding when he told me how lucky I was to have slept in our dirt floored cage last night. To my astonishment I learned Cell Nine, Block Four was the high class neighborhood of Pindi Prison. The other three barracks Ali and I had passed on our way into the prison differed from Char Chuki. There was no attempt to label them as anything but what they were, a combination of dungeon and pest hole. Those barracks consisted of a single gigantic room, one hundred feet long and thirty feet wide, with a barred door at one end. Hundreds of convicted prisoners resided inside on the dirt floor. As in Cell Nine, the government provided nothing for the inmates lodged in these hellish dormitories except a water pot. Prisoners made arrangements for bedding to be brought in or they slept under the coarse burlap blankets provided by their overseers.

Char Chuki differed from the other barracks in several important ways. Like the larger sisters, Char Chuki had a cell running down its middle, only this one was slightly smaller for two reasons. First, prisoners who were awaiting trial were placed there. The length of their stay in this legal purgatory depended on the vagaries of Pakistani justice.

In addition the British had constructed ten cells on the outside of our building. Like Cell Nine, they all backed up to the main wall. There were five cells on either side, each separated from its neighbors by walls seven foot high. A ten foot long courtyard adorned the front of each. The walls and courtyards gave these ten tiny rooms a snug feeling compared to the rest of the prison.

Privacy was a forgotten luxury throughout Pindi Prison, Hans told me. Hundreds of unwashed men lived packed together in warehouse sized barrack rooms where the noise was deafening. For this reason the ten cells of Char Chuki were not just highly prized, some of the most influential criminals in the nation paid to stay in their cramped luxury. Char Chuki hosted a "Who's Who" of Pakistani crooks, ranging from a mysterious, silent murderer next door in Cell Ten, to Karachi businessmen busted for avoiding import duties. Any wealthy and well connected son of sin could thus avoid living in the squalor and noise of the common holding cell by greasing the palms of the DSP and our

Cell Nine – Block Four

warden, Sergeant Shafi. Presiding over the criminal needs of this social elite was the "Dada" or underworld boss of this section of the prison. Residing in Cell Seven, the Dada seldom mixed with the other prisoners, preferring to spend his time living a life of ease in the luxury of his well supplied coop.

"Only the richest criminals can afford to bribe the DSP to stay in the ten cells in Char Chuki. The going rate is 2,000 rupees a month for a cell. I was lucky," the Dutchman said. "When I first got here Babu threw me into the holding cell. I spent three months there until I met Jameel. He was a Saudi busted for selling counterfeit visas. He used to tell me, 'I don't work for the embassy. I am the embassy.' Jameel was so rich he had this whole cell to himself. He invited me to move in to keep him company and practice his English."

"Were you his friend too," I asked Raja in all innocence.

"I was his *bardashti* (servant)," he answered. I could see the truth burning the boy's face with shame.

Hans came to our friend's rescue and resumed his own story.

During the short time the Saudi had stayed in Pindi Prison he had lived with as much luxury as he could afford to have smuggled in. Quilts covered the floor. Fresh vegetables and other food were brought in regularly. Almost anything could find its way into Pindi Prison if you had enough money. In fact Cell Nine's previous rich tenant had escaped using the same principle.

"Jameel bought his way out last week. He paid 100,000 rupees. Officially they called it bail but he almost certainly left Pakistan immediately. Babu came in the next day and took everything Jameel left us. I was afraid he was going to throw Raja and me back into the holding cell next," Hans confided. "The DSP must have wanted to keep us three foreigners together or we wouldn't be in this cell now."

"Or maybe someone told the guard up front we were Muslims," I said quietly, remembering Sergeant Hiyat Mohammad.

Hans and Raja differed in one other very important respect. Hans was serving a three-year sentence for smuggling hash. Raja was an "under trial" awaiting his day in court. Like the other non-convicted men in Char Chuki he had no way of knowing if and when he would ever plead his case before a judge. None of the time an under trial spent in Pindi Prison before trial counted towards any eventual sentence. Despite this hardship Raja assured me he was lucky. There were others much more unfortunate inside Pindi Prison.

There were six distinct categories of prisoners in Pindi Prison. The social order started with trusties, spiraling ever downwards through the ranks of B Class, under trials, C Class, women and "mentals." Every group had its own social rank and rules.

The *nambardars*, or trusties, were recruited from captured army deserters or hardened career criminals. Like Babu, they were serving life sentences, and worked as deputies to the wardens. Some were basically good natured but even the gentlest would not hesitate if provoked to lash out in physical violence against a prisoner. An impertinent remark would result in a resounding slap across the face from a hand as hard as oak. Having ingratiated themselves with the authorities, they looked upon such behavior as the normal function of their job. They varied in age from early thirties to late fifties.

B Class was reserved for political criminals. There was no one currently in the prison afforded that rare distinction. The few prisoners who occasionally met this definition were confined in the hospital.

Under trials were those prisoners waiting to plead their case. They existed in a legal limbo, prisoners held in captivity with no rights until such time as the justice system noticed them. Potentially innocent, they languished in jail, sometimes for years, awaiting their day in court.

C Class, defined as common criminals, were the most numerous. They were squeezed into the other barracks, 150 or more to a room, lying shoulder to shoulder in sardine-like tightness.

Women prisoners were kept secluded in the front of the prison. Special *bajis* (female wardens) guarded both them and the children of the imprisoned women. It was common knowledge many women were imprisoned on fraudulent morals charges brought by husbands seeking divorce. Though Islam had for centuries afforded women legal protection, judicial reality in General Zia's Pakistan was that women were often held captive on the flimsiest of charges. Any male relative could contrive to imprison a female with no more than an accusation of moral turpitude. The women so accused went to prison to await the judge's pleasure.

Rape in Pindi Prison was a whispered reality.

Neither of my cell mates knew how many children were currently locked up in Pindi Prison with their mothers. If a woman had no family to accept responsibility for her children, they went with her to prison. Boys stayed with their mothers until they were ten. Girls remained imprisoned until their mother was released. There was one Pathan woman who had been confined for the past twelve years. Her daughter, now fifteen, had no memory of the outside world.

One female prisoner, who served as a mid-wife, had delivered more than 25 children inside those wicked walls. Like their older brothers and sisters, the "jail babies" were inside because of the sins of their parents. They were accounted the lucky ones. At least they were alive.

A pregnant female prisoner, raped and four months pregnant, was force fed twenty raw eggs. She aborted the fetus and almost died.

The most famous female criminal currently in Pindi Prison was a middle-aged woman known as Jamia. Married, with five children, Jamia had been convicted of having an adulterous affair with a younger man. She was fined 1,000 rupees, sentenced to five years rigorous

Khyber Knights

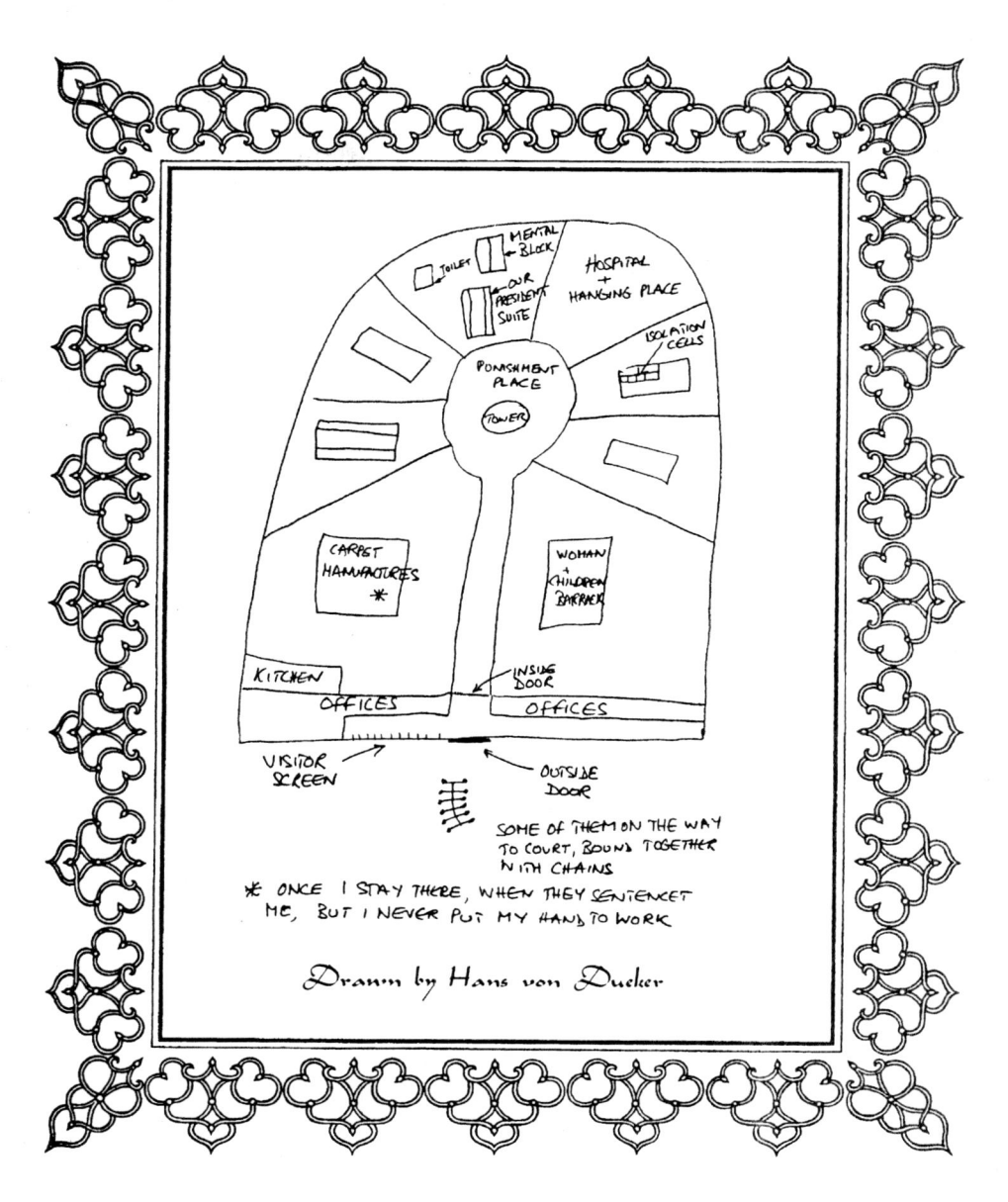

Pindi Prison

Drawn by Hans von Ducker

* Once I stay there, when they sentenced me, but I never put my hand to work

Some of them on the way to court, bound together with chains

Cell Nine – Block Four

imprisonment, and ordered to be publicly flogged twenty times. A female warden had been specially trained for the occasion.

In the other chukis (barracks), convicted male felons were given rigorous imprisonment, known as *mushaqat*. According to the rules laid down by the British, men had to work in the prison shop or kitchen. They wove cheap cotton rugs called darri bunai, or baked bread over hellishly hot tandoor ovens. Earlier that summer one of the *langris* (prison baker) had jumped into the fully fired pit, choosing death by fire rather than face another day toiling in front of the oven.

The pay for inmates at Pindi Prison was 50 paisa, about five cents a day. One prisoner residing in a chuki for convicted criminals had a bulging tumor larger than a football hanging from his abdomen. This emaciated wretch was dressed in only a loincloth. The insidious growth, which weighed almost as much he did, was thus clearly visible. Unable to stand up, the tormented man crawled on his haunches trying to sweep the barrack floor. He had no money either to escape from the labor demanded from him or visit the hospital.

The prisoners who suffered the most, I learned, were the criminally insane. Called mentals, these were truly God's forgotten children. Under the 1912 British Lunacy Act anyone deemed to be insane could be imprisoned by the state. This broad violation of the laws of civilization gave the DSP the God-like authority to lock up a person until such time as he declared the prisoner mentally fit. The small dilapidated building I had observed on my way to the toilet was used to house twenty of these unfortunates. Some had been there for decades and had no recollection of the outside world. The mental cages were basins of pestilence. If you weren't crazy when you went in, you were a certified lunatic when you finally came out. The cages softened a man's brain and aged him prematurely, before finally sending him back into the prison population with an empty mind and a starry gaze like a medium in a hypnotic trance.

"In Pindi you are crazy until you are not crazy. What happens back there is very bad," Hans said.

It was an understatement of the fact that Pakistan had never ratified the United Nations Convention Against Torture or the UN Minimum Standard for Prison Rules.

Babu and Sergeant Shafi used the mental cages to torture not just the mentals but any prisoner who defied their authority. A bold prisoner was overwhelmed by guards and dragged off to the cages. There he were hung upside down by his ankles from a cell door, then beaten into either submission or madness. Men were routinely kept awake for days, had their genitals smashed, burned with cigarettes, gagged with iron balls or had lathis shoved up their rectums. If he was lucky a man came out of the mental cages only a physical cripple. To survive it mentally was a miracle of human endurance.

Raja told me some of the most famous criminals in Pakistan were kept there, including an notorious cannibal known as the Baby Eater, Suliman the mad mullah, and an infamous brigand known as Yusuf.

"Yusuf was the king of the *dacoits* (bandits). Now he is the king of the mentals. He got very rich from kidnapping business men. Last year he led his gang in an attack on a police station to capture weapons but he was shot in the leg and captured. When they brought him here he was threatening to kill all the guards. Babu wasn't afraid of him. He hung Yusuf upside down and beat him with a lathi till blood ran out of the prisoner's ears. Then they fettered him. Now he is mental," Raja confided.

"But Babu and the guards worry Yusuf is faking and only waiting to attack them," Hans added with a mischievous smile.

I told them I was surprised we had been allowed out of the cell that morning, that I had expected to stay locked in all day. They explained this was not out of any kindness but because neither the holding tank nor the ten cells had toilets. Prisoners were allowed out of their cells from 6:30 a.m. until 1:30 p.m. Most days they were allowed out again briefly in the afternoon for another hour. This privilege depended on Babu's mood. Everyone was locked up for the night at 5:30 p.m. After the last lockup, even if the iron claw of dysentery was ripping out your guts, you held the pain and awaited the dawning of the sun. Any man foolish enough not to have used the toilet during his brief time out of the cells was therefore forced to foul his cage before morning. Any prisoner so unlucky used water from the ceramic jug and tried to wash the excrement out the cell door, hoping to clean up the mess in the morning.

All the talk had made Hans hungry. Food was at a premium. One of the few things the prison provided was bread twice a day.

"Come on, we'll go get a roti and I'll show you this place," the perky Dutchman volunteered. I stood up to follow him. Raja seemed content not to leave. For the first time in weeks I was deeply hungry. I asked the Pakistani if he didn't shared the feeling. The quiet young man smiled shyly and shrugged his shoulders.

"I learned to ignore the song of an empty stomach at a young age. You go. I'll wait here for your friend," he told me.

Hans lead me out into the world of Char Chuki.

We left the cell, walked out of our courtyard, and then turned right towards the front of the building.

Immediately outside our cell was a dirt-packed exercise yard. It was hemmed in by walls on three sides but absolutely clean. Three feeble rose bushes had been planted alongside the wall. A large baobab tree, its trunk painted white, stood in the middle of the yard. Char Chuki might be a spiritual sore but there was enough free labor to keep it spotless.

Our route took us past the other four cells on that side of the barracks building. Glancing inside I saw they were opulent compared to ours. Well-dressed men reclined against bolsters, sitting on thick quilts that covered

Cell Nine – Block Four

the dirt floor. Other prisoners acting as servants were busy cooking breakfast for their masters over tiny, hand-built charcoal stoves.

In the yard a host of fellow prisoners were enjoying the autumn morning sunshine. After a night spent in a cage it was hard to believe the sky could still be blue when you emerged. Dozens of men were relishing this small freedom, walking around the chuki and talking to each other. This desire to escape confinement was the only common thread running among the crowd. With the exception of an occasional sweater, there was no evidence of western clothing. I saw one man step out of a cell up ahead. He was dressed in a laundered lilac colored shalwar kameez and polished sandals. His hair was carefully coifed. Further out in the exercise yard wandered one of the mentals, hiding his nakedness under a ragged blanket. His dirty bearded face housed vacant eyes that were no longer able to decipher life. As he shuffled along the mental conducted an urgent conversation with himself, stopping occasionally to fight off imaginary assailants.

We reached the end of the building and Hans lead me directly into the holding tank. I paused to look around uneasily. The little Dutchman had been right. Even though our cell was pathetically bare, it was Paradise compared to this.

The absolute poverty of the scene was overwhelming.

The room was a storage bin crammed full of humanity. It had a cell door made of iron bars and six bare light bulbs hanging from the ceiling. There was nothing else in the room, unless you counted the disease and filth the prisoners resided in. They were expected to live and die on that dirt floor. Many did. There were nearly one hundred men crowded into the room that morning. The population varied from night to night, depending on how many men were admitted to the prison during the day. I saw prisoners lying, sitting, crouching, kneeling, and standing alongside both walls. There was no heating. The men kept warm by huddling close together under the burlap blankets. They froze in winter, roasted in summer.

"Come on, bread's in the back," Hans told me nonchalantly.

The men we walked past looked like they had slept in hell. Their faces were impossibly dirty and many were dressed in rags that defied description. They had been dehumanized, crushed into this old building and then conveniently forgotten. They had come here for justice and found only brutality. Ninety per cent had no concept of the basic laws of Pakistan. At least one third were innocent of any crime. Almost everyone was illiterate. Few had money for a lawyer. Most had been arrested simply because they were close to the scene of a crime. The state prosecuting attorney, anxious to keep its book clean, conspired with the police. The prison administration kept the concept of prisoner's rights a secret, and another scapegoat ended up lost within the walls of Pindi Prison.

Many prisoners were bound in *ara berri*, leg irons. These five pound fetters were another British gift. A man had large iron rings welded around each ankle. A steel bar with an eye on each end was attached to the inside of each ring. Each bar reached up as high as a man's waist. A third ring held the bars together at the top. You either walked around holding the top ring in your hand or you tied it to your pants string. In either case a prisoner wearing the fetters was forced to shuffle in order to move. In addition, the fetters prevented a prisoner from bending his legs unless he first laid the iron bars straight out in front of him.

One of the rules left over from the English Prisons Act of 1894 was the requirement that "prisoners on whom fetters have been imposed shall keep them bright and polished."

The official reasoning behind implementing this cruel device was to deter criminals from escaping. In fact no one had successfully fled from Pindi Prison in living memory. The truth was the fetters were used as punishment. Anyone who showed the slightest sign of rebellion was slammed into leg irons. Once you found yourself encased within those cold iron rings, you had to bribe your way out. Men forced to wear them for years walked around with ankles scarred white from the constant friction of the *ara berri*.

Hans provided a rolling commentary of the men we saw or met on our way. He knew everyone.

He pointed out Anwar who was arrested for stealing a clock from a mosque. The **Shias** (Muslim religious minority) said the thief should have only the fingers of his right hand amputated. The **Sunnis** (Muslim religious majority) argued the entire hand should go. Anwar had been in Pindi for months, with both hands intact, awaiting the outcome of this thorny legal question.

I was introduced to Faiz Mohammad and Qaim Mohammad, two charming brothers who informed me they had done, "Nothing at all."

"Our elder brother, Ali Sher, ran an impostor's den. The police raided his home and recovered 15 forged passports as well as numerous false national identity cards. When he escaped they imprisoned us instead."

Custom dictated the two younger brothers would be held without trial until their elder sibling was captured.

Seven friends from the same Rawalpindi neighborhood were all lodged in Char Chuki, charged with "lethal celebrations". While attending a wedding they had fired their AK-47 machine guns into the air to mark the glorious occasion. Unfortunately a Pakistani national airplane flying overhead had been struck and damaged. Everyone said it would be a long time before the wedding guests even went to trial because the government was determined to make an example of them, showing its displeasure of this long-standing social custom.

We met Zulfiqar from the nearby village of Bashira. He admitted to us he had killed his sister Ashraf Bibi, "due to my suspicion of her doubtful

Cell Nine – Block Four

character." He explained he had no proof of her infidelity but he had observed her looking at a boy in the village. He killed the girl to prevent her from possibly dishonoring the family.

I followed Hans to the back corner of the large room, winding our way in and out among prisoners, stepping over them if they were sleeping, walking around those that weren't. I tried to appear casual but no one was paying any attention to me anyway.

"And here is the bakery," Hans said cheerfully. We found hundreds of sheets of thin unleavened bread. It was delivered to the back of the barracks building twice a day, placed on sheets of old newspaper and otherwise left unattended.

The rear of the holding tank offered me the chance to observe two other things of interest. I could see the rear window of our cell, high up on the wall on the other side of this room. Sitting underneath it was the old man I had heard crying last night. Like me, he was wearing a turban. He appeared to be close to one hundred years old and could not have weighed more than ninety pounds. Thick glasses were perched on his little nose. A snow white goatee and mustache graced a face pinched by starvation. He was talking in a high reedy voice to another prisoner. The presence of such a patriarch in this disgusting pit convinced me there were no rules in the fetid world I had fallen into. The tenets of Islam were carved in stone regarding the respect due to the weak, mentally infirm and the elderly. Only monsters, not men, could condone and govern over such a world as this where all of Allah's weak children were systematically tortured and degraded.

At that moment I replaced my fear of Pindi Prison with hatred.

This was a place unburdened by any remnant of sentimentality. Sadistic by nature, the decaying buildings joined in a happy partnership with a prison administration indifferent to the loss of life. If it was true that the human mind could make a heaven of out of hell, or a hell out of heaven, than Pindi Prison was the ultimate betrayal of human decency.

When I glanced back towards Hans I saw a pile of the burlap blankets stacked four foot high against this wall. The prisoners were required to place them here in the back of the room when they got up in the morning. The blankets were stiff with dirt and body grease. Before I had a chance to pick up my bread I noticed something moving on top of the blanket closest to me. When I held my gaze I saw little gray body lice scurrying across the burlap webbing. My skin started to crawl. Body lice are common throughout Asia. But the thought of those little gray bugs sucking my blood while I slept under these same sort of blankets made me cringe.

I pointed this discovery out to Hans, who told me, "The louse is the pet of this place. We've all got them, even the DSP I hope. The louse sucks our blood just like this prison. Only he is more honest about it."

"You stayed in here for three months," I asked Hans incredulously.

Khyber Knights

The Dutch smuggler stuffed a piece of roti in his mouth and mumbled, "Yeah, some nights it was pretty hard to go to sleep."

"I bet it was tough just surviving," I said as I bent down and got enough bread for Raja, Ali Muhammad and myself.

Hans didn't waste anymore time talking, instead he picked up three pieces of the roti. Despite our surroundings, he looked like he was going to sit down and eat them right there.

"Nice restaurant Hans, but how about going back to our cell to eat?"

"Sure," he said. "I hate coming in here anyway."

He could have fooled me.

We made our way back to Cell Nine. When I walked in I saw my friend Ali Muhammad sitting on a blanket talking to Raja. The former elegant son of New Orleans looked up at me, glad to see the bread, unaware yet of how far he really was from the magnolia scented bayous of Louisiana.

"Find anything out?" he asked.

I shook my head in discouragement, masking my anger and despair.

"Interesting movie we've wandered into," I told him.

15
Naeem

Hunger was the other tenant of Cell Nine Block Four.

The DSP followed the letter of the law by feeding the prisoners three times a day. In reality the portions were so meager they barely kept us alive.

Morning saw each of us served one cup of tea, two *rotis* (bread) and a handful of roasted chick peas. The prisoners called the peas "tooth breaker," an apt name. When you ate the hard seeds it sounded like your teeth were snapping and breaking off at the roots.

The morning tea was delivered to Char Chuki in a shiny copper five gallon cauldron. Two dwarfish prisoners would carry the pot between them, coming to the door and giving each of us a single luke-warm cup of the weak mixture. Ali Muhammad nicknamed Raja, "the father of all usefulness," when the youth managed to beg, borrow or steal each of us a chipped, dirty porcelain cup.

Lunch was two more pieces of roti. The official ration was six pieces of roti per man per day. But it was always possible to obtain more bread. The problem was that the bread left you feeling bloated but still hungry.

Dinner consisted of another two pieces of bread and six ounces of daal. This was a watery lentil soup. The difficulty most days was the daal was ladled out by two p.m. and the bread would not arrive until just before lockup several hours later. By the time the bread came a thick layer of cold orange grease had usually congealed on top of the soup. Adding a twist to this culinary problem was the fact that despite our hunger the daal had to be eaten slowly. The lentils were poorly cleaned. Empty stomachs urged us to eat the daal too fast, thereby running the risk of busting a tooth on one of the many minute pieces of gravel overlooked by the cooks. Not having utensils, we tore off pieces of bread and used that for spoons, scooping the daal up out of our teacups.

Raja assured us once a month the prisoners were also served meat at dinner, but he urged Ali Muhammad and me not to get too excited about the prospect. The DSP and the government meat contractor skimmed off the funds provided to buy decent cuts and provided only "chicras" instead. This was inedible fat, ligaments, gristle, etc., portions not normally served in a Muslim household.

"They give us scraps we wouldn't feed to a dog in my village," Raja told us. "But don't worry you'll eat it and love it."

What shocked me was that despite this starvation diet I continued to heal. Several days had passed since our arrival. October was upon us and the air was chilly at night. The bruises left by Ashgar Ali's devotion to duty were no longer too painful to bear. Plus, though I was still weaker than I had been before leaving Peshawar on Shavon, I knew my strength was nearly back to normal. When I revealed my improving health to Ali Muhammad he chided me, accusing me of arranging the trip to Pindi Prison to recover my health because I was too cheap to go to Dublin.

We joked about our situation but secretly my cellmate and I were both uneasy. It had been nearly a week since we met Eugene Crouch and we had still received neither word nor help from the American embassy. Our case seemed monumental to us but intellectually we understood it was of no importance to the outside world. Experience had taught us that Pakistan knew how to keep time in its place. If you grew restive you were asking for trouble. Things in Pindi Prison moved to ancient Oriental rhythms, not an Occidental doctrine of expedient energy.

We tried to think like Asians, not Americans.

Ali Muhammad wrote Pushtu love songs on scraps of paper. I likewise made notes for a story on the weaknesses of Pakistani justice. We remained guardedly optimistic.

Three days after our arrival we were summoned to go before the prison doctor for a physical examination. Ibrahim, the second and younger trusty, came to get us soon after breakfast had been served. He escorted us out of Char Chuki, across the parade ground where the guard tower sat and into *Paunch Chuki* (Barrack Five), the hospital compound.

The hospital was located in a small whitewashed building with a red tile roof. Ibrahim lead us through the main door, where we saw a large room with six old-fashioned metal beds. Only one bed in the back of the room was occupied and this by a young black man. The Negro prisoner looked shocked to see us. He didn't say a word, only stared at Ali and me with big, chocolate-brown eyes. He was obviously very scared at the sight of the trusty escorting us. The young man's presence was a mystery, heightened by the fact that except for a few diplomats around the country's capital, one never saw a black person in Pakistan. In the southern seaport of Karachi there were rumored to live descendants of African slaves who had taken up residence there more than one hundred years ago. But we were a long way from the sea and my intuition told me this man was not one of those descendants.

I wasn't allowed to solve the riddle. The turnkey lead us through a green door on the left side of the room. Inside we were introduced to the doctor.

The examination was superficial. The medical officer had us remove our shirts, then noted any identifying marks, scars or tattoos on a cardboard card. He next noted our age, weight, height, parentage, domicile, occupation, education, offense, date of incarceration and finally, our prison number. As he was writing all this down I realized he was collecting the information not out of any humanitarian concerns, but simply as a way of describing us in case we escaped. A nearby rolling metal table held a stethoscope, thermometer, blood pressure apparatus and dust. An old scale stood against the wall. The medicine on a nearby shelf all had expired dates clearly visible on the bottles. Those experiencing serious medical problems could expect little or no help.

Before going there, Hans had informed us that the doctor, like the DSP and guards, was involved in getting wealthy at the expense of the prisoners. Milk, white bread, and medicine, supposedly regulated by the hospital, was instead sold to the wealthy prisoners in Char Chuki. The doctor was in on the black market racket that thrived under the surface of Pindi Prison. I was learning not to be surprised.

Ali Muhammad and I were barely back in our cell when the trusty, Babu, arrived at the door. He stood at the threshold, apparently not wanting to lower himself by coming in. His old face didn't hide the contempt he obviously felt for the four of us prisoners. Sitting there on the dirt floor, wrapped in the burlap blankets to ward off the chill, we certainly must not have inspired much confidence.

"I have good news," Babu said.

"What, has your wife stopped being a whore?" Hans interjected and began laughing. We all started snickering despite ourselves.

The trusty gave him a withering look.

"*Mulaqat* (visitor) for you two," he said and pointed at Ali Muhammad and me with his grizzled chin.

It was Thursday, traditionally a day when most official business was only lightly attended to, Friday being the Muslim Sabbath. Yet the trusty wasn't there to give us a choice.

"*Jeldi, jeldi*, (hurry, hurry)," Babu said, snapping out the order to Ali Muhammad and me. We gave Hans and Raja a, "Who knows?," look and got up to leave.

We emerged a few moments later to see Char Chuki going about its daily functions. Prisoners, both sane and otherwise, were walking in the exercise yard. Up at the water tap, Mohammad Siddiq, the little madman, was washing his first load of laundry for one of the rich prisoners.

Gathered nearby under the baobab tree were most of the mentals. They had been allowed out of their cages for the morning. The one known as Suliman was standing up on the mud bench that encircled the tree talking in a loud voice to his fellow mental patients. Suliman entertained a reputation as a political troublemaker. No one was sure if he was in Pindi Prison because he really was crazy or because the military dictatorship running the government was just trying to scare him into silence. Regardless, his congregation that morning was mentally diverse.

Three dirty men sat on the ground in rapt attention, staring up at the noise of the man the guards called the Mad Mullah. Five others stood looking on, their attention coming and going like sea waves. The Baby

Eater lingered off to one side. Another man was busy picking up, then gobbling down, cigarette butts. Yusuf the former bandit was walking around the perimeter of the group. His leg irons were rattling as he paced back and forth. He was carrying a little metal pot with a lid on it. Where the bandit got the metal pot or what secretive concoction it contained only Yusuf and Allah knew. He banged the lid ka-chink, ka-chink, ka-chink, in time to Suliman's sermon.

One of the mentals, a political refugee from Bangladesh, looked our way and noticed Babu leading us into the yard. This young man had a shaved head and a continual grin. His big eyes were bright with both hunger and delusions. He was wearing only an old shirt that reached to his knees and a pair of cast off green socks. Upon seeing us he shouted, "How are youuuuuuu !" at the top of his lungs and started pointing and capering about. This set off the rest of the crowd who began a chorus of noise. Yusuf saw the despised trusty and started banging the lid on his pot furiously.

"Babu," he screamed.

It looked like Yusuf was going to charge. Then Mohammad Siddiq the insane laundry man joined the musical troupe and started yelling, "Nixon, Nixon, Nixon," at the sight of the two foreign devils of Char Chuki.

It was all perfectly normal in that insane asylum with bars.

"Go on," Babu said in a voice laced with boredom and shoved me in the direction of the gate.

At first it felt exhilarating to be outside Char Chuki. Even a drop of limited freedom was a tonic. Yet the trusty's presence leeched away our plebeian pleasure and left Ali Muhammad and me walking side by side, each lost in our own concerns.

Babu strode in front, taking us past the guard tower and onto the road leading towards the main gate. It was easy to see why the old turnkey enjoyed the reputation he did. He exuded a aura of hostility, carrying his hatred of life and other living beings around like an invisible hump on his back.

It didn't help that he resembled a nightmarish grandfather, Boris Karloff wearing a trusty's red beret. The years sat lightly on him, though he was rumored to be in his early sixties. He had a wide slash for a mouth. His short hair was snow white, like the stubble covering his face. His cheeks were sunken. Shaggy eyebrows hooded black eyes that had witnessed an encyclopedia of violence. His sharp nose made him look like some fierce old bird. The long shalwar kameez only accented his height, its white color marking him as a trusty.

Originally a corporal in the army, Babu had been sent to prison after deserting during the 1971 war against India. The judge had given him twenty years to brood over his cowardice. Babu's ability to read, and his fawning, had got him the job as trusty to Sergeant Shafi. As long as the stream of graft flowing out of Char Chuki continued uninterrupted, Shafi was glad to sit under the warden's tree and gossip with the Chief Chakkar, while Babu handled the internal daily affairs of our little world.

The turnkey was not just a local sadist. In a institution where devotion to the degradation of man was an art form, Babu enjoyed a singular honor. The old trusty had been instrumental in the execution of Pakistan's former prime minister, Zulfikar Ali Bhutto. That famous politician's fate changed overnight when his minion, General Zia seized power. The charismatic Bhutto was charged with a contrived case of murder, judged to be a B Class political prisoner and kept on ice in the prison hospital, while a rigged court decided his fate. Outside the walls of Pindi Prison the country and the world howled for Bhutto's release. The accusations against him were riddled with inconsistencies. World leaders, including the Pope and the American president, urged clemency.

Pakistan's new military dictator decreed otherwise.

Zia understood he had crossed the Rubicon of power when he led the military coup. Like Julius Caesar before him, Pakistan's conqueror was thus irrevocably committed to consolidating his authority, regardless of the costs to democracy or human lives. The toppling of the elected government inaugurated Pakistan's degradation. Zia first threw out the hard-won constitution, saying, "What is a constitution? It is a booklet with twelve or ten pages. I can tear them away and say that tomorrow we shall live under a different system. Today the people will follow wherever I lead. All the politicians, including the once mighty Mr. Bhutto, will follow me with tails wagging."

From disposing of a sacred document it was an easy step to the disposal of an inconvenient human life. Zia knew if Bhutto left Pindi Prison a free man, his own chances of survival were infinitesimal. The military usurper believed he must hang Bhutto or perish himself as penalty for his former master's fierce wrath. At first the prime minister reacted to the charges of complicity in the murder of a political opponent with arrogant disregard. Even his incarceration in Pindi Prison had failed to impress on Bhutto the true nature of his ruthless political opponent. It was only after he was found guilty, and sentenced to be executed within the walls of Pindi Prison, that Bhutto, the once mighty ruler of Pakistan realized he was doomed, sentenced to die at the bidding of the man he had brought to power and trusted.

Babu had never lost any sleep over his role in Bhutto's death. He carried that iniquity willingly. As he lead us between the two walls that hemmed in the road, we came upon a bored guard who was overseeing three sweepers. Because brooms in Pakistan do not have handles, the men were squatting on their haunches holding the homemade brooms in their hands. They were painfully duck walking their way down the long road, all the while sweeping the already spotless dirt even cleaner. Traditionally all work of this nature went to the country's tiny Christian minority. This held true even in prison.

The road was plenty wide but Babu kicked the man in the middle as he lead us past. When the trusty saw me look at him disapprovingly he snorted in contempt.

"They were born to be beaten," he sneered.

I didn't have time to discuss it. Within moments Babu was hammering on the Judas Gate that lead into the administrative section of the prison. The portal snapped open and we left the cruel trusty behind. The guard closed the gate and escorted us towards the DSP's office. A crowd was gathered at the visitors area. One prisoner was crying, trying to touch a child through the wire mesh. The world of freedom lurking outside looked like a mirage. The guard knocked on the door, then told us to enter. The moment we entered that room even the illusion of freedom was stripped from us.

The room hadn't changed and the DSP didn't look any less dubious. It was the little man sitting in front of the desk that riveted my attention. When he stood up to meet us you didn't need a reporter's intuition to know you were looking at a lawyer.

Khawaja Naeem looked like the Pillsbury Dough Boy trying to masquerade as Perry Mason. He was short, barely five feet. He wasn't just fat, he was rotund. His straight hair was jet black and greased straight back. He wore an expensive three-piece black suit. His stomach threatened to rebel against the gold vest buttons.

Later, after he had helped destroy Ashgar Ali, I remembered it was the mustache that gave you the subtle clue that this was no overdressed little fat man. He was the only man I ever met who maintained a mustache in the style of Hercule Poirot. When I looked into his beady black eyes I realized the mustache was no mistake. You could almost see his brain spinning like the little Belgian detective's.

I glanced at Ali Muhammad. I didn't have to guess what he was thinking. He rolled his eyes in consternation, as if to say, "Uh oh, we're screwed." But though my dear friend could recite the love poems of Khushal Khan Khattak, he didn't know Sherlock Holmes from Professor Moriarty.

The small man motioned for us to step to the far side of the DSP's office. Three chairs had been pulled up so we could converse. It wasn't exactly private but it was better than trying to talk through the screen outside. I'm glad we sat down, otherwise we might both have fainted when told the news he brought.

"I'm your solicitor," he said and gave us a firm handshake.

Then Khawaja Naeem came right to the point.

"You're both looking at seventy five years to life if convicted on all charges."

We sat there too stunned to respond.

"I'm afraid the man from your embassy made an unintentional mess of things. He sent an official complaint to the government of Pakistan

Khyber Knights

"Babu the Trusty was not just a local sadist. In an institution where devotion to the degradation of man was an art form, Babu enjoyed a singular honor. He had helped execute Pakistan's former Prime Minister."

accusing the narcotics police of beating you. They in turn have pressed charges against you for possession, transportation and manufacturing of heroin."

I glanced at Ali Muhammad for support. He looked like a fish out of water, his mouth was open and his eyes looked glazed from shock. Naeem didn't let up.

"I'm afraid there is no chance now of settling the matter quietly. Things are too far gone. The narcotics inspector, what's his name?" the lawyer said and studied the papers lying across his lap.

"Gilani Khan," I volunteered.

"Yes," Naeem said looking up in agreement, "Inspector Gilani Khan has filed a First Investigation Report with the police which reports that you were arrested entering Flashman's Hotel with two bags of heroin. Of course the inspector denies his men harmed you."

That was the first indication of what we were up against. Gilani Khan's report stated he had received a tip in the late afternoon about two foreigners attempting to smuggle heroin. He and several narcotics officers had driven directly to Flashman's Hotel, arriving at 5:30 p.m. They supposedly spotted Ali Muhammad and me as we were walking into the main gate. An arrest was made there on the sidewalk. Each of us was carrying a small shoulder bag. They discovered the heroin was split equally between us, 500 grams in each bag. While they detained us, five grams was taken from each bag as a sample. We were then briefly taken to our hotel room, where our luggage was searched. After a site plan was drawn, Gilani had two of his men deliver us directly to police custody, where we were handed over to Sergeant Hiyat Mohammad by 6:30 p.m.

It took Ali and me only a few minutes to relate our side of things to Naeem. We explained the discrepancies in time and occurrence, giving enough evidence on the spot to have convinced a blind man of our innocence. Naeem brought us back to reality, explaining to us like two half-witted children that this was no longer a case of mistaken identity or delayed justice. Eugene Crouch's well-meaning complaint had changed the course of our lives and our case.

"They have woven a web of lies to keep you quiet and to ensure that you cannot escape. The accusation of having tortured you is a serious one. Gilani Khan has to prove the narcotic charges or run the risk of being exposed not just to his own government but to the Americans who trained him. Obviously they have falsified evidence and collected witnesses to support their allegations against you," our lawyer explained patiently.

"Can you at least get us out of here on bail," Ali Muhammad asked hopefully.

Our advocate's face took on a pained expression.

"I'm sorry to tell you that the third charge, manufacturing of heroin, is a 1930 British Raj statute. The inspector filed this count against you because it can only be judged in the court at Lahore. You can't go before that court because you can't leave the jurisdiction of the Rawalpindi court. Its a clever move because unfortunately it leaves you inside this prison until your case is settled."

"No bail?" I asked in a weak voice.

"No bail."

"How long before a trial?"

"Long."

"No chance then?" I asked.

"I won't mislead you. The charges are serious and I must warn you not to expect mercy from the court if you are found guilty. But there is a thread of hope. I have discovered that these are the same officers who recently arrested an Englishman on a similar heroin charge. His solicitor is a colleague of mine. That chap was able to prove the case was contrived against his client by proving the heroin in question was in fact Ovaltine powdered milk. The case was dismissed and the Englishman cleared. I believe your case is only the latest justification for the continued existence of Gilani Khan's agency."

"Why don't they just arrest the Pakistani drug dealers responsible instead of foreigners," my friend asked.

"They don't want to upset local sensibilities. Besides it is the American DEA who is pressuring this situation into existence. I'm afraid even if you are found innocent the pretense will go on," Naeem told him patiently.

I took a deep breath and asked, "Is that it?"

The little man stared down at the floor, visibly uncomfortable, then looked me in the eye.

"No. If convicted you will both face rigorous imprisonment. Do you know what that means?"

We nodded.

"We will have to work in the prison shop," Ali Muhammad said.

The lawyer nodded, his mustache twitching nervously, then added, "It also means you will be publicly flogged at the start of your sentence."

I groaned out loud, aware now that this wasn't some misadventure that was going to resolve itself; no reassuring Karl Malden was going to drop in from American Express to help us, no flag waving cavalry from the American Embassy was going to lead a rescue. Nothing and nobody was coming. Zip. Zero. Naught. My best friend and I were trapped in Hell without a visa.

For the first time in my life I was too scared to breathe. I shook with a cold chill. I had witnessed such hellish punishments, knew what to expect.

The night before a prisoner was to be flogged, the whip was stored in a container of oil to intensify its murderous effectiveness. The next morning a government-sponsored mullah blessed the lash by reciting a verse of the Qu'ran over the leather tongued weapon of war. With God's apparent approval in hand, the sanctified sadist who was to dispense the punishment began making practice runs, his half-naked, oil smeared body snapping the whip in anticipation of the arrival of his prey.

When he appeared, the prisoner had been already been stripped, except for a scrap of cloth tied around his groin to hide his withering manhood. The frightened man was immediately chained upright to a wooden rack, the large metal rings snapped around his hands and feet prevented him from escaping the forthcoming blows.

At a given signal, the torturer came running in, stopped a few feet short of his victim, twisted his body in a tight semi-circle, then slashed the whip down across his victim's back with all the strength he possessed.

I had watched brave men not afraid of death broken on the Pakistani rack, had seen white bones peek through torn brown skin, had discovered the dirt around their feet littered with tiny bits of flesh ripped off their backs, had heard non-partisan bystanders finally scream for mercy for the condemned man.

Naeem must have realized we were both too stunned to speak. He took charge emotionally.

"Now that I have done my duty by telling you how difficult things look, I must tell you that you do have a chance. More importantly, I believe your story. I will speak to Sergeant Hiyat Mohammad and the doctor who examined you after the beating. I'll also search for clues at the hotel. But while I'm doing this you must concentrate on making sure you both stay healthy and well," he said and then lowering his voice he added, "You both look like men who've seen a bit of the world. I don't need to tell you unfortunate things could happen to you in this prison as easily as breathing."

Ali Muhammad was the first to grasp the situation.

"The guards took all our money. I think we could make arrangements to get extra food if we could get some rupees," he explained.

"Yes a lack of money is the father of disappointment but we can easily solve that," Naeem agreed. Without a moments hesitation he brought out his wallet and handed Ali Muhammad five 100 rupee notes. At that moment I knew the little man was tougher than he looked. With Naeem's help we started making plans. Ali and I gave him the names of friends in Peshawar who would send us Pakistani funds to cover our living expenses. When we tried to discuss his fee Naeem told us we had more important issues to deal with at the moment. Finally we all rose from our chairs. It had been the longest fifteen minutes of my life.

We walked back and stood before the DSP's desk. The big man looked up from his paperwork. I didn't really know or care how much the jailer had overheard. Naeem didn't stand on any protocol.

"My clients are going to need certain privileges extended to them," the lawyer said.

The DSP smiled. This was a language he understood. Ali Muhammad and I were no longer merely prisoners. We had crossed an invisible line

Khyber Knights

and were now staring at the distinct possibility of becoming long-term paying customers of the Pakistani big house. The jailer assured Naeem many things were possible if discretion were used.

Later that night Ali Muhammad and I found ourselves back inside our new home. Cell Nine Block Four was growing colder with the approach of winter. We had shared our news with our cell mates. Raja exhibited no surprise at anything, the phony bust, the beating, or the false case filed against us. Something seemed to be broken inside him, keeping him from believing there was any hope left in the world.

Hans however was determined to amuse us. He explained how he was the only foreigner in history who had ever been busted for smuggling hash into Pakistan, not out of it. After scoring a large amount of Nepalese hash in India, he had boarded a plane bound for Amsterdam. Unfortunately his Sikh travel agent overlooked the fact that the cocky Dutchman would have to change planes in neighboring Pakistan.

When the little smuggler had disembarked in Karachi, he was forced to board an internal PIA flight for Rawalpindi. There he was scheduled to meet a connecting international flight on to Holland in two hours. Things were going good until Hans observed that all departing passengers were being carefully checked by Pakistani customs agents. Until that moment, in addition to the hash he had secreted inside his belongings, he had been carrying two small balloons full of the drug in his shirt pocket. He quickly swallowed the balloons and then tackled the problem of customs.

The first thing that went wrong was a customs agent discovered the Remy Martin cognac bottle in Hans' luggage. The Pakistani informed the Dutchman it was against the law to have unlicensed alcohol in the Muslim country. Hans told him to keep the cognac but the custom agent's suspicions were already alerted. A closer look revealed the bottle was full of hash. The customs agents started tearing Hans' possessions apart. That is when they discovered the hashish hidden in a Toblerone candy bar box.

Hans' flight back to Europe departed minus one Dutch passenger. He was taken into a small room where he was strip searched. At that inopportune moment the balloons burst in his stomach. Within minutes he was standing there naked, and so stoned he started laughing hysterically. At first the Pakistanis were baffled as to how the smuggler had suddenly got high. When Hans giggled out the details, including the origin of the hash in question, the Pakistanis started laughing too. It was the first time any of them had ever busted a man for bringing dope into their country.

Even the judge was amused. He only gave Hans three years in Rawalpindi Prison.

As usual the little Dutchman was smoking as he related this tale of commerce gone awry. Hans' cheap cigarette had burned down until it looked like he was going to suck in the last burning ember. He took one last daring drag then tossed the ashy fragment out the cell door into the dark night. When he blew the smoke out his nose he looked like a bearded dragon.

He then smiled and said, "I know you think you got bad news today but the Dutch embassy has only visited me once in the year since I've been here. They sent over some big blond fascist. He told me I was lucky to be in prison because the food outside was full of bacteria."

"I guess he thinks this is a germ-free place," Hans said, laughing in that raspy voice of his.

We all smiled but the gloom Hans had been holding at bay came creeping in through the bars. Outside Babu and Ibrahim were making their rounds. Babu yelled out, "Theek hai," and we knew our night had begun. Every hour until dawn the guard in the tower called out the word "Theek hai". This word, "OK," was posed as a question to the different trusties stationed around the prison. One after another the trusties would yell back "Theek hai" in reply. The hateful word was a night time invasion into your soul. You heard it in the back of your mind while you slept. Pindi Prison would not let you escape even in your dreams.

Adding to this aspect of the horror a light bulb burned overhead in our cell twenty four hours a day. The DSP insisted on illuminating all the barracks and cells so the trusties could count us during the night. The bright barrage of light made sleep almost impossible.

Without a word we four cell mates each took our places on the dirt floor, lying on top of one burlap blanket and trying to stay warm under another. Hans, closest to the door, stared up at the ceiling. Raja and Ali Muhammad both lay on their left shoulders. I was last, and positioned closest to the rear wall. Like them I too faced the back wall. Crowded together on the floor, we moved into the confines of our own thoughts, trying to locate the solitude denied us in the world of the prison.

Char Chuki was starting to settle down. The mentals weren't screaming tonight and we four cell mates were beginning to drift into our own thoughts, when the old man in the central cell behind us began choking and crying. It was plainly audible through the cell window above our heads.

"Why is he even in here?" Ali Muhammad asked no one in particular, his question floating softly in the air.

I heard Raja answer.

"He was sent to prison because he is an opium addict."

The people of the Indian subcontinent had been growing poppies and making opium for centuries. When former prime minister Bhutto's extravagant personal lifestyle, including drinking, came under attack from conservative mullahs, he tried to appease his critics by banning domestic consumption of liquor, wine and beer by Pakistani Muslims. The crafty politician's attempt at personal piety never fooled anyone. Yet even after he was deposed the prohibition on alcohol stayed in effect. When General Zia came to power he tried to solidify his power base by appeasing the same persistent orthodox constituency Bhutto had appealed to, only he banned the production, distribution and use of opium. The military regime cited the Qu'ran's intolerance of sharab, all mind-altering intoxicants, a definition which legally banned the products of the grape and hops like wine and beer, but traditionally overlooked the poppy flower or the marijuana weed.

Regardless, at the time of Zia's order Pakistan had more than 700 tons of opium stored, ready for legal export to overseas drug companies. In addition there were an estimated 800,000 opium addicts scattered through out the country. While Bhutto's ban on whiskey had little impact on the average Pakistani, hashish and opium were quietly accepted and widely used. The old man in the holding cell was an unfortunate victim of a new social phenomenon. Under Zia's code of Islamic conduct any concept of narcotics reform was replaced by penal servitude. Instead of spending his golden years at home, the tiny elder was trapped within a prison that joyfully retained a memory of all the cruelty enshrined in its walls.

"They have kept the old one locked up for months without a trial," Raja told us. "He is crying because he knows he is at the end of his life and is going to die here."

At that pronouncement the despair I had held at bay since meeting Naeem took total control. I shivered in my coarse blankets and silently begged Allah to spare my own life from what appeared to be a fate as certain as the old man's.

16
Even Sparrow's Milk

Early the next morning Ali Muhammad and I started fighting for our lives.

Pindi Prison didn't tolerate false hope or self pity. It was carnivorous and desired to consume our faith, our souls and perhaps our very lives. If you weakened you died, and neither of us planned to perish.

Seeking what limited privacy was obtainable my friend and I adjourned from Cell Nine and went to the exercise yard to discuss our situation and devise a plan of survival. Other men were already walking there. Some were solitary figures lost in thought or madness. Some strolled in small groups of twos and threes like us. Regardless, after being locked down in a cage since the previous sunset we had all emerged from the caves where we existed like unwilling troglodytes. A shimmer of warm camaraderie hovered over the yard.

Over our heads was the only visible affirmation available to us that Allah was not dead, that despite the injustice here at ground level, above us still wheeled the unlimited pageant found in the book of nature, a confirmation that man's cruelty was confined only to this world and that a promise endured for some better existence for even such forsaken mortals as us.

The sky was cloudy when we first walked out. It grew gray and colder as my friend and I walked and talked about a life suddenly gone deadly wrong. We discussed the machinations that had plummeted us from a life of exotic ease in Peshawar into the belly of this man eater. Neither of us was the sort of man to wail, gnash his teeth or bemoan his fate. If we had lacked courage we would have stayed at home in our "village" back in America with its comforts, routine, security, and predictability. Neither of us wanted to exist in that sea of conformity where mediocre men took no chances, where every breath was regulated by invisible social, religious and economic legislation. We had come out to Pakistan to live and even here, even now, neither of us shook an angry fist at Allah nor regretted our decision to be free men, though such an initial desire appeared to have stripped us of that very thing we loved, our liberty.

Both of us had been gone from America a long time both spiritually and physically. What happened at Flashman's Hotel we concurred was part of some larger plan. There was an undisclosed purpose to our arrival in Pindi Prison. Yet there was also no guarantee that either of us would live to leave to discover it. Our innocence rested with the court but our survival was our own responsibility. Ali Muhammad and I were balanced on a bridge stretching over Hell, sharper than a sword and finer than a hair. We knew if we were strong we would come through this. Yet a misstep would reduce us to either physical or moral slavery by that vampire of a prison.

As if to guide us, as if to show us we were not alone with our tiny concerns, the skies opened. The clouds rolled in like moving mountains, pouring down a cold hard rain that drenched us to the skin. Big drops were splattering off the packed thirsty earth. Men started laughing and running for shelter. The yard was empty within moments, except for Ali Muhammad, Yusuf the insane bandit and me.

I saw the once-mighty brigand look up at the sky in a silent question that said what every man in Char Chuki was thinking at that moment.

"Oh Allah even if I sinned how could you condone putting me here?"

Then Yusuf threw back his head and howled like a dog that had been beaten. He raised his head and bayed up into the rain. His long black hair and his thick beard were matted with the tears of Allah, as he screamed out a protest that had no need of petty words or lawyers. His was a tuneless song of adversity and tyranny and persecution and oppression. Prisoners were watching him from the cell doors. Like us, they too knew the dirge Yusuf sang. Ali Muhammad and I stood there in the rain, frozen at the sight of him, until Suliman the Mad Mullah came rushing out and led Yusuf back into the shelter of the mental cages.

According to plan my friend and I returned to Cell Nine. We just as quickly departed again, each of us hastening through the rain with one of our cell mates.

Hans and I made our way to the other end of Char Chuki, our mission to petition the Dada for help. The impudent Dutchman had seemed the appropriate companion for this job. Raja had readily agreed to go with Ali Muhammad but had been unwilling even to discuss the idea of accompanying me to visit the crime boss of Char Chuki.

As we entered the courtyard that prefaced Cell Seven I got my first good look at the man who wielded so much unofficial power. His cell door was open, affording me an unobstructed view of this pasha of crime. He was leaning up against one wall, taking his ease, something he obviously did a great deal. In a country populated by lean, athletic men, the Dada was an exception. He was physically corrupt. His body was corpulent and bloated. Thick heavy breasts sagged through his shirt. His head was huge, shiny, and closely shaved. He favored neither beard nor mustache. His jowls hung around his neck like a great greasy necklace. He appeared to be a pustule awaiting our arrival.

"This man looks like a villain," I whispered to Hans, as we made our way to the cell.

"He is a villain," my cellmate whispered back.

We stepped into a private world of comfort unlike anything else in Char Chuki, nor indeed in Pindi Prison. Cell Seven was the same size as

Even Sparrow's Milk

ours. The ever-vigilant light bulb burned overhead. All similarities ended there. All trace of the dirt floor had been removed except just inside the cell door. Here a work area had been set up. Cardboard boxes full of fruit, bread, and other foodstuffs were stacked against the wall. A small stove was sitting on the dirt floor, burning charcoal, giving off a reassuring warmth. Despite its radiant heat, the stove was the oddest thing I had ever seen. It appeared to be made out of a tin can. I had no time for further investigation.

My eyes showed me luxuries I had already lost hope of seeing any time soon. Shoved up alongside two walls were thick mattresses. They were covered in warm green quilts. Large, multicolor bolsters served as low couches. Above this luxury the walls themselves had been covered. The white plaster had disappeared, replaced by lengths of blue fabric that hung in place of more costly tapestries.

I was cold, wet, dirty, and hungry. The room was warm, inviting, soft, and civilized. I longed to sit down and retreat from the world of Char Chuki.

Hans and I stood there in the doorway, dripping and unwelcome. The Dada was leaning up against a bolster. Snuggled up to his fat body was a young man. The older fellow's arm was thrown around the youth in what was obviously more than filial protection. At once I knew why Raja avoided this cell. His good looks would have been an undesirable asset in such loathsome company. My opinion of my quiet cell mate rose but neither the Dutchman nor I had been invited to Cell Seven to volunteer unwelcome social commentary on private sexual practices.

We were intruders.

The Dada however was first and foremost a business man. His pig eyes widened and his nostrils flared at the scent of human prey. He studied me silently. I could sense his mind tossing me up on the block, considering my possible worth as merchandise to be used and resold. The look he gave me was neither cruel nor kind. I was a foreign novelty, nothing more.

He blinked. When a smile widened his face I knew we were in.

"Ah, Dutchman! Who is your friend? Come in. Come in. Here sit down," he said to me, then patted a space close to him on the mattress. "Shonni bring our guests some tea. They must be frozen in this rain."

When I sat down next to the fat man the younger man gave me a sullen look. Clearly pouting, he left his master's side and began making tea over the tiny stove. I thought I would faint from the bliss of feeling that soft mattress. I turned to study my host. He was in his early fifties. But given his transparently ill health I didn't give him long. It was thankfully already chilly. But summers in Pindi Prison would be a torment for a man of his size. As if to confirm my suspicions, in the corner of the cell with the food I noticed a stack of medicine bottles. Obviously my host had already come to the same conclusion regarding the effects such a place could play on his health. The hospital doctor was undoubtedly richer for it.

"Assalaam alaikum," I said and offered my hand.

The Dada's hand though big, was fleshy, his grip weak.

"May you never be tired," he told me smiling.

"May you never be poor," I replied, though I doubted if that problem worried the Dada even in Pindi Prison.

More importantly the fiction of friendliness between us had begun.

Pakistan has a tradition of courtesy inherited from the great Mogul kings who once ruled all of India. So neither of us plunged into our mutual immediate concern, what had brought me unannounced to Cell Seven. Instead the Dada and I discussed safe subjects, this unexpected rain, how long had I lived in Pakistan, when and why I converted to Islam. The obese sultan volunteered the observation that he visualized America as being a perfect country, full of opportunity, streets paved with gold, a land where big men with big ideas were not hampered by petty concerns.

"Petty concerns like the law," I volunteered and smiled.

"Yes, like the law," he said and we both laughed at his candor.

Having arrived at our subject as custom dictated, via the back door, our conversation began to take its true course. I told him someone had informed me a limited amount of smuggling was overlooked if certain officials were rewarded for their patient understanding.

"Oh there is plenty of smuggling going on in Pindi Prison," he admitted, then hastened to add, "but of course I'm not a smuggler."

A smile covered his big face and we both understood the absurdity of it all. He was a corrupt old crook but he had a deep, warm, infectious laugh. When he started his belly roll laugh Hans and I joined him. We were not friends the Dada and I, but from that point on we maintained an understanding. He pulled a cigarette box out of his shalwar pocket. The cigarettes were Gold Leaf, Pakistan's most expensive brand. He opened the box and offered me one.

I held up my hand in a motion of "No thank you."

Hans reached over, before he was invited, and took one gratefully.

"They're bad for you," I volunteered.

"Yes but so many lovely things in life are bad for you," the Dada said philosophically. As if to confirm this, Shonni rushed over to light his master's cigarette. The servant was soon back with a china plate loaded with cookies, followed almost immediately with a tray containing a large pot of chai and cups. The Dada looked on approvingly while Shonni, who looked to be about twenty years old, served us tea like a trained monkey. I had not enjoyed a cup of tea that was actually hot in many, many days. The delicious liquid scored my stomach, warmed my cold body and brought a satisfying sigh from my lips.

The Dada put the plate of cookies in front of Hans and me. My cell mate was literally starving and began eating them furiously. Seeing Hans

Even Sparrow's Milk

was not standing on ceremony, the Dada grew alarmed and raked four cookies off the plate himself before they were all gone. He opened his maw and shoveled them in two at a time.

"This is not my house. This is your house," the crime boss told me with his mouth open, and waved an expansive hand at the cell. Shonni gave me a poisonous look that urged me not to take the Oriental courtesies too personally.

I didn't. I got down to business.

It wasn't necessary to explain what we needed in Cell Nine. It would have been repeating the obvious. Despite his uncouth appearance the Dada was a talented entrepreneur. His contacts could provide rice, sugar, tea, meat, fresh vegetables, charcoal, or medicine. He could send our clothes out to be dry cleaned. Even a woman was possible if I wanted to pay the expense of bribing one of the *bajis*, the female wardens. Hans smiled at the memory.

"I can get you anything except sparrow's milk," the fat criminal said and meant it.

The Dada held court from his little room. It was rumored even Babu came to Cell Seven in search of favors.

"The question in Pindi always gets back to money," he told me "The sooner you make financial arrangements the more likely you will survive. Your lawyer can bring money to you. Otherwise you will starve while the guards fatten, or sicken and die on the prison food, or be forced to become someone's servant like crazy little Mohammad Siddiq. He washes the other prisoners clothes in exchange for table scraps."

The crime boss went on to explain that the jail was a law unto itself. Only credit, muscle and outside contacts gave you a chance to survive. The normal procedure was to receive your money from a lawyer or family member in the DSP's office, secret all except a few rupees in some hidden area of your clothing, leaving a few rupees in an obvious pocket. The agreement with the guard at the Judas gate was he would stop searching once "his" rupees were located and confiscated. The Dada suggested we make a list of supplies. He would have them delivered with his own once a week.

"Of course a slight surcharge can be expected. The affairs of business take precedence even over matters of the heart," he said and smiled.

"What about escape," I asked, broaching a subject I had been silently entertaining.

"Not possible. Hasn't happened since the place was built. Especially impossible for prisoners such as you and I who, how do I say this, have such social prominence," he assured me and laughed again heartily.

Our case was widely known throughout Pindi Prison, I discovered. Hans's guilt had never been an issue. Apparently prisoners in the different chukis were discussing Ali Muhammad and me, not just because of our American birth, but due to our conversion to Islam. It was reassuring to discover that the prison grapevine had not automatically pronounced us guilty.

The Dada's own case was more open and shut. The government had discovered a cargo-ship loaded with 500 new Korean cars about to be unloaded at a Karachi wharf. No import duties had been paid. Impertinent questions had been asked. The previous arrival of similar ships had been uncovered. Millions of rupees in taxes had been overlooked by accident. It was all very unfortunate. The newspapers had exaggerated, calling my host the "King of the Smugglers." The federal government had sent him to Pindi Prison as a consequence of that unwarranted publicity. Yet despite the setback the Dada remained composed, philosophical, a thinker, a man of vision surrounded by the vagaries of life. He assured me his current living arrangement was merely part of the cost of doing business in Pakistan, a temporary setback from the rich table of life.

It had started raining harder. Hans was not anxious to leave and I could tell the Dada was enjoying our conversation. He ordered Shonni to heat water. While this was being done the older man fished into a carry-on bag and came up with a Bic razor that must have been a year old. The cookies had not been to my liking but the offer of a shave was a true luxury. The disposable razor should have long since been retired and the Dada only had a tiny fragment of a mirror. But I managed. I had almost finished when I cut myself. My host quickly smeared the nick with cigarette ash, coagulating the blood and infuriating his jealous servant.

The shave was finished, the rain kept falling and as the last of the tea was poured, Shonni made a point of snuggling back up against the Dada. The thick baby-blue sweater he wore was new. His tan colored shalwar kameez looked fresh. This was no ordinary cook.

As if to scout out my feelings regarding the subject, the Dada hugged the young man close and said, "Isn't he a beautiful boy?"

The callow *kuni* (homosexual) looked pleased at the attention of his fleshy **marvasi**.

"**Buk shah**," the older man whispered, which caused Shonni to giggle.

The Dada gave me a searching look, then asked, "Do you need a servant?"

The air was laced with innuendo.

I smiled, as if in sympathy. Such behavior was certainly not unknown to me. It was common to see two Muslim men walking down the streets of Peshawar holding hands as they carried on a private conversation. This mild affection was however a social practice of long standing that had no sexual overtones, was in fact just a reflection of the brotherhood of Islam. It was one of the few Pakistani traits I was never comfortable adopting.

There was however another aspect of the Pakistani world not so commonly reported. Because of the segregation of women, males found themselves at an early age consorting almost exclusively with members of their own sex. The normal social activities of the Western world, high

Even Sparrow's Milk

school prom, the drive-in movie, the courtship rituals of youth, were nowhere to be found in Pakistan. True, in some cosmopolitan cities such as Karachi and Islamabad, there was a certain amount of mixing between the sexes. Countrywide however, after the onset of puberty a man seldom had any lengthy encounters with women outside those in his immediate family. Weddings were arranged between parents. Grooms traditionally saw the face of their bride for the first time on the evening of the nuptials.

Male friendships remained a strong bond before and after marriages. These boyhood attachments sometimes developed into sexual inclinations. Behavior such as the Dada's and Shonni was an open secret around much of Pakistan. Islam strictly forbade homosexuality. I was of the opinion that a male lover of his own sex was a voluntary eunuch but I had not come to offer rebukes. I had come in search of food. It was for Allah alone to judge whether these men were a reproach to their ancestors.

"They sing an old song in Peshawar," I said in answer to the Dada's prying question. "'There's a boy across the river with a bottom like a peach. Alas, I cannot swim.' I have never had the urge to stray into that stream," I told the Dada and with my eyes told him the subject was closed.

I knew it was time to go. We had learned what we came for. Money could be brought in with discretion. A list would be sent to Cell Seven. Business among friends was a blessing.

When I stood to leave the important man didn't bother to stand with me. He reached up and gave me a weak handshake instead.

"Remember, in this prison my name protects the weak and the innocent. Come and see me if you have problems. I have room in my heart for all the world's troubles," he told me and smiled.

"And room in your stomach for all the world's groceries," I thought to myself.

I thanked him and left. Hans had been right. The Dada was a villain but he had panache. The Dutchman and I ran back through the rain. Our cellmates were waiting.

"The Dada can get us anything except sparrow's milk," I announced with pride to Raja and Ali Muhammad.

"We won't need it. The doctor has agreed to give us each a daily ration of white bread and milk," Raja said beaming.

"How did you manage that?" Hans asked, shaking his head in amazement.

"Ali Muhammad did it. He told the doctor he was going to report him to the American embassy for withholding our rations," Raja explained. "The doctor caved in. I couldn't believe it. He said, 'You come every morning and get it then,' and pointed at Ali Muhammad."

It was the first time I had seen Raja happy.

I looked at my friend. The suave musician smiled and shrugged his shoulders as if to say he bullied corrupt doctors all the time.

"Going to make another complaint to the embassy are we?" I asked him.

"What, and get slapped with another life sentence? Not me," Ali Muhammad assured me.

"They say in my village that a poor man has no friends," Raja said. "I think I have three."

Before I could agree with him, before we could congratulate ourselves on a good days work, before we could salivate and plan meals on food that hadn't arrived, Babu came to our cell door.

"Black man," he said.

It wasn't a question. It wasn't an order. It was a statement.

He reached behind him and grabbed the young black man we had seen in the hospital, then shoved him into our cell.

"Maybe he can share your milk every morning for the next few years," Babu said, then turned and walked away through the rain.

The cell was silent as we five men stared uneasily at each other. Finally the stranger spoke.

"I am from Africa."

17
The Untouchables

A month later we had learned the ropes.

Peshawar did not forget us. Our friend Professor Qureshi had sent us money in answer to my letter. We declined his offer of further assistance, urging him and other friends to stay away for fear they would antagonize the narcotics agents and bring down reprisals on their own heads. Naeem delivered the funds on a brief visit.

After giving the majority to the Dada we still had 200 rupees left, more than $11 held in reserve. Ali Muhammad kept it hidden under the large water jar in the corner of Cell Nine. On the opposite side of the door now sat a small cardboard box containing potatoes, onions and garlic. We had tea in a tin and sugar in a little brown paper sack. A large can of *ghee* (clarified butter) was close by. A bunch of bananas hung from a twig driven into the plaster wall. There was a week's worth of charcoal, two handfuls of salt, more than five tablespoons worth of curry powder, a dented tin saucepan, three ball point pens, some cheap writing paper, a plastic bag, a disposable razor, a piece of hand soap, a scrap of towel, even an Urdu newspaper turned into a table cloth.

We were incredibly rich.

In Pindi Prison I soon learned the truth of the old Peshawar saying that necessity was the mother of invention and the father of Eurasian.

The Dada had ordered Daud, a Persian handyman serving time, to construct us a stove. Daud had shown up in our courtyard with an empty two gallon ghee can. He had managed to cut a small door in the bottom. Part of the round top was folded back to form a crude chimney. With the butchered can in hand, the Persian had gone to our courtyard, where he concocted a mixture of mud strongly laced with coarse salt. This thick compound was spread an inch thick both in and outside the ghee can. After drying overnight, we had a small adobe oven known as an angeethi.

Daud had also suggested we put a brown paper bag over the nagging, ever present light bulb hanging over our heads. The trusties could still see us at night, but the muted light was not so obnoxious. Our fat cat smuggling buddy in Cell Seven even sent over five empty jelly jars as a cell warming gift. These had also been treated by the clever Persian. Daud first tied a string around an empty jar just under the threaded lip. Using a small handmade bow, he pulled the string back and forth rapidly, thereby heating up the circumference of the jar. When it was deemed hot enough, the Persian plunged the jar into cold water. There was a clear line now scored into the surface of the glass. With a little care the threaded top snapped off cleanly. Daud sanded the edges with a stone from the exercise yard and then presented us with matching glasses.

Hans was the scrounger. He had discovered a spoon somewhere. He sharpened the handle on a rock until he had a knife capable of slicing potatoes. He also invented the "Nazi Vegematic," an empty corned beef can which he gave to Raja to chop our vegetables. The smuggler's proudest contribution was a mobile he constructed out of empty cigarette boxes, thread and twigs. Hans spent days constructing It. The graceful "moh-bah-lee" as the Dutchman pronounced it, swung from the light bulb cord, adding a sense of frivolity to our otherwise austere white cell.

It was Raja who took over the little kitchen. He was a natural cook and enjoyed surprising us. Mornings he would heat up the prison tea, adding in the milk Ali Muhammad brought from the hospital. In the evening, Raja would take the weak daal, throw in a few cooked potatoes, part of an onion, plus some spices, and make it taste better than any of us could have believed. More importantly Raja felt he was earning his keep.

I cleaned up the cell, straightening the shoes we kicked off near the door, folding the burlap blankets every morning, helping Raja clean up the kitchen. Ali laughed at my efforts, assuring our cellmates that being tidy was part of my Capricorn nature.

It was a humble beginning. It was still a cell. But it was no longer inhuman. We could not beat Pindi Prison but we could keep her at bay, stopping her at the door like the Dada did.

Ali Muhammad said Cell Nine reminded him of the humorous television series "Hogan's Heroes", but with turbans not Nazis.

Despite the improvements, every morning started out the same. The mentals served as the Pindi Prison version of an alarm clock. They began howling the moment the sun began to peek into their cages. I would stay huddled under my raggedy blanket, trying to exist in the little cocoon of warm air my breath had created. But the lice sharing my clothes and my raggedy bedding were early risers. I would lie still hoping to fool them into going back to sleep but the bugs were all hard working Protestants and bold with hunger. At the first sign of noise they began biting like hell.

Hans, who had them the worst, was always the first one up, screaming and scratching and cursing all insect life, all prisons, all Pakistanis and all Sikh travel agents. The mad mullah would next sing out the azan, the call to prayer. Soon we would hear the holding cell being opened up and then the sound of Babu and Ibrahim unlocking the doors to the ten cells.

Men would come flooding out then, some rushing to the horror of the toilet, others into the exercise yard to take in the sky. Some only walked as far as the end of the courtyards where they would greet their neighbors with a polite "Good Morning" like retired brigadiers leaning over the white fence between trim cottages. The mentals would begin spicing up the morning soup. The little half-naked Bangladeshi would strut

The Untouchables

around shouting, "Hello, hello, helloooooooooo !" into his invisible telephone. Hans would return from the holding cell with the roti and Ali Muhammad would come back with white bread and milk from the hospital. It would be time to go work Pindi Prison style.

Fitting quietly into this new picture was Godwin Mujumba from Bukoba, Tanzania. The son of a Christian minister, the twenty-five-year-old student had been attending university in neighboring India on an athletic scholarship. During school break he came to Pakistan for a short holiday. His passport had either been lost or stolen in a Rawalpindi fleabag hotel. Godwin was arrested during a routine sweep. The passport police responsible for monitoring foreigners neglected to handcuff him, just popped him into a taxi and drove him straight to Pindi Prison.

The young African had no idea where he was being taken. He followed the police out of the taxi. It wasn't until he saw the big blue prison gate and the guards with their rifles and affixed bayonets that the exchange student took fright. As the little Judas gate opened he saw the small black hole waiting to devour him. When Godwin hesitated to enter guards started yelling and grabbing him.

"Inside black man," they shouted, trying to shove him down the throat of the prison.

"I haven't done anything," Godwin screamed in protest.

That is when he resisted, tried to fight back, almost lost his life. Godwin Mujumba, alone and unarmed, lifted his hands to protect himself.

"Kung fu, karate," the guards screamed in warning. They fell on him with lathis, beat him to the ground, kicked him out of his senses, and dragged him into Pindi Prison unconscious.

He awoke after dark in one of the mental cages. He yelled and shook the bars but no one came. It got cold so he sat in the back of the cage, his arms wrapped around his legs to keep warm. It was the most miserable night of his life. The pain from the beating was bad. The cold was worse for a young man raised in the tropical heat of Africa.

Next morning Babu arrived.

"Outside mental," he said, than marched Godwin to the hospital before the rest of the prison was awake.

The doctor gave him two aspirins and told him to stay quiet until the DSP decided what to do with him. Days later he ended up in Cell Nine, Block Four with the other foreign devils.

The African was a man without papers, a serious offense. To complicate matters Tanzania did not maintain an embassy in Pakistan. Godwin's family thought he was in India. He had never been charged with a crime. He would never see a judge. Much later I wrote to his parents, telling them a sanitized version of what happened to their son.

When Babu brought him to our cell that first night the young student was wearing a pair of purple gym shorts and an old brown sweater. A green knitted cap covered his short Afro. Having lost everything, he was also barefoot. Godwin was short, strong, well knit. His face was round and his voice was sweet, even melodious. He was also extremely gentle and was blessed with a beautiful smile. The night he was brought to our cell he voiced his immediate concern.

"Do any of you snore?" he asked. "It's a European disease."

None of us did. It was so loud from all the other noises, the hundred or more prisoners living behind us in the holding tank, the mentals howling, prisoners yelling messages between cells, guards and trusties shouting "Theek hai" back and forth, that I doubted if Godwin would have noticed a little European snoring.

We put him on the floor closest to the door. It was getting cramped but we weren't complaining. Ten Iranians had just been thrown into an empty cell on the far side of Char Chuki. It was so tight some of them had to sleep sitting up.

Godwin was trying to teach me Swahili the morning the younger trusty, Ibrahim, showed up at our cell door. Babu's partner was clearly flustered and wanted Ali and me to come with him immediately. In response to our requests for information he told us only, "*Kachari* (court)," a vague answer at best.

We weren't expecting the early morning distraction. Naeem had visited us once briefly, bringing money forwarded to him by our friends. Our lawyer assured us he was working on several promising leads but urged patience. It was becoming more and more difficult to believe there was another sort of life outside the walls of Pindi Prison. Ali and I lived there in slow motion, suspended in a judicial amber that had no foreseeable end. Other prisoners told us the month we had so far spent in this legal limbo was nothing to whine about.

Ibrahim took Ali Muhammad and me out of Char Chuki and hurried us down the road towards the main gate. Upon approach we discovered we were late arrivals. Ten armed guards were already standing on both sides of two long lines of prisoners. Ibrahim rushed us up and turned us over to a couple of guards standing at the end of the lines. One guard immediately ordered Ali to stand next to another prisoner. I was directed to stand behind my cellmate. I was by myself, the last prisoner at the tail-end of this snake's back. A guard began to immediately confine me in chains. The manacles he bore were a reminder of another age. They were heavy black steel bracelets fully two inches wide at the wrist. Three hand-forged thick chain links bound them together. He placed one of the bracelets on my right wrist, leaving my left hand dangling free. He did not lock it on me. Instead he stuck a long screw into one end of the manacle, twisted it shut, then removed the screw from the end. The manacles were terribly old and dreadfully effective.

Hanging at the end of my archaic jewelry was a four foot length of chain with a large iron loop at the end. My guard took the chain and passed it forward to his colleague standing next to Ali. This man had been

The Untouchables

waiting for me to be confined. He passed an empty manacle through the loop, and only then began locking Ali Muhammad into the last remaining manacle.

While my cell mate was being restrained I had the opportunity to observe that there were forty-eight prisoners in front of me. Locked wrist to wrist and chained by pairs to the men in front of them, they were all now waiting to be lead away. I thought I would be the last man out, number forty nine, when I heard a sound I knew too well. Marching towards us was the music of leg irons. Turning back towards the guard tower I saw Yusuf the mad bandit being escorted up to join our little party.

Though I had lived in close proximity to this outlaw legend I had not been in direct contact with him. As he approached I recalled Raja saying how Yusuf hated the guards. I did not comprehend how that vast understatement was about to influence my own morning.

When Yusuf saw the chain gang he rebelled. The guards were ready for him. The bandit started screaming but before he could flee back towards Char Chuki five men had seized and dragged him forward. Suddenly the mad man of Block Four was being manacled next to me. It was like trying to shove a rhino into a pair of stretch pants. The former bandit was having none of it. Yet the guards were experienced. They overpowered Yusuf and within a minute they had him chained beside me.

The insane bandit was far from through.

"*Behnchodan*! (sister fuckers). *Sta mor banday kharuna wahchum* (I'll let a donkey mount your mothers)," he screamed and with his free right hand he seized the green pull over sweater he was wearing and proceeded to tear it into shreds one handed. He was a cyclone on a chain, pitching, cursing, screaming like an insane animal, and wanting to kill anyone in a uniform with his free hand. The guards were justifiably terrified and fell away the moment he was secured.

No one in a position of authority was waiting for Yusuf to stop his temper tantrum. We all had an appointment with justice. Guards took their places, ringing us with guns. An order was shouted to "Open up." For the first time I saw the two sets of gates, facing both into the prison and out to the free world, swing wide. I was suddenly standing inside Pindi Prison looking at life beyond. The guard leading the detail started us moving. It was a slow dance as many of the prisoners were hampered like Yusuf with leg irons.

My chain mate was still frothing mad. His sweater was hanging in shreds. I feared any moment he would look to his left and notice me. However when we began walking the movement quieted him. Yusuf fell into some secret corner of his mind and staggered along silently in his fetters beside me.

Perhaps he knew what was coming.

The most startling thing was the sound of traffic. The road running parallel to the front of the prison was crowded with people and cars rushing to work. Their noise poured in over us like a flood, its strange, unremembered cadence making my heart beat faster. Far up ahead the ponderous chain gang moved past the outer gate into a dimly remembered outside world. The bandit and I passed slowly beyond the DSP's office and through the foyer of the prison. Then Yusuf and I shuffled through the last gate, chained like dogs but temporarily outside the fortress of grief.

Because of the length of the prison queue, guards stopped traffic in both directions. Far ahead, the front of the line was making its slow way towards the side road where the taxi had dropped Sergeant Hiyat Mohammad, Ali Muhammad and me off so long ago. The feel of the heavy, cold manacle dragging on my wrist had already reminded me I was not free, but that, I reasoned, was only my body. Until that morning my soul had remained my own.

A large crowd of idle pedestrians had gathered on both sides of the road, forced to wait as the prisoners made their tedious progress out of the prison and across the busy boulevard. Though people in the area were used to seeing prisoners marching to and from the nearby court, the spectacle of two *ferenghis* in chains was a conversation-stopper. Voices were stifled in mid-sentence as Ali Muhammad and I walked between the twin rows of the animated throng. At first the mob stared in silence, secretly enjoying the discomfiture of two white-skinned foreigners, grateful for any excitement in their lives of poverty and boring routine.

Then men began pointing and shouting in English, "Hey mister," when my friend and I walked by. Drivers picked up on our presence and horns began honking. The crowd became boisterous. Hundreds of eyes saw our degradation. I began to burn beet red, my cheeks scorching with embarrassment. I saw Ali Muhammad trying to keep his head high, making a futile effort to retain the dignity of his regal Fontaine forebears. It was a fruitless exercise as there was no shelter from the catcalls. My friend and I were a public spectacle, stripped and chained for the mob's amusement.

For the first time I realized we were slaves, degraded, dirty, owned, unwillingly following our masters to wherever they chose to lead us. We had no previous position or social status. Gone were the memories of my nomadic life. I was no longer a proud horseman, only a Pakistani untouchable chained to an insane robber.

At that instant I was crushed with the penalty of shame. Allah had chosen to give me a taste of that moment to come when each man stands before his Maker naked except for the deeds which he has earned. I knew then what it would be like to face the Lord revealed for what little I was. All exterior things given to help in my development on this earthly plane were left behind on that long march. Wealth, property, power, influence, talent, intellect, social gifts, and pride were forfeit to those chains now binding me.

The Untouchables

The great line of men stumbled on and prisoners moaned. On either side of me the crowd jeered. It was a sampling of eternal punishment. It was the angry face of Allah revealed. It was the last thing needed to break me.

It took nearly thirty minutes to crawl in chains three blocks to our destination.

The guards led us across the main road and into a lane that was barricaded at both ends. Two decrepit buildings stood in the middle of this no mans land. The court building rested on the right. We turned left instead and ended up at what had once been a treasury. The forlorn old British building was now the *bakhshikhana*, a dirty, stinking room that served as a holding cell for the *roonumai*, prisoners ordered to report to the adjacent courtroom. Stout walls, a reminder of a paint job, and a mighty door constructed from iron bars were the simple elements of a room twenty feet wide and forty feet long. Two brick blocks stationed in a far corner served as a crude toilet. Two arched and barred windows high up on the back wall let in a little sunlight. It was a cold drafty barn considered fit for prisoners of our low social status.

I finally neared that door. It had taken most of an hour to unlock and toss the prisoners two at a time into the holding tank. Upon reaching the entrance Yusuf and I stopped next to a ankle-deep pile of chains and manacles, but we were ordered inside still bound together at the wrist. The guards were taking no chances with the volatile bandit. Only after we safely locked in did a young guard reach through the bars and unlock our common manacle. When this was done he apologized for leaving me in the room with the madman.

Almost any sort of kind action directed towards a prisoner ignited a feeling of emotional warmth in the recipient, sometimes out of proportion to the value of the kindness. There were many guards such as that one, poor men trying to earn a living who were ashamed to see the condition of their less fortunate countrymen. Such men were tolerant of human frailty. They acted like custodians whose courtesy and good humor never faltered. Babu and his sadistic sort were the exception and never indicative of Pakistan in general.

The room I found myself in was thick with cigarette smoke. The majority of the prisoners sat alongside the walls. This was not only convenient, it was primarily because Yusuf immediately went on a rampage. Though certifiably crazy he was still as strong as an elephant. The bandit went stalking around the middle of the room, his leg irons rattling like mad, cursing and scaring the life out of everybody. Through the haze of his madness he seemed to recognize the place. Yusuf made his way back to the cell door and began to bite on the bars holding him in. When this failed to free him, he started howling and began to shake the door so hard dust started rattling loose from the adjacent walls. The

Khyber Knights

guards became alarmed and started beating Yusuf's fingers with their rifle butts.

"Get back, get back *khunzir bacha* (son of a pig)," they screamed frantically, all the while ordering Yusuf to let go of the door and go sit down.

He did, right next to me.

I had located Ali Muhammad in the crowd, had barely had time to slide down against the wall next to him, when the King Kong of Pindi Prison decided to join us. What could I say? Islam has a strong tradition that madmen and half-wits are to be treated with veneration. Those mentally unfortunate, though lacking reason and wisdom, were under the direct protection of Allah. Woe to the man that abused those with empty heads.

Yusuf didn't need much protection from Allah or anybody else.

He slumped down next to me and without even looking my way began saying, "Tick, tick, tick, tick, tick." Then he turned and looked me in the face, opened his mouth and pointed to a tiny metal ring he had jammed up onto one of his canine teeth. He immediately began laughing. I was too shocked to reply.

Up close Yusuf was a work of art. He had a bent nail jammed through a hole in his left ear lobe. Despite the starvation and abuse he was one of the most powerful men I had ever known in Pakistan. Standing more than six feet tall, he was raw boned, broad shouldered, narrow waisted and a solid mass of muscle. His face had strong cheek bones, a wide nose and piercing black eyes that could have burned a hole though a brick if he were still sane. His black hair was an unruly mess and hung in thick locks down to his shoulders. The dark skin of his face was almost completely covered by a beard that could only be described as once fierce and now turned as wild as its master. A pair of strong hands hung on him. They could have torn off a car door. His shalwar kameez was old but serviceable. His shredded green sweater was hanging on by just the left sleeve. He was oblivious to any of these finer details.

The two of us sat there silently for a few moments, exchanging looks of mutual curiosity. Finally Yusuf reached over and gently touched the red hair that had grown out from underneath my turban. The color appeared to both mystify and soothe him. I seemed to have passed some important test because he pulled a tiny plastic bag out of his shirt pocket and began carefully revealing his treasures; a piece of string, an old ring, a broken bit of glass. He seemed delighted that I was paying attention to him.

Why wouldn't I?

Raja had disclosed the outlaw's history.

Yusuf was a man who was not tame.

He had been a famous badmash, a brigand of rough manners, disdainful of routine, rebellious against the civilized world, committed to a life of adventure. The future killer had been born the son of a farmer.

The Untouchables

When the family lost their land they also lost the anchor of tranquility that for generations had provided them a feeling of security and permanence. The anger of their feudal landlord, a burgeoning economy, it made no difference to the little boy called Yusuf why his family was suddenly rootless. Like hundreds of thousands of other unfortunates they moved to the city seeking work. Yusuf's childhood had been spent in the urban wilderness of Karachi. Its slums were full of families like his who had been ripped from the land they loved. As a youth he had wandered those hostile streets knowing his legacy was economic uncertainty and more misery.

Yusuf grew up like so many others in Pakistan, a heir to violence. He never heard of Muhammad Ali Jinnah's dream of an Islamic paradise, never received a kind word or a worthy look from those above. The little boy belonged to a brotherhood who graduated over the corpses of their fathers, the raped bodies of their mothers, the ashes of their homes. Yusuf differed in one important respect from his schoolmates of the street. Life had not succeeded in crushing him.

The big man had not yielded meekly to life's tribulations. He had taken the path of individual rebellion. Unable to accept the role of the passive, displaced peasant, he left behind the confines of legalities. The gentry had the pen, the courts and the police at their disposal. Yusuf took up a dagger as his darling and a gun as his wife, then set out on the path of armed resistance. By thirty he was a freebooter, a warrior reputed to be as cunning as a fox, as fierce as a lion, as noble as an eagle. He robbed, kidnapped, and terrorized without remorse. Working from a lair in the country, Yusuf recruited similar minded men, other poor peasants who could live without justice but not without hope. Like their bearded leader, his followers were men who refused to accept the role poverty forced upon them. Though promised an idealized Islamic homeland, they realized they were still oppressed by the landed hierarchy, the courts protecting the landlords' interests and the politicians in league with both. Many disgruntled men willingly took up the gun and followed Yusuf instead.

My fellow prisoner made a fortune in ransoms. The family of one wealthy Hindu merchant alone supposedly paid him more than five million rupees ransom. Yusuf grew wealthy and powerful but was driven to do more. He hatched a wild scheme to seize sophisticated weapons by leading his men in a raid against a police station. The outlaw dismissed the constables as landlord lackeys and dog killers, cowards in uniforms too afraid to track him. He had thought of everything, except betrayal.

A special unit of army rangers was waiting, tipped off by an informer. Yusuf's band was ambushed. Some died, many fled. Yusuf was shot twice in the legs and captured.

After he healed they brought the still defiant bandit to Pindi Prison with his proud bearing, his independent spirit, and his martial instincts very much intact. Babu had stolen all of that. The old trusty hung the rebel-leader up by his feet on a cell door in the mental cages, then Babu beat him with a lathi until the blood ran out of Yusuf's ears. The bandit hung upside down, suspended by manacles, for two long days. When they dropped Yusuf his mind had fled, leaving behind the still-strong body sitting beside me.

The big man had now taken refuge deep inside himself, retreating to a place where Babu couldn't reach him. But I saw what he had been, not what he was reduced to. He was a Pakistani Don Quixote silhouetted against the horizon, a solitary tragic figure who had been shaking his fist in defiance at a life that wanted to reduce him to slavery from birth. Well Yusuf was truly only a slave now. The once proud rebel was a *tareekhi* (lifer), chained and degraded at last by a system that had finally caught and crushed him for harboring a dream of individual independence. Yusuf deserved the company of heroes. He got only the mental cages.

Our names were called so Ali Muhammad and I left Yusuf's company.

My friend and I were manacled together at the door and lead outside.

An armed guard lead us across the lane into the old court building beyond. The large room we entered was reminiscent of an overlooked broom closet. It had been painted green fifty years ago. Now its color was hard to describe. Electricity was a recent innovation. A dusty fan hung overhead. Against one side, stuck into a pigeon-hole cabinet, were piles of dusty documents tied off with string. A picture of Muhammad Ali Jinnah hung on the back wall. The country's founder looked wise, elderly and tubercular. On the left side of the room stood a large table. The uniformed Pakistani police officer who was to serve as state prosecutor was seated there.

Overlooking this mess was a large old fashioned judicial bench. There was no microphone on the bench, only a small sign that read, "Magistrate Aurang Zeb."

When the guard lead us through the door of the court, we passed Eugene Crouch standing just inside. Our lawyer Khawaja Naeem was standing in front of the magistrate's bench waiting for us. There was no sign of Inspector Gilani Khan, Ashgar Ali or any of our other antagonists. The guard unlocked the manacles, ordered us to stand next to our lawyer and then retired to take up a position by the entrance to prevent our escape.

"Remember the teeth are the fence of the mouth. Be silent and let me talk," Naeem whispered.

At that moment an adjacent door opened and the magistrate walked in. Unlike his American and British counterparts he was not wearing black robes. In fact he was dressed in civilian clothes, a brown pullover sweater being his only concession to formality. Magistrate Zeb took his seat and looked down at Ali Muhammad and me. The man who was to consider our fate had jet black hair and a thick mustache. Both were sprinkled with

The Untouchables

gray, making him appear older than his 46 years. He had a dignified face and looked like the kind of man for would either give you his last dollar or send you to the salt mines. Zeb rapped his gavel and nodded to the prosecutor, Tanvir Sufwat, to begin.

Our formal accuser was in his early thirties and looked eager. Tanvir held up the challan, the report to the court filed by Narcotic's Inspector Gilani Khan, and informed Zeb that not only were Ali Muhammad and I being held on serious charges, we represented a risk of flight.

"They should continue to be constrained, your honor," he told the court.

Zeb looked at our advocate and said simply, "Mr. Naeem."

The little man launched into a whirlwind of accusatory remarks aimed at the narcotics police.

"My clients were illegally detained and beaten after heroin was planted in their room. The entire episode is a disgrace to this country. I beg the court to release them and drop these unfounded charges," Naeem said.

Ali Muhammad and I stood before the bench, mute supplicants, while the magistrate studied the conflicting reports lying on his bench. Zeb appeared financially prosperous but spiritually unhappy, as if the constant exposure to brutality had wearied his soul. Here was a man who had seen much and long ago come to terms with what fate brought into his courtroom. I could see that the magistrate accepted the idea that men were both truly bad and occasionally good, this conflicting fact being the physical evidence of an inscrutable fragment of Allah's plan. However, even if the magistrate had a trace of the mystic about him, he was no fool.

The dark-eyed man looked up and studied my friend and me with grave, world-weary eyes. It seemed apparent he loved justice but loathed his job. In a dignified voice he sent us back to prison.

"Even though I have strong suspicions this case has been tampered with, the charges are serious ones. The government has expressed its desire to suppress the illegal heroin trade. I am duty bound therefore to hear all the evidence presented by the state. Based on this fact I feel I must waive any humanitarian considerations. I remand these two prisoners back to judicial lockup until such time as their case has been decided. Mr. Naeem, see the court clerk for a hearing date. That is all," Magistrate Zeb said, and rapped his gavel dismissing the court. He then stood up and left the room as if he felt guilty for sending us back to prison.

The guard walked over and quickly began to lock Ali Muhammad and me together again. Crouch chose that moment to approach us. The vice-consul looked sheepish.

"You two must have genetic Lomatil in your veins," he said, trying to sound funny with his reference to the famous American diarrhea medicine.

Khyber Knights

Ali Muhammad, my *muqqudamewal* (co-accused), and I were silent, our eyes fixed on the ground. I felt the manacle bite. I heard the chain rattle as the guard attached us to a loop on his belt.

"I thought you might like something to read," the embassy man said and tentatively held out a bundle of old New Yorker magazines. Under his breath I heard the diplomat say, "I think I would rather kill myself than be held in there."

It sounded like a whispered confession.

"Finished," the guard ordered, then snapped our chain and yanked us back towards the door.

We had no words for the embassy man. It no longer mattered what he thought of us or whether he believed in our innocence. Within fifteen minutes Ali Muhammad and I were back inside Pindi Prison, deep within the primitive colossus that now ruled our lives. Eugene Crouch was soon after transferred back to the States. He never learned of our future fate.

18

When Smugglers Lament

The New Yorker magazines were a godsend.

I pulled out the advertisements for fast cars and traded them for food. The photos of refined, buxom, white American women I gave to Hans, who in turn flogged them all over the prison in exchange for cigarettes.

It was the sixth *Juma* (Friday) we had passed within those walls. The Muslim Sabbath always brought a slight relaxation of tension. I had ventured out of Cell Nine to walk alone in the exercise yard. It was a sunny day with a calm blue sky looking down on my little world. The baobab tree, though devoid of leaves, was full of birds. The crisp autumn weather was a tonic after being locked up with four other men. Even the Dada was outside taking the air. He had ordered Shonni to spread a quilt in the yard. The big man was reclining against a bolster. Sergeant Shafi, the Char Chuki warden, was sitting next to the old crook. The pretty servant boy was serving tea to the two big shots.

On the outside the Dada and Shafi had nothing in common. The warden was all spit and polish, while the fat scoundrel was the very definition of physical corruption. Yet I believed the Dada was the more honest of the two. The crime boss reveled in his sins, never nibbling at forbidden fruit, but gobbling it with gusto.

Despite his starched uniform the warden was the worst kind of coward. He had five children, and with a salary of only 700 rupees a month, was always in debt. Char Chuki was a cash cow for Sergeant Shafi. The moral authority he wore on his sleeve was undermined by the black market money he extracted from prisoner's pockets. In a secretive world were everyone traded favors there was always some reason to slip Shafi a little something, if only to ease up on certain restrictions. The well dressed cop paid little attention to our needs or troubles but was notorious if provoked. The warden just wanted to get along without a thought or a nod, content to let Babu rule the world behind the gate of Char Chuki.

I preferred the fat, honest sinner to the starched, but hidden hypocrite.

When I returned to Cell Nine I found a lively scene. Yusuf and two of the mentals were making a house call. Once they discovered we would not drive them off, the mentals had been gradually coming closer to Cell Nine, easing up to our door like timid birds. Hans insisted they were dirty, saying they brought in more lice than we could kill. But the rest of us had let them know they were welcome.

It was hard to turn them away. After all, they were the living dead.

Khyber Knights

My three cellmates were sitting along the wall watching Pindi Prison's version of afternoon television. The mental known as the Dog Man sat by the door. He was naked except for the vermin-infested blanket draped over his shoulders. He growled to himself, happy to be inside our cell, even if he didn't know where "inside" was.

The little fellow from Bangladesh was leaning up against our water jug. He had found a blue plastic pill bottle. He kept placing the top of the open bottle close to his mouth then shouting inside.

" One, two, three, four. Ha, ha, ha. Hello, hello, helloooooooo!," he would yell, then immediately pop the lid back on to keep his words from escaping.

Overseeing this Pakistani sideshow was Yusuf the insane bandit. I came in and sat down next to him.

The big bearded man was clutching his beloved little tin pot. In order to guard its secrets the bandit always made sure to keep the lid over it. Earlier that morning I had seen Yusuf running around the exercise yard trying to catch a wisp of cigarette smoke inside the small container. When that failed, I saw him successfully snare a moth instead. His deep laugh had shown his pleasure at that recent acquisition.

I had no sooner sat down when Yusuf nudged me and with his eyes beckoned me to study his secretive pan. After noting that he had an old safety pin stuck through his left ear lobe that day, I smiled and gave him my full attention. Yusuf carefully lifted the lid, making sure no one else in the room could see inside. The little crock was awash in old *chai* (tea) and various bits of flotsam, including the deceased moth, twigs, rose petals, cigarette butts and a sprinkling of germs.

When I looked back up from this discovery Yusuf was staring at me intently. Babu had beaten the capacity of speech out of the big man, so Yusuf said nothing verbally. But all the same the bandit tried intently to reach out and communicate with me. I held his gaze and looking back into those wild black eyes caught a glimpse of some little part of the man he once was. It survived far, far behind his physical eyes, a tiny living flame of memory residing so deep it could no longer reach out and touch the world around it. I could sense that this part of Yusuf was trying to tell me something, and even though he was allowed only a few frantic gestures of primitive communication, I was certain Yusuf was waving frantically at me through those thick windows called his eyes. I tried to reach him with my mind, for the first time turning that skill I had with horses on a fellow human being.

The cell was noisy with the talk and noise of the other six men. Yusuf couldn't hear any of that. He just looked at me and lifted the pot in acknowledgment of my silent recognition. I went to take hold of it but he retained control and gently lifting it to my lips, he tipped it back. I took a long drink of that polluted sacrament, then wiped my mouth with the back of my hand. My insane comrade laughed hysterically, clearly delighted at this confirmation of our friendship.

It was little enough to share with a man who once terrorized the same sort of creatures who now imprisoned us both. Yusuf had been an arrogant rebel but he lay broken under the iron wheel of that citadel of shame. He reminded me more of myself than any other man in Pindi Prison. The same sort of rage he once cherished still burned within me. But I knew Pindi Prison didn't tolerate such behavior in her captives. My own future was temporarily on hold. I knew if I was sentenced to spend my life in that prison there would always be room for one soul more down in the pit of insanity where Yusuf and his fellow mentals now resided.

"They hanged the Baby Eater last night," Ali Muhammad said, bringing me back to the situation at hand.

The killer he mentioned was a recognized oddity even in Pindi Prison. For years local children had been going missing from a village up in the North West Frontier Province. On a recent afternoon a little girl had disappeared. The frantic father and his friends rushed to the house of the child's playmate in search of her. There he was told the hamlet's milkman had offered his daughter a piece of fruit if she would accompany him to his house.

A posse of frantic men rushed across the village but arrived too late.

It had proved to be a fatal visit for the little girl.

The child's clothes lay tossed in a bloody heap in the front room. A teapot full of blood was brewing on the stove. Tiny organs were readied for a meal. The tiny missing body was found hidden in a nearby sugar cane field.

The insane milkman was apprehended. During the course of a savage beating he confessed that years earlier he had originally killed and eaten his wife. Having developed a taste for flesh the furtive cannibal began silently scooping up and eating children. His perversity raged unchecked for several years. Sent to Pindi Prison to await execution, the Baby Eater's depravity shocked even that corrupt and jaded establishment. Sergeant Shafi and Babu kept the cannibal locked up in the mental cages prior to his appointment with the executioner. I had peered into that cell once and seen the infamous kiddy gobbler huddled in the back of his cold cell. He was dressed in rags, bearded, covered in unspeakable filth, and clearly quite insane.

"An angry Allah removed that monster from our midst," an outraged Raja told our collected company.

"More likely Babu helped him start the journey by kicking him off the gallows," Hans added.

Ali Muhammad and I took temporary leave from such pleasant surroundings.

On Friday at one p.m. the prisoners were allowed to absent themselves from their individual compounds and gather in front of

Barrack Six for the weekly congregational prayer. It was the only time when we worshipped as a community and together found succor for our souls.

But it was still Pindi Prison. Even our religious rights were reluctantly granted. There was no mosque to serve our needs, only a series of frayed mats unrolled on the dirt in front of the barrack door. Palm fronds had been woven into strips three feet wide and forty feet long. Despite this humble arrangement, the open-air mosque was already crowded when Ali Muhammad and I arrived. Like all Muslims, my friend and I took off our shoes before stepping onto the reed mats. This act was both a sign of respect and a demonstration that we were leaving worldly issues figuratively behind us. Ali Muhammad followed as I led us to an open spot on the second of five rows of mats.

I was unconcerned about the physical poverty of my surroundings. The concept of a glorious building being a necessary vital instrument to funnel our prayers to Allah was abandoned in Islam. Though the religion had the equivalent of many beautiful cathedrals, Muslims knew Allah would hear our prayers in a prison yard just as certainly as He did in nearby Islamabad. There the military dictator, General Zia, prayed in a new multi-million dollar building. The *masjid*, place of prayer, was supposed to be a place of devotion not of ostentatious wealth. The critical beauty of a mosque therefore was not in its architectural magnificence but the spiritual feeling it invoked.

In my short term of years I had prayed in many odd, beautiful, mysterious and holy places. The road of Islamic discovery had begun for me years ago in the Afghan city of Mazar-I-Sharif. Once I entered the serene, blue tiled walls of that city's ancient mosque I knew I had stumbled onto a path of knowledge previously denied me. From then on the trail to adventure ran side by side with the road of spiritual discovery.

Though forbidden by Hindu law, I had prayed inside the white marbled walls of the Taj Mahal. I had prayed in an American mosque that had originally been a ghetto honky-tonk. On that Friday I had been the only Caucasian in a mosque full of black American worshippers, a little room where race made no difference, where all of our mutual attention was directed instead towards hearing a message as old as Adam. I had prayed inside the ancient walls of Al-Azhar, Islam's first university and the pride of Cairo. I had prayed in Europe, North America, Africa and Asia. I had prayed in more road side shacks, mud huts, and nameless mosques than most Muslims knew existed. I had even prayed in Mecca, standing in sincerity before the *Kaaba*, the sacred center of the Islamic world. I had prayed in all those places and on that *Juma* (Muslim Sabbath) in that black-hearted prison, I had come prepared to pray harder than I had ever prayed before.

No matter where you worship you find certain factors in every mosque. Islam is a religion for all people. It does not accentuate one

Khyber Knights

Awarded death sentence for 'cannibalism'

PESHAWAR, March 15: A Special Military Court has sentenced Ahmad Khan s/o Gul to death and his son Shatamand to life imprisonment for murdering an eight year old girls Mst. Safeeda, daughter of Momin Khan.

It may be recalled here that the accused Shafamand charged with the killing, was allegedly labelled as a canibal and a series of episodes had been revealed and published in local as well as national dailies. He was alleged to have killed and eaten the flesh of some other children also.

The accused gave contradictory statements to newsmen from jail, but they established that he had been involved in an act of brutality. The convicts were tried and having been found guilty, were awarded sentences.

According to the prosecution on Feb. 23 1983 Mst Saeeda eight years old daughter of Momin Khan accompanied her grandmother Mst. Said Bibi to attend a marriage ceremony.

Mst. Said Bibi in the afternoon returned home while Saeeda Bib played in a graveyard.

Later Momin Khan, accompanied by Hazrat Said and Wazirzada, went to the graveyard in search of his daughter and then to the house of Mst. Jamroon, the girl who had been playing with the deceased.

She revealed that Gujar Shatamand called Saeeda to his house for collecting some fruit that he had kept for her.

Later, her father, along with other two men went to the house of the accused but Gujar Ahmad Khan and his son Shatamand showed ignorance about the whereabouts of the girl.

During a detailed search, Momin Khan and his colleagues saw accused Ahmad Khan carrying a bundle of 'patri' (sugar cane leaves) on his head.

He threw the bundle in a wheat crop. Suspecting this act of Ahmad Khan, they checked the bundle and saw that it contained the body of Saeeda (deceased) with her head and other organs out of shape.

The accused Ahmad Khan confessed later that he was mentally upset because two of his wives had deserted him.—PPI

"'They hanged the Baby Eater last night,' Ali Muhammad told me. The cannibal he referred to was a recognized oddity even in that hellhole known as Pindi Prison. Having developed a taste for flesh, the furtive cannibal began silently scooping up and eating children. His perversity raged unchecked for several years."

When Smugglers Lament

nationality, tribe, or ethnic origin over another. It is also no respecter of wealth, power, prestige, or influence. It does not care who your famous father was or what legendary accomplishments are cited on your family's heraldic scroll. Islam is only concerned with your own individual spiritual achievement. It does not adhere to the concept of someone else's previous, inherited sins affecting your own purity. In addition, the mosque where Muslims worship does not have pews where one person is favored over another. There is no subtle seating arrangement reflecting the monetary position one retains in the business community. In Islam you kneel before your Creator stripped of social pretense. You find yourself sitting between bankers and blind men, presidents and paupers. All are the same in the eyes of Allah. Islam reminds you that life is temporary, that the trappings and power of this world do not enter either through the door of the mosque or into the next life.

I was never more aware of this lesson than when I sat down to worship with my fellow religionists in Pindi Prison. In that poorest of mosques there was no evidence of a "chosen people," or of Hindu, of Jew or Gentile, of Arab or Persian, Turk or Tajik, European or Asiatic, White or Colored, Aryan, Semitic, Mongolian, African, American, Australian or Polynesian. Gathered around me was the most motley congregation of innocent saints and gallows meat I had ever seen. All the sons of sin were represented there that Friday afternoon.

Men sported black beards, gray beards, white beards, and no beards. They had every type of mustache known to humanity and skin-colors ranging from freckled Irish ivory to Tamil black. They came from widely different backgrounds, with languages as varied as their temperaments and virtues. There were refined Punjabi business men in laundered shalwar kameez. There were ragged Afghan refugees wearing turbans. There were men from the mountains of Chitral dressed in heavy clothes and rolled wool caps. There were fierce Peshawari Pathans. There were Sindis, Multanis, Gilgitis, and Kashmiris. There were Kurds and there were Persians. There were even two Americans. The only thing we shared in common beside our religion was that each of us had been stripped by the pageant of life of all power and possessions. None but our Maker knew our individual soul's spiritual histories, nor understood how each of us fitted into the scheme of life. For gathered around me was the human evidence of the brevity, uncertainty, and vanity of life. We were as physically diverse as the sands of time, yet none could hazard a guess as to what lay ahead of us in the womb of futurity.

There were no statues nor altar in our little mosque. Like Muslims all over the world, we were instead all facing the *qiblah*, in the direction of Mecca, the holy city of Islam located in Saudi Arabia.

From where I sat I had an unobstructed view when one of our fellow prisoners took a seat in front, facing the congregation. I was only mildly surprised when I saw the man leading us in prayer was Suliman, the so called "mad mullah," as his official critics labeled him. If the government had thought to silence Suliman by sentencing him to the mental cages they had sent him to the wrong lodgings.

One unique aspect of Islam is that it does not recognize a religious theocracy. There are no priests, deacons, monks, elders, bishops or popes acting as intermediaries between Allah and Muslims. Every Muslim fills the needs of the congregation based on the gifts of the individual. It is a most democratic religion.

All Muslims are encouraged to not just study but memorize the Quran, the holy book of Islam. The religion recognizes that more spiritual study brings more understanding. A mullah is a low ranking religious authority with a limited amount of such actual study, while an Imam is a man possessing a more in-depth knowledge of both the tenets of the Quran and the finer points of Islamic law. Any Muslim can aspire to either position. The message of Islam initially made its way among the poor and the lowly, the social fringe whose minds were unsoiled by prejudices or false pride. Like Christianity, those earliest Muslims had been slaves and poor men. Because Islam was still such a spiritual meritocracy, no one questioned the authority of Suliman. He had as much right to address the congregation as any of us. And in no mosque before or since have I heard the **khutba** (sermon) spoken so passionately.

He was a middle sized man, strong of bone with a short black beard going prematurely gray. I guessed his age at about 35. Some said he had only learned to read and write within the last ten years. His face was a road map of courage and suffering. Deep lines were chiseled across his forehead and around his mouth and nose. His lips were tight and his jaw shot with tension. His dark, intense eyes were deep set and framed in creases. Though I saw nothing physically unusual about him, Suliman projected an atmosphere of intense spiritual vibrations. Here was a good man if I ever saw one, a man to whom Allah was a reality above all names and forms. Even among this band of hardened prisoners, where strength and boldness were not lacking, we sat in silence before the unspoken power of this imprisoned man. Suliman seemed to be a force of nature, unbreakable despite any hardship.

"Only the mercy of Allah stands between our unhappy few and the vengeance of our oppressors," he said in a deep voice.

We lonely wayfarers fell silent, watching the effort our guide made to say the right words. Every syllable seemed to be weighed before flying free to us.

"Brothers, sin has brought us here today. Sin and oppression are what bind us together in this hateful place. Some of us deserve to be here, some do not. Some of you wronged your own soul and now it suffers the frost of imprisonment. Some of us are held here as captives though our only crime is that we are weak minded. I remind you that those in that condition deserve only words of kindness and justice. Some of us are

Khyber Knights

"Suliman's face was a road map of courage and suffering. Despite the hardships of the prison he was an unbreakable force of nature, projecting an atmosphere of intense spirituality. Here was a man to whom Allah was a reality above all names and forms."

When Smugglers Lament

held here without trial and it may appear without hope," he intoned, his deep, low voice carrying to the back row.

"Regardless of the case, it may feel as if Allah allows evil men the enjoyment of power and good things, while righteous men lose hope and languish in this frightful prison. Brothers, it is our duty as Muslims not to question Allah's universal plan. His justice may not always appear plain to our enfeebled eyes. It is true that we are surrounded by cruelty and can do little against its power. But the Holy Prophet, peace be upon him, told us to take heart, that if through physical or moral incapacity we are unable to defeat evil, then we must rest content with tolerating its presence while concentrating on guarding ourselves against it. In this prison we must remember that though surrounded by evil we must not surrender our souls to its power. No matter what happens to our bodies, only if we lose our souls are we truly lost," Suliman told us.

"In such a case and in such a place as this, Allah's gracious mercy will recognize and forgive our weakness in this situation. He knows your fears. He knows what you have suffered. He knows that if He gave them the power the very stones would shed tears and the walls would weep from what has transpired here," the mullah said with such intensity his face seemed to be on fire.

Not a man moved, not a whisper stirred.

"Allah told us He would try us with fear and hunger and a lack of possessions. That has come true for all of us. But He also told us to remain steadfast in the face of calamity. He told us to say, "Behold, to God we belong, and unto Him do we return.""

Suliman paused and we sat waiting, unsure what to expect from a man who had already surprised us. The mullah looked at us with eyes that were no strangers to horror, murder and debasement. We had all suffered there. Ours was a kinship of pain and fear and melancholy. Any racial or personal barriers now lay behind us. We were united man for man in trying to restore the broken wholeness of our souls, in clinging to our lives.

"Despite what happens, each of you is being tried in a higher court than that one across the road. Despite the crimes for which you are charged, the true trial is inside these walls. Despite the temptation we must not retaliate or return evil for evil against those who persecute us. The hatred of the wicked does not justify hostility on our part. You must instead repel evil with that which is best in you, not pay it back in its own coin, no matter how great the temptation. We have to help one another in piety, not in perpetuating the enmity of our captors. We have to fight to put down evil both in ourselves and within these walls. But in that fight we must not succumb to a spirit of malice. We must act in a spirit of justice and righteousness, even if it is denied us in this earthly court. It is Allah who has sent each of us here. He has also reminded us that despite the hardship we should seek refuge in His mercy. Remember to pray in your cells and to call upon Him during the days of brutality and the nights of silent terror," he told us and then turned to lead us in prayer.

I had known brave Afghan mujahadeen who prided themselves on attacking Russian tanks with little more than a stout heart. But I had never seen a man who stared down into the flaming pit of Hell and showed no fear. Death no longer held any terror for this bearded man before us. He did not seek it, nor did he try to evade it. He had directed his existence into a single purpose and sat before us like a living flame of faith.

The reverberating call to prayer sang out and we stood as a group, standing shoulder to shoulder, all of us sinners bringing our souls collectively before Allah. As Muslims we believed Allah had created body and soul together. This being so, we followed the teachings which instructed us to pray with our bodies, as well as our souls, binding the two elements of our being into one element of worship, and uniting the physical and spiritual aspects of our existence.

As a group we were facing the *Kaaba*, Allah's holy temple in Mecca, knowing that all Muslims worldwide were also turned to it in prayer, and that we joined in one body to worship Him who created us. First we stood upright and recited from the holy Quran, recalling that it is the revealed word of God and helped us to remain steadfast in our faith. Then we said, "Allah Akbar, God is the greatest," to remind us that no one deserved to be worshipped above Him, and then bowed low at the waist in honor of His glory. Then we kneeled in unison, placing our foreheads and our hands on the straw mats because we knew we were as dust before He who created us. Then we lifted our faces from the ground and remained sitting, asking that Allah would forgive us our sins and guide us in this life. Then we again bowed to the ground, touching the dust with our foreheads before the majesty of our Creator. After that we remained sitting and prayed that He would bless the Prophet Mohammad, just as he blessed the earlier prophets including Adam, Abraham, Moses and Jesus. Then we turned our heads to the right and to the left, saying, "Peace and the blessings of Allah be upon you," to the person on each side of us.

Our postures in prayer were beneficial on two levels. They were symbolical of the various vicissitudes in which our souls were tried and tested in life. In addition there were the physical advantages of asking our bodies to stand, bow, and kneel in prostration. How far were the achievements of Islam linked to the benefits of a religion which demanded that its followers stretch and exercise five times a day, abstain from intoxicants, and maintain a yearly fast of four weeks?

Thus we prayed, our prayers directed horizontally towards Mecca and vertically towards Allah, some of us dressed in rags, some draped in fetters, most filthy and all desperate. We were the *ummah*, the local community of Muslims, and like *ummahs* across the world we transcended all ethnic and political definitions as we sought the *quasi*, the invisible refuge of Allah's word. As the men alternately stood and then

When Smugglers Lament

knelt, I could hear the dozens of leg irons clanking and jingling. It sounded like the ghost of Christmas past rattling his chains over our poor frightened heads.

When these group actions were completed each man entered into his private devotions, performing several **raka'ats** (prayers) and asking The One who stood outside time and space to rectify all the problems that plagued us as men in that cruel place. Prayer is a cornerstone of the Islamic faith and is known as the doorway to knowledge. Muslims are required to pray five times a day. They believe that if **salat** (prayer) is offered with a sincere heart and proper devotion, it has the power to clean the soul and change one's life by building an inner sense of peace. Thus we prayed for salvation, for our wives and children left without incomes, for elderly parents abandoned, for justice and most of all for deliverance.

In that prison courtyard I sought an individual hearing before Allah, bowing down in worship as did the heavens, the earth, the sun, the moon, the stars, the hills, the trees, the animals and a great number of mankind. My prayer was not a concession to formalism or a flicker of devotion. I constricted my soul and begged for deliverance from Pindi Prison, repeating the words of an old Sufi prayer.

"Oh Allah, if Thou hast shown mercy to any like me, then be merciful to me. If Thou hast received any like me, then receive me. Oh Allah, Thy pardon on my sins, Thy passing on my errors, Thy covering on the ugliness of my doings, Thy long patience with my wickedness. Whither I did them of error or of set purpose, I ask in hope that to which I have no right to ask. I am thy slave; make me thy freeman," I prayed, making my whole case over to Him, not knowing the seed of truth was already germinating.

Men now began standing up and quietly leaving this momentary refuge, retreating with the promise of hope to their dirt-floored cages and drafty dens. All of us had been insulted and injured in one way or another but for a few minutes we had been temporarily delivered from our troubles. Now we reluctantly readied ourselves to return to our foretaste of Hell.

Having finished my prayers I quietly looked in Ali Muhammad's direction. He was preoccupied in *duah*, a silent individual meditation, his hands raised, his eyes closed, a look of intense purpose and faith spread across his noble face. Lost in complete absorption, praying with his entire soul, my *khaddaywal*, (trusted inmate who sleeps next to you on the floor) was oblivious to his surroundings. The handsome musician of Peshawar had always followed his own path, and if he occasionally erred and went astray, it was because he never tried to be anything except himself. For more than ten years his friendship had provided a warm glow in my bleak life. Yet I saw that the weeks since we stepped off the bus from home had taken their toil on him physically. Though always thin, Ali Muhammad was beginning to look skeletal.

Despite Suliman's admonitions, our faith was tested severely that very night. Ali Muhammad and I returned to Cell Nine to discover that Hans had been busy in our absence. We were all dirty beyond description. The wrinkles in our skin were black from the charcoal smoke in our cell. Godwin was the darkest but not by much. The blankets and our clothes were pestilent and riddled with lice. The little Dutchman suffered from them the worst.

I had mentioned to him that the ancient Arabs had shaved their armpits, pubic hair and often times their heads in order to keep themselves free of the pernicious pygmies. We returned to find, that driven to desperation by the blood-sucking vermin, the Dutchman had adopted a similar method.

"What do you think? Now I'm a beatnik !," Hans told us proudly when we walked back inside Cell Nine. I didn't know what to do but laugh along with him. He had shaved off his pubic hair, as well as armpits. Not being able to resist a touch of the dramatic, he had then recruited Raja into shaving his head into a Mohawk haircut. Added to his wispy goatee, Hans' haircut suddenly made him an altogether startling apparition.

To effect the complete eradication of his insect enemies Hans next enlisted the help of the Dada. A short visit to Cell Seven soon saw Shonni the servant boy outside his boss's cell door spraying Hans' head with Black Flag bug killer. By the time Ali Muhammad and I returned from prayer Hans was convinced he had the lice on the run.

Hans' actions would have seemed radical if I had not understood his torment. It was impossible to ignore the feeling of alien creatures scurrying across your body, running through your hair, shoving their heads into your body and feasting on your blood. No normal activity was free from them. They interrupted conversations, bit us during meals and made us scratch until we bled. They hunted us almost twenty four hours a day. We were living meat lockers. Pindi Prison offered us little hope for relief.

Before the sun was down Hans was complaining of a headache. Babu came to lock us up for the night. When he saw Hans' haircut the old trusty looked through the bars and told the Dutchman, "That is not Islam."

"This stinking prison is not Islam," Hans shouted back.

By nightfall Hans was getting sick and the cell was silent with anxiety and despair. Raja and Ali Muhammad spoke quietly, trying not to bother Hans who was already lying down. I turned inward and wrote a poem, trying to put on paper the feeling of affliction surrounding me. Godwin sat staring at the ground, humming softly, totally withdrawn, his normally cheerful spirit dried up by the misery. Whenever I tried to draw him into a conversation the athletic African would just look at me blankly and say, "What?"

I had more immediate concerns.

When Smugglers Lament

Hans started throwing up in the early evening. There was nothing to give him except water. Ali Muhammad and Raja steadied Hans while he knelt down and vomited through the cage door into the courtyard beyond. There was no doctor available so there was no need to call for help. The prisoners in the holding tank were quieting down for the night. The watch tower guard had already called out to the Char Chuki guards twice.

"Theek hai (OK)," was ringing out into the night sky, but things were far from OK in Cell Nine-Block Four. Suddenly Hans lurched up and scrambled to the cell door.

He started screaming, "Babu, Babu."

It took five or more minutes before the vile old man sauntered into our courtyard and casually approached our cell door.

"What," he asked Hans.

"I have to go to the toilet."

"Not allowed."

"Please, Babu. I'm very sick," Hans pleaded.

"Our sins come back to visit us," the trusty said, and turning away denied our cell mate this primitive biological necessity.

"Please, Babu, please. I'm very sick. Please!" Hans screamed and began shaking the bars in desperation. But the turnkey had gone. We saw him disappear out of the darkened courtyard and then heard him shout, "Theek hai."

The effort was too much for Hans. He grabbed his stomach and doubled over.

Some portions of the world do not even have a word for privacy in their language. The concept was a luxury in a developing country like Pakistan, and Pindi Prison did not even respect the word. We turned our eyes in disgust and modesty while Hans defecated into an old plastic shopping bag. He threw it out into the courtyard and splashed water on himself. The air was foul. Raja was closest. He helped the little Dutchman get under a burlap blanket.

"That whore's son," Hans said through the tears of anger, shame and desperation that overwhelmed him. Raja urged him to rest. It wasn't long before Hans was asleep. None of us knew if he would survive the night.

Deciding slumber was the only escape, the rest of us also retired to our blankets. Many hours later, through the depths of a tortured sleep, I could hear Hans groaning. Even in my sleep I understood there was nothing I could do to help him. Yet something kept nagging me. Some sound kept coming to me, tugging at me, telling me in a whisper that as bad as things were, there was something not right in Cell Nine.

I opened my eyes ever so reluctantly, desperate not to move without just cause lest I awake the damnable lice and never get back to sleep. It was freezing outside and I was huddled deep under my blanket. I lay there for a few moments thinking I had heard nothing out of the ordinary.

Then I heard the sound of running water and I sat straight up.

It was deep within the night and cold as hell.

Godwin was standing completely naked in front of the cell door. He was holding a tea cup in his left hand and was obviously wet from head to toe. My instinct told me this might be an African need for privacy, a midnight bath done away from prying eyes.

"Godwin, what are you doing?" I whispered.

He turned slowly, the cup still poised in mid air. His big chocolate eyes stared at me, not blinking, just peering like a blind man's sightless orbs. His glistening black body was soaked and he made no effort to maintain his modesty.

"What are you doing?" I whispered again.

He looked at me. Then the question seemed to cross the room and sink into his brain.

"I am washing away my sins," the minister's son said in a quiet voice, all the while maintaining his lidless stare.

I got up slowly, more out of duty than bravery, and made my way past the feet of my sleeping companions. When I reached the African I touched his shoulder. His skin was ice cold. The floor was a muddy mess and the big water jug was almost empty. With only the tea cup to assist his efforts, Godwin must have been pouring water over himself for an hour or more.

I tried shaking him, but he only looked at me blankly, naked, freezing and dripping. So I put my arms around Godwin. He was unaware. He would never be aware again. Allah had snatched my friend's mind away from the pain of Pindi Prison but left his body behind to reside with me in Cell Nine.

That was the closest I ever came to snapping myself. Suddenly I feared I would mentally succumb like Godwin had and die marooned there in Pindi Prison. I hugged my cellmate and silently begged Allah, "Oh God, do not let me perish like this!"

19

A Flicker of Freedom

I already had my hands full when the Dada sent word he needed money.

Our African cell mate was now a full-time problem. A month had passed since the Tanzanian had lost his mind. As November grew, then died, I became so busy dealing with the condition of the insane Godwin that I had little time to dwell on my own legal problems.

Godwin had got no better since the night he washed away his sins and his reason. In fact his condition had steadily deteriorated. His eyes were open though his senses were sealed in sleep. His face wore a permanent pained expression of blighted hope. None of us had been able to hold a rational conversation with him since that fateful night. Often times he crouched on his heels, staring at the ground and softly humming. When he did speak it was to himself in sing-song snatches of English and Swahili. In either case nothing he said made sense. No matter, in Peshawar they said if you shared the bread you shared the shame. Kind and patient Ali Muhammad finally got through to some remnant of our cellmate's mind. When my friend asked Godwin what we could do to help him, the former student said, "Nothing. God sent me here because I am guilty."

He didn't say a word after that for five days and never expanded on what possible crime he could be guilty of. It did not help matters that Babu had taken a sudden interest in the African. It was impossible to keep Godwin in our cell. He had taken to wandering around the exercise yard talking to the sky. Such behavior was soon noted by the sadistic old bigot who guarded us.

One afternoon just before evening lock-up Hans had gone out to bring Godwin to the cell. He was trying to quietly guide our cell mate back when Babu stopped him.

"The black man is a mental. Give him to me. I will put him in with the others," Babu told Hans, indicating the cages where he housed Yusuf, Suliman and Pindi Prison's other ultimate unfortunates.

"No, no. He is only sick. He is suffering from spinal pneumonia. It makes you look this way," the little Dutchman countered. "Ali Muhammad spoke to the doctor. He says Godwin will be fine in a few more days."

Knowing our cellmate went to the hospital every morning to pick up our ration of milk, Babu was reluctant to gamble on whether or not this had actually occurred.

"A few days then," Babu warned Hans.

From then on the guard made every effort to try and prove Godwin was either faking his illness or mentally incapacitated. He watched for our cellmate in the exercise yard and shoved or abused Godwin every chance he got. We knew Babu was looking for enough evidence to prove to Sergeant Shafi the Tanzanian belonged in the mental cages. The four of us didn't have to be told our African cellmate would either starve or freeze to death back there.

To complicate matters we feared Godwin was going to die of malnutrition. His once round face was pinched. It became a tiring morning ritual to try and get him to eat. Despite our best efforts this proved nearly impossible.

The morning the Dada's plea for money arrived, we five cell mates were sitting huddled around our little stove, crusty blankets on our shoulders, trying to convince Godwin to eat. Raja had toasted bread for him and swabbed it down with a dab of precious jelly Hans had retrieved somewhere. A cup of chai was in front of Godwin growing cold. But our cellmate had lost all appetite for food and life. He held the toast in his left hand, stared at it, then slowly began pushing holes through the precious bread with his finger.

Hans grew impatient at the sight of food going to waste.

"Give me that," he said, and taking the bread, ate it without any protests from the rest of us. Food was so hard to come by, we could not afford the luxury of allowing Godwin, even in his insane state, to desecrate it

A prisoner approaching our cell door caused us to turn our attentions elsewhere. The Dada had sent the messenger to ask us if we would like to make a civic donation. The new Superintendent of Prisons was coming to make a inspection of Pindi Prison. The rich prisoners in Char Chuki agreed our barrack was in a shoddy state. They were taking up donations so they could pay to have the place painted at their own expense. It was also hoped such an act would place them in a favorable light with the new head honcho.

"It's so nice having high class neighbors," Ali Muhammad said.

We all laughed heartily. It was the type of ridiculous act deemed perfectly normal inside the walls of Pindi Prison. Ali graciously declined on our behalf, asking the bearer to please inform the unofficial mayor of Char Chuki that a lack of funds currently prohibited us from donating to his worthy project.

My musical friend wasn't lying. Naeem had not been to see us for weeks and we were down to fifty rupees, barely enough to buy a few spuds and the charcoal to cook them on.

Despite our lack of a donation, momentum for the big inspection was soon evident throughout the prison. The decay of autumn had turned into the death of winter when the work began. Early one morning a convicted prisoner from Barrack Three arrived in our exercise yard. He was carrying

A Flicker of Freedom

a fifteen foot long bamboo ladder. A guard held a chain attached to the ladder to discourage any escape attempt by the painter. While the prisoners gathered around to watch, the incarcerated painter proceeded to whitewash the inside walls surrounding the perimeter of Char Chuki. After first climbing the rickety ladder, the prisoner splashed on the watery mixture, then proceeded to smear it around with a brush made of straw. He got as much on the ground as he did the walls.

After two days the convict, by now so paint-splattered himself he looked like an apparition, finished the walls and turned his attentions to the ten cells. Despite not having contributed to the common effort, the Dada had sent word that our cell was to be painted too. He said it would be shameful if foreign guests were not treated with due respect. The gracious criminal directed the painter to spruce up Cell Nine as well. When our turn came we eagerly piled our blankets and few belongings into the courtyard outside our door, then lingered anxiously in the exercise yard. The maestro soon emerged with his dripping brush to pronounce our cell was ready to be reinhabited.

Inside we discovered a sodden mess. Whitewash was running down the walls and had dripped all over the floor. The smell was acidic and the cell was more damp than ever. Worst of all, the walls served as our only furniture. We could not lean against them for days without coming away with our backs all chalky.

All this energy concluded in the last week of November. A growing tension was evident among the trusties and the uniformed staff. Babu and Ibrahim shoved and shouted more than ever. What few cigarette butts the mentals did not eat were quickly swept out of sight by prisoners yanked out of the holding cell. Sergeant Shafi actually spent time inside Char Chuki, making sure the place was as tidy as free convict labor could manage.

None of this spic and span mania concerned the prisoners. The news that excited them was that during the *mulahiza* (inspection) the Superintendent of Prisons would consider *sawal* (complaints) from prisoners.

The concept of a *durbar* (open court) was an ancient one in the Indian subcontinent. For hundreds of years petitioners had gone before their kings and personally pleaded their case. The British, as always, had been quick to pounce on a good thing. Dispensing justice gave them a moral and legal authority over the people they had conquered. From busy Bombay to tiny Tirah, Englishmen sat in judgment over natives. The concept of King Solomon, the mighty ruler dispensing justice to lowly peasants, had all but disappeared. The Raj and the native princes who supported it had supposedly been replaced by the rule of democratic law. Pindi Prison was a leftover in this respect as she was in most others.

When the big inspection finally came all I could think of was that Godwin was going to get us all hanged.

Early in the morning Babu had come to our cell to instruct us to place everything we had outside in the courtyard on a blanket. All the meager belongings that defined our miniature world, the tiny stove, the knife spoon, the Nazi Vegematic, our dwindling supply of food, our little cache of spices, our paper and pens, our chipped enamel tea cups, our handmade glasses, and the unused blankets, were carefully placed on a blanket just outside the door. Cell Nine was bare except for the water jug, under which Ali Muhammad had left hidden our last fifty rupees.

The only thing we took with us was Godwin's confession. A few days earlier he had picked up a pen and a scrap of paper. Thinking he was only quietly doodling no one paid him any attention. We were surprised when Godwin informed us, almost semi-coherently, that he had written a confession and now wanted to give it to the DSP. It was Raja's job to distract Godwin, get him to leave the cell, and go outside to the exercise yard. Meanwhile, Hans, Ali and I debated what to do.

The fact that the rambling document made little sense and purported to involve Godwin in imaginary crimes didn't concern us. More importantly the confession was not only an indication of Godwin's deteriorated mental state, the tattered piece of paper was the only document proving the student was imprisoned within Pindi Prison. The three of us finally decided to hide the confession until we could be sure it could be of no help to our sick cellmate. Our collective fear was that Babu would discover the incriminating paper. Ali Muhammad chewed open a hole in the hem of his pants leg and secreted it there.

The little room was then swept clean. As soon as this was effected we were ordered to take two blankets and adjourn to the exercise yard. There we were told to sit quietly on the blankets and wait for the arrival of the Superintendent.

Upon arriving in the yard we found the prisoners from the ten cells lined up on blankets in front of the Char Chuki walls. We five cell mates wedged into a small unoccupied space. From where we sat it was impossible to see the entrance to our cell. What space was left along this wall was taken up by a few dozen of the prisoners from the holding cell. The majority of the holding tank prisoners were similarly gathered in front of a wall on the far side of the barrack. The mentals sat in front of their cages, out of sight at the rear of Char Chuki.

There were 174 men gathered that morning in our section of the prison. Throughout the citadel a total of more than 2,000 souls waited in silence, wearing the yoke of tyranny and harboring a glimmer of hope in their collective hearts. They needn't have bothered. It was judicial humbug, an eyewash constructed to show any snooping human rights activists that Pakistan was treating her prisoners humanely.

I never knew where the Superintendent started his tour, nor exactly what he was looking for. I do know we waited in the cold for more than two hours. Every man in Char Chuki, from the lordly Dada to the naked

Khyber Knights

"The only thing we took with us was Godwin's confession. The false document he had signed was the only evidence we had proving not only our cellmate's deteriorated mental state, but confirmation that he had been inside the infamous Pindi Prison."

A Flicker of Freedom

Dog Man, sat huddled on the ground like shivering chickens in the cold winter air. All eyes were lowered. No one moved, afraid that any sign of impatience would bring the fury of the guards down on their heads.

Hans and I had Godwin jammed in between us. The Tanzanian was oblivious to the situation and the inherent dangers of angering our keepers on such a day. We all understood that any man who embarrassed Sergeant Shafi would suffer the pains of Hell after the inspection was over. Godwin kept trying to get up and walk away. The Dutchman and I kept close hold of his arms.

It was some time after ten a.m. and it was beginning to feel like no one was going to show up when we saw Babu and Ibrahim go stiff.

"Speak of the Devil and he's sure to appear," Hans whispered.

We heard the gate open and saw Sergeant Shafi snap to attention. A short man entered. He was in his early seventies. He wore an expensive light gray shalwar kameez. A luxurious camel colored Gilgiti wool vest kept him from getting chilled. He was going bald, the remaining hair was white. A matching white mustache sat on a face stiff with imperial dignity. He entered the chuki and turned right to inspect our section first.

The superintendent was followed by a line of men in descending order of importance. The DSP was next, his uniform immaculate. The swagger stick he carried under his arm only made him look like an overweight buffoon. Next came Sergeant Shafi, stiff with starch and apprehension. Behind our local lawman walked three *bardashtis*. These were special prisoners serving terms of rigorous imprisonment who were consigned to serve as batmen as part of their labor. One man carried a shovel slung over his right shoulder like a rifle. Next came a trusty with a pick. Last marched a turnkey with a long, stout iron bar. Their job was to use the iron bar to make sure the cell doors were solid or poke around with the pick and shovel for evidence of escape tunnels. All three trusties marched as stiff as a Russian honor guard on duty outside the Kremlin.

Nobody laughed.

The superintendent had barely begun to march slowly by the prisoners when one of the Iranians stood up. The Persian took the opportunity to complain, saying the daal was so bad he couldn't digest it. Could he get something else to eat he wondered?

"You're a young man. You can digest it," the superintendent said and walked on.

Rafiq, a prisoner in the common cell, stood up and pleaded for justice. He had been a driver for a former provincial minister. The politician, along with two friends, had instructed Rafiq to drive them to the country, where they promptly started illegally shooting partridges. When a game warden showed up, insisting the poaching stop, Rafiq's boss flew into a rage. When a heated argument arose between the politician and the game warden occurred, Rafiq had stepped in and struck the warden.

"I gave him a blow on the face and accidentally broke his nasal bone," he explained truthfully to the prison superintendent.

The warden was removed to the district hospital. The minister paid a small fine. The wardens family, feeling honor was not satisfied and knowing the minister was protected by both power and position, had lodged a complaint of assault against Rafiq. He had been imprisoned for months without trial. Couldn't something be done?

"Nothing," the superintendent said and marched on in our direction.

Godwin picked this moment to try and wander away. Hans frantically grabbed our cellmate to keep him from standing up but the African began fidgeting frantically in the Dutchman's tight grip.

"Godwin be still," I pleaded in a whisper, as I too held him tightly, afraid to be seen talking.

After a few seconds Godwin stopped moving. Yet I didn't dare loosen my grip, afraid he would bolt away and bring about our destruction. Then I felt my friend's body relax. He turned to me and said softly, "My brain is sick. I have flown away."

"You will get better," I told him softly.

But Godwin didn't respond. He never heard me. He started humming, which relieved me because I knew he had crossed the borderline again between sanity and madness.

The inspection continued. No one was foolish enough to complain about either Babu or Sergeant Shafi, knowing such accusations would bring certain retribution. But there were other grievances. A one-legged man had been sent to prison to serve two months because he had failed to pay a two hundred rupee debt. He had been hopping around inside Char Chuki for five months. Could he go home now?

The superintendent looked him over with his suspicious, swiveling eyes. A wicked man treated his stepchildren better than this.

"Disobedience is the father of insolence," he told the cripple, ordering the man to stay put until told otherwise.

Another prisoner stood. His brother murdered a rickshaw driver over the amount of the fare. The driver wanted one rupee. The passenger argued it was only a 75 *paisa* (nickel) ride. The driver was stabbed and killed over the few pennies difference. The murderer having escaped, this prisoner, the brother of the killer, had been held in prison for more than a year. Would the superintendent try to at least get him a day in court?

No chance. As custom dictated, he would remain in custody until his brother surrendered or was captured. If his murdering sibling had fled the country or continued to evade capture, the prisoner had better resign himself to a long period of captivity.

So it went.

Almost every prisoner there had originally been subjected to the *mulahaza*, the interrogation. Incoming prisoners were forced to sit bareheaded, bare footed and eyes downcast while they were slapped, kicked

A Flicker of Freedom

and beaten by the trusties, wardens and the chief chukkar. This exercise was supposed to instill immediate terror into a new prisoner. Because Rule 1066 allowed prison officials "to use all force with prisoners who do not behave," such beatings were never recorded or officially condoned by the man walking in front of us.

Everyone had hoped that the arrival of a new prison superintendent heralded more humane treatment. Prisoners repeatedly stood with the mirage of hope dangling in front of them. They sat down dejected.

As he finally neared us the superintendent came in front of the old opium addict who inhabited the central cell. The tiny prisoner was almost motionless with the weight of his years. Having been carried outside he was far too weak to stand and plead his case. When the prison official drew near, the imprisoned patriarch lifted his hands in front of his turbaned head and placed them together in the old Hindu manner of supplication. This gesture of respect spoke of an age gone by. In a reedy voice grown hoarse from pleading to deaf ears, the shrunken prisoner prayed he might be allowed to go home to die.

"Mercy master, mercy," the old man begged.

The superintendent gave the infirm petitioner no more notice than an insect and walked on without a word. All traces of pity had long since fled from his heart. We all bowed our heads in shame at the sight of such injustice. This was retribution not reformation.

"May he burn in Hell," Raja whispered on the other side of me.

He didn't, at least not right away. We watched him walk towards the back of Char Chuki. We knew he had reached the cages because the mentals started howling like the monkey house was on fire. Suliman's voice was raised in protest at the martial law regime but we couldn't make out his words over the racket. The superintendent quickly checked out the other side of the barrack and then left Char Chuki as blind to our grief and needs as when he arrived. He never thanked the Dada for the paint job.

We prisoners sat on without explanation in the cold for another hour, as the superintendent finished his tour of the rest of the prison.

It gave me time to think about the collective life of this nation and the conditions that allowed Pindi Prison to exist.

I could make excuses for Pakistan, could overlook her first few years. She had originally been so harried trying to survive as a nation, it could be argued she did not have the time or resources to worry about those inhabiting the bottom of her social ladder. An unequal division of the riches of the Indian subcontinent had insured that India received a lion's share of the wealth from the departing British Raj. Pakistan was hard-pressed to field an army, build roads, throw together a few schools and maintain a university or two. When the country was formed in 1947 money simply did not exist to spend on such a low social priority as a decent new prison.

Khyber Knights

I could disregard her formative years. She had been physically torn apart in a war with India. That portion of her country, once known as East Pakistan, had seceded and become the new nation of Bangladesh.

I could even condone her early adolescence. She had been busy in her first real peacetime building a new capital, taking pride in her birth, consolidating her place among her sister nations.

I could never accept what I had seen on parade there today.

It could be argued that Pakistan had inherited the sins of her colonial fathers, as well as the penal system and the prison that represented their values.

The Raj had sanctimoniously handed her Pindi Prison as if it were a blood-soaked bone to be proud of. For decades the British had been rattling on about all the progressive works they had given to Pakistan at her inception. They were fond of bragging that their benevolent intervention had left the natives so many miles of railroads or so many kilowatts of electricity. They whitewashed the ugly fact that they widened already existing ethnic divisions among the native population, clearly favored Hindu-dominated India in the 1947 partition and still held the Muslims responsible for the 1857 rebellion that had threatened to drive them home to England. The British cloaked their legacy as mercenaries in the whited sepulchers of a few schools and roads.

The proof of their cruelty was the institution known as Pindi Prison.

In the rush to survive as a nation the Pakistanis had been fooled one last time by their old masters. The moment they were liberated they should have marched on that bastion of foreign tyranny and torn it down with their bare hands, hammering at its walls of injustice until no two stones stood on top of each other. The newly liberated Muslims should have eradicated it as thoroughly as the Romans did the captured enemy capital of Carthage.

Instead they listened to the bean-counters who argued that a young country could not afford a new prison. The arguments of timid economists overruled the hearts of patriots. Pakistan allowed this symbol of despotism to survive. With time they eventually permitted the sadists of their own country to maintain and run it.

Any reasons to excuse Pakistan's allowance for the continuance of this monster were now defunct. What was left was a living lie. If the country had possessed the courage she would have realized she had long ago run out of transparent apologies even to herself. She was no longer threatened. True she still had social, economic and political problems to contend with both domestically and internationally. What developing country did not?

Pindi Prison represented something else. It was a physical evil, a machine of grief now run by Pakistanis themselves to the torment, degradation and horror of their fellow citizens.

The nation who prided herself on being a homeland to Muslims went to sleep every night ignoring the cries of her pitiful prisoners, the howls of the insane or the lament of women and children buried alive in this pit of torture.

The Raj was dead. The imperialists were gone. Their positions had been filled by homegrown fascists. The prison still existed, a sin against Islam, a crime against humanity, a denial of the dream of Jinnah. She represented the dream of a Muslim homeland ruled not by justice and benevolence but by guns and power.

When we were finally allowed to get up my cellmates and I returned half frozen to find Cell Nine looking like a tornado had struck in our absence. Our food was fouled. The spices had been dumped in one pile. The knife spoon was gone and our hand made glasses had disappeared. Inside we discovered the water jug dumped over and the fifty rupees missing. Worst of all Hans' mobile lay smashed on the ground.

Raja said the one word we were all thinking.

"Babu."

Char Chuki simmered the rest of the day in disappointment, despair and resentment. The new superintendent had reinforced the power of the guards and crushed any lingering trace of hope among the prisoners. No one was happy but Babu. He had looted the cells in our absence.

By nightfall Cell Nine was starving. Word had been shouted through the holding tank that to celebrate the superintendent's visit the prisoners were to be given meat in the daal for dinner. We were all faint with hunger and grateful for the small favor. When we heard the two dwarfs coming with the dinner bucket Raja and I went to the cell door, holding our five cups in anticipation.

"Come on," I shouted irritably. I didn't care what kind of gristle they fed us just as long as they hurried.

The two kitchen dwarfs walked up to our cell door. One man held a stack of *rotis* (bread). The other carried the soup bucket. I held out two of the cups through the bars. The big copper cauldron was deep in daal. The smell of dinner made me salivate in anticipation. Even a cupful would slice my hunger in half. The little men hesitated, neither of them picking up the ladle. Before I could ask them why they were delaying Babu walked into our courtyard and stopped next to the copper bucket.

He reached in and extracted a big bone with his dirty left hand, chewed the meat off and then spit the remaining mess back into the bucket.

"I should kill you," I told him coldly through the bars.

"Hunger is the best sauce," the turnkey said in way of a reply. He grabbed five pieces of roti from the dwarf, tossed them through the bars and directed the two kitchen workers to leave. I threw the cups down inside the cell and began shaking the bars in rage. Prisoners from the holding tank began yelling up at our barred rear window, asking what had happened. Raja shouted back, explaining what Babu was doing to the dinner. Outrage flared up like a forest fire.

Hans started yelling, "Lift me, lift me."

I turned to see he had a blanket in his hand. Ali Muhammad and Raja locked hands and hoisted the little Dutchman up by one foot. He grabbed the light bulb and smashed it.

Suddenly Cell Nine was pitch black. It was the first time we had been in the dark in months. Prisoners in the holding tank heard the bulb pop and saw our window go black. The men in other portions of Char Chuki began yelling. The prisoners started cheering as light bulbs began breaking in both the holding tank and the cells. Within minutes Char Chuki was plunged into darkness and the noise was deafening as men shouted and shook their cells doors violently.

"Babu is a pimp's seed," someone screamed.

The mentals joined in. I could hear Yusuf yelling, "*da spee bachee* (sons of bitches)", as well as the little Bangladeshi shrieking unintelligibly in Bengali. Then over the pandemonium came the sound of Suliman the mad mullah.

"Martial law is no law. Free us! Free us! Free us!" the prison chaplain cried.

The vehemence of his protest was so loud it sounded like the force of the cry would burst his ribs. Even General Zia must have heard him in the nearby presidential palace.

Outraged prisoners took up the mullah's rallying cry.

"Free us! Free us! Free us!" began filling the night and threatening to make its way over the walls to the other chukis.

When it seemed like it couldn't get any crazier we heard Ibrahim the trusty yell, "Fire, fire," then saw him run by our cell in the direction of the mental cages.

The silent murderer in Cell Ten, a mysterious man whose victim was unknown, and who never spoke to his fellow prisoners, suddenly yelled out.

"The mullah has thrown his blankets outside and set them on fire."

Standing on the bars of the cell door in Cell Ten, the murderer had been able to see over his courtyard wall and get a view of what was happening at the mental cages beyond. The darkness enveloping Char Chuki was suddenly punctuated by a red glow, all the while prisoners were yelling encouragement to Suliman and chanting "Free us, free us, free us!"

Watching out of our cell door we saw Babu and Sergeant Shafi running by with *lathis* (clubs) in their hands, anxious to confine the infection of riot to our single section of the prison.

Suddenly the silent murderer screamed out, "*Giddar Kut*," and this time Char Chuki went insane with the news. The phrase was originally used when farmers caught a jackal. In Pindi Prison it meant the guards

A Flicker of Freedom

and trusties were pulverizing a cornered prisoner. The murderer in Cell Ten shouted that Ibrahim was stomping out the flames and that Babu and Shafi were dragging Suliman out of his cage.

"You sons of dogs get away from me," I heard the mullah scream, as the prisoners shouted support and encouragement to him.

Then Char Chuki was plunged into total darkness as Ibrahim snuffed out the flickering flames of feeble freedom and Shafi and Babu started stomping out the rebellion. Our shouts of protest began to wane when we heard the song of the lathis. Suliman called down the curses of Allah on the heads of our captors, shouting that they would never succeed in silencing him.

"You bastards leave him alone," the killer in Cell Ten shouted.

But the anger of the guard and the old turnkey were directed against this weakened one of us. We could hear and almost feel the rhythmic throb of the beating they were inflicting on Suliman. Then as the mullah called on Allah to save him, the blows increased in speed and ferocity until his defiant words of protest changed into pitiful howls of agony.

"For the love of Allah and his Prophet, spare me," he screamed.

His attackers remained unmoved, in fact the plea for mercy caused them to strike him even harder. Having heard a host of repentant prisoners call on God to no avail, Suliman's assailants had no fear of divine intervention. They scourged and cursed the mullah all the more, delighted in destroying even the mirage of religious retreat he had dared to harbor in the black depths of Pindi Prison.

One hundred and seventy three men stood listening in the darkness as they beat the man who led us in prayer into a pulp. The soft noise of the lathis sounded deceptively subtle in the total silence that now reigned over Char Chuki. We stood there listening in the dark as they killed him by inches, breaking his bones and busting his organs.

Soon the mullah's shrill screams faded and then stopped altogether. The thump of the deadly sticks continued though, but now not a word of protest was shouted as they finished murdering him. Eventually they stopped the beating. They had quit out of sheer exhaustion, not any concern for their prisoner.

One hundred and seventy three men held their breath in a hush grown thick and deadly. The silence warned us any man who so much as whispered would meet the same fate. At that moment we stood rooted there in the dark. The rebellion in our hearts ran cold and our blood chilled and our balls rose in fear and hid inside our coward's bodies, for every prisoner in Char Chuki knew it could be any or all of us next.

All our bravado and esprit de corps was gone. None of us wanted to die. Every man in Char Chuki was held in check by two fiends with cudgels. There was no longer a whiff of rebellion. We were so afraid we would have licked the broken glass off our cell floors.

Khyber Knights

    We saw Babu and Shafi drag Suliman's limp form past our courtyard by his feet. We heard the gate up front open and then slam shut. Then Ibrahim's voice sang out *"Theek hai"* to the guard tower and the men of Char Chuki sank into the depths of the dark stream that once again ruled their bodies. We never saw Suliman again.

20
Raja's Secret

The tension that marked the short-lived rebellion died as December came and went. By the end of the month things had resumed a quiet normality. The mentals wandered around during the day and ranted like apes at night. The rich inmates of Char Chuki continued to try either to bribe their way out or live in relative comfort until their release. Prisoners in the holding cell merely tried to survive.

In Cell Nine apathy and the smell of charcoal permeated everything. Our faces were so dirty our teeth looked oddly white. Pindi Prison had slowly whittled down our resistance to the point where even our bodies had grown accustomed to the invisible prison clock. Our bowels stayed locked until dawn. At night we would take turns urinating out the bars of our cell door, before settling into our blankets for another night of bugs and noise and the constant light.

Ali Muhammad and I were learning to live quietly with our captivity. Idle prisoners walking by stared at us in our cage. We watched them in their cages. My friend and I were no more than a rare breed of animal in a human zoo. As the days slipped by we marked the slow passing of the milestones of time on the sundial of the prison yard. It was a bleak scene as winter had killed off the nuances and mergings of nature. I now had only the view of the starry heavens through my bars at night or the dim splendor of the winter sun.

Neither of us said it but we were losing hope.

The only thing to be thankful for was that unlike in an American prison, there was no evidence of violent conflict between the prisoners. Even in this monument of misery the tenets of Islam trickled down. Violence between Muslims is severely frowned upon. Fist fights never occurred. A homemade knife was used to slice a potato not a cell-mate.

Despite its obsolescence Pindi Prison stripped away our human dignity. Yet it never managed to crush the camaraderie that existed between prisoners. If there was no sanitation, there were also no all-seeing video surveillance cameras. Outside those towering walls martial law had almost totally eradicated justice throughout Pakistan. This fact only succeeded in making Pindi Prison feel more like a prisoner of war camp than a prison. Despite our individual crimes the inmates rallied as a group if and when they could.

Regardless, events conspired to add to the weight of our confinement. The old opium addict died a few days after the visit by the superintendent. Death had finally been the only way the tiny elder could escape the evils of the holding cell. It seemed strange not to hear him crying and whimpering in the night.

Naeem had come midway through the month to tell us our trial was set for early February, 1984. He balanced the news that we had two more months to wait with a welcome revelation. He had obtained permission from Magistrate Zeb to have the Flashman's Hotel register impounded as evidence. The little lawyer had also interviewed the doctor who examined us. The medico had agreed to testify on our behalf.

Though he was cautiously optimistic about our case, the letters Naeem delivered from our families only helped further the growing depression Ali Muhammad and I shared.

Inspector Gilani Khan's little article in the Urdu newspaper had been picked up and translated by one of the American wire services. A version of the story had made its way via a local newspaper into the home of one of my dearest friends back in America. It had been many years since this good man and I had ridden through the hot California nights on our Harley-Davidson motorcycles. Life had taken us in different directions. Yet friendship has a strange way of materializing in unexpected places. This comrade of my youth had driven to my parents house, taken my father aside and quietly explained the nature and severity of his discovery.

The subsequent letter I received from my folks was full of concern, outrage, and anxiety. That was good news compared to what Ali Muhammad got. Unlike my own parents who had each other to cling to during this time of family crisis, Ali's widowed mother was alone with her fears.

Though nearly eighty she still lived alone in a small apartment in the Garden District of New Orleans. One of the busybody Fontaine relatives had informed Mama of her son's predicament. The petite woman had never understood Ali's need to wander the Earth or to live among the uncivilized marches of Pakistan. Despite years of maternal urging she had been unable to turn her beautiful boy into a clone of her nephews, those hard-working, white-collar employees who enjoyed the beautiful homes and benefits of their more traditional lifestyles. Instead "Beau" had spent the best years of his life immersed in an exotic life in the East, searching for an emotional fulfillment he had found unattainable in New Orleans society. She had always tried to be patient with her son's conflicting impulses, believing that eventually the sensible realism of her own family would triumph over the romantic notions of his Fontaine forebears.

Now Mama was shocked and scared to discover her only child was imprisoned. The letter she sent the errant son was full of tender confidences and motherly worries. It was also clear the old lady did not fully understand the gravity of the situation. She urged "My Darling Beau" to come home at once so they could drink chicory-laced coffee together again at the Cafe du Mond.

Such knowledge brought neither of us anything but grief. It was one thing to lead a life of solitary adventure. It was quite another to unwillingly and unwittingly involve those you love. When my father wrote to say he wanted to come to Pakistan to help us, I responded in haste, urging him not to attempt such a bold measure. He could accomplish nothing by coming to Pakistan, I wrote back. What I did not state was that I already had enough to be concerned about, without the additional worry of having my dad arriving there, perhaps getting physically sick from the food or water, and most certainly going home disappointed. I urged him to stay away and told my mother not to worry.

It was under such emotionally dire circumstances that Hans, Ali Muhammad and I faced the prospect of spending Christmas in prison. Though Ali and I were Muslim expatriates, and Hans a religious freethinker, the holiday represented cherished memories of family for all us. Godwin was another matter.

The son of a Christian minister should have been welcoming the advent of the birth of Jesus Christ of Nazareth. Sadly, Godwin had long since lost touch with his own birth. His mental deterioration had become so obvious that we, his four cellmates, agreed something had to be done on his behalf before Babu carried out his threat to slam the Tanzanian into the mental cages. After a debate about our options, Hans and I were elected to return to the Dada to see if outside help could be arranged. I meant to find out if the fat gangster was only bluffing when he said he protected the weak and afflicted in Char Chuki.

It was a cold gray day when we made our way down towards Cell Seven. The sky over head was full of crows who screamed and mocked us like flying black weeds. We paid no attention to nature's indifference, making our way to the office of the criminal mayor to lay out our concerns.

"The African isn't guilty of any crime but he's so insane he'll die in here without help," Hans told the Dada.

I then explained that even if Godwin had been mentally competent he had no embassy to apply to for help. Ali Muhammad had hit upon the idea of appealing to one of the handful of Christian missionaries who resided in the nearby capital city of Islamabad. Surely, my friend thought, one of them would be interested in assisting not only one of their own flock but the son of a fellow minister.

The pasha of Char Chuki leaned back against a cushion, clearly caught in a dilemma. As Char Chuki's *ghar khorakiya* (prisoner allowed to import food and other luxuries), the Dada's illegal, but sanctioned, activity was a vital link in our bleak world. It was a mutually agreeable business for both parties. He made money. We didn't starve. Clearly the Dada viewed us as valuable customers he did not wish to alienate, but he hesitated to help Godwin, obviously reluctant to get involved with anything as unprofitable as charity. Moreover, asking him to contact Christians was an undertaking so alien to his nature he would have dismissed it out of hand if we had been Pakistanis. When I finally reminded him of his previous promise, he reluctantly agreed to investigate Ali's idea. Meanwhile the glutton of crime told us he would suggest to Babu that the turnkey temporarily leave Godwin alone. This seemed to at least buy us some time.

"Do I have your word on it?" I asked him.

"You have my hand on it," he said and taking my hand in his own, held it tightly and with affection on top of his warm, fat stomach. I tried to remain philosophical about this turn of physical events, not wanting to appear revolted nor wanting to encourage what may have only been a show of genuine concern. Shonni, the jealous servant boy, looked like he wanted to slice out my liver.

In haste I turned the conversation towards Raja, asking the Dada half-jokingly why he didn't go ahead and help our other friend as well. The peevish look that spread over his fat face told me the Dada knew exactly who I was referring to. My cellmate's intuition had not been wrong in avoiding the financial and physical clutches of this promiscuous *gaandoo* (homosexual). Sensing his displeasure I eased my hand free and asked the Dada what kept Raja a prisoner.

"Oh nothing is keeping him here except a lack of money," he said impatiently.

"Could he go free like the Saudi did, on bail or a bribe?"

"Certainly."

"How much."

"Oh I would think a bazaar bug like that wouldn't cost much more than a couple thousand rupees," the rich desperado said and turned towards Shonni, who now took advantage of his master's discomfiture to snuggle up against his tonnage.

On this note I stood to leave. Hans had sat silently through my application for support. The Dutchman now urged me to go back to Cell Nine alone, assuring me he would be along shortly. The Dutchman was his own master. I made my way back to our dirt domicile, which I discovered was now temporarily hosting Yusuf the mad bandit as well. I had not had time to sit down, much less explain the details of my trip, when an obviously pleased Hans came rushing in behind me.

"Merry Christmas," he said and held up a cheap cigarette as if it was of great importance.

"And," Raja asked, vocalizing what was on all our minds.

"And a very Merry Christmas it will be too," Hans said and opening his other hand displayed his prize.

Lying there on his palm was a chunk of *charas* (hashish). It was the size of a quarter and twice as thick, its color a muddy brown.

Raja's Secret

"The Dada thought this might cheer up our holiday and take our minds off our problems," the little Dutchman exclaimed with unrepentant satisfaction.

I slid down and sat next to Ali Muhammad, dubious of Hans' idea, but keeping my thoughts to myself. If the prison population wasn't overly concerned with inmate violence, we did worry about informers who reported back to Babu and Sergeant Shafi. Hashish was routinely smuggled into Pindi Prison but until today it hadn't played a role in Cell Nine.

Yusuf was busy playing near our cell door with our collection of shoes, eyes wide open but otherwise silent. Raja and Godwin were sitting across from me. The young Pakistani was trying to coax Godwin to eat a piece of stale roti. The African was mute. He stared at the ground, showing no more interest in Raja's invitation than a stubborn parrot refusing a cracker.

Hans sat down next to the small stove, his back to the cell door to screen his movements and began the process of making a duc cigarette, the local definition of a joint. Though marijuana grew throughout the country, it was despised as a stimulant by the common man. Smoking hashish was the socially acceptable way of achieving intoxication. The Dutchman now began an exercise as common in Pakistan as seeing a bar tender pour a beer back in America. If there were any little subtleties in the process Hans had long since mastered them all.

"I know what you are thinking," he said to me as if reading the doubt, suspicion and distaste written on my face. "You are thinking hashish is the work of the devil. Nonsense."

As he spoke he laid the cigarette aside on the floor. The *tonka*, or piece of hash, he stuck on the end of a twig he had brought back with him. This piece he now proceeded to hold over the charcoal fire. He did not allow the flame to burn the hash or even heat it so hot as to cause it to smoke in protest. Instead Hans rolled it like a dark brown jewel over the low flame, getting it progressively warmer, until satisfied at the attainment of some invisible degree of perfection he pulled it back.

"I will tell you what I learned from a *sadhu* (Hindu holy man) during my long stay in Goa. He explained to me that opium is certainly bad because it awakens in a man a craving for crazy dreams. It robs him of his life, deceiving him into selling everything he has to buy a little more, a little more, always a little more opium. Ultimately it ruins him, stealing even his courage," Hans told us.

Taking the charas off the fire the smuggler pulled it off the twig and laid it in the palm of his left hand. He then began to press it with his right thumb. Where he had been gentle over the fire, Hans now demanded complete surrender. Using his thumb and palm like a mortar and pestle he was soon able to break the formerly stiff piece of hash into numerous small soft pieces.

"But hash leaves no permanent mark on a man. More importantly it kills greed. If you sit a bag full of money in front of a hash smoker he will not even move his little finger towards it. He will only laugh because he has become indifferent to the things of this world."

Leaving the pieces in the palm of his left hand, Hans now used his right thumb and forefinger to crumble them one at a time into a finer powder.

"Plus while hashish robs a man of greed it makes him as brave as a lion. He is afraid of nothing in this life. Ask him to jump into an icy stream during the height of winter, he would dive in laughing."

Satisfied that the hash was now ground into a fine enough powder, our cellmate picked up the cigarette off the ground. Using only the fingers on his right hand he gently twisted it, being careful not to break the paper, but forcing the tobacco inside to loosen. Under the guidance of his expert fingers he had soon had the tobacco spilled into his left palm on top of the hash. He laid aside the now empty cigarette, its form held intact by the paper and the attached filter. Still using his cupped left palm as a bowl, he began to carefully rub the tobacco and the hash together between his right thumb and forefinger.

"The *sadhu* told me that a man who smokes hashish will learn that to be without greed is to be without fear, and that if a man goes beyond fear he goes beyond danger as well because he knows that whatever happens to him is but his share in this life."

Satisfied at the mixture the Dutchman now began carefully refilling the cigarette. Within a minute he had the project finished to his satisfaction. The excess he stored in a match box. Then holding the cigarette over the charcoal fire he lit it and inhaled deeply. The musty odor of hashish filled the cell. Hans drew the smoke into his lungs greedily. His eyes took on a detached, impersonal intensity. He smiled at us, privy to a secret of his own devising, then passed the cigarette to Raja on his left.

It was as ancient a custom in Raja's country as the five-thousand-year-old ruins at Moenjodaro. Like bread and salt, men had been partaking of it for ages, and unlike alcohol, which was forbidden, Islam only frowned on its usage. None of that mattered to me at that moment. Another perception had suddenly entered my mind. As Raja took a hit off the cigarette I turned to Ali Muhammad and smiled.

"Sorry, no Christmas eggnog but how about a little Pakistani pruno?" I asked, posing the cultural question between us.

At first my friend didn't catch my hint. Then he began laughing.

"*Ah cha, yar* (OK, friend). The night before Christmas and not even a mouse, but certainly a louse," Ali Muhammad said and began scratching to prove it.

Raja passed the cigarette to Ali who took it and inhaled deeply. He had smoked with musicians both in America and in Peshawar. While he settled back I explained to Hans and Raja that pruno was bootleg liquor made by inmates in American prisons. In both countries our actions would be seen as an act of mutiny, not just because we were disobeying the officials, but more importantly because we were escaping vicariously.

It was Christmas eve. A little rebellion was good for the soul.

When Ali Muhammad passed the cigarette to me I inhaled, feeling the smoke sear my throat and expand into my lungs. I coughed violently and they all three laughed, the tension broken.

Without asking permission I passed the cigarette to Yusuf. The bandit chieftain took it in his left hand and inhaled deeply. Then while he still had control of the cigarette, the mad man reached into his shirt pocket and withdrew a ball point pen that was missing both its cartridge and top. He proceeded to place this in his mouth and then blew the smoke out through the pen. This finished, Yusuf tried to turn the pen into a crude cigarette holder.

Hans, disgusted at the frivolous use of his sacrament, snatched the cigarette back. Yusuf just laughed, his thick black beard shaking at his joke.

"These mentals, you give an inch and they take the rope," Hans growled. He took another deep drag off the cigarette and his former antagonism melted. A smile crept over his face. He turned to me and asked, "Any problem?"

"Yes. I'm in prison. Can you talk to the judge for me?"

"If I talk to the judge you'll hang for sure," he said.

We all laughed. Even the feeling of such momentary joy was a forgotten luxury.

In an act of holiday luxury Ali Muhammad threw two little pieces of charcoal on the fire and soon had it blazing merrily.

"There once were three men who arrived outside the walls of Peshawar after dark," he told us. "The gates were locked until morning. None wanted to wait so long to enter the city. 'Let us break down the gates', said the alcoholic. 'Let us wait until tomorrow', said the opium addict. 'No, let us crawl through the key hole', said the hashish smoker."

We laughed again, quicker this time. The cigarette made its rounds, growing steadily smaller but helping us come closer to escape with the passing of every minute. The dope made us warmer. We spoke of life and women and how hungry we were. We grew drunk on remembrances of former meals and former loves.

Poverty of the flesh did not mean poverty of the spirit.

It was at that moment that we all left on invisible wings, some to another place, some to a former comfort, some to a soothing memory, some to an unseen loved one. We each journeyed far and we each journeyed in silence, that dire dirt-floored room the custodian of our bodies but no longer of our souls.

And it was I who finally broke our silence.

"I dreamed my saddle wept," I said. The sound of my own voice shocked me. I had never disclosed any details about my horse trip to either Hans or Raja, and no longer spoke of it to Ali Muhammad. It was the secret place I retreated to when I closed my eyes, but now the hashish had betrayed me by loosening my tongue and disclosing my covert confidence.

"Your dream was trying to tell you something important. Is that all there was?" Raja asked.

Cautiously encouraged, I spoke of Shavon, the trip, the sickness and the disappointment. As I related these repressed events, I closed my eyes and once again saw the world from the back of Shavon's saddle. I told them of the feel of the mare beneath me, the creaking of the warm saddle, and the rocking rhythm that linked horse and man into one. I reminisced about the simple virtues of that other life. I explained how the journey had taken me away from polite and polluted society, slowly changing into a search for something in my life that had nothing to do with monetary wealth or personal gain. I admitted the passion for life I had discovered when I crossed into unknown country, and sitting up there above the palomino, saw the mighty mountains of northern Pakistan for the first time.

I recalled for them how I rode through the shimmering light and dark sickness. Told them of falling from the saddle and how Shavon carried me on. I confessed that I had stumbled onto more than a journey, had in fact stumbled onto a new way of thinking and feeling. I spoke with sad conviction of having discovered this new truth, only to lose it, Shavon, and the lonely course I had been happy to pursue. When there was little left to explain, I went on to reveal how the dream of riding through those mountains had caught some secret corner of my heart and refused to let go. I lowered my voice and whispered of the pain I now felt for something precious, now irretrievably lost. Finally, I said that last night I had had a dream.

"I dreamt my horse was dead and I was in prison and something told me my saddle wept for us both," I said in a low voice, embarrassed at my own disclosures but unsure what it symbolized or signified.

"The soul goes in search of answers and yours went in search of horses because they came from Allah above," Raja told me seriously. I was shocked to hear this young man who seldom uttered five words in a row speaking with such complete philosophical conviction. When none of us spoke he went on to explain.

"Allah created the horse from the wind as he created Adam from clay. He said to the south wind, 'I want to make a creature out of you. Condense,' and the wind condensed. Allah said to the horse, 'I will make you peerless and preferred above all the other animals and tenderness will always be in your master's heart. You alone shall fly without wings. All

Raja's Secret

the blessings of the world shall be placed between your eyes and happiness shall hang from your forelock,'" Raja said.

"The Qu'ran calls the horse El-Kheir, the supreme blessing," Ali Muhammad added in support and took another hit off the hash-laced cigarette.

"Yes and it was Ishmael, the father of the Arabs, who first rode them," Raja explained. "His father Ibrahim (Abraham), the beloved of Allah, taught his son how to call horses. When they came to him, Ishmael took possession of the most beautiful and trained him for racing, the chase and for war."

If I was shocked at my own disclosure, Raja's sudden input left me all but speechless. Before I could ask him more, Hans took a last drag off the cigarette then threw the filter into the little stove.

"Yeah man, I could be a cowboy. Yippee and all that other wild shit," the Dutchman said half mockingly.

Surprisingly, it was Raja who admonished him.

"My father taught me those stories," he said.

The stern look on our cellmate's face, and the sudden warning tone in his voice, said he wasn't about to let that part of his private life become the butt of the Dutchman's jokes. Before the mood could turn ugly, I pulled Raja's attention back to the matter that interested me, bringing the subject around to horses. Thus it was completely by accident that I discovered Raja's equestrian secret. The young man who pulled his weight but kept his own counsel was the son of an army sergeant who had served at a military horse depot. Raja told me about visiting his father there and seeing the best horses in Pakistan. His father had explained to Raja how the government had brought these special giant horses from overseas. Raja couldn't remember the country where they had come from but no one could believe such large horses existed unless they saw them. He held up his hand to show me the size of one of their giant hooves and I was impressed. When India and Pakistan had gone to war these big horses had been used to pull artillery into the trackless mountains of Kashmir.

"Were they all killed in the war?" I asked anxiously.

"Oh no. There are still hundreds of them there at the depot."

"Were you allowed to ride them or go near them?"

"Many times."

"Could you find this place again?"

"Of course," he said. Then a look of pain filled his face and his customary silence fell into place like a silent hood.

When he spoke of horses an aura of gentle kindness had overcome him. Perhaps it was mingled with the memories of his father but now he seemed about to lapse into his customary silence, a situation I would have found intolerable. Having discovered someone who shared my equestrian passion, I wasn't going to remain quietly stoic. Hans had been right. The hash gave me the courage to ask Raja what had happened to his father.

Our cell mate confided he had died unexpectedly, leaving only a small pension to support Raja's mother. The young man had left his village in the North West Frontier Province and come to Rawalpindi seeking work. Soon after arriving he had found employment as a tailor's apprentice. When the older man tried to beat him, a furious fist fight ensued. The police were called. When asked his version of events, Raja revealed he was an Afridi Pathan, a fact he had kept hidden even from us. Even among other Pathans the Afridis were notorious, violent, proud and unpredictable.

"I told the policeman I had no choice. The tailor struck me. A true Pathan believes in giving a punch for a pinch."

When the more docile Punjabi policemen learned of Raja's tribal origin, they didn't hesitate to bring him to Pindi Prison. A spell behind its walls would do him good, maybe even civilize him they said.

Raja, afraid of what his father's family would say, had not written to inform his mother. Being a widow, her position in the extended family was already precarious enough without revealing to the cousins and other relatives that her son was a jailbird. Better to be thought missing, he explained, than to be confirmed as the cause of grief and shame.

The young man had lived without hope since his arrival, too proud to contact home, too poor to rally any help. His perfect charm and natural good looks had been no asset. The only person who offered assistance had been the Dada but that proposal was attached to unspeakable conditions. The departed Saudi forger had given him a place on the floor in Cell Nine in exchange for cooking.

Before any of us could comment on this new information, Godwin looked up. What triggered his interest was unknown, maybe the sound of our voices, or the small circle gathered around him. Regardless, he suddenly began to sing in Swahili. He lifted his round black face and sang with great feeling in words none of us could understand. Perhaps it was a Christmas carol. I never learned. His angels voice began to drift over the bars and as it entered into the holding cell behind us you could hear the men inside starting to quiet down to listen.

At that moment Yusuf joined in by shaking his leg fetters up and down and yowling along in time to the African song. Raja forgot his previous pain and grabbing our only pan began to beat out a rhythm. Hans jumped up and started to dance, his Mohawk head bopping. Yusuf followed him, grabbed the Dutchman's hands and the two of them pipe danced around Cell Nine.

It was unmusical. It was spontaneous. It was Christmas.

We all began laughing at the lunacy of our predicament, delighted to discover that some part of us was still free.

Only slaves did not dream.

21
Stacked Deck

Christmas Day I was hungry. I was dirty. I was thin. I was praying.

I had often turned my soul towards Allah but never with more frequency or devotion than I had since arriving in Pindi Prison. All the mosques and all the prayers that had come before had still not kept me from ending up in that carnivorous prison. I knew in my heart that the Quran said no soul would be asked to carry a burden it could not bear.

Yet I had seen men who led righteous lives die there. I had seen men who had committed some small offense fall prey to realized evil. I had seen innocence ignored and justice raped. I had seen the assault of cruelty from all sides. I no longer maintained the delusion that surrounded by such suffering I would escape unscathed.

If I were to expire I knew the alteration of night and day would follow on in slow succession without me. With the lifting of the veil of midnight's darkness the morning sun would still reveal a country commanded by a tyrant who possessed power without majesty. I was but a tiny fraction of a nation ruled by fraud and wickedness and sin.

At last I understood with complete conviction that I was to be no exception.

It was early afternoon and I was praying next to Ali and Raja inside Cell Nine. I was asking Allah to either release me from the prison or take me from this life. I had no expectation of entertaining either possibility in the near future. Hope had withered on the stony ground of that infamous institution.

Babu came while we were kneeling in prayer.

"*Mulaqat* (visitor)," I heard over my shoulder but I had passed beyond fear of the old trusty and did not bother to turn around.

I heard Hans talking to the guard, seeking information.

Then Babu said, "No, just Asadullah."

I finished my devotions and turned to face him. He could have been there to lead me to the gallows and I would have remained apathetic and felt at peace. There was nothing left of me except skin and bones and spirit wrapped in dirty clothes and a turban. I arose and followed Babu out of Char Chuki. Neither of us spoke on the long walk up to the massive gate. We were both silent captives.

Not that I wanted to speak to the sinister-looking old army deserter. He had long ago proved there was no malignant act he wouldn't perform, including regicide. Among Babu's acts of villainy none was more infamous than his participation in the execution of Prime Minister Bhutto.

After imprisoning his political rival in the Pindi Prison hospital, General Zia moved swiftly. He started by eliminating the rule of law, informing the people of Pakistan that not only would his military government stay in power indefinitely, it could not be called into question in court on any ground whatsoever. Military kangaroo courts, which allowed no lawyers, no spectators and no appeals, would now dominate the legal system. Knowledge was considered a dangerous commodity so its widespread dissemination was strictly forbidden. Newspapers had army officers assigned to their offices as censors. Publications which tried to print the news of massive civil disorder were brought to their knees by being denied access to government imported newsprint. It became a crime under the "Conduct Rules for Civil Servants" for college professors to discuss their political beliefs.

Zia went so far as to hide his political ambitions behind his religious halo. He announced that a voice in a dream had told him democracy was against Islam. Anyone foolish enough to protest was labeled a "disruptionist" and declared an enemy of Allah. But people did protest. There were eight separate incidents of self-immolation. Seven of the men died, their incinerated bodies serving as blackened grievances. Zia had the only survivor, the eighth man, lashed twenty-four times. International organizations estimated two thousand Pakistanis were the victims of political executions during this reign of terror. Thus Zia posed as the Sunni Shogun, cloaking his acts of tyranny in the self righteousness hypocrisy of a Pakistani Pharisee. All the while the country groaned in despair and shuddered in her chains.

After creating the political vacuum used to justify his power, Zia turned his menacing glare on his former boss Zulfikar Ali Bhutto. The legal case brought against him was composed of half-truths cleverly twisted so as to show the elected leader in an evil light. The court's decision was predestined. Bhutto was officially doomed.

Yet even though he had exhausted every avenue of legal appeal and been sentenced to death, the former prime minister still did not believe his "monkey general" had the guts to execute him. Underestimating his deadly rival to the bitter end, the dapper politician believed international outrage would soon force the military dictator to release him. The naive Bhutto was to learn otherwise.

No stay of execution ever arrived at the Pindi Prison hospital where Bhutto was lodged. Finally the failed politician realized he was alone in the dingy little hospital room with nothing but God's grace and the ugly truth. Bhutto's former trusted military advisor was going to butcher him.

The once-arrogant Bhutto, the imperious autocrat who believed he was too important to kill, the nobly born aristocrat who shook a defiant fist, defying the odds and daring his foes to hang him, got his wish, but not before he turned yellow when he smelled the stinking breath of death blowing down on his forsaken neck.

Stacked Deck

Bhutto lost his nerve when Babu and his cronies came to get him. When the merciless trusty arrived at the hospital just before dawn on April 4, 1979 he found Bhutto soaked in the cold sweat of terror. Pakistan's elected official was too weak-kneed to walk, so Babu and his cronies carried the prime minister to the gallows on a stretcher. When the trap door snapped open, Bhutto and democracy both dropped to their deaths, swinging at the end of Babu's rope for thirty minutes. Zia had given the order but Babu had pulled the latch. The sinister old man walking next to me was a confirmed shedder of blood, a man of malice, but the perfect guide through that moaning wound on the earth known as Pindi Prison.

As I walked beside the turnkey I imagined that our lawyer Naeem, knowing it was an American holiday, had come to visit me.

I was wrong.

Allah had been busy of late, but he had sorted through his messages, got to the bottom of the pile and pulled out mine.

My prayers had been answered.

My life was about to be saved.

Babu pounded and the Judas gate opened. I went in without being told. I wasn't handcuffed. It was strangely quite inside. There were no screaming visitors. Even though it was a Christian holiday most of the staff were gone. There were only three guards in attendance inside the corridor.

The guard on duty motioned for me to follow him towards the DSP's office. By now I was as docile as a trained dog. I walked where I was told. He opened the door and told me to enter.

The first thing I noticed was that the DSP was not in the room. It was completely quiet. The lights were on and an American was standing near the desk staring at me.

He was tall and trim, looked square shouldered and about fifty. An expensive dark blue suit sat well on him. His hair was dark and his jaw was square. He looked like George Reeves, the fellow who used to play Superman on the 1950's television show. He had his hands crossed over in front of his waist. It was this familiar stance that triggered a corresponding memory. I had seen this pose before when I was a small boy in church on Sunday. This man used to stand like that in the pew next to me.

I hadn't seen him in more than two years. My father had aged.

It was the only time in my eventful life that I paused, uncertain if what I was seeing was real. Then I saw that familiar confident smile and he opened his arms to greet me.

I walked very slowly to him and we embraced, two men bound by blood and a miracle. We clung together like reunited survivors trapped in the eye of the tempest that raged around our lives.

My father had not ventured overseas since he shipped out in the Korean War. Then he had had a boatload of blue water sailors to back his play. This time he was alone. Typically, he hadn't let that stop him. Leaving behind his family and his business, he had flown for 37 hours to bring me hope and a twisted tale equal to my own.

After a few moments we parted to take a good look at each other.

"I told you not to come here," was the first thing I said.

"That's because you don't know the entire story of what's going on."

We sat down and he painted a picture of Pakistan that shocked me. I learned that this wasn't just a case of Ali Muhammad and me against Ashgar Ali and his cricket bat.

"Your friend Steve brought us the newspaper story about your arrest. We received a letter from you soon afterwards. Your mother and I were still deciding what to do when we saw a television show on "60 Minutes" detailing the Pakistani heroin trade," he said.

The television documentary spelt trouble for my native hosts. It was the first time Americans learned Pakistan was now the world's largest producer of heroin. The so-called "Khyber Connection" was pumping out a billion dollars a year in smack. Estimates said at least 60% of all heroin in the USA and Europe now either originated in Pakistan, or transited through the country from Pakistani-controlled labs in neighboring Afghanistan. Local officials figured there were a minimum of 80,000 Pakistani heroin addicts.

This sudden rise in heroin production was the secret stepchild of the war in Afghanistan. Soon after the Soviet Union invaded that country in 1979, the American ambassador, Adolph Dubs, had been kidnapped by local rebels. Afghan security forces, under KGB supervision, had stormed the Kabul hotel where the diplomat was held. Dubs, an expert on Soviet Central Asian affairs, had been slain in the one-sided gun battle.

Moscow sent its regrets and finished moving more than 100,000 troops into Afghanistan.

At the time General Muhammad Zia-ul-Haq was considered an international pariah because of his execution of Prime Minister Bhutto. The Afghan invasion was to provide the diminutive dictator with a new political lease on life.

The USA declared Pakistan a "front line state vital to American interest."

President Jimmy Carter boycotted the Olympics in Moscow, then offered the Pakistani pasha $400 million in aid if he would support American regional interests against the Soviet Union. Zia had only one word for the amount hung out on a political string.

"Peanuts", he told the man from Georgia.

When Ronald Reagan came to power, the new president was not so parsimonious. Soon after taking office, he sent Secretary of Defense Casper Weinberger to Islamabad to lay $3.2 billion in aid and forty F-16 fighter jets on the poker table. There were only two conditions to Zia's acceptance of the American money and toys. He had to provide refuge and logistical support to the Afghan resistance. With the Russian bear now on his border the local despot was glad to oblige. He also had to promise to crush the heroin trade. Reciting his official Islamic intolerance for liquor and drugs, General Zia easily agreed.

America had a new ally. His former sins forgotten, Zia was transformed overnight from Bhutto's blood-soaked Brutus into Reagan's plucky Pakistani Patton. The fix was in.

"But despite total support from the American Drug Enforcement Agency, the Pakistani seizure rate is less than 10%. For every ton they capture nine more enter our country," my father explained.

The most startling portion of the television story was the revelation that during a recent trip to Pakistan by American officials, local drug authorities had highlighted three drug busts, including one that reportedly confiscated one million dollar's worth of heroin. In fact all three busts were contrived and the heroin turned out to be Ovaltine powdered milk mixed with enough of the drug to give it the correct color. The television show went on to document how in fact the majority of heroin was being smuggled out of the country not by foreigners but by Pakistanis with high-level government connections. Many drug-runners picked up the heroin directly from contacts working in the government-controlled airline. It was handed over in the passenger lounge with a wink and a nod, while cops and customs agents on the take were paid to look the other way.

The only example of local outrage occurred when the Pakistani federal government made a show to impress the Americans. DEA officials complained because a drug lab had been operating in plain sight in a village close to Peshawar. The NWFP governor sent in a 400 man raiding party from the Frontier Corps. Outraged Pathan tribesmen immediately surrounded and threatened to exterminate the national guardsmen. The federal government hastily sent in two-thousand troops to rescue the raiding party.

The lab was moved.
Sensibilities were soothed,
The matter was closed.
The sham war went on.

In a country as poor as Pakistan locals quickly learned it was more profitable to climb on board the heroin gravy train and ignore any unrealistic expectations from the American intruders.

Zia was proof of the pudding. The USA never protested about the smashing of national political resistance and the thwarting of Pakistani democracy, so long as the money and guns flowed into the Afghan resistance and pressure on the Soviet Union continued unabated. In exchange General Zia and his American allies both maintained the pretense the heroin trade was being actively combated.

"Any doubts were crushed after we learned about "Operation Intercept," my father explained.

"One of my friends brought us information detailing how the American DEA had also funded the Mexican drug cops by providing massive funding, training, equipment and manpower. Just like in Pakistan, the American money was tied to results. So the Mexicans started '*La Mordida* (the bite).' There were so many documented cases of beatings, coerced confessions, and bribes perpetrated by Mexican drug agents against American citizens that the protests were soon heard back in Washington. The documented, rampant abuse caused the Mexicans to back off. But the similarities between Pakistan and Mexico were transparent and the DEA is behind them both."

He let all this sink in then told me, "We had intended to listen to you and let you work this out but this new information confirmed our worst fears. You're up against a stacked deck son."

As parents, understanding your son or daughter was in trouble was one thing, deciding where to turn for help was another. The State Department had treated my parents with either condescension or rudeness, acting as if the fraudulent charges alone were proof of my guilt. Eugene Crouch had informed my father by phone that he was leaving for New York over the holidays. The state department official said it was impossible to accomplish anything in his absence. He urged my father to remain in America, assuring him everything possible was being done by American authorities to secure my release.

Amnesty International next offered to send their corporate lawyer to attend our trial if both families covered the expenses. Their man couldn't speak the language, had never been to Pakistan, was prohibited from practicing law in the country and in fact could only observe and make recommendations to our attorney Naeem. It was another blind alley full of disappointment.

"A week ago we thought we had found help at last. Word came that the Pakistani Consul in San Francisco was a British general, retired from the Bengal Lancers. I called him and explained what had happened to you and Ali Muhammad," my father said.

The ex-military man set my parents at ease by letting them know he enjoyed influential contacts through out the country. After the partition of India in 1947, he had sided with Pakistan and stayed on to organize the newly-formed country's military academy. His loyalty had been rewarded by being awarded the political plum at the San Francisco consulate. Most of the top army men now running the country had once been his students. This included President Zia, as well as the general who currently ruled both the city of Rawalpindi and the surrounding Punjab Province. The old Bengal Lancer told my father to give him time to formulate a rescue plan. My mother hoped the Englishman was an answer to their prayers.

The Brigadier called the next day to spell out his conditions.

"Yes, I think I can help you. I know Zia. He was a student of mine and still holds me in great respect. I'll want $50,000 cash from each family up

Stacked Deck

front as my fee. I'll need round trip airfare and accommodations, both first class. Better figure on providing me with $25,000 for my expenses and count on a minimum of a month's stay. Plus you will have to provide a million dollar insurance policy, payable to my wife, in case anything goes wrong."

"Of course none of this came with any guarantees," my father Cordell told me.

"I think I can get your son out but forget about his hippie friend. You know how the Muslims are about misfits. They'll most likely never let him go," the retired cavalryman said.

"We'll never leave him," my father told the Englishman, then realized he needed to tread lightly while he played for time.

"I knew he had absolutely betrayed our trust and was trying to take financial advantage of our emotional emergency. I needed time to think so I told him in a pleasant voice I'd call him back. Your Mom and I were desperate. That night she asked God what we should do. She shook me awake early the next morning."

"When I woke up my head was ringing with the answer," she told my father. "YOU have to go to Pakistan. You can talk to that governor just as easily as that blood-sucking Englishman".

It was agreed that Van, my red haired, hot-tempered mother, would stay home. She was to circulate petitions for our release among politicians, as well as give Ali Muhammad's mother a long distance arm to lean on. With my mother's Irish outlook it was no chore to string along the English general, making the Consul think Cordell was too busy raising money to call him back.

"On my way here I kept asking God what I should do next. My plan is first to meet with the Pakistani governor here in the Punjab. Then I'll call on the American ambassador. I'm going to get you and Ali Muhammad out of here," my father said with absolute conviction.

Back in Cell-Nine Block-Four, Ali and I waited impatiently for tidings from the Southern California dentist who believed he could take on Pakistan single-handed. Hans and Raja shared our excitement. Godwin just sat humming like a broken refrigerator. However after more than a week of silence had gone by my father's glad tidings and the hint of mercy had both worn thin. We were getting worried.

It didn't help that word of Cordell's promise to liberate us had spread among Char Chuki. Ali Muhammad and I were suddenly busy hosting fellow prisoners who wanted to know if "our" father would petition the governor on their behalf as well. Pakistanis dislike solitude. From earliest infancy they are part of large extended families and tight-knit communities. Loneliness is to be avoided at all costs and privacy is a largely western concept. Therefore men we had never met had no problem with coming to Cell Nine. They would wait politely at the cell door until invited in, then sit down and tell us about their individual circumstances. Justice had grown so elusive in Pakistan that it seemed perfectly natural to seek out two unknown foreigners to petition for their help in finding it.

Thus we balanced our social obligations with our own anxieties. According to local legend Allah dipped the sun into the eternal fires of Hell every night in order to rejuvenate its light. That mighty orb swam through the lake of fire nine times before my father came back with news.

When Babu brought word that my friend and I had *moloqats*, meaning more than one visitor, you could sense the excitement in Char Chuki. We made our way with great anticipation up the road, through the Judas gate and to the DSP's door. Upon entering we saw my father and Naeem sitting at the desk, talking to the prison official.

The first thing my father did was give Ali Muhammad a long hug. He and my mother had always been a friend to my friend. After giving me a warm embrace as well, Cordell said, "OK, I've got good news".

Naeem suggested we move to the corner of the DSP's office. While we hadn't been offered tea, the DSP certainly gave Ali and me the impression our social status had taken on a sudden change for the better. The jailer waved us towards four chairs already arranged for the meeting.

"The governor had snake eyes that could look right through you", my father said, and then related his tale of travel and Oriental diplomacy.

Cordell had made his way across the country to the city of Lahore, the capital of the Punjab province and the home of the military governor. Having secured a hotel room, he rented a typewriter and composed a letter. My father explained how he was a friend of the Bengal Lancer general back in San Francisco. He then requested a meeting with General Khan to discuss the imprisonment of his son and a family friend. The governor's personal secretary, an army major, rang to assure my father that the governor would meet with him as soon as his schedule cleared. General Zia was currently in Lahore as well, attending a national women's conference, the secretary said. Governor Khan played host to his boss for a few days and then sent word for my father to meet him the following morning.

"The taxi driver took me to the governor's palace after breakfast. It had been built by the British and reminded me of the White House. We drove past massive black iron gates and a wide grass lawn that was a city block long. The residence was fronted by a series of tall white columns. It was the most regal place I've seen in the country", Cordell said.

The entrance to the palace was on the second floor. It had to be reached by walking up a series of broad steps, passing between the columns and only then approaching two large front doors. The first floor was a solid, white stone facade that added to the majesty of the building by raising it above ground level. Not knowing where to report, my father approached a small, open door located near the immense driveway on the ground floor. Inside, my father immediately discovered an army lieutenant on guard. He informed the officer of his appointment with the governor, then stepped back outside.

"I only had to wait for a few minutes. It was a beautiful morning", Cordell remembered. "Then I heard, 'Dr. Riley,' and turned around to see Governor Khan had emerged to meet me".

"Because he was bald, it was hard to tell how old he was, maybe sixty. He had a round slick head, as if he shaved it. He wasn't a tall man and his face was a little fat. He was clean shaven, almost nondescript, but he had serpent-like eyes that never blinked," my father recalled.

The governor was dressed in a crisp army uniform. Five officers stood by silently, ready to run errands or transmit orders. The major who served as secretary was introduced. The others remained anonymous. The governor offered his hand. The other men remained very much at attention.

"It's such a nice day, let's sit outside", General Khan said in perfect English and then lead his American visitor across the wide expanse of lawn. He directed my father to take a seat on one of four white wrought-iron lawn chairs. Then the military governor and the secretary sat down opposite Cordell.

My father knew the governor had already received his letter explaining the details regarding our arrest, torture and imprisonment. Yet Cordell reiterated his case, explaining how he understood Pakistan was being pressured to satisfy American interests by stopping the flow of heroin, meanwhile trying to control an internal problem of epidemic proportions. My father assured the governor he realized that given the circumstances mistakes were bound to occur. However, he stressed, two innocent men were now in prison.

Then without realizing it Cordell made the correct cultural move. In Pakistan a person needed more than mere merit or even cash to succeed, one needed *sifarish*, a special recommendation. In a country justly famous for its outward belief in hospitality, family connections, and honor, it was the unannounced power of nepotism that usually got things done. The appeal of one family to another made sense to this powerful man. This American dentist wasn't there pleading on behalf of some disinterested government. He was arguing for his son's life. That was the kind of tactic the tough old governor understood.

"Asadullah and Ali Muhammad want to clear their names and remain in your country. Yet I must tell you that I fear if they are found guilty it will kill both mothers. I am told you are a fair man, that is why I have come to you for help and advice", Cordell said with sincerity.

General Khan studied my father with his unblinking eyes for several moments, weighing the evidence before him. Finally he spoke.

"I don't understand why no one from your embassy contacted me. That would have made all the difference. No matter", the general said.

Then he lifted his right hand and pointing his forefinger at my father, stabbed the air to emphasize his point.

"You can rest assured that justice will prevail. My secretary will monitor this case and keep me personally posted of what's going on", Khan said emphatically.

The general then snapped out an order in Urdu to one of his attendants. This officer rushed away across the lawn and into the palace, only to reappear moments later. Trailing behind the officer were four servants dressed in white livery. Each man carried a large box wrapped in white paper and tied with green ribbon, the national colors of Pakistan.

As each servant bowed and presented a box, the general explained that two of the packages bore presents for the British general, one was for his wife, the last was for my parents. The swift appearance of the gifts convinced my father the governor had already made up his mind regarding our case. With typical Pakistani politeness the military man turned politician had seen to the formalities as well.

Things went differently, we learned, at the American embassy. By this time the DSP was making no pretense at not listening. He was just as interested as Ali Muhammad and I in how this was going to affect our fate. The jailer didn't normally have a guy cluttering up his office who met with the regional strong men.

"The American embassy is a new, multi-million dollar complex in the heart of the diplomatic enclave in Islamabad. After I traveled back across the country, I got a hotel room and called for an appointment with Ambassador Benton. I had to wait until yesterday, Sunday, before I could see him", Cordell explained.

When the taxi pulled up my father had discovered the vast, sprawling American embassy complex was surrounded by twelve foot walls. This was to deter rioters like the ones who had destroyed the previous diplomatic compound. That embarrassing fiasco had come about in 1979 due to local response to Iranian-inspired rumors. In a BBC radio broadcast Ayatollah Khomeini had falsely accused the American government of being involved in a deadly hostage-taking situation at the mosque in Mecca, Islam's holiest shrine. Inflamed by the Ayatollah's deceptive message, a Pakistani mob attacked the old embassy, breaking down the doors and torching the place. The besieged staff initially took refuge in a top floor security vault, then later retreated to the roof to await rescue. When Pakistani troops arrived five hours later, they discovered two Americans and two Pakistani clerks had died in the fire.

The American government had gone to great lengths to prevent such a diplomatic nightmare from repeating itself. When my father arrived, he paid off the taxi and then walked a few steps to an exterior security booth located outside the main gates of the rebuilt compound.

Stacked Deck

"When I explained who I was, the Marine guard at the gate buzzed me through and told me to proceed to the first building and confirm my appointment with the ambassador there", Cordell explained.

Though the building itself was huge, once inside my father discovered he was enclosed in a small waiting room. A thick steel door prohibited further entry into the embassy enclave. Staring at him through a six-inch bullet proof window was a stern Marine sergeant. The Americans were taking no more chances. Once again the California visitor explained that he had an appointment to meet the ambassador. He was told to wait. Ten minutes later my father heard the steel door buzz open. A young man in his early thirties, neatly dressed in a gray suit, emerged. He introduced himself and asked Cordell to follow him.

The state department employee lead my father through a maze of long halls and offices, taking several turns. Because Sunday was a work day in Pakistan, things were going full bore. It surprised my dad to see how many Pakistanis were employed inside the sprawling office complex.

After a long walk, the two men entered the ambassador's private chambers, ending up in what could have passed for a hotel lobby. The room was built to impress. White marble floors stretched fifty feet in all directions. Elegant chandeliers hung overhead. The walls were covered in rich wood paneling. At the rear of this elegant room was a magnificent staircase that swept down from the landing above like two perfectly balanced angel's wings. My father and his minder waited patiently, exchanging meaningless chit-chat for a few minutes in the lobby, before they heard someone emerge onto the landing above them.

Looking up my father saw a man walking downstairs to greet him. Concerned with the importance and severity of the situation, Cordell had dressed in a three piece suit for the occasion. Ambassador Benton however was wearing tan slacks, a sports shirt and a pull over sweater. He was in his mid fifties, had a slight build and a receding hairline. His soft voice was as bland and colorless as he was. The glasses perched on his thin nose completed the effect of making him look like an academic on holiday, not a diplomatic majordomo.

The ambassador lead his guest and the employee upstairs to his office. It was opulent, with thick carpet, rich draperies, and expensive paintings. Ambassador Benton took up his appointed place behind a magnificent desk. My father was offered a chair directly in front of the important man. The young state department employee, looking increasingly nervous, was directed to sit slightly off to one side.

A long diplomatic career had taught Benton to use the English language skillfully. He rested his elbows on the desk, put his fingers together and began to explain to my father how sorry he was to meet him under such trying circumstances. He talked, yet said nothing of substance. The diplomat rolled out a patter of tired clichés, his hands were tied, he couldn't rock the boat, he was forced to observe Pakistani customs.

He finished by telling my father in a patronizing tone, "Doctor Riley, I want you to know my staff and I have done everything we can for your son and his friend."

My father had flown half way around the world to answer that allegation

"Ambassador, I only have one word for that. Horse shit"!

The angry doctor then proceeded to administer a tongue-lashing to the unsuspecting, smooth-talking diplomatist.

"Since my son's arrest I have learned that our government is happy to share a bed with this country's military dictator. General Zia and a handful of influential families control more than 70% of this entire country's wealth. The majority of all educated Pakistanis loathe the man. The poor people simply fear him. There are frequent arrests of opposition political leaders. Not content with hanging Prime Minister Bhutto, General Zia now has the dead man's daughter, Benazir Bhutto, under house arrest. All real power is centered with this dictator and his army cronies. They've usurped democracy and our government has continually aided their felonious attempts", Cordell told him.

"As long as President Zia continues to aid the mujahideen resistance and draw the Soviets deeper into the Afghan conflict, you and the US government are willing to support him. Zia's war on heroin is a another hoax. It is abundantly clear to me that this embassy is willing to tolerate the sacrifice of the people of Pakistan, and even the life of my son, if it furthers your mutual political agenda."

The ambassador was unprepared to be verbally accosted. He had expected my father to show up, hat in hand, ask for a update on our condition and then return meekly into the night. That's not how things worked with my dad.

"The governor of the Punjab asked me why no one from this embassy informed him of my son's case. I could not give him an answer, Mr. Ambassador. In fact, according to the Vienna Consular Convention, the police were required to notify the nearest American consulate of the arrest of my son and his friend. That was never done. Plus, under international law neither of them could be tortured. Yet the evidence is overwhelming that both Asadullah and Ali Muhammad were the victims of such state-sponsored treatment", Cordell told the stunned ambassador.

"Yes, well we protested that", the diplomat replied defensively.

"That's right", my father snapped back, "and in retaliation for your misplaced efforts the narcotic's agents slapped my son with a charge of 75 years to life".

"I didn't know that," Benton added hastily, then gave his young employee a hard look.

"Your office wasn't legally required to demand anything from the Pakistanis, but the slightest exercise of your authority would have at least got my son out on bail, not left him to rot in prison. Even if you suspected he and his friend violated local law, you had an obligation to provide consular protection according to the guidelines set out by the State Department. Instead you and your staff chose to play it safe and ignore them. You, Mr. Ambassador, are as guilty as the local drug police in collaborating in my son's false imprisonment", my father told him sternly.

Ambassador Benton had heard enough.

"We're not lawyers", he shot back.

"That's right, you're not. You're cowards"! Cordell told him, then rose to leave.

My father had never been offered any apologies. There had been no hint of hospitality, no offer of even a cup of coffee to a man who had flown 14,000 miles to come to that office. The ambassador had never answered any of the allegations. He ordered his employee to guide my father out through the maze of offices.

"The ambassador was less cordial when I left", my father said with an impish smile.

Despite the story I realized what my dad was also not telling us. We weren't leaving with him.

"Well it sounds like we can at least count on getting a fair trial now", I said.

Naeem chose that moment to help us overcome what had become an awkward moment.

"We have a strong case. With your help, Dr. Riley, I feel confident the narcotics police can no longer tamper with the evidence or the facts. I have a plan that will derail those bastards", the little man said with utter conviction and without a hint of mercy.

I looked at my father and asked the obvious question.

"When are you leaving"?

"Tomorrow. Early. On PIA Flight 786 for London", he said, and stood to go. We all followed his lead.

"I've never been able to make my up mind about what 'PIA' stands for? People tell me it could be 'Pakistan International Airlines', but someone else said it means 'Please Inform Allah', or was it 'Pray In Advance airlines'"? Ali Muhammad asked Cordell in a deliberate slow drawl.

We all laughed, trying to ease the strain.

,"You're going to be free very shortly", Cordell said. I could see in his eyes that he believed it.

He hugged Ali Muhammad hard, slapping him on the back, then told him, " I'll call New Orleans and tell your mother you're fine".

Khyber Knights

Then he embraced me tightly. We held each other, unsure of what life had in store for us. He stepped away and looked into my eyes. I had never been a father. I was his only son. I had no idea what he saw or felt.

"You'll be home soon", he said, posing it as both a statement of belief and a question.

"Yes. I will be now", I told him. "As soon as this mess is cleared up, there is one thing I need to resolve. Then I'll be home. Tell Mom to have the enchiladas ready. I'm dying for Mexican food".

"I love you", he said to me.

"I know".

And then he was gone, and Ali, Naeem and I prepared for legal war.

22
Truth Takes A Holiday

The trial started February 18th with no reason offered for the delay.

As custom dictated Ali Muhammad and I attended the festivities draped in chains. We were accompanied by a single guard. It took only a few minutes to march the two of us across the boulevard and down the side street to the front of the court.

It was very noisy outside the old building. There were close to one hundred men milling about, talking, gesticulating, and scheming. Dozens of solicitors maintained impromptu open-air offices on the steps of judgment. Tiny tables and rickety chairs hosted barristers and clients. Letter-writers pecked out legal petitions for the illiterate. Tea wallahs hustled between tables, delivering the steaming liquid that oiled the wheels of verbosity. Deals were cut, jealousies resolved and plans were made in plain view of the ramshackle hall of justice.

Waiting for us like hungry sharks were the narcs.

I had been linked to Ali's chain. My friend's chain was in turn clipped to the guard's belt. As our escort marched us towards the four brick steps that lead up to the door, I made a pretense of ignoring our adversaries. My play-acting was transparent to the four men who had come to see us legally destroyed. They stood at the base of the stairs, awaiting their chance to finish the job they had started more than four months before.

Inspector Gilani Khan had on a decent brown suit and had left the sunglasses at home. Field Officer Niazi, the fake electrician, was in a traditional tan color shalwar kameez. There was an unidentified third man hovering with them. He was wearing a blue sports coat, slacks and a tie. Ashgar Ali completed the narcotic barbershop quartet. He wore a blue sweater over a lighter colored shalwar kameez. Standing next to his companions it was easy to get a clear impression of how big Ashgar was.

When he saw me being lead up in manacles, the charming loser's big face took on an appearance of arrogant satisfaction. By the time I reached him, Ashgar had lost the look. As I passed we traded a silent exchange of mutual hatred. The other three men remained cold and sly.

Inside we discovered the room had been slightly altered for the proceedings. Two small tables sat at right angles, one on each side of the magistrate's bench. Tanvir the prosecutor was already sitting on the left. He was dressed in a police uniform, complete with pips on his epaulets ranking him as a captain. Though only in his mid thirties, he was already running to fat. He looked sincere, thorough and professional. Grouped beside his table were six old wooden chairs. The prosecutor didn't bother looking up from his papers when we entered.

Naeem however rose from the other table and came half way across the room to meet us. As the guard began the tedious process of unscrewing the antique handcuffs, our advocate took the chance to speak to us quietly.

"Don't say a word, no matter what happens. It is vital that you keep completely still and not reveal a trace of emotion. Display, what you say, only the poker face. Do you understand?" he asked in complete seriousness. His eyes told us nothing.

We nodded in agreement. My chest hurt from the anxiety derived from contemplating spending seventy-five years in Pindi Prison. I didn't need to be told not to talk. I was so nervous. I couldn't have choked out my own name. Ali Muhammad and me were directed to sit in two chairs directly behind our barrister. There were four chairs placed on our side of the court slightly behind us.

No one had bothered to sweep down the room where our fate was to be decided. It was still full of shelves holding withered manuscripts detailing the lives of men long since gone to meet either freedom or their maker. The only hint of grace and dignity resided in the old picture of Muhammad Ali Jinnah, still resting high up on the wall behind the judge's bench. Besides being the father of Pakistan, Jinnah had enjoyed a reputation as being a brilliant lawyer. He stared down upon us from his dusty portrait, looking grave, tubercular and, I hoped, generous.

Naeem had resumed his seat in front of us and immediately began to study a stack of papers placed before him. He was wearing a shiny black suit and a crisp white shirt. A black tie peeped out from behind his customary gold buttoned vest. With his jet black hair slicked back and his waxed little mustache, the chubby barrister looked anything except intimidating.

The guard had barely had time to take up his position near the door, when the side door opened and Magistrate Zeb strode in. Naeem and Tanvir stood to attention in respect for the dignity of the court. Ali Muhammad and I followed their lead. Anyone looking at the man who walked in would have understood why.

Zeb was transformed. The traditional black robes now lent him an air of respect. More importantly, he radiated an air of dignity and formality. Come what may, this man was obviously taking every aspect of our case seriously.

The magistrate walked to his chair and stood looking down at the men standing in his court. Tanvir gave a brief nod in acknowledgment. Naeem however said, "Your honor," and bowed in courtly fashion. The prosecutor looked amused at the older man's elaborate courtesy.

"Be seated," Zeb said, and we all followed the lead of the man who would decide our fate.

Truth Takes a Holiday

The prosecutor appeared confident. When the magistrate gave him permission to start his case, Tanvir laid out the charges and the allegations. He accused us of masquerading as Muslims in an attempt to smuggle a large quantity of heroin out of the country. He assured Zeb there were ample witnesses and evidence to prove the case. The state was asking for an extraordinarily large sentence in order to send a clear message to other drug traffickers. The Islamic Republic of Pakistan would not tolerate such criminal behavior.

When it came to Naeem's turn, he looked nervous, glanced repeatedly at his papers as if seeking support and stuttered out more of an apology than a defense. At the conclusion of the brief statement the magistrate appeared unimpressed. Tanvir was openly amused at our advocate's discomfiture.

Zeb ordered the prosecutor to call his first witness. Tanvir had turned towards the guard standing at the door. He was about to speak when Naeem interrupted.

"Surely your honor won't object if we ask these witnesses to remain in the room after testifying. Despite the preponderance of evidence it wouldn't appear fair if they were allowed to step back outside to discuss the proceedings until after we conclude," Naeem said. He seemed almost to grovel at the boldness of his request.

"Any objections?" Zeb asked the prosecutor.

Shamelessly seeking approval, Naeem gave the younger man an ingratiating smile.

"No objections your honor."

"Fine. Call your first witness."

Within moments the guard at the door called out a name and Inspector Gilani Khan walked in. Zeb did not ask him to state his name or take an oath. The magistrate was also acting as jury and knew all the players.

The narcotic's officer stood before the bench looking confident. Tanvir rose from behind his table and began the questioning.

Gilani's testimony came across as strong and forceful. He recalled how he was in police headquarters when he got a phone tip that two Americans staying at Flashman's Hotel intended to smuggle heroin out of the country. The informant also reported that the foreigners had both just gone out to purchase the drug. Zeb called his office and informed Field Officer Niazi to organize a raiding party and meet him at the hotel.

He proceeded to Flashman's, arriving shortly after 5:00 p.m. Enlisting the aid of a hotel employee, the inspector said he posted his men at the "In" gate of the hotel. At about 5:30 p.m. both defendants arrived and were stopped at that entrance.

"They were both carrying shoulder bags, which we searched. My men discovered each defendant was carrying approximately 500 grams of pure heroin."

Khyber Knights

At this point the prosecutor asked the courts permission to produce the confiscated heroin as evidence. Zeb's approval was quick in coming. Tanvir informed the guard. Within moments Ashgar Ali entered carrying a carton. He placed it on the prosecutor's table and was about to leave when Naeem reminded the magistrate of the agreement to keep the witnesses in the courtroom. Looking somewhat bewildered, the big cop was told to take a seat on Tanvir's side of the court room.

The prosecutor laid two small shoulder bags on his table. One was an old, canvas army issue. The other one was a thick plastic Chinese type commonly purchased in any Pakistani bazaar. Then Tanvir carefully placed two plastic bags on the front of his table. He put the carton on the floor beside his chair. Each clear plastic bag contained the same light brown powder I had originally seen in the dressing room, only now the smack had been neatly divided into two packets, each about the size of a large loaf of bread.

Gilani identified the powder. He went on to explain how five grams were taken from each bag as a laboratory sample as soon as it was seized. The prisoners were then taken to their hotel room where their luggage was searched. After preparing a recovery memo listing our belongings, he made a site plan of the room. When this work was completed, the inspector ordered Officer Niazi to take the accused persons, along with the complaint property outside, and turn them over to police Sergeant Hiyat Mohammad for further investigation. Looking pleased, Tanvir told the magistrate he had no further questions.

Naeem's first question was deceptively easy. The little fat man remained sitting, studying a typed piece of paper. He appeared to be preoccupied. Without looking up, he asked, "What time did you get the tip, Inspector?"

"About four p.m."

"How many men were in the raiding party?"

Gilani hesitated for a moment, weighing his answer, sensing a trap.

"Four. Myself, Mohammad Yusuf, Niazi and a hotel employee, Arshad Shafi," Gilani said, all the while maintaining his look of confidence.

Naeem raised his eyes slowly. Suddenly he no longer appeared flustered. He pointed at Ashgar Ali sitting across the room and asked Gilani, "Is that one of your officers?'

"Yes."

"Was he present at the arrest?"

"No."

"And you took samples of the heroin right away, isn't that correct Inspector?"

"Yes."

"As soon as you made the arrests?"

"That's correct."

"If I understand you aright, you and your men held my clients under arrest, while you meanwhile opened these two bags of heroin, took five grams out of each, weighed the samples, then sealed off both the samples and the original bags. All of this occurring just inside the hotel gate, next to one of the busiest roads in Rawalpindi?"

"Yes. That's how it happened," Gilani said strongly.

"Why didn't Sergeant Hiyat Mohammad sign the witness of recovery memo?"

"He arrived after the arrest and waited outside the hotel room while I was inside drawing the site plans."

Naeem stood up. He looked short, fat, and slightly ridiculous but he no longer looked intimidated.

"Isn't it true Inspector that you took these two defendants to your headquarters on Haider Road where you urged them to falsely implicate themselves?"

"No. That's not true," Gilani barely had time to answer before Naeem attacked him without warning.

"Isn't it true that failing that you resorted to the argument of torture, that you ordered your men to beat them almost to death and then kept them in illegal confinement for nearly six hours?" Naeem said in a loud voice.

Before Gilani could even respond the little lawyer tacked on a clincher.

"And isn't it true the American embassy formally protested the treatment handed out to my clients?'

The inspector looked shaken. Standing as he was before Magistrate Zeb there was no place to hide. The judge snapped him back to reality.

"Answer the questions Inspector," Zeb ordered.

"I believe a letter from the embassy was received in narcotics headquarters complaining about the treatment of the defendants. The matter was not investigated because they were arrested October 30th and the letter stated they had been mistreated on October 29th. No departmental inquiry has ever been held against either me or my men," he answered defiantly.

Tanvir looked shocked at this sudden turn of events. He quickly got Gilani to go on the record as denying Ali Muhammad or I had been tortured or illegally imprisoned. The narc looked visibly relieved when Magistrate Zeb said he could step away from the bench. His escape was short lived. Gilani had barely taken two steps towards the door when Zeb ordered him to sit down next to Ashgar Ali. It was suddenly perfectly clear why Naeem had wanted to prohibit the narcs from returning outside and comparing stories as the trial proceeded.

The look on the prosecutor's face told us he realized he had underestimated the pudgy Perry Mason. He took a deep breath and dug in for a fight. He called his next witness, Field Officer Niazi, and made every attempt to lead him safely through a minefield. Despite his best efforts it was immediately clear the two narco cops had not bothered to coordinate their stories. As soon as Niazi entered the room it was obvious that his boss was upset. The tough inspector was unexpectedly sitting across the room. The junior officer could get no clue as to what was vexing him. The smaller officer made every effort to help the prosecutor's case and inadvertently exposed Gilani as a liar at every turn.

Niazi testified that Inspector Gilani called him at 2:00 p.m., almost three hours before Gilani got the purported tip-off. He said he took the message at their headquarters on Haider Road, a place Gilani had avoided mentioning. Following orders, Niazi had formed a raiding party and gone to the hotel, where he found Inspector Gilani waiting with a Flashman's employee.

"At 5:30 the two foreigners who are present in the court today were arrested and searched. After taking samples from each bag a complaint was prepared and I left to take it to the police station for registration of the case. When I came back the hotel room was being searched," Niazi told the prosecutor.

When it came Naeem's turn to cross examine he didn't bother to act polite.

"Fine words, but they butter no bread," he told the beleaguered cop. Then he stood up and walked around and stood uncomfortably close to Niazi. When he was within arm's reach Naeem started his broadside.

"How many people in the raiding party?"

"Seven. No, eight."

"Did the raiding party split up and cover both gates so the foreigners couldn't escape?"

"Yes."

"And what party was that officer with?" Naeem said, pointing at Ashgar Ali.

"I don't remember."

"But he was there?"

"Yes."

"Where was Sergeant Hiyat Mohammad after the arrest?"

"In the hotel room with us."

"Can you tell the court why the original First Investigation Report says there were was only one group of arresting officers who waited at the "In" gate?" Naeem asked.

"That must be a mistake," Niazi said, looking progressively more uncomfortable.

"Could this heroin have been planted or belonged to someone else?"

"I don't think so."

"Could the excessive charges filed against the defendants have been brought in order to avoid criminal proceedings against the police officials involved in torturing them?" the little lawyer asked.

"No."

Naeem finally asked him if he wanted to comment on the beating the two foreigners received at narcotics headquarters.

Niazi all but surrendered. He avoided the question.

"Inspector Gilani got the tip. I just took his orders," he said and looked down at the floor, nervous and miserable.

Suddenly Naeem had grabbed the ball and was controlling the court. Tanvir realized he was trying to contain the damage. Zeb appeared intently interested with Naeem's line of questioning. My friend and I sat silent, afraid if we so much as whispered we would hex this sudden turn of luck.

Tanvir called the stranger who had been standing outside the door with the narcs. Arshad Shafi informed the court he was employed at Flashman's Hotel as a *mohurrar* (clerk) at the front desk. He had been on duty about 4:30 p.m. when Inspector Gilani asked him to join the investigation. At about 5:30 p.m. the two accused came to the "In" gate and were detained.

He told Tanvir these were the same two shoulder bags the officers had taken off the defendants. After the arrest he had gone with the officers and the foreigners to Room 21. When the recovery memo was completed, he signed it as a witness.

During his testimony I kept trying to place this man who claimed to have witnessed our arrest. There had been a great deal of confusion but I still could not recall seeing him. If I had doubts, Naeem had none. He savaged the clerk.

"What scraps of prosperity have they thrown you, to get you to lie Mr. Shafi?" our lawyer asked to start and pointed with his chin in open contempt at the narcs sitting across the room. Naeem didn't wait for an answer.

We never learned what Gilani Khan had told Shafi to expect. Regardless, no instructions could have foreseen how Naeem attacked the witnesses' credibility.

"What are your duty hours?"

"Eight to five."

"And on the date in question these hours were the same?"

"Yes."

"So you would have been on duty at 4:30 p.m. when Inspector Gilani asked you to accompany him on the raiding party?"

"That's right," Shafi answered, starting to look uneasy.

Had he sought permission to accompany the raiding party?

No, he admitted he hadn't.

"So you left the desk unoccupied for more than an hour while you went to stand outside the front gate?"

He assured Naeem he could see the lobby and the front door from where he stood.

"How long have you worked for Flashman's Hotel?" Naeem asked, glancing down at his notes.

"Two years," was Shafi's rapid reply.

"Are you still employed there?"

"No," the clerk said quietly.

I felt the air leave my lungs in shock when I heard the answer.

In response to a series of rapid questions Shafi told Naeem he did not know why he was let go, then hastened to add that it had not been due to his involvement in the raid. But Naeem was far from finished with him. Because he was standing directly in front of Magistrate Zeb, the clerk kept turning his head back and forth between the judge and our lawyer. With each answer he looked more and more like a man struggling to keep his head above the deep water he had been lured into.

"There was only one raiding party. Right?," Naeem asked.

Anxious to please this nasty little man who kept badgering him, the clerk answered, "Right."

"And was Officer Ashgar Ali there?"

"Yes, he was with Inspector Gilani Khan, Officer Niazi and me when we arrested the foreigners."

"One more question. Can you tell the court which of these two shoulder bags belonged to each of the defendants?" Naeem asked and waited while Shafi physically squirmed, looking first at the bags on Tanvir's table, then back at Ali Muhammad and me sitting there impassively.

Finally the clerk told Naeem he could not recall who carried which bag.

Naeem walked over to the prosecutor's table and without asking permission grabbed the first bag. He took two steps towards Shafi and shoved it at him.

"You do remember that these are the two men who were arrested that day don't you?"

"Certainly."

"You have just told the court you were in the company of my clients for almost two hours, during their arrest, while samples were being taken of the heroin, and later when their room was being searched. You stood next to them for that length of time but you can't tell me which man was carrying this bag?" he said and shoved the canvas bag at Shafi's face.

"I can't recall."

Naeem made no more attempt at pretense or politeness. He tossed the bag back on Tanvir's table and walked back towards his own. It looked like he was done with the clerk. When he reached his chair the lawyer turned to Magistrate Zeb, gave him a long, telling look, then turned to face Shafi.

"Mr. Shafi, during the time of the arrest you must have had ample time to study the features of the defendants. Can you tell the court which is Mr. Asadullah Khan and which is Mr. Ali Muhammad?"

The clerk took a quick glance over his right shoulder.

"I don't recall."

"You stood looking at them for almost two hours Mr. Shafi, surely you know which name goes with which face? They don't look alike do they?"

"No."

"Well then, which is which?"

"I can't say. I don't remember."

"You mean to tell the court you cannot identify either defendant?"

Shafi looked across the room towards Gilani Khan for help but he was dangling on his own petard

"Answer the question Mr. Shafi. Which is which?" Naeem demanded impatiently.

"I don't know."

"No further questions, your honor," Naeem said and sat down.

Prosecutor Tanvir realized he was no longer fighting for a conviction, he was fighting to retain his own professional dignity. He called his last witness, police Sergeant Hiyat Mohammad.

The visual difference between the professional policeman and the previous witnesses was obvious. Hiyat stood ramrod straight. The creases on the sleeves of his shirt were razor sharp. It looked like he hadn't smiled in one hundred years. The prosecutor lead him step by careful step through a series of questions that seemed to confirm our guilt.

"At about 6:30 p.m.," Hiyat said, "Officers Ashgar Ali and Niazi brought the two accused foreigners and registered the case at my police station. Investigation of the case was entrusted to me from then on. I logged in the recovery memos and the case property upon receipt of the prisoners," he told Magistrate Zeb in a dull monotone. His eyes betrayed no emotion. He was a Spartan in a police uniform and appeared utterly incorruptible. Tanvir was very pleased with Hiyat's testimony and sat down looking visibly relieved.

When Naeem stood to question the sergeant, Ali Muhammad looked like I felt, full of nervous tension.

Under our lawyer's skillful cross-examination a more detailed account emerged. The sergeant recalled how as soon as the arresting officers left, the defendants complained of being beaten and tortured. From a cursory examination of the accused he believed there was room for immediate concern. He placed the defendants in police lockup and proceeded to the Flashman's Hotel, intent on questioning the hotel employees. Hiyat told the court he arrived there about 7:30 p.m., only to discover everyone involved had left. He learned the foreigners had been arrested soon after arriving at 11:30 a.m. and departed after lunch time, at approximately one p.m..

In his strong voice the policeman went on to explain that there was a five hour discrepancy where the accused could not be accounted for. The night manager had allowed him into Room 21 and he had made his own site map. Naeem asked him if there were any differences between his map of the arrest site and Inspector Gilani's?

"Yes," he said, "mine shows the armoire where the defendants say the unidentified bag with the single bag of heroin was found. The Inspector's does not."

"Did you ask the night manager if this armoire had always been there?" Naeem asked him.

"Yes. The manager acted surprised and said, 'Of course.'"

Naeem paused for a moment, then carefully asked Hiyat one last question.

"Sergeant, Inspector Gilani Khan has told the court that you were present on the hotel grounds at 5:30 p.m. while the defendants were being questioned and their room was being searched. Is that true?"

"I never saw them before six thirty and never got to the hotel until I went there on my own, which was well after seven o'clock."

When Naeem told Hiyat he had no more questions, the sergeant chose to sit on our side of the court. Tanvir's case was in tatters.

Naeem quickly called Doctor Mohammad Ashraf, who had examined us. He testified we had been beaten by a blunt instrument within 24 hours of the examination. The prosecutor immediately attacked the doctor's testimony.

"Doctor tell us what a bruise is."

"The collection of blood around the tissue or organ after the rupture of a blood vessel inside the human body."

"Isn't it correct that any injured place remains red for the first fifteen to twenty hours, turns bluish after the first day, and then turns brown when it is about to disappear in 14 or 15 days?"

"That's generally correct."

"You didn't mention in your report the color of the bruises on the accused. Isn't it true doctor the bruises weren't red and were in fact at least three days old?" the prosecutor asked, with a look of anticipation.

The doctor hadn't changed since we had briefly met him. He looked busy and impatient with this entire proceeding. Tanvir's question had changed the doctor's attitude with it's implied contempt of his professional judgment.

"Yes, its true they weren't red. However the color could easily be made out. They were only beginning to turn bluish at the time of the examination. They had occurred within the span of the last 36 hours."

"Couldn't these injuries have happened as the result of friendly hands?" Tanvir asked.

"If you mean by that could the defendant had inflicted them on himself, absolutely not."

The trial seemed to have reached an emotional plateau and I suspected it must be coming to a conclusion. The doctor had sat down next to Hiyat Mohammad. Everyone was shocked at Naeem's skillful exploitation of the facts. Tanvir appeared visibly upset at the realization he had been manipulated so easily. Across the room, Gilani, Ashgar and Niazi appeared peeved as they began to realize that Ali and I might have a chance of escaping from their carefully-constructed trap. Yet the game was not over. There were now eleven men in that room. We were about realize that the other ten of us combined were not as clever as little Khawaja Naeem.

Our lawyer stood and said in a loud voice, "Your honor I wish to call Sheikh Fayyaz."

The guard was instructed to call out the name.

I bowed my head and tried to stifle a groan when I saw who it was. The tall man in a well pressed charcoal suit came straight to the bench. When I looked at Ali Muhammad I saw the same sort of bewildered amazement and acute apprehension that I felt. Naeem had called the manager of the Flashman's Hotel who so obviously hated us.

Our advocate wasn't interested in our worries. He launched into a rapid series of questions.

"Mr. Fayyaz what is your job?"

"I am the manager of Flashman's Hotel."

Naeem held up a large book he had uncovered from a stack of papers.

"And what is this, Mr. Fayyaz?"

"That, Mr. Naeem, is the hotel register you had impounded," the witness said, clearly irritated.

Naeem opened the large book and laid it out on the table in front of him. He then pointed to a entry.

"Who does it show occupies Room 21 on October 30th, 1983?"

"Mr. Beau Fontaine of Peshawar."

"Is this written in his hand?"

"Yes."

"What time did he check in?"

"Eleven thirty a.m."

"Can this be verified?"

"Of course. In compliance with the instructions contained in the "Registration of Foreigners Act of 1966," the arrival of both foreigners was communicated to the Senior Superintendent of Police the same day."

There was obviously no love lost between Naeem and the hotel manager but we all knew the advocate was going somewhere with the questioning.

"How much is the room rent?"

"Three hundred fifty rupees a day."
"The register shows them checking out when?"
"At 1:05 p.m. on October 30th."
"How much did they owe?"
"Nothing. They had paid for a full day and left before check-out time on the same day."
"And when is check-out time?"
"Three p.m."
"So they arrived at 11:30 and left before 3:00, is that right?"
"Correct."
"If they had left at say five p.m. they would have owed for two days or 700 rupees isn't that right?"
"Yes," Fayyaz said wearily, looking increasingly irritated with Naeem.
"Is this Mr. Beau Fontaine's signature showing he checked them out?"
"No, that is Inspector Gilani's signature. He signed them out and ordered that defendant to pay the bill," Fayyaz said, and pointed at me.
"Did Inspector Gilani pay for anything else?"
"Yes, he ordered the same foreigner to pay for their lunch?"
"Whose lunch?" Naeem asked.
Across the room I could see Gilani Khan looked like he was going to choke.
"The lunch for the other seven policemen," the manager said, then hastily added, "he offered to feed the foreigners but they refused to eat."
"That's when they were in Room 21 doing the paperwork after the arrest, right?"
"Yes, that's correct."
Out of the corner of my eye I could see Magistrate Zeb leaning forward in his seat to hear everything Fayyaz said.
"Mr. Fayyaz, Doctor Ashraf has already testified regarding the beating given to the defendants. Did you see Inspector Gilani or any of the other officers strike the accused?" Naeem asked.
The manager clearly hesitated. Zeb gave him no more than a heart beat then whipped him back to attention.
"Answer the question. Did you see them being beaten?" the magistrate demanded without a hint of civility.
"No, but I did hear a lot of shouting ...... and the sounds of blows. I heard a lot of noise. I'm not sure what it was. I wasn't in the room."
"And when you entered the room did the defendants look like they had been beaten?" Naeem asked.
"I couldn't say."
The lawyer pressed him, "How did they look?"
"Scared," the hotel manager admitted.
Naeem leaned back from over the register. He seemed to be signaling he was wrapping up. Fayyaz visibly relaxed, thinking the worst was over.

"You've told the court my clients were arrested in their room. Did you happen to overhear where the heroin was located?"

"I wasn't told but I heard two of the officers say it was found in the dressing room closet," Fayyaz reported.

The lawyer pressed on.

"The heroin has been split up into two bags because of legal examination purposes but it was originally in one plastic bag, correct?" Naeem asked.

Fayyaz didn't hesitate in answering.

"Yes, of course. I saw it myself. They had placed it very carefully on the dressing room table in front of the armoire."

Naeem stood up to his full height of five foot five. Thinking his legal interrogation was concluded, Fayyaz turned back to face Magistrate Zeb, obviously seeking release. That was the moment Naeem played his last card.

"Well, that will be all Mr. Fayyaz," he said. The manager hadn't even started to turn before the bull dog lawyer grabbed him one last time.

"Oh, one more thing. When did Mr. Ashraf Shafi come on duty that day?"

Fayyaz looked surprised but did not hesitate to answer.

"He wasn't on duty that day."

Naeem pretended to look confused.

"Shafi wasn't on duty at 4:30 on the afternoon of the arrest?"

"Certainly not."

"Why?"

"Because he hadn't worked for Flashman's Hotel for more than a month at the time of the arrests," Fayyaz said forcefully.

"You're sure you're not mistaken Mr. Fayyaz? You're sure he couldn't have been on duty and just absent from his post, gone to assist the police perhaps as they detained the suspects at the hotel's "In" gate," Naeem asked.

The hotel manager had run out of patience. He looked at our lawyer like he was some sort of imbecile caught trying to pull off an idiotic prank.

"That's absurd. They were in their room at the time of the arrest. I should know because Inspector Gilani came into the hotel lobby and asked me to accompany him and his officers when they went to Room 21 to make the arrest, and Shafi damn well knows he wasn't welcome on the property," Fayyaz said emphatically.

At the disclosure of this news Magistrate Zeb's face went black with rage.

23
Judicial Murder

I could swear I heard the narcs suck in their breath with shock and fear.

The hotel manager's testimony had branded them all as liars and impostors.

Fayyaz was told to take a seat next to the doctor.

Naeem had yielded the floor to Tanvir but the once-cocky prosecutor was a changed man. He made an attempt at summarizing his case, explaining to Magistrate Zeb that even if there was evidence of police mistreatment, the heroin was clearly ours. Ownership demanded that we be punished.

The judge let him finish without interrupting. It was clear Tanvir was embarrassed by the outcome of the proceedings. He refused to look in the direction of Inspector Gilani Khan and his cronies. Once the young prosecutor finished his closing remarks, he sat down, looking weary and shamed.

Our advocate had no hesitation in expressing his opinions to either the man sitting in judgment or the men who had tormented and imprisoned us.

Naeem stood up from his chair and placed his hands on the table. Despite his diminutive size he looked like Samson about to push over the pillars of Gilani Khan's temple of deceit.

"Your honor lying before us are two bags of poison. They represent one of the few truthful things we have seen in this court today, for Prosecutor Tanvir and I both agree on the need to combat this evil plague now ravaging our country. Government estimates believe there are more than 400 heroin labs operating from Peshawar south to Karachi," Naeem said.

"What was once seen as an export has come home with a vengeance. Our country now has an estimated two million addicts, a 46% yearly increase. Pakistan alone is consuming 100 kilos a day of pure heroin. Out of 500 Karachi engineering students recently interviewed, 20% were hooked on the drug. It has become so pervasive pushers are using women and children to make home deliveries. The average addict spends 1,000 rupees a month to maintain his habit. In every city in our country getting heroin has become as easy as finding a meal."

At this point Naeem looked at his legal rival.

"Your honor, do not believe for a moment that the honorable prosecutor and I are at odds regarding the internal dangers facing our country. If anything, we may not fully realize how monumental is our peril. Just last week a Pakistani cargo ship was detained in Turkey, where it was discovered to be laden with ten tons of hashish and two tons of heroin," our lawyer explained.

Naeem choose this moment to walk from behind his table and take a position in front of the bench. He looked up at Magistrate Zeb and continued his explanation.

"The good news in all this is that there are men risking their lives and resisting the black money associated with this evil trade. In the last year the Frontier Corps has seized more than 42 metric tons of heroin and hashish," Naeem said.

He then reached over to his table and lifted up an Urdu newspaper, holding it aloft for everyone in the court to see.

"Yesterday the Peshawar police stopped a truck at a road side haul up. It was bound for the port of Karachi. Inside they discovered two tons of hashish disguised in fake packets of tea and coffee. In an effort to throw off the investigators, the smugglers had even painted the symbol of the Red Crescent Charity Society on the truck doors."

Throwing the paper back on the table, Naeem turned back to Magistrate Zeb.

"As you well know neither the Frontier Corps, nor the Peshawar police, are highly paid. Nor were they trained overseas by the vaunted American DEA. Yet these poorly paid cops on the beat manage to seize hundreds of kilos of heroin a day."

Naeem paused, glanced back at Gilani Khan, then looked up at the magistrate.

"How is it then, your honor, that these men," and he pointed at Gilani, Niazi and Ashgar, "come away unable to prove the ownership of one kilo of heroin? When cops making 500 rupees a month are seizing truckloads of drugs, how can Inspector Gilani Khan and his team attempt to impress this court with either the size, or the importance, of the arrest in question?"

"Your honor, as a judge you know that your first thought must always be to ask yourself what are the speaker's motive. To believe everything you hear will only bring you into difficulties. What we have seen today are circles within circles. The truth in this case has been sacrificed to an atmosphere of falsehood and deceit."

As if to prove that he held no fear of the larger men, Naeem deliberately walked over and stood next to Gilani Khan's chair. He waved his hand to take in all four prosecution witnesses, then said, "To begin with, we cannot believe the allegation that my clients were not seized and tortured by these men. In Lahore the supreme court is currently investigating the death of a twenty-six-year-old defendant who was also illegally imprisoned. He died after being subjected to third degree methods for nineteen days. Only after his family set up a hue and cry did

Judicial Murder

the police admit they had imprisoned the missing man in a torture cell they maintained in a private residence. This scandalous practice of institutional torture was justified by saying they were short of office space at the local jail."

"So please your honor, don't allow these men to impugn the intelligence of this court by claiming that prisoners all over our unfortunate country are not routinely illegally detained and tortured. Police brutality is now viewed by men like Inspector Gilani Khan as a valid method of crime detection. It is an unfortunate if unpublished fact, that police torture has become so commonplace in our country that it has slowly lost its capacity to shock us. The evidence before you is overwhelming that in this case Gilani Khan and his men followed this silent and ugly practice. If my clients are in any way lucky it is in that unlike the young man in Lahore they too did not succumb to custodial death," Naeem said.

Ashgar Ali squirmed uncomfortably. Niazi looked at the ground, while Gilani stared off into space.

"What this case represents is not a search for truth but a search for vengeance. The facts point not towards the guilt of my clients but the men entrusted to uphold the law," Naeem said. "We see the accusers stripped of their disguises. They have attempted to bewilder the court in an effort to hide their own deceit. Their very actions stand condemned and exposed as we see them for the liars they truly are."

The lawyer took a position directly in front of Shafi, the hotel clerk, and pointed an accusing finger at him. Naeem had turned the trial on its head. He had managed to put the prosecution in the dock.

"This witness, your honor, was called to verify the accusations brought against my clients by Inspector Gilani Khan. You heard the hotel manager testify that in fact Shafi was no where near the hotel grounds. Through his lips in fact passes nothing except treachery. His very tongue spews filth on everything it touches, including the truth. Shafi stands exposed and condemned as a perjurious liar who should be driven from the court he soils by his mere presence," Naeem said, looking at the clerk.

Our advocate then moved to face Ashgar and Niazi.

"But Shafi is only a tool of his masters, your honor," the little advocate explained. "How is that Sergeant Hiyat stood before this court and had the courage to denounce the falsehood heaped on these proceedings? I will tell you how, because unlike these two, Sergeant Hiyat never took the law into his own hands. He knew if he succumbed to that temptation he would be breaking the law he was sworn to uphold. Unlike these two unprincipled men sitting before me, Hiyat knows that the law stands above corrupt money and foreign luxuries. The good sergeant has nothing in common with these two jackals, these so-called officers of the law, whose positions of power and prestige became more important to them than either the people they served or the justice they were sworn to represent."

If Naeem had stopped right there he would have accomplished more than I had ever dared hope. Magistrate Zeb looked like a starving tiger anxious to shove through the bars of his cage of self-restraint and tear into the narcs himself. Yet it was the little man in the tight vest who temporarily controlled the emotional high ground. We watched as Naeem slowly turned and looked at Inspector Gilani Khan. The head narc looked back at him, visibly daring Naeem to try his verbal abuse in Gilani's corner of the court. The advocate walked towards our foe and then took up a position directly behind his chair. Gilani was forced to sit up straight, facing off into space, as he tried to pretend to ignore the hail of brimstone Khawaja Naeem then heaped on his shoulders.

"Your honor," Naeem said in a voice grown soft and deadly, "this case is not about heroin smuggling. This is a case of attempted murder. The evidence has shown that not only were my clients not involved in this crime, they were in fact tortured by the man sitting here before me. Failing to force them to sign coerced confessions, Inspector Gilani Khan allowed his ape, Ashgar Ali, almost to kill them. When the American embassy protested that treatment the inspector knew he had fouled up."

With the exception of the four prosecution witnesses, who could not see the little lawyer behind them, every eye was on Naeem.

"And what did Gilani Khan do your honor? His own actions brand him for the primary criminal in this case. Knowing he had to keep my clients silent, he charged them not just with possession of heroin. No, he tacked on transportation of the drug for good measure. Then he deliberately charged them under an obscure 1930 statute, compounding his lie by saying they manufactured the drug. This man, who brags about his foreign training, did this to my clients for two reasons. First he wanted to put them in prison where he could keep them quiet. Second, he realized if the truth about the beatings came out, he and his narcotic's crew would be exposed as the true criminals and torturers that they are."

From where I sat I could see the enraged inspector. He looked like he wanted to swing around and kill the fat lawyer slashing his reputation to shreds behind his back.

"Your honor, Inspector Gilani Khan almost succeeded in making this court an accessory to murder. For you see the inspector was not merely trying to imprison my clients. He was trying to permanently silence them. Prosecutor Tanvir was duped into asking this court to award a sentence of 75 years to life. Why, your honor? Why?" Naeem asked.

He took that opportunity to walk around and stand in front of the enraged cop. What ever else he was, Khawaja Naeem was not afraid. He looked down at Inspector Gilani Khan with the contempt he would have shown a cockroach.

"This man wanted to use the sentence awarded in this court to send my clients back to prison. He wasn't asking for life, this coward was asking for death. He wanted to sentence them to a slow agonizing demise in the hell-hole we all know exists across the street from this very court. He hoped to bury the truth when he buried Asadullah and Ali Muhammad alive," Naeem roared.

He pointed directly in Gilani Khan's face and accused him before the court.

"You were not here seeking justice, Inspector. You came here cloaking murder in the folds of the law."

Naeem turned and walked towards the bench, where he once again looked up at Magistrate Zeb.

"Your honor, these four men are not asking you to convict my clients, in their black hearts they are asking you to substantiate their own shame. They are not policemen. They are cowards and criminals. Their hearts have become twisted, until they seek to emulate the very corruption that destroyed them. Their very words are poison. There isn't a single drop of clean blood among the lot of them."

The little lawyer looked down at the ground. For a moment he leaned against the bench for support. He knew he was walking a thin line in a country where the mere mention of human rights violations amounted to treason. Then Naeem seemed to regain his composure and he lifted his face up, not towards Magistrate Zeb, but the portrait of Mr. Jinnah. He pointed at the picture and spoke.

"Your honor, I will not pretend that either of us do not know our country is currently suffering under a heavy hand. It may be true that justice no longer prevails in the land. That is beyond your personal control. But justice must prevail in this individual court," Naeem said passionately.

He pointed at the narcs, then looked back at Zeb.

"If that is justice sitting over there, then truly our country has lost all justice. I urge you, your honor, to listen to the admonitions of your conscience," he said, and turning from the bench, came and sat down.

Outside the court room door we could all hear the sound of men going about the daily business of their lives. Inside Magistrate Zeb's shabby court I could hear the sound of my own heart beating in my chest. I was afraid to look at the judge. He had leaned back in his chair, had both hands spread before him on the bench and looked like he was trying to control himself. I saw him studying the four perjurers who sat exposed before him. Zeb was a wise man, so perhaps he understood that though moral degradation takes an inner effect at once, its outer appearance may be long delayed. Gilani Khan and his co-conspirators were an example of how evil had taken up a position on a vantage ground of worldly power by assuming a fair-seeming disguise of disinterested loyalty to the law. Yet beneath the narcs' sham efforts lay nothing but spite and selfishness. On the outside they had been quick to cling to the letter of the law, but they had gone from being the chaperones of justice to trying to be its sole owners.

Across the room the prosecutor had picked up a pen and was quietly tapping it on his papers. When I caught his eyes, he looked down.

When I glanced at the narcotic agents who had made my life so miserable, my former rage began to drain away. They were exposed for the slummocky black guards they were; Ashgar the blustering bully, Niazi the grubby coward, and Gilani the moral wasteland.

Magistrate Zeb turned to face Ali Muhammad and me. He looked angry and frustrated.

"Despite what appears to be overwhelming evidence in regards to your innocence, I must remand you back to prison until I pass judgment. The witnesses are dismissed. However I will inform you, Inspector Khan that you and your men are to be present when I pass judgment," Zeb said in an authoritative voice. The narcs looked crest fallen.

"Guard," the judge called out, and our jailer started making his way towards us with the all too familiar manacles. The magistrate stood up and began gathering his papers, clearly getting ready to leave. Chairs legs started screeching against the old floor. Shafi, the hotel clerk, practically ran out of the room. I saw Tanvir go up to the bench. He and Zeb had a hurried and whispered conversation, then the judge departed.

The guard was screwing the hated manacle on my left wrist. Ali Muhammad and I stood silent but hopeful. Hiyat Mohammad chose that moment to approach us.

"Thank you for telling the truth," Ali Muhammad told him.

"I am a Muslim. These others are not," he said and pointed with his eyes at the backs of the departing narcs. "This is my country too. Do not be too quick to judge it on what has happened here. The law cannot prevent evil, only avenge it."

While we being locked up, Naeem and Tanvir were huddled together. Message delivered, the prosecutor made his way back towards his own table. Naeem turned to speak to my cellmate and me.

"I think you will be found innocent. Mr. Tanvir has just told me he has asked Magistrate Zeb to discuss the findings of our case in private. Meanwhile, you should be patient a few more days and not lose hope," Naeem said.

Ali had held his hands out to receive the manacles. He smiled at the solicitor and said, "I think I can eat dal a few more times."

"You knew all the time didn't you?" I asked Naeem. "You realized what Gilani Khan was trying to do?"

Naeem looked at Hiyat Mohammad, then back at me.

"After discussing the case with the sergeant we both understood the dangers you were in. We did not think it was fair to raise your hopes. You've both lived in Pakistan long enough to understand that anything could have happened today. I thought it best to prepare you for the worst and work towards the best. The rule of law still works in parts of our

Judicial Murder

country, despite what certain dictators and narcotic's officers think," he said.

"Will Zeb set us free?" Ali Muhammad asked.

"I think so. Even the prosecutor wants to drop the case quietly."

As Ali Muhammad and I walked back to the nest of despair we still called home, I thought how thankful I was for the clever little man and the honest policeman who had stood by us. At last the truth had come out. Once we were inside the Judas gate even the guards on duty seemed to act nicer towards us. Our uniformed escort had told them what had occurred. We were still frisked but it was a routine pat down. The guard knew the only thing of value left to us were our souls. But the feeling had changed. We were all just guys going to different parts of the prison to do our jobs.

Ali Muhammad and I were feeling guardedly optimistic right up until we reached the door of Cell Nine. Sergeant Shafi was inside Char Chuki helping the trusties lock the prisoners down for the night. It was the usual chaos, and believing I was only going to hear it for a few more days, I was feeling almost nostalgic for the world I had slipped into.

When we walked into Cell Nine the horror of where we were slammed us both back into immediate reality.

Raja was kneeling over Hans. The Dutchman had his left eye shut in obvious pain. A large red mark ran down that side of his face. Raja looked up and saw us enter. Without waiting, the boy explained, "Babu came and took Godwin."

"What! Where? To the mental cages?" Ali Muhammad asked in haste.

"No, they said he was being set free," Raja told us.

"Godwin was so damn crazy he wouldn't leave the cell. He got scared and wouldn't stand up," Hans said. "Babu grabbed him and started dragging him out but Godwin locked his fingers around the bars of the cell door."

"He kept screaming he was guilty and needed to be punished. I tried to tell him they were taking him outside but he wouldn't let go of the door," Raja explained.

The Dutchman finished that ugly story I never wanted to hear.

"Ibrahim started smashing Godwin's fingers to make him let go of the bars. Godwin was screaming and begging us not to let them take him. I started yelling and then Babu hit me too."

"They took him soon after you both left for court," Raja said quietly. "I don't think they really let him go free, but no one knows where he is now."

Raja was right. The Tanzanian had no money, no passport, no sanity. His mind had long ago wandered, a victim to his imaginary crimes.

While my guard was down, the insatiable appetite of that accursed place had claimed the most helpless among us.

Godwin was gone, and as the news set in, outside my cell door I heard the music of Pindi Prison marking his departure; the mentals crying in their cages like tortured angels, the leg irons clanking in accompaniment, the men in dirty cells murmuring in soft chorus, and the guards singing "Theek hai," as an aria of pain filled my ears and crushed the heart within my breast.

24
The Seed of Man

The barrier between life and death, good and evil, sane and insane was a thin one in Pakistan. We waited one last time while Magistrate Zeb pondered our fate in sphinx-like silence. In our hearts Ali Muhammad and I realized that all the effort expended on our behalf was balancing on scales seen only by that one man.

On one side rested my father's promise from the military-governor, the honesty of Sergeant Hiyat Mohammad, and Naeem's brilliant maneuvering. Yet we had never received any official confirmation of the governor's support.

We had instead walked back across the road wrapped in chains, still imprisoned in that black hell-hole. Those facts proved the other side of the scale was far from empty. In Pakistan party politics, family ties and hidden pressures often meant more than an honest cop, a smart lawyer, and a vague promise of official help. My friend and I were just two foreigners in the wrong place at the wrong time, with confirmed enemies now openly bent upon our destruction.

The day they finally took us back to Zeb's court we knew nothing, had no feel of what was coming, walked there almost weeping from the tension of not knowing if we were to go free or return to rot in prison until the year 2059.

We were the last to arrive. Tanvir the prosecutor and Naeem were already standing facing the bench. Sergeant Hiyat Mohammad stood on the defense's side of the court. Standing well behind Tanvir were Gilani, Ashgar and Niazi. When we clanked in the sound of the chains brought them around. The look in the narc's eyes told me they had regrouped, if not professionally, at least emotionally. They looked savagely defiant.

The two lawyers had been talking to Magistrate Zeb. He motioned to the guard to bring us before the bench. While the prison official began the lengthy process of unscrewing the manacles, Zeb impatiently began informing the group standing before him of his decision.

Sitting above us in his black robes he looked stern, disapproving and perceptively acute. As the guard pulled the manacles off my wrists I tried to stand straight and not show how scared I was. It seemed like the weight of all Pakistan was resting on my skinny shoulders.

"I have heard the arguments of both parties and perused the case file and evidence carefully. It was the duty of the prosecution to prove its case to the hilt in all circumstances and beyond all doubt, but the prosecution has failed to inspire confidence in its story because of conflicting testimony and numerous inconsistencies," the magistrate read from a statement held in front of him.

"In my opinion there are ample material contradictions in time of occurrence, persons involved in the raiding team, even who was placed where on the hotel site. These contradictions cannot be dismissed lightly. I believe therefore that much of the prosecution's evidence must be weighed very carefully and viewed with ample prudence. The learned prosecutor has argued that any contradictions in the case amounted to nothing more than misunderstandings among the state's witnesses. He went on to state that even if a beating was administered to the defendants, it occurred after the recovery of the heroin powder discovered in their possession, and henceforth has no reflection on the merits of the other elements of the case. However, the recovery of the heroin powder from the defendants was in fact never clearly established," he said.

The magistrate looked up. None of the eight men standing in front of him so much as blinked.

"I found the testimony between the two parties differed sharply. The defense witnesses proved to be independent and provided documentary evidence to verify their claims. The court believes the hotel clerk Shafi was brought into the case to help the prosecution's attempt to corroborate their story. This witness was unable even to identify correctly the accused persons, making his very presence at the scene of the crime doubtful. Adding further damage to Shafi's credibility was the manager's testimony, based on documentary evidence proving to be accurate and authentic. It reduces Shafi's participation to naught and shatters his testimony," Zeb read, then glanced up to observe the look on our collective faces.

He didn't wait for any sign of approval, just looked back down and continued reading from the long typed document he held in both hands.

"The court also had to consider the defense's claim that the defendants had been tortured. This accusation found strength from the evidence given by Dr. Ashraf regarding his findings that the injuries coincided with the time the defendants were unaccounted for. The good doctor's testimony lends full support to this portion of the defense's story," the magistrate said.

Zeb took this opportunity to glance up at the narcotic policemen standing behind us. The look in his eyes was fierce and hostile.

"I therefore agree with the defense that the partial motive in this case was to implicate the defendants falsely, as a means of concealing the uncalled for acts of torture perpetrated against them. The charge that the defendants may have been unjustly accused on account of some annoyance thus cannot be ruled out."

The magistrate turned and faced the state prosecutor. The look on his face was one of elder teacher to over-reaching student. He looked at Tanvir with admonition, not accusation.

The Seed of Man

"The finding of guilt against an accused person cannot be based on probability inferred from association with the evidence of the case. The finding of guilt has to rest firmly and surely on evidence brought on record. In this case inferences cannot take the place of solid proof required for a conviction. From the evidence on record I find the prosecution has not succeeded in proving the charges against the accused persons," Zeb told the prosecutor.

Then the man who held my life in his hand turned and looked at my friend and me. He locked us in his eyes for the space of two breaths, looked behind us towards Inspector Gilani Khan, then brought his gaze back to rest on Ali Muhammad and me.

"It is my belief the defendants were implicated to hide an act of torture. The Federal Investigation Authority has been requested to make a full examination into the behavior of the arresting narcotics officers. Regarding the allegation of torture to the defendants, I do not find the time appropriate to express my opinion on the merits lest I prejudice the inquiry I have ordered. In light of this, as well as the overwhelming evidence presented by the defense, the prosecution has failed to prove its case," the magistrate told us.

He paused, his face telling me much, then he put my heart at ease.

"You have suffered under a cloud of misfortune. I therefore find you both not guilty."

"*Allah karim* (God is merciful)," Naeem said from next to us.

On the other side the prosecutor answered "Amen" quietly.

Before we had time to react jubilantly the magistrate went on to order Sergeant Hiyat Mohammad to return our passports and personal possessions. Magistrate Zeb also instructed the sergeant to issue us temporary papers freeing us on all charges, until he could present us with certified copies of his legal findings of fact.

It seemed as if we were to leave with Hiyat then and there.

Ali Muhammad took the opportunity to ask the magistrate if we could return to the prison to get our possessions. I knew my friend had quickly realized that if we did not go back now, we would have no chance to bid farewell to Hans, Raja and the others. Zeb explained we had to be officially released from the prison and must return anyway in order to complete that brief formality.

His job done, Magistrate Zeb stood up, gave us a brief nod and walked towards the side door leading to his chambers. As I watched him go, it wasn't easy to reconcile that good man with the narcs, masquerading as servants of the law, who had imprisoned us. When I turned to face my tormentors, they were already making their way out the door. If I thought that Gilani Khan, Ashgar Ali and Niazi were in turn going to be hauled before the bar to face justice, I was only betraying my naive American background. Naeem quickly grounded me back in Pakistani reality.

"I thought the magistrate said he was going to investigate them," I said, a sense of outrage creeping into my voice. I saw Ashgar's broad back disappear through the door. Free at last, I wanted to hurl myself after him, to spend my first moments of liberty smashing the bully's skull against the courthouse wall. Instead Ashgar walked carelessly away, ignoring my silent wish that the minions of black Hell would reach up and seize him.

"What about the FIA?" Ali Muhammad asked, voicing my own thoughts.

"Oh Magistrate Zeb is intent when he says he will have them investigated, but they're slippery. I very much doubt if anything will ever come of it," our lawyer told us.

I could have wept with frustration at the thought of the ruthless inspector and his cronies escaping. Then Naeem informed Ali Muhammad and me that being found not guilty had not solved all our own problems.

"You two had better disappear for a while. Get out of the country or least find some quiet place where you can avoid the very real possibility of the wrath of Gilani Khan and his crew."

"Do you think they would dare do anything to us after what's happened?" I asked.

Naeem gave me a look as if I was the village idiot.

"One accident has befallen you already. Now you're their enemies. Who knows what fatal problem you might encounter. This is Pakistan, not America. Few people would ask any questions if both of you simply disappeared."

"Would Chitral be far enough away?" I asked.

"Nothing any less remote will be safe until this blows over in a few months."

I gave my friend a telling look.

Hiyat Mohammad choose that moment to walk over and shake our hands. The stern sergeant congratulated us, then informed us he was to accompany us to Pindi Prison. He would inform the DSP of the verdict and oversee our release. The guard had joined us and Hiyat was obviously ready to return to the prison, when I remembered Naeem.

"What about your fee?"

"Five thousand rupees for the defense. Seven hundred thirty seven rupees in expenses," he told me, and handed me his business card and a hundred-rupee note. "Use this to come to my office after you get out. We'll conclude our business in private."

It was a ridiculous amount, about $327.00 American. Before I could protest or offer more the little overweight man told me to hold my tongue.

"The injustice done here was to my own country."

We walked back to the jail as free men coming to confirm our departure. Pindi Prison lay there basking in the March sunlight, a vile,

The Seed of Man

shameless pus of corruption, glorying in her arrogant obviousness, smug in the knowledge she had successfully escaped history's notice.

Though our legal trial was over, our emotional ties with Pindi Prison were not yet concluded. Sergeant Hiyat Mohammad walked beside us, ordered the Judas gate opened and then took us directly to the DSP's office. The big man congratulated us and ordered the prison register brought. Because so many of the prisoners were illiterate, we were required to place an inky version of our left thumb prints on the page. By the time the large book was sent for, an ink pad produced and the procedure completed, nearly an hour had elapsed. We were now technically free men. Hiyat left to await our arrival at the nearby police station, where we had met him that dark night more than five months ago.

The DSP ordered one of the guards to accompany us to Char Chuki. For the last time we stepped back into what had been our small world and discovered news of our innocence had spread with exceptional speed. Outside the gate of Char Chuki Sergeant Shafi shook our hands in congratulations. Inside the gate, Babu said nothing but burned me with his eyes. Ali Muhammad and I didn't ask anyone's permission, just started straight towards Cell Nine. When I reached the courtyard of Cell Seven, I told Ali to go ahead without me.

The Dada didn't seem surprised to see me and this time I didn't ask permission to come in. Shonni was busy preparing the important man's dinner over the little charcoal stove. I went over and sat down next to the Pakistani Mafia boss. The clever old crook looked pleased. He gave me a smile and patted my leg.

"The cat weeps that the mice have escaped," he said.

"I have made a few enemies both inside these walls and without," I admitted.

"You got lucky because you're *Angrez* (English)."

"American."

"Same thing."

For a second I got a glimpse inside his cool exterior and saw the longing we shared for a blessing previously taken for granted, the liberty of drawing a free breath. He sensed my intuitive intrusion and lit a cigarette in order to avoid my eyes and keep his hands busy.

"I came to ask if I could send you money. I want to make sure Hans and Raja are taken care of. I know if you handle the funds they will have food and charcoal."

"Yes, the Dutchman could use your help. His government doesn't care if he lives or dies. Our own government understands that. He will stay here a while longer. No one will kill him because he is a *ferenghi*. Of course he could die of disease but then everyone runs that risk here. If he can get decent food he will probably survive until his release."

When I mentioned helping my other cellmate the Dada waved away the suggestion with a flick of his fat hand.

"That bazaar bug was released earlier today, soon after you left for court in fact. I believe you'll find him lingering outside the main gate. At least that's where I told him to stay hidden," the Dada told me.

Before I could ask how or why this had come about the older man explained.

"Surely you now know crime doesn't matter in here. The question is not guilt, only whether a man can afford justice in General Zia's Pakistan. Most of the ignorant men in this prison don't even understand that they have rights. They wait for years until some family member bribes the DSP or some lowly court official makes their case go away. Only in cases like yours or mine, where the government takes official notice, is a quiet departure out of the question," the Dada said.

"And Raja?"

"The police only threw him in here to teach him a lesson, but apparently once he was inside they forgot about him. There was nothing holding him here except the money to pay his bribe to leave."

"Did someone pay his bribe?" I asked.

The Dada just shrugged his shoulders and laughed.

"That is an indelicate question. Besides, he would never have made a good servant," he said and gave me a knowing look. As if to defend his charitable actions he hastened to add "It didn't cost me anything. The DSP owed me a favor. In fact I told him Raja was going with you. I could have thrown in Shonni, but he's so useful."

At the mention of his name, the servant glanced over his shoulder and the two men exchanged a tender look.

I reached over and took the Dada's right hand in both of mine, and without regret squeezed it hard. I knew his reputation was well deserved. He had lied and cheated and committed all sorts of heinous acts in the course of his villainous life. Yet the overwhelming evil of Pindi Prison had shown the Dada that he had met his match. I believed that what little life was left to him he would spend differently than if he were to live to leave those walls, which he never did.

"I am proud to call you my friend," I told him.

He shrugged his obese shoulders, pretending to ignore my affection.

"It is fate that we met in this place. Some of us will live to leave. Some of us will not. The mentals will eventually all die in their cold stone cages and then be replaced by other sweepings from the streets of our country. Some of us will learn nothing from our time here," he explained. But then uncharacteristically he said, "Allah is very wise. He has ordained that all men must die. This way, in time, even their bitter memories will fade and die too. You should leave your bitter regrets here with me, Asadullah. "

I shook my head as if in agreement, silently unsure if that was possible. Nevertheless the Dada smiled.

"When I get out we'll have dinner together," he said, trying to keep up a brave face.

The Seed of Man

We both knew we would have dinner, but never together.

"I must go," I told him. "I wish you well."

When I reached Cell Nine I found Ibrahim the trusty had already ordered Ali Muhammad to grab his few things and leave. Afternoon lockup was due to take place and Sergeant Shafi wanted us out of Char Chuki before it occurred. Hans was waiting, all alone in the tiny room I too had called home. We both knew the Dutchman would enjoy the luxury of the empty cell for only a day or two. As soon as I came in he handed me an envelope.

"Will you make sure this gets mailed?"

I saw "Greta von Dueker" and "Village-Breda, The Netherlands," written on the front. Before I could venture an answer or ask any questions, Hans revealed he had a wife and a two-year-old son he had never seen, back in his homeland. Then, ruthlessly squashing any sense of self-pity, the little smuggler confided he still had a single ace up his tattered sleeve. Unbeknownst to the customs police, there was still a large amount of undiscovered hashish secreted inside a carton of cigarettes, located in Hans' suitcase at the airport police lockup. The scamp put on that cocky smile of his and assured me he would fool them all yet.

I had come back to Cell Nine to say goodbye and to get a single important slip of paper. Reaching under the burlap blanket which had so recently wrapped me, I retrieved what I sought. One side had my writing on it. The other side however was still blank. I located one of our precious ball point pens. Placing the paper against the wall, I put the Dutchman's hand on top the blank side, then traced its outline in order to take with me some memory of my friend, my *handiwal* (cellmate) who I had shared food and danger with. That finished, I explained to Hans how I had made arrangements with the Dada to help him. Finally I looked straight at him, pushing my way past his Teutonic bravado and told him, "You've got to hang on in here. I won't forget you. I'll be back to make sure you're all right."

For a second Hans weakened, then he regained his composure. He nodded his head, and told me in that gravelly Marlene Dietrich voice, "Go on, get the hell out of the Zia Haq hotel before they change their minds."

Then we hugged hard and I walked through the cell door for the last time.

I found Babu waiting for me at the gate leading out of Char Chuki. All around me it seemed like any other day inside Pindi Prison. The hundred or more men crowded in the nearby holding cell were filling the barn-sized room with their noisy chatter. I could hear the mentals yelling from their cages in the back of Char Chuki. Crows were screaming overhead. It looked and smelled and sounded like the place I knew so well.

"Go," Babu ordered abruptly, and pushed open the gate that had held me captive.

Khyber Knights

I weighed the evil old man before me. I knew he still controlled the lives of Hans, Yusuf, even the Dada. To antagonize him meant risking his retaliation against them. But I was a free man. Through the grace of God I had escaped his foul clutches.

"If anything happens to the Dutchman I will hear of it," I told him in a hard voice.

"And?" Babu asked arrogantly.

His eyes were dead black things, reflecting his spiritual nothingness. I stared at him, this warm blooded ghoul who feasted daily on other men's misery.

"Only a dead man does not fear the knife," I warned him, then shoved my way past.

Behind me I heard the key rattle and the tongue of the lock grating, telling me I was no longer a member of that part of the world. I made my solitary way down the long dirt road that led towards the massive blue gate of Pindi Prison. For a few more minutes I was engulfed by this symbol of power over man's natural goodness. All around me I could hear the daily sounds of the Bastille of Pakistan, a place where cruelty was as common as dust.

In my hand I clutched only that single scrap of paper reminding me of my sojourn there. On one side was Hans' hand print, on the other was the poem I had written the night he became so sick in our cell. It read;

Cell 9 - Block 4
Behind, steel door.
Leg irons, so near,
first sound, I hear.
With sun, comes day,
once more, I pay,
The cost, so dear,
my soul, I fear.
No hope, all pain,
inside, my brain.
Dear God, why me,
please hear, my plea.
Sun down, day goes,
night brings, the woes.
Once more, I sleep,
alone, and weep.
Behind, steel door,
Cell 9 - Block 4.

As I neared the Judas gate I knew the wind of Allah blew the seed of man across the world, some to fall on fertile ground and blossom, some

to fall on stony ground and wither. The wind, that herald of change, had come to blow me on.
   At last my heart was free.
   Now I needed the courage to follow it.

Part Three
The Journey

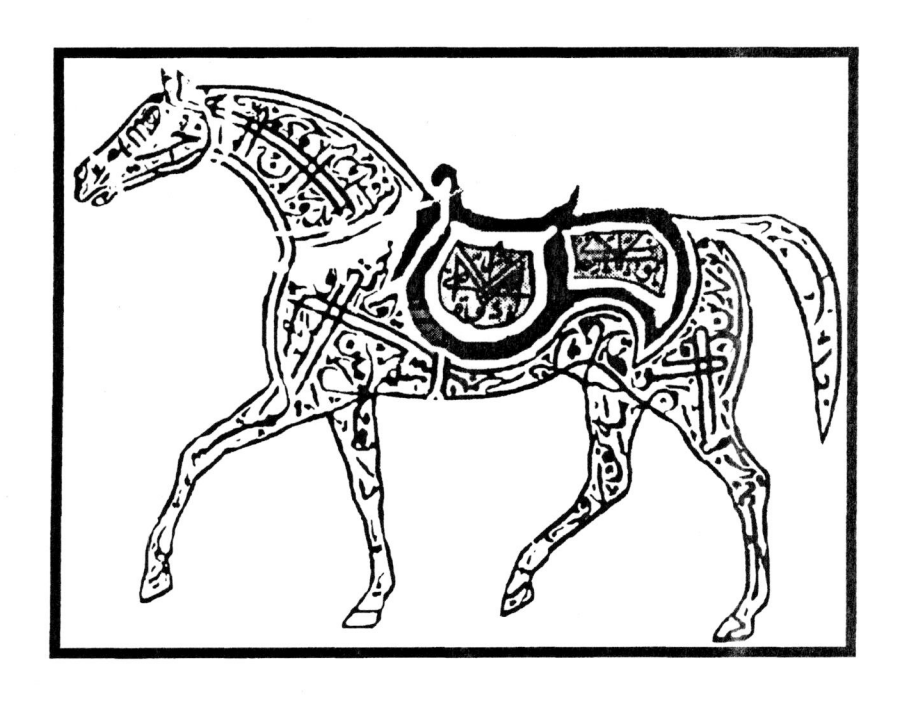

25
Kiss Me Deadly

Raja Bahadur Khan, brave son of the Afridi Pathans, was afraid, and it was Ali Muhammad's fault.

Despite the warm night the young tribesman felt a chill of apprehension as the two men made their way through a section of the city of Lahore. The hour was well past midnight and yet the narrow street Ali Muhammad had led them down was crowded chock-a-block. Excited men from all parts of Pakistan were jostling and chattering, pushing their way through what passed as a Mardi Gras atmosphere in Pakistan. Floating over their heads was the sound of passionate music emanating from a host of small open-faced rooms lining both sides of the long lane. Thick sweet smells, incense, wood smoke, hashish, and cloying perfumes, swirled invisibly over Raja's head and made the night air intoxicating. It was true the younger man knew little enough about the geography of his native country, yet even in his small village the name of this neighborhood, "Hira Mandi" the diamond market, had enjoyed a reputation for exotic wickedness.

As Ali Muhammad lead Raja through the crowd, the naive young tribesman was shocked at what he saw. Inside the rooms lining the crowded street, Raja saw beautiful women, known as nautch girls, dancing wildly in time to live music. As they swayed and stamped their bare feet, excited audiences of men threw handfuls of rupees over the heads of the famous dancing girls of Hira Mandi. To Raja, who had seldom spoken to a woman he was not directly related to, the sight of such shameless behavior shook him to the core of his peasant soul.

The young tribesman stuck to Ali Muhammad's side like an insecure child clinging to a errant uncle, for all around them was the smell of lust and danger. Since our release from Pindi Prison three weeks earlier, Raja had been in almost constant attendance on either Ali Muhammad or me. A quick visit to his home village had laid his mother's worries to rest. He was glad to report to her that he was now employed by two foreigners who were undertaking a long journey with horses. With honest wages in his pocket, and his previous trouble a well-kept secret from his prying family, Raja should have been happy.

He had not counted on Ali Muhammad's zest for life, nor the older man's desire to explore Hira Mandi the night before I met them. My renegade American friend liked what he saw. The raucous music swirling around Ali Muhammad was the perfect backdrop to Hira Mandi's edgy tableau of beautiful women, carefree musicians, excited patrons, street vendors, beggars, cops, and fortune tellers. To Ali Muhammad, Hira Mandi was a hitherto undiscovered treasure from another age, its overt sensuality reminding him of the sexy hospitality of the southern city of his birth. In those crowded lanes Ali discovered an exotic place free of the inhibitions of the new Puritanism raging across Pakistan. The fabled neighborhood was the last remnant of the glittering era of the Mughal emperors and Ali Muhammad loved it.

When two uniformed policemen walked towards my friends, swinging lathis and perusing the crowd for easy marks or signs of public intoxication, Raja wanted to run for cover. Ali coolly ignored the cops, making his way through the crowd as if he were a personal friend of General Zia. My friend was enjoying the sensation of being a free man. He breathed in the carnival atmosphere and cheerfully disregarded any hint of trouble. For as anyone could have told him such a possibility was only a heartbeat away in Hira Mandi.

Raja avoided the searching eyes of the cops and prayed that the foreigner who now employed him knew what he was about.

Lahore, the city known as the pearl of the Punjab, was showing the young tribesman the last traces of a dying cultural practice. Since the glory days of the great Mughal emperors, men from all over the Indian subcontinent had come to admire that city's beautiful women. For more than four hundred years girls had been dancing and sleeping with men who made the pilgrimage to Hira Mandi. The girls had captured hearts and thrones, for a price. They had been called courtesans, whores, concubines, and nautch girls. For one more small breath of time they were still to be seen in Hira Mandi.

The famous nautch girls had now been declared officially extinct.

General Zia, the prudish president, had ordered the famous Diamond Bazaar closed down.

According to plan I was in the capital of Islamabad that night. I had gone there to receive the weapons permits we had applied for. With one free night to spend in Lahore, before I met them the following morning, my bored American friend had brought young Raja out on in search of a fandango. It was to be a night-time stroll, nothing more. Ali had long known of the existence of Hira Mandi from friends in Peshawar. They had told him racy stories about the nautch girls. Wanting to investigate the truth of those ribald tales, Ali Muhammad had brought Raja along so they could get a glimpse of Hira Mandi before it passed into memory.

The great Mughal emperors, who once ruled all India, had cherished the city of Lahore. Each of them lavished treasures and riches on her, but none more so than the famous architect king Shah Jahan. The list of his 17th century works reads like a dream created from stone, including the Palace of Mirrors, the Pearl Mosque and the Taj Mahal. He adorned Lahore, the city he loved, with the magnificent Shalimar Gardens. With its acres of lush greenery, sparkling fountains, and alternating pools of red sandstone and white marble, the Shalimar Gardens were said to be the physical embodiment of landscaped perfection.

Lahore had thus always been a home for beauty, art, poetry, jewels and above all, love. When partition had separated India and Pakistan in 1947, the larger of the two countries had received the lion's share of the

Kiss Me Deadly

loot. The Muslims had been content to come away with the home of romance.

The fabled city had hosted not only the world's largest diamond, the 229 carat Koh-I-Noor, the Mountain of Light, but the seedy side of life as well. Before the Islamic crackdown by the current military dictator, the narrow streets, overhanging balconies, the tiny courtyards, and winding alleys had welcomed liquor shops, gambling salons, opium dens, trained bears, puppet shows, wandering faqirs, fortune tellers, medical quacks, illusionists and musicians. From midnight until dawn the old city enjoyed a second, more tawdry, illicit intercourse for those daring enough to enter her streets and seek out her secrets. It was not all dirt and discourse, rental romance and shady escapade. No less a personage than the Mughal prince Jahangir had fallen in love and left his heart in Hira Mandi. Having seen the enchanting dancing girl Anarkali (Pomegranate Bud), the young man's heart was shattered with desire.

As often happened in those winding avenues, fate was unkind. Emperor Akbar had his son's beautiful lover built into a city wall, alive. The devastated prince, who became a king in his own right, later erected an imposing monument at the site of her execution. Anarkali passed into legend as the most famous beauty of Hira Mandi.

Despite the legends, Raja had already seen enough. Soon after arriving Ali Muhammad had lead him into one of the dancing boutiques. The room was tiny, barely big enough to host two musicians and a couple of second-rate dancing girls. While one man thumped out a rhythm on the tabla drums, the other had twiddled the keys on the squeeze box harmonium. The musicians sat on the linoleum floor, filling the room with pulsing Punjabi music, while the two nautch girls danced for the enjoyment of the men from Peshawar.

The women looked like sisters. In their mid-twenties, both were fleshy, flashy, and wide-hipped, as befitted the common description of beautiful women. They had long thick black hair that reached to their waists. Their cheeks were rouged, their lips red. They also shared a taste for flashy silk shalwar kameez. Raja told them apart by the simple fact that one wore hot pink, the other dark blue. They looked jaded and bored, indifferent to men as a species, unless they were rich.

Both nautch girls were barefoot and wore a pair of large leather cuffs buckled around their ankles. The cuffs contained six rows of small brass bells. As they sang, twirled and danced to the music, the girls slapped their feet, ringing the bells and adding to the atmosphere. If Ali Muhammad enjoyed it he never told Raja. As custom dictated the renegade American stood up during the dance and threw a handful of rupees over the girls heads.

As soon as the covetous tarts saw the notes Ali Muhammad had flung were only one rupees they lost their enthusiasm. They were polite enough to finish the dance, but they were running a business and had little interest in entertaining two Pathan hicks. For with his turban and Peshawari-style sandals, my friend Ali Muhammad now looked just as much a son of the Frontier as Raja did.

His curiosity satisfied, Ali had lead a relieved Raja back onto the street. Hira Mandi was no longer supposed to exist officially. The all-knowing eye of General Zia had passed a decree outlawing its continued existence and then moved on to more pressing matters. The local police, dreading the loss of the illegal income they profited from, kept prolonging the inevitable. An open secret hung in the air as Raja and Ali Muhammad began walking back towards their hotel. A little dancing and music would be tolerated temporarily, but the days of open prostitution and beautiful courtesans were now a thing of the past.

When my companions came to the end of the Hira Mandi neighborhood they agreed that a cup of tea was in order before retiring. An all-night chaikhana was only a few steps away. Within moments they were sitting on the floor drinking their warm sweet chai.

It was a cheap, grimy place. The clientele was what you would expect to see at three a.m. but these things did not concern them at all. To Raja and Ali Muhammad, who had slept on the dank floor of Pindi Prison, any food was delicious, any chai was nectar and the freedom of walking through the forbidden delights of Hira Mandi had filled their hearts with a welcoming warmth. They found no fault with life that night. This smudgy old chaikhana was luxurious compared to what they were used to. Even Raja had to admit that a spring-time night in Lahore was suddenly delicious.

They were discussing the night's heady proceedings when an old man approached them. Raja, who had been in prison long enough to develop an instant sense for his fellow man, felt a foreboding revulsion. He barely replied when the elderly fellow asked if he could sit down. Ali Muhammad on the other hand waved at the floor next to him as if it were a marble palace, not a tea-stained strip of linoleum.

An additional cup was called for. Polite conversation made its course. Eventually the old codger got down to business. He pointed to a woman sitting across the room. His wife sat bundled up in a chador, leaning up against the wall in an effort to remain inconspicuous. They were both heroin addicts the old man admitted openly.

"My wife and I have been slaves of the powdered death for nine years," he told my friends. "We can't go home to the *Sarhad* (Northwest Frontier) with this shame on us."

Seeing two men dressed like fellow Pathan tribesmen he had approached them in the hope he might render them a favor in exchange for a small gratuity.

"I know where there are beautiful Pathan girls, not like these fat Punjabi *meteezas* (sluts) who chill the heat in a man's blood," he whispered.

When the addict saw the look of skepticism on Raja's face he turned towards the older man and made his pitch.

"These girls are **Kaka Khail** (Pathan tribe) and are like delicate pigeons to a tribesman's hungry heart."

Raja leaned in and whispered to Ali, "Be careful, this old sinner is a *dalla* (pimp)." But fate had already interjected her finger into Ali Muhammad's life.

Against his judgment Raja had followed Ali and the old man back out into the dimly lighted streets of Lahore. A ten minute walk brought them into a darkened neighborhood. Their guide then turned down a dead-end dirt alley, went up to a large set of metal gates and quietly knocked. From its darkened exterior the place looked no different than any of the other houses in the old suburban district. As they stood waiting Raja had told himself that as a ferenghi Ali Muhammad must know that this was safe or he would not be risking their recently-won freedom. It was inconceivable to him that his American companion would take them into harm's way with the Hudood Act hanging over their heads like an executioner's axe.

Later, after his life was irrevocably altered by what happened that night, Ali Muhammad admitted to me that he had had no clear idea of the risk he and Raja were running. General Zia's martial law regime had imposed laws that were ripping apart Pakistani society. Under the "blasphemy trap" a person could be punished with death or life in prison for defiling the name of the Prophet Muhammad. Under Section 294 PPC of the Pakistani Public Code it was illegal for men and women to embrace publicly. The Hudood Act forbidding *zina* (illicit intercourse) specified that both parties were to be imprisoned. Obviously visiting a whore-house was illegal but Ali Muhammad had always been a bold traveler in more ways than one.

For centuries Islam had flourished throughout the land known as Pakistan. During that time the people were considered personally very religious even if they seldom participated in public outpourings of Islamic fervor. Now a general was dictating what determined "Islamic" behavior. Though there had never been any doubt as to the immorality of participating in illicit sexual relationships, the loose and easy days of the Mughal emperors were a thing of the past. Whereas before a man's sins were a private affair, under General Zia's regime such behavior was not just a sin, it was a life-threatening crime for consenting non-married adults to enjoy consensual sex.

Hira Mandi's past was dead. The legendary neighborhood's future appeared bleak.

No matter.

When the gate opened, any law, old or new, lay behind my friends.

The old man entered with no hesitation. Ali Muhammad followed. Raja brought up the rear, more afraid of being left behind than of going on. The young Pathan boy found himself inside a typical brick floored courtyard. The one-story house inside the walls was laid out in the shape of the letter L. Various doorways, all hung with pastel cloth curtains, faced onto the courtyard. A teenage boy shut the gate behind them. The sound of the bolt being driven home startled Raja and made him jump with apprehension.

At the sight of his nervousness the three girls sitting on the charpoys in front of the young Afridi began giggling. He was shocked at the sight of them. One was actually smoking a cigarette. The other two were whispering behind their hands, obviously about him.

Nothing in his life had prepared Raja for the sight of those three women. Every molecule of his being, plus the genetic memory of uncounted generations of Pathan ancestors and the laws of tribal custom engraved in fire on the surface of his heart, said that what his eyes were seeing could not exist. The girls were Pathan prostitutes. If Raja had seen a fifty foot genie sitting on the charpoy he could not have been more shocked, because before that moment the Afridi boy would have scoffed at the idea that either mythical creature, genies or Pathan prostitutes, existed.

Everything in Raja's world revolved around the strict observance of *pukhtunwali*, the code of honor observed by Pathans. The underlying bedrock of that code said life without honor was not worth living. Honor demanded the strict maintenance of sexual propriety. Complete chastity among a man's female relatives was essential. Only by ensuring the purity and good repute of his mother, daughters, sisters and wife could a man ensure his own honor. Thus women in the Pathan world were rigidly restricted to private family compounds. They were so jealously possessed by their men that even an innocent exchange of glances would mean death for both offending parties. Custom dictated that a man who broke the Pathan sexual taboo be executed by either his father or uncle. A woman who was compromised, willingly or not, was executed by her father or brother. Thus the honor of both families was thereby cleansed of any shame.

Raja was not merely shocked to see the three beautiful Pathan whores. He was stunned to discover that such a thing could exist in his well-ordered world.

While Ali Muhammad and the old man talked in whispered tones, the Afridi boy stood rooted in place. In Raja's village a man caught staring at a woman, even a woman completely clad in a burkha, was begging to be killed. The mere act of filling your eyes with the beauty of a female was forbidden. And though Raja knew in his heart that the beauty sitting before him was *haram* (forbidden), he suddenly didn't care.

These whores were not like the women of his village, who married at fifteen, bore a child every year thereafter, were old by thirty, grandmothers at forty and withered crones by sixty. Those women, his own mother, his grandmother, every Pathan woman he knew of, endured lives strictly regulated by purdah. They were never allowed to visit the village shop unless accompanied by a responsible male relative. Raja's own mother had taught him the Pushtu proverb, "A woman's place is in the home or in the grave."

He knew from experience that during the 32 years of his uncle's marriage, the older man had never once allowed Raja's aunt to visit the village shop lest it bring shame on the family. His uncle bragged in the

Kiss Me Deadly

hamlet that during the long course of their marriage his wife had never left the house unattended, "even to buy salt."

The only thing the attractive women sitting in front of him shared with Raja's aunt was their common female anatomy. If someone had whispered to him that these laughing creatures had fallen from a star Raja would have instantly believed it. They weren't women as he understood the word, they were wild flowers. They were called Naheed, Sanjeena and Aesha. They should have had names like Peaceful Night, Earthly Pleasure, and Garden of Discovery.

All the concepts he had seen instilled in the village women, fear, subservience, chastity, and labor, lay lost with Raja's innocence outside the gate. These women looked him in the eye as equals, silently informing him they had different functions and responsibilities in life than any woman he had ever seen or heard of. He was unnerved but he wasn't leaving.

The sound of a curtain being slung open brought his attention back towards the house. Walking slowly towards them was a woman of obvious authority. If left to his own devices Raja would have been adrift at that moment, unable to proceed emotionally or financially.

Fate and Ali Muhammad interceded.

Like the majority of American men his age, my friend had been involved in a number of fleeting loves. The Age of Aquarius had thrown open the door to sexual exploration and the former Beau Fontaine had long ago passed through that portal in search of happiness. He had dallied lightly. He had loved deeply. He had both dispatched and received the message of heartbreak. In his raw youth he had been inexhaustible, full of vigor. The beds he had explored in his world-wide travels had hosted women of different colors, races, and religions. Those women had treated him with the same casual approach he showed to them. Now in his late thirties, the creeping realization had dawned on him that the mystery of sex had been muted into a matter-of-fact blandness which often lead to promiscuity.

Ali Muhammad balanced this unwelcome knowledge with the rationalization that he was no libertine, for in all his loves, however flimsy or short lived, there was always the lilt of romantic hope. A vague but insistent instinct whispered to him that the frightful isolation which surrounded his wandering, unhappy heart could be laid to rest if he met a woman who could forge his soul in the depths of her fiery love. He was a fallen catholic that night, desperately wanting to regain his faith in the rapture of the heart, when Shaheen walked across the courtyard and into his life.

The musician from Peshawar was no fool. He had seen a legion of women, both pretty and plain, during the course of his roving life. This woman's beauty had no match from Tehran to Delhi.

She was in her late twenties, with sharp cheek bones, warm wheat colored skin, and brilliant eyes sparkling like two black diamonds. A tad more than five feet tall, her delicate bone structure and full bosom was hidden inside a white satin shalwar kameez. Even from across the courtyard her presence was magnetic and mesmerizing.

My friend watched as his lodestone glided towards him with the deadly, sensuous grace of a female panther. She was drying her long, wet, inky black ringlets on a towel. She had obviously just emerged from her bath. Her bare feet made no more than a whisper as she made her way directly to him. She stopped within arm's reach and looked up into his eyes. There wasn't a hint of subservience in any atom of her being for here was a heart-stopping star who only shone at midnight.

Without looking, she tossed the towel towards the three girls on the charpoys as was her queenly right. Like the old man, they had grown silent at her approach. The dalla *(pimp)* was quiet out of greed, the young whores out of jealously. With all the allurements, all the silks, even all the jewels of Lahore at their disposal, the three whores knew in their tortured souls that they could never compete with this woman's resplendent beauty.

Ali Muhammad's mind was still trying to register the details of this creature's appearance when he began to feel intoxicated. He shook his head, thinking he had imagined he was smelling perfume. Then he saw she had woven long strands of jasmine into her hair. The tiny white blossoms were threaded on string and lay intertwined in her jet black ringlets like angel's kisses. Before he could speak she slowly smiled at him. The effect was as if the moon had arisen for a second time. This was a woman who knew her effect on men. She was accustomed to being both admired and desired.

Then she laughed, a warm, comfortable laugh that told him to be at his ease. She flew down from the lofty throne where her glamour had first placed her and gave him a saucy, reassuring smile, as if to tell him that she was his instant friend and sympathized with the urgent secret only the two of them knew.

The moment she saw that they shared a silent understanding, the air snapped as she took total control of everyone within the sound of her voice. She instructed Ali Muhammad to give the old man 100 rupees. My friend withdrew his wallet and did as he was told. Before the aged heroin addict could begin to express his thanks, the young boy guarding the gate had politely ushered him outside. Naheed, the whore who had been smoking a cigarette, choose that moment to get up and walk over.

"I'll take this one," she informed the woman in white. Raja was too shy to say he would have preferred one of the others. The courtesan in front of him was not as beautiful as Ali's but any water to put out a fire he reasoned. When Naheed took his hand and tossed her head towards the rooms, the young tribesman followed her meekly.

Ali Muhammad didn't have to be told to follow. The woman in white asked him, "Well," indicating with her head that my friend could choose one of the other two if he so wished.

The words seemed to stick in his throat when he said, "I want you."

She smiled as if to say, "Of course you do."

He followed her across the courtyard and entered her room.

"Even with all the jewels of Lahore at their disposal, the other whores knew they could never compete with Shaheen's beauty. This was a woman who knew her effect on men. She was accustomed to being both desired and enjoyed, for a price."

Kiss Me Deadly

There was a charpoy against the wall. A thick quilt covered it. A pillow rested at its head. On the wall at the end of the bed was a single shelf. Her clothes were folded and stacked there. Two simple chairs made up the rest of the decor. Everything was so plainly functional it suddenly left Ali Muhammad feeling apprehensive and embarrassed. In all his many travels, both physical and emotional, he had never paid for his love.

He heard her flick the curtain closed, then turned to face her.

"What is your name?," he asked, in a bid for time.

"Shaheen."

"Shaheen," he repeated softly.

"Three hundred rupees," she told him bluntly, interrupting his thoughts with the details of the matter at hand.

"Is that for all night?" he asked naively.

"Stupid *ferenghi* (foreigner)," she said laughing but without any note of derision. Despite his clothes and his excellent command of Pushtu she had known he was not a Pathan.

She held out her thin hand. He gave her 600 rupees for both him and Raja. Turning her back, she reached up to the shelf, hiding the money there among her things. Ali Muhammad took the opportunity to take off his vest, making sure he folded his wallet and passport well inside. Feeling nervous, he shoved the vest deep under the pillow, then turned around to find her standing, waiting.

She was suddenly so close he could smell the jasmine in her hair.

"You are my first foreigner," she admitted, her curiosity obviously aroused. "Where are you from?"

"America."

The name did nothing to impress her. She was concerned only with the present, not some dim geographical cliché' utterly without meaning or significance in her life.

"Ah-mare-ee-kah," she said quietly, forming the word slowly like an exotic fruit on her tongue.

Ali Muhammad had enjoyed many women. He had spent years in the East, but this was forbidden, this was dangerous, and Shaheen was beautiful. Looking at her he found himself short of breath. For an instant he worried he would not be able to perform, but at the same time he felt a consuming hunger for the woman. He couldn't believe he could buy her beauty.

Unsure of the ground he followed the customs of his youth. He reached out and placed his hands on her shoulders. They were narrow. He could feel the delicate bones under the smooth white satin. He gently pulled her towards him, then leaning over began to kiss her.

She instantly pulled her face away.

"No! Don't do that, its dirty! Don't they teach you in your country that we use our mouth to say the name of Allah?" she told him in reproach.

Shaheen may have sold her love but she had her rules.

He stood transfixed, uncertain how to proceed.

"What do you wait for?" she asked Ali Muhammad, giving him a quizzical look. Realizing she must help the ignorant foreigner unschooled in the ways of love, the courtesan reached down and put her hand on top of his manhood, holding it with hard, unembarrassed fingers. It was painful and threatened to spill under the pressure of her experienced hand.

All hesitation vanished. He reached down and pulled her kameez over her head, exposing her full ripe breasts. Her nipples were purple and dark and stood up to meet his gaze. This time his mouth couldn't be stopped.

"You are a crazy man," she murmured and pulled him towards the bed. She lay on her back and her eyes invited him to follow. He wanted nothing then but to be inside her. He tugged at her loose pants. They slid off revealing she was clean shaven, pubic hair being considered a defilement among Muslims. The sight drove him to madness. In an instant he had tossed his own shirt across the room and stepped out of his native trousers. She murmured at the sight of him. Ali couldn't tell if it was the truth or simply professional courtesy. He no longer cared.

Ali felt himself shoving at the door of her pleasure. Then he was within her trench of fire. She cried, "*Whyee, whyee*, (Oh, oh)," and panting and shoving came up to meet him. The scent of jasmine was in his nose and the feel of her wet hair was against his face. He felt her digging her sharp nails into his back. Then he exploded, better than the first time, deeper than ever before. Every drop of his soul flooded into her and she moaned softly and took it.

Within moments they had consummated the act. No foreplay. No mandatory dinners and movies. Just raw primitive sex unlike anything he had ever experienced in his life. He could feel her heat gripping his manhood and he wanted to stay. But she gently pushed him off and then got up. Her abrupt actions startled him. She pulled on her top and then, looking in a small mirror, began fixing her hair.

For Shaheen it was over. For Ali Muhammad looking at her only confirmed that he was still drunk with desire, a victim of her witchcraft. If he had brought more money he would have demanded more time.

"How old are you?" he asked her.

"Leave it," she said and stooping near a bucket of water quickly began washing herself.

Outside near the gate, Raja waited patiently. The whores had gone to bed and only Usman the gate boy waited to keep him company. Reaching into his shirt pocket, my young Afridi friend took out a packet of *naswar*. He opened the little bag, pinched off a chunk of the strong snuff and placed it inside his cheek.

Unbeknownst to Raja, his own experience had been more indicative of the average customer. Encounters between the sexes, even in a city as historically notorious as Lahore, were usually restricted to a few wistful, sidelong glances. Unlike neighboring India, with its centuries-old traditions of the Kama Sutra and other forms of sexual knowledge, Pakistan was the epitome of prim propriety. In a country where almost all marriages were arranged, husbands were expected to provide children and wealth, not love. Men came there, to the brothel, for the briefest of rendezvous. Neither Raja, nor the courtesan Naheed, had undressed. It had taken but a few moments for the Pathan boy to attain satisfaction with the woman. Though inexperienced, Raja had made no sound.

Not wishing to expose his own innocence before the younger Usman, Raja spit out a green stream of naswar juice, then acting like an old hand, he told the gate boy, "She made a great deal of noise but I was aware that she was only pretending to enjoy an ecstasy of her own."

The boy looked at Raja like he was a moron.

"What do you expect for 300 rupees?"

My Pathan cellmate sat in silence. His young soul told him he had only attained release with the woman, that there was some deeper satisfaction still missing. He was wondering if his curiosity would now cast him straight down into *Jehanum* (Hell).

"*Astaferullah* (God forbid)," he thought. Touching his earlobes with his right hand, he said, "*Toba, toba*, (repent, repent)," softly to himself.

The gate boy scoffed. He had seen plenty of sinners vow to lead righteous lives, after they had sampled the goods of his mistress's bordello.

"*Neeshta khedee* (something is better than nothing)," Usman told Raja, without being asked.

Shaheen snapped open the curtain with a practiced flick of her hand. Ali Muhammad, now fully clothed, was adjusting his turban. His previous worries about being robbed had disappeared. The courtesan had lit a cigarette and was leaning against the door way, waiting, smiling. She was beautiful, sexy, dangerous, corrupt.

"Next time don't bring a *dalla* (pimp)," she told her foreign customer.

Looking at Shaheen Ali Muhammad's heart melted. He didn't have to ask her how she knew there would be a next time.

The American and Raja left.

They walked through the streets, making their long way back to the hotel room they had left a lifetime ago. The smell of dawn was in the air. They passed silently through the sleeping city, together, apart, each lost in the mysteries of what they had encountered. Raja was unimpressed and relieved to be away.

Ali Muhammad was overwhelmed. If he had closed his eyes he could not have shut out what he felt. The memory of the exquisite woman was seared into his mind. Suddenly his dry existence, the loneliness, the big empty house in Peshawar, the denial of love, the agony of the months in prison, threatened to embarrass him in front of the younger man. He choked off the thoughts that had almost brought a cry of pain to his throat.

Overhead the night air had a trace of life. Doves and hoopoes were gently singing in the trees lining the street. A drowsy chaikhana still hosted a few patrons. The aromatic fumes of tobacco drifted over from a bubbling hookah. Sleepy gossip floated across as Ali Muhammad and Raja walked by.

As he made his way through Lahore, Ali knew his world would never be the same. The glowing coal of Shaheen's memory had fallen deep into his breast and burned her name into his heart. A hunger for her body was now as much a part of him as the color of his eyes. For better or worse Ali Muhammad had found his Anarkali.

26
Money, Guns and Horses

I came to Lahore looking for horses not whores.

Though Pindi Prison had done her best to turn my soul musty and extinguish my restless longing to wander, my nomad blood had awakened the moment I was free.

I would lie if I said I did not consider taking my freedom and fleeing to a safer environment. Yet that internal debate was a short one.

In my heart I knew there would be no peace awaiting me in America, the loneliness of a coward's bed, safety perhaps, and certainly all the sensible demands that conspire with age to kill the fire in a man's belly. There were a thousand reasons to leave Pakistan and but one reason to remain.

I wanted to live, not die.

Men, like water, grow stale and muddy if they stand motionless. When they move, both elements become clear and free. My enforced stagnation had driven home how desperately short and uncertain was my own existence. During the days in chains, and the nights in torment, I had dreamed of one last horse trip, one crowning adventure that would stand as a bulwark against the ravages of time.

For more than death I dreaded being old, awake deep in the night, an aged ruin of a man, with regrets and no sunsets. I did not want to lie there with anticipation, awaiting Death's stealthy approach only to say, "Give me rest. I have no cause to linger."

I wanted to listen to my instincts and not my intellect. There was no money to be made from such a horse trip, no fame to be gained. It was solely for the sake of self-applause that I decided to risk my remaining fortune and my life, to remount and not retreat.

From far Chitral I had seen a glimpse of mighty mountains. I had determined to seek out the gypsy ribbon, to draw one long last free breath riding that unknown road before I allowed the responsibilities of America and adulthood to crowd out the dreams that pester all younger men.

So it was that the fear of not living enough overrode the fear of dying with too little. For Pindi Prison had taught me the blessing of the former, and the certainty of the latter. I trusted that Pakistan, the land that had almost crushed me, would in turn heal me.

Luckily the prison had paid dividends at last, for it had toughened me as nothing else could have. The scanty rations, the cheerful disregard for even the most elementary rules of hygiene, had conspired to weather me into a rawhide cord. I was little more than bone, sinew and determination.

It was Raja who sweetened the pudding, providing the vital clue to such an equestrian enterprise.

I had appeared at the agreed-upon hotel early, not knowing my erstwhile companions had but recently retired. That tale unfolded as we journeyed by rickety bus to the military town of Sargohda. The story of their nocturnal adventuring gave me cause to raise an eyebrow in surprise, but I was no saint when it came to the field of love and deemed it not my place to lecture either of them. Allah protects the foolhardy I reasoned, for no apparent harm had been done.

Plus we three had more immediate concerns.

The choice to accompany me on a horse trip had been an easy one for Raja. First, he would be paid for his support. More importantly, the work involved horses, a passion he had inherited from his late father.

As befitted his life, Ali Muhammad's decision to accompany me was based as much on the romantic ideal as on any practical considerations. Though Ali still owned his home in Peshawar, our lawyer Naeem had been correct in advising the two of us to be on our guard against repercussions by Inspector Gilani Khan. Needing a quiet retreat, and unwilling to leave Pakistan, my friend had become infected with my enthusiasm and envisioning some sort of rambling horse holiday had thrown in his lot with mine. The fact that he barely knew one end of a steed from the other was a matter of no concern to him. Ali Muhammad reasoned that teaching him everything required for such a trip was my job, as soon as Raja found us the horses that is.

It was thus that with our freedom realized, we three cellmates shared a collective excitement at the adventure's beginning.

Sargohda proved to be what Raja remembered, forgettable, except for the missile. In the first war with India, an enemy plane had flown overhead and dropped a 500 pound bomb on the sleepy town. The fifteen foot tall metal behemoth now stood upright in the middle of the small town's main street. Painted silver, and for all I knew still armed, it was the pride of a happy populace.

I liked the place.

On the outskirts of town we discovered the army remount depot where Raja's father had been stationed. It was as the young Afridi tribesman had described it, a separate entity, a tiny world devoted to long-dead values, an overlooked oasis, a horseman's dream.

A vast estate was kept separate from the town behind guarded walls and fences. Inside were stables, exercise yards, breeding facilities and every equestrian accoutrement. Originally established in the late nineteenth century by the British occupation army, the Sargohda remount depot had been developed to breed artillery horses. Enclosed within her secrets were the results of years of dedicated effort. Using imported Percheron stallions and country bred dams, the resulting offspring were as strong as their fathers, capable of pulling a cannon into the mountains of Kashmir, and could withstand the terrific heat of Pakistan like their mothers.

Colonel Chugtai, the depot's commanding officer, had but recently been posted there and did not know of Raja's father. However an explanation of our proposed trip was enough to arouse the officer's

Money, Guns and Horses

interest. Journalism had always been nothing more than an vocation used to support my equestrian adventures. I had ridden on four continents and shared experiences of equus with a host of horsemen. The colonel spoke the same passionate language I had encountered among cowboys on the hot plains of Amarillo, Texas and the eloquent chevaliers of the Spanish Riding School of Vienna, Austria. We were all saddle men stranded in an atomic age. Chugtai invited my friends and me to attend a forthcoming army auction where twelve surplus geldings were to be sold off.

Many dreams remain just that, unfilled aspirations slain by a lack of moral conviction. Yet too often I had seen well-planned, well-financed, beloved hopes martyred by the caprice of fate. Life can be cruel and is no respecter of a man's precious passion.

When I saw the horses I knew my luck had changed.

It was a crisp April morning. The many mighty trees surrounded an immaculate green lawn that looked as if it should host an afternoon tea and not an animal auction. The golden lining were the horses standing there awaiting our inspection. I had seen a host of horses throughout the country. Raja had not exaggerated. If I had not witnessed these, I would not have believed such magnificent animals existed in Pakistan.

There were three other bidders. They were looking for polo ponies and quickly agreed among themselves which three horses they would collectively buy. It left us nine to choose from. Our needs were different. We were not planning to race across a level playing field but rather venture into harsh and hostile mountains. A journey such as we were planning was exactly what these horses had been bred for. Where as the polo players choose mounts that favored the smaller dams, Raja and I concentrated on the larger stronger horses remaining, looking for signs of strength and endurance.

They were all fine geldings and at first glance any might have afforded us an excellent choice. The Romans used the word *cantherii* to describe such horses. It was thought that the slow easy gallop now known as the canter derived from their name for geldings. The colonel took me aside and shared a quiet word with me as to which horses he recommended.

"The product will always resemble the sire more than the dam," he confided. "You would never put honey in a jug made of dog hide. Therefore always bear in mind that the mare is nothing more than a sack from which gold will be extracted only if one puts in gold."

He then explained the background and training of each of the remaining nine, reciting blood lines and equine personalities. In the end the auction was a formality. The polo players went away with three of the smaller horses. We purchased four, including a matched set of two exceptionally large roans, a beautiful bay and a small fiery dun.

According to army custom each horse bore two brands. On the right shoulder were the first digits of their identity number. On their left shoulder was the capital letter S for Sargohda Remount.

Khyber Knights

These four horses had been raised like pampered children. Colonel Chugtai ordered a sergeant to collect the money that Ali Muhammad now handed over. My friend and I had each bought one horse and split the cost of a pack horse and Raja's mount. The four splendid animals had cost us $330.00 dollars a piece. We were issued with a receipt stating that Bay #84849, Dun #84104, Roan #8587, and Roan #8068 were now ours.

"Take your horse and may Allah grant that you be happy on him as many times as he has hairs on his back," Chugtai told me. Looking at the dun I now called my own, I thought it a likely blessing.

The remount depot had strict rules and was harshly exclusive. Because of the risk of anthrax and other communicable diseases no outside horses were ever allowed in. Once a remount horse was sold it was not permitted to re-enter. Our four horses had no way of knowing that when we walked them out the main gate they would never return to the world they had known.

Buying horses in Sargohda and getting them across the width of Pakistan to Peshawar was no easy matter. There were no luxuries like horse trailers to be hired. With the exception of sheep going to market, few animals were ever transported further than they could be driven on foot. Everything in the country went by truck.

We lead the horses into Sargohda, away from the regulated environment they had known and made our way to the outskirts of town. There we contracted with a local truck owner to haul the horses, as well as we three would-be cowboys, back home to Peshawar. For the equivalent of sixty-seven dollars the burly, jolly, and very dirty trucker agreed to haul the seven of us starting right then.

What resulted can only be compared to shoving four draft horses into a U-Haul rental truck. There were no ready-made large trucks in the country. No imposing Chevrolets, no gigantic Mack diesels, nor mighty Peterbilt trucks ever rolled down the pot-holed roads of Pakistan. The only source of trucks came from the old motherland. The Bedford truck company of England supplied Pakistan with the bare necessities. Four giant wheels and tires held up a bare steel frame, a sturdy motor and a transmission. A steering wheel drove the naked components of what would become a 32-foot lumbering lorry off the ship at the port of Karachi. It was up to the Pakistanis to build the required body. This they did with an intense national pride.

Sitting before us was such a motorized expression of art, an exercise in vivid color and a lack of restraint. The cab consisted of hand-carved sandalwood doors attached to a bright blue steel body. Brightly-colored gold tassels hung from the windows. The single bench seat that served as both bed and throne for the owner was upholstered in sky blue plastic. Various Islamic mottoes were plastered around the inside of the windshield obstructing the driver's view, but assuring him of Paradise should he crash and kill us all.

Behind the operator, eight-foot tall steel slabs were welded together to form a giant three-sided steel box in which to haul cargo. Vertical

Money, Guns and Horses

wooden slats slid into place between grooves to serve as a back door. A steel floor was laid across the bottom. To finish its exterior the truck builders constructed a wooden crow's nest which jutted out over the truck's roof. This open air box served to carry any extra baggage or passengers the trucker might wish to haul along.

It was the rear cargo section of the vehicle where an owner's personality was truly reflected. Every Pakistani truck was a rolling work of art. This one was no exception. The outer steel walls provided a surface on which the painter had provided a fantastic menagerie of both real and mythical beasts, flowers, birds, jet airplanes, Islamic citations and arabesque designs. The rear wall depicted a giant pastoral scene of an old-fashioned steam locomotive making its way through an idyllic countryside as a benign Mount Fuji looked on wisely.

We paid 150 rupees to cover the slick steel floor in thick dry straw. Lacking a ground-level loading ramp, the truck was backed up against an adjacent embankment. Using this slope as an access ramp, Raja and I loaded our new charges. We placed three of the horses, the bay, the dun, and the larger of the two roans head first and shoulder to shoulder, facing the front of the truck. Their lead ropes we tied up above to the crow's nest where Raja and I planned to sit. The smaller roan we tied crossways across the rear of the truck. Though none of the animals had ever been in a truck, they all reacted quietly as the big motor fired up and we rolled out of Sargohda with the setting sun.

Ali Muhammad had chosen to sit up in the cab. Within minutes Raja and I could hear the sounds of a cassette tape playing a Khayal Mohammad song about unrequited love.

It was a fine night, balmy and the horses, though intrigued, were by no means reluctant travelers. The small two lane road kept our speed to a sedate forty miles an hour. Raja and I agreed it was going to be a long haul to Peshawar. We had been traveling three hours, and the night air was just beginning to take on a chill, when the driver pulled off in the small village known as Khusab Junction. My companion and I climbed down to discover the trucker wanted to have a tire changed before proceeding further. He urged us to walk down the street to a chaikhana where we could get dinner, while he oversaw the needed repairs. My stomach was growling and it seemed like a reasonable suggestion. We walked away to the sound of tire coolies grunting and groaning as they started breaking the big lug nuts loose by hand.

Ali Muhammad, Raja and I were soon sitting around a wooden table sharing a common bowl of sheep meat swimming in oil painted red with chilies. We dipped in pieces of bread, alternating between the greasy meat and a platter of rice placed alongside. Such a meal might have been deemed by many as being plain and ill-cooked, but to us who had known the kiss of starvation the rich, spicy food tasted ambrosial. We found no fault with life and discussed the horses and our plans.

As we divvied up the dinner, reaching and eating and talking, we agreed upon the division of the horses as well. Though he was the most inexperienced, Ali Muhammad was to ride the largest of the roans. This gentle giant we named Pahlwan, meaning "strong man" in Pushtu. The beautiful bay went to Raja, who dubbed him Pajaro, after an expensive imported four-wheel-drive vehicle. The younger roan was to be the pack horse. We agreed to call him Pukhtoon to honor the tribes whose land we would cross. The dun I named Pasha, meaning king.

In the weeks since our release from Pindi Prison, I had told them of my own experiences on Shavon. I had given plenty of thought to the mistakes I had made and the equipment I should have taken. Considering the fact that we were planning on riding more than 1,000 miles through some of the most desolate portions of northern Pakistan, we still had a great deal of preparation to accomplish before we could set out. There was equipment to be bought, as well as training to be undertaken for both us and the horses. Raja was up to the task but Ali was experiencing some understandable trepidation.

"Don't worry Ali Muhammad," Raja told him. "Just remember that the horse means you no harm. He recites three daily prayers. In the morning he says, 'Oh Allah let my master love me.' At midday he adds, 'Oh Allah, do good unto my master so that he will do good unto me.' At night he prays, 'Oh Allah, allow my master to attain Paradise on my back.'"

The musician mumbled something about not wanting to reach Paradise in the next few weeks. We laughed, finished our dinner and returned to the truck to find a disaster in the making.

Having a different set of cultural values, and no understanding of the nature of horses, the driver had ordered all the wheels taken off the truck. We discovered the horses standing quietly in a vehicle that was sitting four feet up in the air with an assortment of wood scraps serving as precarious jack-stands. If the horses had become spooked and started to act up, the truck would have certainly come crashing down and most likely flipped over in the process.

Strong words were passed. Threats were made guaranteeing the short duration of the driver's continued life and career if the situation weren't immediately remedied. Wheels were hastily retrieved and we set out in the dark on bald tires, but at least with live mounts.

Our route took us in a north-westerly direction back towards the North West Frontier Province. Instead of heading due north for Lahore and the Grand Trunk road, the truck diverted onto a short cut, taking us through the lesser traveled mountains known as the Salt Range. The road was softly lighted by a full moon, so sitting up in the crow's nest Raja and I had a good view of the barren, boulder-strewn plain that prefaced the mountains.

The Salt Range ran in a westerly direction across Pakistan, ending at the Indus river hundreds of miles away. That was the same mighty river that had left vast deposits of rock salt behind in these hills 100 million years ago. As the truck shifted gears and started to slowly climb, I pointed out what I thought was a plane hovering far ahead of us over the crest of the black topped mountains.

"No, that is where we are going Asadullah," Raja was quick to point out, and he was right for the light I saw was indeed another truck

Money, Guns and Horses

crawling along high, high above us on the darkened mountainside. For the road led us ever upwards through the dark, over the bones of these dead, salty mountains. The early Arabs had believed that the crest of the Salt Range was where Noah's Ark rested after the deluge subsided. Inside the mountains were salt mines that had been in existence since the 13th century, as well as a mosque rumored to be cut into the red and pink salt deposits deep within the mountains.

We traversed the entire mountain range before dawn, pushed on past the ruins of Taxila, crossed the Indus river under the grim shadow of the Attock fort and pulled into Peshawar by late morning. The city of my heart was wide awake, noisy, an intoxication, a deep delight. It was wonderful to be home.

Following Ali Muhammad's directions the driver brought us to Sherqi Tanna, the police stables and the home of Peshawar's last mounted patrol.

Ali Muhammad and I had experienced our share of problems of late but we were by no means friendless. Police Inspector Akbar Ali was a case in point. A round-faced, gregarious, warm-hearted man, he would have seemed out of place in a police barracks if it had not been for his love of horses. I had met the former army cavalry officer when he was in charge of a secret program designed to deliver Tennessee mules to the Afghan freedom fighters. That experiment had been short lived. The mujahadeen worked the giant mules to death on brutal arms caravans quicker than the naive but well meaning Americans could supply them. My friendship with Akbar Ali, whose participation in the sad attempt was limited, was still going strong.

Akbar now maintained the last mounted police unit in the North West Frontier Province. Dressed in mirror-bright, knee-high black boots and jodhpurs, he was the very image of a dashing old-world cavalier. He had agreed to stable any horses we might find.

By lunch time we were relieved to have the horses unloaded and stabled under his care. For truckers in every country, time meant money. The driver was on his way back to Sargohda within minutes after being paid.

Raja and I headquartered in Ali Muhammad's house. The fourteen-room, four-story dwelling had cost my friend all of $12,000 and was largely empty, unless you counted the various musical instruments, recording machines, microphones and cassette tapes that filled the many rooms of the rambling affair. It wasn't a matter of saving money on my room at the Amin Hotel. We needed the space to gather and prepare the equipment necessary for a trip of that magnitude.

The route I proposed would take us in a 1,000 mile circle, north from Peshawar, past Chitral, east as far as Gilgit, then south through Kashmir to Islamabad and finally west back home to Peshawar. Lying in between were four of the largest mountain ranges in the world, including the Karakorams and the Himalayas. There was an odd desert or two, at least ten rivers, pockets of vicious sectarian violence and more than a dozen different languages between start and finish.

It sounded perfect.

"One does not cross the mountains smiling," is what they say in Peshawar and despite my enthusiasm I did not believe we could set out with frivolous hearts and poor equipment.

The world revolves around money and the old city of Peshawar was no different. Going to the bank there, however, was. Since the days of the ancient caravans men had frequented the Peshawari money bazaar just as they would attend to any other specialty need. Money-lending and foreign exchange had been major local activities for centuries, dating back to the era when the great Silk Route passed that way on its way to faraway Cathay. Even in such modern times there was no American Express to see to our financial needs. No Bank of America waited to offer us lines of credit. Instead we went to that portion of Peshawar known as Chowk Yadgar and transacted our business with one of the private money dealers who exchanged foreign currency for Pakistani rupees. We were small potatoes, exchanging our measly handful of American hundred dollar bills for a briefcase full of red, 100-rupee notes. The war in nearby Afghanistan had driven that country's currency down so badly that men were reduced to selling off their native money by sheer weight, offering bundles and bundles of nearly worthless notes in exchange for a handful of Pakistani rupees.

With money in my pocket I took a lightning one-day trip back to Rawalpindi, where I visited a well known saddler, the only shop left of its kind in that portion of Pakistan. A few hours later I made my discreet exit and returned by bus the same night. I brought along two refurbished 1896 style British military saddles for Raja and Ali Muhammad. This was the same style saddle I had saved from my trip with Shavon.

The saddles were fashioned from twin steel forks making up a high pommel and a fantail cantle which were nailed to wooden sidebars. The undersides of the sidebars were lined with felt, the upper ends covered with leather. The seat was supported from underneath by stretched webbing. Originally the British army used American bison hide for these saddles. The ones I bought had the seat and skirts made from native water buffalo hide. Years of rigorous campaigning had proved how tough and reliable they were.

No one ever claimed they were comfortable.

In addition I came away with a serviceable pack saddle, two deep canvas panniers to carry our supplies, as well as the breeching, new halters, bridles, bits, saddle blankets, cruppers, breast plates, horse brushes and two rifle scabbards.

Though years of haggling with avaricious Oriental shop keepers had sharpened my skills, I was but a raw beginner beside Raja. He had grown up in the school of destitution and had an exact knowledge of the most insignificant objects and the most wretched coin. The young Pathan was a shopkeeper's nightmare. I made sure he accompanied us when we went to get guns.

Ali, Raja and I left Peshawar early one morning and journeyed 30 miles south to Darra Adam Khel. The small one-lane village was over the

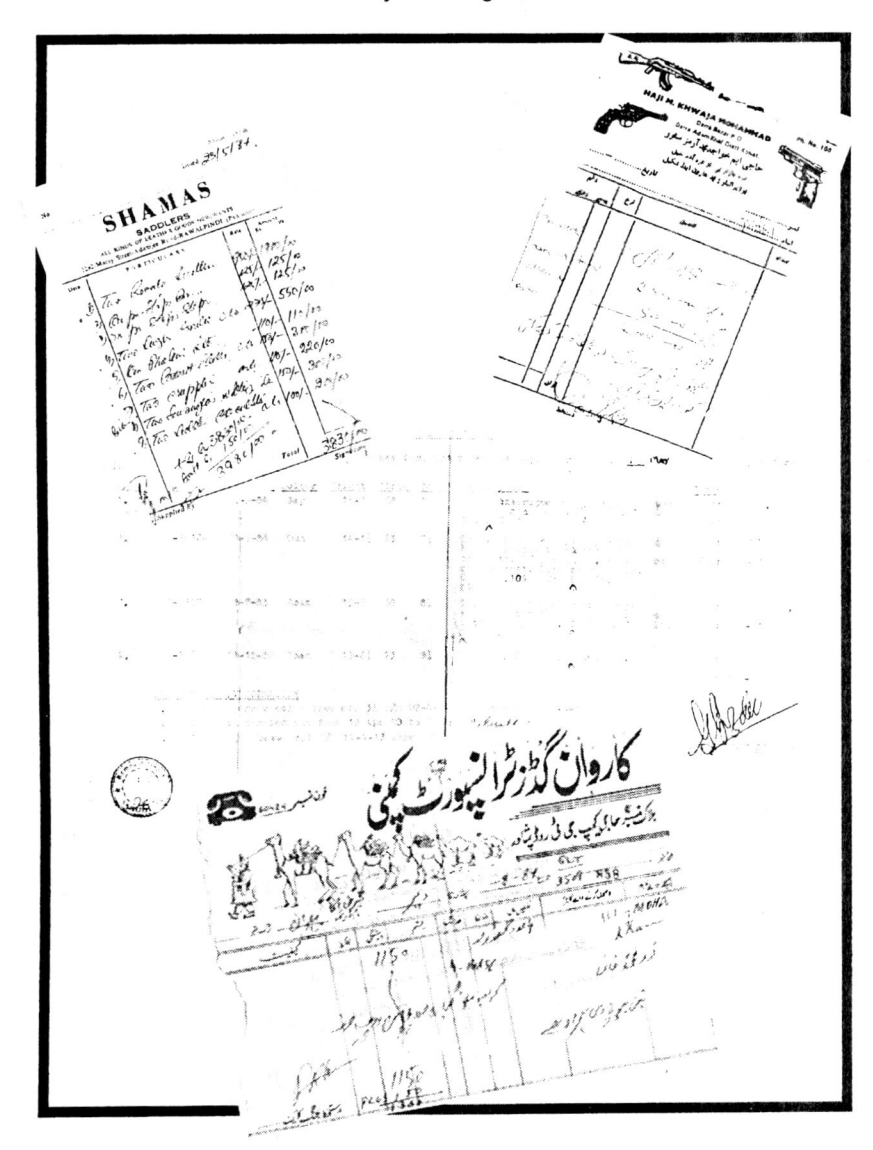

"The route I proposed would take us and our horses in a 1,100 mile circle north from Peshawar. Lying in between were four of the largest mountain ranges in the world, including the Karakorams and the Himalayas. There was an odd desert or two, at least ten rivers, pockets of vicious sectarian violence, and more than a dozen different languages. It sounded perfect."

Money, Guns and Horses

border in tribal territory and so technically off-limits to foreigners. However with our turbans and native dress Ali Muhammad and I didn't look out of place on the crowded bus. Anyone who took an interest, including police, waved us on when they learned we were converts to Islam.

In a country full of excitement and intrigue Darra stood alone. It was home to the world's least-known arms industry, and a gun buff's dream. For more than one hundred years the Pathan tribesmen had been running the country's most infamous cottage industry. Starting out with the rudest of tools, including wood rasps, knives and hand-held drills, the tribesmen had learned how to reproduce a passable copy of the Enfield rifle.

Oddly enough the mighty British Raj did not interfere. They rationalized that these unreliable copies were easier to battle than genuine rifles stolen off their soldiers. In the late 19th century a pilfered army rifle sold for $192.00, while a bootleg version only cost $26.00. The new arrangement seemed to make everyone happy. It wasn't long before the industrious Pathans were also soon selling every type of weapon known to the civilized world. Within a few years the lethal flotsam of the Western world was showing up in Darra, including Winchester repeating rifles and broom-handle Mauser pistols.

As the armament in Europe and the United States changed so did the fashions of well armed tribesmen. In the macho North West Frontier Province the village of Darra Adam Khel served as the Pathan tribesmen's Tiffanys.

When I first came to Pakistan, Pathans were still proud to own an English Enfield rifle. The Afghan war had ended all that ordnance innocence. I had been to Darra many times for various reasons. I had seen mujahadeen both buying and selling the scourings of war. I had witnessed the famous AK-47 machine gun spiral downwards from the status of being a tribesman's unobtainable dream to that of common everyday appliance. Shops which once proudly sold laboriously hand made shot guns now openly displayed boxes of live grenades, rocket launchers and state-of-the-art machine guns. Even the big fifty caliber Dashika machine guns, mounted on tripods and used as anti-aircraft weapons, were readily available.

Darra looked like Dodge City when Raja, Ali Muhammad and I showed up. If it shot a projectile or exploded, someone in town owned it, smuggled it, or could locate and always sell it for more than it was worth. As we prowled around we saw both sides of the street were lined with sophisticated weapons. If rumors were to be believed there was even a Stinger missile or two stashed away. Hundreds of men and boys were either selling, making, or repairing a potpourri of small arms. It was a terrorist shopping center and you could smell the money. The sound of gunfire periodically interrupted our inspection tour. It was no cause for alarm, merely a customer trying out a new weapon.

Those with good manners went behind the shops with their prospective purchases, shooting into the nearby hills. Anyone in a hurry to get down to business could step out a shop door and fire off a pistol clip without raising either an alarm or an eyebrow. It was considered courteous however to walk away from the immediate vicinity of the shops before lobbing a hand grenade or popping off a rocket-propelled grenade.

The little town had helped change the political face of Pakistan. What had once been primarily a tribal rite of passage had become a national obsession and had given birth to what was deemed "the Kalishnakov culture." Because of the nearby Afghan war, Pakistan was awash with guns. Drug lords, sectarian murderers, kidnappers, political assassins, renegades and rebels all had access to weapons that most European police forces did not own. Pimply faced kids now packed the latest fashion in captured Soviet weaponry. Pathan home owners considered it fashionable to keep an anti-aircraft gun on their roofs. In the mountains where we were headed, to carry anything less than an AK-47 was to acknowledge poverty.

Poverty aside, we weren't licensed to carry automatic weapons.

While Ali Muhammad and Raja had been exploring the Lahore night life, I had spent my time in the nation's capital pulling in a few favors. We were in Darra shopping with the full authorization of the federal government, which had issued us weapons permits. These important little green books allowed us to purchase and carry pistols, single shot rifles, shotguns, swords, daggers and ammunition for our horse trip.

But not only was foreign-built armament prohibitively expensive, my contact in the government had not authorized us to buy AK-47s or other automatic weapons. Instead we were looking for lightweight caravan protection, not enough fire power to arm a long range army patrol. The object was to deter, not outgun any opponent.

The task at hand that day was to test-fire the usual Pakistani choices.

Raja, though the youngest, had more experience with the arms of the country than either Ali Muhammad or I had. We wandered from shop to shop, taking our time, learning what our options were. The deeply experienced traders tried to mislead or tempt us. Luckily, our own Afridi knew the game. He was unyielding, decrying this rifle's quality, that pistol's longevity, jeering at the prices, ridiculing the offers made to us. In short he bargained with crafty patience, holding his own against the greedy shopkeepers.

Eventually after fingering, hefting, test-firing, arguing, leaving, returning, arguing some more and threatening to leave for good, we eventually settled on a shopping cart of your basic equestrian needs. Lying in the bottom of our basket were five guns, several hundred rounds of assorted ammo and a few odds and ends.

We each had a chunky .30 caliber semi-automatic pistol. These guns were direct copies of the American Colt 1911 .45 caliber automatic and packed the largest handgun round civilians could legally buy in Pakistan. In addition we had a bolt-action, clip-loading paratrooper rifle that was sighted in at 1200 yards. Lying beside it was my little baby, a sawed-off, double-barreled, twelve gauge shotgun. Each of us would carry 40

Money, Guns and Horses

rounds of pistol ammo in holsters round our waist, as well as a 100-round reserve for the two long guns in the pack saddle. All the guns were locally manufactured, which meant we couldn't trust them absolutely. They were handmade from inferior steel refined from ships salvaged off the coast of Karachi. Consequently, we knew the guns might jam when we could least expect or afford it.

I took that problem, as well as some advice, into consideration before I left Darra. My government friend in Islamabad had known both of my recent troubles with Ashgar Ali and the earlier kidnapping when I was riding Shavon. He had given me some sound counsel regarding any future trouble I might encounter on the new horse trip.

"Don't bother taking along any sort of guard. Three mounted men who can keep their wits under fire are better than an armed rabble. Besides, bad shots eat as much as marksmen. If anyone attacks you, kill them yourself. We'll sort it out when you get back to Islamabad," he said in a serious tone, then slid me the weapons permit as proof of his sincerity.

As the sound of guns echoed around me, I rounded out my shopping trip in Darra by buying a serviceable Persian sword for my hip, and a small dirk to wear around my neck underneath my shirt.

I was nearly ready to ride north on Pasha.

27
Sargohda's Secret

Sometimes it happens in life that we receive a faint resonance from our instincts. Standing there in the thick, gray fog of non-understanding, a flash of light will momentarily slice through as if from a far away lighthouse, briefly illuminating the path we are to follow.

Such a dimly perceived communiqué came to me about the dun.

In the pantheon of horses that had shaped my life, including Choctaw Red, Irish Music and Shavon, some muted message told me the dun-colored gelding was to be special.

Pasha on the other hand thought his mission in life was to either maim or kill me.

Over the next two weeks he tried both.

Colonel Chugtai and the Pakistani army had provided us with physically superb specimens. They were however far from being ready to set out on a lengthy expedition. They ranged from being nearly ready, such as Ali's mount Pahlwan, to being nearly berserk, such as Pasha. The other two geldings were calibrations in between.

What became immediately apparent was how ignorant of the world our new horses were. They had lived in an equine sanctum and were devoid of common day knowledge. They knew naught of cars, nor any distracting device from the 20th century. They were in effect equestrian time travelers who had stepped out of their 19th century time capsule into the hustle and bustle of modern day Peshawar.

Because they had been kept in large groups of horses on the army base, our new mounts had no trouble fitting into the social life of the police horses. There were a dozen of these stoic, well-mannered creatures, most of which had been quietly stabled at Sherqi Thana for years. The police horses were kept under cover in an open-aired stable. The long building was really only a roof overlooking a single dividing wall. On either side were brick feeding bins built up off a brick floor. A shallow gutter drained off at the rear of each side. It was an old but serviceable structure. Several Christian converts were in constant attendance, keeping it swept clean and occasionally seeing to some minor need of the horses. The mounted police men, though lowly paid in the extreme, acted as their own grooms, keeping their horses in perfect order.

When our army horses were unloaded and tied off, they were plunged into another world. Hunger taught them to adapt to what was fed to them at the stable and they were soon eating the chopped feed served at the police lines. Yet they tossed their heads and ignored carrots, apples and other treats we brought them from the bazaar. Having no knowledge of these things they were uninterested in such culinary oddities.

Their knowledge of man was similarly limited.

Khyber Knights

Close by was an unfinished army stadium. The concrete grandstands were in place but the work had come to a halt due to a lack of funds. I quickly decided the hard packed, level playing field in its center was a perfect arena to work both the men and horses of our team into collective shape.

Pahlwan at seven was the oldest. His Percheron blood ran almost pure. Only the army could have afforded to have kept a horse of his immense size. He did not fill your eye so much as blotted out the landscape. Seen from the front Pahlwan resembled a high mountain peak. With legs like trees, the massive horse had powerful haunches, firm flesh, and heavy bones. His mane had been roached, which in turn made his thick neck look even stronger. His forehead was like that of a bull. He had nostrils as big as a lion's den, beautiful deep black eyes and the air of a kindly monk. Though officially designated a roan, his coat was a soft white, the color of a wild pigeon. The moment he started to sweat he turned a darker gray.

Looking at him you knew you could count him as on your own heart.

His half brother Pukhtoon seemed to be a smaller version of the same picture. Whereas Pahlwan turned gray under exertion, Pukhtoon's white coat revealed his mother's sorrel inheritance. A glance in his direction would have revealed his strength and grace. He had slender mobile ears, lean jaws and a long clean belly. His withers were prominent and his breast strong and broad. He carried a thick white mane and tail that had a whisper of rosy red to it.

Pukhtoon doted on and hated to be parted from Pahlwan. Though far stronger than his other two stable mates, Pukhtoon was the most emotionally needy of the bunch. He was the younger, smaller child anxious to be noticed and liked. He was also an unrepentant glutton. At four years of age he was the youngest of the army lot and had never had a saddle on his back or a bit in his mouth. It was for this reason that I decided to cast him as the pack horse, thereby taking advantage of his physical strength and not taxing his emotional weaknesses.

Raja's mount Pajaro was the most interesting. All horses have some inner need in life. Some, like Pukhtoon, wanted to eat. Others, like Pahlwan, wanted to quietly serve. Pajaro wanted to be left alone.

He was a horse who carried an inner sadness. The hardiest and yet the most gentle, if someone had said a horse had leapt to the bottom of an abyss to please his master, I would have believed it of Pajaro. Of all the four horses he was the most strikingly beautiful. He favored his dam and had the look of a thoroughbred, with his deep chest and elegant lines. He was long legged, sleek and lean. His coat was a shiny cocoa brown, his mane and tail jet black. A white blaze rested between his kind brown eyes. Regardless of the dangers we later faced, the hardships we suffered together as a group, even the loss of life, this noble animal never misbehaved or ever gave less than his all under the most dire circumstances. He was quiet, withdrawn, even timid but there wasn't a mean bone in his body. Only a monster could have laid a whip on his back. It would have been like beating a baby.

Sargohda's Secret

Which left me with Pasha.

He needed none of us, not man nor horse. He could have run independent of the world and not stopped until Samarkand, where he might have lingered for a hasty drink. His sole mission in life was to breathe and run and be free.

Like his stablemate Pajaro, he was five years old. Pasha however had inherited none of the calm demeanor of his Percheron father. He was a son of perdition, an unrepentant sinner who never wore a saddle out of meekness. Though he tolerated me, and I believed later learned to love me, I never for a moment thought he would not desert me. For Pasha never lost his noble bearing, nor the look of regal sufferance he carried in his eye. He was but freedom held on a temporary rein.

Except for the army paper proving his birth, there wasn't a trace of civilization or French breeding apparent in him. Where as Pahlwan stood for everything the army breeders had been hoping to accomplish, Pasha was a unashamed son of the Pakistani desert.

Of all the horses we had bought, he was the smallest, standing at fifteen hands. While lacking Pahlwan's massive strength and Pajaro's elegance, the smaller Pasha was perfectly proportioned. His legs were strong and boasted sinews of steel. His hooves were black flint. The broad chest sprang from shoulders that could have held up Atlas. His powerful flanks were rounded grace.

He was a classic dun. With his soft beige-colored hide and the darker dorsal stripes decorating his legs, Pasha was what was known as *el-khedeur* (wolf colored). A solid deep brown stripe ran the length of his back, ending in a silky gray-brown tail that reached the ground. His elegant mane had been left long and draped over the left side of his neck. The nostrils on his dark muzzle were close set and flaring. He had inherited his dam's head, with a clean, light jaw crowned by intelligent black eyes that only confirmed his impudence. He sported one white sock on his right rear leg and stepped so light he could have danced on my beloved's heart.

The first day Raja, Ali Muhammad and I walked the four horses to the army stadium we quickly learned all these secrets of their personalities. To have shoved them out onto the traffic thick roads of Pakistan would have risked their lives and ours. Though Pahlwan, Pajaro and Pasha were broken to the saddle, they had no concept of the world as we understood it. The ten minute trip revealed screaming cars, overcrowded buses and blaring trucks. It was the usual mix of old world animal traffic, mixed with mechanical madness, that defined the larger roads of Pakistan.

Pasha reared almost as soon as we started walking next to the traffic. He rolled his eyes and nearly snatched the reins out of my hands. It was all I could do to control and walk him to the stadium successfully.

Inside the quiet walls of the stadium we got down to the matter at hand.

The saddle looked like a postage stamp on Pahlwan's broad back. I put the big Percheron on a lunge line, got Ali Muhammad aboard, then put them both out on a trot. The slow moving giant was perfect for Ali, who hung on manfully. My old friend was soon taking a terrific bouncing. When he got off he remarked naively that the saddle seemed hard and that the inside of his legs hurt. I assured him this was only a temporary trifle.

Raja not only knew horses, he loved them. While he was waiting, he would stroke Pajaro's black mane like a lover caressing his mistress. He had no formal training but lacked all fear, seeming to communicate his utter confidence and trust to the dark gelding. Knowing that neither of my two friends, nor the three riding horses, had any experience with neck reining, I had bought snaffle bits. Raja tended to be heavy handed but his confidence and exuberance soon had him and Pajaro cantering. He was never going to make the Olympics but he was going to make that ride.

When he came to a halt in front of me I asked him, "Are you pleased Raja?"

He patted the horses neck and beamed.

"He is a bird without wings. Don't ever say this is my horse. Say this is my son," the youngster told me.

We hit our first snag when I asked Raja to put Pukhtoon to the test. I had thought it unwise to bring the roan to the stadium with the pack saddle on his back until after I had seen how he would react to being lead by another rider. The Afridi had not dismounted, so I handed him the lead rope and told him to slowly walk the pack horse away from the others.

Pajaro, the ever patient, was glad to oblige. The bay stepped out in a clean walk, but the further Pukhtoon went from his stable mate Pahlwan, the more anxious the small roan got. He no sooner left than he began glancing over his shoulder. When it looked like Raja was heading the two horses out of the gate and back to the police lines, Pukhtoon starting whinnying his distress. The big horse standing next to us answered and Raja's problems started increasing. Before Raja could turn the horses back in our direction, Pukhtoon began biting Pajaro's flank. The young rider suddenly had his hands full trying to steer his mount, control his pack horse, and retain his seat. Pukhtoon took that opportunity to stop dead in his tracks.

Pajaro kept going and Raja, not realizing what was happening, was almost yanked out of his saddle. More from luck than knowledge, he dropped the lead line and kept himself from falling off. Pukhtoon turned on his heels and ran back whinnying in delight, clearly pleased with himself. Raja came thundering up, ready to inflict Pathan revenge on this disgraceful creature. I waved aside the suggestion and told Ali Muhammad to mount up on Pahlwan instead.

I almost felt sorry for the musician. It was the first inkling he had received that talking about going on an extended horse trip was not like actually confronting the reality. With great nervousness he swung up onto his big horse and then looked down at me from the great height of his charger.

"OK, take them both out in a slow walk," I told him and thrust Pukhtoon's lead rope in his right hand.

"Where do I go?" he asked indecisively.

"You're the boss. That's up to you. But I suggest you walk them in a circle and stay close to the other horses."

To give Ali Muhammad credit he was no coward. I'm sure I would have been just as nervous if he had shoved a sitar into my hands in front of a crowded auditorium and said, "Here, play this." He clucked to the big horse, who stepped out in a sedate fashion, ready to go in a circle or go to Kashmir, which ever pleased the man on his back. Pukhtoon thought it was some sort of swell game and thinking Pahlwan was leading him somewhere fun, perhaps to food, followed sedately along behind.

Ali was stiff with apprehension. I went over and walked alongside him.

"Remember seeing those mechanical horses outside the grocery stores when you were a kid? Did your mom ever put you on one?" I asked him.

He admitted that like every little boy our age, he had shared that moment of Hopalong Cassidy fantasy. I got him to recall how that horse rocked back and forth, front to back. Ali Muhammad didn't know how to spell equestrian education, but he remembered the feel of that dime store horse in the faraway Garden District of New Orleans. After that explanation I let Pahlwan do all the teaching. The big horse gave him the movement and Ali Muhammad, relaxing more and more by the minute, was soon visibly rocking up in the saddle faster than Pahlwan was walking.

I had gone back to stand next to Raja and the other horses.

"What do you say?" I shouted at Ali Muhammad as he rode by.

"What do you mean?"

"Yahoo cowboy," I yelled back.

My friend was so pleased with his progress he had forgotten he was leading Pukhtoon.

The sun was high overhead before it came my turn to ride.

Pasha had been standing by idle and bored, paying little attention to the other horses, day-dreaming it appeared about some privy secret. Ali Muhammad and Raja were talking and the other three horses were standing in a close group resting. With everything else under control I turned my attention to the dun.

The moment I reached for the girth his ears flicked back. He turned his head back towards me and I halted my movement, anxious to see his next move. Yet he was only testing the waters, as was I. We circled like wary heavyweights unsure of the skill of our opponent.

With the saddle tight, the bridle snug, and my heart in my mouth, I walked Pasha away from the group. Everything I knew about horses told me this one was about to blow up like Mount Vesuvius.

I pulled the reins up in my left hand, put my left foot in the stirrup and mounted in one smooth movement. Nothing happened. Pasha stood stock still. I centered myself in the flat military saddle. This wasn't my old high-backed Heiser western rig. No bucking rolls here. If the horse starting pitching there was next to nothing holding me on. I took a deep breath, found that quiet space I reserve for horses, then with my heels down and my seat secured, I started putting him through his paces.

Someone at Sargohda Remount had taught Pasha his lessons, they just hadn't got around to reminding him of his manners. He walked out, taking the bit, listening to his cues like a well-trained gun dog. He responded to the subtle pressures from my leg. I had left off my spurs but the barest touch of a heel was enough to get him to move forward well. He knew his circles. He responded to the bit, cutting across the arena in a clean trot and giving me lovely, full figure eights. I was beginning to think I had misjudged him when the equine devil destroyed me.

Though I had no walls to work him against I was putting Pasha through the paces of a dressage test. I had turned the gelding and was sitting him in the trot, coming across the arena well, when he started to act up. I felt his attention slipping, felt him start jigging on the bit, felt my trust starting to slip. As we neared the far corner I whispered to him through the reins, urging him to behave. He obeyed with a bad grace, then started to toss his head impatiently. I reached out to him with the tools at my disposal.

"Come, I am not a dotard. Do not try to intimidate me," I warned him with a quiet voice, all the while soothing him through the reins and holding him steady with my legs. When I turned him into the far corner I thought I had charmed him. We circled left, and came up on the new diagonal. I slid him into a canter and he exploded.

Pasha hump-backed so high I could see into Afghanistan, then came down stiff legged, trying to pile-drive my spine into dust. The instant we landed he became a squealing, sun-fishing, bundle of concentrated fury. We battled for control as he twisted and bawled and bucked his guts out. He was a grave-digger and a flying demon bent on my destruction.

The art of riding is not the art of winning. Many know the outer technique who never learn the inner way. I never struck Pasha. I was not trying to break his spirit or vilify him. I clamped down harder with my legs, kept my balance over the center of the saddle and followed his every twist and turn as he hop-scotched over the arena. My main worry was that my turban would come unwrapped and fall over my eyes. I did not count how long the battle lasted but I knew I was weakening. It felt like he had dislodged my liver. Then we passed some invisible marker whereby he knew of the two of us, I was the master and he stopped. He was breathing hard from his exertions. I immediately took up the reins and urged him into a collected walk.

His pace was rough but more importantly the horse obeyed. The time for play was over. I asked no more. It was enough.

Turning him back towards the others, I gave him a long rein and a pat on the neck. Pasha and I had formed an understanding. Though he lacked the power of speech, the dun understood me as well as any son of Adam.

Sargohda's Secret

Back at the stables we encountered some gentle ribbing from the policemen. They mocked Pahlwan's size and color, saying that only a fool would set out on a long trip on a white horse.

"The sun will melt him like butter," one said to Ali Muhammad.

"This is not a horse. This is a cow with a saddle," said another, though both were smiling.

Taking up the brush and hoof pick, the police riders were both soon teaching my unskilled friend how to attend to his big Percheron.

There had already been talk around the stable regarding our decision to buy geldings. We had not had a choice in the matter and purchased what was available. Yet the talk was of whether mares or stallions were best. One group said studs caused too much fuss. Others believed that mares were not dignified. Everyone agreed that both were better than geldings. This was an ancient prejudice among most riders in that part of the world. It was believed that because he did not mate, a gelding would live longer. However the same school of thought said the gelding lost speed and vigor after the operation because he was reduced to the condition of a mare and it was reasoned women were weaker than men. Many Muslims prohibited the operation.

I thought of Shavon and kept my opinions to myself.

For two weeks we worked and trained ourselves and the horses. We led them by degrees closer to the traffic. The three biggest accustomed themselves to the sounds of the blaring mechanical devices rather quickly. Every episode was a circus with Pasha. Finally, in desperation, I haltered and tied him to a tree and sat nearby, all the while reading a book for hours. The dun grew bored and ultimately resigned himself to accepting the noisy mechanical animals speeding by.

When we weren't riding, we were fitting equipment, saddle-soaping the leather goods, cleaning the weapons and making last-minute purchases. Raja found us three Turkoman saddle bags. The brightly colored wool bags were woven like the famous Afghan carpets they resembled.

One long hot day was spent shoeing the horses. This time it was Pahlwan who surprised us. With his unbelievable strength it was impossible to outfight him. My hands were raw, my back was breaking and the blacksmith was ready to quit. I rigged up a crude twitch, something the Pakistanis had never seen, and soon had the big horse standing quietly. It only made an impossible job a little less difficult. Each of Pahlwan's shoes was bigger than a saucer and weighed in at more than a kilo. The blacksmith also supplied us with four hand made *mugays* (picket pins) and four extra sets of horseshoes.

In addition to corn for the horses, we were carrying their brushes, our clothes, food, some simple cooking gear, a small tent, light blankets, and the ammunition. We had all three spent many hard days, training in increasingly hot weather, before going home to Ali's filthy and tired. Every night our clothes reeked of sweat and were caked in horsehair but we had reached a point of achievement. Even Ali Muhammad learned the wisdom of the old saying that a nobleman may do manual labor without blushing for the benefit of his horse.

Both my companions had made good progress in the saddle. I had not bothered to teach them to post, the wearisome custom of bobbing up and down like a jack-in-the-box. It was a gait suited to the Englishmen who once rode hard trotting breeds that forced them to rise in their stirrups or be pounded to death. Other nations who copied it were slaves to fashion rather than intelligent horsemen. Like the Arabs, I seldom employed it except as a brief transition before cantering.

Ali Muhammad still bounced in the saddle but what he lacked in grace he made up for in grit. Big-hearted Pahlwan seemed to sense it was he, not Ali Muhammad, who was in charge. The horse and I silently agreed to keep the secret between us. Pukhtoon displayed a sense of vigor and surprising dependability regarding the pack saddle. He never bucked or carried on, and as long as he was close to the bigger white horse, he was happy to follow along and obey the few orders we gave him. Raja and Pajaro were a team, both quiet and dependable.

I had learned to never take Pasha for granted. One of my earliest riding teachers told me, "One does not become a horseman until one has been frequently thrown." The dun made me a true believer. He had a mouth of velvet which taught me to avoid all violent gestures with the reins. I kept my voice low and avoided fighting him, fearing a struggle would only result in my winning at his expense. Instead I rode him with a constant recognition of his fiery temper and his need to retain his own self-respect, while trying not to let him throw me off in front of an oncoming truck. He was either an angel or a devil, with no warning in between.

The day of our departure was nearly upon us. The horses were in excellent shape. When we weren't attending to them, the police men were. Their coats rippled like silk from all the attention lavished on them by the attentive cops. Their artful hands had brushed, combed and curried the horses they had originally scoffed at. It had taken a while for the length and difficulty of our proposed trip to settle in among the mounted policemen. None of them knew anyone in their country who had ever ridden so far. Suddenly they wanted the big white horse and the other geldings to make the collective dream a reality. Once ridiculed, the army horses were now pampered mascots.

We went to the police stables to take a last ride, planning on putting the horses through their paces both in the arena and in nearby traffic. When we arrived the first thing we saw was Inspector Akbar Ali and one of the Christian sweepers standing next to the pack horse Pukhtoon. When he saw us walk up, the equestrian policeman left off and walked over to meet us.

"Joseph has found something very bad," he said, indicating the dark-skinned sweeper standing next to the pack horse.

Like the majority of Christians in Pakistan, Muslims considered Joseph and his fellow religionists dirty because of the jobs they performed. These usually included cleaning streets, lavatories, stables, etc. Yet these were the only jobs allowed them. Most had been low-caste Hindus, "untouchables", before the 1947 partition. By staying and converting to the foreign religion, they had thought to escape the prejudices of class-ridden India. They had been sadly mistaken. They were still doing the dirtiest work of Pakistani society. Though never numerically strong, Peshawar's Christian minority worshipped in their own cathedral, St. Michael's Roman Catholic church on the Mall in Peshawar.

I feared the worst.

Akbar Ali pointed at the roan's rump.

"Look," he exclaimed.

The big horse was eating green corn stalks and to my eyes looked like a happy, slobbering mess. I saw nothing amiss. Akbar put his hand on the left side of the horse's rump then looked at Raja for support.

"Don't you see this?" he said.

Raja admitted he too was ignorant.

"The whorl," the old horseman said, and placing his finger directly on the horse's white skin, I could see where Pukhtoon's hair turned in a tight circle. It lay partly hidden under the left side of his tail and had never given any of us the slightest hint of any significance.

The policeman, realizing he was dealing with two foreign idiots and a village simpleton, began explaining the problem.

"A horse can have any one of forty whorls. Of these, twenty eight are considered neither good nor bad. But twelve have a definite influence on horse and rider. Six indicate an increase in wealth or good luck. While six others bring on ruin or cause adversity," Akbar told us.

The sweeper had seen the whorl while working around the gelding and rushed to inform the mounted policeman. Whatever I thought, it was clear the two men in front of me were totally sincere in their belief in its strange power.

The look on Ali Muhammad's face was evidence to Akbar that my friend at least did not understand the significance of the discovery.

"The tight whorl on the side of the neck is known as the touch of the finger of the Prophet. It means that horse's master will die in his bed, a good Muslim. The whorl of the Sultan is longer and runs the length of the neck. It will bring love and riches," Akbar said patiently.

"The whorl on the flank is known as the whorl of the spurs. It will save the rider from any mishap in battle."

"So which one is this," Ali Muhammad inquired, misreading Akbar's drift.

"This is none of those. It belongs to the other six. The whorl above the eye means the horse's master will die from a blow to the head. The whorl on the cheek is the whorl of lamentations. It will bring the rider debts and financial ruin. The whorl of theft is found on the fetlocks. The worst is the whorl on the withers. That is the whorl of the coffin and means the rider will die on the horse," Akbar said.

"But what about this mark on his butt?" my naive friend asked.

Khyber Knights

"The whorl to one side of the tail presages trouble, misery or loss," the policeman said, then turned to look at me. I knew that the subject of horses was full of prejudices and traditions often motivated by distant family memories of lucky and unlucky horses. I also knew that I was far from the Occident, with its belief in science and logical rationalism. Other forces helped steer the course of Pakistan, sometimes even superstitions.

"The army sold the big horse because his white color is a sign of weakness. They sold the bay because he is a coward and the dun because he is crazy. But," and Akbar patted the pack horse, "they sold this one because of his whorl of ill fortune."

"We can do nothing but tie this on him and hope for the best," Akbar said and opening his other hand he displayed a tiny tin box. It measured only an inch long on all sides and was less than half of that in thickness. The top was clearly stamped with a crescent moon and star, the symbols of Islam, as well as a border of interlocking flowers. The ends had been folded over to hide its contents. Two small rings were welded above its center. It was a *ta'wez*, an amulet containing verses from the holy Qu'ran. Each little box was the repository of verses designed to combat specific evil effects.

Akbar ordered the sweeper to hold the horse's head. Without asking permission, Akbar then tied the amulet securely onto the halter, admonishing us to never remove it. It was the first indication I had that everything was not going to work out smoothly on the trip.

Ali Muhammad provided more obvious evidence the following morning.

28
The Garden of Fire

When we got up Ali was gone, bound by bus for Lahore. There was a brief note saying he would be back shortly. He hadn't spelled out where he had headed. I didn't need to be told.

During the course of the last few weeks his speech had made it abundantly clear that invisible chains were tying him to Shaheen's memory, making him a willing slave to both his passion, and her beauty. As the sun rose over Pakistan, my friend looked out the window of the speeding bus at the fleeing countryside, knowing in his heart he had tried to put Shaheen out of his mind.

It had proved to be a futile attempt.

He would be riding Pahlwan, and would remember her face.

He would be playing music, and the smell of jasmine would jar his memory.

He would be talking about the upcoming trip, and the recollection of her body sat him on fire.

He had tried.

He had lost.

He was hunger with a name on his way to Lahore.

Ali Muhammad was many things but he was no fool.

The pain of Pindi Prison was too raw, too recent, not to frighten him and he knew by going back to Shaheen's arms he risked re-entering that hell hole. So he made what preparations he could for the task at hand. He had started by not informing either Raja or me of his intentions. He didn't want a lecture. He wanted time alone, plenty of time, with the woman he couldn't forget.

In the breast pocket of his shirt he carried a 500 rupee note, to be used as a bribe if the police stopped him. A sizable wad of rupees to buy her favors was hidden in a smaller inner pocket. Inside his waistcoat he carried his weapons permit. Riding concealed under his left arm in a new shoulder holster was the big .30 caliber pistol. He had left his passport at home, along with anything identifying him as a foreigner. If he was stopped in Hira Mandi he intended to try and bluff his way out of trouble. If he could.

Regardless, Ali had known he was coming back. It had been a severe trial of his self-control for several days. Finally, with the horses trained, he knew I would want to depart immediately. He picked that moment to journey to Lahore, determined to confirm his heart's suspicions regarding Shaheen.

It was early afternoon when he pulled into the city. His arrival was uneventful. The Queen of the Punjab had watched, passive and bemused, as star-crossed lovers came and went through her streets for centuries. This was an ancient city and the follies of humanity were nothing new to Lahore. There were some who said she was built by slaves left behind by Alexander the Great. If I had been along for the ride I would have told Ali Muhammad that some historians even believed that this was the city where the Greek warrior king had entombed his beloved horse Bucephalus.

The big horse's name meant "bull headed" but was no insult. It referred to his small ears and wide forehead, both marks of fine quality among Greek horses. Born on the same day as his master, after riding the stallion during seventeen years of constant warfare, Alexander had founded the missing city of *Buchephalia* over his equine companion. Many thought this ancient link to a famous horse was the cornerstone on which so many Lahore legends now rested.

My friend was not interested in horses that day. His life was narrowing down to one desire. Though Ali Muhammad cared for his own mount Pahlwan, horses would never be anything to him but animals. They had nothing to do with the passions that drove him, nor his reason for journeying all the way across Pakistan to seek Shaheen's favors.

When the bus door opened, my friend got off quickly and started making his way through the city, walking through the old streets on his way towards the Hira Mandi neighborhood. Overhead the sky had turned cloudy. It seemed to share his anticipation. He could smell the oncoming rain. He walked rapidly, giving no notice to the things that normally intrigued him. In more recent years the city of Lahore had been familiar to the English who once ruled there. The famous author Rudyard Kipling was employed in Lahore as a journalist. His boy hero, Kim, was portrayed at the start of his career clambering over the great cannon named *Zam Zama* which stood nearby.

Of course the British seldom mentioned that close by they had also overrun the famous Badshahi mosque, turning part of it into a horse stable and a public toilet for their soldiers.

Ali Muhammad paid no more attention to the history all around him than he did the screeching green parakeets flying overhead. The noisy streets were crowded with pedestrians, buses, *tongas* (horse carts) and motor-rickshaws. It was a diverse city full of human endeavor, sprawling out over the Punjabi countryside.

Lahore had never been strictly crammed inside tight walls like her smaller sister Peshawar. In 1947, at the time of partition, the inclusion of Lahore into Pakistan was a near thing. If the city boundaries had not been extended a few years previously there would not have been the Muslim majority necessary to warrant its inclusion into the new Muslim country. As it was, Lahore saw some of the worst street fighting of that terrible time. Both countries had huge segments of their populations ripped up whole and cast out onto the roads. Hindus were forced to flee for their lives towards their official homeland of India. Many left behind homes and lands in Pakistan where their families had lived for centuries. Muslims living in India were likewise obliged to leave that country, fighting their way westwards through the killing mobs, towards the new

The Garden of Fire

Islamic state. The Sikhs, residing on the border of the two new countries, were crushed in the process.

Lahore lay caught in the middle.

The city of romance became the abode of madness.

Sikhs fought Muslims, who fought Hindus, who fought Sikhs. It was religious insanity running rampant over the land. Half of Lahore's citizens fled for their lives as bitter street fighting raged out of control. On the road leading out of the city were 150,000 refugees spread out for 60 miles. It was one of the greatest caravans of human misery ever witnessed. Those suffering souls were the lucky ones.

All across the rich farmland of the Punjab province lay burning villages. Agony and mutilation overtook the homeless. Neighbors who had lived together in peaceful harmony for generations, fell on each other in a sudden explosion of savagery. One of the Muslim refugees was a 23-year-old cavalry lieutenant named Mohammad Zia-ul-Haq. During World War Two Pakistan's future dictator had served with the British army in Burma, Malaya and Java. There his brother officers had described the middle class son of an army mullah as being austere and dignified. Mohammad Zia ul-Haq had been born in the city of Jullundur in 1924. However the great and tragic partition of 1947 was no respecter of future dictators. As chaos, murder and political instability swept across his hometown, located in the eastern Indian portion of the Punjab province, young Zia fled for his life with his fellow religionists.

Back in the city of romance madness reigned.

Lahore's beautiful canals were choked with the dismembered bodies of former peaceful citizens. Trains pulled in from India awash with blood, with everyone on board, men, women and children, butchered and only a gibbering engineer left alive.

As Ali Muhammad made his way through the now-peaceful streets he could have found no trace of that ugly episode in Lahore's past. Her history had been swept clean. The Hindu history and all traces of that sublime culture simply did not exist. Lahore was a city gutted of her Sikhs and Hindus. She was now home to Muslims only, who endeavored daily to forget the blood shed in those lanes. There were gaps in the street where my friend now walked. A Sikh temple had been closed. A Hindu shrine was turned into a shop. All traces of religious toleration which had once bound the entire subcontinent together were wiped clean.

Like the current citizens of Lahore, Ali Muhammad had thoughts of his own troubles and not those of the recent past.

For more than a year my friend had recognized the signs of his own growing dissatisfaction. The thought of his big house in Peshawar no longer brought him happiness. Before the Partition it had rung with the sound of children's laughter. For years the old Hindu house's sole occupants had been their ghosts and Ali's lonely soul. For the first time in years he was restless, had even secretly thought of leaving Peshawar because his heart ached for love. However his search until that day had been a brittle failure.

Ali Muhammad had made the decision months before his imprisonment to take a Pakistani wife. He reasoned that nothing could bind him to his adopted homeland more than the benefits of a family. Having toyed with the idea of paternity, he was now anxious to join the ranks of his friends who all enjoyed the respectability of home and hearth.

Unfortunately he had not foreseen the complication of who would be offered on the matrimonial altar. An assortment of friends had rallied to his decision to seek a spouse. His gentle spirit and artistic ability would be better served, they reasoned, if he was not preoccupied with the upkeep and daily chores of the big house. Consequently they brought him a parade of village girls. Strictly speaking the demure virgins were not supposed to talk to the future bridegroom. The concept of dating was a Western abomination not to be tolerated in prim Peshawar. However due to Ali Muhammad's foreign upbringing concessions were quietly allowed. Discreet meetings, with prospective parents in tow, had occurred on several occasions. Each time with the same regrettable results.

Dumpy girls with downcast eyes had assured him they would gladly cook and clean and wait on him. He knew none of them could ever be his friend or lover. They were a product of an environment that relegated their purpose to that of servant and child bearer. He sent polite regrets to those village girls and gradually lost hope of finding a woman who could arouse his heart. He did not understand that the portion of him known as Beau Fontaine was clinging tenaciously to the western belief that stated a man had to love his wife, not simply reside with her.

That was one reason why Ali Muhammad had guarded his secret meeting with Shaheen so jealously from those closest to him in Peshawar. Not only was a relationship based on romance alien; with the burden of centuries of accrued prejudice even Ali's closest and most broad-minded friends would have been horrified to discover his beloved was a "taxi," a whore.

For days he had felt the ground falling out from beneath him. His adopted life, his beloved Peshawar, he might have to surrender both voluntarily if it meant winning Shaheen.

His steps took him through the cloudy city and ever closer to her home. Overhead blue jays tumbled and scolded. In the daylight he discovered there was a canal running close by her house. Children were floating by in its turgid waters, sitting on a charpoy raft, blissfully unaware of the adult problems all around them. When Ali Muhammad entered Shaheen's alley he passed a blue car full of men sitting at the corner. He saw the gate to the brothel. His steps quickened. He put behind him all doubts and forgot any future criticism from his Peshawari friends.

"He laughs at heartache who has never had a wound," Ali reasoned, just as the rain started.

Ali Muhammad pounded on the gate and threw away tradition.

"Shaheen your *Angrez* is here," Aesha, one of the whores shouted and waved him in out of the gently falling drops. He didn't wait to be

The Garden of Fire

invited but began walking impatiently towards the courtesan's door. He longed for her animal pleasures, for her soft rippling voice, the glitter of her garments, the sound of her laughter as light as cat steps, and most of all the smell of jasmine.

The curtain flicked open and his heart's heart stood revealed.

Her shalwar kameez was flamingo pink. Her long black ringlets lay like the curtain of night on her shoulders. She was barefoot. A smile revealed her white teeth. Shaheen's eyes were amused at the sight of Ali Muhammad's transparent need.

"Have you come for a program?" she asked him coyly.

"Is that the term for it?" he said, and walked into her room without asking permission.

The musician had grown blind to the world around him, his tunnel vision revealing only this woman he would have walked across Pakistan to retrieve. He pulled her into his arms, and before she could resist, began to kiss her passionately. This time it was different. She allowed him the liberty. Her lips were warm and sweet beyond belief. He kissed her over and over until he felt her becoming aroused in his arms, until at last her own lips parted and he felt her shiver with the fire he had brought her. Her mouth was burning and he thought he would swoon, when he heard shouts and screams coming from the courtyard he had just left.

He tried to hold her tight against his chest, to ignore the repeated shouts of "Shaheen! Shaheen!" The courtesan broke free and went running out of the room. For an instant Ali Muhammad hesitated to follow, thinking he would sit on the charpoy and await her return. Then he heard his lover screaming and the sound of men's voices raised in anger. His first thought was that the police were raiding the brothel.

When Ali Muhammad ran outside Shaheen's door he saw turmoil and terror. A warm, light gray rain was falling. The car he had passed at the corner now had its nose shoved inside the gate. The driver was revving the engine, trying to ease the car further into the narrow, confining space. The three dark-skinned male passengers had grabbed the young whore Sanjeena and were trying to drag her towards the automobile. Naheed and Aesha, her two companions, were attempting to stop the abduction. They were hanging onto her arms, making a losing attempt at dragging her back towards safety. Everyone was screaming, Shaheen loudest of all.

She had become a raging tigress dressed in pink. The diminutive madam seized a hefty length of firewood and started beating the hood of the car. She was screaming *kunzil* (obscenities) in three languages and heading towards the invaders when Ali Muhammad shot his pistol into the air. The automatic spat out the big brass shell, which rattled when it landed on the brick courtyard. A cloud of blue smoke hung in the rainy air around my friend's head like an ominous warning.

Everyone froze in surprise at the roar of the big gun. The men looked shocked to see this man in a turban suddenly appear. Before they could react and release the girl, Ali Muhammad shot the pistol into the air again, then dropped the barrel, taking deliberate aim at the driver.

The driver slammed the getaway vehicle into reverse, scraping blue paint off its side as he screeched out of the gate. The passengers, seeing their retreat being cut off, let the girl go and began running after the car. As they fled, Shaheen smashed one of them in the back of the head, then threw the firewood after them as a parting insult. She and Naheed quickly slammed the gate shut and throwing the bolt, locked it securely. Sanjeena was crying, scared, afraid her abductors would return. Shaheen told her to stop her blubbering, then turning to Aesha, gave the fourth whore a resounding slap across the face.

"You imbecile", she shouted at her, then began berating the prostitute for allowing the raiders inside. Shaheen gave instructions not to open the gate to anyone, then came walking purposefully back in Ali Muhammad's direction.

She pushed her long hair impatiently out of her eyes and walking past him, went directly into her room. Ali Muhammad holstered the automatic, followed her into the room and closed the curtain behind them.

Shaheen had lit a cigarette. She took a deep drag and blew the smoke up into the air. The room was small and suddenly humid. Her shalwar was soaked from fighting outside in the rain. She smoked her cigarette unaware or uncaring that her dark nipples were shoving through her rain soaked top.

"Who were those men?" he asked her.

"Punjabi pimps. Business is bad because of the government. The local pimps want to drive us out because we are Pathans."

"Weren't you afraid?"

She filled the room with a hearty, honest laugh that mocked his innocence.

"No. Wasn't I in the movie "Assassin?" she asked him.

When Ali Muhammad confessed he had never heard of it Shaheen looked astonished, explaining that it was a Pushtu film.

"Was it famous?" he asked.

Shaheen smiled at his ignorance. She didn't truly understand this foreigner but he amused her. "*Aao kana* (it sure is)," she told him confidently.

Ali Muhammad had known many other women, including plump white American virgins who made a man pay in subtle ways then whispered threats of rape or marriage, and exotic Europeans with unshaved legs who took his love and seed before moving on to the next forgettable lover as easily as he did. This creature before him was raw, energetic, sharp, illiterate. She was Kali the goddess of danger and death come to life and dressed in pink. Nothing in his life had prepared him for either her intensity or the love he suddenly bore her. Looking at her beauty he felt as if his clothes were on fire. He could feel the sweat standing out on his forehead like a stallion's. The adrenaline rush of watching her attack the pimps had aroused him. He was stiff in her presence. When they made love his intensity transmitted itself to her.

As Ali thrust his sword into her garden of fire Shaheen cried, "*Whyee, whyee* (Oh, oh)," long and deep and wet him in her passion.

The Garden of Fire

Afterwards she lay beside him on the charpoy. It was quiet outside. He could hear the rain splashing down in the courtyard. He held her warm, naked body as close to his own as possible. He had never, never, experienced the emotions and the sex that Shaheen brought up from the depths of his body. The traveler had been looking for someone for a long, long time. Before today he had never known her name or how she looked. Now he knew.

The courtesan seemed content to share his warmth, to allow him to rest in the berth of her temporary love. She asked him various questions about his existence. Who he was? What did he do? Why had he come back?

Ali Muhammad smiled at her obvious attempt to fish for a compliment.

He got up off the charpoy. Walking across the room, he picked his vest off the floor where he had hastily tossed it. He withdrew a small cloth bag and went back to the charpoy. Sitting down beside her, Ali handed Shaheen the gifts it contained.

When the young woman opened it she first found an imported watch. Ali Muhammad watched as Shaheen attempted to fasten it upon her wrist with the numbers facing upside down. He posed the indelicate question of whether she understood its usage. In answer Shaheen tossed the watch on the charpoy in disgust. As she had never been taught to tell time, the mechanical bracelet was nothing more than an oddity to her. Like many of her Pakistani sisters Shaheen was ignorant of any of those basic elements of formal education. The men ruling the lives of Pakistan's women had long been opposed to putting the power of the pen into the hands of creatures deemed already cunning by nature.

The prostitute had no difficulty understanding the delicate silver ring set with a deep blue lapis lazuli stone she found in the bottom of the bag. She slipped it on her finger, clearly delighted.

On the way there, Ali had worried that he would be too shy to present her with his gifts. Now, sitting beside her on the charpoy, sharing her nakedness, he knew he would never be embarrassed for her or in front of her again. His only regret now was in not having brought her a bagful of gold coins to prove his love.

She humored the foreigner for a brief while, leaning back and allowing him to feast his eyes on her ripe body and her warm, wheat-colored skin. Then, without wanting to hurt his feelings abruptly, she let him know they should dress. There had been no talk of money. His display with the pistol had convinced her this was a repeat customer who could be trusted to pay, and he willingly did.

When he had regained both his clothes and his composure, Ali Muhammad handed her three hundred rupees and his heart. He then tried to explain the upcoming horse trip to Shaheen. She certainly knew what horses were but she had no conception of his mission or its purpose. The idea of traveling through the hostile mountains without setting off after material gain was so alien as to be indecipherable.

"Can I take your picture?" he asked her, and showed her a small camera he had brought along.

"No. Leave it. I will get in trouble if they find out."

He did not know who she was referring to, so he did not push the issue.

Ali Muhammad knew love was clouding his reason but he stood close to her.

"I love you," he told her quietly, sincerely, bravely.

She looked at the tall foreigner. He was handsome, perhaps rich, but there were a lot of men in the world and this was only one of them. She smiled at him, her black eyes melting any last remnants of Ali Muhammad's resistance and told him just enough.

"I cannot love in return," she whispered. "My life is no good. I do not like this work. But I am compelled."

"Would you marry me?" he asked her.

The question shocked Shaheen. She had not expected this effect or this response to her beauty so quickly.

"I will think on it," she told him and smiled, anxious now to conclude their business and to get him on his way.

"It is not easy for my heart to look on your beauty," Ali Muhammad told her truthfully.

Shaheen moved away. The foreigner had told her many odd things which she had not fully understood, but she had heard him say he was going to Gilgit. The beautiful woman knew it was in the distant north, close to China. That much she used to her benefit.

The courtesan reached out and placed her hands on Ali Muhammad's chest, then looked up at him with her warm, black eyes.

"When you go to Gilgit will you bring me a red tea pot?" Shaheen asked him softly, making no attempt at hiding her cupidity.

The question startled Ali Muhammad. He thought she would want to discuss the details of how to get her out of her current situation. Instead she seemed not to comprehend most of what the American had confided in her.

"Yes. Certainly," he assured her.

"Will you come back with it next week?" Shaheen asked naively.

My friend knew then that his lover did not understand the trip he was setting out on, or that he would be gone for many months, or that there was a danger that he might not ever return. Yet in his love Ali Muhammad forgave what he believed was her lack of understanding.

"It won't be next week."

"But you will bring me a red tea pot from China?" she repeated anxiously.

"Yes," he said, and saw a look of pleasure spread across Shaheen's face.

At that moment the only thing the lonely Ali Muhammad wanted was for Shaheen to send him away with a memory of her love. He longed in his heart to see a reflection of his own devotion mirrored on her face. He wanted to hold dear some trace of her burning beauty. The mercenary whore was interested in more practical matters.

"You had better go," she told him.

The Garden of Fire

"Goodbye," my friend said and then throwing aside his pride he told her, "I will think of you every hour of every day until I return."

Shaheen took him by the hand, lead him outside, assured him she too would remember, then closed the gate behind him.

Ali Muhammad stood there in the gathering twilight, staring at nothing, thinking of nothing. His heart was as empty as his arms. Slowly the sounds of Lahore began to filter in. The road was muddy. He saw people walking by, glancing his way. He did not want to arouse suspicion, so started stumbling like a sleepwalker in the direction of the bus station.

It was a long ride back to Peshawar. All he had of Shaheen was a memory of her vivid soul. The disappointed lover sat in silence on the returning bus, lost in the darkness of his thoughts and the Asian night.

29

Through Tribal Territory

The Peshawar sky was as black as a smuggler's heart. The only exception was a sliver of dim yellow moon. That tiny light resembled the Islamic crescent I loved so well. I wondered if Allah had hung it in the sky as an omen to bring me luck.

At 4:30 in the morning there wasn't much else to get excited over. Our hometown wasn't turning out to say goodbye. As we three horsemen made our way through the sleeping streets, the only noise was the sound of our heavy riding boots clomping on the cobblestone streets.

We were a day late leaving.

The delay had been unavoidable. Ali Muhammad had returned from Lahore too tired and late to consider pulling out on time the previous morning. Raja had discreetly left yesterday after breakfast, ostensibly going to check on the horses, in reality to allow my friend and me the privacy needed to discuss this new wrinkle in our mutual situation. Ali Muhammad didn't hold back and nether did I. In addition to telling me what had transpired, his account revealed the emotions that swirled around Shaheen. The musician turned equestrian explorer finished by informing me of his romantic intentions, determined as usual to let his heart override any practicalities.

"This is no time to get messed up with a woman, especially another man's woman. And she's a prostitute! If you're caught you'll be deported or end up back in prison," I told him.

"It could have happened to anyone," he told me with a look of defiance.

"Yeah, but things like this always seem to happen to you."

"I'm going to marry her," Ali Muhammad announced with finality. The look in his eyes told me not to cross him on the issue.

We had four trained horses and hundreds of dollars-worth of equipment sitting a few blocks away. Or rather I had all that gathered there. I wasn't sure about Ali Muhammad. The idea of riding horses had always been my vision not his. At that moment of disclosure I knew we were both weighing the years of our friendship, the shared adventures, the legacy Peshawar had woven through both our hearts. There was a lot to value, on both sides.

I opted to trust him.

"When are you marrying her, before or after the trip?" I asked, trying to sound convincingly casual.

The bastard let me hang there and stew in uncertainty. When my discomfiture became transparent, he smiled and drawled, "After."

Khyber Knights

So it was that the four of us, Raja, Ali, me, and the ghost of Shaheen, locked his door and walked through the darkened streets of the Hasht Nagari neighborhood on our way to adventure.

The police were waiting.

Six of them had turned out early to feed and help brush the horses. Even Joseph the Christian was at the police paddock. Hoping to assist, he thoughtfully carried all of our gear out of the tack room and stacked it within easy reach as we began saddling up. It was an old stable and with the exception of a single kerosene lantern we all worked in the dark. I went from horse to horse, checking to make sure hooves were cleaned, shoes were tight and backs were properly brushed.

Despite our numbers, a sense of solemnity kept us almost silent. We worked in the dark in whispers.

As the sun slowly arose our joy came up with it. It was then that Raja's innocent exuberance revealed itself. Ali Muhammad had come to grips with his decision to play it safe and leave town for a while. I never had any doubts about the course of my life. As Raja started cinching his saddle onto Pajaro he began quietly singing. Ali was soon smiling and I in turn felt relieved that we were all leaving on a happy note.

The moon really had brought me luck.

We three were dressed for hard travel. Like me, Raja and Ali Muhammad wore locally crafted knee-high riding boots. Made by an Afghan cobbler from an ancient design, the boots had a tough walking foot equipped with a thick sole. The legging was made of two layers of soft deerskin. Long cotton ribbons, tied off just under the knees, held the supple boots up in place. Our shalwar kameez were new and had been left intentionally loose. We all wore large turbans to shield us from the threat of the sun.

Ali Muhammad and Raja each carried a holstered pistol high up on their right hip. My own wide belt bore the pistol on the right, as well as my sword on the left. The thin dagger I carried hung on a cord around my neck, hidden from view underneath my shirt. I slipped the sawed off shotgun into Pasha's saddle scabbard. Ali's rifle was already stowed aboard Pahlwan.

None of the armament was a fashion statement. We wore our weapons in deadly earnest. I had run out of patience and was taking no chance on being involved in any more cases of mistaken identity. Whatever happened, I wasn't planning on going anywhere quietly, or without an armed struggle.

When the sun lit the sky the horses stood saddled. Raja and two of the policemen were adjusting the pack saddle on Pukhtoon. Guns were in scabbards and bedrolls were lashed down before Inspector Akbar Ali made his appearance. He walked around quietly checking cinches, running his hand under saddle pads, making slight adjustments in bits, carefully looking each horse over by turn. Like me, he adjudged the crew of men and horses ready and told me so with via a nod of his head.

"Right! Tighten the cinches and empty your weak bladders. Time to see if you're horsemen," I barked.

Khyber Knights

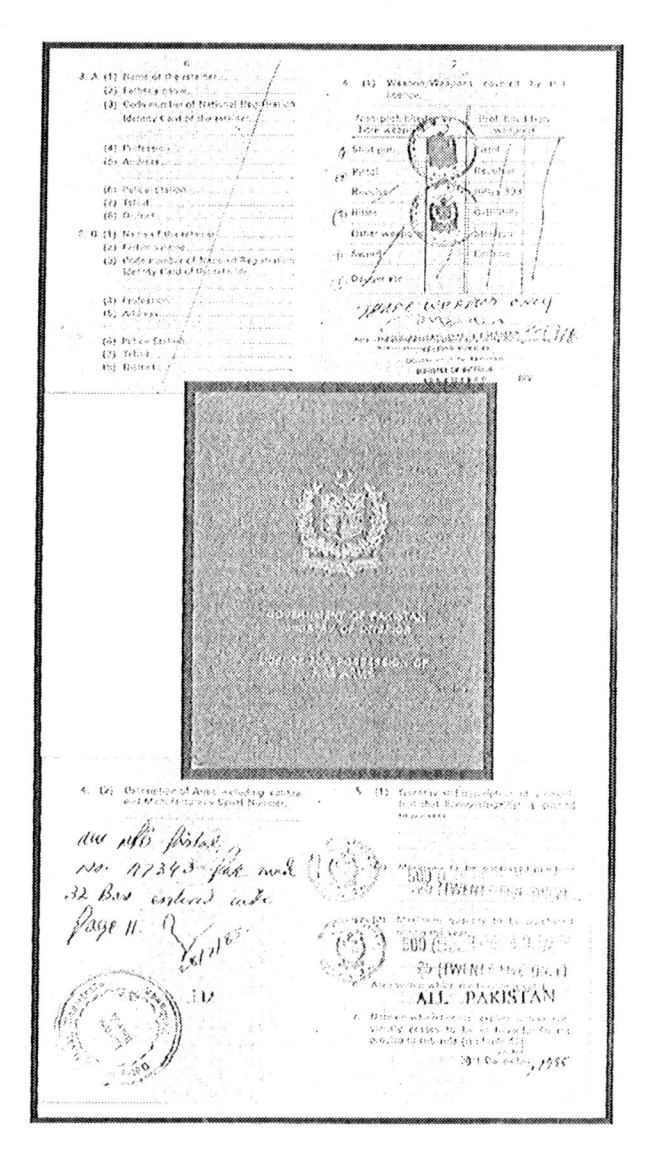

"We stood dressed for hard travel. Each man carried a pistol on his hip. The sawed off shotgun and the rifle hung from the saddles. None of the armament was a fashion statement. I wore my own weapons in deadly earnest. I was taking the advice of the government official who had authorized my Pakistani firearms permit. 'If anyone attacks you, kill them. We'll sort it out when you get back.'"

Through Tribal Territory

A few minutes later I swung up onto Shavon's old saddle.

Our friends gathered around, their faces reflecting our own excitement.

Akbar Ali stood in front of the men we were leaving behind, these riders who had overlooked subtle differences like race, religion, and national origin. Only one thing bound us, our animals.

The police inspector held his hands together in front of his chest, palms facing towards him. The others, including Joseph the Christian, as well as my friends and I, did likewise. In a strong clear voice the inspector recited a blessing over us before we departed.

"*Bismillahir Rahmanir Rahim.* (In the name of Allah, the compassionate source of all mercy). Remember that Allah made the horses on which you ride in order that you may sit firm and square upon their backs and from there celebrate the kind favor of your Lord. So say, Glory to Him, Who has subjected these horses to our use as a blessing, for man could never have accomplished this alone without the guidance of Allah," Akbar said, then dipped his hands in front of his face in token of surrender to the Almighty.

"Amen," we all answered.

Akbar Ali came and stood looking up at me. Reaching out, the old horseman shook my hand solemnly.

"Remember to be careful. The grave of a horseman is always open. Take no chances and beware of trusting this horse," he warned me as he patted Pasha's neck. The gelding seemed to sense his disapproval and pulled away.

We rode out the gates of the Sherqi Thanna police station with bells jangling and spurs jingling. I was surprised when Raja rode Pajaro out front. One of the policemen had handed Ali Muhammad Pukhtoon's lead rope. The amateur rider pulled the pack horse up close to Pahlwan, then fell in without comment behind Raja. Pasha danced insolently. I soothed him through the reins and we settled into a rhythm of our own at the rear of the caravan.

There were many things I thought of as we rode through that gate. All the worries and fears that had gone into putting together that expedition still rested on my shoulders. Should we have trained longer? Would the horses hold out? Would their riders?

The moment the gelding started gliding down the road I surrendered my soul to Allah. I knew we would only return alive if He so willed it. Pasha jigged his head in silent agreement. So I put my trust in the kismet that had brought us all together. The difficulties that had plagued me I left behind in the courtyard of the police station. I no longer troubled my mind over unskilled horses and weak riders, giving myself up instead to the journey that now dominated my soul.

Outside the stables walls we were plunged into the terrible traffic that led out of Peshawar. With the sun had arrived hundreds of busy people, coming and going to the events of daily importance that dictate lives in all parts of the globe. Within the first few minutes I knew the training program had paid off. Crazy drivers in screaming cars flew by. Over loaded lorries tipped and swayed, threatening to fall over on us before rumbling past. Men on bicycles rang little bells and waved cheerfully, for in all this sea of motion we were the only ones on horseback. An illegally overloaded bus passed beside us. Two dozen men and boys were sitting on top. It had been years since Peshawar played host to mounted nomads. When they saw us the merry bus passengers began screeching like parrots.

"Where are you going?" one of them shouted.

"Some place I've never been," I yelled back, but by then they were gone and we three rovers were left with the wind of northern Pakistan blowing in our faces.

As agreed, Raja took us on a heading into the edge of the Frontier Region. The road we chose was forbidden. Though it had much less traffic, it sliced through the edge of the semi-autonomous tribal zone. Traditionally the tribes allowed first the British Raj, and later Pakistan's federal government, to maintain rough control over the roads and a few dozen feet on either side. In exchange gratuities were issued to tribal leaders. Yet even this close to Peshawar, the governor of the North West Frontier Province seldom dared to delve into matters that lay outside a few limited official affairs. Here, where we rode, the law and the tribes lay in uneasy harmony. Within rifle shot lay a land beyond even the hint of any federal control.

Off to our left lay Afghanistan. In between our road and that forbidding country lay the FATA, the Federally Administered Tribal Areas. Up there, in the secretive foothills, the Pathans lived like they always had, democratic but deadly. No one, not even Pakistani government officials, entered that undeclared country without good reason. Seven reservations made up a tribal belt separating the madness of the Afghans from the semi-sanity of the North West Frontier Province. From Bajaur in the immediate north, to Waziristan in the far south lay more than 10,000 square miles of what was designated "Pakistan" on the maps. In actuality it was an uneasy alliance of fiefdoms and villages who bore only a grudging acknowledgment towards the capital in Islamabad. We skirted the FATA's edge, heading through the rich farm lands that defined its border.

By mid-day we were boiling and the early morning traffic seemed an illusion. On both sides of the lonely road were vast fields of sugar cane. Green walls higher than the horses heads waved far off into the distance. The heat and isolation combined to dispense the initial excitement of our morning departure, a pleasant memory that had already lapsed into the recent past. We rode strung out in determined silence, while the sun turned the blacktop soft and seared the air we breathed.

I welcomed this timid torture if it meant being back in the saddle that I loved.

Raja's morning song was left behind in Peshawar. All he had to listen to now was the sound of the caravan, the creaking of the saddles, the clip-clopping of the tiring horses and the music of the bells.

Through Tribal Territory

Before leaving I had attached two small brass bells to the halter of each horse. I had taught my companions how to fit the bridles directly over these halters, which were to be left in place, cavalry-style. With lead ropes tied off around their necks, the horses could be quickly staked out to graze without having to dive into the pack saddle for halters.

The soft ringing of those golden bells now provided the melody of the road. We were following a tradition almost as old as that of riding.

The use of bells on horse trappings is noted on the pages of time. Many are the tales of how the tinkling music adorned the mounts of various riders, from the steppes of Mongolia to the deserts of Arabia. Our geldings transferred that age-old practice across the wide expanse of history onto that hot, forgotten Pakistani road. We rode in companionable silence, my saddle-pals and I, as that symphony of antiquity played us a soothing jingle to ease the tough miles of our first day.

By early afternoon we had reached the Kabul river and seen hardly a soul. Once across the small bridge we pressed on, every step marching us further and further away from clocks, motor transport, and Western influence. The sun was loosing its grip on the sky before we realized we were nearing our first destination.

Pajaro seemed to notice the change in the day before the rest of us. The bay had set a steady lead for the other horses for hours. Pahwan and Pukhtoon were quiet gray brothers of the road. Even Pasha realized we weren't going home, ever again. Something was different and we all sensed it. The many low-lying fields were starting to be dotted by the occasional mud house when the bay picked up his gait. It was subtle, but he instinctively knew that we were nearing that day's destination.

He quickly transmitted the information to his rider.

Raja reached down from the saddle, and picking a tiny, white roadside flower, stuck it into the edge of his turban. Pasha perked up. Ali Muhammad sat up straighter in the saddle. We rode into the market town of Charsadda pleased and proud and in trouble.

The single chowk (junction) was crowded with farmers. Imported red Massey-Ferguson tractors shared the narrow lane. It was an important wide spot in the road with a single inn. The misnamed Venus Hotel we found there promised to provide three charpoys for the riders but no stabling outside its pink walls for the horses.

Luckily, I had anticipated such a problem.

I walked back to the outskirts of the town, where I entered the local police fort. Here I presented my firman to the captain in charge. This official letter from the federal government identified my companions and me as legitimate travelers. The document instructed the servants of Islamabad to assist us in our travels, provide shelter when possible and protection when necessary. In Pakistan, with its legacy of Mughal graciousness, the scrap of paper represented a link with the past. A police captain returned with me to the Venus Hotel, and that night the four horses rested safe and well-fed inside the walls of his fort.

After a hard day in the saddle the pink-walled hotel was close to Paradise. It had a common room, a pitcher of water, two tables and an overhead fan. Riding across country sounds pleasant and easy enough, but let anyone try marching twenty five miles over a grueling road at a foot's pace, throw in the labors of unsaddling four grumpy horses, plus their care and feeding, before rounding up a few local scraps to call your own dinner, then tumbling into a bug-ridden rope cot for a few hours before arising at dawn and I believe most would-be equestrian travelers would say, "No thank you!"

After serving us dinner, the hotel owner locked the door behind him and went home. We lay at rest in the darkened room, enjoying the reprieve of evening. Ali Muhammad and Raja confided they were sore in unaccustomed places but admitted they liked the ride.

Overhead the old fan stirred the air, clicking so fast it threatened to spin off and fall down on us. To Hell with the danger we reasoned. The cool air felt good and we were all too tired to move the charpoys into a safer, albeit hotter, part of the room. The conversation lagged. Our bodies were exhausted, even if our spirits were still strong.

Something in us was responding to the primal urge that beckons men over the wide, free horizon. This had always been particularly true of horsemen. Throughout history they had ridden over the rim of the world in search of bold adventures. Prison had tried to lull the longing that civilization had thought to tame in me. We fell asleep to the murmuring of wilderness and wild gods lurking up ahead.

We awoke before sunup, still idiotic with fatigue.

The absent owner of the Venus Hotel had assured us he would return before our need to depart. Having collected our money the night before, he was apparently in no hurry to rush back. With no regular way out, Ali Muhammad crawled through an unlocked window. Raja and I handed the guns and saddlebags out, then followed. The majority of our equipment we had left with the horses. Charsadda was still sleeping but we were anxious to make as many miles in the cool morning hours as possible. At the police station we found our four chargers anxious to see us.

There was no hay. We gave them the left-over ration of green corn stalks saved from their last night's meal. While Pasha was busy eating I started brushing him. I worked the last traces of dried sweat from yesterday's ride off of his coat, then went through his mane just as thoroughly. When I started to handle his tail with care he looked up from his meal and gave me a look which plainly said, "Stop playing the fool and get on with it." Thereafter he stood patiently when I took the hoof pick to his feet. That was the moment I realized Pasha and I were starting to trust each other.

The distance between Peshawar and Charsadda may not have been great in terms of mileage but in that short stretch the horses had recognized that we three men were the emotional threads that bound our herd together. As the seven of us went quietly about our work, brushing, saddling, eating, each took up the responsibility we individually bore. We men looked to our chores. The horses were equally serious, eating as if they understood the importance of preparing for what lay ahead. When they stood saddled and ready, Ali Muhammad, Raja and I walked across

Khyber Knights

"The lighthearted Raja reached down from the saddle, picked a tiny white roadside flower and stuck it into his turban. His horse Pajaro never slowed down. The big bay gelding seemed to realize he and his master were never going home again."

Through Tribal Territory

the street to a chaikhana. There we feasted on fresh unleavened bread, washed down by sweet chai. It wasn't much. It was going to have to be enough.

Our luck changed and some of the hardships eased. The road took us along the Lower Swat Canal most of the day. The waterway was thirty feet across and deep green in color. The air along its banks was humid. Great tall trees grew along its banks for miles. Going in and out of the shade gave us a chance to relax in the saddle. The farm land was rich, the villages not much more than a few huts, the people curious but friendly. Following the dirt road we came to a hamlet that boasted an outdoor barber. An ancient chair, an old mirror, a few rudimentary instruments on a rickety table were sitting beside the road underneath a shady tree. No sign, no advertising, just an obvious statement of fact. We took it in turns to allow the local tonsorial artist to give us a shave. I unhitched my sword belt before sitting in the creaky old chair. I doubt the barber had ever performed his art on a red headed foreigner. The dark-skinned little man graciously overlooked the accident of my birth. He leaned me back and told me to relax. It was an easy order to follow.

The shade was a delight. The big tree rustled softly in the warm mid-day wind. With my head inclined far back I could see birds singing and flying in the branches overhead. Village children scampered around barefoot and happy. Pasha stamped his foot behind me, then shook his saddle. Raja and Ali sat their horses, talking quietly. I closed my eyes and let the little barber run his old cutthroat razor across my throat and around my face. It was the most peaceful shave of my life.

By evening we reached the rich village of Tangi.

It had been a pleasantly uneventful but long day in the saddle. The only occurrence of note had been when we stopped to observe a crew of men harvesting wheat. The big thresher was painted in bright pastels and bore the name "Enemy of the Wheat" in bold letters.

In Tangi we discovered a government guest house. Once again our firman paved the way. We were shown into a clean room furnished with a few charpoys. Because these rest houses are maintained for traveling government officials, they often stand vacant for weeks at a time. Though we had to find our own dinner in the village, there was no charge for the room.

The horses were let loose to graze inside a walled in field adjacent to the guest house. Their free demonstration of equine athletics delighted the local children. A swarm of them hung on the walls shouting, "*Shahbash, Shahbash* (bravo, bravo)," at the scampering horses.

That was the last carefree night any of us ever had together.

The next day brought the beginning of hardship, at first in subtle increments, then later in bucketfuls full of grief.

We left behind the shady canal and ventured northeast. There we hit the main road leading north to Chitral. By skirting through the tribal zone we had missed most of the traffic crowding the road out of Peshawar. Late afternoon found us in Dargai. It was still a miserable place and had not changed since I passed through on Shavon. No one would give us a room, a charpoy or a helping hand. In desperation I presented myself at the court, the only government building where I thought we might find help. There we discovered the local judge about to go home for the day.

Qadir Khan was a kindly man and listened with sympathy to my tale. Looking outside the door he could see my six tired companions, human and otherwise. They were all dirty and hungry. I stood like Joseph petitioning a stable bed for a weary Mary. The firman lay on the judge's bench as proof of our reliability and our need.

Though the judge granted our request it was a mixed blessing.

If there is a Hell it must have a section called Dargai. What a foul little town it was. It was so hideously inhospitable the judge ordered three policemen to guard Raja and Ali Muhammad when they shopped in the bazaar for horse food. Judge Qadir informed me we would be safe only if we locked ourselves inside the court house for the night. The horses we could tie to trees growing inside the walls of the courtyard. He said all our equipment must be brought inside his court or considered lost before dawn. Knowing we were less than twenty miles from where the Afghan refugees had kidnapped Shavon and me, it didn't take much to convince me that Dargai was indeed a lousy neighborhood.

When Ali Muhammad and Raja returned they looked crestfallen.

They had been unable to find any hay, corn, corn stalks, or chopped feed for the horses. Raja looked ashamed when he showed me that the big sack on his back contained only bhoos, chopped wheat stalks. Ali carried a smaller sack of flour. The judge resumed his interrupted trip home, leaving us to tend to ourselves.

While Ali Muhammad and I carried the tack inside the court house, Raja set about making dinner for the horses. It was little better than starvation fare. When I confided to the young Pathan that I had never heard of this trick before reaching Pakistan, Raja gave me a knowing look that said he thought me very nice, if indeed very ignorant. The Afridi tribesman spread out an old piece of borrowed canvas. Dumping the wheat straw in the middle of the canvas tarp, he poured water on the pile, then mixed in the flour. The result was a lumpy gruel fit only for an equestrian Oliver Twist.

To give Raja credit it was all he could manage with what little we had. The horses simply hated it. But gone were the days when uniformed attendants fed them lush rations at the Sargohda Remount Depot. We gave each horse a share in his feed bag, then watched and worried. They may not have liked it but the big horses ate it quick, then begged for more. That scanty ration would have to hold them until morning.

"My father always said, 'For the love of God be not negligent to your horse for you will regret it in this life and in the next,'" the young horseman told me, all the while shaking his head in self recrimination.

I reminded him that we had our own problems as well.

Even with the door open, and the overhead fan going the old court room was already oppressively hot. We spent a tormented night. Following the judge's orders, we locked the door when the sun went down. The room became suffocating. The sweat-stained horse blankets reeked. We smelt no better. Though we placed the charpoys directly under the ceiling fan, the sweat poured off us in our sleep.

Plus the charpoys were flea-ridden. The invisible, blood-sucking little vampires fed on us until we cried out in our sleep. Late in the night I fled my vermin-ridden bed in despair, preferring to rest on the table standing at the foot of the judicial bench. It was hard but at least I was its only occupant.

The sun didn't have to tell me to wake up. I went outside while it was still dark to discover the horses hated the vile village as much as I did. Pahlwan, who once turned his nose up at apples, had stripped and eaten the bark off the tree he was tied to. We fed the horses the lumpy rations saved from the previous night, then swung into our morning routine without problem or comment. Raja and I started brushing the horses, while Ali Muhammad packed personal gear into saddle bags and caravan equipment into the panniers. There was little enough food to cause us to delay. By sun up we seven had put the wretched place behind us.

Before us lay our first serious obstacle, the Malakand Pass. In a way Shavon and I had been lucky to have traveled its stony heights during the night. With no street lamps to light the way there had been almost no traffic to plague my previous ascent. That morning with Pasha was far, far different.

The dun gelding was scared and I didn't blame him. Driving in Pakistan is an exercise in either folly or delayed suicidal tendencies. In all my travels in various portions of the country I had never met a licensed driver. Like genies and Pathan whores, they were a rare bird. Few women got behind the wheel except in the major cities. In the country an equestrian explorer encountered macho male drivers with the mentality of a "Top Gun" pilot and the formal training of a monkey.

That morning we discovered the slick, uphill road was crowded with massive Bedford trucks, desperately overloaded buses and swarms of impatient automobiles. The conditions were fearful. The problem was not that the road wasn't wide enough to accommodate two lanes of traffic. It twisted and turned up above our heads, leaving the plains behind and winding up through the jagged, stony teeth that sliced across the top of the horizon. The problem was that no one going in either direction cared a whit about anyone else on the road. Other travelers were obstructions to be passed or swept away.

Initially I led us, with my hands full and my heart in my throat.

Pasha had been doing fine with the traffic since leaving Peshawar but that stretch of road was different. The twists and turns of the road put us in blind spots to oncoming drivers. To augment my difficulties I had taken Pukhtoon in tow behind my own mount. As the three of us made our way up the mountain we were presented a terrible choice. We were traveling uphill on the outside of the road. I reasoned this way the oncoming traffic could see us and slow down.

It was a bad choice. We found ourselves looking over the brink. There was no guard rail, just a straight drop hundreds of feet down to the canyon floor. Far below I could see the rusty remains of unlucky trucks and buses who had plunged with their screaming passengers to a fiery death. With the oncoming vehicles pushing us to the very edge of the cliff, I realized we had to change to the other side of the road, even if it meant being hit by speeding drivers.

When we saw a break in the traffic I shouted to Raja and Ali Muhammad to follow me across. Pukhtoon choose that moment to pull back and in the mix-up Ali ended up in front of us, with me in the middle, and Raja bringing up the rear.

"Hug the sides or we're lost," I screamed at Ali Muhammad.

The musician didn't need to be reminded. The big horse and his frightened rider were doing the best they could. The novice horseman already had Pahlwan so close to the mountain his saddle bags were scraping. It still wasn't enough. As he neared a blind corner, an over loaded bus came lumbering up behind us. I watched as disaster kissed our caravan. The horseman and the bus went into the corner at the same instant. A small Toyota truck appeared rushing downhill. It forced the bus to squeeze the big white horse. I thought it was the end of them both but at the last moment the bus avoided crushing them to death. It clipped the saddle bag, almost throwing Pahlwan off his feet. The impact would have certainly thrown one of the smaller horses under its wheels.

Ali Muhammad, the amateur equestrian traveler, was shaken but alive. He continued to lead us over the time-worn flanks of the Malakand mountains. The only floral decorations were a few scrub bushes that had evaded the local goats. We were glad to leave behind the uninviting and dangerous mountain and reach a safer passage on the plains beyond.

After that experience ordinary trotting was nothing, going up rocky roads nothing, avoiding pits and potholes nothing. By the time we reached Timargara, many miles and some days later, we were a smoothly functioning seven-member team.

It was with high expectations that we rode into the beautiful government rest-house. The recently-built, one-story stone building sat high above the Panjkora river, looking across that watery expanse at the oncoming mountains. Raja rode Pajaro through the gate, so Ali and I naturally followed him. The three of us didn't have time to dismount before we were accosted.

The caretaker, a Christian named William Bill, informed us that firman or no firman we couldn't stable the horses on the well manicured lawn. We obliged by riding the horses back outside, tied them off and then reentered to discover an unexpected source of bigotry.

"No servants allowed," William Bill informed us, and looked down his nose at the Pathan tribesman who had shared our cell and ridden with us so faithfully.

I was in no mood to brook interference from a fat, middle-aged gatekeeper. Recalling my government friend's advice, I informed the Christian we would agree to stable and feed the horses outside the compound. In addition, I was taking his best room. I kicked open the closest door to prove it.

Through Tribal Territory

"Either get the police or shut up," I told William Bill.

He choose the latter.

It put a damper on what should have been our first good rest. We had no sooner tossed our smelly gear into his clean room, when the custodian showed up at the door with a peace offering. He proudly bore a tray on which rested a book and a bottle.

The book, I discovered, was the guest register. It contained a long list of signatures, with accompanying occupations and comments. Almost all of William Bill's recent guests had been American narcotics officials. The DEA men had stopped in Timargara on government-arranged tours. Next to their names were insipid remarks about how they were winning the war on drugs up there amongst the wild opium fields of Pakistan. Without exception the only other subject matter dealt with was how witty and invaluable William Bill had been during their tiring stay in his primitive country.

After reading these remarks I glanced up to see the would-be butler smiling as he held out the tray with the proffered bottle. It was a Johnny Walker Red whisky bottle full of clear liquid. I was mystified.

"What is that?" I asked.

"Why boiled water, sir. I always offer it to our foreign guests."

I threw him and his damnable water out the door.

We ate in town that night. Raja was quiet. None of us discussed the issue that was at the heart of his unhappiness. William Bill had correctly classified him as a servant and it ate at his proud heart. Though Ali Muhammad and I paid Raja, that had only been a formality. He was our friend, our cellmate, a brave tribesman of the Afridi Pathans, and most importantly a fellow horseman. He was no servant.

Early the next morning Raja pulled on his clothes and boots, strapped on his gun belt and donned his turban without waking us. He cracked open the door and slipped out as quietly as a cat, the only sound being the tinkling of his spurs.

Outside the air felt cool. The guest house still lay wrapped in sleep. The sound of the river caught his ear and thinking he would peek at what he had scarcely noticed the day before, Raja strode across the grass and stopped at the brief wall that marked its edge.

Sixty feet below him ran the broad Panjkora river. It looked nothing like the gray, sullen watery course he had followed yesterday. Instead its surface shimmered with a pale magnificence. Looking up, his eyes were enraptured by the sight of Allah's signature strewn wide across the sky. Exquisite lilac-colored clouds lay above him. From the mountains in the north, to the Malakand Pass in the south, the heavens stretched unbroken in one long swirl of pastel purple paint. As if it too were in love with that sky, the river rippled quietly by, its surface mirroring the colored stream of air that ran above them both.

Off to the north, at the edge of his eyes, were mountains crowned in deep blues and regal purples. As Raja turned his head slowly to the south, he saw the crags turn from rose, to pink, to amber. He knew nothing of culture, that Pathan boy with little education. Yet he was wise enough to know that only in nature, and never in art, could he see the hues of red butterflies wings, green sea mists, and yellow wild flowers. He knew somehow that the blue color of those far-off mountains now beckoning him was something he would never reach. No matter how fast he rode Pajaro, the mystery of those colors would recede into the distance, as if to remind him that the perfection of such beauty was never to be attained in this world, but could only be reached at the end of the long journey known as life.

Raja stood transfixed. The colors had bewitched him.

He saw the beauty and knew in his heart that this was why he had come on the trip, to see mighty mountains, strange people and Allah's work. He understood that this moment in his life explained the unexplainable. The view from that ledge justified his abandonment of all the sensible things he could have done when he regained his freedom.

Surely such beauty required a price? Nothing comes free, Raja reasoned.

Here before him was Allah's divinity laid out in more beauty than any mullah had ever described. The secrets of the ethereal magic lay revealed and the tribesmen's soul sang in silent praise to the miracle of one common day's dawning.

No birds peeped. No dogs barked. No people stirred to disturb this evidence of Allah's glory. The world, and Timargara, lay in a breathless trance at the sight of such subtle beauty. The first rays of silver sunlight began to pierce the sky. Their brightness shot spears of white light through the delicate colored clouds. Within seconds Raja's secret was dissolving. He tried to memorize each shade, to recall the look of each cloud, to remember the stillness of that moment, never to forget the calm tranquility that evidenced Allah's love of the corrupt world.

The sight of that sky removed the lurking pain left in Raja's heart by Pindi Prison. He threw his original plan to leave us over the wall and walked away in silence to see to the horses.

30
Pukhtoon

We shook the dust of Timargara from our blankets and rode away.

Raja was anxious to leave. Something had stirred within him that proved love of adventure was not simply an occidental affliction. In Ali Muhammad I wasn't so sure.

The road north ostensibly lead us to Chitral and beyond. As Pasha pranced away from Timargara I realized that where I was heading was no longer a mere direction. All day the mighty gelding ate up the road, taking me further and further from the former clock-oriented life I had been a part of. Far behind lay the hot plains of Peshawar, ahead lay unknown mountains.

That day I threaded Pasha through the small rocky precipices which were a promise of larger things to come. Yet while handling the reins I was cognizant of the slow methodic swaying that bound horse, saddle and rider into one mute and mutual creature. As Pasha journeyed on I saw Pakistan sliding slowly by, inch by dusty inch. The sound of his iron shoes on the rocky road, the low creaking of the hot saddle, the jingle of bells, those sounds were the missing mantra of my life.

Bygone cavalrymen, cowboys and Cossacks already knew what I had long suspected. Those bred-in-the-bone horsemen could have told me it wasn't important to reach Chitral, or Samarkand, or any tangible place. The maps all lied. Borders shifted. Towns were renamed. History moved on. Fabled Constantinople was no more. Alexandria was reduced to ruin. Balkh was inhabited by ghosts.

Those saddle-trained specialists of another age could have explained that the magic of the journey lay in recognition of the bond that lay between the rider and this prince of animals. Where the dun took me was no longer as important as the freedom I experienced as we journeyed there together. While the equestrian voyage lasted I would share with my horse the pangs of separation or the delight in the union that had forged us into one new animal.

Sitting up there on Pasha's hurricane-deck I had an excellent view of the world. From where I sat I could see that, unlike Raja, my friend Ali Muhammad had not grasped this essential fact about the nature of horses. I feared for him it would never come. His mind was preoccupied with other matters. More than just a few horse lengths separated us old friends. Pahlwan remained for Ali Muhammad no more than a lovable beast.

By late afternoon when we reached the village of Warai we had other matters to attend to.

A crowd of children followed us as we rode in, entranced at the sight of armed men and big horses. In their eyes the circus had come to town.

"Are you going to the Jihad?" one little boy asked Ali Muhammad.

"No! I'm going to Lahore," he shot back angrily.

As we made our way along the only street the crowd of men and boys grew. Surrounded by a host of these idly curious, we stopped in front of the local version of the Ramada Inn.

The nameless chaikhana had nothing to brag about except its air of dignified poverty. No door had ever graced the fine establishment. It was an apology cast in concrete, with a single battered samovar and two weary benches stationed inside a two-walled open-air room.

My friends and I stabled the horses in a narrow alley between the tea house and the shops next door. At first my main concern was that Pahlwan would back his rump into the samovar behind him. We unsaddled under the intense eyes of dozens of idle onlookers. Raja was busy answering questions, while Ali Muhammad carried the tack into our temporary quarters. We had unintentionally brought a carnival atmosphere to the drab village, and normally I would have been glad to share in the excitement, when I discovered the saddle sores on Pukhtoon's withers. A small hard patch on each shoulder marked the spot where the old military pack saddle had rubbed him through his blanket.

I told myself it was a curable problem but all that night I worried.

The music of the horses' hooves sounded on the road early the next morning. Ahead lay a stretch of ever-growing mountains. Tall brown hills marched first before my eyes, becoming green, cedar-covered peaks. At the edge of the sky, and the top of the world, lay stern gray granite massifs, devoid of trees, stripped of men and skeptically awaiting our arrival. The tarmac road we were traveling on soon became a dirt affair which took us ever higher into the clear blue air.

The cool early morning was soon replaced by a warmer afternoon. We left behind the brooding rocks surrounding Warai and entered low lonely mountains where we saw no other people. Hour after hour, mile after mile, we rode on through this desolate unnamed stretch of Pakistan. Slowly it became a grueling endurance test for horses and men. We humans shared few words. The distance between riders became too great to shout back and forth. The only occasional noise came from the slow-moving horses. As the miles began to mount we riders became increasingly grim. The sun was starting to droop, and so were we, before we sighted Dir.

Before leaving Timargara, William Bill the Christian gatekeeper, had passed on a special confidence. Most travelers to the notoriously unfriendly hamlet of Dir stayed in its decrepit hotel. Unknown to almost everyone was the government-maintained rest-

house located beyond the edge of town. The Christian had never seen it but assured me it was worth the extra effort.

Pajaro didn't like William Bill anymore than his master Raja did. When we came to the outskirts of Dir the big bay stopped in front of the first building he came to. After a forty-mile day, he was clearly ready to halt and avoid taking the gatekeeper's advice to press on.

Pukhtoon

    I tickled Pasha's rib with the spur and urged him to take the lead. We weren't fooling anyone in town. We looked like saddle sore gypsies. It had been our longest and hardest day yet. Despite my years in the saddle, it felt like my bones were breaking with fatigue. My right knee was on fire. I hung on, ground my teeth and prayed for the end of the day. Pasha reluctantly left town behind and continued up a road that lead between pine-covered rocky-ridges. I was so tired most of the natural beauty was lost on me. Following an ever higher path our little caravan came at last to Pani Kot, the former rest house of the Nawab of Dir.

    I dropped the reins of a tired Pasha onto his neck and swung out of the saddle. My joints ached. My fingers still wanted to grip the reins. The phantom sensation of the saddle lingered with me. Like my friends, I was hungry and near exhaustion.

    "God's holy trousers," I quietly exclaimed at the sight awaiting our little caravan.

    Before us lay a lapse in time, a perfectly preserved nineteenth-century British hill station. William Bill had lied. This wasn't a rest house. It was heaven.

    We tied the horses to the pine trees that edged the road. With spurs jingling and my sword slapping against my leg, I entered the compound through a neatly-painted red garden gate. Directly before us was a wide expanse of grass that resembled a putting green. The lawn was crowned on both ends by two matching gazebos. Inside each structure was a large cannon aimed at the road we had just ridden up.

    To my right lay a magnificently preserved single story building. Its walls were spotlessly white. The wide verandah, with its stately posts and extensive wood trim, was ornamented in bright red paint. Carefully-maintained antique lawn chairs sat outside the doors of each guest room. Delicate rose bushes were blooming nearby, perfuming the evening air.

    A chowkidar came out to greet us. Our firman cleared the way into expansive three-room suites consisting of a sitting-room, bedroom and bath. The front room boasted ceilings nearly twenty feet high, crowned by ceiling fans. The furnishings were rich and included a twin bed, a dark wood armoire, several handsome chairs and a writing desk. Each large bath was laid out in turn-of-the-century tile work and fixtures.

    Our horses could be grazed on the nearby grass-covered hills, the chowkidar informed us. The only drawback was we would have to supply our own food, which could be purchased in nearby Dir. There was however a large kitchen available for our use. We would be expected to take our meals in the formal dining room. The best part was that unlike Timargara, which was frequented by a steady stream of guests both foreign and domestic, Pani Kot was a forgotten Shangri-La. No one had visited the place in months.

    After seeing to our mounts, we went back into Dir in search of our dinner. The main street in town was almost totally dark but we managed to find a chaikhana that would serve us a meal. Our culinary experience that night was more indicative of Pakistan in general than the genteel surroundings we had just left behind in Pani Kot.

A kerosene lantern threw a haphazard light over what served as a tiny dining room. We were three tired horsemen and almost anything would have sufficed. A chipped wooden table gave us something to lean against. Two hard benches kept us up out of the dirt. While we awaited dinner a servant boy brought us a metal pitcher of water to assuage our thirst. The single tin cup he left was designed to serve our collective needs. Because Dir was a frontier sort of place there was no silverware or dinner linen.

I poured myself a drink of water, took a deep swig, and gagged. It was so full of silt a spoon could have stood on end. Ali Muhammad gave me a look of questionable disbelief. When he tried the artesian delight he too recognized its vintage excellence. We left it on the table however, thinking if it was good enough for the locals we could stand to drink it as well. Within five minutes an Afghan mujahid came in seeking dinner. His face was as delicate as an unshaven log. One look told me he probably spent all day killing Russians with both hands. Upon drinking the water, he promptly spat it on the dirt floor in disgust, proof it appeared that we had chosen a dive even by local standards.

Supper merely confirmed my suspicions.

The cook brought us a big platter of grainy rice decorated with large lumps of raw, lukewarm fat. The local sheep boasted a club-like tail that often weighed more than ten pounds. This deformity was a solid mass of fat, and though a genuine burden to the animal, was considered a culinary delight by everyone in Pakistan, including Raja and Ali Muhammad.

I groaned when I saw what they served us. I hated sheep fat. The practice was to serve pieces that resembled little ice cream scoops of pure protein. To Raja the native meal was as ordinary as a hamburger and French fries encountered on Sunset Boulevard. And one of Ali Muhammad's many talents was his ability to consume anything with gusto. Having developed an adventurous palate eating crawdad gumbo at a young age, the son of New Orleans was not only a student of the culinary science, but a connoisseur of supposedly edible items that passed beyond Western belief. Sadly, my own skills started at the saddle and ended at the table. I was a timid eater but knew better than to back down, or worse yet, go hungry.

When I picked up a piece of the yellow fat it quivered and trembled repulsively on the end of my fingers. Raja was eating his way into my part of the rice and paid me no attention whatsoever. Ali Muhammad gave me a look of supreme impatience, so I popped the ghastly gobbet into my mouth without chewing and felt it slime its way down my throat. Even after swallowing the disgusting taste lay on my tongue unbidden. But having jumped the first hurdle I carried on in silence, never exactly enjoying the meal but at least not choking with repugnance. I washed it down with a swig of the gritty local champagne and congratulated myself on having chosen such a wonderful country to live in.

Khyber Knights

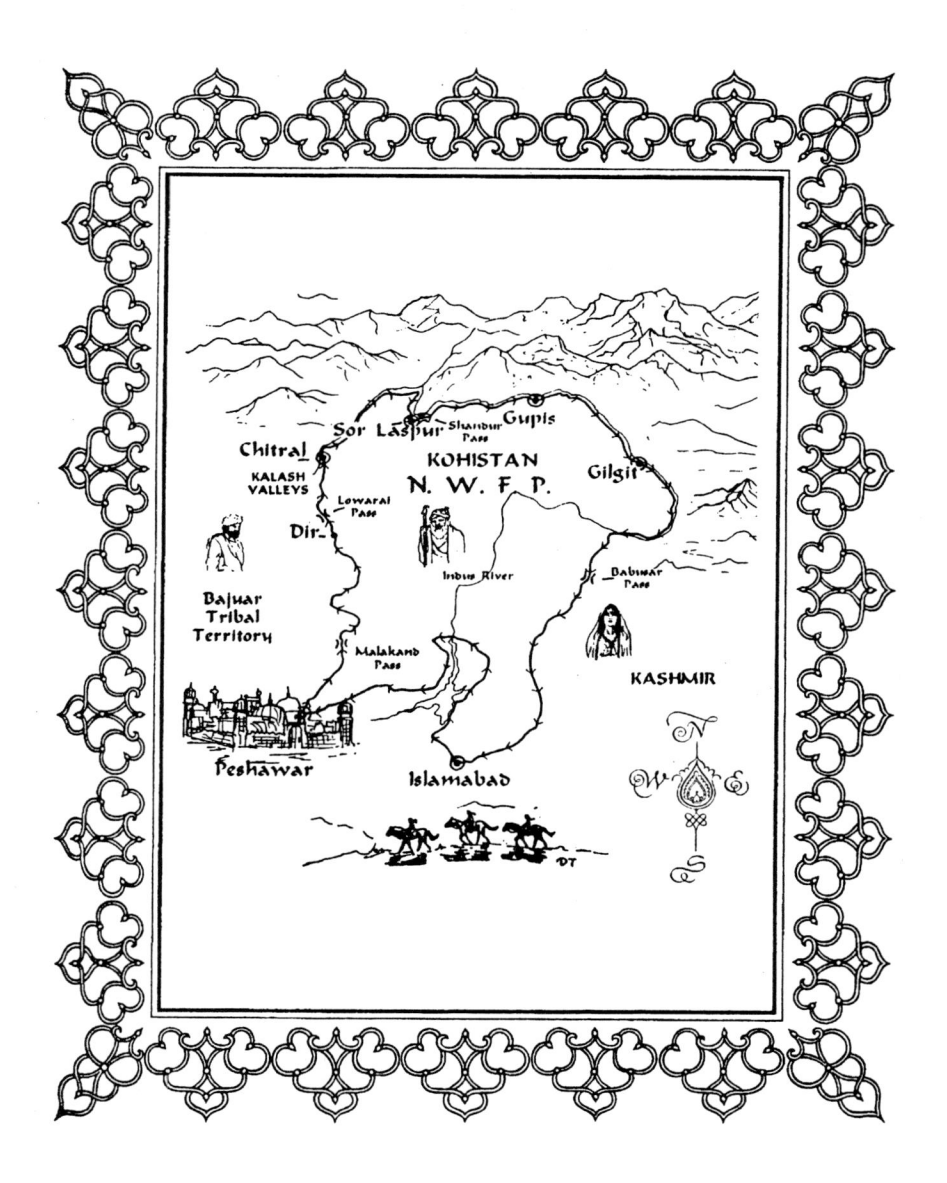

The Long Ride

Pukhtoon

With such an excellent restaurant and a so-so rest house at our disposal, it was decided to allow men and horses to rest over for a few days.

The next morning found me smoking my pipe as I sat in the Pani Kot garden. After providing us with a delicious breakfast of fried eggs, bread and chai, Raja had taken Ali Muhammad and departed for the bazaar. I was left alone to ponder, rest and watch over the horses.

At 5,800 feet high Pani Kot's pine-covered hills were decidedly cool. Lying there in the immediate distance was the Lowari Pass Shavon and I had climbed together. While I was thinking how good it would be to reach Chitral and see the palomino mare again, guests arrived. The local *Qazi* (judge) and the Assistant Commissioner of Dir District had received word of our touchdown.

A new four-wheel-drive Pajaro, complete with driver and armed bodyguard announced their arrival. Introductions were made. The chowkidar quickly brought chairs for the two important men. They joined me there on the lawn. The view was seriously magnificent, the two light-hearted Pakistanis not at all. Both were from down country, articulate, university educated and bored. They had lived together in mutual professional exile for so long they resembled an old married couple. One would barely start a sentence before the other finished it for his colleague. They squabbled and squawked like two starlings arguing over a shiny bug. In no time my pleasant morning resembled a tea party where the Mad Hatters all wore turbans.

Thinking they had come to check on our papers, I offered to retrieve the firman. Explanations were quite unnecessary. We were guests of Pakistan. That was enough for them. I quickly learned they had simply come on a social call.

"I remember seeing you and your yellow horse," the local judge told me. He went on to explain how he had passed me in his car the morning I was riding up the Lowari Pass on the palomino. He was sad to hear I had left her in Chitral, and paid no attention to my explanation that I had not retrieved her because I later became preoccupied in Rawalpindi for many months. When he asked me what I had been doing in that city I said simply, "Government work."

While the attentive chowkidar served us cups of tea, my guests solved the mystery regarding the origin of Pani Kot.

"The old Nawab lived in his fortress overlooking Dir. He had this guest house built at the turn of the century to house his British guests. This way he could keep his visitors close at hand, without having actually to allow them inside his castle," the Qazi said. The look he gave me was a reassurance that he considered himself the local expert on the subject.

"After one of his trips down country he brought back that German-made Krupp cannon," he continued, pointing at the artillery piece closest to us. "It had been captured by the British from the Turks during the first World War. The Raj gave it to the Nawab for his services to the government. Of course they only intended it to be used for decorative purposes. The Nawab not only had it made operational, he had it copied.

The other cannon is an exact duplicate that was forged right here in Dir by his local gunsmiths. Both guns fired black powder and bags of nails. The Nawab was a true Asian tyrant, more concerned about making guns than taking care of his own people. When he lifted an eyebrow men fell at his feet trembling."

"Oh don't be absurd," his companion challenged him. "The only thing the old Nawab got was a one-way ride into banishment. The government swooped in with a helicopter full of commandos and whisked him away to Lahore under armed guard. Even though his family had ruled this country for generations, the Nawab was never allowed to come west of Rawalpindi again. The truth was the chaps in Islamabad even stripped him of his hereditary title and gave it to his son because they knew the old man could snap his fingers and raise 10,000 men at arms within a matter of days," the Assistant Commissioner informed me with equal conviction.

It was a story like so many others in Pakistan, full of devious turns, half-told truths, baseless rumor, a handful of evidence and some moldering bones to spice the soup. I knew better than to rake through the ashes. I would have had to open graves to find the answers to their debate. I kept my peace and let the two friends gossip on. The only confirmed fact was that on either side of me two serviceable field guns still pointed at the road, their sullen black eyes testimony of the Nawab's social preoccupations.

Later that day I went to town seeking veterinarian assistance for Pukhtoon.

What followed was a disappointing journey. Situated as it was on the threshold of the mountains, Dir was never much of a horse town. What little knowledge I might once have discovered there was now lost. Horse doctoring was a special profession, a vanished science. The pack horse's withers had started to worsen, discharging a small amount of pus. What he needed was rest. I reasoned I could provide that in the nearby pastures of Kafiristan, only a few days ride from Dir. I had come to town to try and find any sort of medicine that might ward off infection until then

Sitting in a shop not much bigger than a closet, the town's only pharmacist offered me a cup of chai and some sound medical advice. As a boy he recalled hearing his father and uncle discussing why horses traveling over the rugged Lowari Pass returned with saddle sores. The old man assured me he could remember what had once been common knowledge.

"The illness is caused by the bite of large flies, who after having feasted on serpents, have become impregnated with the venom. Their bite deposits it in the flesh of the horse," he told me with complete confidence.

I left with a box of boric acid powder to sprinkle on the horse's back. With the mild antiseptic in hand I made my way along the main street. Dir remained a suspicion-ridden place, inhabited by people more apt to give you a hard look than a friendly hand. Modernization had skipped over this depot of unfriendliness. No down country liberal values had been allowed to infiltrate. No woman dared show her face. The spirit of the old Nawab still ruled decades after his banishment.

Many of the yeoman farmers who shared the street with me were opium growers. It was hard to scratch a living out of the stony ground in the nearby mountains. The brightly-colored opium poppies had been providing them with a lucrative cash crop for generations. The hardy red and white flowers grew as high as a man's chest. At the top of each stalk was a bulb that resembled a small green tomato. When the ripe bulb was slit a brown gum began oozing out. After allowing the sticky secretion to congeal on the sides of the bulb for a few days, farmers would scrape off the brown opium gum with a small, specially-crafted knife.

In a country where the annual yearly income for a farmer was $300, opium growers around Dir were getting $1,000 for a few donkey loads of the intoxicating sweat of their sweet-smelling flowers. Buyers from any of the hundreds of secret heroin labs would then discreetly move the opium paste to their "factories" hidden along the border deep in the adjacent tribal country. The poppy scrapings would there be easily converted into raw heroin using nothing more complicated than a few large boiling pans and some tubing. Ten pounds of Dir opium, which could be bought locally for $250, would be distilled down to one pound of high grade heroin. The same pound of pure smack would be sold direct from the factory to a smuggler for $2,500. The dope-runner could expect to be paid $250,000 for his uncut pound of heroin when he delivered it to New York city. Within a few days the same heroin would have been diluted numerous times with various other ingredients The final value of the Dir poppies was estimated to be worth roughly $3 million dollars on the American streets.

Due to the high amount of American aid flowing into Pakistan, the opium farmers were coming under direct pressure to curtail their ancestral growing habits. Yet, much like the moonshiners in the American south, Dir's backwoods capitalists resented any governmental interference, foreign or domestic, into what they viewed as an inherited right. At first cash incentives had been offered if they would switch to maize or wheat farming instead. Failing that, the outlaw farmers had become the subject of raids by the Frontier Constabulary. Front-page photographs often appeared in the Peshawar newspaper showing a large group of policemen burning a pile of seized opium poppies.

In actuality it was a sham war provided for the entertainment of visiting American Drug Enforcement Agency officials. The Pakistanis would drive the visitors up into the nearby hills, where they would observe some of the flowers being destroyed. After spending an uncomfortable night back in Timargara on one of William Bill's lumpy beds, the Americans would scuttle back to Washington convinced they had seen the end of that year's poppy harvest. They were unaware that the Pakistani Narcotics Control Board agents were cutting deals with local growers to destroy the opium crop in one area in exchange for ignoring another.

Khyber Knights

The locals viewed the American interference as a plague to be endured like that of locusts. If someone's field had to be sacrificed for the good of the community, then next year that man's crop would be inviolate. Everyone in Dir, that rough old cob of a town, knew this tit-for-tat appeasement was part of the price of doing business. Besides, they smugly reasoned, history was on their side.

In 1926 the Mehtar of Chitral, a local prince related by blood to the Nawab of Dir, accepted 15,000 English pounds as a bribe from the British Raj in exchange for curtailing the production of hashish in his kingdom. The grateful Mehtar took the English money and of course his farmers carried on as usual. It was a simple lesson the Americans never learned. No outside foreign influence was ever going to restrict the rebellious men of Dir, especially when such astronomical sums of money were involved.

The American Congress had provided between $20 and $50 million dollars, to be distributed over a period of three years, to directly combat poppy production. Those funds were funneled to the same outfit that had tortured and illegally imprisoned Ali Muhammad and me.

Yet when Attorney General William French Smith was taken on a tour of a Pakistani village, one of his assistants observed heroin being openly sold on the streets. Renegade Afghans were pumping the dope out of their war-torn country as fast as they could boil it down. Two of Pakistan's world-class squash players had been busted trying to smuggle a million dollars-worth of the powder into New York. Even the Soviets were suspected of peddling the infamous drug. A Russian freighter had been seized in Holland after twenty kilos of heroin were found on board. Diplomatic sources quietly agreed that it would have been impossible for such a large shipment to have slipped by without Soviet acquiescence. The poppy farmers of Dir were only small fry among the nouveau riche of the Pakistani drug world.

After three days' rest we departed from the forgotten paradise known as Pani Kot. We rode out at sunrise with the songs of the awakening birds over our heads, their chirps, cheeps and twitters falling out of the pine trees to mark our departure. Raja and Ali Muhammad soon learned the hard lesson Shavon had showed me. The Lowari Pass was very different from the Malakand. Though rugged and steep, the Malakand is a desert pass like the not-so-distant Khyber. Both could prove formidable when defended, but were too low to pose altitude problems. The Lowari is a true Himalayan pass. Its single-lane road lay buried beneath the snow for more than half the year. Its avalanches were legendary and lethal.

We were rested and fed however so went laughing up the Lowari, traveling across her tree-covered flanks all day. Before us was a great wall of ice and stone, beyond: the promise of new horizons and fresh countries. Reaching the top spelled more than mere height attained. It symbolized the leaving behind of the monotony of the flatlands.

One of the curses of modern civilization is that such a premium is placed on life that it ceases to be worth living. Risk was the price we

Pukhtoon

three travelers were willing to pay to capture that view. From the beginning of time man was made for such endeavors. The effort to reach the top of the Lowari was to our hearts the wish to surmount the places hard of access, whether of physical surroundings or spiritual point of view. It was the wall of rock separating us from the divine spark that made our lives different from that of other men.

By sunset we had achieved our goal.

As if to confirm man's bold self confidence, we discovered a tiny encampment inhabited by half a dozen men. These hardy souls lived in four surplus army tents on an alpine meadow adjacent to the road. Four of them were busy setting up a log cabin which would serve as a future truck stop. The other two graciously offered us charpoys, pasturage and food. Ali Muhammad and I staked out the horses in the short grass. Raja meanwhile set up our gear in one of the tents.

Night found us tired but happy. The rough-looking innkeeper surprised us with a culinary delight. He handed each of us a round cake of freshly baked coarse bread. On top he had melted goat cheese. Slices of roasted goat meat adorned the thick Pakistani pizza. The hosteller was proud of his skill as a cook. We did not mention all the bits of grit, goat hair and straw that infiltrated the meal. That was just the Pakistani sauce. The delicious dinner was followed by sweet, hot chai. Soon afterwards our small group of pioneers and horsemen sat around the campfire enjoying our tea, talking softly and smoking.

Lowari tolerated us but she would not let us slide into comfortable denial. It made no difference to her how hot they were down in Peshawar that night. Each man sat wrapped in everything he owned to keep out the cold. Nearby, the horses stood picketed close together to stay warm. When the moon arose it resembled a white ice cube. It made me freeze just to look at it. As the talk subsided I glanced up. There above our heads was a bright constellation. It was called the Big Dipper, or the Chariot, depending on who was looking and whom you asked.

With nothing keeping us from the warm quilts on the charpoys, we all retired early. I was tired and shouldn't have had a care. I had reckoned without Pasha. The impudent rascal was full of mischief. I no sooner settled into my bed, when the dun pulled up his picket pin and went charging off into the night. From our tent I could see him running around the meadow, delighting in his freedom and daring the other horses to follow him.

To the sound of Raja and Ali's snickering, I hauled myself up, pulled my boots onto the wrong feet and stumbled out after my errant charge. He tore past the tents with his bells ringing like Satan's stage coach come to get us. He never ran far from his stable mates, thereby telling me he was only playing. I was swearing, cold and mad before I managed to grab his rope and haul him in. I pounded the picket pin in as deep as the stony ground would permit, then tied him with every knot known to man. When I was satisfied, I stood up to find Pasha looking at me.

The happy gleam in his eye clearly told me, "I enjoyed the trouble I created far more than the few mouthfuls of grass I snatched."

Khyber Knights

Next morning I checked him for stone bruises but not surprisingly discovered he was unscathed from his great escape. Though the sky overhead dawned a brilliant blue, we horsemen waited around the fire for the morning to warm up. With tea and bread in our bellies we then rode the short remaining distance to the top of the pass. We stopped our horses there on the 10,000 foot crest. Clouds came from their nostrils. The air was bitter cold. It gnawed at our fingers and clawed at our faces. It bothered me not at all. There before me lay the long-remembered sea of mountain peaks. I had carried that scene in my mind like a secret icon throughout the dreadful days of my imprisonment. Mighty fingers of stone, with names like Nanga Parbat, Masherbrum and Rakaposhi now awaited my arrival.

I was lost in my contemplation when Raja turned to me.

"What are you looking at?" he asked.

I couldn't answer. It was too private.

The Afridi smiled in understanding and said, "Your blue eyes must come from watching the heavens overhead."

Before I could answer, he clicked to his bay and started the long descent.

The climb down was still as steep as I remembered. It took us four hours to negotiate the forty two switch-backs representing the north face of the Lowari. Only the croupers kept the army saddles from sliding down around the horses necks. We often rode with our legs straight out, practically lying down on the backs of the horses. It was a snake-back road and gave us several bad scares.

At one point a Chitral bound truck came growling down behind us. We dismounted and pulled the horses as high up onto the mountain as we could to give the driver room to pass. When he pulled even with us, shifting and sliding the massive vehicle by in low gear, I could see that despite the brave face he looked pale under his dusky complexion. The sound of the close-passing truck frightened big Pahlwan. He refused to lead after that, preferring to fall in behind Pasha, Pukhtoon and me.

Eleven hours later I led us into the town of Drosh. We were all tired, hungry, and stressed. The dinky chaikhana we discovered at the village's edge was a Godsend for us and a cruel disappointment for the horses.

We had to stake them out in a hard-dirt parking lot. The geldings had called some barren places home for the night but that was the worst. There wasn't even a blade of grass. Additionally, the bazaar was long since closed. Once again the worthy horses went to bed on a dinner of straw, flour and water. We riders faired slightly better. The inn keeper gave us a decent room, then informed us he could provide a bucket of hot water for each man to take a bath with. At least we went to bed cleaner.

Immediately upon rising we set out to feed the horses. We managed to locate barley and news of a local veterinarian. While our mounts ate, we moved our gear out of the inn. Though we were legally cleaner, our clothes still reeked of horse sweat. Added to the smell wafting off our pile of tack, the little room had taken on the odor of an airtight barn before morning.

Gone was the soft sighing of yesterday's cold mountain wind. We found ourselves once again in hot weather. As soon as we were saddled up we lead the horses to the far side of town. Here we met the government employed vet. He had a pleasant practice. His little office was situated under shady trees. The local farmers brought him an occasional sheep or cow to treat. I suspected Pukhtoon was the first horse he had investigated. We pulled off the pack saddle and let him examine the animal's sore withers. He agreed with Raja and me that rest was the ultimate cure. Meanwhile, he thought an injection of a strong antibiotic would help ward off infection. A boy was dispatched into the office. He soon returned with what looked like an old bottle of medicine and a syringe big enough to draw blood from a bull.

The vet jabbed Pukhtoon in the neck, swabbed down the spot with alcohol and told us not to worry. There was a minimal charge for the medicine which the medico assured me was worth every cent.

"Money spent on horses is in the eyes of Allah like giving alms," he assured Ali, Raja and me.

We set off thinking that by the end of the day we would be in nearby Kafiristan, where the loyal pack horse could rest and recuperate like Shavon had. It was a route and a routine known to me. We rode through drab, burnt-out countryside, until crossing an old iron bridge took us over the river separating us from our destination.

It was a hot ride that day and we could not believe we had ever been cold. When we stopped at a spring to let the horses drink, Pasha, Pajaro and Pahlwan pulled in long deep draughts of the sweet water. Pukhtoon oddly ignored his chance. I looked at him perplexed. His soft brown eyes had a far away look I had never seen before.

We bent our backs to the task at hand and began marching through the thick dust marking this point of passage. The air grew deathly hot and utterly still. No birds sang. Pasha lead us into that portion of the world where Allah dumped the rocky refuse from his earthly creation.

Late afternoon found us at the entrance to Kafiristan. We had left behind the village of Ayun and begun threading our way through a canyon as skinny as a key hole. I had taken Pukhtoon behind me. He followed quietly but kept bumping into Pasha. When I stopped, what I saw scared me. The normally white pack horse was now a dirty gray from the dust and perspiration. Yet on the left side of his neck, where he had received the injection, he was drenched in sweat. His skin there was scalding hot to the touch. Worse yet, the big horse was weeping.

His eyelids were partially closed but the tears were running down his cheeks in mute agony. A feeling of helplessness swept over me as I saw his tears splash on the ground. I reached out and scratched him as I had done so many times before when he, Pasha and I rode together. He rubbed his sweaty head on my leg as if to reply that he too recalled the long miles we had shared.

Khyber Knights

We only had one choice, to make for the closest inhabitable spot, the village of Boumbaret. With Pukhtoon following me half-blind, we set out with what haste we could muster. The sun was setting before we drew close. Ancient mulberry trees began to appear, then small patches of delicate green grass, and finally fields of ripening green corn. Night was threatening to enclose us completely by the time we reached the outskirts of the village.

Once again I saw the picturesque inhabitants, the women with their distinctive black dresses, the men wearing wool caps. Ali Muhammad stopped the first Kalashi man we met and asked where we could stay. Up ahead we learned was a small hotel with pasture and running water.

I reasoned we were saved.

I reasoned wrong.

Within sight of the Kalash Hotel Pukhtoon collapsed. When he fell the lead rope ripped through my hands, nearly dragging me out of the saddle. I let go and scrambled off Pasha.

I knelt beside the big gray. Pukhtoon had settled down with his feet underneath him. He wanted desperately not to move. That option wasn't open to us.

"If we leave him here some fool in a jeep will run him over in the middle of the night," I told Raja and Ali Muhammad. "We have to get him on his feet and move him to that pasture."

Though only a few hundred feet away, it looked like an eternity. I urged Ali to ride ahead and tell the hotel owner we were coming in with horses. Handing him Pasha's reins I told him, "Go. Go now. Hurry."

The once amateur horseman galloped off on his mission.

"Get down," I ordered Raja. His normally kind face was a mask of apprehension. Slipping the thick leather quirt I carried off my right wrist, I handed it to him.

"When I pull on his lead rope you must whip Pukhtoon," I told the boy.

"Asadullah, I cannot."

"If we don't get him up he will die like a despised dog in the middle of this road. Do what you must," I told him in a stern voice that gave no hint of my own growing fear.

Reluctantly, like a condemned man, Raja fell in behind Pukhtoon. Pajaro's reins hung limp in the boy's left hand, as did the quirt in his right. I walked to the pack horse's head, aware of what needed to be done and dreading it. I pulled on his lead rope, urging him to rise. He ignored me. I pulled again harder. Nothing.

"Whip him," I yelled in frustration at Raja.

He laid a light mark across the stricken horse to no avail.

"You cowards!" I screamed at both of them, and turning my back, leaned into the rope until I thought my spine would snap. Behind me I heard Raja sob, followed by the sound of the lash and the big horse reached deep into his big heart and rose, not out of fear but from the same blind loyalty that had lead him this far with me.

I never looked back. I heard Pukhtoon breathing hard, breaking his back to reach that pasture. I would have carried him if I could. Together

Pukhtoon

we walked the few hundred feet that separated us from safety. As soon as I stopped, Pukhtoon sank gratefully to the ground.

Ali Muhammad came running up with a Kalashi. Abdul Khaliq was a shifty eyed little squint but he said we could picket the horses anywhere we liked. I wasn't waiting to ask permission. I was stripping the pack saddle off Pukhtoon. Within minutes Raja and I had the gear off of him and two of our blankets draped over his once strong body.

When I looked up I saw with surprise that standing on the balcony of the nearby hotel were a number of Caucasian foreigners. None of them made a move to come to our assistance. From where I stood I had no idea of their nationality, nor did I care. Perhaps our uninvited martial air had discouraged them from investigating. The sweet odor of hashish came floating over from their way. It didn't matter. Nothing mattered, except saving Pukhtoon.

Life intrudes even into emergencies. The other three horses had to be staked out on their picket pins. We took it in turns to carry our tack to the room provided for us. A Kalashi teenager was sent to fetch fresh corn stalks to feed the horses. An old Afghan serving as hotel cook rustled us up some fried eggs and bread for dinner. While all of this was happening Pukhtoon stood up and the sun went down.

Our caravan was soon dining together. The three healthy horses were close by eating a hearty supper. We three famished men were mopping up egg yoke with pieces of the cook's homemade bread. The dishes were soon cleared .The food killed the pangs of hunger, but not the pain of the day. We stayed on duty, talking in low tones, afraid to leave the sick horse, watching the night advance. By the time the old cook joined us, the hotel's patrons had long since gone to bed. He and Ali Muhammad sat squatting on their heels in the grass, quietly discussing the pleasures of Kabul that everyone remembered but no one would ever see again.

Pukhtoon seemed to be slowly rallying and had risen to his feet after a short while. We had kept him warm, yet he had refused both food and water. His breathing was short, shallow and despite the cool night air, his neck was still hot and damp. His eyes were haggard but I knew in my heart he would recover. Tomorrow, I reasoned, I would journey to Chitral and if necessary kidnap a veterinarian to save the big roan. I was in no mood to be trifled with I thought, when I saw a convulsion ripple through Pukhtoon's body.

I jumped to my feet but before I could reach him the pack horse collapsed, falling on top of Pahlwan's picket rope. The bigger horse started screaming in fear and tried to rear. I reached under my shirt, pulled out my dagger and fought to locate Pahlwan's rope in the dark. When my hand found it, the line was as taut as a piano wire. The sharp knife slashed through it in an instant. Feeling the rope go loose, Pahlwan turned and ran into the darkness. Ali Muhammad started to follow.

"Leave him," I shouted, "he won't run far from the other horses."

Sliding the dagger back into its sheath, I turned back to help Pukhtoon.

Khyber Knights

I got down in the dirt, picked up his head and placed it in my lap, willing him to live.

"Maybe if you cut a hole in his belly he will breathe better," the old cook volunteered.

The advice went unheeded. I held my horse's head and told myself the big roan with the childish spirit would pull through, that he would be back on his feet by morning.

Fool that I was, Pukhtoon died to prove me wrong.

I was sitting with his head in my lap when he gave one last twisted, tormented gasp and expired in my hands. It was 12:07 a.m. I noted mechanically. His big brown eyes started glazing, something I had always read about but never in my sheltered life seen. At that moment, as if to illustrate my agony, the full moon rose behind us, shining down through the limbs of the large mulberry tree overlooking the meadow.

My tears, those vagabonds of woe, arrived unannounced. Through the loss of Shavon, and the horrors of Pindi Prison, I had held the despised watery weaknesses at arm's length. Somehow I had always successfully waylaid my growing grief, ignoring the adversity that humiliated my soul and the misery oppressing my neck. No more. Stoicism deserted me and I wept long and hard, holding the warm head of that gentle creature who had fled without warning from this perilous life.

31
Horseman's Horror

I dreaded the dawning of that next day.

My tiny hotel room was still black. The gentle blush of dew was but barely in the air and if sleep had graced my eyes I could not recall. During the night a constant spur jabbed my mind. The most intelligent man can make a mistake. The sharpest sword can fail to cut. Even the most noble of horses can stumble and die, I rationalized through the long hours since my life too had stopped at midnight.

Say in silent defense what I would, in my heart I knew I was reduced to nothing, no one, less than an ounce of dust. In such hatred introspection had I laid awake, waiting for the sun to confirm my crime of ignorant neglect.

Under my charpoy's thick quilt, wrapped in warmth and grief, I heard a woeful sound. The tinkling of children's laughter came seeping through the thick log walls of the hotel, presaging vexation and grief. Dawn or no, I knew Kalashi children were early risers. Having slept in my clothes, it was easy for me to slip on my boots and call myself dressed.

Stepping out onto the hotel verandah I discovered a glorious morning full of promise. The valley we had traveled up last night fell away to the east, rolling down between two giant gray massifs. Between these stone walls lay a hidden Eden. The left side of the valley held the road, which lay guarded on both sides by a marching line of walnut trees. Rustic wooden houses could barely be seen, their flat rooftops peeking shyly through the trees. The right hand portion of the valley was dominated by the jolly sound of an unseen river rushing by. It rambled and tumbled downhill just beyond the hotel, running its course in a sunken stream bed that lay hidden to my eyes but not my ears. Crowning this beauty was the long sloping pasture laying directly in front of me. Nearly five acres of rich green grass rolled gently away. At the top of the pasture, next to the base of the hotel, ran a smaller sparkling stream. Its pure waters rushed by like a living crown.

My eyes feasted on this beauty. My ears took in the jingle-jangle music of the stream. I could smell the faint aroma of wood smoke and baking bread coming from the cook shack. It was a still mountain morning and my heart should have soared like a hawk.

The idyll was ripped to shreds by the macabre scene confronting me.

Picketed on the far side of the pasture stood the surviving horses. They huddled there in a group, Pahlwan, Pajaro, and Pasha, their heads hung low, staring in nervous anticipation at their dead companion close by.

Pukhtoon blotted the landscape like a dormant sack of death.

Khyber Knights

Seven little Kalashi boys and girls were scampering around him, poking, prying, and peeking at this strange addition to their normally serene valley. As I watched the sound of the jolly river was lost, its lovely tune eaten by the crass laughter of the curious children. My heart took in the surrounding beauty only by accident. It was too busy breaking at the sight of my lost companion.

While I hesitated, unsure what to do, one of the little boys crawled up on Pukhtoon, standing there proudly as if he had conquered a mighty peak. I could no longer remain an impassive observer.

"*Bachas, za, za* (children, go away)," I said, and waved my hand in their direction. I must have looked a fright with my wild red hair, my strange looking clothes and my tall riding boots. The oldest girl pulled the boy off Pukhtoon and they all scurried away, running towards the closest of the houses.

I walked across the pasture and stood looking at the dead horse. My eye came to rest on the silver amulet still faithfully tied to Pukhtoon's halter. Inspector Akbar had been right. The young roan had been unlucky. I pulled the dagger from beneath my shirt and reached down. The sun dried string tied to the halter was as fragile as Pukhtoon's life. I cut off the amulet which had failed to protect Pukhtoon from the unlucky whorl in his hair. Maybe it was just a horseman's ancient superstition. I didn't know or care. The shock of what the death of the packhorse meant to the expedition at large was just beginning to set in.

"How will we go on?" I asked myself.

Until now we had journeyed through well settled ground. What lay ahead were mountains beyond measure, scattered villages and few foodstuffs for either riders or horses. Beyond Chitral was when I had counted on using Pukhtoon to carry the supplies that would see us all through to faraway Gilgit. I was lost in such contemplation when my host crept up behind me.

"Such a tragedy. Such an error," Abdul Khaliq said.

I had no idea he was even close to me. I turned and for the first time saw the hotel owner in full light. At close range he was more than mildly repellent. A small, well-knit man, he wore the national costume of shalwar, kameez and a dirty vest. A pair of green socks confirmed his rustic sophistication. His ready smile, in which his eyes played no part, disclosed rotting teeth in a face that was both unshaven and unwashed. He had large, soft hands that looked out of place in this farming village. His manner was altogether full of courtesy and concern. Yet he struck me as insidious, unreliable, decayed.

Despite his odious appearance I had a problem on my hands that could only be solved with the innkeeper's help.

"My pack horse died last night," I said in a flat voice, trying not to reveal my depth of emotion.

"Yes, the cook came to my house and told me."

"What can I do with the body?"

Horseman's Horror

"You have three options," Abdul Khaliq said and with each succeeding word lead me by stages into a delicate trap in which who I was fought for control with who I thought I had become.

We could, he explained, hire ten men to haul the carcass away in a jeep and bury Pukhtoon "in the jungle." We could hire men to push him over the nearby river bank and bury him intact close by. Or we could hire Kalashi butchers to cut him up and haul the pieces away for burial. The first option was the most expensive, 1,000 rupees, a fortune by local standards. The other two were more reasonable, 500 and 300 rupees, but unacceptable.

Pukhtoon had brought me to an unforeseen junction in both my journey and my existence.

Years of experience had taught me that many people on the Indian sub-continent were utterly callous with regard to the sufferings of horses. I had often observed that even those few who did not actively ill-use their horses in an effort to get the maximum of work out of them, would seldom take the trouble to put a mount out of its misery by the use of a charitable bullet.

The average Pakistani would have scoffed at the idea of negotiating over the burial of a dead horse. They would have casually gone about the normal affairs of their morning. Any discussion with a lowly pagan Kalashi hotel keeper would have only been to inform him to ride the dead horse straight to Hell for all they cared.

Abdul Khaliq, the intuitive villain, sensed that my roots would betray me on this issue. Despite my turban, my adopted religion and all the adaptations, both external and internal, I was still carrying in my heart the supposedly forgotten influence of my American community of culture. At that moment I could have easily confirmed my Asian identity by laughing at the innkeeper and going in search of breakfast.

Instead all the lessons instilled into me by those childhood western TV heroes said I could not ignore my duty to this animal. If their siren song had lead me to find myself that morning on a faraway frontier, I could not now betray the same lessons they taught me and allow Asia to harden my heart in regards to my equine comrade.

I stood there, locked in a silent struggle, unsure of who I was and what I stood for. For years I had sought to push down the invisible walls imprisoning me within the restrictions of my existence. All the experiences I knew, the cultural, spiritual, familial boundaries that defined my limitations had supposedly been left behind, as I ventured not only into the mountains of the unknown but into the mountains of my own limiting definition of who I was.

Pukhtoon was that test for me.

It finally came down to one issue, one morning, one horse.

In truth I may have killed him. I was no judge of that. He died on my watch and I would always live with that shame. It was what I did for both of us that morning that would justify which route we shared from that moment on. I knew it was not about justifying the money to bury him. It was the rejection of Pukhtoon's worth if I denied him that last respect. It was about the derogation of the dignity of Allah and the animal who He had allowed to share my life and my road.

I did not know what had slain Pukhtoon. I could have read a book on veterinarian medicine and it would not have mattered. I was in Kafiristan where not murdering your neighbor was still considered a novel idea. It was about believing he was more than a slab of cold meat.

Asia lay rejected.

"We are different from you people," I told Abdul Khaliq. "He was a friend and not just an animal to me. Hire the men and take him away by jeep. Then bury him intact, and with respect."

"And the money?" he asked.

"The money will be paid when the job is done," I answered.

With the arrangements settled, I returned to the hotel where I found my companions awake and anxious. When informed, they agreed with the decision to bury Pukhtoon with what little grace we could manage. Raja took the calamity better than either Ali Muhammad or I. He had a deeper reserve of unfettered philosophy to draw on. His touching faith in Allah was his strength and standby in all hardships, trials and disappointments.

While our horses breakfasted on grass and green corn stalks, we men tried to put on a brave face by eating fried eggs and bread. The morning was wearing on and we had turned to grooming the horses. The foreign guests had started to dribble out of the other rooms. Ali Muhammad and Raja spoke to them. I remained aloof from outside contact, lost in thought and worry.

By ten a.m. there had been no sign of ten men or a jeep to haul away our dead charge. Ali and I approached Abdul Khaliq about the delay. Every minute we looked at Pukhtoon's rigid mass was a tear in our hearts. Where were the men and why the delay we asked?

"I sent a servant to the village but all of the men are busy in the fields and refuse to come," Abdul Khaliq said smoothly, his face smothered in a cheesy smile. "I also looked at the river bank. Its too rocky to bury him there. Plus our people will be angry if we put him so near the water. We will have to cut him up and then take his parts away to be buried in the jungle."

The idea appalled us. Butchery, added to an untimely death, seemed too much to consider. We had no choice. Logic dictated Pukhtoon be removed from the pasture as soon as possible. His metamorphosis from valuable teammate into a jarring reminder of death was complete. The lovely valley was jaded by his presence. We opted for the unthinkable.

"Bring the men. Do it quickly," I ordered.

Raja shook his head and Ali Muhammad was silent at this turn of events. With the decision made, we three decided to go in search of better pasturage for our remaining horses. The meadow adjacent to the hotel, though large, had been severely cropped down by goats. Trying to feed the big horses on such scanty fodder would be self defeating.

Before any of us had a chance to set out, Abdul Khaliq corralled our team into helping dispose of Pukhtoon. The wily inn keeper had managed to secure two local men to carry out the repellent task of butchering and burying the horse. Their plan was to drag him to the embankment, a distance of forty feet, and slide him down to the river bank below. The actual bloody deed would then be done below the vision of the hotel and in close proximity to the nearby water.

It was one of those impossible situations that occasionally occurs in Pakistan. Despite our loathing to have anything to do with that morbid operation, necessity forced us to partake in this carnival of death. As if sensing our predicament, several of the children had reappeared. They hovered nearby, as the six of us, Raja, Ali, Abdul Khaliq, the two butchers, and I, took up positions around Pukhtoon.

There is no graceful way to drag a 1,200 pound dead animal forty feet. Here was no longer our cheerful friend. The cadaver resembled that departed companion in name only. His once bright eyes were glazed over with a strange blue film. His inquisitive face was twisted in a grimace of pain. His light gray coat was caked in mud.

Gone was our friend. The only thing left was this final disgrace.

We positioned ourselves around the corpse and on Abdul Khaliq's signal tried to push it. The obstinate dead thing refused to budge. Pukhtoon's great bulk lay there, a massive, immovable tonnage that defied our puny efforts.

The inn keeper ordered us to take up positions around the horse's body. While Abdul and I grabbed the tail, the other four men each took up a leg. When everyone was in position, we threw our backs into the effort. The children screamed in excitement as we began moving the big horse towards his final trip over the cliff. Once we had him underway the end of our labors came quickly. We stopped just short of the edge and stood behind his back. Then with a mighty shove we managed to tip his body into the waiting void.

I was unprepared for what followed. Pukhtoon did not slide down gracefully to the riverbank below as I believed he would. Instead the air was rent with the sound of his legs and ribs snapping like great, dry tree limbs, as he rolled end over bone breaking end, smashing up against the merciless rocks twenty feet below. He lay there, a heap of unrecognizable white carrion. I held my stomach, calmed my nerves, forced myself to act casual, as the Kalashi butchers slid down after him like excited Comanches. The children followed, intent on witnessing the horrid butchery. I stood frozen, not wanting to believe what images my eyes were delivering to my brain, telling my ears not to remember the sounds of his breaking bones, trying to recall what a good horse he had been, until I saw the flash of the long knives.

I turned and gave Abdul Khaliq a look of contempt.

"Horsemen do not traffic in the meat and skin of their mounts," I told him. Then turning to my friends I said, "I am not a cannibal to watch this," and walked away.

Raja, Ali Muhammad and I saw to our other horses and soon left to find grass or other feed for them. What we discovered was only more disappointment and regret. Boumbaret was the largest of the three

Kalashi valleys. It was in such an Arcadian valley that Kipling had set his famous story, "The Man Who Would Be King." The story of Daniel Dravit and Peachy Carnahan related how the former British soldiers came seeking the lost treasure of Alexander the Great, supposedly secreted among his Kafir descendants. Though initially deified by the Kalashis, the soldiers of fortune were discovered to be spiritual impostors and executed.

As we walked through the Boumbaret valley we saw history repeating itself, however this time the execution was of a culture, not two adventurers. Commercialization was creeping into Kafiristan. Tourists, both domestic and foreign, had learned of the forgotten valleys and none was more popular nor easier of access than the one we had unfortunately chosen. The rumors of promiscuous celebrations lured in Pakistani men anxious to ogle the unveiled Kalashi women. The rumors of a hashish haven lured in the foreign hippie element. Though they had long abhorred Muslims and outsiders, the Kalashis had become wise to the ways of the world.

Their traditional wood carving, which included embellished floral designs on homes and temples, was a thing of the past. The life sized wooden statues that decorated their tombs had either been stolen or sold to unscrupulous foreign art dealers. Even their famous dances were now largely performed only when a crowd of tourists agreed to pay. Kalash women, dressed in long black dresses and picturesque jewelry, shoved out a greedy hand and demanded money at the first sign of a camera. Children were becoming beggars. Men had grown sullen. Paradise had become sullied.

What had been an island of independent thought was surrounded by a girdle of gradual annexation. Free since the days of Alexander the Great, the once fiercely independent Kalash of Kafiristan found themselves residents of a game preserve in which they were the main attraction.

This new set of circumstances affected our decision to stay.

For hours we three horsemen tried unsuccessfully to negotiate for a field of grass for our horses, as I had previously done for Shavon. Farmers were unwilling to part with forage, citing their need to prepare for the winter. Our sense of determination turned into gradual dejection. As we made our way through the valley the only note of hospitality we located was at the Frontier Hotel. Unlike our current residence, this smaller establishment was owned and run by one of the few Muslims living among the Kafir population.

My friends and I stopped there for a cup of tea and discovered an ally in Ishaq Khan, the owner. Though less charming than the more picturesque Kalash Hotel, there was a sense of humble honesty about this hostel, whose presence we had inadvertently overlooked during our hurried march in last night. The hotel had three rooms and a decent kitchen. A large walnut tree threw shade over a serviceable wooden table and benches. We drank the chai provided by Ishaq and discussed our options in regards to continuing the trip.

Horseman's Horror

Sitting nearby, practically unnoticed at the time, was a jeep owned by the hotel. Though it plied back and forth to Chitral as the need arose, our concerns were equestrian not mechanical. Yet our options were almost as limited as those early Christians who were forced to ride through Muslim countries bareback as a penalty for the profession of their religion. Should we go on at all? What to do with the pack saddle? Should one of us sacrifice our mount and walk alongside? Could we find another pack horse? Perhaps Shavon in nearby Chitral could be bought back?

There were no longer any easy answers. Gone were the days when the Shah of Persia would penalize a horse owning subject for appearing in public on foot.

We paid for the chai, thanked Ishaq for his hospitality and returned to the Kalash Hotel still discussing our future. The one subject on all of our minds lay unspoken, a denied grim secret.

Was Pukhtoon buried by now?

Our steps took us off the dirt lane into the pasture where our horses stood waiting. As we came close to the stream that rippled in front of the hotel we discovered the grisly answer to our unasked question. Stretched out on the grass like a gray flag of grief was the flayed remnant of our departed companion.

"Those sons of dogs invite us to eat our own filth," Raja yelled and started running towards the hotel bent on murder.

Abdul Khaliq chose that moment to appear, coming out of the nearby cook shack to meet us.

"I'm sorry," he said, holding up his hands in token of surrender before either Raja or I could slay him. "I have already reprimanded the butchers and told them to take the skin away and bury it with the rest of the offal. It was a simple mistake, nothing more."

It was Ali Muhammad who defused the situation. He stepped between the Kalashi pagan and Raja, gently pushing the Afridi boy back in my direction. I put my hands on the younger man's shoulders and restrained him. Raja did not try to push by, but he spat on the ground at Abdul Khaliq's feet.

"You spay zoi (son of a bitch) may your father's grave be polluted and your mother abased in Hell," he told the Kalash with pure Pathan hatred.

I walked over and looked down the embankment. The rocks were splashed red. A pile of partly digested barley lay on the ground next to a pile of guts, and Pukhtoon's head. All other trace of him was gone. I saw the blood covered butchers coming back to gather up those last grisly remnants. Revolting as it was, I was thankful that I had managed to at last lay the big horse to rest.

The hotel owner fled for the safety of his kitchen but the discovery of Pukhtoon's skin was the final straw for all of us. Despite the hotel's beauty it was agreed that none of us could stay another minute without brooding over the horrible occurrences of the last twelve hours. While Raja and I saddled the horses, Ali Muhammad packed the few things we had scattered in our two rooms. My old friend advised me to take Raja and the horses to the Frontier Hotel. I agreed to send the jeep back for Ali and the pack saddle.

Our retreat almost became a rout. Suffering from delayed shock, that afternoon became the emotional low point of our collective endeavor. While Raja and I were still pounding in the picket pins, trying to stable the horses under the walnut tree for the night, Ali Muhammad arrived in the jeep with our gear. What had been a bad day became worse.

The Kalashi hotel-keeper had taken advantage of our separation to deceive my trusting friend. Swearing to Ali Muhammad that I had already agreed to the prices and terms, Abdul Khaliq suckered him with a bait and switch routine. The weary traveler was charged an outrageous amount for the two rooms we slept in. Abdul Khaliq over charged for our food and the few corn stalks the horses had eaten. In addition, he hit us with a tax to clean up the area where the horses had been picketed. Khaliq even charged us for the kerosene in the lanterns. Yet these were trifles. The final blow came when Ali informed us that he had paid 1,000 rupees to have Pukhtoon buried, instead of the 300 rupees Khaliq had quoted me. Altogether we had just dished out almost 2,000 rupees to the avaricious pagan.

There was no Better Business bureau to complain to. In northern Pakistan if you lost your money, you lost, and woe betide your tears. Our expedition was in danger of foundering. We were exhausted, brain dead, emotional wrecks. For the remainder of that dire day we hovered around our horses, brushing them, paying thanks to Allah that at least we retained these precious three. They sensed our distress and tossed their heads anxiously, unsure why Pukhtoon was gone. Pahlwan was the most noticeably upset. The big roan kept looking around, whinnying, waiting for a reply from his little brother that would never come again. When dusk began to fall our spirits became as black as the night gathering around us.

Ishaq Khan gave us a simple dinner and left us alone. We retired early, saying little, sitting in our new room, unable to speak, unsure of anything except that we were all determined to leave in the morning. Our future it seemed could not be reconciled with our present until we reached Chitral and tried to find Shavon. Well after dark the drums of Kafiristan began to beat. I was not interested. I had seen the dancing. I had witnessed the frolics of the light hearted children of nature but fearing the noise might frighten the horses, I arose and went outside. I did not fancy chasing Pasha on such a night.

The lane, dark as it was, had people in it. The moon was still hiding. The curtain of night was pierced solely by pinholes of starlight tumbling down from the sky. Through that inky darkness I could see the Kalash making their way towards the far end of the valley from where the music originated. They were all cheery, laughing folk, dirty perhaps but joyously quaint to the western eye. Pasha and his stable mates were resting quietly at last, their weary senses sealed in sleep, so I turned my back on the Kalash of Kafiristan and went back to an uneasy bed.

Next morning found us up early, anxious to leave. The jeep had already departed with our extra gear. We were riding straight through to Chitral with nothing on the horses except guns and a canteen. Everything else was sent on ahead to the hotel in town. Though no fault of his own, Ishaq Khan had apologized for what happened in the valley. We paid with thanks and money for his hospitality and generosity, then turned the horses to leave.

Raja trotted ahead and I was close behind on an impatient Pasha, when I saw Ali Muhammad lingering at the Frontier Hotel. I reined in my horse, and turning in the saddle, saw my pal leaning over and talking to the old Afghan cook who worked for Abdul Khaliq. Thinking it no more than a farewell between acquaintances I gave Pasha the spur and cantered after Raja, glad to be away.

The same road lay awaiting us. Only this time we longed to leave the misery soaked place as anxiously as we had entered it. We rode spaced out, each lost in our own recollections of what had occurred and the part we played. Eventually after more than an hour of riding, we neared the canyons end leading out of Kafiristan. I knew our road north lay down at the end of that narrow gorge. Once we reached the emotional safety of Chitral, I reasoned we six men and horses would regroup.

As if some silent signal had been passed Raja slowed down. I caught up and the two of us reined in, waiting for Ali Muhammad. He rode slumped over like an old man. His hand held the reins but his horse walked without direction. Pahlwan was trudging along. Ali Muhammad just happened to be aboard. When he drew up I saw a look of sorrow on his tanned face. I did not have to ask what was wrong. He voluntarily divulged the heavy secret he had carried alone out of beautiful Kafiristan.

"The cook came to tell me he liked us because we became Muslims and had visited Afghanistan. He doesn't want to work for Abdul Khaliq but he has a family in a refugee camp and work is hard to get," Ali said, all the while looking down at his hands resting on the saddle and studiously ignoring us.

"That's nice," I said impatiently, unsure as to why he was relying this apology. "Is that all he wanted?"

Ali Muhammad looked up, his eyes rapidly filling with tears.

"He told me Abdul Khaliq and the Kalashis did not bury Pukhtoon. Last night when they were drumming, the tribe gathered together and ate him."

32
Dr. Ali Muhammad

It was a pitiless crime that defiled our hearts.

Not only had they robbed us, Abdul Khaliq and the pagan Kalash had devoured Pukhtoon in a dark orgy of debased gluttony. The traitorous savages had misled us only long enough to carry the meat and skin away. Pukhtoon's once-white hide was hidden on the roof of the guest house. His meat was distributed among the ravenous locals.

We had inadvertently aided this mischief by removing ourselves to the other hotel. While we sat locked away in grief, Abdul Khaliq led his Kafir neighbors in an orgy of drink, dance and debauchery.

Though that news was bad enough, the old Afghan had also confided to Ali Muhammad that the sly Kafir innkeeper had lied to his foreign guests. Khaliq had invited the dozen hippy tourists to a traditional Kalashi feast. There they had been introduced to a banquet of what he said was cow meat. Not only had these unsuspecting ferenghis helped eat Pukhtoon, they paid Abdul Khaliq for the privilege of doing so.

Thus while we wept, Abdul, his friends, and guests, had been dancing around the cook pot in the starlight, stewing the horse we had paid to bury.

The evil news lay between us, an abortion of our equestrian ambition.

It was treachery most foul and I screamed with rage when I heard it

My initial thought was to gallop back and kill Abdul Khaliq, to slice off his verminous head, then ride berserk through the valley that had flaunted its depravity by betraying the sacred tenets of hospitality. One look at Raja told me I would not ride alone.

"After I murder him I will pound Abdul Khaliq's grave into dust," Raja said quietly with utter conviction.

Ali Muhammad startled us both.

"He may already be dead," he told us.

"What? How?" I asked.

"The Afghan reported that many of the Kafirs and the foreign tourists were violently ill this morning. They and the villagers are all sick."

Then it dawned on me.

"The injection," I said.

"I believe so," Ali Muhammad replied. "Pukhtoon was mildly ill from the saddle sore but that wouldn't have killed him. He only became critically sick the afternoon after the veterinarian gave him the injection. Who knows how long the medicine had sat on the shelf. Maybe years. But it was almost certainly toxic."

"That would explain why his neck was so hot where he received the shot," Raja said.

"And why his eyes were closed and weeping," I added.

The big horse had been dead for twelve hours before Abdul Khaliq's men butchered him. In that time his blood had grown as cold as the Angel of Death sitting on his chest. If Ali Muhammad was right the tainted medicine that slew Pukhtoon lay waiting to wreck its vengeance on the irreligious heathens and the foreign hedonists who later devoured him.

"Evil indeed are the deeds they have done. They respect not the ties of kinship or of covenant. It is they who have transgressed all bounds," Raja whispered.

We all knew the verse from the Qu'ran spelling out the misdeeds of the ancient pagans of Arabia. They too had scoffed at the laws of God and man and were destroyed for their arrogance. A chill ran down my spine. I had seen too many supernatural things occur in Pakistan not to believe in the direct intervention of the Almighty in the puny affairs of men.

All three of us were aware of the strict requirement observed by Muslims to make sure any meat was "halal" before it was eaten. Like the Jewish kosher practice, an animal about to be slaughtered by a Muslim first had to have the tasmiya (prayer) said over it, both to invoke the name of God and to remind us that our act was not done out of any wanton cruelty but only to satisfy the basic need for food. Without this solemn invocation mankind was apt to forget the sacredness of life and misuse the power Allah had given him over the weaker, mute creatures of the earth. After the prayer was intoned the animal's throat was quickly cut and the blood allowed to drain from the body. Only then could the flesh be consumed. The eating of dead flesh full of coagulated blood was so repugnant a taboo to Muslims that I had never heard of it being broken in Pakistan under even the most dire of circumstances.

What had occurred last night at the village was so beyond the scope of accepted Pakistani and Muslim values that it left me speechless. For long silent seconds I sat in my saddle torn between anger and disbelief. I had no answers to the why of what happened, except to believe that there is a reward, either good or bad, to be gained for every act done to animals. I was a nomad and a horseman, that is all.

"The crows of doom could be circling the village as we speak. Everyone who ate that carrion could be ill or worse," I said quietly, **remembering the primitive state of medicine I encountered in Kafiristan when I was sick there with hepatitis.**

I knew then that the same distance that allowed Abdul Khaliq to rob and deceive travelers without fear of repercussions might prove to be his carnivorous undoing. I looked at Raja and saw in his face that he understood there was nothing we could or should do. Though poor, the pagans could not have pleaded hunger. Their valley was rich in produce, fruits and goats. They had viewed Pukhtoon as a thousand-pound feast provided by providence and naive outsiders. The Kafirs had broken a sacred trust. The poisoned blood they so wickedly ate would course through their bodies, bringing with it retribution and revenge.

Dr. Ali Muhammad

"Leave them to Allah's judgment," Ali Muhammad said quietly, and looking at his eyes I saw the burden he must have carried until he shared this truth with us.

Pasha knew it was time to go. He gave an impatient toss of his head, urging me to leave my sorrow behind. Our own troubles were far from over, he seemed to say. I heeded his advice, spun the big dun and cantered away from that blood-soaked valley, leaving the pagans of Kafiristan to their fate, never knowing nor caring what became of them after their act of treachery was exposed.

At first we rode in mutual silence, men and horses tied together by an invisible thread of distressing regret. Pakistan was no respecter of our grief. Like a cruel step-mother she seemed to know that only a dose of strong medicine could cure our sorrow. She quickly obliged, gladly teaching us in the process that strength of character is learned from the travails of travel, as is bravery in battle.

What I had failed to see on that previous trip with Shavon was now revealed in all its desolate glory. Pasha led us through a landscape that resembled the moon in its wretched barrenness. By riding through unconscious on the palomino mare I had missed nothing but an agony of landscape devoid of even an insect. It was a minor desert, unnamed, empty, and wickedly hot. Within a few hours our early-morning rage had been replaced by early-afternoon resignation.

I missed the feeling of Pukhtoon's big head rubbing up against my leg. I missed looking down from the saddle at his childish eager face, anxiously awaiting the next meal, the next rub on the head, the next hug around his big gray neck. Yet Pakistan did not let me miss him for long.

Within hours the sun had baked our brains and roasted our throats. I could feel my tongue swelling and my lips cracking from the heat. I pulled the tail of my turban over my fair-skinned Irish face. The horses plodded on, sending up a cloud of dust that filled the air and threatened to suffocate us. We were soon six gray gypsies from this unwanted dusty overcoat. With our white eyes squinting against the glare, Ali, Raja and I resembled three dirty raccoons.

That stretch of hellish road lead us between a high range of mountains on our left and the Chitral river on our right. This was a singularly unappealing body of water, being sixty percent fluid and forty percent silt. Its wide rushing waters rolled by, tempting us with delightful daydreams of swimming and cool drinks. That's all we did was day dream, as we rode mile after tedious mile next to a torrent of water that looked like it had been thrown out of a dishpan.

In the early afternoon we stopped to refill our canteen and eat the bread we had brought for our noonday meal. The horses were just as hungry as we were, so each rider shared his meager lunch with his mount. It took only a few moments for Pahlwan, Pajaro and Pasha to make it plain to we three supposedly superior creatures that in fact we had been idiots for not packing more food.

Men and horses were all thirsty so Ali Muhammad scrambled down the steep, rock-strewn riverbank and refilled the canteen. Drinking the glutinous stuff proved nearly impossible. The water was swirling with dirt. I took off my turban and sucked the water through the thin silk cloth as a strainer. I could still feel the dirt tumbling down my throat and gritting up my teeth. Despite a long drink my thirst was only intensified with the effects of the liquid mud sloshing around in my stomach.

Pasha was not so discerning. He eagerly sucked it up out of my turban cap and gave me a look that said, "Ahhhhh."

That road twisted and turned through the nameless mountains, with we six captives following faithfully. As I rode I understood why Shavon had not stopped until she reached Chitral. Neither did we.

It was an arduous day that began and ended on a note of sorrow. As we approached the outskirts of the mountain fastness called Chitral, the last mile of the road lead us directly through a new Afghan refugee camp. The poor people were literally caught between the perennial rock and a hard place. Rising on their left was a great gray mountain on which grew no tree, no flower, no blade of grass. It was a slag-heap of dust and rock, threatening to fall down on the human misery camping on its ugly skirts. A short distance away rushed the muddy Chitral river.

Squeezed between the rock and water lived life's unfortunates. The Afghan fugitives resided in square little adobe homes made of gray mud topped with canvas roofs. A fine gray dust filled the air. A feeling of sadness and weeping dogged our weary steps as we rode through. The only song I heard was that of isolation, grief, homesickness and despair. They called it a camp. It was an apostasy against humanity.

Chitral had never welcomed me. Unlike Dir who would have kicked my corpse and walked away singing, this northern town was more subtle in her cruelty. Shavon and I, thinking we had discovered a safe haven, had our dreams snatched from us there. Once again Chitral stood by in arrogant silence as this time Pasha and I pleaded for help.

The morning after arriving I hurried to locate Shavon, only to discover her new owner was gone out of town. The teenage boy minding the rug shop remembered me however. He had no reason to lie about the whereabouts of the palomino mare. His master had sold her to the first bunch of Afghan freedom fighters who had flashed their money. Shavon had never played polo. She had instead been cruelly overloaded. The mujahideen then headed her over a mountain pass notorious for killing horses. If the tales were true, part of the trail crossed stretches of ice where the living walked over the decomposing bones of horses who died passing that way the year before. This year's slaves trudged over the frost holding last years equine victims.

My golden friend was gone, and so was just about everyone else in town, including the town blacksmith. Every man in the community who could leave town was heading off for the Shandur Pass, more than 100 miles away, to witness a sporting event of gigantic local importance.

We three riders held a powwow and discussed our options. Everyone agreed we were on the razor's edge of the wilderness. The problems we had initially encountered, heat, sharing the road with crazy vehicles and sullen tribesmen were behind us. Ahead lay a new set of obstacles including hunger, treacherous trails and mountain passes high enough to make the Lowari look like child's play.

None of us denied the dangers ahead. Pukhtoon's death had rammed home the fact that our mortality was sometimes swinging on a delicate thread. Oddly enough it was the death of the pack horse that bonded us and gave us the strength and courage to continue. To have turned back would have classified his sacrifice as being worthless, would have branded us as cowards in our own eyes, would have forced us to abandon our three remaining horses to the unkind hands of cruel men. Speaking just for myself, I told Raja and Ali Muhammad I was not turning back. Pack saddle or no pack saddle, I would never agree to leave Pasha in Chitral, fated to suffer the same lingering death as Shavon.

In Pakistan they say warriors and journeyers must both suckle from the well of courage if they would succeed. We weighed the consequences, took a deep drink, and voted to continue.

Historically the Chitralis had a reputation for cupidity, lying and slander. They were never really happy unless they were sitting in their shops spreading some petty intrigue amongst themselves. Boredom and isolation had undermined their manhood. They would take your money and start their whispering campaign before you cleared the street. Some said we were agents for the CIA. Others boasted they knew we were riding to the lost emerald mines in Afghanistan. Everyone believed we were involved with the Afghan resistance.

We used Chitral like the northern whore she was. For two days we spent most of our time in a large chaikhana, feasting on rich lamb kebobs, drinking steaming chai and listening to an Afghan refugee play sweet tunes on his rebob. When the horses were not filling their bellies on grass and grain, they were resting. Raja searched the bazaar and returned with what foodstuffs he thought we could carry in our saddlebags, mostly dried fruit and walnuts. Despite what nature and man had thrown in our way so far, we knew we were going on.

On the third day I rode back to the Afghan camp in search of a blacksmith. The local expert, if such a creature existed, had left Chitral for the Shandur Pass. Men from all over northern Pakistan were gathering on that alpine plateau to watch an upcoming polo game of Olympian proportions

For uncounted hundreds of years the horsemen of Chitral rode northeast and scaled that frigid mountain pass. Waiting for them there on the crest of the frozen waste were the horsemen of faraway Gilgit, who had in turn traveled hundreds of miles due west to meet their traditional rivals. The Shandur Pass polo game was the stuff of legend and now occurred only every few years. Like all Pakistani equestrian traditions, no one knew how long this one would last.

Our trail was going to lead us that way but not unless we managed to reshoe our horses. Following a lead, I discovered the old Afghan who tended the mujahideen's horses. I found Mullah Gulzar sitting inside his mud house, waiting for his country to be freed or the sun to set, whichever came first. No one really knew how many Afghan refugees were living in Pakistan, though the number was said to exceed three million. Yet local government officials exaggerated this estimated number by as much as 30% in order to justify the massive amounts of relief money being sent to Peshawar. Everyone knew the foreign generosity was dependent on continued Soviet discomfort on the Afghan battle fields. Japan alone had funneled an estimated $200 million in aid through Pakistan. The old man in front of me hadn't seen a dime of the money.

When I told him my need, the *nal band* (horseshoer) reached into a crate behind him and withdrew a ready-made horseshoe. The tiny rim of iron would have fit inside Pasha's worn horseshoe. I informed the *nal band* we could provide what was needed at the hotel. He was glad to gather his simple tools and meet me back in Chitral.

Though Mullah Gulzar used the shoes we had brought from Peshawar, once again it was a tiresome affair, trying to convince Pahlwan we weren't trying to hurt him, urging Pajaro to stand up straight and not lean on our backs, and watching Pasha's teeth to make sure he did not sink them into our unprotected backsides. We paid the old man fifty rupees a horse for his efforts, a reasonable amount. Then we sent him home in a hired jeep, loaded down with the pack saddle and all the extra gear we were jettisoning in Chitral. It would have been considered little enough in Peshawar, but in that squalid refugee camp every bootlace and button would be gratefully used or sold. Either way we stood rested, reshod and ready.

Raja and Pajaro led us out of Chitral the next morning in a blinding rain.

We were wrapped in surplus army ponchos. Our weapons rode on our hips or in their scabbards. A handful of small personal possessions, a hoof pick and brush for the horses and the dried fruit rode in the saddlebags. Along with the three blankets lashed behind the saddles, this was now our world. If we were to eat it would have to be from supplies we purchased on the way. The emotional and physical baggage we had carried with us from Peshawar was staying behind.

That morning the clouds hung over our saddles but not over our hearts. Not a strand of sunlight could be seen. The road leading to faraway Gilgit disappeared into a tunnel of mountains topped by a pitch-black sky, yet we refused to be delayed.

Chitralis peeked out of their shops as we rode out of town in the storm, murmuring that there went proof that Pathans and ferenghis were all mad. I no longer cared. The deluge washed away the last traces of my grief. Shavon and Pukhtoon were part of the past. Ahead lay a new country and new horizons. Everything I had previously known and experienced in Pakistan ended in Chitral. So I welcomed the rain and rode a fiery Pasha headfirst into the watery fury of that storm.

Thunder rolled through the dark skies as we passed through the edge of town. Raja turned in the saddle. His face was dripping wet but happy. Looking back he shouted, "Thunder is a good sign. It's the sound of genies fighting on horseback."

Dr. Ali Muhammad

It was a liberating madness that boiled our blood and set us to laughing. We threw caution to the wind and cantered out of Chitral without so much as a backwards look at her muddy street and timid citizens.

Within a mile of leaving we found ourselves utterly alone in the world. No trace of man remained except the thin line of dirt road down which we rode. The rain soaked our turbans, ran down inside the legs of our boots, and trickled past the necks of our ponchos. We were resigned to that discomfort before we left Chitral.

That first day's journey was a taste of what was to come, for if that portion of Pakistan we had ridden over already was not tame, this new land was a testament of trial. Behind lay mere travel, ahead began survival. It was the beginning of weeks of riding wherein we saw no hint of civilization, no electricity, no canned food, no telephones, no foreigners, nothing on wheels except an occasional battered jeep. Ahead lay only starlight and peaceful, sparsely-settled wilderness. The visual hint of a mountain refuge I had glimpsed from atop the faraway Lowari Pass was about to become a reality. Shavon and Pukhtoon had not been sacrificed on the bloody altar of equestrian exploration for nothing.

The dirt road lead us into the narrow Mastuj river gorge. Its introduction was a wet one. What water was not pouring down from the skies was roaring through the canyon. The river was a wild beast. It ran so close to the base of the trail that stormy waves were tossed up onto our path. Our initial laughter was drowned out by the sound of this disorderly torrent. With more than three hundred miles behind us we knew the look of a long day. We settled down for a tough ride and reined in the horses, urging caution. A slip off that slick trail would have spelt death for horse and rider. A rock wall loomed over our right shoulders, part of a gray wet mountain of stone that disappeared above our heads in the rain. A few hundred feet off to our left lay another matching mountain. In between ran that untamed snake of a river.

The Mastuj was never more than fifteen feet away. It lashed and snapped at the mountain, trying to consume the trail and anything on it. The river hit the foot of the road like a lion lunging against its leash, spraying us with water, anxious for us to fall in so it could sweep us away to oblivion. The horses splashed stoically through the soft squishy mud. We rode relying on their instincts as much as our near-useless eyes. Occasionally they would slide and then a rider's heart would start pounding as he saw the river waiting to receive him. The steadfast geldings ignored the treacherous waterway and with brave hearts carried us away from our former troubles.

In such pleasantly interesting conditions did we ride, until the rain finally slackened in the early afternoon. Then the gorge opened up and we finally left behind the feeling of being trapped inside a stone envelope. The rocky walls fell back to a decent distance, far enough away so that they were not smothering you. Long ago our early morning chatter had turned into a feeling of determination. Each man now rode with his horse, three sodden teams of two, one caravan, with home 700 long, long miles ahead.

With Pukhtoon gone the dynamics of our herd had changed. The two smaller horses now looked to big Pahlwan for direction, though he was a reluctant leader. The mighty giant had always allowed the smaller gray not only to misbehave like a spoiled child, but to dominate the entire group. Pukhtoon was missed but he had often been a bully. Pajaro was content to quietly follow whoever was in charge. Pasha retained his independent, mischievous nature. Yet all three remaining horses sensed something had changed. After leaving Kafiristan none of them ever again strayed far from his stable mates.

I had long ago learned that they were as different as we three men. If I had a secret to confide I would have gone to quiet, dreamy Pajaro. If I wanted a shoulder to lean on I would have sought out good natured Pahlwan for support and advice. If I was stepping out on the town I would have turned to that hot-blooded hidalgo Pasha to lead me to trouble.

Two days after leaving Chitral we knew our instincts about pressing on had been correct.

We started that day traveling with the turbulent river on our left and the inaccessible cliffs on our right. As we rode on the landscape opened up and we emerged into a country of mountains, mountains and more mountains. The road was leading us in a gentle north-east arc towards the Shandur Pass. As we rode along we passed small hamlets of mud houses. Apricot trees and corn fields ripened in the alpine sun. Yet these were only dots of humanity in a sea of stone.

Everywhere there were two landscapes, one reaching ahead, another reaching up to Allah. Pasha never noticed that we were now surrounded on all sides by titans. They stood looking down as we rode deeper and deeper into their secretive sanctuary. There in the world's emptiness we might have been riding at any time in history since horses were tamed. Our former lives fell away as new needs expressed themselves. The sun dictated our movements. The moon urged us to rest. We were no longer Ali Muhammad, Raja and Asadullah. We were reduced to our simplest needs, three rootless saddlemen looking for food, fire and pasture.

In fact any kind of food would have been welcome. We were almost starving. Our small portions had run out after the first day.

The second night saw us staying with a poor farmer who shared his family's Lilliputian portions of rice and yogurt with us. The three pieces of bread he handed us for dessert didn't go far in filling the corners of our empty bellies. The tiny teapot we shared was refreshment big enough for a child. Three famished horsemen saddled up with high expectations the next morning.

"You can get plenty of food at the next village which is very close," the farmer assured us. We thanked him for his hospitality and thinking a big meal was but a mile or two away we put the spurs to our horses and started a mile-eating trot.

The road starting winding almost immediately, climbing steadily over the next several hours. It was rough, hot going with no sign of a village,

Dr. Ali Muhammad

another traveler, or any trace of human culture. We did the only thing we could. We rode with our bellies grinding under our gun belts. Hours later, still no people, no shops, no chaikhana, nothing, just ever higher mountains. Finally, after being in the saddle for six hours, we met a farmer coming towards us. He agreed with our former host's description of what lay ahead.

"In Harchin you can get EVERYTHING!" he emphasized.

It sounded like Paradise.

We hurried on, all of us hungry, even the horses.

Almost an hour later we entered the outskirts of a village that looked anything but prosperous. A few mud houses lined the road. There was no sign of a shop or a chaikhana. We had ridden almost all the way through town before we realized there must have been a mistake. The road ahead looked exactly like the deserted one we had just left. At the edge of this wilderness a man sat in the shade of a tree next to a small wooden pushcart. With no one else to ask for directions, Raja pulled up under some trees across the road.

I was stiff when I dismounted but that was nothing compared to the pain gnawing a hole in my belly. We left the horses tied to the trees and walked over to ask directions to the village shop.

"Is this Harchin?" Ali Muhammad asked.

The man was friendly but clearly surprised at my friends question. He gave my hungry friend a look as if to say, "You yokel, of course this is Chicago."

"Certainly," the villager answered.

Ali Muhammad followed up with, "Where is the shop?"

Another stunned look.

"Why this is the shop."

"This is the shop?"

"Of course. This is the shop!" the proud store owner said and waving his hand invited our disbelieving eyes to rove over the six dusty boxes of Pakistani cigarettes, two cartons of battered cookies, some matches, razor blades and ball point pens that proved his point.

Needless to say we first purchased, then devoured the two boxes of cookies. As we were searching the cookie boxes for crumbs, Pahlwan ripped a six foot strip of bark off the tree he was tied to. Like us, the geldings were almost dizzy with hunger. They gnawed the bark between them like an old bone.

Learning that no one in Harchin had so much as a seed to spare, we left the northern Gotham and rode on like hungry orphans.

The trip had shown us how to suffer. We had weathered bad weather, hardships and loss. That afternoon as the sun rode over our heads we learned that all the other lessons had been but a prelude. Mountains reared up on all sides of us and we had only the Harchin shopkeeper's word that a short way ahead lay a rich village. Three hours later we were hungry, tired, dusty, and disoriented.

In such conditions are mistakes made.

Khyber Knights

The sun was warning us that he was thinking of leaving, and we three riders were clearly worried. I called a halt. The country was deserted for miles in all directions, a vast panorama of beauty and barrenness. On my right I thought I recognized a peak. While Ali Muhammad and Raja sat on top of their tired horses, I pulled our map and my reading glasses out of my vest pocket.

Maps resemble treacherous lovers. They peddle deceptions. The chart's little lines tell you that here is a mountain, there a village, but their wavy linear impressions are delusions. They are mute about washed out roads and bad weather. They are smugly content to pass off their limited wisdom, telling you what the condition of the terrain will be, but wisely ignoring the condition of the traveler when he gets there.

My map told me that looming off to our right was 21,000 foot high Buni Zom. Next to it was another massif just as large but unnamed. Using the named mountain as a point of reference I calculated we had at least six miles, or about two more hours, to go before we reached our destination, the village of Sor Laspur.

The information put me into a foul mood. I began folding the map. Pasha, until now totally placid, began to walk towards the other horses, who were slightly ahead of us. I grabbed the reins and yanked him up short. The gelding halted but ended up facing into the mountain side next to us. Without me realizing it, he had planted his feet slightly higher than the trail. I was too preoccupied to remember Inspector Akbar's advice that a horseman's grave is always open and waiting.

Still messing with the map, short-tempered, unthinking, when the dun moved again I reached down and gave his reins a sharp and painful pull.

When the hard steel bit hit his sensitive teeth the formerly quiet horse reacted like an angry rattlesnake. He pulled back from the undeserved punishment, threw his head up into the air and smashed me.

My world exploded in pain, blood and glass. The impact from Pasha's head hit me squarely in the right side of my face. The shattered glasses ripped into me like shrapnel from a grenade. Then the momentum from the blow unseated me, throwing me backwards out of the saddle. I flew through the air blinded, landed on my back and heard Pasha coming to get me. He was screaming and stomping, ready to ground me into the dust for tormenting him unjustly. I covered my head with my arms and rolled instinctively away from the sound of his deadly hooves.

I had no way of knowing if I was going to roll off the other side of the trail but I knew I could expect no mercy from Pasha. I rolled blind until the sounds of his anger moved away. At the last moment I heard Raja and Ali Muhammad screaming a warning, so I stopped. I was on my back in the dirt. Slowly I opened my left eye. The right side of my face was quivering uncontrollably. I reached up and touched my face. My hand came away smeared with blood.

Suddenly my saddle-pals were there, the horses forgotten. Ali Muhammad helped me sit up. For a few moments I was too stunned to speak. Finally I whispered, "How is it?"

Dr. Ali Muhammad

Judging by the ashen look on Raja's face I figured it must be bad. Ali handed me a small pocket mirror. Looking in the little glass circle I saw a hole just beneath my right eye big enough to swallow up the end of my little finger. The sight knocked out the numbing shock of ignorance. Tears of pain began to stream down my torn face. They burned with the salty fires of Hell when they ran into the ragged bloody hole now dominating my features.

The only surprise was the discovery that Raja, the brave Afridi Pathan, was blood shy. I've no doubt he could have killed his man, but the sight of the red gore would have later made him faint. So it was Ali Muhammad who tended to me. Sitting there in the middle of a nameless piece of dirt trail, my friend used a pair of tweezers from his Swiss Army knife to extract the glass shards from my face. I had given him that knife as a joke shortly after I bought my sword in Darra. It was plain to see who was the fool that day. Ali then laid two of our Band-Aids across the gaping hole, temporarily pinning the jagged edges of my meat together.

There was only one option, and we all knew it.

I squeezed my face tightly shut, wrapped the end of my turban around it and stood up. The front of my clothes were blood soaked. Raja had tried to catch Pasha, but the arrogant cuss would let no one else near him. I held out my left hand and walked toward my horse slowly.

"You bastard, I should beat your hooves off," I told him, but he knew I didn't mean it. The dun held still, glad to see me, wondering what all the fuss was about. I swung onto the hurricane deck. My face was on fire, but I knew I depended on that horse like I depended on my own heart. It was my temper that had started the accident, and his that ended it. But Pasha got me to Sor Laspur as night fell.

Morning found me in a chaikhana. I sat up on the charpoy. The log walls were black from a hundred years of smoky cooking fires. The air was thick with the smell of mutton cooking. Empty charpoys littered the rustic lodge. Across the room a bearded *chai wallah* was sitting watching the cook-fire burn. Steam was pouring out of the top of a samovar. Everything was silent and peaceful. I remembered very little of last night, except stumbling through the door and collapsing through a wall of pain into a deep pool of exhausted sleep. The *chai wallah* noticed I was awake.

"Where am I?" I asked him.

"In the temple of the passing traveler," he told me and smiled in jest.

"I must see to the horses. It is only right," I said, thinking out loud.

"Your friends are doing that now. Rest," he ordered, and I obeyed, falling asleep again.

The sound of my friends' return awoke me. They brought news. The horses were picketed nearby in a field of grass. Sor Laspur had a shop with various supplies. We had come much further than we suspected. The chaikhana sat at the foot of the trail leading up the Shandur Pass. All this they related to me as we enjoyed a delicious breakfast of chai, bread and mutton. It was the same monotonous meal we had been eating for weeks, but after the last few hungry days I would never begrudge its appearance again.

By mid-morning I knew it was time to get down to the task at hand. When Raja learned Ali Muhammad was going to operate on my face, he diplomatically excused himself to go look after the horses. This left Ali the pleasant task of repairing me.

It was a toss-up where to perform the operation, outside in the open cleaner air, or inside in the chikhana where it was warmer and semi-private. The light was bad in there, just what sunlight could filter in through the door. Plus there would doubtless be loads of exotic germs. Ali Muhammad gave me my choice.

"Allah protect me. We are horsemen and require dignity. Certain things should not be performed in public view," I said.

I chose to stay inside, preferring warmth and a cup of chai nearby as we worked. The chai wallah had temporarily left. The germs could watch out for themselves. Just inside the door, Ali Muhammad laid the surgical necessities on a dirty table, two cups of chai, a large needle, a roll of black thread, the scissors on the Swiss Army knife, a couple of questionable rags, plus a bottle of alcohol and some extra Band-Aids he had bought in the village shop. He placed a three-legged stool in the sunlight steaming through the doorway, then ordered me to take a seat.

Having some fundamental idea regarding the theory of sterility in the operating chamber, I expected him to douse his hands in alcohol. I had no sooner sat down when he instead bent over as if to peer at the wound. Without warning Ali ripped off the previous day's bandages. I yelled in shock and agony but he was already busy examining the wound.

"Hummm," he said as he peered into the open hole.

"Will it scar?" I asked, as he set about scrubbing off the dried blood and grit with a rag soaked in alcohol.

"Knowing your luck probably not," he said, as he attacked it scrupulously, each motion of the rough cloth sending a wave of pain through my eyes and across my face.

"Bugger yourself. How bad is it?"

"I can't see any bone. Let me make sure. Nope. No bone. No glass either. Just meat. I think you're all right. Shall I sew it closed?"

"Can you do it?" I asked, trying to hide my skepticism.

"Maybe. I sewed up an Afghan blanket once in Kabul," he recounted reassuringly.

"I hesitate to accept such qualifications," I said.

The amateur sawbones studied the length and depth of the facial crater.

"Sewing it closed will undoubtedly hurt," he told me.

"Undoubtedly."

"Such pain might cause some men to scream in pain, perhaps even loose self control and thrash about."

"A worthy consideration," I admitted.

I drank my chai, pondering my options. I could taste the bitter rubbing alcohol on my lips.

"Perhaps another alternative?" Ali suggested. "Instead of sewing you, lets just glue you shut."

Before I could object he strode outside and returned within moments with my leather quirt.

"Here, use this," he ordered and thrust it at me.

Following Dr. Ali's orders I bit down hard on the salty, sweat-stained leather whip. When I saw him pick up the alcohol bottle from the table, I hastily grabbed the sides of the stool as well. Ali Muhammad held my head steady with his left hand, carefully placed the lip of the open bottle next to the bottom of the wound, turned the bottle straight up and held it there for an eternity. The alcohol ripped into my open flesh, sent flames racing through my body and tensed my spine like a rod of steel. I managed to hold still, but moaned in pain.

Seconds later the quack removed the bottle and I spat out the quirt. My right eye was screwed up tight with pain. Ali Muhammad began to immediately pinch my tortured cheek shut between the fingers of one hand, as he applied sticky bandages to close the wound with the other.

"I thought you were a man of stronger bones?" he said calmly as he taped my face shut.

"And I thought you were a friend and a doctor, not a butcher's assistant?" I replied hotly.

The bandages in place, Ali Muhammad stepped back to admire his handiwork. My face was alternating between blinding pain and terrifying numbness, and my right cheek was a patchwork of white adhesive strips.

"I think it would be a good idea to continue covering your face with the end of your turban. That will help keep the wound clean," he informed me authoritatively.

"It will also stop people from wondering who has misused me."

"This is gratitude?" Ali asked.

"No, this is relief at having survived both the accident and the treatment," I told him in a huff and hurried outside.

I found the morning sunlight anxious to warm me inside and out. My eyes, though tortured, still functioned. Waiting there to greet them was the Shandur Pass. The great mountain filled my vision. Far above on its crest I could make out the notch where men, jeeps and horses passed through to the alpine plateau hosting the world's highest polo game. The dirt road leading up the mountain was spotted with tiny black dots, travelers hurrying up there from all over this portion of northern Pakistan. They were rushing to reach the windy top before the match began between the legendary champions of Gilgit and Chitral.

I fell in with Raja and Ali Muhammad, anxious to depart, eager to press on, impatient to see this great gathering of the best horsemen of the north. The pain of my wound was already a thing of the past, excruciating to endure, easy to forget.

33
Among the Centaurs

From that morning on we rode blind, with only rumors to lead us.

If we had left behind our previous troubles, we had also jettisoned everything we recognized. What lay ahead were meaningless names on an outdated map. None of us knew anyone who had traveled beyond Chitral. The Shandur Pass was the portal to a part of Pakistan that was terra incognita.

To differing degrees all three of us were children of Peshawar. Though none of us had been born there, her history and values had shaped us. The way we reacted to people and events were based on the rules of the *Pukhtunwali* (Pathan code of honor) and the North West Frontier. After the Shandur those rules were to prove largely valueless. Our clothes, our customs, even our religion were soon to be the source of controversy.

We got a late start due to Ali Muhammad's medical experimentation on my face. Raja had busied himself bringing the horses up from the pasture. All three mounts were tied to trees in front of the chaikhana, a look of bored resignation on their equine faces. I found Raja taking the hoof pick to Pajaro's feet, so I grabbed the brush and set to work giving Pasha a good cleaning.

While I brushed and saddled my gelding, I looked over his back at what lay in store for the two of us. At the end of the verdant village of Sor Laspur rose a curtain of sheer stone. Three great zigzags tattooed the face of the nameless mountain waiting for Pasha and me. It was miles to the top of that snake's back and loomed like a trudge up the escalator of Hell.

The bells on the horses rang merrily as we six travelers left Sor Laspur. On both sides of us were rich fields of green corn, gold wheat and fruit orchards. Tidy square mud-brick houses dotted the agrarian landscape. As we rode through the village I had the uneasy feeling we were swimming out of the shallow end of Pakistan into deeper waters.

My instincts were not wrong.

Nothing on four continents had prepared me for that ride.

One minute we were talking and cantering across flat ground, the next we were climbing, as the mountain slammed us into a new reality. Compared to that ascent the Malakand Pass was a joke and the Lowari Pass fit for children. We did not scale the Shandur Pass like arrogant caballeros, we crawled up her flanks like lowly insects, one slow painful step at a time.

From the moment we put hoof and foot on that road our legs and lungs complained. The little village of Sor Laspur lay 6,000 feet above sea level. Horses and men took one burning step for each of the 6,500 more feet that lay between us and the crest of the cruel pass that loomed over the hamlet.

Our horses were forced to go slowly due to the angle of the road and the ever-increasing altitude. After a short while we three riders got down to relieve their burdens. With their four legs Pasha and his stable mates already knew they were standing on an incline. As we walked beside our mounts, we two-legged creatures discovered that each step forward was one step higher as well. It became not a noble ride but plodding labor.

Two hours into the attempt we stopped to rest. Sor Laspur looked like a toy town laid out below us. Mounted again, we rode, but gave the horses their heads, letting big Pahlwan set a slow pace for all of us. Pajaro put his back into the effort. Pasha kept his eyes on the ground. Raja, Ali Muhammad and I said little, this new set of circumstances grounding us in quiet concern.

As the day grew longer the air grew thinner. One thousand feet to the hour is reasonable progress for laden horses. Yet we were soon stopping every ten minutes, letting the horses suck in great draughts of increasingly cold air. We rode, then walked, rode, then walked, all of us panting like dogs as we crawled towards the top.

The only noise on that great, long road were the jeeps.

News of the Shandur Pass polo game had filtered down to every village, hamlet, and eye-blink outpost. From Passu to Pingal, Gakuch to Gupis, a vast multitude of men were rushing from east and west to reach the top of this mountain.

Normal motor traffic retreated hundreds of miles back in both directions. Even Pakistan's daredevil bus drivers could not negotiate this far north. We were sharing the domain of the mountain taxi, a jeep that in any other country would have been classified as derelict decades before, but was here an honored veteran. As we inched our way up the mountain we were passed by vehicles looking like a highway patrolman's nightmare, many carrying ten to fifteen men hanging on like ripe grapes.

Because the Shandur Pass was barren of so much as a single tree, everything needed by the spectators, participants and horses was being hauled in by jeep. Food, firewood, hay, cooking oil, tents, blankets, you name it, was being brought up that mountain for the greatest sporting event of the far north.

A vehicle would first be loaded down with several hundred pounds of supplies, rice, tea, firewood, etc.. When the springs looked flat the personal baggage of the passengers was piled on next. At least six pilgrims were then allowed to position themselves on top of the cargo and baggage. Commonsense urged them to grab hold of any metal protuberance. Some favored bigwig was placed in the sole passenger seat up front. The driver, as well as his helper, known as the "rear mirror," squeezed themselves into the space remaining in the front seat, and everyone was off.

Because of the excess manpower available to push, starters were often non-existent. Tires were always old, usually slick, and sometimes sported rags shoved into holes to protect the inner tubes. Brakes were

Among the Centaurs

mandatory. An emergency brake was a large rock placed behind the rear wheel by the helper.

As we made our slow way up the Shandur we were repeatedly passed by these east-bound wrecks. The usual procedure was to kill the engine and coast down hill to save gas. This mountain would allow none of that. As we walked or rode, the jeeps went by with springs groaning and motors grumbling in protest from both the unreasonable load and the killer road. Even in a country known for its bad motorists, the jeep drivers held an esteemed position in the pantheon of automotive lunacy. The passengers were either white-faced with fright or certifiable maniacs like the drivers. Having only limited control, it was not unusual for an overconfident daredevil and his helpless passengers to plunge screaming off a cliff face to a crushing, fiery death on the rocks below. Five such jeeps were lost around Gilgit in the space of one month.

Pasha, Pajaro and Pahlwan paid little attention to the noisy vehicles. They were too busy, like us, trying to breathe. The dust thrown off by the battered jeeps would hang in the air, then slowly settle, once again leaving us surrounded by silence. As the hours passed we made our way like six ants across one giant turn on the road, then up another. By late afternoon the cold had become so severe we halted the horses.

It was impossible to believe I had ever been too hot in Pakistan. That was a dream from somewhere long ago. As we neared the top the mountain road widened. Ali Muhammad and Pahlwan had led us into a great field of boulders. Across this rocky pasture we could see yaks grazing. Tiny yellow alpine flowers covered the ground between the stones. We riders shook like dogs in the cold as we dug in our saddle bags for our vests. Though the sun was still up the air was already frigid.

Our late start had guaranteed that night would find us on the mountain. Yet Allah showed a little compassion even for nomads like us. The horses labored as they carried us up, up, up, with every breath an effort and every step a victory. At last the sky was so close there seemed to be nothing between us and Allah. I could have touched Him, if I had possessed the courage to look up and reach out.

The evening we crested the Shandur Pass will go down in my memory as the quintessential equestrian moment of my life. We six wanderers stood 12,500 feet above the faraway sea. Laid out before us was a vast alpine valley, a giant green bowl of wind-blown grass. In the middle rested a dark blue lake never sullied by boat nor man. On all sides, save for the notch where we stood, were lofty, jagged peaks edged with snow and forming a protective ring around this sacred, secret place.

None of us needed to be told to rein in. What we saw would have halted a world-weary king. The last rays of the sun were coloring the sky like a rainbow. Great clouds overhead were the color of orange sherbet. The mountain tops surrounding us were a delicate shade of blue. The sky itself had turned rose. Yet breathtaking as that was, it was the vast grassy arena that riveted our eyes. The giant camp lay spread out before us like a carpet of fire. Lantern lights and cook fires beckoned and winked, urging us to join the great multitude gathered below.

I drank in that vision, then shut my eyes tightly, storing the image of that valley behind them forever.

When I opened them, we rode down a sandy track into a Babylon of voices. The green grassy valley floor was full of shelters of all descriptions. Local farmers were camping out next to bigwigs from Chitral and Gilgit. Patches of ragged canvas sat next to proud felt yurts. Rich and poor alike had journeyed to watch the world's highest polo game. Stone huts with canvas roofs had been erected to serve as rude restaurants and stores. It was a wild west town come to life overnight.

The inhabitants were equally wild and woolly.

Without being told, we three riders brought our horses close together and rode three abreast. What few rules normally existed in Pakistan seemed to have been left at home by the hundreds of men gathered up there on holiday. The giant encampment had the feeling of a Mongol hunting camp, where the boisterous behavior of men is to be accepted as normal. It was at once invigorating and dangerous. We rode slowly through the crowds, looking for a place to stay.

The sky was black when I drew Pasha up in front of a burrow. The track ran straight ahead, but the fire inside this humble shelter had forced me to make a decision. We had wandered slightly up onto the hillside, away from the flat polo ground now behind us. An enterprising merchant had located a soft spot on the flank of the mountain and dug a large hole. Having squared off the floor plan of his enterprise, he threw a canvas roof over it, put large stones along the edge of the roof and hung out his shingle for business. A single hole in the back served as crude chimney and barometer.

Our initial exhilaration at having conquered the mighty pass was giving way to hunger, cold and weariness. Around us were a sea of tents, but none obviously advertising public lodgings. We had stayed in many places on that trip yet none was ever so welcome as that fire-warmed hole in the ground.

We picketed the horses and put our saddles inside the burrow. While Ali Muhammad stood guard over our equipment, Raja and I spent the next hour locating hay and blankets for the horses. Both were available for a high price. We watered the horses in the stream that fed into the nameless lake. With the demise of the sun, it had become cold, cold, cold, bitter nut-shrinking cold. With shaking hands we cut small holes in front and bottom of the wool blankets, then threw them over the horses' backs. We used scraps of string to tie the blankets in place, then picketed the horses close together near the door of our hostel.

The last thing I did was warn Pasha that if he made a nuisance of himself during the night, I would let him freeze to death before I came back out. He looked like he could have killed me for bringing him up there. I reminded him of the painful hole in my face and we agreed to call it even.

By the time I followed Ali Muhammad and Raja into the dugout I was so frozen I was babbling. There were four other men sharing our little sanctuary, the cook-cum-owner, his half-wit assistant and two farmers from the faraway village of Brep. Though wrapped in my blanket and everything I owned, I was still shaking. I huddled as close to the fire as I could manage. Being the last one in I was the furthest from the warmth and closest to the door.

Though I had slept on everything from a judge's table to a feather mattress on that trip, the den we called home that night had naught to offer except an earthen bed. We never stayed in more humble lodgings. Being poor, Mirza the owner did not have a kerosene lantern or even candles to brighten his lodgings. The fire served as warmth, stove and illumination, its faint light diluting the otherwise omnipotent darkness.

Mirza may have been poor but he had a nose for business. He had journeyed from his village near Chitral to the top of the frosty pass accompanied by his nephew, arriving a week before the start of the polo game. A jeep had brought them and the cooking pots, tea, milk, sugar, bread, fire wood, and three goats it took to make this hole a home and a hotel for the duration of the short polo season.

The farmer-turned-innkeeper explained that men had been arriving for days. He had made a tidy sum selling simple meals and a place to sleep, but Mirza admitted he wasn't going to be sad to leave. We were dining on the last goat. He would be glad when the polo game was over tomorrow. If it was this cold on the Shandur Pass during summer he reasoned, it must be truly terrible in winter. Everyone murmured agreement at such wisdom and hunched closer to the fire.

The goat meat and bread kept me alive. The steaming cups of chai sent heat coursing through my veins. The crackling fire poured warmth into my puny bones. Within an hour I had thrown open my blanket and was growing relaxed.

The fire crackled, burning in strange colors because of the high altitude. I brought out my pipe. Ali Muhammad and Raja each put a large pinch of naswar, the green Pukhtun snuff, inside their lips. Neither of the two farmers sharing the dugout had seen a man smoke a pipe before. Their village was so isolated that no foreigner had visited it in more than fifty years. Ali Muhammad and I were the first Americans either of them had ever met. They had heard of Pathans, and had even seen a tribesman like Raja once in Chitral, they told us proudly.

We gossiped as men do when they are relaxed, speaking of God, and horses, and women, and the vagaries of life. The small cave sheltered, besides us, a primitive odor, half animal, half man, a combination of horse sweat, wood smoke and men grown stale from honest labor. There was no trace of the outside world to distort that evening. The seven of us were beyond the reach of time. Outside the doorway I could see my horse standing in the cold bright moonlight. Campfires twinkled like living rubies in the darkness beyond. It was only men and a fire that night, huddled together against the dark, obedient to custom, at peace with the simplicity of life.

Khyber Knights

With such thoughts did I retire, only to be awakened before dawn shaking like a dog in my blanket. The fire had gone out during the night. Condensation dripped down off the low canvas roof, hitting me in the face, reminding me where I was. I had drawn up into a tight ball and pulled my head under my blanket, hoping to use my breath to keep myself warm, all to no avail. I shook so hard, I thought I would expire before sunrise. As soon as Mirza arose to start the fire, all of his guests immediately joined him. Like me they had been awake and shivering. I was never so glad to see the sun.

When I stepped outside that morning it was bright and cold. Down country in Peshawar they were frying in their own grease, while up there on the Shandur Pass men and horses were struggling to keep a warm heart beating in their chilled bodies.

All my life I had lived for horses.

That day I was proud to be a horseman.

While Mirza got the fire going, and Raja and Ali Muhammad saw to our own horses, I took the opportunity to wander through the great camp and marvel at what lay around me. The brilliant blue sky looked like a giant lid flipped over the top of a stone-lipped cauldron. Men walked among the tents, shelters, stone huts, yurts and burrows they had called home for a night. Cooking fires were snapping. Chai was brewing. Bread was warming and everywhere I went I heard the same words, "horses, Gilgit, Chitral."

The mighty Shandur Pass stood as a cultural, as well as a geographical boundary between two ancient kingdoms. Two hundred miles further east lay Gilgit. It straddled a caravan route that was ancient before Marco Polo wandered through in the 13th century. Gilgit's influence reached out to Tibet, China and Kashmir. For centuries the northern metropolis was a critically important staging post in the surrounding Karakorum mountains. Gilgit had reason to hold her head high. Compared to the stony savages surrounding her, she was rich and cultivated.

Chitral meanwhile looked to Afghanistan, Russia and Peshawar for her contacts with the outside world. She had always been a xenophobic kingdom, ruled by a local king known as the Mehtar. While that smaller city reigned as the most influential place in the Hindu Raj mountains, she had a history of murder, slavery and fratricide. It was a time-honored custom for the Mehtar to blind or slay his male rivals for the throne. The concept of legal punishment did not exist. Law breakers were sold into slavery, as was anyone unfortunate enough to be seized by the Mehtar's men. The bloodthirsty Borgias of Italy would have loved Chitrali politics.

No one could tell me when these two great northern rivals first met on the windswept Shandur plateau to wage symbolic battle on the polo field. As I wandered I heard different accounts, yet no year was certain. Like the origin of the game itself, the beginning of this localized equestrian warfare was lost in the dim recesses of man's genetic memory. What was agreed upon by Chitrali and Gilgiti alike was that polo had been played longer than any other game known to man, and that the Shandur Pass had witnessed its birth.

I made my way through the two opposing camps. Hundreds of impatient villagers, shopkeepers, farmers, and businessmen were awake, mingling, talking, betting and waiting for the sun to warm the sky enough for the game to begin.

Originally the polo horses had come from the nearby Afghan province of Badakhshan. It had been many years since those cat-footed, nimble mountain ponies had played there. War had so decimated the Afghan equine export, no one was sure if any Badakhshi ponies even survived.

Both teams now relied on horses purchased down country in the hot Punjab province, then brought up to their respective mountain kingdoms. The horses were to my mind too thin-chested, as they were all directly descended from the Australian thoroughbred stock imported so many decades ago. Nevertheless, with the distinctive twist to the top of their ears, the Kathiawari-Waler half-breeds were long-legged, high-stepping, bright-eyed athletes. Only stallions were employed and on each side of the field I heard horsemen exclaiming the merits of their respective horses.

"When he gallops he brings tears to your eyes," said one, as he brushed a white faced sorrel from Chitral.

"No one has ever ridden his equal," said another, as he examined the legs of a glistening black from Gilgit.

The spectators were far from mute, pointing and exclaiming in excitement as men do in all countries at the sight of a famous sports figure.

"That one was raised like one of his children," they whispered with pride about a Chitrali horse.

"He says to the eagle, 'Descend, or I shall come up to you,'" bragged the Gilgitis of their favorite.

It was well that these horses were the best Pakistan had to offer, for this was no polite match between Argentine and British gentlemen playing with Marquis of Queensberry rules on a warm summer lawn. The British were fond of saying they "discovered" polo when their officers were stationed in these mountains in the mid-nineteenth century. They overlooked the fact that the root word "*pulu*" was an ancient Tibetan term for willow root, from which the earliest balls had been commonly made. What we gathered to watch was not the civilized version of polo played by Prince Charles, because this was not sport for rich men, this was war between fierce rivals. This was about honor and courage and daring and defying destruction, because Death was watching too and made his presence known soon enough.

When the sun reached its zenith the vast arena was at fever pitch. Jeeps had been pouring in all morning. I estimated the crowd had grown to more than two thousand strong. The cold never let up, so Ali Muhammad, Raja and I stayed wrapped in our wool blankets when we went in search of a seat. We chose to sit on Chitral's side, though they were underdogs, and we owed the place nothing more than a scrap of geographic loyalty.

The playing field was perfectly level. Rocks had been laid out to form three sides of an immense rectangle. Police, and enlisted men from the Chitral Scouts, were stationed behind the lines to keep the spectators off the field. Being a musician himself, Ali Muhammad thought it fitting that we take seats near the band. Even before the game began this six-piece ensemble was engaged in a musical duel with their Gilgit rivals sitting on the opposite side of the polo field.

Four gigantic *dadang* (drums) beat out a roaring beat, while two *surnai* (oboes) added a steady stream of ear-splitting tunes. This was a carryover from bygone days when the Mehtar directed his troops in battle by signaling his commands via different tunes. The band now played musical messages from the coach, as well as signature tunes for each player, indicating who had scored. These tunes were well known to the crowds on both sides and only added to the growing hysteria.

When the twelve players appeared at the end of the field the air was electric with anticipation.

There were six riders on a team. Men and horses were expected to play through to the finish without replacements. Despite the bitter cold the horsemen were too haughty to don warm clothing. They were attired in light cotton polo shirts, red for Chitral, blue for Gilgit. Three sported helmets. The others were disdainful of injury and rode bare-headed. All wore white riding breeches and glossy knee-high black boots. Two had heavy leather pads strapped over their right knees, all the better to ram into their foes. Safety and warmth lay disdained, and rightly so, for within minutes they were as soaked in sweat as their mounts.

Sitting on their magnificent horses, those twelve chevaliers represented one of the major differences between India and Pakistan, between horsemen and pedestrians.

India, lacking a dramatic equestrian class throughout much of its existence, was the only important eastern nation to show no notable active leadership in recent historical times. While true that it had a horse culture for many centuries, this was primarily seen in the use of chariots. The few outstanding horsemen who appeared within its borders had been transplanted foreigners from nearby horseback nations. India had largely viewed the horse as the prerogative of royalty and as instruments of religious ceremony. Not so these mountaineers, these sons of caravan raiders, these horsemen.

Since her inception in 1947, little Pakistan had fought two wars with her bigger neighbor. That cold afternoon much of the country stood shackled in the chains of General Zia's martial law. Many of her founding concepts lay stillborn. She had few things to be proud of. This was one of them. That bright afternoon, witnessed by a mob of shouting illiterates on top of a forgotten, windswept mountain, Pakistan held her head high. What we saw was that nation's contribution to an international equestrian brotherhood. No one else in the world risked their lives in the saddle as did these twelve horsemen. No other horses belonged to this exclusive band. These twelve stood alone.

The polo players sat their horses impassively, giving the crowd a long look at both the teams and their local heroes. The rival bands filled the air with their wild competing music and men were shouting before the ball even touched the field. It was the magic of the horse, not just the game, that had brought thousands of strangers together.

Historically, men on foot seldom strayed far from their village, or ventured off to view the far horizons that drew their equestrian brothers. Being immobile, footmen were more apt to accept an overlord and his taxation. On horseback, a man lived as lord of all he surveyed. He may have been a unlettered barbarian, but he was independent, superior, not a member of a subject race. His mobility and his courage were marked in the pages of history. He was not earth-bound. Such were these Pakistanis, such were these proud horsemen.

The white ball hit the field and the horsemen battled, not played, battled up and down the length of that long, long field for possession. Their horses' breath came ripping out like dragon's smoke in the freezing air, clouds of steam following them as they raced by. Their great horse eyes were as mad as the men who rode them.

Chitral was first to score and the band went insane, pounding the drums till they threatened to burst, blowing on the oboes until they screamed for mercy. All the while the spectators were being pushed back by the police, who were intent on keeping the crowds behind the simple line of rocks. In their excitement men would stand, and be shoved down by the police, or be grabbed by spectators who couldn't see from behind them.

Points were scored and tempers flared and the crowd was becoming unmanageable in its excitement. They screamed, roared and wept as Gilgit and Chitral fought like centaurs for honor and a polo ball.

"For Gilgit," the other side yelled, as their music roared in agreement and another point was scored.

Then the horses came charging our way, coming so close that the earth shook and dirt clods came pelting over us and I feared for our safety as the horses screamed in rage, grappling and fighting with their enemies from across the mountains. Then the ball became entangled beneath their feet and the game became a milling mass of wild men and wilder horses directly in front of us. The air was ripped with sound as the horses spilled over into the seating area. We all fled for our lives, while the men on horseback took no notice and fought on, polo sticks flaying friend and foe alike.

Some bravo from Chitral cracked the ball, which went soaring back onto the field, and we were safe, and they were gone like a memory which has terrified you but you love all the same.

God those were men! They would have charged Hell with a bucket of water.

"For Chitral," our side screamed as the music roared again, and we danced and sprang in the air from excitement, while the field grew sloppy and treacherous, horses reared and men fell, and one horse died in his tracks and one player collapsed, falling from the saddle with a heart attack in a world so high even eagles could scarcely breathe.

It was pandemonium.

It was glorious.

Gilgit won three to two.

By nightfall all trace of it was gone.

The victors were lifted from their saddles, the surviving horses were rubbed down and loaded into two trucks, and men ran for jeeps, and motors screamed to life, and the crowd began to flee the harsh world we had all called home during those short hours of sweet madness. Tents were hastily pulled down. Caverns abandoned. The denizens of both sides of the north country abandoned cold Shandur to her lonely glory.

We too saddled up and left the frozen heights of the plateau to await the next invasion of polo players. With the few hours of sunlight left we eagerly took to the road in search of a warmer bed. The trail narrowed as we left the vast arena, leading us down gradually until we descended into milder weather and found a small, secluded valley. The road passed nearby, otherwise it was an untouched green jewel, nestled between mountain tops, clothed in rich grass, alpine flowers and blessed with the secluded head waters of the Ghizer river.

The jeeps had passed through already, so we picketed the horses and made a fire. Nightfall found us lying beneath a stream of wild stars. The only sound was the soft murmuring of the tiny river and the tinkling of the horse's bells as they slowly grazed their way across the darkened grass. My companions lay nearby on their backs, wrapped in their blankets, gazing up at the panorama of Allah's paint brush splashed above our heads. The brilliant beauty of the night had left us all speechless.

On the map the place was called Burbolango Shal, a ridiculous name for such a beautiful place. With the memory of the polo game still recent, I sat there and thought about the effort that had gone into bringing me to that little valley. Sitting near the fire I could feel its heat on my face and the cold at my back. Pasha's bell rang softly in the dark. I could taste the night wind. I realized I was utterly content.

If it is true that when men died their spirits returned to the place they loved best in their lifetime, then I knew I would find myself with Pasha, there again in Burbolango Shal.

I knew my restless spirit would drive me on in the morning, to journey down to Gilgit and then beyond. It no longer mattered. From the next morning on I would travel only from necessity and not out of longing. That night I knew I had discovered the moment and the place when I no longer suffered from the gypsy curse that had cast me out onto the road to wander. In Burbolango Shal I had discovered my own restful place in the world where my inner and outer lives rested in complete tranquillity.

My friends perhaps thought similar thoughts.

"Allah must have grown tired when he made this place. He was so busy making it beautiful He forgot to make men to go with it," Raja said softly, and we let it rest.

Khyber Knights

34
Religious Difficulties

We entered into a strange country as one should, on horseback, and with a sense of reverence.

The dirt road we traveled on towards Gilgit was thought to be the one Marco Polo used to reach Cathay. Those who believe Jesus Christ survived the cross, and later died in Kashmir, attest that this was the same route he took after passing through Persia and Afghanistan.

I hope Jesus got better treatment than we did.

Everything seemed the same to us. The horses moved well. We were hungry. The sun shone. Yet we had crossed an invisible border into a likewise invisible kingdom.

Oddly enough, the only news I had been able to garner from other travelers about our upcoming route east was that the road, though wide, was prone to avalanches. Of the natives there was little word. In fact I met no one at the polo game who lived close by to the other side of the Shandur Pass. Everyone seemed to have traveled over from the Gilgit region. Thinking that the daily requirements of subsistence farming gave the villagers between here and that faraway town no opportunity to attend, I gave it no thought.

Early that morning we had said a reluctant adieu to our camp in Burbolango Shal. The horses were well rested and the road lay alongside the banks of the little Ghizer river. According to the map we had an easy day in front of us, no more than twelve miles. Additionally, the British Raj had built a string of bungalows between the Shandur Pass and Gilgit to shelter travelers and troops. Our federally issued permit authorized us the use of these rest houses, though we had no idea what condition they would be in nearly fifty years after Partition. The first one was located in that day's destination, the village of Teru.

It was impossible to get lost. We found ourselves trapped between two giant walls of stone. We rode alongside the river with unnamed mountains on both sides. The sun made the journey pleasant and we three horsemen were chatting and light hearted. Almost immediately the little stream began to widen considerably. Being fed by snow-melt it was soon too broad to cross.

Almost five miles down that relaxing road we came upon a great loop where the river hugged the edge of a mountain, leaving exposed a large widening of the valley. Here we discovered more than twenty local men busy digging up a vast peat bog.

At first I thought I was mistaken. Yet I had witnessed similar operations in Ireland and recognized the actions of men slicing and stacking turf. Only I had never heard of this fuel being either found or burned in Pakistan. Upon asking I was told that indeed this soil did burn after it was allowed to dry. Raja thought them all mad, his skepticism plain to see. It was our first hint we had left his part of Pakistan far behind.

The men were working in teams of two. While one dug, the other stacked the slices of wet peat into wicker panniers resting on nearby donkeys. No one could tell me how long they had used peat for fuel or who had first discovered its fiery nature. The bare foot, busy villagers gave me a look of skepticism in turn for asking such a useless question.

This new revelation only added to the country's growing charm, for by late afternoon we had come onto the outskirts of a village. It was not Ireland but it was strikingly beautiful all the same. The valley here was half a mile wide, rich in lush crops, green pastures and apricot trees dripping ripe fruit. All around us was a peaceful bucolic Shangri-La. The air itself was warmer, and except for the sound of the river, it was tranquil and quiet. We had ridden over the pass and entered a place devoid of all hurry, embraced by restfulness.

Teru was lovely and the bungalow was perfect, whitewashed walls, shady trees out front, grass for the horses inside spacious perimeter walls, even a porch where I could smoke my pipe. The only problem was we couldn't get in. Having arrived at the guest house in the early afternoon, news soon spread to the *chowkidar* (night watchman).

To say we were in a pleasant mood would have been an understatement of our emotional condition. I handed the bungalow's guardian our firman, explaining who we were, only to be told we couldn't stay there for the night. At first I thought there was a mistake.

No mistake, we couldn't stay he informed us. The bungalow was already occupied by two engineers. Seeing no sign of anyone else I began to suspect the man was lying, but for what purpose eluded me. Raja was impatient and voted that we seize the dwelling.

"Can't he see my mustache?" the hot-blooded tribal demanded, referring to the common expression of Frontier manliness. I didn't tell the youngster that I could barely see his newly sprouted statement of facial vigor.

"We'll wait to see if the engineers return, otherwise we will sleep here tonight," I informed the chowkidar.

His immediate agitation was instant proof of his conspiracy. If evidence was lacking, by dusk there was no sign of any other travelers. By now we had lost patience and demanded the stubborn guardian open the door. He did so with complete reluctance.

Inside we discovered a serviceable room with four charpoys and a fireplace. A villager agreed to supply us dinner. The price was high, five rupees a plate, but our hunger overrode our pocket book. We were pleasantly surprised to find three large fried trout on our plates, next to bread and curried potatoes. Our chef explained that the Ghizer river had such fish to spare. Pajaro and his friends dined quite well on the tall grass growing up around the bungalow.

The next day brought new revelations.

"Pasha and I found ourselves trapped within two giant walls of stone. Otherwise everything seemed the same. We were hungry. The sun shone. Yet we had crossed an invisible border into a likewise invisible kingdom.

Religious Difficulties

We departed early. The treeless mountains on both sides of us closed in even tighter. The little stream we had seen at Burbolango Shal was now a raging torrent. There was no path except straight ahead on the horses or to fly away with the eagles. All that day we rode through mountains that made us feel like were dolls who had wandered into a giant's house. Our eyes could not become easily accustomed to the new proportions of that massive landscape.

Nightfall again brought us only disturbance.

Stopping at the next rest house we were rudely told by the chowkidar that we could not stay. He dismissed our slip of paper out of hand.

"I take my orders from Gilgit not Islamabad," he told us rudely.

"Don't you call yourself a Pakistani?" I asked astonished.

"No," he snapped back and stood there looking sullen and defiant.

The situation was at an impasse when a well-dressed Pakistani man came out of the bungalow, took the *chowkidar* aside, and spoke to him quietly. The stranger's influence immediately swayed this local version of Norman Bates. We were reluctantly shown a room, as well as told where we could picket the horses. That night we learned from the chowkidar that the other guest was an employee of the Aga Khan Foundation. Like our hostile host, the other man was an Ismaili, a minority sect of Islam holding widely differing views from the majority of the Muslim world. Though the stranger had obtained us a room, he made no effort to meet us, only furthering our feeling that not only mountains, but cultural taboos now walled us in as well.

As we moved further on next morning we found the country becoming increasingly beautiful in the bright sunshine. The mountains had a light lavender tint to them. The sky overhead was robin's egg blue and crowded with white clouds. Around us as we rode were little villages transparently rich in produce. Even the river was bountiful.

At one section the Ghizer had flooded over her banks, creating a warm, shallow pond the size of a football field. Though no more than four feet deep, the recently-flooded fields were teeming with schools of trout. The fish had rushed in with the trespassing tide and could now be seen swimming lazily in clear view. None of us were anglers but we sat there in our saddles hungrily wishing we owned fly rod and tackle. With no natural predators the trout had been left largely undisturbed for fifty years. They circled lazily in the sun-drenched water, eating an occasional bug. Some were longer than a man's forearm and as big around as his calf. I could probably have waded in and slain them with a stick. Instead of getting wet we filled our bellies on ripe apricots picked from trees overhanging the trail, washed down by cool, clear ditch water.

Soon after we rode on we saw our first Jamat Khana. This religious facility of the Ismailis was unlike the traditional Muslim mosque with its distinctive minarets and star and crescent. The Jamat Khana sat by itself away from the village. It resembled a traditional stone-walled square building, in that it gave no outside clue in either decoration or script as to its religious function. It had no minaret to call the faithful to prayer and in fact boasted a large stone wall that seemed to advise people to stay out.

Khyber Knights

Over its roof flew an orange and aquamarine flag. In all my travels through Islamic countries, this was the first Muslim house of worship that was altogether secretive and inhospitable.

The riddle of our new environment was beginning to be solved.

Our road east was an unsurpassed landscape of color, vista and visual pageant. We however were uninvited, unwanted, and unacceptable. Even our horses were disliked. The men ignored our greetings. The women, though unveiled and in plain view, made sure to turn away. A wedding party we encountered on the road pointedly passed us with no more than a curt nod from the groom and no hint of an invitation to the celebrations. It was hard to stay in conformity with Islamic custom, we learned, when traveling among the hardhearted Ismailis.

Gone were the rough but friendly people we had encountered from Peshawar to Chitral, with their poor farms but generous hearts. Instead we found ourselves in a churlish land where despite rich fields and fat-cheeked children, the people thrived on avarice and deceit.

Evening found us on the outskirts of the large village of Phander. The government-owned bungalow was impressively maintained and visibly empty. In answer to our request a young boy ran off to locate the *chowkidar*. We stayed in our saddles. The day's events had left us increasingly annoyed. None of us had ever seen or heard of such blatantly rude behavior as we had encountered the last few days among the Ismailis. It was apparent members of the local religious minority had either boycotted, or more likely been unwelcome, at the Shandur Pass polo game.

The horses were stamping their feet with impatience before the boy returned with an bearded old man in tow. During our wait a group of idle villagers had gathered around. The dozen men looked bored, but made no effort to open a conversation, preferring to keep their distance. The crafty-looking *chowkidar* seemed to have graduated from the same school of discourteous impudence we had encountered the last two nights. I palavered with him from Pasha's saddle, thinking I wasn't explaining the authorization slip correctly to his simple farmer's mind.

All this time the *chowkidar* had been keeping a close eye on his fellow villagers, waiting to see if they would stay to support him. Perhaps he thought we were penniless Afghan refugees? Perhaps he believed us infidel Franks who had wandered in from the unknown reaches of the west? No matter. He did not accord us even the basic courtesy afforded to tired travelers.

That was a mistake.

The rude old man shoved the paper back in my hand, not interested in either its message or my plea for mercy.

"I don't have to let you in," he told me in a loud voice dripping with disdain.

"Are you deaf? This paper orders you to open the door to us," I told him, at the same time trying to hold my temper.

Religious Difficulties

Seeing I wasn't going to accept his argument the *chowkidar* played his last card.

"I don't have the key," he told us and crossed his arms to signal the end of the discussion. The villagers were starting to snicker and the old charlatan looked delightfully smug, when Ali Muhammad pulled his pistol. The tall horseman leaned down from his saddle and shoved the black gun into the *chowkidar's* face.

"I brought the key, you ignorant rustic," the out-of-patience musician said in a surly voice. He then deliberately cocked the big pistol in the old man's face.

"No need to show your fangs. Look, look I have found it," the *chowkidar* stuttered, and immediately pulled the missing key out of his vest pocket, holding it in a shaking hand for all to see.

"Your lucky day. Now open up," Ali ordered, as he pushed the pistol closer to emphasize his point.

While the old fraud scuttled off, I urged the angered American to cool down.

"What's the point of carrying this thing if I can't shoot anybody?" he said loud enough for his intended audience to hear.

The crowd immediately started drifting away, though the angry looks they shot our way relayed their message. Their manner of behavior was unknown to me in Pakistan.

The country was poor, yes. But inhospitable? Never!

From Karachi to Karimabad I had never seen the laws of hospitality so bluntly trashed. Though the country suffered from a multitude of problems, including sectarian violence, massive illiteracy, corrupt politicians, a soaring infant mortality rate, etc., the average Pakistani family prided themselves on placing what little they had at the disposal of guests or travelers. They may have been unwashed or unlettered but no one ever broke this first and greatest rule of the road. It was a tradition predating the arrival of Alexander the Great, a custom reaching back to the cloudy, ancient days of the Medes. True, Pakistan was an oftentimes dangerous country, saddled with sin, but none of her children broke this inviolate law of antiquity.

Across the ages even a starving family traditionally gave their last crust of bread to a traveler, knowing the same rule of hospitality would also secure them from distress if the roles became reversed. Pathans believed so strongly in the sacred law of hospitality they even offered it to their confirmed enemies. The Quran itself specifically confirmed that alms were to be given to the poor, freed slaves, those struggling in God's cause by teaching, and travelers.

The Ismailis glaring at us were heavy-blooded, sullen, lacking gaiety, grace and the common courtesies of man. We stepped down from our saddles into a vale of tears. The *chowkidar* had unlocked the door and rethought the importance of his guests. Thinking that such violent gentlemen could only be important, he was suddenly transformed from obstructionist into toady. In answer to our needs he smacked the boy and sent him in search for grass for the horses, then promised to see to our own dinner himself. Despite his transparent turn of heart, looming over his head on the bare mountainside above all of us lay ample evidence of the real problem.

"*Khush Amadaid Hazir Imam* (Welcome our Present Leader)," had been written out in painted white letters, almost one hundred feet high, on the barren mountainside above. The letters were a gigantic environmental offense to the eye and the last missing piece of the inhospitable puzzle. The words spelt out a salutation to the spiritual guru of the Ismailis, as well as plenty of trouble for our caravan.

By nightfall even the horses had been fed but offended. We paid an exorbitant amount for their hay and our dinner. The sullen village refused to provide us with so much as a candle, so we three travelers sat outside in the warm night air hoping to shine the rays of truth into the dark corners of ancient prejudice. With the horses' bells as background music each man threw into our pot of talk every scrap of knowledge individually dredged up about our reluctant hosts.

What we all agreed upon was that what distinguishes a person in the eyes of God was their deeds and individual righteousness. God made no distinction between man over woman, Arab over non-Arab, white over black, English and American over the rest of the world. In Peshawar it was said that hearts and souls had no color. This fundamental belief was the foundation of Islam, an all-embracing brotherhood claiming more than one billion adherents worldwide.

Islam was also a legalistic religion with no clerical hierarchy. It was anathema in the majority of the Muslim world to bestow the roles of pope, bishop, priest or monk on a fellow religionist. The traditional view of Islam held that by personal prayer, anyone could communicate directly with the Almighty. No religious intermediaries were either required or tolerated.

Muslims, like Jews, were presented with a set of God-given laws that they were required to use in everyday life. The two religions differed in that the Mosaic law was presented to a well-defined people in Judaism, but in the case of Islam was given to any man or woman who would accept it. Both religions taught that all human behavior was to comply with God's will.

After the death of Muhammad, the Prophet of Islam, upon whom be peace, a question immediately arose as to who his successor should be. The majority of Muslims, known as Sunnis, believe the Prophet instructed his followers to elect a "Caliph" after his death. These traditionalists believe religious issues should be resolved based on reasoning and personal knowledge of the Quran. Abu Bakr, a close friend of the departed leader was democratically chosen to lead these Sunnis, based on his proven leadership and traditional religious beliefs. The majority of Muslims in the Arab world followed this early decision.

An offshoot, known as Shias, believed that Ali, the Prophet's cousin and husband of his daughter, Fatima, should have been chosen to lead the Muslims. The reasoning of these devotees was that a religious dynasty based on male descendants of Muhammad and Ali were

Religious Difficulties

uniquely qualified to lead the Muslim community and represented a designation of spiritual authority based on the will of God.

This question remained a theological one during the formative years after the Prophet's death. However as Islam expanded geographically it took with it this problem of succession. In newly-conquered Persia, already an old and proud civilization, the people rebelled against the elected Arab successor. While to all appearances' sake they held true to the new religion introduced to their country by Arab conquerors, the Persians theologically revolted, siding with the minority view. Unlike the fiercely independent Arab nomads who brought Islam out of the hot deserts, the Persians had a long tradition of monarchy that they looked back upon with pride. It was an easy step psychologically for them at once to reject the Arab claim of leadership, and adapt that of religious king in its stead.

Though in fact Ali was eventually elected to lead the Muslims, he was murdered on his way to pray in the mosque. Additionally, soon afterwards his grandsons as well as their followers were brutally massacred after a ten-day battle on the sandy plain of Karbala, located in present day Iraq. The death of these kin of the Prophet has divided the Islamic world like a bloody curtain ever since, with the Arabs and the majority of the Muslim world still on one side, and the present day Iranians and Ismailis of northern Pakistan on the other.

The Shias in essence became the Catholics of the Islamic world, with a priesthood and a religious mystery surrounding the teachings and activities of their first twelve Imams.

Growing like dragon's teeth from this hate and dissension came numerous religious leaders among the Shias, known as Imams, who purported to be descended from the murdered Ali. As religious persecution took hold, the belief grew that even though the Arab Sunnis had driven the Imam, or true leader of the Shias underground, he would one day return to reveal himself to his devout followers. Thus appeared the myth of a spiritual leader who would one day reappear to lead the oppressed Shia underdogs to victory over their Sunni oppressors. Over the next thousand years one of the world's bloodiest religious feuds remained unresolved, as a series of Imams were no sooner revealed, than they were killed or chased off the pages of history.

In the early 1840s a new Imam once again appeared in Persia. This current "reappeared" religious leader was the Prince Imam Agha Khan Mahallati, the first of his clan to carry the distinguished title "Agha Khan" and the ancestor of the same "Agha Khan" these local farmers so slavishly worshipped on their painted mountainside.

Mahallati had been granted his honorific title, as well as the post of governor of the province of Kerman, by the Persian Shah. Yet the new Agha Khan rewarded his rightful ruler's generosity by foul treachery. After signing a secret treaty with the British in nearby India, the Agha Khan raised a covert army and attempted to conquer Persia. Despite British cannons and money the revolt was an abject failure. With his head nearly in the Shah's noose, this first Hazir Imam fled into Afghanistan one step ahead of his Persian captors.

Here he once again offered his mercenary services to the British, this time offering to conquer and rule Afghanistan for a price. Typically the xenophobic Afghans made short work of this religious pretender by killing his imperial British advisors and driving the apostate back onto the road.

His next stop was into recently-conquered Sind, where the Agha Khan rewrote the definition of the word traitor. The British were busy consolidating their stranglehold over the native Amirs in that previously independent kingdom. Always a survivor, Mahallati at first sided with the British against his Muslim brothers, stating he did so because the foreigner conquerors were "the true People of God." Soon the Agha Khan switched sides to the rebellious Amirs. Then in an act of base treachery, the Persian Quisling changed sides a third time, reverting to his British masters, and revealing the Sindi battle plan "for the sake of God's pleasure."

The native troops were slaughtered and the Ismaili Judas was rewarded with a lordly sum of blood money by his grateful foreign employers. Basking now in official favor, the Agha Khan and his retinue turned their backs on the chaos of Persia and Sind and moved to richer, more urban pickings. The leader settled his cult in the safety of British-ruled Bombay. Here he was safe from the fratricide of Persia and more importantly, able to expand his congregation.

Over the next few decades the Agha Khan's infamous avarice and greed would have made a Washington politician blush in shame. Reinforcing his claim to divinity, the Agha Khan saw to it that the hitherto-sporadic religious contributions paid into his coffers by devout Ismaili followers became a steady stream of uninterrupted wealth. Hindu converts were encouraged to send donations to this new incarnation of their god Vishnu. Ismailis in forgotten corners of his rapidly-spreading religious empire were instructed to contribute to a lifestyle that included jewels and palaces. Before his death, the first Agha Khan's wealth and insidious influence began emanating from his spider's web into the politics of the Indian sub-continent.

As one Agha Khan succeeded another the Ismaili political influence reached though history until it colored the birth of Pakistan itself. By 1947, the year of Pakistan's inception, the third Ismaili Agha Khan exerted an extraordinary amount of influence over both the Muslim League political party, as well as Muhammad Ali Jinnah, himself an Ismaili, and the founder of Pakistan. Ismaili gold poured in every year, not just into the coffers of the Bombay court of the Agha Khan, but indirectly into the campaign chest of the Muslim League, the organization dedicated to creating a separate homeland for Muslims on the Indian sub-continent. Despite the enormous expense of financing a project as costly as the birth of a nation, there was enough wealth left over still to support the Agha Khan in a lifestyle that would have suited the tastes of a Pharaoh.

Religious Difficulties

The Agha Khan presiding over the Ismaili court in 1947 was a man of tremendous wealth and girth. In a yearly display of religious devotion and servility, the Ismailis counter-balanced their Persian pope's 300 pound plus body against an equal amount of gold, platinum and diamonds that had been collected from the unwashed masses who believed in his divinity. What the majority of these trusting followers had no way of knowing was that the son of their leader was leading a life of such celebrated debauchery, that it scandalized even the notoriously hedonistic Agha Khan. That son's ultimate act of folly was to marry the famous Hollywood starlet Rita Hayworth.

Even the permissive father couldn't overlook the wild oats sown with the sexy, redheaded Rita. In an act of insight the Agha Khan passed over his son, choosing his infant grandson to be his religious successor instead. Thus the rise of Pakistan and the current Agha Khan had walked nearly hand in hand through history.

Unlike his overweight granddad and his star-struck father, the reigning Agha Khan devoted much of his inherited wealth to public works. The Agha Khan Foundation had an immediate positive affect on the same followers who still worshipped him as a living incarnation of Allah's majesty. A vast network of Agha Khan services, including rural hospitals, public schools and agricultural research stations, now dotted northern Pakistan. For as the wealth of the first Agha Khan in Bombay grew so did his empire. The Ismailis now reached from old Persia, through Afghanistan and across that section of northern Pakistan.

The current Agha Khan, believed by the Ismailis to be a direct descendent of the Caliph Ali and the Prophet Muhammad, preferred to live in a multi-million dollar chalet in France, raise thoroughbred horses in Ireland, run his religious empire from London and present himself before the United Nations as the voice of moderate Islam. Yet despite his respectability, the religious rancor that had plagued the Sunni versus Shia conflict for centuries was still very much alive not just in Pakistan, but in the village where we found ourselves lodged that night.

While the present Agha Khan might be skiing in the French Alps, his followers in northern Pakistan were more likely trying not to be butchered by their intolerant neighbors. While the Sunnis are the power that rules Pakistan, the government in Islamabad was realistic enough to court the mind-boggling money and worldwide influence of the Agha Khan. That translated into concessions for the Ismailis and official government tolerance of this otherwise commonly despised sect.

Yet what Pakistani politicians said in public was often vastly different from what they voiced in private as devout Sunnis. The double standard led to an unwritten feeling that the Ismailis were wealthy by duplicity, therefore to be enviously admired, but beneath the surface still Shias and not to be trusted. This distrust translated into ill-will and oftentimes murder between Ismaili and Sunni neighbors.

Being a European in all but name, the Agha Khan encouraged education for all of his subjects, including females. This added to the Ismaili reputation of being progressive and industrious. The original wealth had been collectively spread back among the believers, bringing with it many wonderful results in the way of much-needed programs and facilities. Ismailis were self sufficient, educated, and liberal. In the Ghizer river valley they were also poor hosts. In an effort to survive persecution, what had evolved religiously over the last hundred years was a secretive belief, based in Islamic tradition, that now increasingly looked to the West for many of its guidelines.

Many Sunnis in the surrounding areas were resentful and jealous, not just of the apparent Ismaili wealth, but the unorthodox views that went with it. The differences in belief only widened the breach between outside-looking Ismailis and inward-looking Sunnis, who tended to see things through rose-colored glasses back to the glory days of Islam. Consequently the same envied contact with Europe and the West that had benefited the Ismaili's daily lives had also brought the sword of Sunni religious retribution down on their necks. This intolerance had lead to pogroms by the more numerous Sunnis surrounding these isolated Ismaili valleys. Though Islam urged its followers to use reason to interpret the faith, all too often it had become fossilized. In their misspent piety the Sunnis had lost sight of the fact that Islam, as defined by the faith in a man's heart, was different than the Islam they claimed as a political ideology. As history and the village of Phander had shown, a wonderful lesson was being torn apart in the name of faith by the actions of misguided men.

The age-old conflict over the question of who ran Islam was still very much alive that night in Phander. We had stumbled into a part of Pakistan where only the currency reminded these people of their nationality. Being isolated for more than half the year, the Ismailis were in essence an inaccessible nation shut in between the snowbound passes of the Hindu Raj and Karakorum mountains. In these mountains they governed themselves according to their own customs, free to worship as they chose. They were as cut off from the rest of their country, and the world, as if they lived on an atoll in the vast Pacific ocean. Yet they led the lives their fathers had led. The historical pattern of worship was laid out, all they had to do was follow it. The letters were painted on the mountain to highlight a recent whirlwind helicopter tour by the visiting Agha Khan.

Decades of historical persecution had forced the Ismailis to formulate a belief unique in Islam known as *taqiyya*. The term literally meant to hide one's face under a pillow. In practice it gave Ismailis the authority to hide their religious practices and beliefs from all outsiders. Their rites stayed secret. Their beliefs were veiled from inspection. What little was known was that Ismailis had incorporated components of Judaism, Christianity, Aristotle, gnosticism and the Manichaeans into Islam. Unlike other Muslims, the Ismailis did not allow outsiders to enter one of their mosques. Their Jamat Khanas were closed to Raja, Ali Muhammad, and me. The Ismailis were as exclusionary as Masons.

What this centuries-old conflict between Sunnis and Ismailis unfortunately did for us was turn those solemn beautiful mountains into a

Religious Difficulties

toxic dumping ground of religious animosity. Having been exposed to generations of ridicule and slaughter, the Ismailis were pitted against us before we ever stepped down from our horses, lumping us in automatically with the most bigoted of our Sunni co-religionists. There were pious bigots on either side of the issue who were so busy preaching their interpretation of the religion they forgot to practice it. The only thing both factions were managing to do was give out the wrong image and the wrong message. They had laid aside the fundamental truth that it was not about practicing Islam on the outside, but practicing it within, that mattered. It was mankind who had mistakenly broken up God's unifying message. Each party rejoiced in its confused ignorance, its narrow views, its jarring camps, its sectarian sects, instead of taking refuge in the brotherhood of universal truth that had never changed throughout the ages.

The actions of the Ismailis were a blow to me for a personal reason.

They represented the first time anyone in the Muslim world had ever slammed a door in my face, either physically or spiritually. I could not help but wonder how different my own life might have evolved if my first introduction to Islam had been through these unsociable, religiously constrained, Muslim papists.

During the course of my life's adventures my external journeys mirrored the religious quest I was also on. From the day in 1977 when I visited the great blue mosque in Mazar-I-Sharif, Afghanistan, I knew I had stumbled onto a faith whose very definition had been previously denied me.

I was no different from a multitude of other Americans raised in the hedonism of the 1970s. I was a disaffected Christian, spiritually hungry, starving for succor, yet too prejudiced by my world view to know where to look. Christianity for me had been an exercise in degradation and hypocrisy. The church I attended as a boy was populated by either those who clung mindlessly to the wooden ritual of their recently-invented dogma, or those more liberal skeptics who considered religion an outmoded superstition that they outwardly clung to for its social values but were secretly ashamed of it as being intellectually indefensible.

During my youth I had squirmed in discomfort for years, sitting on a hard pew while I listened to a series of red-necked preachers rant from the pulpit about how only the congregation of our particular church was going to be saved. Like other self-righteous guardians of that sect, the preachers were busy devolving God into nothing more than a tribal deity. They misused the New Testament to justify their actions, in the meantime arguing venomously with other congregations in their own faith, classifying Christians in other denominations as little better than misguided agnostics, and taking smug satisfaction in defining everyone else world-wide as unwashed, unrepentant, unsaved sinners doomed to Hell.

Those Bible thumpers and their co-religionists had happily conspired to adjust all creation in order to classify themselves alone as God's new "chosen people." To have said the people of my childhood church believed the entire American Bible Belt was going to be saved would have been a vast overstatement. My boyhood church was a mere tiny notch in the Bible belt, a religious junta of proud zealots who gloated and denied the rest of humanity any portion of God's grace, while translating the accumulation of material wealth into a sign of spiritual progress.

It was a religious view barren of any attempt at a universal message. So parochial was its misspent energy that by their definition 99.9 percent of humanity had been created by an act of Divine accident.

As a young man in spiritual despair I dabbled in a superficial examination of Eastern religions, but found their ideas too distant from my Western world view to either effectively challenge my American heritage or to offer me any practical day-to-day guidance and knowledge. It seemed I had hit the limits of my ecclesiastical vacuum. I had not yet learned that if you find no God it is because you harbor none.

My initial travels to Afghanistan took me not just to that country, but into the heart of what once made it special. As I journeyed through the last remnants of that pre-war society I encountered Islam for the first time. No one pushed it on me. Nor did anyone deny me a good look through the door. The longer I was around Muslims the stronger became the impression that I had arrived in Afghanistan with a deep-seated egocentric cultural outlook that automatically defined these people's religion as a worthless, second-rate superstition. Though I was myself spiritually bankrupt, in my arrogance I disdained to examine a religious system accepted by a major portion of humanity. Though my body was traveling through the country, my thinking still began and ended in America.

In my defense I was a product of an educational system that taught me Islam was a phony religion, founded by an Arab who forced people to convert at the sharp point of a sword. This misanthropic bit of religious chauvinism had its basis in the well-spread misbelief that the Greco-Roman-Occidental doctrine was superior to any other. The collective consciousness of my country's impression of Islam was still rooted in the racial and religious biases formulated in the Crusades. My own reactions still bore traces of that die-hard ghost. Though Islam had abandoned any idea of conquering Europe, and Christendom had given up her hope of converting Islam, little moral sympathy existed between the people of the two great faiths who worshipped the same God.

I was unschooled in the ways of men, and still unable to perceive that many of the raging political issues commonly associated with Islam were a legacy of the world's colonial period, and not in fact religious in origin. Man hands himself to evil. Those political terrorists who mislabeled themselves as Muslims were instantly thrown up by the western media as examples of Islam, though they were imbued with the same poison of their former masters. They were desperate fanatics lost in the trap of nationalism who had forsaken the Islamic message revolving around God's love for the universality of mankind. In my stupidity I lumped those bomb-throwers in with the saints, forgetting that Hitler considered himself a devout Christian, losing sight of God's message in the gunsmoke of

Religious Difficulties

mankind's politics. Plus my primary education and American culture did not allow me to see that misdeeds done in the name of God by either a Palestinian Muslim nationalist or a German Christian fascist were both still evil.

Consequently I arrived in Afghanistan with an American's natural tendency to believe that the cultural and religious experiences of the West had to be superior to the Muslims in the East. Like many of my countrymen I rejected as absurd what I couldn't understand at once. I was like the ancient Gothic savages in regards to the subtle mysteries of the Quran. The Goth drank water, washed in it perhaps, but never reflected on its qualities as ice or steam. I also failed to recognize the higher truths lying unexplored in the Quran. Because of my religious and national background I was unable even to theoretically concede a positive role to Islam. It was a religious option dismissed out of hand, and out of ignorance.

If that was the case, I finally asked myself, how come the Afghans were praying all the time, living in a spiritual harmony I had never seen in America, and willing to accept me, a total stranger, into their mosques and their discussions?

When I finally laid aside my cultural prejudices and started asking questions, I started finding new answers. Once I learned to separate the universal message Islam offered for all mankind from the stereotypes of Arab terrorists and Aladdin cartoons, I began to change my world view. In time it became a wholehearted transference of allegiance from one cultural environment to another. I came to the point where I approached my problems from a Muslim perspective. I thought that the religious intolerance of my youth was a thing of the past, that my Muslim brothers were a mislabeled group of sincere devotees, that I had stumbled onto a message largely devoid of hate, intolerance, and bigotry.

I had forgotten that though God's message was perfect, humanity, no matter in what country or on what continent, remained flawed creatures. Traveling through the beautiful Ghizer river valley I had overlooked the reason behind the need for God's mercy and kindness. It lay rooted in man's inhumanity to himself and his brothers.

In the land of the Ismailis I soon discovered my beliefs were not only still naive, they were soon revealed to be hideously, murderously, inaccurate.

35
Shakra the Killer

Pasha took me away from Phander soon after sunup. The Gordian knot of religious misunderstanding still lay untied despite a long night of talking. As was to be expected from a conservative Pathan, Raja was shocked and offended at the Ismaili's behavior. Ali Muhammad said little that morning, his thoughts locked away on other issues as we all rode away.

The grinding daily routine of equestrian travel soon gripped each of us. We traveled inside a straitjacket of mountains, following the river as it lead us, the landscape's only movable objects, through a stone shroud that hemmed us in and reached up to the skies at the same time.

There was no need to have worried about Ismailis, as we did not speak to another living soul during the course of that long day in the saddle. The farms and villages fell behind us as the day advanced. The land became a sandy brown wasteland, studded in places with boulders bigger than houses. I had to remind myself that the turbulent torrent running next to our road was the same merrily tumbling clear stream we had discovered only a few days earlier. It was now wide, tragic and savagely intense. When we stopped the horses to rest, we could hear rocks and boulders grinding beneath the water's surface, rolling towards Gilgit almost as slowly as we were.

We alternately either rode in companionable silence, taking in the scenery, or passed the time in the idle chatter that affects travelers in transit. The low cantle on our saddles was a source of much discussion as we all suffered from back pain. The sun would rise and we would once again grit our teeth and swing into our saddle, either loving or cursing the journey which demanded so much physical effort from us and the horses.

When the sun at last began to set we felt as if we had covered 500 miles, when in actuality we were averaging 25 miles a day. Our daily routine however gave us the sensation we were covering as much distance as an airplane traveling from Lisbon to London. Unlike the jeeps that still occasionally roared by, we were seeing Pakistan inch by slow, hard-won inch. We rode next to mountains of staggering height, only to discover they didn't even rate a name. The world we now inhabited was measured by standards other than time and mileage. The rocks ignored us. The mountains took no notice. The river never gave us a glance. We were truly alone with our animals and our faith in a landscape that classified trivial men next to tiny insects.

In circumstances like these mistakes made. After such a lulling day are oddities encountered. If the map did not lie again, the village of

Pingal lay not too far ahead. With the day nearly done, Raja sang to relieve the monotony.

"*Charta gerzee pa baran shpae pa biabon shpae musafara,*" the young Afridi asked the cooling night sky.

"Where are you wandering on this rainy night in this desolate place, oh traveler?" he sang again in a melancholy voice. Looming out of the gathering darkness was his answer.

Pingal was the home of forlorn hope, the abode of abandoned empire, the forgotten outpost. We reined in the horses and stared at a place full of visual grief, a rocky opening in the narrow mountain valley where in days of old weary travelers rested their tired mounts before pressing on to Gilgit. Our map showed Pingal as being a village of importance on our march east. Unlike Phander, which showed no rest house on the map but clearly had one, Pingal's accommodations were surely of note, as they were the only ones marked on the map.

A short distance away rose a wall of living rock. Running along its base ran the Ghizer river, though we had temporarily climbed too high above its bed to hear its mighty music. No, all we could hear was the sigh of our tired horses and the whisper of a lonely wind singing us the song of forgotten Pingal.

"This is it?" Ali Muhammad asked incredulously, as the three of us sat our horses staring in amazement.

I was too stunned by the weathered wreck in front of us to know what to say. Before us lay a long, long rocky field covered with stones ranging from microscopic pebbles to giants weighing tons. Forget the green lushness we had become used to. It looked like we had wandered into Death Valley by mistake. There was no grass, no trees, no shade, no water, just an old stone building.

It must have been a graceful place at one time, back when the British officers and their native orderlies rode past on their way to Chitral. In this area, where local uprisings were common and travelers butchered in their sleep, such accommodations had to serve as impromptu forts as well as lodgings. Perhaps that is why some long-dead stonemason had spent so much time constructing the building to withstand a siege. The well intentioned fool had done his job too well.

Pingal had fought off the clutches of time.

Her strong stone walls stood without a blemish. Overhead the earthen roof was intact, though bleached white by decades of exposure to the burning sun. A raised porch was reached by climbing three wide steps of square cut stone. A wooden door sat back within the shadows.

It wasn't the building's structural integrity that held us back, it was the feeling emanating from it.

You could sense its presence from twenty yards away, watchful, vigilant, half crazy with loneliness. It was obvious what had happened. In the days before motor transport, the stages between rest houses were set up according to how far a horse could safely journey in one day. Despite her rocky ground and nearly waterless condition, Pingal had taken her place on the pony express route leading east and west through these mountains.

Then the motor car killed her.

She was shut by the British, forgotten by the Pakistanis. Local natives shunned her, at first half afraid of official retribution if they pried her door open. Later, as the years passed and she aged, they avoided her out of a growing sense of unease. She was a relic of a colonial past, a glancing eyeful of interest to a rushing jeep full of east bound passengers.

No one stopped.

Officially she no longer existed.

Physically she could not die.

Unlike our motorized cousins, we equestrian travelers were forced by the constraints of time and weariness to accept conditions and accommodations as we found them. I eased Pasha off the road and reluctantly headed him towards the building. As we passed through the rocky field I could see some of them were carved in ancient petroglyphs. Outlines of men with spears chasing deer were etched into the ancestral stones. It only added to my growing sense of unease. As my gelding brought me close to the door I half expected to see a lone, wounded British survivor stumble out from inside the old building, more dead than alive.

Instead a man with a rifle stepped out of the door and took aim at my chest.

I remember meeting a lot of people in my life. No one ever introduced himself like Shakra. I brought the horse to a halt without being told. At that range the bullet from the .303 caliber Lee Enfield rifle pointing at me would have punched a hole through my chest big enough to accommodate a freight train.

The light was getting poor but I could clearly see the bearded man standing on the porch aiming at me. He was in his early thirties, had a trim black beard and a huge handlebar mustache. A wool *pakul* (cap) was on his head. Muscular, but thin as a sapling, he stood there in a dark brown shalwar kameez. His arm was rock steady. His left eye was squeezed shut. His right eye was looking at me down the length of the rifle barrel. It wasn't blinking. The biggest O in the world was staring at me from the rifle's ugly metal eye.

He didn't say a word. I sensed Raja and Ali Muhammad had stopped behind me. Slowly I laid the reins on Pasha's neck, then carefully lifted both my hands into the air. The rifleman held his aim. I was wondering what to say or do when Pasha entered the equation. I had taught him long reins on his mane translated into a pat on the neck and a job well done. The dun gelding ignored my issue of interest holding the gun and decided the free reins meant he was done for the day. He gave himself a great shake, which set the saddle to rattling, forced me to grab up the reins and brought a yelp of fear out of me as I waited for a bullet to punch me back to Peshawar.

Instead a smile cracked across that coal black beard. I saw bright white teeth as the rifle barrel slowly lowered. The guardian of Pingal chuckled at my expense. I got the distinct impression he liked Pasha.

"Sorry," he said.

His voice was deep, low, as black as that beard masking his face.

"When I heard you ride up I thought you were those damn *dushman kafrots* (enemy pagans)," he said in way of explanation.

"No just travelers. We hoped to spend the night here?" Raja asked from behind me.

I was glad the boy could speak. I was too busy wondering if my saddle was wet.

"Anyone with you?," the stranger asked.

By now the rifle was aimed at the ground, the man relaxed, the question a formality.

Raja assured him, "Just us."

"Mujahid?"

"American Muslims and a Pathan," Raja explained.

"Mussulman?" the gunman asked, meaning were we Sunnis.

The Afridi Pathan needed no encouragement to declare that we may have been dirty but we certainly were not Ismailis.

"*Alhumdulillah* (by the grace of Allah)," Raja said, as much a confession of traditional faith as a rejection of our recent hosts.

The gunman gave us all a nod which signaled we could unsaddle and enter, then turned and went back inside himself. I sat there for a moment, trying to regain my composure. Raja paid me no mind, just headed Pajaro straight towards the hitching post placed in front of the bungalow.

As Ali Muhammad rode Pahlwan past me he said, "Oh yes, that is a VERY smart horse," and began laughing heartily.

That night the horses suffered. A small stream gave them a long drink of tepid water. No dinner. No grass. Just a good brushing and an apology. We did little better.

With saddles in our arms Ali Muhammad lead us up the stairs. He stopped at the open door before shouting, "*Assalaamu aleikum* ," to the man inside.

"Enter wayfarers," came back.

I followed the others in to find a good-sized room, barren of everything except dust and memories. A stone fireplace sat off to the left. It hosted a small fire, barely big enough to boil the tea pot hanging over it. Low flames cast a flickering orange light.

"May Allah give you life. This house is your house. Come eat in the name of God," said the man I had met on the porch. He was squatting on his heels next to the fire. His blanket was spread on the floor close to the fire. A large loaf of rough bread sat waiting. A simple wave of his hand bid us lay down our tack and share what he had.

Raja and Ali leaned their saddles up against the back wall. Coming in last I placed mine in the corner closest to the door. I would be the one watching the horses tonight. A dive into the saddlebag and I got my tea cup, joining the others. Our host wrapped a rag around the handle of the pot and poured out four cups of tea.

The liquid was steaming but we each took a sip out of politeness.

It was immediately apparent our host was a man of exceptions.

Pakistan was like many portions of the Orient. You got used to seeing physical deformities that had disappeared generations ago in the west. A walk through any Pakistani bazaar would likely show you an old man with a goiter the size of a baby's head hanging off his neck, a legless man dragging himself along the scalding hot pavement, a beggar child with scabby face, snotty nose and eyes smeared shut from infection, or a starving war widow draped in the shroud of her bourka holding out a bony malnourished hand in a silent request for alms. A fat man was a rarity. A stranger passing on the sidewalk was as likely to have one eye, no teeth, and be missing a limb or two. Pakistan was a country where the main concern was survival, not physical appearance.

If our host sported any disabilities they weren't apparent.

This close it was easy to see that he would have been considered strikingly handsome by western standards. Even in the low light I could see his deep brown eyes. They looked kind, which later surprised me when I learned what nature of man he was. His skin was the color of creamy coffee, from birth or the sun I could not discern. The strong hands were long fingered and looked like they could snap a stick or a neck with equal ease. A tender mouth hid behind a jet-black handlebar mustache as wide as Texas.

Shakra looked dreamy, a poet, a philosopher, a boon companion.

He was a devotee of violence, a shedder of blood, a friend of the Furies and the nightmare of the next village, Gupis.

None of us spoke during the course of our short meal. Neither Raja nor Ali Muhammad said anything, but I was sure they were just as shocked as I was when they discovered the tea was flavored with salt, Tibetan style. The drink was hot and the bread was fresh. Not much of a meal but we knew we would have gone hungry but for this stranger. Whoever he was, his culinary habits and mannerisms clearly told me we had not stumbled into another Ismaili. I was wondering about feeding the horses when our host spoke.

"I was glad to find you were *dosotani* (friends)."

He eyes kept darting to the door while we ate. The Lee Enfield rifle, his constant mute companion, was leaning against the wall within immediate reach. Her wooden stock was shiny from the polish of decades of blood-soaked but tender hands. She looked like she was World War One issue. Originally carried by a British Tommy, she had probably been a renegade for most of this century. A good marksman could kill with her from a mile away. I shuddered to think how many men had dropped from her lethal kiss.

When I asked our host if there was any way of getting anything to feed the horses in nearby Pingal proper, he rebuffed me.

"Not a chance. The villagers won't unbar their doors until morning when someone tells them a fire was seen burning in this old house. The

Ismailis will be telling stories tomorrow about ghosts on horses riding through their hamlet," he said derisively.

He leaned back against the wall, his shoulder touching the rifle in subtle salute.

"Of course you can walk down and try if you want. But this is a poor village even in a good year. If you want anything worth while you have to travel on to Gupis."

The look on his handsome face said there was meat on that bone if we cared to chew it.

Raja leaned over and rested on one hand.

"Is that where you are headed in the morning?" he asked casually.

"I'm going there right now."

"Now? In the dark? Isn't it too far?" Ali Muhammad asked surprised.

"Oh, I have made the trip before."

And therein lay a strange tale.

Once Shakra, for thus did he introduce himself, lay his suspicions regarding us aside he was completely candid about both his past, and more importantly, the uncertainty of his immediate future.

He was a citizen of Kohistan, though the concept of citizenry would have offended him. Known officially as the Land of the Mountains, its whispered moniker was Yaghistan the Land of Murder. It was a country roughly 100 miles wide in any one direction. Only its perimeters were known. It stretched from the Indus river to Afghanistan, from Swat to Gilgit. The Pingal bungalow sat on its northern border. What lay south of us no one in that room except Shakra would ever know.

One of the last white spots on the world's map, cartographers did not lie when they wrote, "Unexplored" across Kohistan's unknown features. No Pakistani in recent memory had ventured deeper than a toe-step inside her borders. I knew of no European who had dared travel there since Alexander the Great made an armed foray in 320 BC. The Greek scholars accompanying that bold conqueror had described the country as "Agrapha - The Unwritten," because even their master had been unable to count, tax or govern the ferocious inhabitants.

More than two thousand years after Alexander died, the descendants of the primitive alpine pastoralists he encountered were still holding the outside world at bay. They stayed locked away in their high mountain valleys, farming in isolated but fertile valley bottoms. After all the centuries, theirs was still a rebellious country, independent of law, disdainful of government, contemptuous of civilization. Their natural mountain defenses still locked out all outsiders. The Kohistanis were the last warrior tribe left in the fortress of the Hindu Kush mountains, a pocket of pre-industrial stone-age men surrounded by a world intent on their destruction.

When I asked Shakra if he had any desire to visit that outside world, he rolled out that deep, low laugh of his in response.

"What could be more beautiful than my village,' he asked me in return.

Shakra the Killer

I had no way of knowing as he hid the name of that secret place from us. His world ended at Gilgit, where foreign goods could be bought after making a long trip on foot. The known universe stretched to Peshawar, where guns came from. In the dim beyond were stars called Karachi and Lahore, who lay beyond local definition. Further still were misty legends, places of no relevance, hosting unexplainable names like America and Germany.

He had never heard of the 20th century and would have been contemptuous of it if he had. His people were nearly self-sufficient. They built strong log homes, grew their own food, wove their own cloth. They had maize, potatoes, timber, cattle, sheep. The only thing they were short of were women. He was headed to Gupis that very night to get one.

"Last year I took a woman from among the Ismaili kafirs to be my wife," he explained as he poured the last drops of salty tea into our cups. This done, he reached in the pot and scooped out the dregs, throwing them across the room into the far corner of the floor. He tossed a few more sticks on the fire as a courtesy, though it was obvious he was packing up to leave.

"The men of my valley have always taken Ismaili women to wife when our village ran short. There was no shame in it. By marrying them we made them Muslims and no longer accursed Shias."

Shakra's beard looked like a black spade in the dim room. His voice remained detached, as if he was describing a stroll to the corner market, not a mission to kidnap a mate.

"I had arrived in Gupis late that afternoon. I drank tea in the chaikhana. It is run by a Pathan," he said and looked at Raja approvingly. "That night while the village slept, I broke into the house I had chosen. The father resisted so I shot him. Dahzoo! Dahzoo!"

The Kohistani gave his rifle a look as if to remind the hungry huntress of that previous kill.

"The girl was too frightened to resist much. I cuffed her several times, then she followed me well enough out of the village," he told us as he began slowly to fold up the blanket previously serving as a table. The dark brown eyes were bent on his work. The long fingers carefully swept off the bread crumbs. His calm voice continued.

"Of course, I already knew what path to take home through my mountains, but I had been foolish and picked a young girl thinking of other things except her weak legs. She made my progress very slow, though in fairness I beat her more than a donkey to try and hasten her progress. Yet she was a stupid, crying creature. I considered leaving her, but not wanting to waste a bullet, decided to allow her to rest. Her fate would be decided at sunrise I told her."

He reached back and picked up a small canvas sack. Opening its drawstring neck he put the teapot inside.

"I had not counted on the Pathan policemen. You have not been to Gupis so you do not realize it has an Assistant District Commissioner. He is sent up from Gilgit to oversee the needs of the Ismailis. We free men pay him no mind. But because he dwells close to us, the Pakistanis keep a group of Pathans there to guard that coward and his *kafirs* (infidels)," he told us.

Neither Ali Muhammad, Raja or I said a word. We three horsemen were still wearing pistols. That did not matter and he knew it. We outnumbered him but were of no concern. His senses told him we were only shocked dinner guests, not killers or kidnappers. Shakra tied off the neck of the little canvas bag, laid it at this feet, then leaned back against the wall and recalled his defeat.

"I wasn't expecting the Pathans to follow me over only one woman. I later learned the Ismailis ran to the Commissioner. Those dogs were too afraid to follow me themselves but they got that big man to put his police on my trail. They surrounded my camp, swept down on me unawares with the dawn, disarmed me, rescued the girl, took me back to Gupis in chains," Shakra recalled, but his voice had taken on a hard edge and his eyes were glazed with hate. His strong hands reached up and squeezed the rifle by the barrel.

The Kohistani explained how the local politico promptly sent him to Gilgit for imprisonment. What happened there remained a mystery. He would not say if family members had bribed a jail guard. It was clear his fellow mountain men viewed Shakra's capture as a shame on their community. His rescue was a point of honor, another log thrown on the centuries-old fire of religious hatred blazing between Sunnis and Shias. Regardless of how it was arranged, after many months in jail he was loose, gone like a malevolent wraith back into the wilds.

Gupis trembled at the news.

It would be a misconception to believe Shakra and the Kohistanis knew nothing of law and order, or that they were obsessed with plunder and murder. That would have been a simplified modern view. If the Kohistanis had a collective obsession it was not murder, it was honor, and the people of Gupis had unwittingly offended the honor of this dark, brooding man before us.

Shakra possessed a world view that had changed very little since Alexander the Great left that country. Like the other men of Kohistan, the rifleman believed he was born with *ghrairat*, which roughly translated into a sense of personal honor. Shakra's integrity and reputation were more important to him than life itself. Without honor there was no purpose to his existence. This most precious of God's gifts was thus a great responsibility and a fragile gift. It could be polluted by enemies.

If the women of his family were insulted, if anyone murdered a kinsman, if he was assaulted or verbally abused, then his *ghrairat* was publicly stained and drastic action was necessary.

A man's honor was different from and more important than even his social prestige. *Izzat*, social prestige, was an artificial condition bestowed upon a man depending on personal accomplishments, such as wealth, education, piety, or elected position. All these conditions brought a man merit and respect in Kohistan, but they could also fluctuate in the turbulence of life. Shakra could have lost his social prestige without losing his honor. They were separate issues. One was a regrettable loss. The other was a matter of life or death.

When the gleeful Ismailis sent Shakra to Gilgit in chains they thought it was the last of him. The peaceful followers of the Agha Khan had not reckoned on the handsome man's loss of *ghrairat*. They had insulted his honor, which in turn lead to an even more dreadful event.

As he sat there before us I could see that behind those soft brown eyes burned the heart of killer. He finished his story by reminding us of what he believed was an obvious statement of fact.

In the world which we four shared that night, Islam was the single most important factor in any personal or public decision. Muslims function in a religion that offers no separation between the concept of church and state. Regardless of the issue, Islam colored the consequences. This was no Sunday morning religion. Muslims didn't trudge into the mosque only on Christmas or Easter. It was a daily experience that existed over, under, in front of, behind, within, without, throughout every aspect of the Pakistani culture. Nothing escaped its impact.

"When the Ismailis arrested me they were guilty of *kafirano kar karant* (pagan mischief)," he said. Even in the dim firelight I could see his knuckles were white where they gripped the rifle. Every sinew in his body looked taut.

In his view of the world Shakra believed the Ismailis had stripped him of his personal honor. His individual religious interpretation allowed him to rationalize that this desecration was in turn an attack on Allah, who had initially bestowed honor upon Shakra. An attack on Allah, he believed, was an attack on Islam itself. Shakra told us he was headed back to Gupis that night to restore his loss of *ghrairat*. He wanted us to understand that he was not returning to the unsuspecting village merely to steal another woman. He was primarily going to defend God, and to regain his self respect in the bargain. If he got a wife as well, fine and good.

"I am no *aman pasand* (friend of peace)," Shakra told us and no one disagreed.

This was a man who learned vengeance in the cradle and sucked up revenge from his mother's milk. What had started as a mere wife search had escalated into a deadly vendetta. There were no ambiguous answers in Kohistan. Outside we heard the hungry horses stamp impatiently. The sound brought the raider into action. He stood and began to wrap his blanket around his shoulders in preparation for travel.

"Aren't they expecting you? How can you think one man can attack an entire town and live?" Ali Muhammad asked.

Shakra shrugged.

"I have no choice. Their attack on me must be answered in bullets. By guarding their women they prohibit me from redeeming my honor. Only death or success will satisfy me," he told Ali Muhammad, with a look on his bearded face which said he was stating the obvious.

Khyber Knights

Being a Pathan, Raja was more at ease with the philosophy behind Shakra's proposed actions. He was only curious how the lone gunman could hope to survive.

Shakra was non-committal about his chances. He wore an amulet around his neck on a string to protect him. The little leather bag contained a magic formula of verses from the Quran. More than that he counted on his ability to put many miles between him and the police. He fully understood that the wild existence that gave him liberty, pride, and honor could also demand that he surrender his life before morning. Shakra wasn't a man living in the torpor of the modern world. He inhabited a mountainous realm where similar creatures all lay hidden and insulated in their ignorance. Even if he did not succeed, his death would make him a legend in Kohistan.

He was setting out to fight with the no more logic than a toreador stepping into a bullring, simply going to Gupis to demonstrate his courage and retrieve his honor. Though Shakra's views had fallen out of fashion in the modern world, there were once others who shared his view. The Cossacks of Russia, the Banditti of Italy, the Bushrangers of Australia, the Pistoleros of Mexico, the Ronin of Japan would have all left the fire in Pingal and gone with him to rape and pillage Gupis. He was one of the last of their kind.

The Kohistani was packed, the blanket wrapped tight around his shoulders, the little sack ready to be carried until it could be hidden later. He had draped a heavy bandoleer of .303 Lee Enfield bullets around his chest. They were real ammunition, not the dreadful homemade stuff, and worth their weight in gold. Lastly he reached down and picked up the rifle like a faithful lover. Shakra might squeeze a mate out of Gupis but any fool could see that the lethal, time-worn Lee Enfield would always be his true love.

"I have waited many months to return. Undoubtedly the Ismailis have grown lazy and think I am no longer coming. Better to eat them for breakfast before they turn me into dinner. Don't worry friends, Ismalis will weep in Gupis this night. I'll widow a few women and make a few orphans before sunrise," he said casually, as if he were setting off to catch a train to work.

Seeing he was ready to leave, we stood to say goodbye. None of us were stupid enough to ask him to reconsider. It would have been as fruitless as arguing with Geronimo. As custom dictated we each hugged him twice, sending him on his way with equal politeness and assurances of mutual respect.

He walked as far as the door, then stopped as if perhaps he was reconsidering his actions. He turned and faced us, his brown clothes making him almost invisible against the darkness awaiting him outside. It startled me when he softly began a song in that low, deep voice of his.

"What are you hunting in the night Shakra? Who knows what the night hawk may take home to his nest?" he crooned to us, then grinned like a ghost and was gone.

I waited a few moments, then following him outside, went to check on the horses. It was a cloudy night. The moon was a conspirator in all this. I patted Pasha, checked the picket pins, made sure the knots were tight, then hastened back inside.

Ali Muhammad had thrown the last of the wood on the fire. Raja was already in his blanket. I picked out what looked like a soft part of the floor, rested my head against the saddle and pulled my blanket over me. The firelight flickered and danced. We horsemen said nothing. What do you say after meeting a man from another century?

Lying there I glanced up and noticed in idle curiosity something written on the wall over my head. I sat up. Drawn in pencil was the following inscription.

"Traveler, do not stay the night in this place. - Kirpal Singh 1948."

On that cheerful note I went to bed.

36
Gupis Pays in Blood

That country, that Pakistan, God she was a rigorous lover. She stripped me bare of emotions that summer's day, leaving me as naked as the mountains rearing overhead.

I was still in my blanket when Ali Mohammad's voice roused me from a lingering slumber.

"Get out here quick," he screamed from beyond the bungalow door.

Raja ran out the door before I was even up. My boots were barely on when I heard them both crying in distress.

"Hurry," one of them shouted.

When I got to the door I saw them standing next to their horses, waving their hands in some pantomime of distress. Thinking they might be playing me for the fool, I walked down the steps of the bungalow slowly. It was still early. The air was gray and damp with dew. Pasha stood listless. Within seconds the reason for his unusual demeanor, and my friends' antics, were revealed.

As soon as I stepped next to my gelding I could not accept what message my eyes delivered. Pasha's belly was a moving black curtain of tiny foul flies and blood. The inky oozing mass was literally eating the wretched animal alive. Shouts from behind me only confirmed similar discoveries regarding Pahlwan and Pajaro. The winged cannibals were burrowing into them as well. Looking down I saw the insects had eaten all the hair off Pasha's belly.

The dun moaned, a deep exhausted animal groan that spoke without words of a long, long night spent trying to shake off the vampires. His tired red eyes said what his mute voice could not, of hours spent swishing his tail until he was left too tired to even lift it. My gelding now stood exhausted, dejected, too fatigued to fight.

Still incredulous I tried to slap the insects away. The flies barely moved. They were contemptuous, and so bloated with blood and horse meat they barely buzzed off, before immediately coming back to burrow in again. Disgusted, I ground my hand across the arrogant black horde in anger. They never moved, thousands of them dying satiated. When I lifted my hand it was sticky with Pasha's blood and covered with a black fly pulp. The survivors flew off, only to return with new hungrier replacements. They wanted Pasha and did not fear me. I slapped them away again and again, trying to get him some relief.

Instead they attacked me like battle crazed veterans, biting me all over my face.

The air-borne vermin assailing me were the size of dust particles yet stung like snakes. I too started waving them away. They paid no attention whatsoever, running instead up my nostrils, crawling inside my ears, crashing into my eyes. When I started to shout, they rushed into that unsuspecting aperture. I could not speak, being too busy grinding and spitting the filthy pests out of my mouth.

In pain I shouted to my companions. Similar noises told me they too were under attack. Suddenly we were in disarray. The flying pestilence never retreated, in fact we did.

We forgot about brushing the horses, ran back inside long enough to shove gear into saddlebags, threw on the saddles, tossed in the bits, shoved the rifles down their scabbards and fled that accursed place, that forgotten Pingal.

With flies and that wretched bungalow behind us, we pushed on through the everlasting mountains, around one gigantic turn, then another. The Ghizer river was always on our left, a wild wet horse that no man would ever ride. It was a tough morning. We could feel hunger pushing our bellies into our backbones. The horses walked with drooping heads. We once-proud riders rode slumped and weary.

As the sun rose higher the land continued to grow even more stony and desolate. The trail brought us to a cleft in the mountains. On our right appeared a larger river, the untamed Gilgit, roaring out of the hidden mountains of Kohistan to meet and dominate her smaller sister the Ghizer. A forty-foot wooden bridge spanned the Gilgit. The middle of the bridge was missing. Lying in the raging water below our feet was a tractor and a large attached wagon. I had heard of this incident.

The driver had been racing to the Shandur Pass polo game with a wagon load of cheery passengers. He took the bridge too fast. The old timbers gave way. Everyone was lost in the torrent below.

I dismounted and led a tired Pasha across the narrow wooden remnants that rimmed one edge. His head hung low like the reins in my hand. All of us were running on empty. Once across we mounted back up and pushed on slowly.

Raja took the lead, so Ali Muhammad and I rode alongside each other. Our talk was of food. Once we got to the colossal village of Gupis we would order hot bread, sweet chai, juicy kebobs, maybe even a fried egg. My impatient stomach urged Pasha to pick up his pace.

In a short while the mountains began slowly to open. At first it was barely perceptible. Then they fell further back until it was clear to see we were in the mouth of a wide valley. The river, now larger than ever, still rushed by on our left. Above it on both sides rose sheer walls of high gray stone. Yet on our right the mountains were retreating. Another half hour's ride found us still hungry but happy. The stony wasteland lay behind us. Pasha, Pahlwan and Pajaro had brought us to a rich verdant farmland hidden from the world's prying eyes, subject only to the gaze of eagles. The womb of the earth was rich there, the valley clad in all directions with the green and golden ornaments of growth and life.

Seeing amber fields, tended orchards, stone walls and tidy homes brought peace to my heart. Ali Muhammad was silent as we entered this rich Eden. He looked hungry, uninterested and preoccupied. We rode

Gupis Pays in Blood

through an unfolding vista that had sprung genie-like out of the stone bottle of the mountains.

It was still early but I had no intention of riding further than the first chaikhana. I was going to take care of Pasha, then eat everything not tied down in Gupis. But as we passed house after house, field after field, the same calm that had at first lain like a mother's hand on our hearts began to seem too quiet. In fact it seemed eerie, unsettling.

Where were the farmers I asked Ali? The day was early, the sun hot. The fields called out for attention. Where were the wives? No washing by the river. No fruit being picked from ripe trees. Where were the children? No mischievous shouting from behind stone walls as we began to enter the outskirts of Gupis. Something else was out of place in that beautiful valley. At first I couldn't place it. I stopped Pasha, and turned to Ali Muhammad, who brought big Pahlwan to a halt beside me.

"No dogs," I suddenly said. "Not a barking cur to warn against strangers on horses."

"Something is dead wrong here," he agreed.

Truer words were never spoken on that trip.

We put the horses into a trot, picked up Pajaro and Raja, and headed towards the rapidly approaching village. An occasional house soon became several. Yet still no people. The lone road we rode along began to branch out into other directions. Still no other travelers came our way. When we heard rifle shots coming from up ahead, we spurred the horses into a heart-pounding gallop.

Bells ringing wildly, saddlebags flapping, we came racing into Gupis, only to discover chaos, murder, kidnapping, a mob and the bloody fruit of Shakra's black revenge.

The road led us between a narrow row of shops. Even at the canter I could see their steel shutters were slammed shut and locked tight. If that was the extent of town it took Pasha only a couple of seconds to pound me through it. The big dun gelding came up short when we exited from among the buildings.

The road ran straight ahead. We did not. The crowd gathered ahead of us kept Pasha from going any further. Raja and Ali Muhammad reined in beside me, trying like myself to make sense of the boiling mass of confusion rolling towards us.

Sitting on a slight knoll off to the right was a Raj-era building that could have only been the residence of the Assistant Commissioner. Seven policemen were standing in front of the door, obviously guarding a well dressed Pakistani who cowered behind them. The resolute-looking cops still had their rifles snapped to their shoulders. The thick smell of cordite, and the gun smoke hanging lazily above their heads, was a clue to what had just occurred.

The second piece of evidence were the dead and dying villagers lying on the road in front of us.

A screaming mob of more than one hundred men were falling back in panic in our direction. Men began pushing by us. So great was their fear, they took no notice of the horses or armed strangers standing in their midst. Pasha reared as the men pressed around him. I pulled in his reins and held on as he reached up and screamed in anger and fear. But by now Pajaro and Pahlwan had also got a whiff of the blood and gun smoke. They began whinnying and backing up in distress and fear at this unexpected turn of events, trying to maintain their balance as men shoved wildly into the bottleneck behind us.

The mountains around us were still echoing from the rifle shots. Adding to that symphony of violence was the chorus of the men of Gupis screaming in fear and anger as they ran past. The crowd stopped their retreat in front of the shops behind us. They quickly regrouped, shouting dire threats at the policemen still defiantly standing their ground.

"Asadullah fall back," Raja shouted, as he headed Pajaro towards safety.

I didn't need to be urged twice. The moment I spun Pasha he charged after his two companions. Like the men of Gupis, we three riders sought safety in numbers at the end of that short lane. The policemen had not followed our retreat. They kept their rifles aimed at our backs. They seemed to be content to maintain their elevated position on the knoll above the road. I eased Pasha up in front of the crowd, turning to look back in their direction.

"You Pathan killers!" one man next to me shouted, and waved his fist at the cops.

"Brave enough to slaughter unarmed men but not brave enough to go after Shakra, you bastards," someone yelled from the rear of the crowd.

Turning my head I saw Ali and Raja had gently ridden their horses through the crowd, emerging on the far side. Taking their lead I started guiding Pasha in that direction. There were two hundred eyes looking towards the police and not at me. For once the dun behaved himself, sensing this was no time step on toes or sensibilities. I was relieved to draw rein next to Ali Muhammad and Raja, and observe events unfold from the rear of the crowd.

"So we took out a protest to demand the Assistant Commissioner send his damn police after that *behnchowd* (sister fucker)," I overheard one of the villagers telling Raja.

"What's happening," I asked Ali quietly when I drew Pasha up next to him.

"Shakra. I think the less we say about knowing him the better," my friend said and gave me a look I agreed with.

Behind me men at the front of the crowd were shouting and pointing.

"You heartless bastards let us have our dead."

I spun around in my saddle and saw three older men, obviously respected villager elders, separate themselves from the crowd. They began walking slowly back towards the scene of carnage, their hands held high in the air.

"*Salaam* (Peace)!" the one in the middle shouted. "Let us come and retrieve our men in peace."

None of the cops bothered responding, but neither did they shoot the unarmed men advancing towards them. Perhaps they were done slaughtering ducks in a barrel that day?

The elders cautiously approached their fallen friends. It was one of those remarkable moments of courage never recorded in the history books. Despite the size of this valley I didn't need to be told that everyone there was either related to or intimately associated with the men lying wounded, dying or dead on that blood-soaked road. It was their fathers, sons, brothers, or nephews slain from the barrage. The shouts had dissipated. Tension grew. Even the horses were quiet as those three brave old men walked towards the rifles still pointing in our general direction.

As soon as they grew close each of the elders bent over a man on the ground. One quickly moved on, his chosen subject obviously dead. I heard a cry of grief go up from behind me at the visual relay of this mute message. A second elder stood and spoke quietly to the well-dressed man hiding behind the policemen. The government man held a soft conversation over the shoulders of his uniformed protectors, setting out terms and conditions. The bearded old man agreed, then called back for volunteers to come and help retrieve the casualties.

Immediately the front wave of the crowd started running in the direction of the outrage. The policeman in charge shouted that only half of the men could advance. The others were ordered to fall back or be shot. Twenty-odd men slowly walked up and began bending over their comrades. I counted eight bodies waiting for bandages or a hole in the ground . Some were obviously moving. At least three appeared ominously still.

Behind us the crowd parted, and men came running through with charpoys to bear the bodies home on. As the men of Gupis began to attend to their wounded I saw the policemen slowly lower their rifles. They still maintained their alert position on the knoll but the crisis seemed to have passed.

As the Assistant Commissioner disappeared inside his residence, I heard men close by throw a few half hearted shouts in his direction.

"Murderer."

"You Sunni butcher."

When I heard the last epithet I snapped my head in the direction of my companions. We didn't know all the details, but it was obvious we had ridden into a pot of boiling sectarian violence. Ali Muhammad gave Raja and me a quiet nod of the head to signal us to follow him back. Most of the crowd were breaking up into smaller groups, afraid to go forward, unwilling to abandon their friends and family. Yet the once-compacted group was cracking into smaller units as conversation, not violence, once again gained control over men's emotions.

There was grass growing at the end of the shops. Raja directed Pajaro into this welcomed free treat. Ali and I joined him with our own horses. We held a hushed conference, unsure of what to do or where to go. We needed food and rest. Gupis was too preoccupied to attend to our needs. When two villagers stopped close by we listened to their conversation until it seemed polite to interrupt and ask for details. Their tale was what we expected.

Shakra had hit Gupis at dawn, first setting fire to several houses as a distraction. While the men ran to fight the blaze, the Kohistani outlaw had swooped in like a hawk, kidnapping a fourteen year old girl. Someone had seen him fleeing. None of the Ismailis were armed but several of them trailed him. He was observed heading into the mountains at the wrecked bridge, by the Gilgit river gorge.

When I learned the outlaw's route had nearly crossed ours, I wondered if he would have shot us that morning, forgetting his hospitality of last night?

"Why didn't the police go after him?' I asked one of the two men, a slim built fellow in his mid-thirties.

The answer to that riddle, he told us, lay buried between layers of regional differences. The outlaw was Kohistani, the villagers Ismaili, the Assistant Commissioner a recent appointee sent up from the Punjab, the policemen all Pathans from the North West Frontier Province. Regional and religious differences quickly raged out of control. The only thing everyone agreed upon was that all three ethnic groups represented in Gupis despised each other.

As the morning wore on, the villagers waited for the government man to respond. They finally marched on the bungalow in unarmed but vigorous protest. Their patience at an end, angry threats were shouted, the older of the two villagers explained to us.

Why hadn't Shakra been tracked down and killed before he was allowed to return to attack Gupis a second time? Why had be been allowed to escape from jail in Gilgit? When were the police going to capture him? Were was the girl? Who was safe in town when children were kidnapped from their beds? What use was this Punjabi coward? Who were these damn Pathan policemen who served him anyway? Weren't they outsiders too and little better than the Kohistani outlaw who had stolen the unfortunate daughter of Gupis? Why shouldn't the villagers beat them for letting Shakra escape, to use them as a scapegoat for the folly of the fools in faraway Gilgit?

Neither man had to tell me what happened next. No one insults Pathans, not even distraught villagers. When the local men made a rush to attack the police, and seize the Assistant Commissioner, the Pathans calmly opened fire with devastating effect.

It all seemed to be just another senseless Pakistani tragedy. It was only what we learned next that made it personal.

"We can't even call out for help. That damn Kohistani disruptionist cut the phone lines to Gilgit. That's why the Punjabi coward panicked. When he discovered he couldn't call out, the Assistant Commissioner thought the Kohistanis were going to attack Gupis. He told us that's why he refused to let the police men follow Shakra," the smaller man told us. The villager's face was contorted with rage. He beat his little fist into his other hand to emphasize his point.

Gupis Pays in Blood

"That's right," the other fellow added. "The Commissioner said we were already cut off and he couldn't risk sending his policemen into a trap by letting them go after the kidnapper. He said he was protecting the town but he's only protecting his own skin."

Ali Muhammad looked puzzled.

"Cut off by phone, right?" he asked, seeking confirmation.

"No," the small villager answered angrily, and began waving his arms in frustration. "Cut off. Cut off! The road to Gilgit is gone. Wiped out."

I could hear the horses eagerly ripping up the grass behind them but they were otherwise temporarily forgotten.

"What do you mean? Is the road out?" Ali Muhammad said in a voice bordering on panic. "We need to get to Gilgit. I have to get to Gilgit!"

Raja and I exchanged a knowing look, suddenly aware that confirmation of a unsaid concern we had each shared was at least now out in the open.

The older man looked at Ali and shook his head in a strong negative response.

"Well, you're not going on that road unless you want to wait a week or more. Traffic is stopped both ways further down," he told Ali Muhammad.

"You don't mean to say Shakra destroyed the road?" I asked. I gave the outlaw credit for bravery but this seemed too much for one man. I was right, no mortal had seasoned this pudding. It was fate, kismet, a force of nature, the will of Allah, call it what you will, that threatened to trap us in that blood-soaked town.

"Avalanche. Took it out three days ago. We don't know if Shakra knew about it or not. If he did know, he realized no one could get through to help us. Doesn't matter. No one's coming, going, or getting out. My advice is for you three to head back to Chitral," the local resident explained.

Ali Muhammad looked crushed and distraught at this new revelation.

"Have you seen the road?" I asked, "Are you sure there there's no way we can get across? If it's only boulders on the road keeping jeeps from driving through maybe we could ride around them?"

Both men looked at me like I was the slow learner in the back row.

"I don't see any wings on these horses. Unless you're willing to take them over the *parri* you better head them back the way you came."

Ali Muhammad was quick to grasp that some local alternative existed.

"*Parri*? What's the *parri*?" he asked but never got an answer.

A group of men were beginning to pass by carrying the wounded on charpoys. Though they were walking slowly, the victims were bleeding profusely and moaning in agony. I didn't give any of them much chance of seeing sunup. Suddenly our two villagers were once again rooted in local reality. Their full attention was devoted to the men passing by. Ali Muhammad wasn't willing to let matters rest. He pressed the younger fellow, ignoring his previous signs of anger, shoving his way next to him so eager was he for a response.

"Is this *parri* another road?"

"Yes, yes. Now leave us alone."

"Is it far? Can we reach it today?"

The villager turned to Ali, his patience at an end.

"Skirt the village," he said, pointing at a road leading out of Gupis but running in the general direction of Gilgit. "A short ride ahead you'll find a tent set up. Its on this side of the avalanche. Ali Daud is there selling chai and food to the stranded jeep drivers. Now go away," he said and turned his back on us.

"Can we get anything to eat in the local chaikhana before we go?" I asked his friend.

The man gave me a hard look, then pointed at one of the victims being carried by in front of us.

"The chaikhana is closed. The owner is dead. You can get food at the tent."

Like the kidnapped girl, we had no choice. We swung into our saddles, pulled the hungry horses away from the free grass and starting making our way carefully out of Gupis. The lane we followed avoided the soldiers. At the other end of the valley we passed three smoldering homes. There was nothing to be said about that poor child who had been stolen from one of them. Shakra had fled like a silent cat, dragging her into the heart of a country where only weapons spoke. Her rustic life in Gupis would soon seem elegant compared to where she was headed. When she found herself at last in the outlaw's unnamed village, she would learn she was expected to take her place in a way of life beyond the definition of time, a place where only the sequence of days, nights and seasons had any bearing.

My own concerns soon drove that unfortunate girl from my mind.

An hour's ride brought us within sight of the ruined road.

The horses brought us over a rise. Our previous route had been through the last remnants of the valley system that the people of Gupis called home. Below us lay the end of that ribbon of road. It ran like a thread to the base of the valley where it came in direct contact with a wall of rock reaching thousands of feet high. At that junction, where valley met mountain, the road became blurry.

Looking further on we could clearly see a line of tiny jeeps parked around the far side of the mountain. They could have been backed up all the way to Gilgit for all we knew. Lying closer to us, at the base of this rise, a similar gaggle of stranded motorists were gathered around the tent we had been told about. There were at least twenty jeeps parked close by. From where we sat I could see sixty or more men walking, sitting, and lying around the vehicles or the tent.

With no reason to delay we headed the horses straight down the rise. Drawing near the tent we saw the jeeps were piled high with cargo, parked at all angles. Men were sleeping in the shade of their vehicles. Others were gathered in clutches under the ragged canvas awning that served as emergency headquarters. Curious faces turned our way as we rode straight past the tent and up to the reputed obstruction. I remember being unconvinced that the problem might not be solved by determined horsemen.

Would that Allah had not heard my thought.

"Stop. Road closed. Go back," a dirt-encrusted man screamed at me.

I didn't need the reminder. Only a blind man would have proceeded.

Pasha came to a halt without being asked. I was speechless, my former confidence fading when I saw the severity of the obstruction. My gelding had brought me to the edge of a crumbling precipice. It was clear that now there were two roads, the one we were trapped on, the other matching bit of dirt highway a distant stone's throw away. Nothing lay between the two but air and memories. A mountain goat couldn't have crossed what was left.

Neither Ali Muhammad nor Raja said anything. From my saddle I could see past Pasha's head. The avalanche had smoothed out the mountainside. The Gilgit river rushed by fifty feet below. The view made me shiver. I had been afraid of heights for years. Remembering my bad experience on top of the Bamiyan Buddha back in Afghanistan still sent me into chills. Yet I made myself dismount and look over the edge. It made me giddy to peer into the rushing water roaring by. Far away on the other side I could see similar stranded travelers looking in my direction. One of them waved and shouted to me but I could not hear him over the roar of the river.

On our side there were ten men armed with picks and shovels attempting to chop a rough trail along the mountainside. Based on the unhurried pace of repairs, it was going to be a long time before anyone managed to effect even a footpath across that divide. Three fellows were carrying stones off the road, exhaling with exaggerated breath after each small load was deposited. They wiped their foreheads and stopped to chat before heading back to tackle the debris again. There were two shovels in use, each mutually operated by two men. The boss on the handle end would shove it into the dirt. His companion would then assist him in extracting the load by pulling on a rope tied just above the shovel's blade. These two-man teams were nibbling at a nameless mountain bigger than anything on the continental United States. It was one of the pickax men who had ordered us to turn back.

By talking to this fellow Raja had discovered the Pakistani army was supposedly sending a bulldozer and a crew of army roughnecks up from Gilgit to solve the problem before us. However I doubted the man with the pick knew what day of the week it was. I was certain he could not give us an accurate estimate of how long it might take before we could expect to cross on this road. It appeared we were indeed trapped.

I remounted Pasha and started to turn back towards the tent.

"Is this the *parri*? Where is the *parri*?" Ali Muhammad yelled at the pick man. But he had crawled back out on the edge of the cliff, returning to his work, ignoring my friends entreaty.

Only a few hundred feet back from the crevice sat the canvas awning serving as the disaster command station. Directly across the road from the tent was an unoccupied stretch of decent grass. None of us needed to be told to head our horses there. We slipped the bridles off and left them free to graze. I reasoned they were all too hungry to want to run away from the free meal. With so many strangers around, Ali and I slung the rifle and shotgun over our shoulders. It would have foolishly irresponsible to leave them hanging unattended on the saddles while we were preoccupied with other affairs.

"I'm going to look around," Ali Muhammad informed Raja and me, then left without a word, heading off towards the men and jeeps gathered up on the far edge of the mountainside.

When I looked at Raja he just shrugged.

"Let's get something to eat," I suggested.

"Praise God! I thought you would never ask," he said smiling.

We set off for the awning with empty stomachs and high expectations.

It was a sunny day and every square inch of shade under the awning was occupied by angry, impatient men. They were squatting on their heels cursing the disruption in loud voices. The road leading from Gilgit to Chitral was the lifeline for every village for hundreds of miles in all directions. To have the road go out was similar to having the Pacific Coast Highway being destroyed, then watching the motor traffic from Seattle to San Francisco pile up on both sides. Goods were rotting. Passengers were fuming. Drivers were running short of cash waiting. No one was happy but the owner of the tent.

Our travels among the Ismailis had been unpleasant ones. They had been ill-mannered, suspicious, offensive hosts, squeezing us for every rupee, shaking us out of our beds at the crack of dawn to hasten our departure, inhospitable to the last small child. Yet everyone we met up until that point was a saint compared to Ali Daud, the owner of that worthless stretch of canvas.

In his early forties, bearded, stocky, short, dark haired and beetle-browed, the Ismaili had sniffed opportunity the moment disaster struck. He rushed to the closest inhabitable wide spot in the road and set up shop before the dust settled. With the other villagers of Gupis occupied by the nocturnal visit of Shakra, Ali Daud's monopoly was the only game in town.

Glancing around, the culinary options didn't look too promising. In fact all I saw were men drinking chai. My stomach was so empty I could have sucked the salt out of my saddle pad. Before I could make my way to the back of the tent to ask for a meal, an altercation broke out between a white-bearded old man and the proprietor.

"A hundred rupees? I'll give you only gunpowder," the old man shouted and began shaking his fist at the visibly impatient owner of the makeshift restaurant.

"If you don't like it go back to Chitral *chacha* (uncle)," the younger man said with a sneer.

Raja and I had eased our way up next to the small table separating the two men. I did not mean to interrupt, was in fact waiting my turn, when Ali Daud abruptly ended his former conversation, turning to me instead.

"What do you want?"

Gupis Pays in Blood

"We want to eat and we want to picket the horses across the road while we rest."

"We only have chai. No food until tonight," he told us. Looking up he saw the horses for the first time. A look of rapacious pleasure crossed his face.

"Five hundred rupees per horse per night. You owe me two hundred rupees for what they've already eaten," he said with complete self-confidence.

From the moment we had ridden down the Shandur Pass I had not met a soul who respected the sacred Islamic teaching that travelers were to be offered hospitality, given the last crumb in the house if need be, but at the very least offered respect. I would have been willing to pay extra considering the extraordinary situation. However Raja and I were not dealing with an emergency, we were dealing with an extortionist.

Ali Daud was charging ten rupees a cup for chai, fifty rupees a night to sleep on the dirt under the awning, weighing out food by the crumb on a scale to these hungry, weary, stranded travelers. The villainous knave would have billed us for the shade if he had thought of it.

I was tired. I was worried. I was hungry. I was sick of Ismailis taking financial advantage of us. The *chai wallah* could have tried to rip me off for a meal or a bed and I might have let it slide. Instead when he tried to take advantage of the horses I finally snapped. My sight narrowed down into that tunnel vision which affects me when I lose control. All I saw was this greedy insect enriching himself on the misery of others.

Reaching across the table, I snatched his shirt collar with my left hand, then shoved the barrel of the sawed off shotgun so far into his throat his head bent backwards. The tent went deathly quiet. I could hear the tea bubbling on the nearby fire. Ali Daud's formerly confident eyes were suddenly as large as saucers.

"Are you hungry?" I asked him.

When he didn't answer I shouted, "Are you hungry?"

"No," he weakly whispered.

"Like the old man says, maybe I should give you some bullets to eat?"

I shoved him backwards so hard he stumbled into a tent pole, almost lost his balance but came up facing me. I saw the thought of resistance cross his mind. I cocked both barrels, took careful aim at his chest and told him, "If you move I'll cut you in half."

In that half-mad state of mind I would have not hesitated to do it if the old man had not tapped me on my shoulder.

"Leave this *kafir* (pagan) dog my son. He is not worth going to jail over. Come with me," he said, then turning, he spat on the floor to emphasize his contempt for our host.

"Yes, leave him," I heard from one of the men behind me.

Someone laughed, then shouted, "Don't kill him you fool. He's an Ismaili but he's the only cook we've got."

Lowering the shotgun I waited to see what Ali Daud would do. He remained silent. I then turned to the assembled men in the tent.

"Who owns that grass?" I asked no one in particular.

"Allah," one man yelled.

"The Angrez with the shotgun," said another and everyone laughed.

I reached into my shirt pocket, peeled off a fifty rupee note from my money, and tossed it on the table in plain view.

"That is to pay for my horses. I prefer not to break bread with such a man," I said and tossed my head in the direction of Ali Daud. No one stopped us as Raja and I left like we came, hungry.

The old man was indeed from Chitral. He led us to a jeep parked close by our mounts. With one eye on the horses and another watching out for a vengeful Ali Daud, Raja and I sat in the dust and gladly accepted our new friend's poor hospitality. Old Kamran Khan was on his way to Gilgit. Having arrived two days before, he was watching his meager traveling funds disappear while he waited for the road to clear. As he explained this to us he offered Raja and me a raw onion and a chunk of coarse brown bread. Neither of us argued, instead we began devouring the meal voraciously, taking turns eating the onion like a succulent fruit, gobbling chunks of the bread as if was manna.

"In my father's day we would have killed off that criminal and sold his wife and children into slavery," explained the furious old man. He went on to explain that in his youth an able-bodied Ismaili male slave could have been purchased for 200 rupees, likewise a healthy woman swapped for a decent horse. Kamran derided the modern age that tolerated such rude treatment to travelers.

Before the elderly fellow could relate any more details of the good old days, Ali Muhammad came walking up. Four haggard-looking men were following him. Each of them was carrying a large wooden tea crate on his back like a primitive rucksack. A length of rope was used to balance the load around their shoulders. None of them put down their burden. They seemed anxious to move on.

Ali Muhammad didn't bother asking us any details, he just launched into his discovery.

"They've just come from the other side on the parri," he said, clearly excited.

The onion finished, I stood up slowly and wiped my mouth with the back of my hand. This was suddenly turning into a day full of snakes and scorpions.

"They're on foot," I said, observing out the obvious.

My musical friend was not going to be discouraged. He turned to the closest backpacker, a grizzled man who looked like he slept in a cave all winter. I dreaded to think what was so important he would risk his life carrying it across that mountain in a crate.

"Can horses make it across?" Ali Muhammad asked the caveman anxiously.

Looking over his shoulder the hiker pointed towards a barely discernible trail that led up across the face of the mountain.

"It is the high *parri*. All I can say is that men once did."

Before I could put a question to the caveman, he cut me off.

Gupis Pays in Blood

"You travel across on the forgotten road or you go back to Chitral. Come on, let's go," he said to his companions, and without delay they all departed.

"They say we can make it," Ali Muhammad repeated eagerly.

I was tired of pretending. The deeper we had ridden into the north, the more melancholy my friend had become. At first I thought I was only imagining it. After the polo game failed to rouse much interest in him, I knew his problem lay in Lahore, not with the trip. The truth had lain between the three of us like an untreated sore until that moment. Now Ali Muhammad had chosen the wrong day to cross me. The crook operating the chaikhana tent had already robbed me of my good humor.

"You'd risk all of our lives because of your impatience to see a prostitute in Lahore?" I snapped.

"You said you were the horseman. If you can't ride over it I'm walking out alone," he said, his anger matching my own.

I felt my face harden like my heart. In order to satisfy his wave of selfish passion Ali Muhammad's treasonous lust was cutting him off from all reason. I knew my friend was naive, over-confident, and most importantly, wrong. True, Ali Muhammad had more than five hundred hard-won miles under his saddle. He had scrambled out of the way of crazy truck drivers, had clawed his way with Pahlwan over three mountain passes, had ridden until he was so sore he thought he would break from fatigue, had come as close to being a horseman as he ever had.

It wasn't enough.

But Ali Muhammad had managed to drive a dagger into my greatest weakness. Like an idiot I had let him insult my most precious vanity, my equestrian skill. In all the years we had been friends we had never shared a cross word. That day was no exception. Rather than argue with the fool I gave him what he wanted, and almost killed him in the process. If he had been wise Ali would have weighed the tone in my voice and backed off. Somewhere back down the trail Ali Muhammad had lost that wisdom. He was fixated on reaching Shaheen at the possible expense of all our lives.

"There is a difference between the horseman of the summer and the horseman of the winter, between him who rides a horse well over dry terrain and he who rides skillfully over dangerous ground," I told Ali Muhammad in a cold voice laced with warning.

He ignored me, his face defiant, his actions clearly determined if I did not give him his way.

"Come then. Let me finish your apprenticeship," I said and walked towards the horses without waiting to see if he would follow.

Khyber Knights

37
Where Horses Fear to Tread

I was in a foul mood.

As we made our way towards the horses, in my heart I was asking myself who was the bigger idiot, the fool or the fool who followed him? I never had a chance to answer my own question. Suddenly the valley was filled with the sound of thunder. Looking up I marveled at the sight of a cloudless blue sky, wondering how a storm could blow up on such a crystalline day. The sound continued, becoming a deep throated roar. Then I heard voices screaming in terror.

Glancing behind me I saw the road crew running for their lives as a heavy rain of rocks came pounding down the mountain from up above. Loosened by their smaller brothers, fragments the size of houses paused in momentary indecision. Then they too rumbled and began falling like ten-ton snowflakes from Hell. The stony shower came cannonading down in great leaps, hitting the Gilgit river with terrific explosions, blasting the water into geysers high enough to reach up and drench the already-raped road.

Then, as soon as it started, it stopped.

For several minutes smaller stones whizzed down like bullets, further frightening men and horses into bone-shaking silence. A long, low cloud of gray dust began drifting down the slope like a slowly descending shroud, covering us everyone with its gritty reminder of our own limited mortality.

The nameless peak looming above me stood at the apex of four titanic mountain ranges; the Himalayas, the Karakorams, the Hindu Kush and the Hindu Raj. From that unnamed corner of the map I could see a forest of 20,000 foot peaks in any direction. The old planet was crashing together above my head from all directions. While men ran for their lives, competing mountain ranges tried to grind their rivals into dust. Geologists had estimated the highly unstable region suffered an earth tremor every three minutes. No one bothered to count the landslides and their associated deaths.

It was Pakistan, where such trivialities were of limited local interest.

Instead, there on the destroyed road to Gilgit, we frightened travelers observed the bones of Mother Earth crumbling in decay.

Ali Muhammad had chosen a poor day to try and ride over the crow's nest of Asia. The previous pathetic attempt at road repair was swept away. The crowd of marooned men had gathered around the tent, seeking comfort in numbers like a flock of frightened chickens.

I gave Ali Muhammad a questioning look, asking him silently if he was still determined to proceed. When he yanked Pahlwan's head up to fit the bridle into his horse's mouth, I turned to Pasha and did likewise.

The hot-blooded dun was angry at being pulled away from his meal. He tried to outmuscle me, reaching back down to the grass. My first reaction was to lose my temper. Then I felt the itching hole still healing in my face and remembered my previous foolish attempt at losing my self-control with Pasha. Suddenly it dawned on me the lunacy of what we were attempting. I knew what a *parri* was, or rather had once been. The thought filled me with dread. In that instant I knew this horse trying to gather a last mouthful of God's green grass was the only thing standing between me and death on the hideous precipice Ali Muhammad was forcing us to cross. I pulled Pasha's head up gently, hugged him around the neck in appreciation of the miles he had brought me so far, then gently slipped the bridle into his mouth, prepared to risk both our lives. That finished I turned to Raja and Ali and gave them quiet orders.

"Check your saddles. Inspect every buckle. Clean the horses hooves. Tuck the tail of your turbans up. Wrap the bells in rags. We ride silent if we expect to live."

While I went about my end of this business, our fellow traveler Kamran Khan stood nearby. The old Chitrali had his hands held up before his chest in a *dua*, a silent prayer offered up to Allah. Having lived his life in these mountains he knew we needed the extra help.

I wasn't content until I carefully checked each horse myself, running my hands under each cinch, yanking on the stirrup leathers, jamming the long guns deep into their saddle scabbards, making sure the bridles sat snug. Pahlwan, Pajaro and Pasha were ready. If we riders were remained to be seen?

Swinging into the saddle I carefully settled in, pushing the pistol belt securely down around my hips, making sure the sword hung well out of my way, shaking my turban to make sure it fit snug and tight. The last thing I needed was thirty feet of blue silk fluttering loose and spooking Pasha. When I felt comfortable I turned and looked down at Kamran Khan.

Pakistan is like that. You make friends on the side of the road you remember the rest of your life. I never saw that old man again. I still believe his prayer saved my life. He gave me a firm handshake and said he would pray for us. I nodded in silent appreciation. We were going to need it.

I looked at Ali Muhammad.

"Where?" I asked.

The foolhardy lover pointed behind the tent at a pencil thin slash of slightly different colored earth. It curled up across the face of the mountain like a joke in judgment. I followed it with my eyes. The *parri* rose in a long steady line of ascent until it disappeared around the shoulder of the mountain high above our heads. The local people were intrepid cragsmen. Additionally they had been riding their surefooted Badakhshi ponies over these same mountains for centuries. Nowhere in the world did men habitually ride their horses on such life-threatening trails. Traditionally, no matter how awful the road, the horsemen between Gilgit and Chitral stayed in their saddles and stuck to their mounts.

Where Horses Fear to Tread

Those horsemen had spent their lives riding over the *parris*. I had only heard vague rumors of these tortured trails

The *parri* was a system of dual roads that ran around the face of the mountains.

The lower *parri* was constructed solely for pedestrians. It was never more than twelve inches wide. That footpath followed the natural fault lines in the rock. Where all evidence of the trail disappeared a crude facsimile was constructed. The self-taught engineers took advantage of ledges and cracks in the rock to drive pegs into the face of the mountain. They then laid bundles of tamarisk or a single shaky plank across the gap. If a height needed to be scaled, a notched tree trunk would be laid against the mountain side as a rough ladder. Often polished by generations of use, the lower *parri* was impossible for horses, and was used exclusively by men on foot, both carrying loads and without. It often ran hundreds of feet above the rocks below.

The upper *parri*, though never more a than couple feet wide, was a highway compared to that lower twisted torment reserved for footmen. The upper course worked its way laboriously, rising in slow turns until it conquered the cliff, then dropped in a gut-wrenching descent down the other side.

When a new road capable of sustaining motor traffic had been created, it had largely destroyed the need for the *parris*. However large sections still existed throughout the mountains, used by local residents on various occasions as the need arose. I wondered what we were about to encounter, knowing the *parris* had never been considered safe in the old days, dreading to think what condition they may have deteriorated into a hundred years later.

Looming immediately above us was that colossal mountain, so obviously indifferent to our plight, so contemptuous of our puny efforts to scale her heights. Her sides were a glaring slope barren of trees. Studying the massif I could see gigantic fragments of stone suspended on the mountainside by the merest trace of gravity. Each boulder weighed many tons and was surrounded by long expanses of shingle slope. Above my eyes, above my comprehension, the towering summit was sheathed in snow and arrogant isolation.

The *parri* trickling across this mountain's flanks looked like an impossible rock staircase. While I was brooding over our chances Raja reined his bay gelding in next to me. I didn't turn to look at him, my eyes still trying to weigh the scant evidence before me.

The young Afridi said in a quiet voice, "My father always said the angels have two missions in life, presiding at the birth of a child and protecting horsemen."

I looked at Ali Muhammad. My friend's mouth was set, his face cut in stone. I knew if I hesitated he would dismount and try that accursed mountain alone and on foot. I turned to Raja.

"Before this day is over you'll tell your children you rode with the Angel of Death breathing on your cheek," I told him.

"Let's go," I said and spurred Pasha into a canter straight at the tent. Seeing the horse charging towards him, the wretched *chai wallah* Ali Daud dived back inside.

It was only a brisk bit of bravado. As soon as we passed the awning I stopped at the trail's base. Pasha was excited, anxious to go on. Before I let him start up the mountain I turned to Raja and Ali Muhammad.

"These are my orders. Me, Raja, Ali in that order. Keep one horse length between each rider. Not a sound lest we bring the mountain down on top of us. If I fall, dismount and save yourselves. If you can't turn the horses around, shoot them. Don't leave them to plunge off the trail and die in agony on the rocks below," I said, remembering the sound of poor Pukhtoon's snapping bones when he crashed off the river bank.

The look on their pale faces told me they understood the seriousness of the venture. I lifted my hands in supplication to Allah.

"*Bismillah Al-Rehman Al-Rahim* (In the name of God the compassionate)," I said trusting my soul to Allah, and my body to my horse. I choked back my fear, clucked quietly to Pasha, and told him to walk on.

The path was a horseman's agony from the first step. The moment we began I could tell Raja believed I could see far enough ahead to judge the route we traveled was safe. Ali Muhammad rode behind, lost in his own thoughts, too preoccupied not to trust me. Riding up front I had no delusions about what lay ahead. The *parri* had decayed into an almost impossible state. Never more than two feet wide, I could tell from the start that the hideous shelf was the worst excuse for a road I had ever crossed.

From the beginning Pasha was in charge. I sat absolutely still in the saddle as the dun gelding climbed the gravel-covered trail like a mountain goat. He lowered his head, scanning the ground carefully, placing every foot down like a ballerina. He was a combination of courage, endurance and skill. I thought of all I had taught him on the long journey and knew the time had arrived when I had to trust him totally.

Though I knew we were climbing, I was not trying to keep track of time. It wasn't until I looked back that I realized Pasha was making steady progress. The men we had left behind looked tiny. The tent resembled a doll's handkerchief. I was thinking that perhaps I had been overly cautious when a rock came tumbling down that cruel mountain. Pasha shoved himself back onto his haunches to avoid having the giant stone slice his front legs out from under him. I felt Pajaro bump into us from behind. The impact almost knocked all four of us off balance and over the side. Pasha held his grip, slowly eased himself up and waited for me to tell him what to do next.

I did not dare turn to look at Raja. With my right hand on the reins, I held my left hand facing back towards Raja, slowly waving at him to keep his distance. Once again the dun climbed. He was leaning into the mountain. I leaned with him, hoping Ali and Raja were watching how I was staying centered over the saddle. We traveled like that for several thousand feet, the path sometimes shrinking to no more than eighteen inches wide. I was worrying about how big Pahlwan was managing to place his giant hooves on the skinny ledge, when Pasha brought us to a the last stretch before the summit. It was a villainous length of smooth rock.

If left up to me I would have lacked the courage to continue. Pasha came to a halt, sniffed the shiny gray stone before him, then tenderly put his right forefoot onto the slick surface. His shoes were worn thin but that didn't make a difference. Out of the corner of my eye I could tell we were hundreds of feet above the roadway. We had passed the point where anything but kismet mattered.

I could hear Pajaro breathing hard behind me, out of fear or exertion I couldn't tell. The only other sound was the pounding of my own heart in my throat. Suddenly Pasha pushed himself off, climbing, sliding, pushing with his slick rear shoes, scrambling for traction as he fought to save our lives by taking us both to the top. It was the most anxious moment of my equestrian life.

Our reward was to have passed that nameless stretch of accursed trail too unworthy to grace with the name "road." I did not dare linger, hearing the other two horses scrambling up behind me. The *parri* turned around the shoulder of the great mountain and blessed me with a view of a descent just as cruel as the one I had just ascended. If I entertained an urge to turn and wave goodbye to those fellows left behind so far below at the tent, it was now too late. We had passed out of view from their camp. Suddenly even the company of Ali Daud, that greedy criminal with all his faults, was preferable to the rugged inhuman force of nature playing with our lives.

I risked my life by glancing back. Raja was pale. Ali Muhammad looked like he wasn't breathing. Both their horses were following Pasha's example, walking with their heads lowered as a way of maintaining their balance. The quick turn of my head lasted less than two seconds. That brief look told me my human comrades understood every breath brought constant danger and that they were on their own.

Pasha had no relief from his duties. While I was looking at his stablemates he was starting to make his way down. The *parri* had reached its greatest width, a little more than 24 inches. Yet the route lay covered with the stony debris from countless rock slides from above. The gelding managed to negotiate his way over the various sized rocks, making his way as carefully as a cat.

I estimated we had been traveling for more than an hour without a word spoken between us. Not being able to look back, I could only imagine that Ali Muhammad and Raja's sense of tension was as overwhelming as mine. I thought my head would burst from the effort of living through the exercise. The *parri*, that hideous snake, lead us around a fold in the mountain that now obstructed our view back. Though we were high up on the mountain, and far beyond the point where the avalanches had taken out the jeep road, we had seen no sign of the motorists on this side of the obstruction. I could only guess that our route had taken us above and beyond them. It was while I was considering why we had not seen the other travelers, that a terrifying thought came to me. Like a complete fool I had neglected to ask the caveman pedestrian and his friends if anyone else was coming in our direction on foot. If we met anyone heading towards Chitral everyone involved was out of luck.

I was sick to death of that mountain, wanted to forget the misbegotten pile of rock had ever entered my life. Even though we were riding in the shade, Pasha's neck was soaked in sweat from his efforts. I didn't need to be told that he was dripping sweat from his flanks as well. I could feel the evidence of my own anxiety soaking through my shirt.

At last it seemed I could see the *parri* starting genuinely to descend. I suspected the jeep road must lie somewhere below us but didn't dare look down to confirm my hunch. No one needed to tell me we had come out over the Gilgit river. Without turning my head I could see it running five hundred feet below us. If the rocks didn't get us, the foamy brown waves far below promised us a quick demise. The *parri* no sooner threw this bit of information at me than it narrowed again, before heading downhill across a ledge of polished rock. There was nothing to do but continue. My right leg scraped the cliff. My left leg hung out over eternity. I think Pasha just closed his eyes and walked across, too weary any longer to fear that impossible mountain.

The gelding half walked, half skated across the slick-faced rock. I could hear Pajaro sliding down behind me, further back still came the reassuring thumps of Pahlwan's big hooves scrambling for traction. The *parri* started dropping quickly, widening once again. We were only a couple of hundred feet up and for the first time I could see the empty jeep road waiting below us. Then the trail once again took us around a fold in the mountain.

Pasha took me around the edge only to reveal a sharp ninety-degree corner straight ahead where the trail turned back on itself, before heading down at last to the road waiting below. As I drew nearer I saw the *parri* ran under and around a massive tan colored rock that was projecting out over the trail. The dun slowed to a crawl as we approached this final difficulty. I didn't dare stop and study the obstacle. At the last moment I decided I could not safely lie down in the saddle and hope to pass under it. I grabbed the front of the saddle, leaned far out into space, felt the rock scrape my right shoulder, and managed to slide by.

Immediately my gelding kept walking, taking the corner and giving me a view of Raja approaching the same problem. Though Pajaro looked calm, I could tell his Afridi rider was scared. Raja hesitated as he approached the boulder, started to lie down on his horse's neck, thought better of it, and came up in an attempt to copy my move. His quick action brought him into instant contact with the rock. Not understanding his rider's distress, Pajaro never slowed. His forward movement smashed Raja's right shoulder into the rock, flipping the boy up and out of the saddle. As Raja went flying through the air he managed to let go of the reins, otherwise he would have pulled Pajaro over on top of him.

Where Horses Fear to Tread

I yanked Pasha to a halt, watching Raja turn a complete somersault in the air, then come smashing down with his body hanging over the side of the cliff. The chance landing of his arms on the edge of the *parri* was the only thing keeping him from tumbling into the river far below.

Pajaro had stopped the moment he felt Raja fall from the saddle. I looked across the short distance separating me from the Pathan tribesman.

"You're fine. Do you hear me, Raja? You're fine. I can see the end. Pull yourself back up onto the trail," I told him. Behind Raja I could see Ali Muhammad unsure of what to do. I gave him a look which said, "Stay still."

Raja was still too startled to move.

This time I yelled at him.

"Get back on the trail!"

He dug his heels into the soft dirt and by a combination of pushing and pulling managed to scramble up onto the *parri*. We couldn't afford the luxury of letting him sink into shock.

"The ledge is too narrow for you to mount. I want you to walk behind Pajaro. Raja, do you hear me?" I shouted at him.

He nodded numbly. Looking back at Ali Muhammad I told him, "Hold on to the front of your saddle and lean out away from the rock. If you have to, lie down on the outside of Pahlwan's neck. But go slow and let him make his own way around it. Do you understand?"

Ali Muhammad looked sick with fear. If I had wished a cruel revenge on him for this exercise in stupidity I would have been satisfied with the look of dread and trust he sent my way. But I did not wish him ill. In fact I did not see how he and the big horse could manage to scrape by that merciless stone and live.

"Are you both ready?" I yelled. Weak nods signaled affirmation. I whispered to Pasha and he started walking slowly. Pajaro fell in behind without being told. Raja stumbled along, watching the ground as if he feared it would once again fall away from beneath him. I tried to keep my eye on the *parri*, on Pasha, and glance back at Ali's progress. Finally unable to do both, I cursed the *parri*, gave Pasha his head and turned my head to see how Ali Muhammad fared.

Pahlwan edged up next to the boulder, then slowed to a crawl. The giant horse knew he was in charge. When the big roan passed his head under the rock the massive bulk of his body came into contact with the stone. He moved so slowly I heard the rifle hung on the far side of the saddle grinding against the unforgiving stone.

Ali grabbed the front of the saddle with both hands, dropping the reins around the gray horse's neck and relinquishing any pretense at control. With the rock looming over his head, the terrified rider had no choice except to lift his right leg and bring it up alongside the back of his horse. He clung to Pahlwan, left foot jammed deep into the stirrup, hands locked in a death grip around the front of the saddle, balanced like a butterfly over the precipice yawning impatiently below him.

Khyber Knights

The big gray horse scraped the two of them through, took the corner and came up behind Raja. It had been a narrow escape.

After that Pasha lead us down the final stretch to safety. When we emerged onto the jeep road, I stopped him. My four companions followed me, all of us grouping close together like stunned survivors. Neither Raja nor Ali Muhammad could speak for a few moments. I pried my fingers loose from the reins, only to discover they were soaked in sweat from the palms of my unsteady hands. When I dismounted my legs were trembling. Raja could not talk, only kept blinking at me. Finally he managed to utter a hoarse whisper.

"My father would have been ashamed to know I fell off."

"Your father wouldn't have had the guts to ride that road," I told him.

Looking up at Ali Muhammad I gave him a grudging smile.

"You lack style but I must admit you may now call yourself a horseman."

Pakistan loosened her grip on our necks. Oh, she still beat us unmercifully for several more hours. We shared a drink of water from the canteen, then did the only thing we could do, headed down the rediscovered wide, flat road until we could find food and shelter. Yet we rode with lighter hearts because we knew that at last we were on the Gilgit side of Pakistan. Everything we knew and understood about Pakistan lay behind us, behind the mountain passes, behind the inhospitable Ismailis, behind the *parri*. We couldn't go back. Not ever.

Instead we rode east praising our mounts.

"For these horses nothing is far," Ali Muhammad said.

"A loyal horse honors his master," Raja added.

"On Pasha's back Death was afraid to touch me," I concluded.

Yet such are the ephemeral things of this life that our fear was like the greening of the fields. It lasted but a season of our hearts, passing away when that cool light of beauty, the moon, rose to guide us in at last to a *chaikhana* in the tiny village of Beyache.

The evening wind had filled my mouth with dust. Every atom in my body ached. I feared Pasha was dying from exhaustion. Even my spurs were too tired to jingle. When we reached the village we were reduced to one goal, to just stop and rest from the grind of putting one foot in front of the other.

Allah blessed us there with the only corral of the trip. The horses were let loose inside with ample fresh hay, the first they had seen in many long days. We stumbled into the low-ceilinged, log-walled chaikhana, threw our saddles into a corner and slumped down onto the dirt floor after them. Food was ordered. The little room was full of travelers. I was too tired to take part in the conversations. I had already learned the mountain we crossed had no name. The hard-won miles of that day's journey were significant only to we three men of the saddle. There was no need for public acclamation. Ours was a private reward.

As the waves of exhaustion began to take control of my body, I knew I had at last slipped into a slower life. Leaning against the rough teahouse wall I looked at the river of Asian faces surrounding me and

Khyber Knights

"I yanked Pasha to a halt in time to see my friend disappearing over the edge."

listened to the different languages filling the little room. Outside I could hear the sweet music of the horse bells singing, as the geldings ate their well deserved alfalfa in the dark corral beyond. And then I rested, knowing that this moment in my life was where I had always longed to be.

Khyber Knights

38
Hunza Water

It was no pony holiday.

Our gelded responsibilities were ringing their bells impatiently soon after sunrise, demanding their breakfast and our dutiful attendance. We three servants hauled our tired bodies out to the corral to feed those demanding masters.

Pasha was one of those disgustingly cheerful morning types, awake at once, full of vinegar, eagerly shoving me with his nose, or slobbering all over my shirt sleeve. Regardless of the early hour, he was already dusty, muddy, filthy and otherwise disreputable. Whereas gentlemanly Pajaro looked elegant despite any hardship, and even blue-collar Pahlwan never needed much cleaning except where his saddle left sweat marks, my wild bully-boy had started that day by trashing the corral, rolling till he was an equine mud ball, and kicking his heels up at the sun. Feeding the dun his hay, before my own eyes were barely open, only reaffirmed the symbiotic emotional relationship I shared with Pasha. It was an open question as to who was leading whom across Pakistan.

To think our movements were free of timetables and deadlines would be to admit ignorance of equestrian travel. Our days were as restricted as any businessman rushing through the course of a Manhattan morning. The scramble began the moment we were awake, bringing a bustle of preparation and an urgent compulsion to depart without delay. The question never revolved around our desire to see the next pretty patch of Pakistan, but rather the length of the next stage of the trip, and the condition of the horses.

We travelers, both men and horses, were but six little cogs in a bigger wheel. Each had his part to play. No one of us could delay or all would suffer accordingly. Though we had no bus to catch, no freeway traffic to beat, every morning found us in a hurry to depart, for we had a far more important appointment to keep than most ordinary commuters. If we prolonged our departure too late, sundown would find us between villages and meals.

That particular morning there was a heightened excitement. We knew certain comfort and ease awaited us at the end of that day's effort.

Even if we had felt so inclined, there was little enough reason to delay. The *chaikhana* was poor. We three friends had chai and yesterday's bread for breakfast. No matter. Better than nothing, and ahead lay Gilgit.

Outside it was raining. Despite the army ponchos, by the time we saddled the horses we were soaked. As I shoved my shotgun into the scabbard I noticed it had begun to rust since last night. Well, I told myself, there were a host of chores to attend to once we arrived at that great northern terminus.

The moment I swung into the saddle the rain-washed leather soaked through the seat of my pants, leaving me sighing at the prospect of a cold, wet morning. Ali Muhammad took us out of the corral and back onto the road. The rain pounded us, running down our necks, blowing through the cracks in our ponchos, turning our turbans into sodden lumps. The road was a muddy ruin. No one spoke. Men and horses bent their backs and pressed ahead. The first six hours were thus spent crossing many dreary miles in a rain so thick we could barely see further than our horses' heads.

Too often a journey deteriorates. The once joyful quest into the unknown becomes poisoned by the realities of the road. Endless delays, arguments, unforeseen catastrophes, weary the traveler and slay the innocent image of a poetic mountain ride. The dream becomes a struggle. The struggle sometimes comes between friends.

I was the only one not anxious to reach Gilgit. True I longed for the physical comforts I knew awaited me. Yet I was sad to be arriving, sad to think that every step Pasha took brought me once again closer to the dull routine of civilization. Ahead lay electricity, telephones and the ugly woes of the 20th century. Behind me were rumors of the Dasht-I-Taus, the Desert of the Peacock, and portions of Pakistan so dim and aloof I could not find even local travelers who had penetrated their mysteries. Left to my own devices I might not have proceeded on to Gilgit, might have happily turned back to wander even deeper into the mountains falling behind me.

Ali Muhammad gave me no choice.

If there was a fascination to the nomad equestrian life, my old friend had missed its meaning. If I rode in silent contemplation of the many places left unseen, my companion sat his saddle as if he were cut from stone. He was not interested in looking back. His eyes were ablaze from the anxiety of searching the skyline for what lay ahead not behind. He spoke no word. I knew if I suggested we turn aside on some errant mission, Ali would lose all sense of self control. The look on his face said he might slay anyone who stood in his way.

As we rode through the rain, the country itself decided things for me. The grand mountains we had been following since the Shandur Pass had deteriorated into ugly gray hills. The Gilgit river still ran on our left, untamed, brown, in a hurry like us to reach her namesake. By early afternoon it felt like we had been riding forever. Luckily the rain stopped. Thereafter we all rode swaddled in a steaming, aromatic group of smells composed of sweet leather, rancid man sweat, salty horse sweat, bitter wet metal and moldy, dirty clothes.

It came as a complete surprise when cresting a hill we saw the long-sought town far ahead in the distance. Suddenly there were no more mountains. Below us lay a vast valley, a great green blur that filled my eyes and rendered me speechless. After seeing so many rocky hard

Hunza Water

places, here was a quiet windy greeting to tired travelers, a sea of trees with slow green leafy waves lapping in the gentle breeze.

I was overcome with emotions at the sight of that little city. We had floated through the mountains like shipwrecked sailors on our three little equestrian rafts. Lying now before us was an azure island of relief and refuge. I could have wept with pride and joy at our accomplishment.

When we started down the hill a change set in. The stony arms of the Hindu Raj mountains had held me for so long, I suddenly felt naked and exposed when I left them behind. We set off with growing anticipation. Though we had seen the dim skyline of Gilgit, it took us several hours to reach our goal. The vision of Gilgit brought an anxiety to our hearts and every step was suddenly one too many. Though it seemed the city had temporarily disappeared from existence, lost in the trees all around us, our talk was of nothing else.

Our tired eyes were the first to be refreshed. Everywhere we looked we saw quiet farms, irrigation canals, and busy people. The fertile sight told me it was time to temporarily leave behind the unseen desolation and my desires to journey there. Our road moved away from the river, winding us into a lavish land, past billowing apricot trees whose white blossoms perfumed the air. Stopping next to an overhanging orchard, Pahlwan reached up and began eating the ripe fruit off the tree limbs. Pasha and Pajaro immediately joined him. The hungry geldings were delighted, busy slobbering and spitting out apricot pits as fast they could gobble them. Gone were the days when they were picky eaters.

Huts turned into houses. Outlying fields became interlocking green expanses lining our road. Then at last the horse's hooves were making a hollow sound on a defined dirt street instead of tapping along some nameless stony path.

To our unaccustomed minds it seemed we had stumbled into the wonders of Babylon. Gilgit's main street was half a mile long, filled with shops, restaurants, hotels, barbers, confectioneries, bakers and more produce and meat than we had seen since leaving Peshawar months ago. Plus, we once again had to negotiate through traffic of a sort.

A human potpourri had gathered from all the various ethnic areas of Northern Pakistan. Uncouth tribesmen from Baltistan, furtive raiders from Kohistani, purse proud Dards from Hunza and hard-eyed Sunnis from Chilas were all making their way along what passed as a sidewalk. Regardless of where they originated, they were all forced to dodge the overcrowded buses coming in from faraway Rawalpindi and the big red Massey-Ferguson tractors grumbling to and from the nearby fields. Gilgit was a busy, thriving city full of faces representing economic interests from Karachi to Kashgar.

It did not take us long to determine on a place to stay.

The single story Vershinghoom Inn was close to town, close to the river, and close to succulent grass. Bul Bul Jon the owner was a pleasant, curly headed, handsome fellow, ready to serve up an omelet, or a smile, as the situation required. Armin Baig, his twelve-year-old son, was enlisted as groom for the horses. The quiet little place had four rooms, only one of which was occupied. We soon had our horses picketed and brushed. While they made their way through the fresh hay Armin Baig was delivering, we three dirty equestrian travelers walked back into town to take care of other important business.

Bul Bul Jon assured us it was safe to leave the saddles, rifle and shotgun locked in our room. We walked down the main street of Gilgit still wearing our holsters though. Coming to the first barbershop and bathhouse we did not hesitate to enter.

The small front room had the luxury of sporting two barber chairs. That however was not our first destination. The barber was delighted to see three customers. A flick of a curtain revealed the bath house lodged in the back beyond prying eyes. This larger room had four small cubicles. Each of us was presented with a towel, a bottle of shampoo and a bar of green Chinese soap. A rough wooden door allowed each customer entrance to his own stall. On the back of each door were two hooks, otherwise there was no luxury of any kind.

Low to the floor were two brass taps. Underneath was a galvanized five-gallon bucket and a plastic dipper. Before entering I had observed the large wood-burning boiler used to supply the hot water. The only thing extraordinary about the Gilgit set up was that the barber was burning a pile of surplus army snowshoes as fuel. I didn't care where the hot water came from. I turned the taps and began filling the bucket.

While I waited for the water I undressed. My sword belt and clean clothes I hung up on one hook. The clothes I took off were so dirty I was tempted to throw them over the door and order them burned. The sight of my own body distracted me away from that thought. I had not washed anything but my hands, feet and face since leaving Chitral. Except for my red hair I was as dark as a coal-mining coolie. My normally fair, freckled Irish skin was black and leathery, every pore filled with minute grit. The dirt did not surprise me, the condition of my body did.

If I had been thin after escaping the clutches of Pindi Prison, there was little left of me now except bone and sinew. My joints resembled great bony knots. My tendons flexed like taut bow strings. I could count my ribs like so many survivors. If I once had a belly, no more. Here were the hard results of the healthy life of a horseman.

When I heard the rushing water, I quickly turned off the tap. I poured the delicious hot water over my head, feeling it envelope me like a warm glove, and began scrubbing away the travel dust of many miles.

Bathing from a bucket did not surprise me. I had been doing it for years. Most people in the Indian sub-continent considered the idea of washing in a bath tub barbaric, a disgusting habit where the patron wallowed in his own watery filth. The principle, both in Pakistan and Gilgit, was to use fresh running water to sluice off the body as you washed, as opposed to sitting in progressively more stagnant and polluted water. As custom dictated I worked my way downwards, cleaning the private and dirtier portions such as the feet last.

I could hear Ali and Raja blowing like happy seals in their stalls. Clean at last, I made a vow never to see that precious commodity, hot

Hunza Water

water, spilled or wasted again. I then exited to meet the barber in the clean clothes I had brought.

My face was a covered by a red bristly mess of whiskers. My hair resembled wild, wet, red plumage. Sitting myself in the old chair, I leaned back and looked at the thin face staring at me from the mirror.

"Leave the soup strainer on my lip. Shave off the rest. Cut my hair short for travel."

Seeing a row of multi-colored bottles of ointment, cologne and hair tonic arrayed on the counter before me, I decided to go for the full Gilgit experience.

"Perhaps I will even indulge in a splash of your tincture," I told the fawning barber, then settled in to await the results.

It was an unadorned place full of old practical items that fit a barber's hand or a customer's face. Luckily for me this was a master of the razor. Tucking a crisp white sheet around my neck, he began the ballet of shaving. Leaning back, I felt him use his brown left hand to hold my face firmly in place. Then he started drawing the straight razor slowly across my throat. I didn't resist. I stretched my neck back and gave myself up in trust to the stranger, all the while the razor sliced the offending beard and the accompanying grime off my face.

An hour later we emerged looking like new men.

That was a happy day. We were rich in fodder for us and the horses.

We walked no further than the first restaurant. After stuffing ourselves on mutton, pilou, rich custards and chai, we staggered back to the hotel, too tired to see the rest of the town. Little Armin Baig had tended the horses well. The sun was barely sinking and already they were dozing. Their masters were not long in following. No one who has not ridden for long, hard months can fully appreciate the luxury of a real bed and soft sheets. The unaccustomed sensation was too much. I felt almost destroyed by the effort to reach Gilgit. The moment I stretched out I was seized with a longing to rest deeply. The 600 miles between me and Peshawar lay like a weight upon my lids. Within moments I was lost in the dark arms of sleep's embrace.

The sun was well up the next day before I went to check on Pasha.

The horses had become used to sleeping in rough conditions, eating vile rations, and living under the most dire circumstances. Like little children the only thing they understood about the trip was that every day their world changed. Every sunup we traveled on. Every day was a crap shoot where they did not know what they would eat or where they would sleep. Despite all that, in silent loving trust they had brought us to Gilgit. We three men were the only emotional stability in their lives.

Picketed under trees behind the hotel, all three horses were resting comfortably.

Looking at their thin bodies I knew it was time to head them home to Peshawar and the rest they deserved. If they made it that far.

For the first time in weeks there was leftover hay, but Pahlwan looked like a giant, gaunt gray skeleton. Gentle Pajaro was still beautiful but the fierce sun had bleached out his previously-dark hair. Pasha had been down on the ground sleeping. When he heard me coming, he opened his eyes, then rose slowly to his feet.

Oh, my once proud Pakistani mustang. I ran my hands over him. His skin was warm from the sun but was loose from effort and malnutrition. He too had ribs showing. Only his unconquered black eyes reflected the wild pony who had tried to buck me into Kabul so long ago. The horse standing before me was too tired to fight.

"This trip is destroying the two of us," I thought and reaching up I scratched him above his forelock. He sighed, a contented, exhausted sound expressing how deeply he had labored on our mutual behalf.

"We are feathers from the same wing," I told him, thinking I was alone.

"I believe you care more for that son of Satan than anyone else," Ali Muhammad said from behind me. Turning I saw he was holding his saddlebag, obviously ready to depart.

"It is not right to give one's love to an animal who has no soul," he added sanctimoniously.

"Or to a soulless whore," I answered.

His kind face instantly became a mask of anger. I stepped away from Pasha, ready to meet Ali half way if he attacked me. I saw his fists clench. I prepared to meet his rush. Then his face drained of strong emotion and he looked down at the ground. When he glanced up there was pain written across his features. I could almost see the invisible wire reeling him back to Lahore, could almost glimpse the red hot hook sunk deep in his heart, could see him struggling against the emotions binding him to Shaheen.

I lost all my anger. He would always be my friend. I moved away from Pasha and grabbed Ali Muhammad's right forearm tightly. I offered him my sweetest words, full of anxiety for his well-being and honest concern about his future. He pretended to listen. But how can a deaf man hear? It was impossible to offer counsel to one who rejected guidance. The anguish on his face revealed the agony of having the wide world constrained within the narrowness of his ruddy heart.

What more could I say or do?

If a man goes wrong is it not because he wrongs himself?

"The horses are done in. I'll rest them three days then I'm pushing on to Peshawar with Raja," I told him quietly, not sure if I really meant it or not.

He gave me no smile, offered no false promise about his return, entertained no illusions regarding his destination.

"I better be going. Hell will be itching with impatience at the news of my impending arrival," Ali Muhammad told me, then rushed off to find a bus going down country, oblivious to anything except the need to satisfy the fire consuming him.

"*Khuda hafez* (go with God)," I wanted to say, but by then he was gone.

There was nothing to do but take my clue from Pasha and rest. That first day Raja and I did just that, slept, ate, and tended quietly to our

Khyber Knights

"I felt almost destroyed by the effort to reach the town of Gilgit. To our unaccustomed minds it seemed we had stumbled into the wonders of Babylon. Here was a busy thriving city whose pleasures beckoned. No one who has not ridden a horse for long, hard months can fully appreciate the luxury of a hot meal and a soft bed."

Hunza Water

horses. The second day Bul Bul Jon brought the horse shoer I had requested. This time I did not even attempt to help. It was humid in Gilgit. I sat under the trees and watched a man old enough to be my grandfather shoe the three equine travelers. By sundown of the third day Raja and I were feeling fed and rested.

The pleasures of the town beckoned.

Both of us had ventured into Gilgit, visiting shops, attending to simple needs. But between the demands of our tired bodies and the required errands, none of those sojourns had been for aught but business. That night was different.

Raja and I sat under the verandah awaiting our dinner. The sun was setting. The air was cool, the horses safe and content. When Bul Bul Jon made his entrance from the kitchen he was greeted with loud sighs of anticipation. The succulent pilou he carried would have satisfied a Persian shah. The savory dish of boiled rice was laced with tender chunks of roast beef, then topped with sliced roasted almonds and raisins. No one needed to urge Raja or me to dig in.

As custom dictated we were using our right hands to scoop up small balls of rice, before popping them into our mouths. The fresh-baked bread was broken off one small piece at a time and then used as a crude spoon. Otherwise there were no utensils.

Our faces were greasy, our hands more so. We were smacking our lips like only starving men can, when the other two residents of the hotel walked in. The English couple appeared to be in their early fifties. They wore the khaki Banana Republic-style safari clothes fashionable at the time. Both their pants and matching vests had a plethora of pockets. Bul Bul Jon had already informed us the Englishman, Nicholas, was a university professor studying dried apricots. His wife, Priscilla, kept busy complaining to the hotel owner how poorly run Pakistan was since the departure of the Raj.

One look at the two greasy, turbaned diners eating with their fingers was enough to send the English travelers straight to their room. Intent as I was in not letting the rapacious Raja eat all the pilou, I gave the tourists no more than a cursory look.

Every other meal in Gilgit had merely been to satisfy the effects of near starvation. That platter of rice was rapture. We left not a grain. At the conclusion of the culinary battle Armin Baig came from the kitchen bearing a lota of warm water. The boy poured the steaming water over our outstretched hands, allowing us to wash the grease off our hands and faces. His father, Bul Bul Jon, stood nearby with a old but serviceable scrap of towel. Within a few moments we were stuffed, cleaned and satisfied. I was thinking about making an attempt to shove back from the table, when the propitiator leaned over in a conspiratorial manner.

"Khan sahib, would you like to try a local delight?" Bul Bul Jon asked in a low voice laced with conspiracy. There was no one within hearing distance except his son and Raja, so I did not understand the need for this secrecy. Thinking I comprehended his subtle message I rejected what I perceived to be his offer.

"I do not care to smoke hashish."

"No, no. I am speaking of Hunza water."

"Ah," I said, as a smile crossed my face.

"Ah," he repeated and playfully wagged a finger at me and my ignorance.

"Hunza water." I said softly, "is such a thing available?"

"I would not allow others to know of it," he said glancing in the direction of the English couple's room. Then looking at Raja and me, he said, "But diligent and discreet travelers who have ridden so far should have something better to swallow than water from a brook."

"Will you try some?" the hotel owner inquired again.

The look on Raja's face left no doubt that he was sitting there in the dark. He shrugged his shoulders in innocence when I looked his way for confirmation.

"Wine. Hunza water is the name of the local wine," I said softly.

"Oh," Raja replied in shocked surprise. The look on his face couldn't have been more revealing than if I had suddenly slipped a Playboy magazine across the table.

"Well, shall we explore this local delight?" I asked my youthful friend.

"I had an uncle once," he started to say.

"So did I," I replied and started laughing at the idiocy of our attempted conspiracy. It was an indictment of the religious situation in Pakistan that we were whispering about breaking one of the country's greatest social taboos. The law against drinking alcoholic beverages was especially harsh under General Zia's fascist regime. Though the people of Gilgit, and the surrounding countryside known as Hunza, had been making wine for centuries, the heinous crime suddenly carried the promise of a prison sentence and a public flogging of eighty lashes. Bul Bul Jon had been right to play it safe until he determined which way the wind blew.

"No, I'm serious," Raja told us, "I had an uncle who once drank **sherob** (liquor) in Peshawar. He later told me he absolved the sin by saying "*Toba, toba* (shame, shame)" before and after the course of his actions, thus becoming a good Muslim once again."

"This is not whiskey only wine," Bul Bul Jon hastened to add. "Shall I bring it?

The look on Raja's face told me the time for indecision was over.

"Only if you bring three glasses and join us," I told him.

"Gladly."

The innkeeper disappeared into the kitchen but was back within minutes with three glasses and a two-gallon plastic kerosene can. Armin Baig cleared off the dishes while his father poured out the forbidden liquor. When he handed me my glass I sniffed the concoction suspiciously. Though I was no authority on bouquet, the smell greeting my nostrils was the first warning. I wondered if Bul Bul Jon had not grabbed the wrong container.

"In a kerosene can?" I asked skeptically, unsure if the wine I was being offered had not been combined with the other liquid to fortify the mixture.

"What better way to disguise it but to leave it out in the open next to the fire?" the hotel owner assured me. Then without another word he tossed off his full glass like it was Kool-Aid. Raja was clearly waiting for me to advance. I gave the young man a lying smile, pretending to be confident, then said "Allah forgive me. All men occasionally sin," before taking a long drink.

No one could have convinced me Bul Bul Jon had bothered to rinse out the kerosene can before drafting it into use. The mulberry moonshine had an oily taste but it slid down easy enough. The result was no great wine. Its miracle lay in the mere fact of its existence and its incredible kick. I waited for only a second before I felt its deceptive delivery hit my stomach and set off a small explosion of warmth. It tasted terrible but worked admirably.

Bul Bul Jon saw the look of understanding flood over my face.

"Ah," he said, holding up his empty glass and smiling.

"Ah," I answered with the forbidden proof of discovery warming me already.

We clinked our glasses hard and began laughing.

Raja was holding the glass in his left hand like it was full of tiger's milk. He quickly reached up with his right hand and gently pulled down on each of his ear lobes, saying the magic words, "*toba, toba* (shame, shame)," as if to dispel something sinful he had overheard by accident. Lifting the glass he timidly sipped the forbidden liquid. He made a sour face and started to lower the glass quickly. When he saw we two older men looking at him with undisguised misgivings, the Pathan took a deep breath and drained his glass.

We all waited. Within a few seconds a smile began to creep over Raja's face.

"Ah ha," Bul Bul Jon said loudly. "He knows."

Our host laughed as he refilled the three glasses, splashing some on the table by accident.

"Careful, you'll burn the furniture," I told him.

"No, only our heads," he replied laughing.

"First my head," Raja said and shoved his glass forward for another shot.

An hour later we were best friends for life, comrades who understood the others' woes, privy to their secrets, a befuddled merchant prince and two woozy warriors who had also long since lost the urge to hide their forbidden activity. What the English hiding in their room thought of our increasingly loud activities I never learned nor cared.

Perhaps it was because we were besotted with the charms of life that we let Bul Bul Jon lead us into town. Discretion should have dictated that we stay quietly in our rooms. The giddy Gilgiti wouldn't hear of it. He insisted we take up his invitation to accompany him to see "The Well of Death." Suspecting nothing more mysterious than some watery pit akin to Lourdes, I grabbed Raja. Little Armin Baig was left to watch the horses and attend to the needs of the sober English guests.

His father was busy leading us to the far end of town. Neither Raja nor I had ventured out in that direction. An excited look crossed Bul Bul Jon's face when he heard the noise of engines racing.

"We'll have to hurry," he urged us, without revealing the reason why.

Exiting from Gilgit we discovered a hard-trodden waste ground at the edge of town. Even though it was by now completely dark, a noisy generator was running a series of flickering bulbs that illuminated both the field and the crowd of men gathered in it. Still thinking we were heading for a well of water, it did not dawn on me that this was our destination. Bul Bul Jon stopped at the edge of the dim white light thrown off from the strings of bare bulbs hanging over our heads.

"Well," he asked impatiently and held up his hands as if he were revealing the Eiffel Tower to an hick from the French countryside. In truth I did not know what to say.

Before us was a wooden structure that resembled nothing more than a two-story circular water tower, minus its peaked roof. Even from this distance I could see a rickety staircase winding up its side from the ground to a catwalk running around its circumference. Men were climbing down. Others waited in line to replace them at the top.

"Hurry or we'll miss the show," the drunk hotel owner told us over the noise of the crowd.

"What is this?" Raja asked me.

I had no answers. The only clue was a large wooden billboard hoisted over the staircase. A gigantic painted figure of a man on a motorcycle, his arms crossed, his face sporting both a fierce mustache and a look of disdain, only added to the enigma. Like dutiful boys following our Scout leader, Raja and I got in line and bought tickets.

Even if I had not been knee walking drunk, the climb up that staircase would have scared me to death. To say the fool who built it had spared the nails would have been an understatement. It was barely wide enough to accommodate one man and yet it groaned under the human load shoving their way up its concourse. Telling myself not to look down, I followed Bul Bul Jon up to the catwalk.

He had made his way halfway around to the far side, shoving a hole among the group of men already peering over the edge.

"Here, here Asadullah," he yelled at me, urging me to hurry.

The walkway was too narrow to have placed two cats tail to tail. Raja and I had a hard time easing our way between the buttocks of the locals and the flimsy board serving as a handrail. After numerous apologies we took our places beside our host. Bul Bul Jon was out of breath with excitement and peering down into the "Well of Death." The series of lights strung over our heads illuminated nothing more than a gigantic empty bucket, forty feet deep and nearly that wide. I was perplexed and not a little perturbed.

"What is this?" I asked the hotel owner, making no effort to hide the note of irritation in my voice.

He gave me a look of astonished disbelief.

"Its the Well of Death. It visits here every summer," he shouted over the noise. He then patted me on the shoulder, giving me a compassionate look as if to say he understand I was too drunk to comprehend the obvious. Before I had time to follow up with another question, a previously-hidden door opened in the bottom of the wooden receptacle. Two men walked over to the center of the deep enclosure. The crowd started cheering wildly, at what I had no clue.

When a third man entered through the hole pushing a motorcycle I understood the crowd's anticipation was about to be rewarded. While the motorcyclist began kick-starting his machine, his two attendants carefully closed the trapdoor. Suddenly all three men were enclosed within the wooden barrel. There was no preamble, no singing of "God Bless America" before the show. The crowd wouldn't tolerate any delay.

"That's Zareel," Bul Bul Jon shouted, pointing at the rider climbing on the motorcycle.

Clearly Raja and I were supposed to recognize the name of Pakistan's version of Evel Knevel. When I looked at my Pathan friend for help, he shrugged his shoulders, as lost as I was regarding the meaning of all the excitement. Suddenly the engine grabbed. The air was full of white smoke, engine exhaust drifting up to us mixed with the perfume of motor oil. Zareel climbed aboard and began circling the motorcycle inside the bottom of the Well of Death.

The intrepid motorcyclist really did have a big mustache. Suddenly he showed us why he was also famed for his look of disdain. In the dim light I had overlooked the fact that the bottom of the well slanted in. While the walls were perfectly circular and flat, the first two feet were pitched in at a steep angle to give Zareel both a ramp and a runway. Without warning, he gunned the motor and shot the motorcycle up onto the walls of the Well of Death.

Before our amazed eyes Zareel began climbing, every circular trip around the Well bringing him higher and higher. Men began shouting in anticipation.

"Zareel, Zareel," they screamed like adolescent girls swooning over Elvis Presley.

But this was no "King of Rock and Roll." This was clearly a madman.

Before I had time to shut my amazed mouth, Zareel was spinning his motorcycle so close to us I could feel the heat blowing off the exhaust. Raja and I both yanked in our hands in alarm as the stunt man ripped by. Bul Bul Jon had no such qualms. Like his neighbors he held out his right hand. Zareel roared by, driving with his left hand, slapping the outstretched palms or the spectators with the other.

There was no letup. The motorcyclist did in fact look disdainful of death, riding in circles, ignoring the crowd until they pulled out their money. Men began holding out different denominations of rupees. Zareel swooped around like an eagle, snatching the money like so many lambs out of the field. When the money ran out he began circling to the bottom.

When Zareel reached the half-way mark, he circled the Well with both arms crossed over his chest, then pointed both hands into the night sky, daring gravity to grab him before finishing his descent.

The moment the daredevil stopped the motorcycle the crowd roared its approval. More money floated down. I watched Bul Bul Jon throw handfuls of rupees over the edge. The air was raining money onto brave Zareel. His two attendants hastened to pick up the notes. When the clean-up was over, they held up their arms, urging the crowd to calm down. As the motorcyclist climbed off, I thought the performance was coming to a close. Bul Bul Jon grabbed me and pulled me back to the edge. Following his finger pointing down, I saw that Zareel had climbed on the motorcycle backwards.

"That's impossible," I shouted to Bul Bul Jon, but he wasn't listening, and suddenly neither was I.

I never learned what town Zareel grew up in, regardless, brave men must be as common as cabbages in that village. He gunned the motorcycle, giving less regard to his safety than ever before, then began climbing to meet us once again. This time he shot the green motorcycle straight to the top of the Well of Death. He came so close to the edge men almost fell backwards over the rail behind them.

Like my fellow patrons, I had been gripping the top of the Well. The motorcycle came so close to my fingers I snatched them back. Zareel had ridden so near I could clearly read the word "Triumph" on the side of the World War Two era military machine. It looked like the suicidal maniac was going to fly over the edge like a cannon ball, releasing himself at last from the confines of gravity. The motion of the motorcycle looping so close to the edge of the barrel was so violent, it set the old wooden structure into a groaning protest. Suddenly I could feel the Well of Death rolling back and forth like a huge hula-hula hoop, as Zareel roared by, punishing spectators, the motorcycle, even the structure itself with his arrogant disregard for Death.

When he finally rolled to the bottom, everyone, including Raja and I began screaming. I thought the catwalk around the Well of Death would collapse from the abuse of men jumping up and down in excitement. More money flew through the air.

"*Shahbash, shahbash* (bravo, bravo)," they were shouting to Zareel and each other.

He looked up and waved once, then prepared to depart. The door was again opened, but no sooner was the motorcycle gone than a small table was carried in. One of the attendants soon ran in an electrical extension cord and set up a phonograph. Our excitement had no chance to evaporate. The bottom of the Well of Death was suddenly filled not just with music but four dancing girls.

Their silky shalwar kameez glistened in the hot Gilgit summer night. They were four pink, blue, yellow and green blossoms swaying and singing beneath the crowd. If the men were not hot to begin with, Zareel's performance, and now the sight of these maddening beauties drove them to new heights of excitement.

Each of the singers picked a quarter of the crowd, then began working the men above. When the girl in yellow beneath us saw Raja, she smiled. Even from that height she was clearly unattractive, a big-shouldered village girl if I had ever seen one.

"Hello, pretty boy," she yelled up at Raja, then blew him a kiss. The men near us roared in appreciation.

"Throw her some money boy," yelled the big bearded man standing on the other side of Raja. My friend cautiously threw her down a green-ten rupee note. She snatched it out of the air before it could touch the ground. The woman was clearly delighted at the attention. To show her appreciation, she began grinding her hips lewdly up in Raja's direction. Looking uncomfortable, Raja turned to Bul Bul Jon and me. Leaning across the edge he had to shout to be heard.

"She's as ugly as a turnip," he yelled at me, as the ribald laughing went on around us.

"Well she likes you," I shouted.

If Bul Bul Jon had lacked amusement so far, he now surrendered himself to mirth. He pointed to Raja and laughed uproariously.

"You Pathan yokel, she is a he," he yelled.

A look of shock flew across the boy's face.

"*Hijra?*" I asked incredulous.

"Of course," Bul Bul Jon yelled back.

Suddenly the joke was as plain as the dancer leering up at Raja.

"Oh yes, what a pretty boy," I yelled and slapped Raja on the back in delight. I waved down at the dancer. "Wait by the door madam. I will send him down to you."

The *hijra* was clearly pleased at the prospect.

"Come, let us force this groom to leave his lady love," Bul Bul Jon said.

I waved goodbye at the hijra and followed the hotel owner to the stairs.

We talked and joked at Raja's expense as we walked home through the darkened town. In all fairness, his had been an easy mistake to make. The well-dressed *hijra* looked like a young woman from the top of the Well of Death.

The Indian sub-continent was the only place left in the world where the caste known as *hijras* still existed. They were the sexual untouchables of Pakistan and India, eunuchs, hermaphrodites and transsexuals. Some were cursed at birth with a sexual deformity, others fell outside the accepted sexual norms. In either case the *hijras* lead a sad and desperate life.

History had once allowed them to fulfill a worthy social need. Considered free of sexual desires, they were originally employed as harem guards. Under various kings clever *hijras* sometimes even rose to political power as chamberlains and generals. They were considered to be such excellent and incorruptible guardians that at one time the shirt of the Prophet Mohammad was guarded in Cairo by *hijras*.

They had fallen on hard times since the 1947 partition.

With the demise of their former employment, these sexual outcasts created a new role for themselves. No longer discreet, they now flaunted their outrage, earning a living by crashing weddings or births, singing bawdy songs and dancing until they were paid to leave by scandalized home owners. If the money was slow in coming, the *hijras* would threaten to expose their mutilated genitalia for public inspection. Money was always produced for these uninvited guests. They were forced by circumstance to become vulgar and sometimes violent.

Only a few were true hermaphrodites. Most were homosexuals thrown out by their scandalized families. Unlike in the West, where gender-change operations were available, hijras did not have access to such technology. Finding they could not return home, they followed an ancient custom, allowing themselves to be sexually deformed in order to win a place within the hijra community. The applicant would be heavily dosed with opium, a string tied tightly around his genitals, which were then sliced off with a razor. Many did not survive the horrific operation. Those who did took a new feminine name and joined their clan of sisters.

Having been jeered at and often attacked, the *hijras* banded together for protection. No census had ever been made, but government figures estimated there were more than a million *hijras* living in both countries. Though they professed no single religion, many openly preferred Islam over Hinduism, finding it less exclusive than the latter caste-ridden religion.

Regardless, neither community accepted them. They were reduced by circumstances to the role of petty magicians. To the poor the *hijras* promised to dismiss the evil eye or make barren women pregnant. They blackmailed the rich by their mere appearance. They made clever use of their legendary occult power to curse or bless, wielding the threats that were their only power.

They also acted as homosexual prostitutes.

Though the men of Gilgit had been responding lewdly to the *hijras* dancing, community propriety demanded that no one openly accept their favors. However I had no doubt the "girls" would find a few customers for their favors before the sun rose.

The practice of "Le Vice," as the English explorer Sir Richard Burton called sodomy, was an open secret in Pakistan. From Iran to India the sexual repression of women went hand in hand with the unwritten practice of homosexuality. In Pakistan, where the sexes were forbidden to mingle, one of the resulting events was homosexual behavior. Young college chums could be caught necking in many major cities.

Even the Afghans, those macho mountaineers and puritanical Muslims, concealed a strong homosexual subculture. Olden travelers used to keep "*kuchi sarafis*" or traveling wives with them as they moved across Afghanistan from city to city on business. These seductive Afghan boys would be dressed in women's clothes and be sporting long attractive hair, rouged cheeks and hennaed hands. The angry wives were left to sulk at home.

Hunza Water

One of the reasons given by the Afghan mob for killing the British officers visiting Kabul in 1841 was the strangers were carrying on illicit sexual relationships with the women of that city. What is seldom reported is that the Afghan women, having discovered foreign men not addicted to homosexual practices, made themselves readily available to the heterosexual outsiders.

The Afghan city of Kandahar was still considered such a hotbed of homosexual rape that its reputation compared to the legendary city of Sodom. The Afghan journalists I had trained to report on the war used to joke that the danger of covering assignments in Kandahar came not from the Russian bullets but from their mujahideen hosts.

Because of all the merriment I was in no condition to greet the sun's arrival.

I stumbled out of my room late in the morning, only to find Raja already sitting on the verandah. He was leaning his elbows on the table, his head propped up in his hands. The look of misery on his face reflected how I felt. When he saw me, he raised one eye lid in weary recognition.

"I've been poisoned," he said in a husky whisper.

I sunk into the chair next to him.

"Don't talk to me. I'm dead," I responded weakly and groaned to prove it.

Armin Baig brought us chai and bread. His father, we learned, was in no shape to join us. Luckily the sweet tea was coursing through my veins when the uniformed policeman arrived less than an hour later.

"You're to come with me," he rudely informed me.

"And you're to go to Hell," I told him.

"Official business."

"I wouldn't get up to go see General Zia," I said bluffing.

"You're close. ISI (Inter Services Intelligence)," he said. "Let's go."

He wasn't joking. Raja wasn't required. I walked through the hotel gate alone and got in the waiting jeep.

The cop drove me through a bustling Gilgit to the end of town.

Here the driver headed the jeep across the Gilgit river bridge. The rushing torrent we had followed through the mountains had entered the valley and looped around the town. Most of the newer government offices and buildings lay on the other side of the river. Within minutes we stopped at an army post where ISI, the Pakistani version of military intelligence, was headquartered.

I was still wearing my pistol and sword, the cop having made no effort to suggest I leave them. Consequently, I was hung over but armed when I met Major Changez Wali in his little office. It didn't take long to discover that if the cop who came to fetch me wasn't bluffing, his boss the major was. Despite his official capacity, Changez had dragged me in on a fishing expedition, trying to discover why people were crossing through his area on horseback.

"There are so many foreigners traveling through Gilgit it's hard to keep track of them all. You naturally drew attention to yourself. Going by

431

horse you pass through very slowly. This is a very sensitive area. We are close to several borders this far north. Are you sure you're not taking pictures of bridges or other off-limits installations?"

I knew what he was hinting at. India and Pakistan had already mauled each other in two wars. Paranoia was ripe on both sides of the border. My head ached. I hadn't brushed the foul taste of the Hunza water out of my mouth, and the man in front of me inspired no confidence. He was swarthy, chubby and stretched his uniform in all the wrong places. Unfortunately he was also a major. I was sure my friend's advice to kill offending strangers did not extend that far up the chain of command. Rude Ismaili *chai wallahs*, yes. Majors, no.

So I told Changez the truth. I didn't even own a camera. Then the discussion took a new, unexpected turn, one that sent a cold chill down my back and sobered me up in a heartbeat.

"Nevertheless one can't be too careful. Not all fingers are equal. Things may not be as they seem. I checked you through Interpol. You appear to just be travelers. So?" he said and let his voice trail off.

"So?" I asked in return.

"So go easy, and goodbye."

I was immediately ready to leave that office and Gilgit. If this snooping military spy had got wind of my run-in with the Rawalpindi narcs he could have imprisoned me on the spot, holding me until he was satisfied the horse trip was really not camouflage for a more sinister purpose.

It was my turn to bluff. I scraped the chair back from his desk and stood to leave.

"Good, if I'm not under arrest I'd like to be taken back to my hotel. I don't feel well."

"Too much of our Hunza water?" he asked smiling, giving me a look that convinced me he knew all about last night's forbidden activities.

"*Toba, toba* (shame, shame)," I replied and touched my earlobes as if I did not understand, but at the same time I played a guilty smile across my face, as if that was my worst secret.

"No reason you can't depart."

I didn't wait to be told twice.

Changez stopped me before I managed to get through his door.

"Where's your other friend?"

"He went back to Peshawar to get horse shoes for the big horse."

"Really?" the major said. It was a question not a statement. He smiled like he knew something and my heart hit my stomach.

The errand boy cop was waiting to drive me back. Gilgit was the same bustling town I had seen four days before. It had been a welcome sight from the distance but upon closer examination its beauty was suddenly vanishing. When the jeep dropped me off at the Vershinghoom Inn I rushed inside. Raja was where I left him, hung over, though he had never heard the word.

"Get up, we're leaving," I told him.

"What about Ali Muhammad?"

The question angered me. How much longer should we linger I wondered, waiting for a man who may not want to return or may not be able to?

It had been four days since my friend left. In the back of my mind I knew I had got drunk and waited the extra day to give him plenty of time to come back. I had waited a day longer than agreed. Now my generosity might have led Raja and me into an unsuspected trap. There was no way of knowing if Ali Muhammad was in transit, in Shaheen's bed or in a Lahore jail. The look on the major's face seemed to imply the latter.

If Ali Muhammad was in trouble I didn't want to learn about it in Gilgit from Major Changez Wali. Knowing my luck I'd get handcuffed over a chair and beaten with a polo mallet instead of a cricket bat. Plus if Pindi Prison had been bad I shuddered to think what the local correctional facilities would be like, especially during winter. My mind was decided even before I heard the wailing police sirens heading our way.

"Hurry. Help me get the horses ready. We're not waiting," I told the Afridi tribesman.

Khyber Knights

39
Pakistan's MacBeth

Ali Muhammad started that bus ride with a hopeful heart.

After leaving the Vershinghoom Inn he walked down the dirt street to the end of Gilgit. An hour later he was southbound on the first portion of a dog-legged journey that would lead him first to Rawalpindi, then due east to Lahore. Even in his emotionally intoxicated state it was impossible to ignore his new physical environment for long.

The impatient lover boarded a typical Pakistani bus, part utilitarian object, part rolling artwork. Like the imported trucks, the Bedford company in faraway England supplied only enough to drive the bare-bones frame off the ship.

To have said the bus was one color would have been a mistake. That queen of the road was a rainbow on wheels. True enough, the enormous hood of the bus was the color of snow, but three wide, bold stripes of bright color flowed back along her sides like yellow, pink, and green wings blowing in the wind. The words "Wajid Flying Coach Pindi" proudly adorned her flanks, revealing both the owner and her destination.

There were no doors, only two six foot tall gaping holes on the left side of the vehicle placed front and back to allow passengers access coming and going. Hanging under the rim of the bus were chains from which draped small sheet-metal diamonds. These baubles were intentionally allowed to drag on the ground, thereby adding to the noisy roadway ambiance. Four big windows on each side were shoved all the way open, thereby permitting the passengers some small amount of ventilation, but also allowing in every bit of dust and smoke encountered on the interminable journey.

A gigantic blue luggage rack was welded along the top of the vehicle. Crates, suitcases, cardboard cartons and roped-up parcels were piled two feet deep and twenty five long inside its tubular depths. It was a warehouse on wheels up there. Perched in front of the rack was a eagle, its multi-colored sheet-metal wings spread in decorative defiance of the onrushing wind.

Lower down but no less important was the vehicle's proud crown.

Placed proudly above the windshield was a metal facsimile of a F-16 jet fighter, Pakistan's strongest totem of national pride. Thrusting forward from her body, just below the plane, rested a large half-moon of bright green sheet metal. Painted on that crown in graceful white Arabic letters was an invocation from the Quran asking Allah's protection over the people inside.

They needed all the help they could get.

Khyber Knights

No one in Pakistan willingly made the trip from Gilgit to Rawalpindi by road. Not only was it considered one of the most dangerous motor trips in the country, it lasted at least eighteen grinding, boring, uncomfortable, life-threatening hours. Anyone with political connections and real money bought or bribed a seat onto the prop plane that sporadically flew in and out of the northern capital. The flight was always booked weeks in advance. It only lasted one hour but, because of the surrounding mountains, landing safely in Rawalpindi was never a certainty. Nevertheless most foreigners chose to risk their lives for sixty hair-raising minutes in the air, and forego traveling in a motorized steel cocoon down the narrow road.

When Ali Muhammad climbed through the vehicle's front door he quickly took the unpopular aisle seat closest to the driver. Not only was it the smallest seat, barely big enough for two adults, it was also considered the most dangerous. Most people reasoned the further back you rode the safer you were in case of accident. Ali wanted to see where he was going, even if it was over a cliff into the raging Indus River far below.

He groaned the moment he sat down, remembering why he hated Pakistani buses. Pahlwan's saddle was more comfortable. To conserve space the back of the seat was built almost straight up and down. Like the bottom, it was covered with the barest minimum of foam padding. The sheet-metal floor was sticky from orange peels, spit, baby vomit and assorted other organic materials too rank to classify.

Like all private buses plying the roads of Pakistan, this one had both a driver and conductor. That exalted figure, the driver, never appeared until the conductor had filled the bus to its maximum capacity.

The two rows of seats, and the long bench across the back, could technically hold twenty five passengers. The Pakistanis delighted in ignoring such niceties. That polite and totally imaginary number had nothing to do with the reality of how many people the conductor shoved inside the rattletrap bus.

The young man was eager to impress his boss, Wajid the driver. In road-stained and greasy clothes, the conductor stood outside the door, yelling at the top of his lungs in an effort to attract as many passengers as possible.

"Pindi, Pindi, Pindi, Pindi, Pindiiiiiiiiii," he yelled repeatedly and with total abandon at the top of his voice.

Because passenger comfort was neither an option nor a consideration, it was nearly an hour after Ali had taken his seat before the bus was judged to be full. Of course it had been legally stuffed five minutes after Ali Muhammad sat down. The energetic conductor was still finding space for passengers long after that myth was dispelled. First a third person had been shoved into each of the other two person seats. Then extra baggage was brought in to fill up the center aisle. This lumpy surface provided seating for older children and unfortunate late arrivals. Women and babies were crammed across the bench, as well as the back two seats. The interior became so crowded the poor passengers could barely move once they were lodged into place. Finally another twenty men were allowed to climb on top of the luggage rack and grab hold as best they could. Only when the springs were groaning, and there were nearly seventy-five people on board, did the conductor proudly inform the driver they were ready to leave.

Personal economic interest having set aside civilian propriety, Wajid climbed aboard like a visiting dignitary. He was in his early thirties, a swarthy, skinny little runt who did not inspire immediate confidence. The biggest thing about him was the flaring black mustache covering his weak-jawed, pinched face. Without a glance at his lowly passengers, this matador of the road started the bus, ground it into gear and pulled out of Gilgit. The old vehicle was so overcrowded, the conductor was forced to hang out of the front door. Yet he was still screaming, "Pindi, Pindi, Pindi, Pindi, Pindiiiiiiiiii," in a vain attempt to attract one last passenger.

The moment the bus started down the road the uneven load shifted. Suddenly the bus leaned precariously to the right, so much so that the passengers on the left side of the bus were thrown several inches higher than their comrades on the right. The upcoming Karakorum Highway suddenly tilted and Ali Muhammad groaned at the thought of looking at the country sideways until sometime the next morning. He was impatient to get to Lahore.

"Ah, Jesus," he said quietly in English.

If my friend had any doubts about the grueling nature of the trip they were immediately confirmed. The chance remark in his native tongue was picked up by the other passenger sharing his seat. At the sound of the foreign language the young man next to Ali Muhammad quickly turned and started eagerly practicing his hard-won English on the resigned American. At first Ali nearly escaped the trap of polite conversation. He confirmed his foreign birth and nationality by shouting but insisted it was too loud to talk further. The equestrian traveler was not lying.

Like many of the drivers plying Pakistan's roads, the bus driver was a Pathan. The moment he pulled out of Gilgit, the skinny driver slid a cassette into the tape player. Suddenly the bus was as noisy as it was crowded. Pathans are an exuberant race. The driver cranked the volume up full blast. The cassette was playing a recording from a new Pushtu movie. The passengers' din subsided as they listened to this reaffirmation of *Pukhtunwali*, the Pathan code of honor. Badar Muneer, Pakistan's answer to John Wayne, was yelling in mock rage at yet another enemy. This villain had caused a grievous loss of honor to Badar. The accompanying sounds of a momentous battle then filled the air, complete with screams, shouts, and blows. This confirmed the old Pushtu adage that a Pathan will always give a blow for a pinch. The violent uproar gradually subsided, to be replaced by the film's heroine singing a love song to the accompaniment of a wheezing harmonium organ. As her clear voice sang of her lost love, Wajid enthusiastically yelled, "Der kha (well done)," to no one in particular.

Khyber Knights

The music was so loud Ali could barely hear the old engine straining, the ancient gears grinding, or the nearly bald tires screeching around the curves of the twisting hairpin turns that made up the mountain road.

No one cared.

An unwritten law said all their lives were in Allah's hands anyway. The driver would have had to be legally blind before anyone would have complained. Like his counterparts, he was not licensed, had no formal training, and possessed no conception of the term "traffic safety." His only job was to transport as many people as possible, as quickly as conditions allowed, back and forth along one of the world's most treacherous roads.

The Karakorum Highway was proudly called the "Eighth Wonder of the World" by the Pakistanis. If not a true wonder, it rated its place as the world's highest road. Far to the north where it crossed into China, the KKH, as it was locally known, crested the 16,000 foot Khunjerab Pass.

As it twisted and turned its way south, the KKH followed the path laid out for it by the Indus. Originating on the frozen plains of Tibet, that mighty river rivaled the Nile and the Amazon in social importance. Too wild to carry human riders this far north, the brown torrent tolerated the bus crawling along at thirty slow miles an hour above its banks.

The walls of the mountains looming above the travelers were almost totally devoid of all traces of human habitation or influence. Except for an occasional tiny village no bigger than a bug spot, the two-lane strip of asphalt could have been taking Ali Muhammad through the lonely mountains of Mars. Everyone breathed a sigh of relief when sunset began to color the sky and the bus reached the small village of Dassu.

Gilgit was Paris compared to the little place, but it boasted a chaikhana and a barren field where the male passengers could squat and relieve themselves. Ali Muhammad did not stop to wonder what isolated corner the women discovered to suit their own needs.

When the American heard the call to Maghrib, the sunset prayer, coming from a tiny mosque situated next to the road, he too washed and took his place in the line to pray. He didn't worry about losing his seat. The driver was praying next to him. As Ali Muhammad recited the familiar Arabic words asking Allah to forgive him for his sins, he tried to hide in his heart what had become most important in his life. He was afraid to reveal his secret love to the Almighty, thinking he could somehow manage to control both his heart and his destiny by this unspoken denial.

Dassu was the closest thing to a break Ali Muhammad and his fellow travelers would get. The passengers were given time to quickly empty their bowels and fill their stomachs. Then the bus prepared to pull out and push through the darkened mountains non-stop to faraway Rawalpindi. Though the interior of the bus was still uncomfortably crowded, the male passengers on top the luggage rack had all disembarked at the various villages preceding Dassu. With the sky grown jet black, the bus roared to life and the passengers scrambled back on board.

The interior of the bus was now lit with dozens of garish red and yellow lights. They helped illuminate the many Islamic stickers plastered over the now-closed windows. The mottoes not only proclaimed the faith, they helped inspire the man who controlled their mutual destiny.

The bus driver was an audacious, tough little mutt trying to avoid an unpleasant fate. On the KKH fatigue was common, and so was death. Buses went crashing off the road on a regular basis, killing or maiming anyone unlucky enough to be on board or close by. If the driver escaped alive he always "absconded." This was a common ploy not only to keep him out of prison, but it also gave the parent company an excuse to avoid any blame. Everyone involved, the driver, the owners, and most of all the passengers, were fatalists.

Ali Muhammad was no exception.

When the music ran out so did his luck.

"Have you seen this," the young man sitting next to Ali Muhammad asked and held up a local English-language newspaper in search of a reply. The banner headline stated "Vice President Bush visits Pakistan."

It was news to Ali Muhammad and he couldn't have cared less. Whatever his faults, Ali Muhammad did not possess a political bone in his body. He hadn't paid any attention to American politics since avoiding the Vietnam war, didn't know Khomeini from Kennedy. Regardless, the young man next to him had been waiting patiently to flex his foreign language skills.

"My name is Salman Rashid, but my friends call me Bugi," he said and thrust his hand forward, eager to shake Ali's.

The manner in which Bugi was dressed should have warned Ali he was being towed into deep waters. Over the normal shalwar kameez the young student was wearing a dark gray, pin-striped suit coat. Wrapped conspicuously around his thick neck was a gray and white ascot. In a land full of Moses-length beards and valiant mustaches, Bugi's big square jaw was noticeably bare. His black hair was neatly combed. Completing his attempt to appear foreign were the large square-rimmed glasses covering nearly half his face. Their lenses had an expensive brown tint. If the young man was trying to appear bookish, he had certainly succeeded.

Bugi was that rare Pakistani breed of animal, a "domestic tourist." When his country's wealthy upper-class traveled, they impatiently fled to Europe, or the United States, in search of foreign sights and forbidden pleasures. The nation's poor traveled only out of necessity, and never far from home. Because of social tradition the Pakistani middle class usually kept their families at home. Not only could traveling expose their female members to possible insult, or worse, there were few facilities available to shelter and entertain families.

Ali Muhammad's fellow passenger was the son of such a new minority. Curious about his own country, financially comfortable, and most importantly single, the engineering student informed Ali Muhammad he had spent the last week in the Gilgit area looking at glaciers, foreigners and unveiled women. It had been a delightful trip, even before he found himself sitting that night next to an American.

"What is your President Reagan up to now? He's clearly sent this clerk ,George Bush, here on a reconnaissance to check up on his creature General Zia. Oh, what *behnchowd* (sister fuckers) they all are," Bugi told Ali Muhammad, not bothering to wait for a reply or making any attempt to hide his strong contempt for all three politicians.

It didn't surprise the American to hear the vice president spoken of in such harsh terms. Pakistanis in general had little respect for American fame. That unseen world had small impact on the average citizen of Ali Muhammad's adopted country. Unlike Mexico, which stared hungrily through a barbed-wire fence at the glittering glory of the unattainable First World, Pakistan's distance and culture isolated her from the full dose of material envy felt by the Mexicans.

Plus Islam prompted Pakistanis to wear shalwar kameez instead of tee-shirts, a small but contributing factor in maintaining the Muslim country's self respect. The Mexicans aped the values of their wealthy northern neighbors by wearing slogans, automobile logos and names of American sports teams on their tee shirts. Pakistan was almost entirely free from that sort of cultural pollution and advertising endorsement.

Besides, most Pakistanis could have only named four famous Americans anyway; President Ronald Reagan who sent massive financial funds to keep the war in Afghanistan afloat, his errand boy Vice President George Bush, the singer Michael Jackson and the boxer Muhammad Ali. Because he was a Muslim, the latter was the only one who garnered any wide range of respect.

"Tell me the truth, isn't your vice president like the Prince of Wales, a powerless figurehead? If that's the case how can he say these things about that butcher Zia? What was Reagan thinking? Here you must read this," Bugi said impatiently, and shoved the newspaper into Ali Muhammad's unwilling hands.

From a distance the red and yellow lit bus must have looked like a low flying UFO to the primitive people inhabiting those coal-black mountains. The queen of the road groaned and swayed, but pushed resolutely forward through the night. Ali squinted to read the text of a news story he was utterly uninterested in. Yet he was a captive of Bugi and the bus.

Years of living in Peshawar had inured him to tales of visiting American bigwigs. The only difference was that Bush was the most important representative of the United States to step on Pakistani soil since 1969. Reporting for the Frontier Post in Peshawar, a local journalist spelled out how the Zia government had given the vice president the "Peshawar Package Tour." As soon as his bulletproof limousine was unloaded at the municipal airport, Bush was rushed to the nearby Naseer Bagh Afghan refugee camp. Here a chorus of elementary-age children sang "Mujahadeen," to a beaming vice president.

Without a backward glance at Peshawar, the politician was quickly loaded back into the limousine and headed towards the nearby Khyber Pass. Just before reaching that fabled rocky battleground, Bush's car

Pakistan's MacBeth

entered the notorious village of Landi Kotal. Normally everything from Japanese washing machines to a donkey-load of opium could be bought from the bustling Pathan smugglers who called the corrupt hamlet home.

The Frontier Post reported that every shop in Landi Kotal was locked that afternoon. With the exception of the American sharp-shooters stationed on the roofs watching Bush pass through, the place was a ghost town.

When the vice president asked about the noticeable lack of people his Pakistani translator quickly assured him, "The local people must all be home saying their prayers."

A quick look through a borrowed pair of binoculars gave Bush a hasty peek at both the Khyber Pass, and that forbidding war zone known as Afghanistan. It wasn't much of an inspection considering the American government he represented had reportedly spent $400 million last year alone, supporting the fight against the Soviets who were bogged down on the other end of the pass.

No matter, the vice president had bigger fish to fry in Islamabad. He and the trusty limousine were soon back in the air. Their plane landed in Pakistan's capital before sunset. Here Bush got down to the real meat of the tour, a well-photographed visit with the military dictator who so efficiently and ruthlessly ran the country. Even in the bad light Ali Muhammad could read that Bush had given General Zia a ringing public endorsement.

"American support for Pakistan transcends the current Soviet problem," the smooth-talking politician told Zia. Then the vice president hastened to add that Washington fully endorsed the general's handling of domestic affairs. Bush concluded the interview by stating for the record his "praise of General Zia's unique qualities as a leader." My friend knew our mutual vice president didn't support Pakistan's dictator because he was a war hero like de Gaulle or Eisenhower. The only foe Zia had conquered was his own people. Even Ali Muhammad understood George Bush had come to Islamabad because General Zia promised to follow American orders.

Ali Muhammad didn't need to be a politician to know that what was of real interest in the Zia-Bush tea party had not been reported in the heavily-censored Pakistani newspapers. The Punjabi dictator had gone from being an international pariah to poster boy of the Reagan anticommunist war machine. Like Marcos of the Philippines, and the Shah of Iran, Washington had made it clear they would overlook any amount of repressive domestic tactics so long as their strong men followed the anti-Soviet party line.

The local jewel in the crown was Afghanistan. So long as both President Reagan and General Zia looked at that ongoing conflict through the same rose-colored glasses, there would be no letup in the plane-loads of guns, money and euphoria flying from Washington to Islamabad. The fabled "Great Game" was still very much alive, with Soviet tanks on one side of the Khyber Pass propping up Moscow's puppet, while American dollars accomplished the same task on the

Islamabad side. Meanwhile the people suffered on both ends of the Khyber Pass, as the opposing politicians fought over a country as dry as a dog bone.

According to the newspaper, Bush postured in Islamabad, using his visit to denounce Ayatollah Khomeini's religious regime in Iran. The vice president neglected to tell his American voters that his host, General Zia, had allowed fellow general, Saddam Hussein of Iraq, to open a recruiting office in Karachi. Unemployed Pakistani men and boys were being signed up and quietly shipped off as cannon-fodder to fuel that country's war with Iran.

"Look," Bugi said and jabbed the bottom of the front page. "Bush is here and he ignores the evidence before his very eyes. Can't he see we are suffering under this man he supports, or is it because he doesn't care what happens to us?"

Ali Muhammad glanced down. The article was yet another carefully-worded but evasive story about the growing civic unrest raging across the country. In one massive demonstration against the denial of their basic human rights by Zia's government, 4691 people were arrested, 200 were injured and 61 were shot and killed by the police. In Karachi students were flying black flags in protest. In Hyderabad doctors and nurses had gone on a hunger strike. In Lahore lawyers had barricaded themselves inside the High Court in protest. Any lawyer caught making a political protest was subjected to fourteen years in prison, forfeiture of all personal property and 25 lashes. Ali Muhammad didn't give any of the protesters much chance of success but kept his opinion to himself.

It was tough being an American in Pakistan under such conditions. None of the $3.2 billion in US aid earmarked for the country had been allocated for literacy programs. In fact they had been specifically eliminated. Washington believed much of the aid money would be recycled back into United States coffers anyway, through weapons procurement for the government, or college tuition for the children of the ruling elite. Ali Muhammad knew that American ideas such as integration, freedom of the press and individual rights were widely admired in Pakistan. The shame was that many Pakistani's believed the teachings of Patrick Henry, that legendary American advocate of freedom, were not being exported. They believed that instead of liberty and equality they were the recipients of an electronic-based imperialism which propped up the domestic thug in power and made their country a technological and financial client state. Though supporting the Afghans bid for freedom, Vice President Bush denied the Pakistanis choking on Zia's tear gas the same desire.

"This is a dark time for my country. Under the iron fist of marital law we are forbidden democracy, self-rule, free thought, even individual expression," the student told Ali Muhammad over the sound of the bus motor.

"Don't the people of your country know not a single general, feudal landlord, or political ally of Zia's has ever been arrested, much less

Pakistan's MacBeth

punished for corruption or dishonesty? Can you blame us for thinking we are being crushed not only by that tyrant but his American masters?"

"Look," Bugi said, pointing at the photograph of Bush and Zia smiling together. "My country bleeds, while Zia sits on the throne laughing. He hides behind a fig leaf of respectability pretending to be Reagan's viceroy. Surely Allah will hear the cries of the people!"

The bus gave the young man no answers, nor did the black night pressing in around him, nor the emotionally-preoccupied American. But of all the crimes committed by Pakistan's ruler his new "Islamization" policy was considered by many to be far and away the worst.

Not satisfied with the military domination of Pakistan, General Zia had set about imposing a moral invasion of his own country. Having robbed them of democracy, Zia next looted their religion, bankrupting the fundamental factor holding the country together. When the new country emerged on the map of the world in 1947, it was Islam that unified the diverse ethnic factions, Pathans, Punjabis, Sindhis, Baluchis and Mohajirs into one country. Created like Israel as a homeland for the subcontinent's Muslims, Islam had always been above the fray of politics and retribution.

The man Vice President Bush dined with had now started the alteration and adulteration of the very bedrock on which Pakistan was founded. General Zia was attempting to dictate his specific ideal of what Islam was, an version in stark contrast to what many Pakistanis viewed as correct. Worse yet, the unexpected outcome was that by relying on a domestic policy grounded in one man's interpretation of Islam, Zia had stripped the religion of its former unifying factor. Instead it was now used to highlight tensions between diverse groups, a tactic the wily general used to further his policy of divide and conquer.

Under his Islamization program Zia had transferred many types of criminal cases from civil courts to newly-appointed religious courts, where defendants had no legal representation nor right to appeal. Draconian punishments were inflicted in the name of a merciful God. Pakistan's judicial system was being dragged from the 20th century back into the dark ages, as General Zia became caught up in the public trappings of religion, meanwhile degrading it into a heartless ritual. Like the reigning family of Saudi Arabia, Pakistan's dictator was a classic example of a Muslim ruler who had sold out to worldly wealth and power.

The founder of the country, Muhammad Ali Jinnah, had been pro-modern, not pro-western. He had foreseen the need for Pakistan to reconcile her fundamental Islamic structure, which he would not have changed, with a combination of the best strengths of the Western world. The progressive Jinnah had wanted roads, not Elvis. This should not have presented any problem for a religion that was not only practical, but destined for continued growth. General Zia was intent instead on enacting his version of Islam from the top down. Unlike the Prophet Mohammad, who surrounded himself with the weak and poor of early Arab society, the Islamabad dictator rubbed elbows with generals, robber barons and feudal landlords. Zia's historical role model had been the

Mughal emperor Aurangzeb, known as the "Prayer Monger," who used Islam to rule India with a rod of iron.

With her limited resources Pakistan should have been bending all her efforts towards lessening poverty, curbing disease, building roads, schools and growing more food. Instead Zia maintained a lavish ultra-modern military machine, complete with F-16 attack jets, guided missiles and a burgeoning nuclear weapons program, meanwhile maintaining a religious police mentality that punished the poor, the uneducated and the politically oppressed. It was farcical.

The mighty general had never learned the difference between Islam the personal faith and Islam the political ideology. He couldn't grasp the difference between religious dogma and spirituality. He was aping the imperialists, who had said religion was a segment of life, not a way of life.

In his effort to crush the very people he supposedly served, Zia overlooked a critical historical fact. Islam taught that truth is worked out in the consciences of individual people, not imposed from above, that moral sanctions could only come from the *ummah*, the community, and never from a head of state. He had managed to thrust his people into a fire of religious contradictions. Their religion, principles and values were being rendered meaningless as despair and defeatism set in across Pakistan.

If Ali Muhammad was no politician, he was equally no theologian. He was a musician and a man in love. He knew what he knew and had a hard time expressing it. The news about Bush reminded him of a place that had almost no emotional hold over him. He would have been happy to spend the last breath of his life looking at the skyline of his beloved Peshawar.

As he handed the newspaper back to the young man next to him, Ali sought for the right words, tried to say what it was like to not fit into either world, never truly a part of Pakistan, never emotionally able to ever return to his previous existence in faraway New Orleans. The look on Bugi's face said he was waiting for an answer to the complicated moral and political questions that bound the two countries together as effectively as the small seat holding the two men shoulder to shoulder. For a moment Ali Muhammad sat silent, rushing through the night to embrace the sea changes in his life.

The driver was starting to nod off over the wheel. Ali reached over and shook him on the shoulder. A grateful smile was his reward. The wheels kept rolling and Ali Muhammad looked through the open front door for answers. They had been traveling for more than twelve hours and Rawalpindi was still a long, long way off. Ali Muhammad was no Alexander the Great, able to slice through the Gordian Knot of Pakistan's problems. He didn't know what to say except he was sorry for the sense of betrayal he knew Bugi felt, sorry he couldn't explain the vast difference between the average American and a slick professional politician like George Bush, sorry he couldn't offer some advice regarding the ongoing attack on the religion that bound them both together.

Ali Muhammad knew many people felt General Zia had disgraced Islam. Religion used to control people was never true religion. It was empty. It was knowledge without fire, dogma without belief. It was fascism cloaked in Islamic robes.

Not content to rule the country, the ruthless despot had turned the people's religion into part of his war machine. Thus on an international level, the teachings of the Prophet were being prostituted to bring in American dollars ostensibly to fight communism and heroin production. Meanwhile it provided the general with the domestic moral justification needed to destroy his political opponents and choke the life out of the country.

Zia was more than a mere usurper residing in the mansions of the former colonialists, and willingly assuming their heavy-handed role in crushing his own people. He lay like an entrenched serpent on the bloody throne he had seized from the murdered Bhutto. The executioner of Pakistan's Prime Minister had draped himself in the robes of a Pharaoh's piety, while spitting in the eye of God. General Zia had unwittingly assumed the role of Pakistan's MacBeth, arrogant, cursed, unknowingly rushing towards his own doom.

How could simple Ali Muhammad have answered all of that?

Khyber Knights

40

What Price Love

The road to Shaheen was a winding one, proof that the heart does not always lead a man in the most sensible of directions.

Sunrise found Ali Muhammad red eyed and emotionally alone.

He and Wajid the driver had been the only ones capable of seeing the journey through to its bone-grinding conclusion. The other passengers had dropped off to sleep from either exhaustion, terror or both. Even the insistent Bugi had finally surrendered to the song of Morpheus, leaning his tired young head in gentle, unsuspecting sleep on the older man's patient shoulder.

That irony did not escape Ali Muhammad as he watched the outlines of Rawalpindi finally begin to fill the tilted windscreen of the old bus. Late in the night and nodding from exhaustion, Bugi had come to a parting of the way with his fellow passenger.

Though he had no hesitation in denouncing what he perceived as American interference in the domestic affairs of Pakistan, Bugi was equally unashamed to ask Ali Muhammad if he could help the student manage a visa to visit the United States. Ali was not surprised to encounter such an apparent dichotomy. The hunger to escape Pakistan to that hazy, ill-defined source of Coca-Cola, free love, and Hollywood starlets was all too real to an intellectually curious bundle of energy like Bugi. Boys his age did not dream of running away to the circus. They dreamed of Los Angeles, New York and Miami as though they were unattainable planets. If presented the chance they would have left Pakistan with a grieving heart, but they would have left.

Unable to help, and unwilling to mislead his fellow passenger, Ali Muhammad had stared through the windshield into the night's inky darkness, wishing Bugi would leave him alone and not pester him with his repeated request.

"Why do you even live here? Why? Why? When you could live there," Bugi finally asked Ali in frustration and anger.

Tired and impatient, Ali Muhammad turned to Bugi and expressed out loud the burden he was carrying in his heart.

"I am in love with a Pathan prostitute."

Even in the badly-lighted bus, Ali saw Bugi's eyebrows arch in total shock. Yet the younger man said nothing, asked no questions, demanded no details, just turned and looked out the window as if the previous conversation they had been carrying on for hours had never occurred. Despite his sincere attempts at Westernizing his outlook, the truth so stunned Bugi he never spoke another word to Ali Muhammad during the course of the trip.

Twenty hours after he boarded, Ali Muhammad stepped off the Wajid Flying Coach in Rawalpindi. Bugi rushed off, never saying goodbye, acknowledging what Ali Muhammad already suspected, that no self-respecting Pakistani would condone or understand his love for Shaheen.

The weary lover gave it no mind, just immediately made his way to a connecting bus to Lahore. The madness of the Grand Trunk Road seemed positively refreshing after the two-lane horror called the Karakorum Highway. By 1 p.m. Ali had reached the city of his desire.

To say he was tired would have been an understatement. He trudged through Lahore until he located a *musafar khana* (cheap traveler's hotel). He paid, then stumbled like a sleep walker to his rented room. Inside he turned on the overhead fan, locked the door and fell onto the bed exhausted. It was his impatient heart that soon awoke him from a sound sleep. Stripping naked, he stepped inside the concrete floored-cubicle that served as a bathroom, ran a bucket of cold water, and promptly dumped it over his entire body.

The bracing shock of the chilly water brought his lethargic body to attention. In less than an hour he was shaved, bathed, wearing clean shalwar kameez and on his way to Shaheen.

Under his arm he tenderly carried a small bundle. As Ali Muhammad made his way across the busy city he made sure no one bumped it. In his shirt pocket were lodged two purple five-hundred-rupee notes. He hoped to bribe any policeman curious enough to stop him. All around Ali were the traces of former civilizations. Many of the old streets still hosted the same crafts and guilds that had graced their cobblestones since medieval times. The past was alive in beautiful Lahore that late summer afternoon. Part of her heritage was still flourishing in that intoxicating living museum patrolled by a cast of colorful actors. Even if Ali Muhammad had not been preoccupied, it would have been easy to forget America ever existed.

As he made his way past buildings that were old when the British arrived, Ali Muhammad sighed a breath of relief, glad that he had made the choices he had. He loved the old buildings and the twisting streets, even if it was a romantic luxury on his part and a hardship on the people who had to live there. Lahore, Peshawar, all Pakistan were harsh and often dirty, but Ali knew he was at least free from prostrating himself before the almighty American dollar. His life was driven now by something more important than financial gain.

When his footsteps at last took him past the canal, and into the dead-end alley that contained Shaheen's house, he knew he was as close to Paradise as he had ever come in that lifetime.

Life is no respecter of lovers, and the thorny path to Shaheen's heart started at her gate. As soon as he turned the corner Ali Muhammad saw a man already standing at the portal of his hopeful romance. An imported Japanese car was parked nearby. The American Muslim made his way cautiously up to the gate, still afire with desire, but unsure if he should advance or flee. Hearing footsteps behind him, the other visitor turned, saw Ali Muhammad and sent him a smile in way of greeting.

What Price Love

Without hesitation, the unknown stranger knocked loudly at the gate, then turned to face the equestrian traveler.

Ali's fellow petitioner was six feet tall and well built, the broad shoulders and slim waist making him appear graceful and virile. He appeared to be in his late twenties. His skin was shiny and dark. The color of cafe au lait, Ali thought. The man's face was a composition in extremes. A generous nose rested beneath laughing, coal-black eyes. The large jet-black mustache twirling across his face touched deep dimples in either cheek. A cruel mouth sat in the middle. He was crowned with a mass of black curls that swept down past his ears and nearly reached his shoulders. He looked like a dark angel.

Whoever he was, he was not only handsome, he was obviously well-to-do. His shalwar kameez were freshly tailored and primly starched. An expensive gold wristwatch graced his left wrist. He appeared rich and arrogant, a preening peacock of a man who took great pride in his good looks and expensive apparel.

Before Ali Muhammad could say so much as "Hello" the other man took the initiative.

"Khan sahib I can get you a beautiful girl," the unknown stranger told Ali Muhammad. A leering smile told the American that his mission was no secret, and though well dressed, that this fellow must be a pimp.

"I've come to see a special girl. Another one won't do," Ali Muhammad countered.

A smile played across the man's face, revealing stained teeth. Despite his handsome countenance, his breath was rancid, a hint it seemed of the corruption hiding inside the handsome exterior.

The Pakistani was clearly amused at Ali's attempt at conjugal fidelity. The stranger did not argue, only beat on the gate impatiently as if he were expected. Ali was just deciding that he disliked this man intensely, when he noticed the stranger was wearing Shaheen's ring. The small delicate silver band, set with blue lapis lazuli, that Ali had given her was now riding on the little finger of the stranger's right hand.

Several things suddenly happened at once. The gate opened, revealing Shaheen. At the same moment the pimp saw Ali Muhammad staring at the ring. The dark-skinned man smiled at Ali, delighting in my friend's combination of recognition, ignorance and innocence. The stranger then reached up and squeezed Shaheen's chin in a rough greeting, handling her like a servant. She shook off the man's advances but said nothing in protest.

She was even more beautiful than Ali Muhammad had recalled. Her long, shiny black hair had tiny silver bells laced into her locks. Her full bosom was covered by a tight-fitting, cranberry-colored, embroidered top that left her midriff bare. The pants were a billowing match. A shiny gold silk scarf hung around her neck like an afterthought. She was barefoot. She was gorgeous.

Ali felt his throat constrict at the sight of her. There before him was the bewitching mirage that had led him to risk his life by riding over the perilous parri. He stood mute in Shaheen's presence, aware that he had no shallow feelings for this woman. Seeing her breath rise and fall, observing her full red lips, smelling the subtle perfume wafting towards him, Ali knew he was in the presence of physical beauty so nearly perfect it could make sick men whole. He was starving for the feel of her body, would have charged Satan's legions if it meant she would embrace him in welcome.

Only Shaheen's eyes bid him a guarded greeting. She who had so fiercely attacked the car-load of Punjabi pimps on his last visit was uncharacteristically sullen at the sight of the other man.

"Is she not like a soothing balm on a wound?" the pimp said softly. Yet his voice carried no trace of deep emotion. Instead the dalla weighed Shaheen in his eye like a man does his mare before a race, wondering if his investment of capital will repay his expense. When he turned to look at Ali Muhammad the pimp's smiling face said he knew he had found his mark.

"I'm Shaheen's husband, Maroof. Come into my house. I want to talk to you."

The American froze with shock. Seeing the impact of his news, Maroof slapped Ali Muhammad on the back as if to allay his fears. As he walked through the gate Maroof tossed off a curt command to his wife.

"Feed us," he ordered, then made his way inside without glancing back to see if he was obeyed.

Ali Muhammad stood speechless, unsure if he should obey his heart or the pimp's command.

It was Shaheen who decided for him. A look of tenderness and understanding played across her delicate features. Though ignorant of formal education, she knew the effect her beauty had on men, the ability it had to strike them dumb, or freeze them in place.

"So Ali have you come from Gilgit to see me?"

He held out the package in mute testimony of that truth.

"Come inside," she said softly to her suitor, and, like a schoolboy, he obeyed.

Three charpoys were pulled up in the courtyard.

Lounging on the string beds were the three whores Ali Muhammad remembered, as well as a an attractive teenage girl and an older woman. The American was given no more than a moment to glance in that direction. Shaheen closed the large metal gate, then lead Ali towards a room that sat off from the rest of the house. She motioned him to go inside, then, without waiting or speaking, made her way across to the kitchen located on the far side of the courtyard.

Maroof was waiting for him. It was a good sized-room with an overhead fan. It also possessed a hitherto unseen door. From its direction Ali could tell this door exited from the house into a different part of the neighborhood than that which the main gate served. A real bed, with a foam mattress, was shoved up against the far wall. Linoleum had been laid on the floor. Large red pillows were propped against one wall. A series of built-in cabinets lined two of the walls. Through their glass fronts Ali could see folded clothes.

What Price Love

The pimp leaned up against the red pillows, smoking a cigarette, taking his ease under the whirling fan. He motioned with his hand for Ali Muhammad to take a seat beside him on the floor. The house was quiet except for the sound of the five women laughing and talking outside. Yet Ali Muhammad sensed that the air felt tense, as if some previously-ignored secret were about to be revealed and everyone in the house dreaded its dawning.

"My father recently died in Swat," Maroof told his visitor. He looked up at the ceiling as if contemplating that loss. Ali noticed the pimp was smoking a Gold Leaf cigarette, Pakistan's most expensive brand.

"Shaheen was only temporarily in charge during my absence. Now that my mother and sister have returned with me from our village, my wife will once again resume her place. I heard of your visit from my other girls. Shaheen seemed reluctant to share either that news or her blessings with me," Maroof said. He held up his hand to admire the slender ring gracing its finger, then smiled at Ali Muhammad, clearly contemptuous of the other man's deep-seated emotion for his wife.

Ali Muhammad had no chance to inquire as to what Maroof meant before the dapper host began complaining about General Zia's efforts to drive the Hira Mandi prostitutes out of business.

"Zia is threatening my livelihood. The house is quiet tonight because the police are crawling around the neighborhood scaring off my customers. Even before his death, my father told me to beware, that times were changing. I need to start thinking about steering my business into a new direction, but in order to do that I'll need money."

Maroof paused, then took careful stock of Ali Muhammad. The smile the pimp was so fond of played across his face, as some hidden thought or agenda obviously amused the flesh peddler.

"Why don't you marry Shaheen? I'll take five lakh for her. That's 500,000 rupees, about $25,000," Maroof asked.

Seeing the doubt crossing Ali Muhammad's face, the pimp hastened to dispel his concerns. He didn't hesitate to recount a vibrant description of Shaheen's bodily charms, her deep technical skill, and her intimate secrets.

"She's not really my wife, only my cousin. Besides, one woman's not enough for me," the entrepreneur of lust bragged, and took a deep drag of his cigarette.

Ali Muhammad had come to see Shaheen with expectations that appeared penniless compared to such news. His mind raced at the offer, as well as the mechanics involved in making it come to pass. Obviously his original concern regarding Maroof had been largely misplaced. Emotional jealousy did not enter into the pimp's reasoning. It was the money that counted. The plain-dealing villian saw Ali not as a romantic rival, but rather a wealthy overseas buyer of valuable property. Maroof's blunt offer reminded Ali of purchasing the horses at the Sargohda Remount Depot. The pimp showed no more sign of emotional loss than had Colonel Chugtai when he sold the geldings. Maroof wasn't a husband, Ali realized, only the owner of a beautiful mare.

"Five lakh?" Ali repeated quietly.

"You've seen her beauty. Five lakh is a bargain."

"Five lakh?"

Ali Muhammad knew he would have to sell his house in Peshawar. He would have nothing left, but if he had Shaheen that would not matter.

"What if she won't agree to marry me?" he asked.

"No need to ponder if unpoured milk will spill. She will do as I order," Maroof replied confidently.

The negotiations were cut short at the sound of the azan coming from a nearby mosque. The call to the evening prayer came floating over the wall of the house, reminding all men, even those two, that their allotted time on Earth was brief and that other issues must take precedence over that unresolved matter of the heart. They stood, then withdrew together to the courtyard, where Maroof showed Ali where he could perform **wuzu** (ritual ablution). Once their ablutions were completed, the two men stood shoulder to shoulder on two small prayer rugs placed in the courtyard for their use by one of the prostitutes. At the completion of the normal prayer, Ali Muhammad joined Maroof in offering up a *janaza* prayer for the soul of his father, the dead pimp.

"Put the rugs away, would you," Maroof asked Ali Muhammad, and pointed to the room closest to the courtyard. After shaking off the dust, the American carefully folded the rugs and carried them into the bedroom of Naheed. He felt embarrassed to see where the young woman plied her trade. Unsure of where to put the rugs, he laid them on the end of Naheed's charpoy. No sooner had he done so than she entered behind him.

"No, no. Not there. That is where I work. It is dirty," she explained patiently, and lifting the two little rugs, placed them on a shelf near the door.

Despite her depravity, the whore was very attentive to the duties of her religion.

When Naheed lead him back outside, Ali Muhammad saw Shaheen carrying a large covered pot into the room he had so recently vacated. With Raja's former lover leading the way, my friend crossed the courtyard and re-entered Maroof's private chambers.

A large plastic table cloth had been spread out on the linoleum. Seven plates lined the edge. Maroof sat on the floor at the far end, clearly placed at what served as the head of the table. His mother, a stout woman in her fifties, occupied the opposite end. Ali was told to sit next to Maroof. The pimp's sister, a dark-haired teenager with passable good looks, sat opposite. The three whores were spread along both sides. They chattered like magpies, taking little notice of the American. Shaheen had placed the pot in the middle of the tablecloth, then sat down demurely next to her mother-in-law. She carefully avoided looking at Ali, keeping her eyes on the piece of bread lying in front of her.

Maroof leaned back on one hand, waiting for Aesha, the closest prostitute, to pass her master's plate down to his mother. The older woman had meanwhile lifted the lid off the pot, and taking up a ladle,

What Price Love

portioned out a generous serving to the son she so clearly adored. When Ali's plate was returned to him, he saw it contained slices of water buffalo stomach. The gray tripe swam in a rose red chili sauce. He had little appetite, from the effects of love sickness and Shaheen's proximity, not from any culinary weakness. Yet the American tore off pieces of the bread laid in front of him and scooped up the repast with no hint of aversion.

The conversation was light, the atmosphere relaxed. Ali wondered if he was being sized up as a potential son-in-law? Though his host and hostesses were occupied illegally, he otherwise felt at home. Muslims were unlike Hindus. They were prepared to accept converts, and had no inhibitions about eating or drinking with anyone, regardless of their creed, national origin or social status. Ali's foreign birth only made him an oddity, not a pariah.

When the meal was completed, Shaheen brought her husband and Ali Muhammad two bottles of Bubble Up. Ali sipped the lemon-lime drink to be polite, while the women scurried about cleaning up. They were clearly intent on leaving the two men undisturbed to further their previous discussion. When they were alone again, the pimp spoke confidentially to his prospective customer.

"I must go. I'm driving down to Karachi, won't be back for several days," Maroof told Ali.

He ignored the cold drink, instead placing a large leaf of paan inside his mouth. The mild narcotic had stained his teeth beet red. The wad swelled out the man's left cheek until he looked like dark-skinned squirrel. He stood to go and Ali Muhammad followed him.

"The Prophet said women are either millstones or gemstones resting around a man's neck. Shaheen is a diamond I am prepared to sell to you. Think on my offer," he said, then hugged his guest goodbye as custom dictated.

When the American started to follow him towards the door, Maroof stopped him short.

"Oh no, I know the way out," he said laughing. "You stay here and sample the delights of my house."

Then he was gone and Ali Muhammad did as he was told and stood there while he heard Maroof take leave of his mother, and bid the whores goodbye. If he spoke to Shaheen, Ali Muhammad did not hear it. A few minutes after the gate was closed the object of Ali's desire came into the room alone. She closed the door behind her softly, running a large deadbolt across to secure the entrance.

Once again Ali Muhammad found himself unsure of the protocol. Something in his soul urged him to keep Maroof's offer secret until Shaheen mentioned it. He stood there looking at this woman he had traveled across Pakistan to find. If she had beckoned to him from the far side of a pit of fire, Ali would have leapt in without hesitation to reach her.

Instead Shaheen glided across the room on her silent bare feet. Coming up next to Ali she placed her hands around his neck without hesitation. She held him fast with eyes as soft as a gazelle's. Without waiting for permission, she surprised the traveler by kissing him. Her saliva was sweet like honey. He thought his heart would burst through his chest at the touch of her body. Then she pulled back and looked at him carefully, her full lipped smile burning him like the sun.

"So, what have you brought me Ali Muhammad?"

Reluctantly he stepped away, retrieved his burden and brought it to her. When she unwrapped it, a delicate white tea pot was revealed. Its snow-white surface was covered with tiny red roses that climbed its shiny walls.

"From China like I requested?" she asked him.

"Yes, from China. I discovered it in Gilgit and brought it away with me."

The courtesan placed the delicacy into one of the cabinets, then walked towards the bed. With her back turned to Ali, she reached up and pulled off the cranberry top, then stepped out of her loose trousers. She hung her head back and shook out her thick tresses, when she did the tiny silver bells laced into her hair sang a little song of impending ecstasy. Then she slowly turned and faced the American.

Loving Shaheen was no light burden. The sight of her drove two daggers into him, one into his burning eyes, the other into his smoking heart. Patience was bitter but here was its sweetest fruit. Her perfect body would have insulted the most flawless marble.

"*Jahnanna* (beloved)," he whispered then walked towards her, followed her into that deep bed and let his body, that runaway servant, surrender at last to the tyranny that had whipped it impatiently since last he lay with her.

Shaheen soothed the weary traveler, pulling him down into the deep rest that only she could give, jangling her bells as she allowed him to penetrate her secrets, pretending that she cared for Ali Muhammad, lover, traveler, sincere man and fool.

When he had spent himself, he lay beside her, radiating heat, dizzy, gasping for breath, unsure if he still occupied that mortal shell binding him to earth. At last he grew at ease. Her kiss and her own passion had emboldened him. Ali Muhammad believed that Shaheen must know and approve of Maroof's plan to wed her away to the American. He reached up and touched her cheek with utter tenderness. In all his travels he had never encountered even the suspicion of this depth of feeling.

"It is not easy for me to look upon your beautiful face," he told her.

Shaheen lay curled alongside him, her head resting on his left arm as a pillow, looking off into space and pondering their mutual future he thought. Sensing her approval he broached a question.

"I want to sleep with you."

"You just have."

"No, not this. I want to sleep beside you. To hold you."

She did not argue. Some premonition seemed to have gripped Shaheen. She rose in silence and began dressing, bidding him do likewise. When they were decently attired, she walked to the opposite side of the room and opened the previously-unseen door. Though there

Khyber Knights

"'The Prophet said women are either millstones or gemstones resting around your neck. Shaheen is a diamond I am prepared to sell to you,' the pimp told Ali Muhammad."

What Price Love

were no people currently passing by, he knew it was unseemly to handle her physically in plain view. When she told him to return to that same door after midnight, Ali Muhammad took his leave with no more than a look at her sad-eyed radiance. If he had needed further proof of her blessing, he walked away knowing she had not asked him for money.

If there was a tide in the affairs of Ali Muhammad's heart, it reached its peak that night. He struck out boldly from the shallows, leaving behind the shore of his fears, braving the strong currents in the hope his effort would bear him to either the woman he loved, or a loss of that venture that burned his heart but denied him peace.

He left his tiny room after midnight with his few possessions slung in a shoulder bag. The city streets were dark. During the hot summer months there was not enough electricity to service the entire city. Consequently "load shedding" caused the eager lover to tread his careful way through a temporary black-out. He went cautiously, trying to avoid attracting attention, as well as holes in the road. Ali Muhammad's heart was his compass and Shaheen his dark-haired guiding star. He could have found her blindfolded.

Yet he knew his mission was the cause of great peril. Though Maroof had offered to sell the woman like the family cow, the husband would be within his rights to slay Ali Muhammad if he discovered him in her bed that night. Her fate if discovered did not dare be thought of. Though Maroof did not love Shaheen, he was fanatically jealous of his property to the point of insanity. And jealousy, as Ali knew, was not a meaningless word among the Pathan tribesmen.

When he reached the darkened doorway, Ali felt his heart beating in his chest. From base fear, or anxious love, he did not know. He was sweating and scared. With shaking hand he timidly knocked thrice.

Before his heart had beat twice Shaheen had opened the door and pulled him within, quickly closing and locking the door behind him. The room was empty and he saw the bolt on the door leading out into the courtyard was also locked.

More importantly, though the room was dimly lit by only a single candle, he could clearly see Shaheen was blazing with fury. The woman's face was distorted with anger, reminiscent of the time she attacked the kidnapping pimps at her front gate.

"Are you here to pick up your goods?" she hissed at him in contempt.

The undisguised disdain she flung at him caused Ali Muhammad to freeze in shock. Here was a woman who worked only on animal instinct, and that instinct said she had been wronged by two men, one of which unfortunately had returned unawares to see her.

"I thought Maroof told you?" Ali Muhammad said weakly. "He said he wasn't married to you."

"He's a black liar. He is my legal husband and my first cousin," she whispered, then turned her back towards him in an act of total rejection.

Ali became desperate. He hastily stepped next to her and tried to turn her around but she shrugged off his hand in protest.

"Shaheen I didn't know. I thought you wanted to come away with me. Maybe to Peshawar, or if need be even America," he said and groaned inside at the thought of returning there, but prepared to visit Hell itself for this scornful lover.

He stood there ignored, rejected, foreign, contemptuous in his own eyes, hating his own uncertainty. On a small table between him and the bed he saw a photograph. It showed a younger Shaheen, smiling, happy, unlike this trapped and sorrowful creature who refused to even look at him. Next to her in the photograph was an attractive older woman and a smiling, handsome young man. Denied a chance to look at the real object of his desires, he picked up the photo instead.

"Is this your family?" he asked softly.

She glanced over her right shoulder, then turned back to face him. He could see the anger starting to ease. He swore at that instant that should he ever in fact win her love he would try to avoid the rough side of her tongue. This was a woman who would slide a dagger between your ribs and twist. He held the picture towards her in mute supplication of his sincere innocence. When Shaheen saw the image dangled before her like a talisman, her features softened. She reached out and gently took the frame from Ali's hand. The sensation of her soft fingertips gave him hope. Shaheen stared down at the photograph, then replaced it on the table, but kept her eyes on the images before her.

"That is my mother and my only brother. They live in Swat, in the same village as my husband's family."

"What does your mother think of what he is making you do?"

Shaheen gave him a look of pity, saying without words that she understood he was only an ignorant, half-witted Angrez who did not comprehend the workings of the world.

"What can she do? The old woman you saw today, my aunt, as well as my mother, they were both born to this work, as am I. Whichever I bear, sons or daughters, they too will be a part of this *dumann* (caste). We are like the musicians and *dacoits* (bandits), a low caste without hint of escape," she told him gently, and touched her family's photograph in token of surrender to the fate that crystallized in such ancestral evil.

When she turned to face him, Shaheen's face was devoid of anger. In its place was another look, that of guarded hope.

"Would you really pay that much for me?"

"Yes. I would sell everything precious to me to take you from this place. Haven't you ever heard of AIDS?" he asked and tried to explain the plague.

She grew impatient at the discussion of the foreign disease. Its symptoms frightened and confused her.

"Leave it! Allah will take care of Shaheen," she said brusquely.

She stood there then, looking at him, weighing him, deciding of what further use he could be in her limited understanding of the world. Finally, her mind made up, she issued a single order.

"Don't offer Maroof more than two lakh rupees to start," Shaheen told Ali Muhammad, then blew out the candle.

What Price Love

Once again she permitted him to lie with her, but in the humid darkness he found only relief from his itch, and no comfort for his soul. Shaheen allowed Ali to hold her, but she kept her own counsel. They lay there in Maroof's bed, staying quiet in that darkened room, two people who knew the ins and outs of each other's bodies, but nothing of the secret chambers of the other's heart.

Her jealous reaction to Maroof's rejection still bore down on Ali. He wanted some snatch of honor in regards to Shaheen. He knew his Peshawari friends would deride her as a "taxi", a whore to be ridden, then disposed of. But Ali's *niyat*, his intention, was pure despite the circumstances surrounding Shaheen's discovery. He believed that the world had served the beautiful young woman ill. Yet he knew enough about Pakistan to wonder if Maroof had not swindled other lovers, setting a honeyed trap using Shaheen's beauty as bait?

In the dark, and in desperation, he tried to trust her.

"If you lived in the city or in the forest, you would always live in my heart," he whispered to her, repeating the words of a famous Pushtu love song. She gave him no answer, breathing softly as though she was asleep. She snuggled up against him, the movement of her warm, naked body causing the silver bells to tinkle in the dark. He fell asleep thinking that the sound of her bells was sweeter to his ears than the songs of pious angels.

During the depth of the night his need came on him again. In the darkness he moved his manhood into her secrets. She accommodated him, never really awakening, letting him use her body as his needs must, then moved away across the bed. Ali was sunk in a deep slumber when he heard a pounding and a screaming from outside the walls of the house.

"Shaheen!" filled the night, followed by another series of poundings.

"Shaheen! Open up," rang a harsh cry through the night.

"Maroof," she said and shook Ali Muhammad to wake him. There was no need. He was already tearing into his clothes.

"Shaheen, wake up you worthless *meteeza* (slut)."

"Hurry," she urged the American.

She had pulled on her shalwar kameez and already opened the back door, whipping him in whispers to hasten his departure lest his laggard behavior get them both killed. Ali grabbed his shoulder bag, rushed to the door, but stopped short of leaving, turning instead to whisper to Shaheen.

"Kiss me goodbye," he said and held her arms in order to force her to obey.

"OK, goodbye," Shaheen replied, kissed him briefly, then shoved him through the door, locking it behind him.

Ali Muhammad stood in the doorway, trying to soak up her departing essence, but then he heard her open the other door and he knew she had left him. When he turned he found himself in the obscure dirt alleyway. He was miserably alone, except for the pain in his heart, and the bittersweet knowledge that in theory he could buy Shaheen's freedom. That is if she agreed to leave. Reluctantly he began walking through the sleeping city. The red wings of dawn were spreading overhead and a gentle breeze blew the tears off his face, as my friend made his way back towards the horse trip and the hellish juggle now dominating his life.

41
Music of the Nomads

Ali Muhammad was not the only one with problems.

The sound of the sirens threw Raja and me into a perfect frenzy of activity, as we rushed about grabbing saddles, weapons, hoof picks, clothes, and the minutiae of equestrian travel. Ours was not an orderly departure. We were in fact heading towards the horses with our arms straining under their loads, when little Armin Baig came running into the hotel.

My anger and anxiety were increasing by the minute. Hung over and furry-tongued, I was loath to be captured, detained, or seized, had in fact no desire to discover what polite term the authorities would use before throwing us into the local lockup. Head aching and paranoid, I was unprepared to hear either the sirens pass us by, heading on out of town, or for Bul Bul Jon to pop his head out of the kitchen with the answer to the all the hubbub.

"The plane went down," he said anxiously, then pulled his head back into the kitchen to pry more news from his son the informant.

"It disappeared on its way to Rawalpindi," he shouted to us, and both Raja and I stopped dead in our tracks, knowing now that the noise roaring by outside was not directed towards us.

If my heart stopped beating as rapidly, my curiosity however was piqued. I threw my load onto the hotel table. Raja did likewise. We then walked into the kitchen to find father and son in an eager exchange.

PK303 was gone from the clear blue skies without a trace.

The 43 passengers and crew had taken off from the tiny Gilgit airport in the twin engine Fokker prop plane with no hint of trouble. Owing to the short runway, and the towering mountains looming dead ahead, the pilot had braked the plane, all the while revving up the engines until they were screaming in protest. When it was apparent not another ounce of energy was forthcoming, he released the brake, flinging the fragile craft down the runway as fast as it could go.

It was barely airborne, when it was forced to bank sharply to the right, in order to avoid crashing headlong into a sheer wall of rock. The aeronautical daredevil then traditionally flew south above the Indus river gorge, gaining altitude, until he managed to raise the plane at least close to the mountain tops. Owing to the extreme heights of the massifs on either side, the Gilgit to Rawalpindi route was considered one of the world's most dangerous flights.

News of the mystery spread quick. PK303 had flown off, called back once to report that everything was fine, then disappeared. Outside, we could hear people running by on their way to the airport at the edge of town. In a place as small as Gilgit, I knew everyone would lose a friend, neighbor or relative.

If Raja and I had not already decided to leave, there was now no hesitation left. Neither of us looked forward to remaining in the grief-stricken town. We set about preparing the horses, brushing them well, saddling them slowly, packing our gear carefully. We shared the job of getting big Pahlwan ready for the road, making sure that Ali Muhammad's gear was safely stowed. After thanking Bul Bul Jon for our headaches and a good rest, the Afridi and I swung into our saddles and rode out of the town we had been so anxious to reach.

The main street was full of confusion. Tractors were racing by. Women had come out of their houses, and, along with their menfolk, were making their mutual way towards the airport. Grief was rippling through the populace. These were mountain people who understood the cruel caprices of their harsh environment.

Pasha could sense the excitement and acted up accordingly. Luckily Raja had offered to take Pahlwan behind the never excitable Pajaro. I sawed back and forth on the snaffle bit, urging my mischievous gelding to settle down and attend to his business. I could hardly blame him. All around us were the growing traces of a coming emotional eruption. The ugly reality of the 20th century had come to sleepy Gilgit.

For centuries it had been an isolated place. Towering mountains guarded the approach to the site many travelers believed was the model for the fabled Shangri-La. During the brief summer Gilgit's citizens had traditionally busied themselves growing, drying and storing enough food to fight off the frightening winter. When the wind died down, the men of the area took up their famous pastimes of plundering caravans, kidnapping and slavery. In those olden days the fun-loving Gilgitis were fond of capturing foreigners and using them as human firecrackers. Then the outside world started arriving in stages. The first British officer was stationed in Gilgit in the 1860s. He often went ten months or more without seeing another European.

When the first cargo plane landed in 1944 it disgorged a jeep. Thinking the plane had given birth to a child, the people ran to give fodder to the jeep, fearing the baby would fly away unless it was immediately fed. Even up until the mid-1960s the people of the region were famous for their health. A man who lived to be a hundred was no oddity in Gilgit. Once renowned for their longevity, the people were recently starting to be treated for mental illnesses caused by the disruption of their lifestyle from the intrusion of the outside world.

Even without a prying military cop, Raja and I knew it was time to go.

It would have been hard to get lost. We rode south on the Karakorum Highway. At first the great road ran through miles of farmland. Yet soon the tidy little houses petered out, the tractors stopped passing, and we riders and horses were alone on an increasingly lonely road.

The highway had taken fifteen years to build and claimed the lives of 900 men, one for almost every kilometer of its length. It threaded its

Music of the Nomads

narrow path between the Karakorum and Himalayan mountains, a collision belt of geography rippling with tremors every few minutes.

We had only been in the saddle an hour. Gilgit lay far enough behind us to have eased our previous concerns, when a bus heading in that direction at first slowed down, then stopped in front of us. When the door opened, a grinning Ali Muhammad stepped off. The bus passed on without delay, as our friend walked over to his horse.

"Thought you might be too busy to come back?" I said casually, secretly relieved to know he was safe.

Ali checked Pahlwan's cinch, took the reins from Raja, then swung into the saddle as casually as if he had only just dismounted.

"You need me to guide you home to Peshawar," he told me.

"Guide me to a whorehouse more likely," I replied.

Ali Muhammad smiled and nodded, not attempting to hide either his proclivities nor emotional ambitions. As we rode he told us both of his adventures, and his plan to purchase Shaheen's freedom. His kind blue eyes were brimming with dreams. Raja was unsympathetic. The tribesman only grunted.

"My father told me never trust a snake or a whore," he said, the sour look on Raja's face clearly reminding him of his own moral failings in Lahore.

I too was equally unsympathetic. It was wrong, I thought, to pursue a woman who would neither marry or bed you except for money. Ali Muhammad was running after Shaheen like a puppy begging for scraps I thought. However I kept my counsel, glad to have him back, and even happier to have escaped from Gilgit without incident.

Our friend's trip was not without its benefits for Raja andme. Ali had been delayed in returning on time by a rock slide far down the Karakorum Highway. Though not as severe as the one which we had previously encountered, Ali had known better than to sit on the other side and wait. A bulldozer was already on the job. But when a group of Gilgit bound men suggested making climbing over the boulders and through the rock slide, the impetuous Ali Muhammad had promptly joined them. The rock climbers were rewarded when they managed to locate a driver on the far side of the avalanche who agreed to drive them back to the northern city. When I asked Ali Muhammad what the country up ahead looked like, he had one word.

"Hot."

We stopped early that day, glad to find a village that would feed us. There was little to choose from in the way of food, only corn or okra. Local independence was withering, replaced by that modern idea "commuting." Many villagers now traveled into Gilgit to purchase supplies. That night Pasha managed to wedge his picket rope under his right rear shoe.

The next day the Sunni villagers gave us a kilo of dried apricots as a going-away gift. Though we had left behind the gloomy Ismailis, we now had a new set of difficulties to consider.

Khyber Knights

Our loyal geldings had brought us so far from home, that the year itself had changed. Summer now stood in full flower. Plus the greenery we had grown so used to fled, replaced by an aridity that grew more harsh with every southern step. That second day out we rode only a few hundred feet above the rushing Gilgit river, grown now into a reckless, terrible brute. Suddenly our road brought us to the confluence of the Indus and Gilgit rivers.

That gorge was a terrible place. This was no frothing playful stream hosting fly fishermen and picnics. Passing along under our left stirrups was a thundering discharge of mud, rock and brown water intent on destroying anything that stood between it and the sea. Even the colossal Himalayas were being battered into defeat for daring to try and encompass Neptune's savage stepchild.

The torrent was so loud we had to shout to be heard above the roar of the insatiable monster. We found ourselves encased on all sides by mountains that reared up like dragon's-teeth. Sandstone cliffs and gray granite boulders were evident everywhere. Yet the river road lead us through a landscape that resembled the desert landscape of the Grand Canyon. Not a blade of grass lived down in that gorge. No tenacious tree ever sunk a hopeful root into that sun-blasted blight. It was a suffocating, rock-bound desert ruled by a watery Titan.

A long day in the saddle finally brought us back into the world of men. As evening fell we reached the village of Thelichi. It was a lovely oasis of green and gold offsetting the wilderness around it.

Here we discovered an old British rest house. A stone wall surrounded the adobe bungalow. Tall trees provided shade. The grass underneath was knee deep and succulent. We riders fared less well. There was no chaikhana and the only shop was a tiny affair. Our choices for dinner were scanty, some grapes, or walnuts, either a handful of apricots, or apples, and for desert, a single box of mislabeled crackers instructively entitled "Salty Titbits." We bought and ate everything.

Looming over the hamlet was the mighty mountain, Nanga Parbat, the "Naked Mountain." First seen by a European in 1835, it reared up for 26,660 feet. All around us was a jungle of stone, a portion of the world where 10,000-foot-high peaks were merely childish dots on the map. There were more than 30 mountains nearby in excess of 24,000 feet. Many of them were nameless.

Nanga Parbat differed however. She enjoyed a nasty reputation as a killer. More than 30 climbers from various countries had died trying to scale her inhospitable glassy walls. The villagers of Thelichi believed the mountain was now responsible for the disappearance of PK303. The mountain was so large it normally took the missing Fokker ten minutes to fly around its perimeter. A massive rescue operation had gone into effect, complete with military helicopters combing the route, and mountain guides searching for wreckage between Gilgit and Rawalpindi. A substantial reward was offered for clues, and rumors abounded as to the whereabouts of the aircraft, some people even speculating the plane had been hijacked and taken to neighboring India. Yet no trace of the aircraft had been found.

In Thelichi they had a different idea. The villagers living in the shadow of Nanga Parbat told us the mountain had reached up and devoured the plane. Others confided that the fairies residing on Nanga's summit now had the passengers hidden inside the monster's frozen embrace. The only thing certain was that somewhere in that frozen, stony wasteland 43 people were at the mercy of a landscape too brutal to describe.

Though picturesque, Thelichi was infested with flies and fleas. By morning we had been eaten alive. Our bellies were raw, our ankles swollen, even our eyelids were bitten. Ali had 32 bites on the top of his right hand alone. The musician swore he couldn't affix a postage stamp to any part of his body without covering an insect bite. Scratching and complaining, we left the village thinking it would be a tough day. That was an understatement.

Pasha took me into the unforgiving Diamer Desert, an high altitude wasteland that received less than four inches of rain a year. Overhead loomed that icy slag heap, Nanga Parbat, while underfoot we rode through an unforgiving vise of desolation. The dun trudged up sugar-white sand dunes never kissed by monsoon rains, past boulders bigger than three bedroom houses, over glacial garbage, and across hot lava rocks untouched since Creation.

To add to our pleasure a hot, suffocating wind blew into our faces all day, filling our eyes, ears, and noses with sand. Along the road the government had placed signs for the comfort of rich motorized tourists heading towards distant China via these wretched mountains.

"Stop worrying. Slide area over. Enjoy your trip," one such encouraging billboard read.

The traffic flowing by was evidence that the road was again opened. However we never encountered another traveler. Buses and lorries flew by, bound for either China to the north, or Rawalpindi to the south. Villages lying in between now relied on flagging down a ride. No one walked or rode anymore, and the isolation between villages had increased accordingly as foot traffic diminished.

Raja lead us off the road at sunset into what the map told us was the village of Jalipur. Here we discovered a total of six families living in a pleasing rustic Arcadia. Tall trees, cool shade, and thick grass welcomed the horses. The people however were surprised to see Raja, Ali Muhammad and me. The rest house was standing empty and it was some time before anyone could discover the key. Everyone was pleasant while we waited, offering no hint of the antagonism we had encountered among the Ismailis. Once the creaky door was finally opened we discovered the bungalow was stripped bare of so much as a cobweb. A old register sat on the fireplace mantle. Inside was written an inscription.

"The rest house is in loss hence no proper arrangements can be made. Sorry to visitors."

It was dated almost ten years earlier. No outsider, including Pakistanis, had stopped in forgotten Jalipur since then. The villagers were kind, giving us *mustaki*, a coarse, stomach-filling brown bread for our dinner. With the horses safely picketed near the door, we saddlemen talked quietly in the dark about such people as these who were born, lived, and died in one tiny place. Never knowing what was over the horizon seemed to us inconceivable. We all agreed that something had happened to each of us, even Ali Muhammad. Our lives were now grown accustomed to the differences in the world, each roll of the mountains, each subtle new taste in the brooks, each hard-won meal. We were many things, we three, but we were no longer manageable villagers.

That rugged road brought us next into the Devil's Anvil, a two-day ride through a brutal and unforgiving landscape we covered inch by painful inch. Between Jalipur and the town of Chilas lay a savage, soulless place full of burnt cinders, towering black rocks, and the shifting dazzle of blinding white sunlight.

"When Allah was done with creation He obviously dumped all the extra rocks and sand here," Ali Muhammad croaked.

Raja added, "In Peshawar they say the sun burns up its precious fuel on its long journey across the heavens, but that Allah ordained that in order to rejuvenate it, the sun should be dropped every night into the eternal fires of Hell that rage beneath the earth. I am sure the door must be close by."

I didn't bother to disagree with the obvious, just rode on in grim silence, further away from the shade of mountain or cliff, deeper into that abomination of desolation. The only sound was the steady beat of the horse's hooves, the creak of the saddles, and the soft jingling of the brass bells.

The hot sun beat down on the poor horses like red hot hammers. Pahlwan suffered the most cruelly. The gentle gray looked like he was trapped in a sauna, his pale coat grown dark with sweat. Pajaro did not complain, but even Pasha was at last subdued.

We rode with our eyes blurred and our backs and knees aching. We would have died if not for our turbans. Like the caravans of old, the sight of Chilas caused us to break out in hysterical jubilation. Man had come crawling across the unrelenting hostility of the Diamer desert to this stubborn town since before Christ walked the world. Tired travelers from all parts of Asia, along with their thirsty camels, ponies and donkeys had scanned the wasteland anxiously for a welcome sign of the Chilas caravanserai. The ancient town was compressed tightly between the mountains and the Indus river. The rocks nearby bore many hieroglyphics, inscriptions from ancient Buddhist pilgrims, pictographs, and samples of the various languages, including Hebrew, that had been spoken on this portion of the famous Silk Road.

As was to be expected among religious rivals, the Ismailis inhabiting Gilgit had referred to the rival caravan town of Chilas in the most disparaging terms. We had been assured that the inhabitants of the desert oasis were notoriously intolerant Sunni bigots who would rob us, or slay us, as the mood struck them. Nothing could have been further from the truth. True, as per traditional custom, every man in town sported

Music of the Nomads

a massive beard as a sign of religious piety. Yet they were neither fools nor fanatics, just products of their harsh world.

Chilas was hot, ugly and windy. The awful ambiance burned away the trappings of civilization. Just to survive in such a harsh environment was a daily reminder of the fires of Hell. Men who lived there spoke bluntly, and prayed often.

We found lodging in a decent hotel, bedding the horses in a sandy wasteland behind that building. News of our arrival soon spread among the inhabitants. We had been the first men to ride from Peshawar to Chitral in fifty years. No one however could remember when horsemen had last arrived in Chilas. The geldings had taken us out of the reach of recent memory.

Our animals were invited to graze within the confines of the local electric plant. This fenced-in compound was rich in untended grazing. For two days we let the tired horses rest and eat. Our only problem occurred when I came out one morning to find Pajaro gone. Fearing he had been stolen, I quickly set off in search for him, only to discover the clever horse had untied his picket rope and already strolled down the road to the power plant in search of breakfast. I discovered the easy-going bay eating contentedly. After that Raja made a point of rubbing red chili pepper all over the end of the rope's knots to discourage Pajaro from wandering.

When the horses were not grazing they were filling up on apples or dal. We men slept or ate as well. Knowing we were about to travel up into the mountains once again, we visited the bazaar in search of supplies. The reportedly cruel-hearted men of Chilas laid the lie to the malicious tales spread about them by the Ismailis of Gilgit. In every single instance no shopkeeper took our money, without first offering to give us all of our purchases for free. As travelers from faraway Peshawar, they appreciated how hard our trip had been. Even in the post office our money was at first rejected. Though we knew none of them personally, the denizens of Chilas proved they had passions like ours, and more importantly, respected the bonds and burdens of the road.

Despite such generosity, we longed for the cool green mountains that reared up behind Chilas. Leaving at sunrise, we once again rode through a wasteland of rocks, wondering why everyone had repeatedly assured us of the close proximity of a new type of country. By noon we discovered the bottom of the Babusar canyon, a twisting dirt track wide enough to accommodate a jeep. Single pine trees began to appear, sentinels it seemed of a cooler clime. The horses began to strain as the climb became steeper. Looming up ahead we knew was the infamous Babusar Pass, but we had reasoned incorrectly that our first day's ride would be an easy one.

As the day progressed the occasional splotch of shade became long continued stretches under dark, blue-green pine trees. At one point a crowd of angry men came walking downhill to meet us. A murder had occurred not far ahead. These armed men were hot on the trail of the escaped killer. The numerous guns they carried provided ample evidence that the miscreant could expect no delay in justice from this nest of angry hornets. Ali Muhammad assured them we had so far seen no one, so they let us pass.

I had never met anyone who had journeyed over this forgotten road. Once a well known caravan route, the track over the Babusar Pass was now seldom traveled. Unlike Chitral and Gilgit, everything up ahead was dim and aloof, a barely perceived slice of the Himalayas riddled with strange-sounding names, and whispers of other nomad travelers. We rode on, figures in a tapestry of increasing woodland luxury. It soon became apparent that the air was cooling as our horses took us higher. A rushing river helped chill the air. As the sky darkened we grew increasingly cold eventually having to stop and bundle up in clothes left packed since the faraway Shandur Pass.

After experiencing the thirsty wastes of the Diamer Desert, this new land was a refreshment and a reassurance. We managed to reach the tiny village of Babusar just before the last light of day left the sky. Our overnight home consisted of one little lane, some cedar built cabins, and a single shop. A very dilapidated rest-house stood nearby.

Despite its isolation, the people were cheerful and exceedingly friendly. The men wore embroidered blankets, thick sweaters and wool caps to keep out the cold. Children scampered around the horses. Sheep and goats grazed in the rolling pastures surrounding the village. It was quiet, bucolic, very cold and utterly peaceful.

A chowkidar let us into the bungalow without a murmur of dissent. A large room soon provided us with bedsteads, a rugged table and several chairs. Best of all was the strong aroma of the sweet resin given off by the pine logs burning in the fireplace.

When I went outside to feed and brush the horses I found myself surrounded by a beauty I could barely survive. The mighty mountain looming over the village was bathed in rose-colored light. As a hungry Pasha nudged me, I watched the warm color slowly fade to a cool lavender. Then that too disappeared and the darkened massif touched the black sky above. Here was a sure cure for old age and sorrow, I thought. Regardless of the hardships and the problems, Pakistan had sunk her claws in me. I knew no matter where I traveled, only she could heal the wounds inflicted by such a sunset.

We were up with the dawn, eager to get an early start over the Babusar Pass. While the horses ate, Raja, Ali Muhammad and I attended to our own culinary needs. The town's only chaikhana soon presented us each with a cup of chai, and three plates containing one fried egg and a piece of bread apiece. Still starving, I asked the chai wallah if I could have another egg, only to learn that we had eaten the only three eggs in the village. After paying a few rupees to these kind people, we started our ascent.

There were no signs stating that this was one of mankind's oldest caravan trails, though in fact that is where the horses took us. The dirt track led us away from any trace of human habitation, into a pine forest where the air was so clean it snapped in your lungs. Though we climbed steadily, the Babusar was a gradual ascent like her sister the Lowari, not a lung-busting effort like the Shandur.

We were surprised when we met two herdsmen coming down from the pastures further above. Each of these Pakistani cowboys was riding a miniature pony, urging their black-skinned cattle to move along. It was the first clue that the rumors regarding other nomads was no exaggeration.

As we kept going higher the trees began to struggle to survive, then died off at 11,000 feet. Instead we found ourselves in a high alpine meadow that covered the shoulders of the mountain. The green grass was colored with small flowers resembling forget-me-nots. Their color ranged from snow white, through pastel pink, to a delicate blue. The meadow was exquisite, the air thick with the scent of the flowers.

We could not linger. Overhead we could see the glaring sunlight reflecting off bare gray stones that lay between us and the peak. Pasha took me ever higher, until we reached the summit at two o'clock in the afternoon.

The dun and I stood near our friends, all of us, men and horses, dumbstruck by the secrets revealed before us. The Babusar Pass was 13,696 feet high. The summit was uneven but vast. Surrounding us in all immediate directions were acres of small slate gray stones. A cairn had been raised to mark the summit, though a blind man could have discovered it. Roaring up to greet us was a wind so cold I thought it would strip the meat off our bones. Though the sun burned down, the crest was a cold place, magnificent in its desolation, unwilling to tolerate any life form except the wind and elements. We stood there shaking in bone-chilling misery, unable and unwilling to depart from that mystical place, the severe glory of that vast vista being as brilliant as a frozen dream. Looking about me I wondered why anyone was left in New York, New Orleans or New Albany? Why would one linger there, disaffected with the strains of modern life, when the Babusar offered air so cold and clean it was like wine on one's palate?

The world we knew and loved was laid out before our feet. Turning in my saddle and looking back I could see the snowy white top of Nanga Parbat close behind me, further off still lay the beautiful mountains we had crossed through on our journey from faraway Chitral. Facing front again, I discovered the great Himalayas stretched like a blue line of stone off to the left, on my right ran the mighty Karakorams. When I looked southwest I saw the magic mountains gradually descending into a white mist. In that direction, past those stony ripples, lay my heart's evasive oasis, beloved Peshawar.

A wise Sufi once told me that a man retains an image inside himself that never ages nor changes. During that heady period of his life when he burns hot with the fires of youth, and has not yet tasted the ashes of defeat, he hangs a secret, sacred image of himself in his mind's eyes.

Pasha and I sat there on top of the world together in wind-blown silence. A sense of harmony existed between my mind and body, my horse and myself. Understanding does not always come between man and mount, arrives only after experience and a sometimes painful process. The great dun stood looking into the cold, bitter squall, no trace of servitude in his proud head.

It was that moment with Pasha that I hung with reverence in my mind' eye. Though age would eventually track me down, though love might come and go, friends desert me, and wealth be a forgotten luxury, so long as I breathed I would have the memory of my shared experience atop the Babusar Pass with Pasha.

All the pain that had filled my soul, from war-ravaged Afghanistan to the inhumanity of Rawalpindi Prison, was blown away up there. No prisons. No police. No war. Just sitting in my saddle atop my friend, as high and as close to my Maker as I would ever achieve in this physical life.

I knew I had found what I had sought that long ago day on Shavon, knew I was ready to go home to Peshawar.

To rest our weary bones on that summit was impossible. Despite the bright sunlight it started snowing, so we headed the horses onto the stony track. There was nowhere to go but down. The road took us lower and lower, as the sun also descended and the snow finally stopped. We had been advised that after crossing the summit we could expect to spend the night in the village of Gittidas. We had been expecting a repeat of our last night's accommodations, a small village, a rough meal, an old rest house. We were sadly, naively, mistaken.

For three long cold hours our horses headed in that descending direction, never being asked to sway left or right on a track that went but one way, either straight up or straight down. The sun was almost gone and we were getting worried about finding the village in time. On our left was the humble beginnings of a river. On our right was a mountainside covered with stones or close cropped grass. The millions of gray rocks camouflaged the village until we were almost on top of it.

The first clue was the sheep, a vast host of the fat-tailed variety that looked delicious to three cold, hungry equestrian travelers. Then we made out the figures of men, women and children making their way around a gathering of small stone huts. At more than 12,000 feet high, Gittidas had no trace of trees or firewood. I was thinking how cold and forlorn a place it looked when the dogs attacked.

I was riding out front, wondering what sort of village we had discovered, when six great dogs came charging around the end of the last hut. They had lain in wait for us, neglecting to bark lest they warn us, taking us by complete surprise. Three of them attacked Pasha and me without hesitation, snapping at his face, springing up at me to grab my legs and pull me out of the saddle. Pasha reared, and I went up along with him. He slashed down at the huge, vicious brutes with his hooves, while I beat at them with my quirt. They were nimble devils. Their ears and tails had been sliced off to make them harder to grapple with in a fight. The effect made them look like black bears intent on eating us.

While Pasha and I were thus occupied, I could hear Ali Muhammad, Raja and their horses, screaming behind me. Before we managed to

Music of the Nomads

draw our pistols and kill the brutes, their owners came running from the nearby village. The obvious leader of the group of men was carrying a Kalishnakov machine gun. His fellows were armed with stout sticks. The sheep herders waded in, clubbing the gargoyles in an effort to control them. They managed to repulse the savage attack. The dogs however only slunk off a short distance, giving us hate-filled looks, saying they would rip our throats out if given the chance. At last, unable to stop our advance, the fanged brutes paralleled our course as we were escorted by their feeders into Gittidas.

The forgotten village of Jalipur was Paris compared to what we found. In Jalipur time had stood still. In Gittidas it moved backwards. Twenty stone huts were built on a rise just above the road, making it impossible to approach from either direction without being seen from afar. With the exception of the nearby stream, all around us was an unforgiving desert of cold stone. Situated at 12,000 feet, no tree could grow, nor could any flower last long among so many ravenous sheep.

There were no streets, just walkways in between low stone buildings resembling Indian huts. Without being told, we followed the man with the machine gun until he stopped in front of one of these humble dwellings. When he turned to address us, I got my first good look at our host.

He resembled a bearded tree, with a stout oak for a body, thick redwoods for legs and strong junipers for arms. His long, coal-black beard was so thick birds could have nested in it. The facial hair climbed up his craggy face, meeting eyebrows that stood up like angry bushes. His eyes were deep set and utterly merciless. His name was Hajii Batool and he looked mean enough to beat a baby with a rose bush. He did not address us in the traditional Arabic salutation shared amongst Muslims, preferring instead the ancient greeting used between nomads.

"May you have a road," the dark man growled.

I asked him if we could find shelter and food for ourselves and our horses?

For the horses there was nothing he said. The sheep had played out the pasture so badly they themselves were leaving in the morning. The geldings could be watered, then picketed, that was all. As for our needs, something could be arranged.

Despite our host's tender appearance, we had only two choices, accept his limited and grudging hospitality, or ride on into the freezing mountains with the dogs trailing us in the dark. It was the children that decided us. A flock of urchins surrounded us. They stared up at the strange horsemen, their dirty little faces smeared with snot and excitement, their little backs covered with tossed off coats, their little feet wrapped in broken down rubber shoes. Regardless of their woe-be-gone appearance, their mere presence reassured us enough to stay. Hajii Batool cuffed them away as effectively as he had done his murderous dogs, then motioned for us to dismount and follow him into a hut.

"Dear God above but this is a stone age place," Ali Muhammad whispered, and neither Raja nor I dared to disagree.

Khyber Knights

The threshold was so low we had to stoop to enter. The ceiling was barely tall enough to accommodate us. A tiny fire was laid in the middle of the small round room, a few pieces of precious wood giving off a flickering light. The struggling blaze threatened to choke the inhabitants quicker than warm them. Overhead were smoke-stained timbers. The walls were rough stone, too harsh to lean against, otherwise the hut was devoid of any trace of human habitation.

Our host and two other men had already seated themselves on the cold ground close to the fire. We did likewise, the six of us saying nothing. The red flames were ignorant of the tension and did their job, heating us partly through regardless of our national origin. Within a few minutes a teenage boy arrived with a plate, a cup and a pot.

Our dinner was three small pieces of bread and a pot of warm goat milk. Hajii Batool and his men made sure we had eaten everything, before he spoke. He urged us to bring in our saddles and gear. When we exited the hut we were plunged into a world so cold it made the icy Shandur Top appear luxurious. While Raja watered the horses, Ali Muhammad and I drove the picket pins in next to the stone wall which would separate us from our horses. When the geldings returned there was no course left except to wrap them in their blankets and bid them be patient till morning.

It was a cruelty to leave them cold and hungry. It was worse to see the murderous dogs lurking nearby. Even in the gloaming I could see the canines' black coats were covered in battle scars, both old and fresh. The fiends weighed as much as a small man.

When we reentered the hut our host laid out the rules.

"My dogs have no respect for guests. If you leave this place during the night they will tear you to pieces before I can reach you. Better that you should block the door with your saddles after we leave and not emerge before the sun rises," said the undisputed warrior king of Gittidas.

The dying fire barely lit his dark bearded face. The only thing twinkling in that dim light was the shiny black metal on his Kalishnakov. Raja assured him that we would do as we were told and with that our hosts departed.

Our hut had grown so smoky we thought it might be a blessing when the fire died out. In the remaining light we hurried to construct a door using our saddles as blockage and our two rifle scabbards as props. In the last glow of the embers we unrolled our blankets and without saying a word lay down next to each other, our weapons primed and close at hand.

When the little fire expired we were plunged into a darkness so complete it was comparable only to that experienced in a cavern. The stone hut allowed no hint of starlight to penetrate into its secret depths. Only a few beams of stray moonlight played through the chinks in our saddles. Otherwise we were surrounded by a medieval silence reflecting off the iron coldness of our icebox hut.

Oh, that night lasted an eternity.

Music of the Nomads

I never managed to do more than doze. There was a large rat in the room and he kept scurrying around in the inky darkness, perching on top of our bodies, or rummaging through our hair. But worse than that were the sounds of the poor horses. Only the thin stone wall separated them from us. They stamped their great feet in the blood-killing cold, whimpering, and starving, and begging the sun to rise.

The half-heard noise of movement brought my eyes open. Aware that I had napped, I lay there freezing in my blanket, keenly aware of why the old Tibetans thought Hell was a frozen wasteland. Outside I could hear the sound of low voices and soft footsteps. Crawling carefully to the make-shift door, I peered out through one of the cracks between the saddles. The sun was just rising, sending the first red traces of warmth sprinkling down like heated rain drops. Even in that dim light I could see that the path leading back up towards the Babusar Pass was now astir with people and animals.

We never learned why Hajii Batool and his people left so unexpectedly, without a greeting or a goodbye. Perhaps as they said the pasture was played out, perhaps the sight of three armed men unnerved them. Regardless, the people, the children, their flocks, and most importantly their wretched dogs, were gone by the time I could pull on my boots, tear down the door and emerge dumbfounded into an utterly empty village.

The only living things left were three horses huddled next to each other in order to survive that bitter night.

There was not a crumb of fodder or food amongst any of the huts, so we did not bother brushing the horses. When we took off their blankets, their hair stood away from their bodies in the freezing air. The buckles on the cinch were so cold they burned my fingers. The bit was so frigid I had first to warm it with my breath before I dared put it into Pasha's mouth. Under such circumstances did we leave Gittidas, journeying downhill in search of warmth and pasture.

Then at long last did Allah ease our burdens.

Our road took us into the glorious Kaghan valley. We celebrated our deliverance from danger by riding through countryside both pleasant and hospitable. The horses took us to the forgotten Lulasar lake. It was so enchanting a place I expected to see the sword Excaliber held aloft from its reflective aquamarine waters. Once again we were in pine trees and pastures, nor were we alone.

At first we traveled for days amongst the Gujars, a race of nomads who had inhabited those alpine pastures for 2,000 years. Supposedly descending from the hard-riding Scythians, it made my heart pound to be among these mounted men. The Irish too were thought to be cut from the same branch. Many thousands of years later, we horsemen from the same distant root met there in those mountains, they on their tiny ponies, I on Pasha. Men and horses, distant equine cousins both, now shared nothing more than those blessings of the road; food, fire and fable.

The country was otherwise thinly populated. Further down we encountered Afghan koochis, gypsy folk originally from the Gardez area of that war-torn country. Like the Gujars and ourselves, they too were in search of grass and rest. The men sported large turbans and embraced us when they learned we had converted to Islam. Their women were unveiled and proud, adorned in multitudes of thick silver bracelets that were the families' mobile wealth. We stayed in their camp along the Jhelum river, our horses blending in with their crowd of children, goats, sheep, dogs, donkeys and camels.

That night we men ate goat meat and bread, onions and mulberries, as we discussed what once was, and what might have been. All the while our tiny human actions were watched over by a patient full moon.

Yet while these kind people were all traveling up into the mountains, we three weary travelers were heading in the other direction.

For many days we rode the horses, watching Pakistan slowly change. The things that at first delighted us, food, fire, water and grass, were soon replaced by the gradual realization that with the ending of these mountains, so too was our mighty journey approaching its natural death. The fairy forests were replaced by banana trees. The babbling brooks gave way to motorways.

Pasha took me into Kashmir, where the mountains were not so far reaching, and my eyes had to again become adjusted to the smaller proportions of mankind's accomplishments. He brought me down through the pine-covered slopes to fair Murree. He carried me through the Margalla hills, until at last we six travelers stood on the outskirts of Islamabad, the nation's capital.

The air was warmer down there on the plains. It was also congested with the exhaust of vehicles. I sat on my horse taking in a scene whose exposure I had long dreaded. To any passerby I must have appeared as a gaunt red wolf. My mustache hung over my mouth. My face was covered by an equally unruly red stubble. My cheekbones jabbed through my starved and tightened skin. A slight shiny scar graced my face where Pasha had ripped me open back at Sor Laspur. My clothes hung loose. My leather gloves were in shreds. My saddle was shiny from the constant rubbing of my legs.

Raja and Ali looked no better. Like me, they had drawn up silently, the horses standing in check while we three saddle-hardened men stared at this new obstacle before us, our first traffic light.

I sighed in my saddle, knowing that whatever lay ahead, from then on I would hear the recollected music of the nomads only in my dreams.

42
A Strong Dose of Sin

His heart, that wretched, rash, intruding fool, led Ali Muhammad back to Shaheen. What he saw at the brothel blistered his admiration and sowed the seeds that later poisoned his love for the ravishing courtesan.

We had barely managed to picket the horses in Islamabad when my old friend informed me he was immediately leaving. He ignored my anger, criticism and any concerns for his safety, simply handed me Pahlwan's reins and walked away, swearing he would be back within twenty-four hours. Raja and I had our hands full with the needs of three tired, hungry horses. Muttering our collective curses on all Pakistani strumpets, the Afridi and I turned our attentions to the caring of our animals. Pasha was, if anything, as impatient as Ali Muhammad.

It was a short two-hour bus ride to Lahore from Islamabad. The brothel had no phone, and of course took no appointments. Otherwise Ali Muhammad might have had some idea of what he was walking into, might have been told he had picked a bad night to show up unannounced.

The eager lover came fresh from the saddle bearing gifts. If he was expecting to be met with tears and roses, he had forgotten the nature of the people he was dealing with.

Ali Muhammad arrived at 8 p.m. It was *Juma* (Friday) the Muslim Sabbath. Unbeknownst to him, Ali's previous visits had come during lulls in the brothel's normal activity. As he made his way to Shaheen's house, the American noticed the low profile of the police patrols and the consequent increased activity in Hira Mandi, the word having filtered down that it was once again safe to speed up the illicit businesses in the area. My friend never suspected what such a discovery would mean to him personally.

A discreet knock on the gate brought a nearly immediate result. Maroof's old mother pulled it open so quickly it startled Ali Muhammad.

"Angrez! OK, come in," the matron of crime said. Visibly pleased, she motioned for him to enter. When he did so, Ali Muhammad was surprised by the scene that confronted him. The three charpoys sitting in the courtyard were filled with men. The teenage errand boy Usman was running back and forth between these clients, serving them bottled drinks, or lighting their cigarettes. Once Ali Muhammad was inside the old woman snapped out an order to the youth, telling him to bring a chair for their foreign guest. Within seconds Ali Muhammad was sitting alongside the other men waiting to be serviced.

There was no sign of Maroof. The large front bedroom where they had all eaten was firmly shut. Even without that clue, the direction of the other men's eyes would have given Ali Muhammad all the evidence he needed, to know where the women of the house were operating. The four small rooms that ran along the back wall of the courtyard had lights showing through the thin cotton curtains serving as doors. Though there were no amorous noises coming from that direction, the American did not need to be told that Shaheen and the other three whores were on their backs, busy practicing their trade.

This information had barely sunk in when Usman handed him a Shazan. He wasn't thirsty but Ali Muhammad took the mango-flavored drink from the servant boy to be polite, and to have something to hold in his suddenly shaking hands. A glance down the charpoys told him there were ten men either awaiting their turns, or for their friends to re-emerge. The sound of splashing water snapped Ali's head up. Within moments a practiced flick of the curtain revealed Shaheen standing in the doorway of the last room, the same room Ali Muhammad had shared with her the night he and Raja discovered that snake-pit of vice and villainy.

The object of Ali's desire stood in the doorway, giving a final smile to her latest customer. He was a fat, dark-skinned, clean shaven Punjabi old enough to be her father. He tickled Shaheen under her chin and whispered endearments to her. She smiled in return. The satisfied customer was no sooner on his way out the door than the man sitting on the charpoy next to Ali Muhammad eagerly arose to take his place.

When she looked in his direction, Shaheen saw Ali Muhammad. She smiled at him, her eyes seeming to say, "Patience, I will soon be yours alone." Then the next customer entered her crib, and she flicked the curtain shut with the finality of a doctor going back into surgery. Ali Muhammad felt a poisonous rancor threaten to seep into his heart. Before he had a chance to digest the situation, Shaheen's recently-serviced client threw his bulk down onto the charpoy's vacated space next to the impatient lover.

"She is such a good girl," the fat man muttered more to himself than to Ali Muhammad. Shaheen's fat customer then sighed at the recollection of her body, clearly enamored with the woman Ali Muhammad adored.

"An answer to a prayer," Ali said softly.

"Yeah. Pray as much as you can, so you can sin as often as you like," the fat man replied cheerily, laughing at his own joke. When he offered the American a cigarette Ali declined. The fellow was utterly normal looking. In fact all of the men grouped inside that courtyard could have been classified as such.

"Any one of them could have been sitting next to me on the bus and I would never have suspected," the musician thought sadly, and took a drink from the Shazan bottle. Even the normally sweet mango juice suddenly tasted bitter and sickly. When the fat man started making small talk to Ali Muhammad about Shaheen, it dawned on the impetuous foreigner that the older man sounded as if he too were in love with her. That thought struck him like a bolt of electricity. Besides Maroof, Ali had never considered the possibility of other suitors. It made his stomach

A Strong Dose of Sin

knot to wonder how many other men were smitten by his lover's soft flesh and warm charms.

In a few minutes Shaheen was back in her doorway.

Watching her flick open that curtain Ali knew why she was the object of such intense desire.

Shaheen wore a soft yellow shalwar kameez the color of ripe apricots. It contrasted against her long black hair, which shone like raven's wings. Her full bosom thrust against the tight material. She was barefoot. Her lips were painted the color of a light red wine. Even the briefest glance at her breathtaking beauty was enough to make any man wander off the path of discretion.

His fellow clients stared at her like thirsty men leering at a soothing mirage. Though they differed in outward appearance, Ali Muhammad saw them all lusting for a taste of Shaheen's beauty, their eyes glaring, their nostrils trembling, their breaths panting. She floated mermaid like before them, the promise of her gorgeous body obscuring the ulcerous contagion of her brutal truth. For a price Shaheen would give each of them a sample of her sighs, her pleasures, and her forgeries of love. All the parties involved spoke the language of lust, that misleading dialect of the heart that was filth condensed, and shameful ardor hastily revealed.

That was a busy Friday night and Ali Muhammad got an eyeful. It seemed the charpoys were no sooner almost empty, than they were refilled again with a new set of anxious customers. As my friend sat there he wondered how many other busy Friday nights Shaheen had catered to, wondered how many countless men had trod her silky path. That was the moment his great love for her began to turn into even greater misery.

The old woman let in the clients with increasing regularity, all the while Ali sat and waited, taking an occasional glance from Shaheen like a drop of gravy tossed to a loyal dog. All four prostitutes were running the men through their cribs as fast as possible. Some customers arrived with pimps. Ali Muhammad reluctantly admitted to himself that most came without need of outside assistance, further heightening his suspicion that many of the men were repeat clients. Though all the girls were busy, it was obvious Shaheen was the preferred choice.

During one brief interlude Naheed came over to greet him. Of all the whores Ali liked her the least. Little Sanjeena was a victim of the primitive, unwritten code of the brothel. Aesha was a submissive, idiotic slave, glad to execute the pimp Maroof's every command, be it ever so crazy. Naheed was the jaundiced survivor.

She sat down on the charpoy next to him and lit a cigarette. Ali Muhammad remembered how shocked Raja had looked when Naheed had led the Pathan boy away into her room. With her rough, crude style Naheed had promptly destroyed Raja's illusions. If Ali had any lingering romantic doubts about the true nature of where he was, Naheed immediately laid them to rest. She lit her cigarette and took a deep, grateful drag before turning to speak softly to the American.

"I'm still the champ," she whispered, a look of smug satisfaction splashed across her face.

Khyber Knights

When she saw the lack of understanding on the foreigner's face Naheed leaned forward to confide in him.

"Most of them are so inexperienced sometimes all I have to do is run my hand up their leg. I hate to spend more than five minutes with any of them. My record is two minutes, in and out the door," she told him softly and laughed at the memory.

To prove her point Naheed handed Ali her cigarette, then boldly grabbed the first man waiting in line by the hand. Before the cigarette had burned more than half way down, the hard-boiled trollop had collected her money, plied her trade, and stood waiting in her doorway for the next passionate sucker. Naheed was lust in its most primitive form of execution, never working for love, only hard cash. Occasionally she wouldn't even bother to get up from the charpoy between clients. The mercenary harlot figured time spent on her back was money earned. She was often too lazy to speak to her customers, when she did open her foul mouth it was usually to berate those in close proximity.

"Give me the money. Come on hurry up. I haven't got time for amusement. Get out. Usman, quick quick, the next!," she would scream at the gate boy.

Prospective clients waiting outside her door were lucky if they heard the splash of water before they entered. A bit of old rag floated in a pail of fouled water, the same rag and water sufficing for the entire night, made cleansing a simple, if sporadic, formality for the tough whore. Naheed didn't care. She understood the mentality of the men who came to her charpoy. She was depraved vice disguised in female form, a withering soul rotten to the marrow in her bones.

Though Ali Muhammad did not admit it at the time, later he remembered that this was the instant he went to war with himself, that the colors of his heart began to change, that every flick of Shaheen's curtain stabbed him without a blow, that he asked himself why he was running the risk of the life-threatening Zina Ordinance for such a woman.

As he sat there waiting, watching the men go in and out of the rooms, Ali Muhammad had plenty of time to contemplate the suicidal action they were all so eager to embrace. In General Zia's Pakistan only treason was considered worse than illicit sexual relations. One of the first things he had done after seizing power was to enact a series of draconian laws designed to control public morality. The diminutive dictator had not just outlawed dancing girls, he had tried to eradicate all types of sexual promiscuity. In his efforts, Zia, who prided himself as being a champion of women's rights, had thrown them back into the Dark Ages.

Female literacy was estimated at a bare 14%, while only 5% of women were part of the compensated work force. Less than 3% held civil service jobs. Women in Pakistan were more likely to be subjected to constant motherhood and poor health than any chance at social advancement. Women had also been withdrawn from competing with the nation's international athletic teams.

However it was in the judicial theater of events that Pakistani women truly suffered. An illegal and undemocratic body of men and women had

A Strong Dose of Sin

been chosen to impose Zia's new regulations dealing with theft, rape, adultery, fornication, slander and consumption of drugs and alcohol. The newly contrived "Hudood Ordinances" were widely criticized both at home and abroad. Yet if it could be argued that the new laws penalized men, they crushed women wholesale.

One of the worst of the new laws was the Zina Ordinance. This law defined Zina as "willful sexual intercourse between a man and a woman who are not validly married to each other." Designed to curb prostitution, the Zina Ordinance was quickly seized on as a way of exploiting the women of Pakistan.

In order to prove that an act of adultery, fornication or rape had occurred, it was necessary for four adult male Muslim witnesses to have observed the actual act of penetration. For a woman to prove a case of rape, it was necessary to have four men thus testify on her behalf. If the witnesses could not be found the woman found herself being punished instead, since by her very actions she admitted illicit sexual intercourse had occurred. Consequently, when a woman filed a complaint of rape, instead of seeking justice, she was placing herself at the mercy of a court who would decide if in fact she had been a consenting party.

Furthermore, the woman was often then charged as being the rapist herself, since it was assumed if she could not prove her case she had seduced the man. Often times in a case of rape the families' fear of disgrace kept them from reporting the incident. If the woman became pregnant she could be promptly punished.

Safia Bibi, an eighteen year old blind girl, had been raped by her landlord and his son, as a result of which she became pregnant. Fearing social repercussions, her father did not at first report the crime. When it was discovered Safia was pregnant, the father filed a complaint against the landlord. Both men were found innocent as there was doubt as to whether the young girl had been a willing participant. Safia was convicted however under the Zina Ordinance, since she had given birth to an illegitimate child and was therefore guilty of fornication. She was sentenced by the court to be publicly lashed fifteen times, as well as serving three years in prison. The decision attracted so much outrage that the conviction was set aside.

Under General Zia's new regulations even a hint of scandal was enough to ruin a woman. Any man could have any woman arrested for zina by simply accusing her of the offense. Thus an innocent woman could find herself suddenly arrested and instantly subjected to injustice and degradation.

In Karachi Mohammad Sarwar had divorced his wife, then promptly remarried. Believing herself a divorced woman Shahida remarried as well. She had no way of knowing her first husband had deliberately failed to register the divorce documents with the court, thus never legalizing their separation. When his second marriage failed, Sarwar registered a case of zina against his former wife and her new husband. The unsuspecting newlyweds were both found guilty and sentenced to death by stoning.

When a woman filed for divorce she was expected to move away from her husband's house. If she had no blood relatives who were willing to take her back, she might be forced to move into the house of friends or neighbors. There had been many cases when the husband promptly filed a case of zina against his former wife, as well lodging a case of abduction against her protector. Both implicated defendants would naturally go to prison until the case was settled.

Rahima, one such accused woman awaited trial for four years. When finally convicted, her sentence was four months' imprisonment. Sakina Hyder was still awaiting trial after being imprisoned for nine years. Her father had filed a complaint against her when she refused to be sold for a third time to a man in exchange for a hefty bride price. Her two small children had been imprisoned along with their mother. Two-thirds of all women imprisoned in Pakistan were being held on similar charges.

A woman arrested on the charge of zina was not usually released on bail, and even if the court allowed it, she could only be released legally to either her parents or husband, often the same people pressing charges against her. It was also a common ploy for disgruntled husbands to blackmail a wife's friends or relatives. Being accused of being co-conspirators in an adultery complaint was a quick way to force them to hand over family property as a bribe, or accept a proposed divorce from a intolerant husband.

In Zia's Pakistan even consenting adults were liable for prosecution. In Peshawar two young lovers had eloped and married, flaunting tribal tradition which stated that all marriages must be arranged by the parents. When the newlyweds were discovered, they were both promptly convicted. While an estimated 15,000 people watched, the young groom was publicly lashed 15 times. His bride received the same treatment in private.

Even if the lovers escaped the kangaroo court, someone else close at hand would be punished instead. When sixty year old Naiken Bibi's son eloped, the police arrested the mother as an accomplice to her son's crime, thereby making her liable for his lashes or punishment.

The Zina Ordinance was only another example of how General Zia had twisted the people's religion against them. Though the founder of the country, Muhammad Ali Jinnah, had been socially progressive, his murderous successor had ushered in an era of fear and humiliation. In Zia's court it took the testimony of two women to equal that of one man. In a case of murder a payment of blood money could be made to avoid punishment. It was seldom reported that only half the amount had to be paid if the victim was female. There were documented cases where children who were victims of rape had been punished instead of their attackers. Even the mosques were under the sway of this harsh and unjust yardstick.

Women and men prayed shoulder to shoulder in the great mosque in Mecca, and many countries around the Islamic world allowed women to attend the mosque to worship, providing screened off sections for them and their small children. In his zealous but misplaced piety, Zia had

A Strong Dose of Sin

misinterpreted the idea of giving women equal access to the wisdom of God, denying them that opportunity, and oppressing them instead.

Pakistan's dictator resembled the sacred cows of India who wandered the streets gobbling up scraps of paper. Though both digested the holy words of the Quran, neither Zia nor the cows understood the message.

The idea of a political ruler using Islam to justify his own chokehold on power was nothing new. Unlike the Christians, who adapted the legal system of the Roman Empire, the early Muslim empire did not have any coherent judicial strategy at its inception. To rectify this problem an all-embracing legal system which ideally governed all phases of Islamic life was adopted. Known as the *Sharia*, the Way, it was based on an understanding of the teachings revealed in the holy Quran. While Islam prided itself on having no official priesthood, the scholars and custodians of the law acquired great social and religious prestige.

Even in its infancy the Muslim community was confronted with a moral dilemma surrounding the importance of the *Sharia*, a debate to which no acceptable solution has ever been found. Some Muslims viewed strict performance of the law as all important, emphasizing increasingly rigid traditionalism and the mechanical repetition of official ritual prayer. Others viewed a formalized, state religion as bondage to *dunya*, the ways of the world. This crisis in interpretation highlighted the difference between outward obedience and interior devotion. Many Muslims believed that the guidance of the Sharia must be united with an inner search. A Muslim traveled down the river of the law, they reasoned, in order to reach the ultimate goal, the ocean of God's truth.

History however had repeatedly proved that the spirit guiding Islam was in danger of being overruled by the activities of worldly kings and religious lawyers. Within seventy years of the death of the Prophet many of the basic tenets of the religion were being ignored by the so-called Muslim rulers of the expanding empire. Separation of men and women into different parts of the home began under an early caliph residing in Damascus. In order to screen his licentious activities with dancing girls from his wife, the caliph had his home physically divided and spiritually separated.

No one better exemplified this corruption of religious authority in recent years than Pakistan's illegitimate ruler, General Zia. The glamour of Muhammad Ali Jinnah's Muslim dream had withered under the dictator's oppressive regime. The vitality of the government had been sapped. Corruption was rampant among the bureaucracy. The army had been debased into a state police-force whose main concern was preserving the status quo. Under such conditions it was easy for Bhutto's executioner to exploit the nation's growing spiritual stagnation.

Islam is reminiscent of a colorful carpet, with threads running through it from the mystical words of the Quran, the traditions garnered from the life of the Prophet, and the legal system which provided a daily framework for the people's lives. Despite differing personal opinions on the varying importance of these issues, Muslims were tied together in their unifying belief that knowledge of God was all important. Yet General

Zia taught Pakistan that the purpose of humanity was not to know God but to obey Him. His was the argument of military violence, the difference between exploits and wisdom. The love of God had been lost under a military regime repressive in nature, since it carried to the extreme conclusion any dictate of the Islamic law.

Ironically General Zia, who publicly claimed to support the cause of equality for women, dismissed the teaching of Rabi'a al-Adawiya. This former slave woman and early Muslim mystic wrote, "It is a bad servant who serves God from fear, or terror, or from the desire of a reward."

The army chief who had promised to rule Pakistan for only ninety days was still basking in worldly glory and drunk on his own power. He had manipulated the symbols of Islam, overlooking the kernel of the Quran's truth and settled on the husk. In his desire to force the Pakistani people to accept his definition of the outer law, Zia had lost sight of the totality of the Islamic message, the belief that only when a person's inner and outer needs are both met will there be a fulfillment of the human soul. While preaching that outer conformity of Muslim orthodoxy, Zia neglected the inner qualities of the people. The necessary balance between Pakistan's outer law and its inner enlightenment was thus weakened and harmony was lost throughout the nation.

The righteous example of Muhammad Ali Jinnah, and those martyrs who had given their lives that Pakistan might live, were therefore sacrificed so that Zia and the men who supported him might continue preaching their religious forgeries. Islam taught that all humanity was equal in the sight of God. It offered hope to the millions of people trapped in the caste system that sickened the Indian subcontinent. How sound had been the religious roots of the country, and how rotten had become its branches when a tyrant judged as he pleased, put his opponents to death in anger, and took the law of Islam out of context. No one in Pakistan's history had so severely misused the lamp of God's universal light. The core of spiritual truth, which is the real illumination of Islam, was thus covered by layers of injustice.

No one delighted in abusing this misconception more than the Pakistani police. Under the Zina Ordinance they could arrest anybody, anywhere, at any time, and charge him or her with zina without any proof. As he sat there observing the proceedings going on around him in the brothel, Ali Muhammad knew everyone, from Maroof's old mother, to the boy serving the soft drinks, could go to prison for years just for being within those walls. The male customers could probably eventually bribe their way out of trouble. The hookers could expect only grief. That is if they even bothered to think about the consequences of their actions.

Ali Muhammad watched the four women taking the men into their cribs, observed as the old madam tried to keep the customers happy while they waited. All five women were all fatalists, ground down deep in a rut of sin. The look on their faces clearly showed they were beyond hope, pity, and most of all, fear. Ali watched as Shaheen took another man into her room. She showed no desire for repentance, just went about her job in that prison full of wickedness and despair. Shaheen was

A Strong Dose of Sin

like so many others, not just in the brothel but all over Pakistan, who plodded along in the groove they were born into. They believed it was natural to accept their parent's burdens, that redemption was not to be contemplated.

Despite the inertia of her life, Ali Muhammad was determined to offer Shaheen a chance to change. He wanted to give her a choice between a repentance that offered only starvation, or a life based in sinful prosperity.

Plus Ali had no fear of Zia. Pindi Prison held no mystery. The American knew no single rational reason existed to love Shaheen except to stop the torment he felt when he was separated from her. Ali understood his passion had killed his prudence but he no longer cared.

If Ali Muhammad and Beau Fontaine shared one common trait it was not that the soul driving both men could never be satisfied with polite affections. Regardless of what name you attached, my friend longed to burn with fire for the woman he loved. Even as he watched the sordid acts going on around him, Ali Muhammad told himself his love could grow even on such barren ground, with few rays of promise, amidst such pensive gloom, so long as the soil of Shaheen's heart did not prove too stony, nor the seeds of his devout love be rejected.

He sat there for hours, watching eight men come and go from within Shaheen's room. Some were in and out faster than you could tie your pant's string. Others stayed for long, heart-breaking periods of time. Watching the sordid proceedings, Ali Muhammad found himself wishing he only shared her with Maroof, her husband, and not any man in Lahore with three hundred rupees in his pocket.

During the long wait Ali considered lying with one of the other prostitutes instead, in an effort to hurt Shaheen and allay his own jealousy. Then he rejected the idea.

"They're loose character women," he said to himself and then began to laugh, knowing he was guilty of the same hypocritical prejudice affecting all the other men gathered in that darkened courtyard. For eager as they were to pleasure themselves with Maroof's tarts, none of them would ever have lowered themselves by considering marrying one. Ali well remembered the case of the young Peshawari who had eloped with his lover. When the two young people were imprisoned, the police asked the fellow if he now wanted to marry the girl.

"Certainly not," he quickly replied, "she is a slut or she wouldn't have fled with me."

That protracted night had grown old before the other men had all departed. The birds lay long since hushed in their nests. Even the stars were at rest. My friend watched the three prostitutes, the old woman and the boy quietly go about the business of closing shop. Everyone was weary.

When Shaheen at last stood in her doorway, looking tired, alone, and beckoning to him, Ali Muhammad did not hesitate to hasten. He was consumed with the pain of longing for his lover. Simple separation from her had become a torment. Water lifted from the deep sometimes fell away as individual drops, yet retained a memory of that former bonding. Therefore he disregarded the sordid events he had witnessed, sought no escape through the unguarded gate, hurried instead towards the source of that flame which was blistering his heart, that blazing candle called Shaheen, though deep inside he knew he was flying like a moth towards emotional immolation.

He was barely inside the room when he heard the flick of the curtain behind him. When he turned around he saw Shaheen leaning up against the wall near the door, clearly tired of playing the coy hostess to a string of strangers. Perhaps if he had known more about women, more about Shaheen, he would have known that was not the night to press her with his emotional needs. The look of near exhaustion on the woman's weary face stirred his jealousy. He tried to ignore its origin by bringing a small package out of his vest pocket and giving it to her.

Shaheen unfolded the bag and dumped its contents into her hands. Revealed there were dozens of glittering crystals, frozen stars of clear light lying in her warm golden palm. A look of complete puzzlement crossed her face.

"What are these?" she asked, not bothering to hide the irritation in her voice.

Her skepticism took Ali Muhammad by surprise.

"They are crystals. I brought them from Nanga Parbat. An old man found them on the side of the mountain," he said, and his voice faltered then fell away.

She looked at them with no understanding.

"Are they glass beads? What are they for? I have never heard of a Nanga Parbat?"

"I thought they were pretty. They reminded me of you. I hoped you would like them? I didn't see anything else to bring you," he added hastily, feeling foolish and embarrassed.

Shaheen looked resigned to having to deal with her endearing but half-witted foreigner that late at night. Considering the situation she did what came naturally. Closing her right hand over the crystals, she reached over with her other hand and pulled on his pants string, trying to reward Ali Muhammad's patience by granting him the precious gift every other man in her life sought so avidly.

"Come here. This one is for free," she said, and laid a practiced smile across her tired face, attempting to maintain the illusion one last time.

Ali Muhammad gently pushed her back.

"I didn't come here just for your body. I came here because I love you."

"For you too there is some love," she said quietly and looked down at the floor as if the revelation brought her no joy.

"Then marry me?" he asked eagerly.

Shaheen's mood shifted immediately, suddenly she was the furious whore who had attacked the car load of pimps. A glittering warning burned deep in the depths of her black eyes.

A Strong Dose of Sin

"Leave it. I cannot marry you. It is only business. Give me the money," she said angrily and shoved out an impatient hand.

The American became livid with rage. He both hated her and loved her, could have destroyed her and died in her at the same moment.

"Bring in Naheed if it is only business. You only want my money and my gifts," he shouted.

The look on Shaheen's face told him as clear as day she would have carved out his liver if she could have grabbed a knife. Instead she screamed in rage and threw the crystals at him with all her strength. Ali Muhammad dodged the missiles but she was immediately upon him, pounding on him with her small fists, trying to inflict back onto him some of the hurt and woe poured onto her by an unreasoning world. He grabbed her hands and held her, all the while she struggled impatiently. Finally she began to cry in sheer frustration at being out-muscled by the lean horseman. He loosened his grip, then slowly put his arms around her, drawing her to his chest, where he held while she sobbed in grief and rage and weariness.

"Change is not possible. I am compelled," she told him through her tears.

"Kiss me."

"No. It's dirty. We say the name of ...."

But he never let her finish, just held her by the back of her hair and forced her head back. At first Shaheen resisted, then began kissing him passionately. When she at last stopped, Ali Muhammad gently kissed her eyelids, tasting the salty tear drops gathered there and on her cheeks.

"I'll take the tragedy from your eyes Shaheen," he whispered.

For one brief instant he thought of the Pakistani women he had been introduced to as possible wives. They had invariably been one of two kinds, virgin daughters carefully paraded out in front of proud parents to parrot a few English phrases, or frumpy village girls who cast transparently greedy glances at him as if they were sizing up his American passport and not him. In either case both bored him and offered him no more than passive pulps.

Then he felt the female panther in his arms who was light years away from all the other women he had ever met in his life. The sheer lunacy of his actions appealed to his "Devil take tomorrow" attitude.

Ali Muhammad stood there holding the woman he loved and knew no one else in Pakistan would support him. Tolerance was a rare flower in that country. It grew in few places and withered easily, even in his beloved Peshawar. In his heart Ali Muhammad understood he could not take Shaheen back to his home. She was never going to be the chaste wife required by polite society to dribble out male children and hold her tongue.

Despite the sacrifices she required, when he looked down at her tear-stained beauty he saw a future without her presented only a picture of more empty years. It trailed off into a bleak distance leading into loneliness. The courtesan turned her face up towards him. Even in her present condition she was beautiful. Her black hair was hanging partly over her eyes. The color was thrown up into her cheeks by the flash of anger and passion.

A cold chill ran down his back, a premonition that he ignored. He remembered an old saying, "I stood at the gates of Paradise and saw most of its inhabitants were paupers. I stood at the gates of Hell and saw most of its inhabitants were women."

So long as Allah put him in Hell next to Shaheen, Ali Muhammad could find a balm for his pain.

"I love you," he said quietly.

"Thank you."

"But you are public property."

"Leave it," she said in return and guided him to her bed and into her soothing body.

Their love-making seemed hurried. The thought killed him and he threw himself into it with a sense of desperation, trying to memorize the feel of her body for fear there might be no tomorrow. So once again he drank her potent poison, spending himself as had so many others that night in the lie between her legs, believing his love was not a mischance, nor accidental judgment, was gold not dross. When they were finished she did not get up, rewarding him by letting him hold her soothing soft nakedness.

"Do you love me?" he asked her, staring up at the ceiling and dreading the answer.

"Love isn't important. It comes and goes. Forget it."

"I could take you to Kashmir or even to America."

"I wish I could be what I am not, but there is too much difference between us. Why don't you find a clean girl in Peshawar and marry her?" she told him, clearly unwilling to discuss leaving her thralldom.

"I want to help you. This work is bad. You could get sick and die," Ali told her sincerely.

"Only Allah is without sin. Besides I may be leaving," she said, and for some unexplained reason, perhaps because he was foreign and therefore to be trusted, she confided in him.

Shaheen sat up on the charpoy and whispered that she had many admirers and that several of them had offered to take her away. Ali Muhammad looked up at her, took in the golden glory of her curvaceous body, and doubted every word. He tossed around the information in his mind, weighing the possibility that this was another story invented to pry more money or gifts out of him. Any other time he would have urged her to leave with him that very instant, to flee with him to a place where he could give her a life of love, respect, safety and devotion. But after watching her take money off eight johns, he reluctantly began to wonder how deep her own corruption ran.

Ali Muhammad trusted his knowledge and experience of Pakistan to tell him that no woman, not even a whore, would run the risk of deserting her husband. The penalties under the Zina Ordinance would almost certainly be death by stoning for her and her lover. He believed Shaheen was too ensconced in the brothel to leave without his help.

Instead Ali told her to be patient, that he would return within two weeks from the horse trip to begin negotiating with Maroof to buy her freedom, still believing in his heart that circumstances were the cause of her condition. A look of silent withdrawal came across Shaheen's face as she retreated to the other side of some invisible barrier.

The pendulum of Ali Muhammad's affections had not yet changed. He still loved her with an undivided heart. Only now the lovers lay apart on the charpoy, two halves of a broken pitcher full of lies.

43
Pasha

Islamabad was a city in search of dignity.

Founded in 1961, the nation's capital sat with her back against the green Margalla Hills and her straitlaced bosom unwillingly touching her warm-blooded sister city, Rawalpindi. The original seat of national authority had been in faraway Karachi. It had not taken long for the Pakistani power brokers to determine they needed to be closer to the geographic center of their new country.

Lahore, despite her cultural importance, sat directly on the border of antagonistic India, and was therefore considered too perilous. No one gave wild-eyed Peshawar any serious consideration. Rawalpindi, though once the seat of imperial British power, was now considered too tattered to pose as the show-piece of the new country.

A series of foreign architects were hired to construct a model city.

Instead they concocted a sprawling, featureless, concrete monstrosity that managed to do nothing more admirable than to gather the country's parasitic bureaucrats into one forgettable place. It's very name was ironic, for instead of emulating Islam, the city epitomized what Pakistan had garnered from the west, namely a worship of federal power and personal isolation. Nowhere in the country was it more apparent that a promise of tomorrow's heaven was not going to dispel today's problems.

Wide featureless streets led Pakistan's generals, admirals, air marshals and pencil-pushers past strip malls, nameless government buildings and gated residences. Everything in Islamabad was a repudiation of everything Pakistani. It was a sullen, silent place arrogantly aping the foreign ideals of the West.

Shops proudly displayed imported junk from Japan, China, America and Europe. Greasy attempts at foreign cuisine catered to the legions of bored diplomats, corrupt local politicians or foreign drones who called the imperial city home.

All traces of Pakistani life were rooted out like a virus. The scraps allowed to remain had a side-show feel to them, allowed to survive quietly so long as they politely entertained the water boilers.

Gone were the tongas and the street vendors, the call of the muezzin and the lowing of cattle, the laughter of children and the chatter of neighbors. Islamabad was populated instead by men in suits and ties who despised poverty and the common unwashed humanity of that populous nation. There was no place in Islamabad for poets or the poor. Those lacking dignity were told to stay in the warrens of nearby Rawalpindi. Even the animals so commonly encountered throughout all other parts of the country, the sheep, goats, camels, water buffalo and donkeys, were banished, nowhere to be found in that soulless eyesore. The only animal life to be seen were those flying weeds, the crows.

It was no place for a horseman.

We had no choice, our road lead there, for many reasons.

The first was grass, lots of it.

Islamabad had pockets of civilization juxtaposed against acres of urban jungle. Level building sites, mile-long traffic meridians, and acres of federal lawns were all overgrown and overlooked. It was unlike the barren north, where every blade of forage had been carefully hoarded. Following directions, Raja and I rode our mounts to a federally owned campground near the center of town. It was a small place with showers, toilet facilities and camp sites maintained for more traditional travelers, including a Japanese fellow bicycling to Europe and a Dutch couple driving to China.

For once we did not have to show our federal permit authorizing our stay. The friendly chowkidar told us to take any spot we liked. A giant tree, plenty of free grass and running water, soon had both the Pathan, the horses, and me set for the night.

The other reason was more sinister, Pindi Prison.

I knew I had to go back there.

True to his word, Ali Muhammad returned the following morning from Lahore looking tired and emotionally distressed. He located us, curled up on a blanket and fell sound asleep. With the horses free to graze within the spacious confines of the camp, I left Raja in charge and made my way back to Rawalpindi.

If there was one thing Islamabad had plenty of, it was beaten up taxis. The roads were teeming with old Morris Minors. The diminutive automobiles were invariably painted black with a taxi yellow roof. Their doors rattled. Their engines smoked. You were lucky if you didn't get jabbed with a broken seat spring when you sat down. It only barely beat walking.

One such reeking wreck responded to my signal. A brief argument about the fare, then I was on my way. Even considering traffic we made good time. In less than thirty minutes the driver had exited Islamabad, entered Rawalpindi, wove in and out of various streets and finally deposited me in front of Khawaja Naeem's office.

When I walked in unannounced, the fat little lawyer looked like he had seen a ghost. He quickly regained his composure, invited me to sit down, then proceeded to tell me I had wasted my time by coming there.

"Your friend the Dutchman, I forget his name?"

"Hans von Dueker."

"Well, whatever they called him, he's gone."

"Dead?"

"Nearly. Got hepatitis. He was sent back home on compassionate release."

"Did his embassy request that?" I asked, recalling how indifferent they had always been to Hans' dire predicament.

"Oh certainly not. I kept him supplied with the money you left with me. Two months ago I discovered he was in the prison hospital. In fact he was nearly dead already. A brief conversation with the DSP, and then a phone call to the Superintendent of Prisons, convinced them it was not going to help anybody to have a dead European on their hands. Some paperwork was quickly arranged and he was quietly allowed to fly out of Pakistan," the lawyer recalled.

In answer to my questions Naeem informed me Hans departed on a KLM flight to the Netherlands, the destination of his original ticket, and that his luggage had been released to him. Knowing the Dutchman still had Nepalese hashish stashed inside various portions of his possessions, I suspected the gravelly-voiced anarchist had wasted no time getting rich at last in Amsterdam.

"If you're thinking about going over there to the prison for a visit, forget it," Naeem informed me sternly. "Out of sight, out of mind is the best way to handle your situation. All charges were dropped against Inspector Gilani Khan and his men for lack of evidence. You can't fix Pakistan. Nor can you save any of your former cell mates by sticking your head back into a noose Asadullah."

He unlocked a drawer, counted out some money and slid it across the desk towards me.

"That's the balance. Take my advice, get out of Rawalpindi before you bump into Ashgar Ali."

I sat there for a moment, secretly relieved, then stood to go. The little man gave me a long and careful look, thought about something, then asked me, "Are you low on funds? I can advance you some money if need be."

"No. I'm fine. Thanks. Why do you ask?"

He tried to hide his embarrassment, then couldn't help laughing.

"You look terrible. I think if I ever get serious about losing weight, I really must consider taking a horse trip. You're an absolute advertisement for an equestrian diet plan."

We shared a parting laugh, then shook hands. He was the kind of good friend you found all over Pakistan, and seldom in Islamabad. I promised to take his advice and leave Rawalpindi, then went outside and immediately proved I was a liar.

There was only one other reason to stay in that dangerous city, a certain gelding I knew from Sargohda named Pasha.

Another nameless taxi, and an even shorter trip brought me to the Saddar Bazaar. Not wanting to be seen, I paid the driver off inside the car, then quickly darted inside the adjacent shop. Shamis Din the saddler remembered me. No one came in nowadays preparing to ride across northern Pakistan. He was surprised my friends and I had made it to Islamabad. In fact he admitted he hadn't thought we would get past Chitral. The portly man assured me he knew of no one who had ridden as far as we had before the fall of the British Raj, certainly not since the inception of Pakistan.

Khyber Knights

Once the niceties were discussed, Shamis told me what I needed to know, where to find a horse shoer. He agreed to send a local man up to Islamabad the next day to see to our horses. The shop smelled of rich leather. Shiny polo boots were stacked against the back wall. The noonday sun streamed through the window onto a row of lovely, locally-made saddles. You could close your eyes, and your nose would take you back one hundred years, to a day when such a shop was a necessity not an anachronism.

When I opened my eyes I saw the modern, noisy, mechanical world looming outside the door awaiting me. The crowded Rawalpindi streets seemed even more boisterous than normal. In answer to my question, Shamis Din informed me it was Maharram, a fact I had overlooked due to our travels. With the saddler's promise to send a shoer, I made my way into the streets.

Even at the best of times there were few Afghans wandering around the old city in turbans. Though the communist-inspired terrorist bombing campaign had never taken hold in Rawalpindi, it was the same old story of guilt by association. Now that I found myself down country old problems would increasingly re-merge.

My main concern was to leave Rawalpindi before I bumped into any of my old acquaintances from the Narcotics Control Board. After what seemed like an eternity, I flagged down a taxi and gratefully headed back towards the anonymous sanctity of Islamabad.

The driver was a talkative sort. My turban seemed to classify me automatically as a Sunni to him. He threaded the motorized heap past tongas, around buffalo carts, between children, down narrow lanes and finally onto the main road leading back to the capital. Along the way he talked nonstop about what he labeled as the disgraceful behavior being displayed that day by his religious rivals, the Shias.

Once a year the Shia community commemorated the lamentable death of their religious martyrs, Imam Ali, and his two sons, Hasan and Husayn. Once a year Shia men and boys from various parts of the Muslim world, gathered together in their respective communities to weep over the tragic events of thirteen centuries ago. Long processions of bare chested men would lead parades of fellow Shias through Pakistan's various cities. At predetermined spots along the way these leaders would stop. Then as the crowd loudly chanted the names of their martyred leaders, the Shia leaders would begin to beat themselves rhythmically, slapping their bare chests as hard as possible with their fists.

After this initial exercise was concluded, select members would unfurl sets of special knives. Each participant would hold in his right hand a wooden handle. Attached to it were six short chains, at the end of which hung a set of long, double edged knife blades. As the crowd's chanting became hysterical, the religious mendicants would begin flaying themselves with the knives, slicing their backs into bloody ribbons in the process.

The previous year I had written about this strange destructive ritual. While thousands of men and boys screamed the names of the Prophet Muhammad's grandsons.

"Ya Hussein, Ya Husayn," the crowd screamed, as I watched the most religiously devout among their group whip themselves with the cruel and vengeful blades. While covering that story, I had got so close that my face and camera had been splattered with hot blood from a raw-backed old man who successfully transformed his body into hamburger.

It was this pervasive melancholy that was the dominant note among the Shia's interpretation of Islam. They collectively mourned over past events, giving more emphasis to what had occurred then, than to the message of hope and universal truth still found in the Qu'ran today. This was one of the contributing reasons for the increasing sectarian violence running across Pakistan. The two communities were apt to use fire and sword to resolve their religious differences.

Their undying hatred could only be compared to the venomous hatred expressed between the Irish Catholic and his Ulster Presbyterian neighbor. The majority Sunnis believed that the Shia had an even deeper place in Hell than either the Catholic or the Protestant, since the Christians were not Muslims, as were the so-called heretic Shias.

I was glad to see our camp and Pasha, to pay off the driver and avoid any more references to bloodshed, religious or otherwise. That night we three travelers sat around our small fire discussing the news of Hans's escape, and that wretched prison which lay like an open wound just over the horizon. Despite our close proximity, somehow I felt safe, if overlooked, camping there in plain sight next to my horses.

With the sun came the answer to the last of my worries.

Farooq, the *nal band* (horse shoer), was as good as Shamis Din had promised.

Even though the worst of the terrain was behind us, the geldings still had to carry us almost 300 miles before we reached Peshawar. There was no way we could ask them to push on until they had new shoes.

Big Pahlwan was barefoot up front. My horse, Pasha, had only a couple of metal remnants nailed on. Pajaro, Raja's dapper bay, not only looked like he just left Peshawar, he apparently put down his feet more carefully than his stable mates. His shoes were paper thin but intact. Farooq was used to taking care of the tonga horses in Rawalpindi. He clicked his tongue in concern when he saw the condition of our horses' feet, then set to work with enthusiasm.

If Islamabad had one blessing it was that it was generally quiet. From our camp we could hear the light sound of passing motor traffic, however it was not the mind-numbing noise of most Pakistani urban centers. The imperial bureaucracy that ruled the city quietly supported General Zia's policies. Their official job was to raise revenue and help maintain order. Unofficially their common goal was to preserve their own privileged position. In Peshawar people whispered, "Seek sanctuary with the Devil if the alternative is a bureaucrat."

These civilian autocrats had quickly fallen into line when they discovered that the only one of their ranks who dared resist had been hanged in nearby Pindi Prison. The joke around town was that General Zia's official title, CMLA or Chief Martial Law Administrator, actually stood for "Cancel My Last Announcement." However Pakistan's bureaucrats were masters of political survival, they knew not to jest too loudly. Besides, theirs was an easy existence. Pakistani's worked six days a week. But between the Muslim Sabbath on Friday and the international time zone differences, their country was actually in working communication with the western world for only three and a half days a week.

Raja, Ali Muhammad and I sat in the shade and watched as the shoer went about his business. It was a peaceful interlude in our lives, a scene I knew other horsemen had witnessed for centuries.

For more than two thousand years equestrian travelers had been periodically forced to stop their wanderings, as they too watched the same ancient treatment being applied to the same ancient problem. In all those long years the age-old solution had been a crescent of iron, nailed on to cover the rim of the hoof. The tap, tap, tap of Farooq's little hammer sounded that song of yore, a reassuring message that never changed for those whose successful ventures depended on the feet of their horses.

While we were waiting I asked Raja if he had ever heard of St. Dunstan, a Christian bishop and a horse shoer of great skill. While working on a particularly dangerous stallion, the learned man recognized that Satan had assumed this shape to deceive him. Having securely tied the animal, the saint proceeded to pare down his Satanic majesty's feet, ignoring his screams of protest. When the Christian horse shoer began driving nails into his feet the Devil finally begged for mercy.

Before agreeing to release him, Saint Dunstan managed to extract an oath from the wily Devil. In remembrance of their mighty battle Satan agreed he would never enter or disturb any building on which a horseshoe was hung. A horse shoe over the door had been a symbol of security ever since that day.

The Pathan youth grinned and pointed at how the gigantic Pahlwan was fighting the horse shoer as usual.

"I don't think Pakistani horses ever heard of this Christian holy man. They are still full of the devil," he said and indicated the struggling horse shoer to prove his point.

We didn't need Saint Dunstan to tell us to leave the neighborhood before we were discovered. Early the next day we rode south-west, avoiding Rawalpindi altogether and cutting through flat farm lands, until we arrived at last on the great Grand Trunk Road.

If our journey had started, instead of ended, along that ignoble byway I doubt we would have ever seen the majestic mountains of northern Pakistan. I reined in Pasha and looked aghast at this artery running east and west across the face of the country. There was no doubt that it was the most direct route home to Peshawar. Yet even a blind man would have hesitated before riding out into that mechanical melee. The din from the chaotic stream before us was so loud we had to shout to be heard.

Swarms of trucks, buses, cars and motorcycles roared by, spewing hot exhaust into the air. In addition, the sides of the narrow motorway contained bicyclists going to work, wagon-loads of bricks drawn by trundling water buffalo, bleating sheep being moved to pasture, and pedestrians trudging into Rawalpindi. If it moved in Pakistan you could find it traveling on the Grand Trunk road.

The once humble, ancient camel track known to the mighty Mughal emperors was now a asphalt-covered monster. We six travelers stood at the edge of the noisy river of movement, until an impatient Ali Muhammad headed Pahlwan into the free for all. We edged out into the confusion, joining the chaotic stream that was heading back to that dim and distant love, Peshawar.

Pasha and I soon learned that there were no rules on the great road. We had wandered onto an ugly two-lane world inhabited by motorized savages, a place where fierce pride and fickle fate ruled the outcome of your arrival. Trucks screamed by shoulder to shoulder, passing within inches of our saddlebags. Buses threw up gravel and covered us in filth. Cars blared their horns intentionally to scare the horses.

By the end of the first day we men all suffered from severe headaches, a result we agreed of the noxious exhausts. We spent the night at a truck stop, sleeping on bug-infested charpoys, listening to the never-ending sound of trucks growling by throughout the night.

The next day was worse.

We had journeyed beyond the reaches of Rawalpindi and Islamabad. There were no lone travelers that far out. No other nomads shared our wretched path. Plus, the old GT road bore the marks of her age. Millions of tires had worn her pavement as smooth as glass. Even if we had not feared for our lives by venturing onto the car-crowded blacktop, we would have avoided riding the horses on such treacherous footing. Instead we hugged the shoulder of the road, staying as far off to one side as possible.

Noon found us stopped under some convenient trees. The free grass was too rich to pass up. The horses grazed alongside the busy motorway, ignoring the mechanical monsters that no longer terrified them.

As the day progressed our route became increasingly difficult for psychological, as well as physical, reasons. We passed out of the farmlands and entered great barren tracts of flat, arid earth. That is when we started riding by the numerous brick factories.

They should have been called slave pens not factories. Despite a distance of a few miles between them, they invariably boasted the same few physical trophies. A tall metal chimney stood slammed into a burning hole in the ground. Smoke as black as Satan's heart spewed out from the top. A fire was kept burning day and night, baking the bricks inside.

On the perimeter of the brick field a few shacks could be seen. Those hovels were the residences of the miserable creatures who toiled in the brick fields. During the day the men and women who made the small red building blocks of Pakistan worked relentlessly under the watchful eyes of the factory wardens. The worker's children did not go to school. Their only education was in pain and suffering, abuse and degradation. The little ones were forced to bring their parents water so that the adults might mix the mud for the bricks.

The brick system was geared to keep the workers continually in debt. They were so poor they might only eat meat twice a year. Despite working nearly every day of the year, they never came any nearer to clearing off their family's financial obligations. Children inherited their grandparent's debts. If the workers fled they were hunted down and hauled back. Men who ran away were frequently tortured, often had their legs broken as a punishment. Women escapees were gang raped by the factory owners and their wardens.

We rode by and shook our heads silently. The condition of the brick workers was a well known secret in Pakistan. No one wanted to break the system because of the country's dependency on bricks. Plus the ruthless factory owners were invariably wealthy and politically well connected. Their savage feudalism had been unaffected by either the departure of British imperialism or Pakistan's independence. They were generally not interested in national politics. Their interests were primarily local. The current military dictatorship was content to give the feudal brick lords a free hand, so long as any local government offices were manipulated to their mutual benefit.

Nor did it help that many of the workers were Christians. Despite the injunction in the holy Qu'ran to respect "the people of the Book," meaning Jews and Christians, the money-worshipping slave-drivers ignored both their religious and humanitarian duty. They prospered by violent wrongdoing, believing the temporary power of this world could shield them from the consequences of their evil.

Every man's hand was against those poor people and their unfortunate children. In a country often devoid of pity, the condition of the brick workers could draw tears from a stone.

Riding past mile after mile of the hot, sun-scorched factories threw me into a funk. The heat being reflected off the black top began baking both horses and riders. By late afternoon mighty Pahlwan seemed done in by the unaccustomed heat. The big gray was drenched in sweat and close to collapse. We managed to reach another roadside truck stop where we quickly stripped the gelding and bathed him in numerous buckets of cool water. Yet I knew the Grand Trunk had at least two hundred more miles of such hatred in store for us. I made what I thought was the obvious suggestion.

"Tomorrow we have to get off this road. We can circle into Peshawar via the foothills that lie to the north. It will take us a few days longer but it will be safer and easier on both us and the horses," I told Ali Muhammad and Raja.

The Pathan youth was indifferent, happy to be on the adventure, willing to go where I led. For Ali Muhammad, however, the Grand Trunk road still beckoned, holding out a message of reaching Peshawar, and hence Shaheen, sooner rather than later. For me every step on that bleak road took me closer to a life I no longer respected. When Ali Muhammad tried to argue his point I stood my ground. The sight of Pahlwan was enough to convince me of my friend's selfish motives.

I told him he could run any risk he wanted with his own safety in a Lahore brothel. He could even choose to leave Raja and me if he wanted to go home by bus. But come tomorrow I was going to lead the horses off a road I had unwittingly steered them onto, a road that risked their lives needlessly. This wasn't the parri. I wasn't going to be shoved just to satisfy Ali's haste. Journey north on horseback, or ride the bus alone I told him.

The next day at dawn the sullen American joined Raja and me as we headed away from the nauseous paved reminder of the 20th century.

Our luck changed immediately.

We entered a country that was already old when Cleopatra reigned in Egypt, the legendary kingdom of Taxila. A quiet road ran under cool trees and past fertile farmland. Gone was the roar of the paved monster, replaced by the soothing whispers of history. We left behind the parched Grand Trunk road, quivering and swaying in its own sun-baked heat, and ventured into an unexpected oasis of shade and story.

Once the main university town of the fabled land of Gandhara, the now-small village of Taxila had rested at the crossroads of the ancient world. It linked Central Asia with China and Europe. Despite its current Islamic demeanor, for more than one thousand years Taxila was a treasure house of Buddhist theology. From 600 BC until 400 AD the vast, lush valley was home to Buddhist monks who diligently studied the wonders of the world around them. Besides religion they delved into mathematics, astronomy, law, medicine and military science. Taxila was a showcase of humanity's early achievements. Traders and scholars treasured it alike.

Alexander the Great conquered the inhabitants in 327 BC, but allowed its people to work on. The famous city, renowned for its pacifist inhabitants, was ultimately destroyed by mounted barbarians. In 450 AD the White Huns of Central Asia descended on the peaceful valley like a swarm of blood-sucking locusts. The great city was looted and destroyed, never to regain its former educational or cultural importance.

Centuries after the dispersal of Buddha's disciples, we rode through a land that was lush, but quiet, rich, but withdrawn into herself. The British Raj had departed but an eye-blink before our arrival. Alexander the Great was here only a few heartbeats ago. We rode through that landscape slowly, pushing our way through the molasses of time and the lingering heat, sensing on all sides the lost wisdom of mythological men, our horse's hooves stirring up the dust of three thousand years of human effort.

That night we camped in a tiny village, fed the horses well on corn stalks and slept badly, the effects of past horsemen invading our dreams and looting our peace of mind.

Khyber Knights

The next day I was riding along lost in thought. Peshawar was a week away. I had used up all my fat, then my nervous energy, and was down to only determination. Though the journey was threatening to come to a close, I realized I had achieved a longed-for state of mind. I thought now only in terms of basics; pasture, shelter, food, and water. Pasha bore me quietly through that day, leading me and my companions into the town of Haripur, and unexpectedly bringing the dun and me to the beginning of the end of our long sojourn together.

It surprised us to find ourselves in a rich market town. Though close to the busy GT road, Haripur was a rich but overlooked little place. Right away I noticed that the streets were filled with some of the best tonga horses I had ever seen in Pakistan. We located a hotel with hot water to cater to our own needs. However finding suitable stabling for the horses proved more difficult. Following the advice of the hotel manager, we went to the local government bus station, thinking we might be able to picket the geldings on their vast parking lot.

We were disappointed to find this was not possible. All six of us were tired, hot, dirty, hungry and worst of all, thirsty, when we were approached by a dark-skinned Punjabi. He introduced himself as Riaz, a *syce* (groom) employed by a local *zamindar* (wealthy landowner). Seeing our predicament, the groom invited us to seek his employer's hospitality. On the outskirts of town we discovered Riaz was indeed telling the truth. He lead us to a large house with an attached stable. A beautiful black stallion was the sole occupant.

The pampered beast immediately began creating a loud fuss at the unexpected sight of three strange horses. Within a couple of minutes the stud's owner emerged to investigate all the noise. Riaz hastily informed his master who we were, as well as the problem of stabling the geldings.

Anyone would have known Ishaq was rich just by looking at him. In a nation full of skinny, hungry people, he was chubby. His ivory-colored shalwar kameez was spotless and stiff with starch. An expensive linen vest covered his immaculate clothes. In his early thirties, he looked the part of a country squire. Our host immediately informed us he was the nephew of General Ayub Khan, the former military dictator who had ruled Pakistan prior to Zulfiqar Ali Bhutto's election. Though we certainly had heard of Ishaq's uncle, this was no cause for celebration. It was like meeting a nephew of President Richard Nixon, someone you've certainly heard of but are unsure if you want to brag about knowing.

Ishaq's stable however was tidy. Our fellow horseman urged us to let Riaz attend to our horses as honored guests, assuring us we could spend the night in the unaccustomed comforts of the nearby Haripur hotel without fear or worry.

Any kind of bed sounded wonderful.

We unsaddled the geldings, then returned to the hotel with our saddlebags.

That night we each had two buckets of steaming hot water to bath in. After getting cleaned up, we retired to the restaurant downstairs. There we feasted on ginger chicken, *palak* (spinach), and *pilou* (rice). Knowing

Pasha

the horses were being equally well treated I slept like a babe, never dreaming what the next day was bringing.

The care of animals sneaks into your sleep. Even in the deepest slumber the back of your mind is aware that you have other concerns. Your body is at rest, but your mind wanders to the horse who has carried you so far, and bought with his own exertion and sacrifice the soft bed you now repose in.

I awoke early, uneasy, worried about Pasha.

At the stable I found nothing amiss. Pahlwan, Pajaro and Pasha were already fed and were standing comfortably in a large holding pen. Unlike the geldings, the stallion was restless. He swayed back and forth in his stall, anxious to get out and fight the strange horses who had invaded his space. Pahlwan and his stable mates were three battle-hardened veterans of the road. Eight hundred hard miles had taught them to waste no energy in fancy displays of temper or testosterone. They stood together, an intertwined band, an equine family, wise and simple pilgrims enjoying the luxury of not having to move.

I was enjoying such quiet thoughts about the horses when their host emerged. The British riding togs Ishaq wore were tight fitting, and though designed to be dashing, only succeeded in highlighting his soft body. In my rough, travel-stained Afghan clothes and scarred riding boots I was out of his league. The gracious landlord came to stand beside me, resting his well heeled boot on the bottom fence rung. Without being told, Riaz quickly began to groom the stallion in preparation for his master's departure.

"Would you like to join me on my morning ride," Ishaq asked politely.

It was an innocent question, riddled with a dozens reasons why I should say "No." Pasha and I were both tired. Neither of us ever had much time to rest. I had planned on letting the dun gelding stand undisturbed until we departed the next morning. I was about to decline the offer when Ishaq made the mistake of insulting my horse.

"I paid 17,000 rupees for Dark Cloud," he said with great satisfaction.

The stallion he referred to was busy resisting his groom in the stall, trying to nip him while being saddled. I didn't need to walk any closer to see the beautiful black horse was as spoilt as his pudgy master.

"Your horse is only a heavy breed, isn't he?" Ishaq asked me.

Before I could answer, the nephew of the former dictator stuck his custom made boot further into his mouth.

"He doesn't look like much, appears to be weak after all the hard traveling," he said with open contempt.

I don't know what made me speak up. I should have kept my mouth shut but Ishaq didn't know when to stop.

"But after all he's only a gelding," the rich man said derisively.

I slowly turned and looked over this cream puff in fancy clothes. He would never have lasted through the grueling conditions Pasha and I had endured, and yet he had the gall to insult my splendid horse. I was no humble backwoods peasant afraid of this preening peacock. I looked at his over-rated horse stamping and snorting.

"Perhaps a small wager might change your mind," I suggested.

"You would race that gelding against Dark Cloud?" Ishaq asked, seeming to think the idea ridiculous in itself.

It was not hard to settle on the terms, a mile race, winner took the other fellow's 1,000 rupees.

While an eager Ishaq rushed to the stall to oversee the saddling of his own mount, I went into the pen. Pasha calmly walked over and began to nudge me with his soft nose, pushing my vest pockets looking for treats. However before I fed him I took care to give Pahlwan and Pajaro the two apples I had brought them. They slobbered out their thanks. Then I turned to the impatient dun and fed him his fruit. He stood close to me, his mouse colored head leaning against my chest, as content to be near me as I was him. No money could buy that sort of hard-won affection.

With no trace of hurry I began brushing the dun, ignoring the increasingly impatient Pakistani waiting nearby. Saddling took the usual amount of time, no more, no less. When I finally judged Pasha to be ready I turned around to discover a dozen men had gathered around the pen. They were clearly my host's friends and supporters, come to cheer him on. Ignoring them, I walked Pasha through the gate.

Ishaq was already mounted. Dark Cloud was high strung even before he sensed his rider's excitement. The long legged black was turning tight circles, tossing the bit, wild eyed, eager to fight or fornicate. I continued to ignore both him and his rider. Instead I checked my cinch one last time, adjusted the bridle, made sure the bit sat smooth, then swung into the well polished saddle that I called home.

"Shall we trot to the starting point," I asked, and without waiting for an answer, heading Pasha out onto the level country road that was to serve as the race track. I had no watch, knew no landmarks, but I did not need to be told where a mile ended and began. I could count my heartbeats and clock off the miles in the dark. Like me, the dun was uninterested in the tranquil landscape surrounding us. It was flat farm land with an occasional mud hut denoting the residence of Ishaq's tenant farmers.

Yet the morning was still deliciously cool and the footing firm, the only two things that concerned me. Pasha and I were thus engaged, he covering the ground in that long, quick, clean-cut pace of his, I rising and falling with the gait, when Ishaq and Dark Cloud came pounding up beside us.

The stallion's neck was shiny with sweat. I didn't have to glance back to know he must be dripping from under his fancy English saddle. His rider looked angry. As Pasha and I trotted hard down the road, Ishaq had his hands full just keeping up. The stallion was chomping at the bit, trying to push his head out and seize the irritating metal wedged between his teeth. Ishaq was barely in control. He bounced like a sack of potatoes, jamming his spine every time he smashed into the stallion's back.

We traveled that way until I judged we had nearly reached our destination. When I slowed Pasha into a walk several things happened at once. Ishaq looked utterly relieved. Pasha realized Pahlwan and Pajaro had not accompanied him. The stallion tried to bite the dun, for which I gently slashed him across the shoulders with my quirt.

"Mind your horse," I told the Pakistani. Suddenly I was busy with my own problems and had no time to tolerate his mount's bad manners.

Pasha started whinnying in frustration and fright when he realized he was separated from his stable mates. From back in the distance we could hear the deep bellow of Pahlwan calling Pasha home. The sound drove the dun nearly mad. He tried to turn back but I continually kept him facing down the road away from his comrades. His mouth had grown so sensitive to the bit I barely had to move the reins to keep him on course, but I could feel his fear growing as I asked him to leave behind the only emotional support he knew.

The stable was distant but still in sight when I reined in. Ishaq looked pleased to be stopped. Just getting to the starting point had been an effort for both him and his horse. The rider had rings of sweat under his arm pits. His unschooled horse looked blown just from the excitement of being so close to another animal.

"Sometimes I think he is going to kill me," Ishaq confided. I knew then that he wanted me to call off the race, to give him a face-saving solution in front of his friends.

But the air was clean and pure and purred over my skin like the back of a deerskin glove, and besides Pasha was anxious to go home. I momentarily felt sorry for the popinjay beside me, then reasoned that he had pretended to be a horsemen in front of the local farmers for too long.

I turned the dun's head, pointed him back towards the stable, and barely said the word, "Ready," when the Pakistani seized the initiative, jumping ahead of Pasha and me by three horse lengths. The stallion was showing us his heels before my gelding ever took off.

Without a word, without the spur, without the quirt, I simply let out Pasha's reins and quietly told him, "Za (go)." His mighty Percheron hindquarters dug into the ground, then pushed us off like a rocket leaving the restrictive confines of mother Earth. I was suddenly in the front seat of a symphony of sound as Pasha's strong legs pounded the ground and the wind blew by me. The long tail of my blue turban hung suspended behind us like a battle flag and my clothes snapped against the breeze as my "weak" gelding began to catch up with the other horse.

Ishaq glanced behind and saw Pasha coming on strong. He began flailing the reins and kicking the sides of the black stallion. His efforts were pointless. The expensive animal was out of condition, had no chance of winning. I had known it before we left.

We had raced a little more than half way when Pasha overtook the fancy black horse. The dun never paid any attention to the heaving stallion, ignored the foam blowing off his lathered black sides, just stretched the long legs his Pakistani dam had given him and passed the stud in four long strides.

The sound of Ishaq's feeble curses grew faint as Pasha and I raced on alone. When big Pahlwan sounded his deep bugle cry of a whinny, the dun had enough wind left to answer him as we ran. It was at that instant when I finally gave him the long rein, then laid down along his neck and galloped flat out with my Pasha. Our bodies became one. My heart sang in rhythm with his hooves. His long mane blew up into my face, stroking my cheek. The race and the journey now meant nothing, all that counted was that brilliant shared moment in our mutual lives.

Some ancient Sufis teach the concept that if a man is lucky he will discover his *ijtihad* in his lifetime. This seldom-taught belief says that a person should seek to express his Islamic convictions through an everyday act. Instead of wearing his religion on his sleeve, the Sufis believed the wise man could take a humble material or a daily event and turn it into something valuable. That by addressing your attention to your garden, your music, your kitchen or perhaps your children, a man could turn his humdrum existence into a shining testament of faith.

I was an accidental Muslim. I knew little theology and had always struggled to find any mystical meanings. All I knew at that moment in my life was that Pasha and I were wind-borne pilgrims going home together. That feeling brought me my only glimpse of *ijtihad*. I knew that this alone I did well. The pounding of Pasha's hooves was my chorus, the sound of the wind in my ears the beating of angel's wings, as the gelding brought me closer to God than I had ever achieved in any man-made building.

Pasha was not privy to any lofty philosophy. He only wanted to place his muzzle up against those of his friends. I never hid my spurs in him. I let him cover that firm ground like a dun colored bird. He came in sliding, stopping just short of the fence. He was barely breathing hard. I had already dismounted when Ishaq and his exhausted Dark Cloud came struggling in behind us.

The Pakistani was barely out of the saddle before he came over and offered to buy my horse. In a low desperate voice the landowner began making entreaties. At first I was taken aback by this unseemly advance. Riaz the groom was seeing to the man's mount, while he was trying to soothe his pride by buying the toy that had bested him.

At first I gave the idea no serious consideration. Then I remembered another fine horse, a golden mare who had not been lucky. I sighed, my former exultation evaporated by the reality at hand. Ali Muhammad and I had never considered selling the geldings on the open market in Peshawar. The truth was that Pahlwan was so gigantic no private party would have been able to afford to keep him well fed. Pajaro and Pasha though smaller, were still large compared to their civilian equine cousins. Besides there was the problem of daily abuse among tonga drivers and cart wallahs.

Before leaving Peshawar I had discussed donating all three horses to the mounted police patrol, in order to assure them of a safe future. However Inspector Akbar Ali had been unable to get confirmation for this arrangement before we departed. I had made the journey thinking I would resolve the domestic needs of our horses when I returned to Peshawar. Suddenly the their future was staring me in the face.

Ishaq was an option I had never considered.

Pasha

I told him I was not interested in selling one horse. As he had seen, the three geldings were stable mates. I was only interested in selling them together.

The man had many flaws, however the situation in Haripur was not without benefits. The stable was more than large enough to shelter three more horses. They would never want for feed. Riaz would be close by to attend to them and serve as groom. When the anxious Pakistani assured me he would buy all three Sargohda geldings to use as riding horses for his friends and family, I felt trapped by harsh circumstances.

Once the talk turned to money Ishaq began to regain his confidence. His main desire though was to own Pasha.

"How much do you want for him?"

"What is written by God," I told him.

"Seven thousand rupees," he said slyly.

I could feel my anger threatening to rise. I turned a cold eye on this merchant prince and expressed my contempt.

"Do you think I am in want that you make such a proposal? I might give you my children if I had any, but I warn you, this horse is as close to me as my own heart. He makes a fool of your horse and proves he can travel a distance of five days in one, yet you dare to insult him. I am not a shopkeeper nor a pimp to be bargained with," I said, and turned back to unsaddling my dun.

Yet things were against me and I knew the ground that Pasha and I shared was slipping out from underneath my feet. In the end Raja, Ali Muhammad and I agreed to sell our geldings to Ishaq for twice what we paid for them. In the cruelty that sometimes defined Pakistan that was the closest thing we could manage to a sure thing.

The *zamindar* was anxious to take immediate possession but that was out of the question until we finished our ride to Peshawar. Ishaq agreed to meet us in seven days time at the police stables. We shook hands to seal the deal. Funds would exchange hands in a week. I let him keep the bet.

With a sad heart I left that town on top of someone else's horse.

Oh that was a weary portion of our journey. For the next five days we rode mostly in silence. Ali Muhammad and I had decided to give Raja the money from the sale of Pajaro. The funds for our own horses would be ours to do with as we saw fit. Yet our trip had never been about money and now that subject hung over us like a polluting cloud.

The countryside was pleasant enough, full of villages, farms and simple folk, and it was the journey herself that eventually cured my aching heart. A quiet country lane brought us back at last to the banks of the mighty Indus River. We had not seen that watery brute since we left her in the desert outside of Chilas, on the other side of the faraway Babusar Pass.

We six travelers came to a halt there. Our route lay across the top of the Tarbela Dam. This was the largest earth-filled dam in the world, three times bigger than Egypt's Aswan dam. Looking at the river trapped behind this mighty wall I knew that our trip was drawing to a close. Even the Indus River had been tamed.

Once we showed our tattered paper from Islamabad proving our identities, we were issued a chit authorizing three horses, two American Muslims and Raja Bahadur Khan to ride across the Indus river. We were the first horsemen ever so honored. The narrow road stretched for more than a mile and a half on top of the dam.

We were utterly alone up there, just three nomads and their horses. The river's transformation had been unbelievable. There was no sign of the muddy brown monster from the north. Crashing out of the twin spillways on our left came a torrent of pure white water. A gigantic tidal basin lay five hundred feet below us, its surface sparkling like a beautiful aquamarine jewel.

Though we were still several days from Peshawar, that crossing seemed to be the final parting with the wild north. Gone were the untamed rivers, the grand mountains, the forgotten spaces on seldom-traveled maps. But we left our grief behind as well. Those last few days we no longer suffered, no longer complained about the hard saddles or the burning sun. We spent most of our time watching our shadows slipping by us. The black flickering pictures on the ground showed hazy men in turbans riding, riding, riding.

A day out of Peshawar we came to our last barrier, the Kabul river.

Circling out of the north, we had approached the river through a strange land of eroded hills and vast sugarcane fields. People had warned us it was too dangerous to ride through this area, that we should travel west two days more and cross over a bridge further on. Having heard of a local ferry up ahead, we ignored their warnings and pushed on, discovering a seldom visited section of Pathan territory.

That final day had grown late. Pasha had taken me through vast stretches of lonely sugarcane fields, before finally emerging on a half-hidden dirt trail. We rode down through tall reeds until the wide river brought us to a halt. Little shepherd boys were driving their cattle home from the river banks. A small village sat on a bluff overlooking the calm Kabul river. There before us was the ferry.

It looked like a boat used by Alexander the Great. The great wooden craft was thirty foot long and ten feet wide at the beam. A giant paddle in the stern served as a rudder. She was bleached white by long decades spent in the blistering sun. I doubt if they had used a single nail to construct her. She looked like she was held together with pegs and prayers.

Before we could go looking for the ferryman, he appeared. The white beard and lean frame revealed his age. The horny hands and knotted muscles bespoke his years on the river. Five younger men accompanied him. The sun was setting and the patriarch of the river wanted to get us across quickly so he could be home in time for the Maghrib prayer.

For one hundred rupees, less than six dollars, the ferrymen agreed to make the three trips required for our six member team. Not surprisingly, Ali Muhammad volunteered to go first. His attitude about the trip had suddenly altered when he realized that his time with Pahlwan was now concluding. Yet his haste to reach Shaheen was ever foremost. The big gray stepped over the gunwale and the boat pushed off. Raja and I watched it drift out into the current. Then the five men began pushing the awkward ship towards the far shore with their long poles.

It took twenty minutes for the ship to deposit Ali and come back. Raja went next, Pajaro making no protest. I watched them slide away across the still water. When Pasha saw both his friends on the far shore he began neighing in worry. Our turn came soon enough.

Off to the west the sun was setting over the river and our trip. Swallows wheeled through the air like silent acrobats. When the boat softly docked on the muddy bank, I led Pasha next to the strange object. He blew and snorted in fright at the wooden creature confronting him. I stepped over the low gunwale. The boat men had laid thick straw across the wooden floor. Once I was aboard, I gave Pasha a gentle tug on his reins.

"Come Pasha," I said quietly.

He stood there, the horse once afraid of cars, once so sheltered by his army life, once unsure of who I was. His eyes searched mine, then he stepped into the old ship. A thousand shared miles later a deep sense of trust bound us together, and always. If I had pointed him toward a mountain, Pasha would have climbed it. If I had asked him to cross a desert, Pasha would not have hesitated. If I had climbed onto the saddle, and aiming him at the far bank asked him to swim that treacherous current, Pasha would have launched us into the river, trusting me to guide us there.

Yes, there were all the other horses of my life, and then there was Pasha.

The captain directed his crew to shove off.

Our world had grown silent except for the tiny noises of the river. The boat groaned quietly like an old man on a cold night. The five sturdy boatmen were mute. Only the sound of Pasha's bells gently ringing in time with the boat's rocking broke the stillness.

The Kabul river had grown gold in the sunset. The sky overhead was dissolving into different shades of pink and lavender. Our watery road was still and peaceful. Its soft colors began to ripple like living pastels, casting a shiny translucence in our path. I held my breath, unwilling to believe such an effect could exist. Then the sky in the faraway west flared up in a scarlet red farewell, casting the shore where we landed in a final rosy light.

We travelers did not linger on that far riverbank. Men and horses traveled silently through the gathering dark, moving willingly without need of spur towards our adopted home.

Pasha and I rode on under the full moon, her silver light brightening that collective road. The fleet dun and I shared our last contentment, passing through that final nocturnal phase of our mutual existence. I yearned to retain my dual destiny with him and childlike, knew I could not, knew some fulfilled purpose had pervaded our lives. So we journeyed on to the sounds of his bells, and the lapping of the moon's waves on our last road.

I was filled with longing to hold that night, to capture that moon, to never dismount from the gelding who owned my heart. All around me was a sleeping, silvered Pakistan. I tried to guard myself against the beauty surrounding us. It was a futile attempt. God himself had conspired against me, throwing one last visual challenge at the horse and me. That was no familiar night-time beauty. Pasha and I made our way past flickering trees and drowsing villages, treading softly through a beauty that knew no calmness nor control, that threatened to shake us in her silvery arms and leave us barely alive.

In the early morning hours Pasha brought me home at last. The sleeping streets of Peshawar echoed softly as the sound of his bells tinkled in the remnants of that final night. What use are definitions at such a journey's end? There was still so much we had not done, Pasha and I. Looking inside my heart I saw again the mountains we had shared, the parri we had crossed, and knew in the long distance of my life this was the horse I would remember, that such a horse was only on loan from God.

Part Four
The Rescue

44
A Transitory Love

It is never the same horseman who rides home from a long journey, returning from weary miles in faraway blue mountains where magic holds no mystery. Nor did I try and justify my equestrian accomplishments to men who in my absence had never ventured past the end of their narrow streets, their pedestrian routines, or their pinched everyday existence. My secretive inner rewards could not be explained to house bound poltroons who never felt the sting of thirst, nor savored the perfume of alpine breezes.

Peshawar however neither questioned nor disappointed me.

Often when one returns to a city that has nestled safely in one's mind, there is an initial feeling of disappointment and shabby smallness, and it is several days before you can renew your intimate acquaintance. That shiny morning the old city seemed ten times more magnificent than the image I had kept locked in the saddlebags of my memory. Here was a vibrant, storied place that was almost a grief to the mind. How happy I was to see the sun rise on those little streets, to hear the Paris of the Pathans sing her morning song. It was good to be home within the cobblestone arms of a city fit to have poems written about her.

By early morning we three riders sat in the Kabuli tea house in Hasht Nagari bazaar, feeling shattered from exhaustion, but proud of our accomplishment. The difficult journey with its litany of dangerous obstacles, hazardous marches, and daily privations lay complete. We were all three lean on account of our journey through deep and distant mountains, our bones clothed in little flesh. Yet like any horsemen worthy of the name, we had seen to our mounts before looking to our own comforts.

No more wretched beds for the three remaining geldings. Their precarious journey over, the weary horses were led away by police Inspector Akbar Ali and his mounted officers. For the first time in many a long, long day Pasha, Pajaro and Pahlwan had rested in decent quarters.

With the chargers safely fed and quartered, their fatigued riders took the last cup of tea from that trip together. Peshawar was too busy to give us much notice. We drank our sweet chai and watched school children march off to class, saw women in chadors slip away to the vegetable market, observed men opening their shops, saw the colorful human tide of Asia ramble past our table.

What do you say at the end of such a journey to the travel-stained, saddle-worn rovers who have shared your life and your road ? I drank my tea, too numb to talk, thinking that this trek was like all my earlier ones, occasions where I had wandered through foreign lands, always returning to the same past I had left behind.

How was I to know that the direction of all our lives had changed forever, that the brief moment we shared over that cup of tea was not the end of our adventures, but the windless calm before the storm.

With chai in our stomachs Ali Muhammad led Raja and me through the winding lanes to his home. Though invited to linger, I picked up my gear and returned to the relative luxury of the Amin Hotel. The thick concrete walls of my room were soon busy keeping out the noise of the nearby Grand Trunk road. Within the hour I was stretched out on a real bed pondering which was the greater luxury, not having to share the room with my mates and a pile of smelly horse gear, or the extravagance of taking a bucket bath with all the hot water I wanted. Exhaustion laid the argument to rest as I tumbled into a deep pool of slumber.

I awoke late that evening, rang down stairs to the little restaurant for dinner, and after eating in my room, promptly slept the rest of the night away. It was late morning before I emerged, bathed yet again, shaved and wearing clean clothes and turban. The walk to my friend's house was just long enough to stretch my legs. When Raja answered my knock the news that greeted me wasn't reassuring.

"Ali's gone."

"Back to Lahore?"

Raja nodded his head in agreement.

"Left early this morning," the Afridi told me.

The look on his face reflected my own bleak feelings.

The horse trip was over. Any obligation Ali Muhammad felt towards us was fulfilled. His only desire now was to marry Shaheen. He had therefore lost no time. Ali had no way of knowing the Flying Coach was hurtling him across the country not into his lover's arms, but into a spider's web of deceit and betrayal.

If the American thought he was going to the Lahore brothel to buy the freedom of his lady love he was sadly mistaken. He got off the bus in the neighborhood of the city's great fort. It had been built by the great Mughal emperors. Its once beautiful fountains and pools had been destroyed by Lahore's English conquerors, covered over by tennis courts in the 19th century. The anxious suitor ignored the past. By walking in great haste, Ali reached the dead-end alley where Shaheen lived before lunchtime. He had intentionally come as early as possible, wanting to avoid the crowd of evening clients he had encountered on his last visit. The American needn't have worried about any romantic rivals, at least not in Lahore. The gate was opened by the prostitute Aesha. A sly, smug look crossed her round little face when she discovered the identity of the caller.

Upon stepping inside the courtyard, Ali Muhammad saw the charpoys were occupied by Maroof's mother and younger sister, as well as the other two whores, Naheed and Sanjeena. There was no sign of Shaheen. The American had no chance to ponder her absence. He was being directed by Aesha to follow her to the doorway of Maroof's parlor.

A Transitory Love

The husband of his lover was reclining against pillows placed against the back wall. He was staring up at the ceiling lost in thought when Aesha knocked lightly on his door. Any irritation at being disturbed disappeared when he saw who was standing behind his employee.

"Come in, come in," Maroof said, the smile playing across his handsome face giving no hint of the situation at hand.

Ali Muhammad stepped in, left his sandals at the doorway and walked over to meet his romantic rival. Maroof immediately stood up in greeting. Before Ali could shake hands, the other man embraced him sincerely, then immediately waved for him to sit down next to him.

"What brings you to see us?" Maroof asked innocently.

The question stunned Ali. His first thought was that this was a ploy to rise the asking price on the woman in question.

"I've come to discuss my marriage to Shaheen," my friend said, hoping his voice sounded steady, trying to keep his face devoid of the anxiety he felt rippling through his stomach.

Ali felt his heart start to pound even harder when he saw Maroof grin.

"Oh no, the price has gone up," Ali Muhammad thought in a panic.

The love-struck musician had already figured his finances out to the last rupee. After selling his house and possessions to raise the dowry he knew he would be nearly bankrupt. The money was not as important to him as the prospect of a gloomy future without Shaheen, yet he knew the previous asking price was as high as he dared go. Considering what was to come to pass, it would have been a blessing if Ali Muhammad's only worry that day was a doubling of the original bride price.

"Didn't that simpleton Aesha tell you?" Maroof asked innocently, toying with the American.

The look of perplexed ignorance on Ali's face was answer enough.

"Shaheen is no longer here."

A cold chill constricted Ali's throat. His first thought was that Maroof had killed her. Before he could ask where she was the pimp volunteered the information.

"The slut ran away with a customer from Bajaur a week after your last visit," the husband said.

Maroof immediately picked up a pack of cigarettes lying on the carpet next to him. Ali Muhammad noticed the pimp was now smoking cheap Red and White cigarettes, not the more expensive Gold Leaf brand he preferred. The American did not bother to comment on this subtle indication of Maroof's economic distress. He was too busy feeling the accumulated weight of his universe crashing down upon him. The news would have driven him to his knees if he had not already been sitting down. His mind reeled with shock and he felt a cry of disbelief choke itself in his throat.

Before he could speak a single thought raced across his mind.

"Don't let this be true. My *niyat* (intention) was pure. How can You take her away," his withering soul called out to Allah.

But if God heard, or cared, no sign came. Instead the pimp added fire to the flames, explaining how Shaheen had slipped off with one of her many repeat customers, a handsome, short-bearded Pathan tribesman from the border territory known as Bajaur.

Aesha, the prostitute who had been beaten for letting in the Punjabi pimps, had never forgiven or forgotten her mistress's abusive behavior. She was the one, Maroof explained, who afterwards revealed the clues to his wife's escape. Though not privy to Shaheen's plans, Aesha had overheard snatches of a conversation that later proved to be prophetic. The whore would have gladly betrayed Shaheen to Maroof, delighting in watching any cruelty he might have served out. But Shaheen was gone before anyone suspected she was even planning to escape.

No one, that is, except Ali Muhammad.

He hid his face in his hands and felt his world imploding as the thought set in that he could have stopped her, that he could have been more insistent on making her understand he loved her, on explaining to her that he really was going to return and buy her freedom from the debauched rake sitting beside him.

The room was silent except for the soft click, click, click of the *punkha* (fan) whirling overhead. In the blackness curtained behind his closed eyes Ali Muhammad felt his guts contract with pain and his heart scream in silent agonizing grief. When he opened his eyes he was a changed man. If Maroof had bothered to study him, the pimp would have seen that the American was tottering on the invisible line between rational thought and madness. Ali Muhammad's first question was an indication of how radically different the two men perceived Shaheen's importance to be.

"Didn't you look for her, or try and bring her back?" he asked Maroof, making no attempt at hiding the desperation in his voice.

The look of surprise that crossed the pimp's face should have been answer enough but Maroof spoke nonetheless.

"Go into Bajaur? Not even another Pathan would venture in there after her," he quickly told the American.

The well-pressed and expensive shalwar kameez Maroof wore was ample evidence that this was no primitive tribesman ready to go crawling through the rock-covered wasteland known as Bajaur. He saw himself as many things, including a business man and a cunning opportunist, but the pimp knew he was no frontier type, ready to grab a rifle and hunt through the mountains for either his ex-wife or revenge.

Despite his years on the North West Frontier, Ali Muhammad realized he knew very little about Bajaur. All he could remember was that it was rumored to be one of the most backward and remote tribal areas in Pakistan. He could not even remember ever meeting a Pathan tribesman from Bajaur in Peshawar. The snippets of information attached to the geographic term centered around natives resistant to any outside interference.

"Is it as bad as Kohistan?" Ali Muhammad asked, remembering the kidnapping proclivities of Shakra the outlaw.

Maroof leaned back against the cushion and weighed the question carefully.

A Transitory Love

"No. The men of Bajaur are not savages like the Kohistanis. They are Mohmand tribesmen who have no fear of either General Zia or God Almighty. They are rebels against every law known to heaven and earth, notorious smugglers and ruthless kidnappers. They are famous for kidnapping rich merchants. Everyone knows to pay the ransom quickly or you'll see *Abu's* (father) fingers start showing up in the daily post," Maroof explained and nervously began lighting another cigarette.

He made no attempt to hide the shudder that ran down his back. If Ali Muhammad had given it any thought he would have understood that Maroof was not going to risk his fingers, or his life, going into the trackless wastes of Mohmand territory in search of Shaheen. However the pimp maintained his male pride by lying about the financial importance of the beautiful missing courtesan.

"Besides," Maroof added, trying to sound casual, "I don't know where she is and really don't care. She wasn't important to my operation."

He was still a crooked dog and could tell as many lies as four men.

Shaheen's two lovers sat there in the room, the one lost in thought, the other spinning a web of candid observations, brilliant insights and grandiose fabrications about the part he played in Pakistan's prostitution industry.

Maybe Maroof was just talking to hear himself talk? Ali Muhammad was in no condition either to leave or listen. My friend sat there lost in thought, wondering what he should do, where he should go, who he could turn to for help in a country that would condemn Shaheen to death without hesitation?

If the pimp understood that Ali was not really interested he never let on. His ego was too enlarged to admit to any mistakes, and in the secret parts of his heart he knew as soon as the American left his venomous bile would gnaw at him again. For despite his protestations of indifference Maroof knew better than anyone what a gold mine Shaheen had been. Until Ali appeared Maroof had been dwelling on the loss of income Shaheen had represented on a daily basis. The American's presence had only confirmed the loss of even more money. Maroof had never planned on allowing Shaheen to actually leave with her ardent suitor, had in fact thought to separate the American from his money, then scare him off with threats of police reprisals.

Shaheen's unexpected departure had spoiled all those plans, and while he chatted as if he didn't have a care in the world, Maroof knew in the bottom of his black heart he would have gladly killed Shaheen for shaming him.

"She was a mercenary bitch who always used me and my family," Maroof said, shaking his head for emphasis. "I tell you trying to find truth in a man is like looking for a hoopoe bird in a dark wood, but finding the truth in Shaheen was like looking for the echo of the hoopoe's voice."

"This used to be a good life," the pimp confided to the American who, though sitting next to him, was mentally miles away. "In my father's day they used to say. *'Lahore da shahano au mashukarm kor deh'* (Lahore is a city of lovers). The courtesans of Hira Mundi once attracted clientele from as far away as Persia. But that *spay zoi*, (son of a bitch), General Zia has done his best to kill off Hira Mandi. Now they whisper a new saying around here, *'Hujai nano ta chad Lahore'* (If you have money get out of Lahore)."

Every man has his complaints, and though he was a pimp, Maroof was no different in that regard. Having been born into a family that had prostituted its women for generations, he was a ethnological and cultural goldmine of information. He talked as much to himself as to Ali Muhammad, explaining to the American how these drab faded houses once housed rich and beautiful women of fabled manners and redoubtable sexual charms. Maroof told the story of Ghulan, once considered Hira Mandi's most gorgeous prostitute. Men had to first play cards with her. If they lost the game they forfeited not only their money but any chance of further favors. Yet most were satisfied to leave without experiencing Ghulan's many talents, being content to feast on her visual beauty.

"My grandmother was kept to her dying day by a rich *zamindar* (landlord). She had several children by him. He never married her but provided for her generously. Growing up I heard stories of how he used to come riding in from the country in his own tonga with liveried servants in attendance. My mother told me he once gave her a pair of shoes worked in gold thread," Maroof recalled wistfully.

"Before he died, my father told me there were at least 40,000 dancing girls working in the port of Karachi alone during the big war with Hitler. I tell you this bazaar has seen better days," he said and let out a long sigh of disgust at the turn of recent events.

If Ali Muhammad had been listening he would have realized that despite his faults Maroof was a born survivor. Shaheen's disappearance was a pivotal event to her husband, who had decided to adopt new tactics in General Zia's aggressively religious society. Maroof saw the handwriting on the wall. Traditional dancing girls now had as little to do with prostitution as democracy did with Pakistani politics. The pimp realized the dizzy throb of musical Lahore nights was being delegated to the past. Many of the ancient customs he and his family practiced had been dispatched to oblivion. Running a brothel had gone from being a discreetly profitable business into a enterprise fit only for daredevils.

In the past the city's whores were contained within well known boundaries. This not only gave the cops an idea of how large the problem was, the centralized flesh market also presented an eyesore and offense to Pakistani moral pretensions. When the puritanical Zia came in charge Hira Mandi simply had to be done away with.

At first Maroof's family had lain low, thinking the trouble would blow over. Soon after his father died, the heir-apparent realized the glory days of Hira Mundi's *lal bazaar* (red-light district) were a thing of the past, never to return. There would be no more rich *zamindars* (landlords) coming to the gate to woo courtesans and play cards. The rules of love had been permanently changed. Dancing girls might linger on to a tiny degree, looked upon as a quaint cultural oddity, but the prostitutes of Lahore were either going to jail or going to change.

Maroof was ready to close the traditional shop and move his girls into greener pastures. He had decided to keep the house open only for discreet and trusted clients. Taking his cue from America, the flesh-peddler had determined that the prostitutes working for him were going to spread quietly throughout the suburbs and no longer remain confined in their distinct, if fabled, neighborhood. Maroof was going to have the hookers start posing as respectable office equipment representatives, insurance agents, and ad procurement agents for imaginary college publications. By moving into the mainstream workforce his prostitutes would not only have greater camouflage, more importantly, their increased social mobility would make him more money.

The most important bonus of this new method was Maroof believed such a discreet business would allow him to recruit girls from previously unsolicited sources, and not rely on the traditional families that moved in such circles, including some Pathans from Swat and the Marchroon tribe of Gujrat.

"Not only are these new girls going to be harder for the police to catch, I won't need to marry one to get her to work for me," he said and began laughing at the thought of his own missing wife. His only regret, though he kept it to himself, was that he had not been able to separate Ali Muhammad from his money, in order to bankroll this new operation.

A discreet knock drew both men's eyes towards the door. Maroof's younger sister stood in the doorway, hesitating to bring in the tray bearing tea and cups until the undisputed master of the house gave his permission. The curt nod from her brother told the girl she could enter.

The yellow shalwar kameez Saira wore was dull but contrasted well with her long black hair. Overall she was a rather plain girl. Her most attractive feature would have been her quiet modesty, a rare and subtle gift in that household. A man would have to have studied Saira to notice it.

Ali Muhammad never did.

He barely glanced at the apprehensive girl as she carefully sat cups, saucers, as and a tea pot in front of her brother and his guest. If Ali had bothered to glance in her direction he might have realized Saira was avoiding his eyes. The American never looked in her direction and the girl left hurriedly.

Her brother took no time in drawing Ali Muhammad's attention to his sister.

"She is very pretty don't you think?" Maroof asked as he poured the tea for his guest.

"What?" Ali asked, his mind adrift.

"My sister. I said she is very pretty, don't you think?" the pimp asked.

Ali took no warning from the eager look on Maroof's face. He had missed the anxious inflection in the other man's voice, had no idea it was a loaded question posed by a master manipulator. When Ali hesitated to answer, Maroof quickly jumped in with additional information.

"She's fifteen you know," he said and let the statement hang in the air as if was explanation enough. When the American still said nothing, Maroof threw his last card on the table.

"Would you like to try her? You could forget Shaheen in no time," Maroof urged him.

Suddenly Ali Muhammad understood both the reasoning behind Maroof's invitation and the girl's nervous behavior. The heart-broken suitor snapped out of his state of shock. He blinked his eyes several times, seizing mental control and coming to grips with the issue at hand. The cup of tea Maroof had poured for him sat steaming on the adjacent tray. An unspoken invitation to drink, to linger, to sample forbidden carnal pleasures hung in the air. Ali Muhammad stared at the pimp as if he were dog dirt discovered on the bottom of his sandals.

Though he had not paid much attention to Maroof's grandiose plans of changing the face of Pakistani prostitution, enough of the details had drifted in for Ali Muhammad to recognize that here was a man whose selfishness lay beyond definition.

Maroof rationalized his vile actions like the ancient pagans of Madyan who said, "It is our tradition to sin like our forefathers, so do not reproach us."

Sitting next to Ali Muhammad was a man who took delight in his obstinate love of vice, who wove a spider's web of wickedness, every strand of which was wrung from the blood and souls of the women he used as chattels. He was a peddler of evil passions, a schemer with no respect for any laws, divine or human.

Without a word of explanation Ali Muhammad stood up to go.

Seeing his prey about to escape, the pimp urged Ali to stay. Maroof was a well-dressed monster, capable of any corruption. He offered the American his unwilling sister and more. Ali Muhammad never answered the summons, only stared at a person he knew was so deep in sin nothing could reclaim him.

The American walked out of the room without a word of explanation or goodbye. With Shaheen gone Ali Muhammad knew he had no reason to linger with her husband, a villian who had long ago cast God behind his back in contempt. Immersed as he was in decadence, Maroof believed that by concealing his frauds from the world he could escape his eventual consignment to misery. Ali Muhammad left the unrepentant violator wallowing in sin, luxuriating in abomination, waiting to take his place in the regiment of the damned after coming face to face with a patient and angry Allah.

Ali Muhammad returned to Peshawar, informed Raja and me of the recent developments and promptly retreated into his house. Two days later I went to visit him, urging him to come with me to the stables to visit the horses.

Ishaq was due to arrive shortly at the police stables to seal our bargain to sell the three geldings. As Pahlwan's owner Ali Muhammad needed to be present to sign the papers transferring title to the new owner. My friend made no attempt to hide the despair gripping him. His

A Transitory Love

face was wan, his eyes bloodshot from weeping, his demeanor a mixture of impatience and detachment. He was working on composing a new tune to play on his rebob. I didn't have to be told it dealt with the loss of Shaheen. I gently urged him to come outside into the vibrancy of Peshawar's streets and accompany me to see his horse one last time. He shook off the suggestion, my plea having no more effect on him than music on a dead man. Then he relented, assuring me he would be at the stables in time to fulfill any legal obligations.

"Go ahead Asadullah. I will bring him shortly," Raja whispered to me.

I had long ago learned to have complete confidence in the Afridi. I left Ali Muhammad's home on Gari Syeddan street, flagged down a tonga and rode out to the police stables to confront an ancient problem.

Wise men say that horses have carried men on their backs for more than six thousand years. As I walked into the old stables I wondered if during all that time it had ever been easier to say goodbye to a horse you love, for to part with a horse who will not miss you is bad, but to part from a horse who loves you in return is as bad as anything I know.

Pasha heard my step and turning, whinnied in recognition when he saw me. Big Pahlwan and stoic Pajaro both bobbed their heads in way of a silent greeting. Their mangers were full of succulent chopped feed. Their coats were shiny from the attention lavished on them by the mounted policemen.

When I stood next to my dun gelding he placed his smooth head up against my chest, waiting for me to scratch him in way of a greeting. This done, he nuzzled me as though he sensed something was wrong. There are no secrets as close as that between a horse and his rider.

Waves of loneliness washed over me. When a man has lived with a horse, eaten with a horse, survived dangers with a horse, traveled hundreds of miles with a horse for months on end ----- the horizon of my life suddenly appeared empty without the continued companionship of that loyal animal.

I stroked his satin-smooth neck, felt his long mane slide through my fingers, saw the kindness and courage I had come to know of him flicker in his deep brown eyes. On the one hand there were all the other horses of the world that had passed through my life. On the other hand there was Pasha, brother, child, friend, warrior, imp. Did Alexander weep for Bucephalus? So in turn did I grieve for this horse more than any other.

"We should have died on the trail," I told him softly, "and been buried at Burbolongo Shal like those great Scythian chiefs whose bones lie mingled with their chargers beneath forgotten funeral mounds."

Pasha nuzzled me, sensing my distress.

"You'll be OK Pasha, you'll be OK," I whispered huskily, then hugged his strong neck, hoping to God that what I was saying was the truth, and that where he was going was as safe as I prayed it was.

The big dun nuzzled me, then nickered softly in reply.

I heard steps behind me and turning saw Inspector Akbar Ali walk out of the bright sunlight into the shadows of the stables.

"The truck is here," he announced.

The older man saw the look of indecision on my face, read my mind and knew I was holding back, undecided if I trusted this fine animal to even a pampered prince.

"Best to remember the transitory nature of horses and men," Akbar told me. "You are richer for having shared your life with him. Understand the time has come to let him travel on."

I nodded mutely, my eyes silently streaming tears, unembarrassed to display the tenderness I felt for Pasha in front of this wise old horseman.

"Yes, I recognize the moment," I managed to say and untied Pasha's lead rope to prove it.

Akbar lead out Pahlwan and Pajaro. I followed with the dun.

Ishaq was waiting close to the main gate of the police compound. A large Bedford truck was parked nearby. It looked like an old-time circus wagon, with its brightly colored scenes of landscapes, animals and religious lettering painted along its sides. Riaz the groom, the truck driver and a helper loitered close by their rich boss.

I handed the lead rope of my horse to one of the several mounted policemen who had come out of the barracks to help load the geldings. The police inspector did the same, then walked over to inspect the truck bed.

The passing of time had not taught the wealthy landlord any additional manners. We had no sooner shook hands than he informed me he was eager to pay me off and climb back into the air conditioned Mercedes Benz sedan he had arrived in. I explained that we would wait for Ali Muhammad and Raja before completing our arrangements.

A wave from the Inspector allowed me to leave Ishaq's questionable presence. It was plain to see the reason Akbar had called me aside. The steel floor of the old Bedford was shiny with age. Either through neglect, or ignorance, no one had bothered to place any straw in the bottom of the truck as footing. It was already late to send someone off to the bazaar, and it was technically not my concern, but that of the new owner. Anyone could see the horses would slip, fall, and most likely hurt themselves on such dangerous footing. The situation reminded me that the harsh realities of Pakistan were already exerting control over my horses. Yet this last thing could at least be set right before they left my protection and care. Akbar and I concurred that we did not believe the matter would be resolved unless we forced the issue.

We did not ask Ishaq, rather we told him the horses would require proper footing before they were sold or loaded. The zamindar screwed up his face in anger. He was clearly used to having his wishes instantly obeyed. After screaming at Riaz, who he blamed for the oversight, Ishaq reluctantly gave the groom and the trucker's assistant a few rupees and ordered to them to return with enough straw to cover the truck bed.

The landlord then walked over and began to stroke Pasha's neck. All three geldings were grazing quietly on a large expanse of lawn that lay within the police compound. My dun paid little attention to the stranger. He was too busy, like his stable mates, eating as much of the succulent grass as he could get his teeth into. Watching the three geldings eat, I

A Transitory Love

knew they still did not understand that their days of scant rations were finally over.

Pasha's new owner made a few complimentary remarks about how well he looked.

"God hung happiness from his forelock," I said quietly.

I watched the three horses, each unique, all three an integral part of a tiny, self-contained equine society . They were the closest thing to a family I had ever had in Asia, my beloved vagrant comrades of those northern roads.

"They were never victims of human tyranny under my watch," I said to myself.

No one heard me, nor would anyone there except the Inspector have understood such an outlandish foreign concept. I was glad when a tonga full of straw came wheeling in with Ishaq's men on board.

For the best part of an hour I oversaw the preparation of the truck. Finally Pasha's new owner would be delayed no longer. He was anxious to get back to Haripur, insisting that I accept the money and sign over the horses. I kept glancing out the gate, thinking I would see Ali Muhammad and Raja come running up any moment, but I was wrong. The rich man's impatience only added to my own nervous indecision. In the back of my mind I knew I still had not completely made up my mind to sell Pasha.

Most horses only tolerate the men on their backs. They have no love nor confidence in those who ride them, nor should they. Such horses are not noble companions of the road, they are equine slaves, they are agricultural products, they are objects of no passion possessed by men of no honor, who buy and sell them like furniture, dismissing at a whim an animal worthy of grander considerations.

A horseman's honor begins in the stirrup and ends in the saddle. I had made a dreary mistake when I sold Shavon. Looking at Ishaq's pudgy face, I did not want to be rushed into repeating my error.

Eventually he lost patience. There was no sign of my friends. He gave me an ultimatum to either sell or let him return home. With a sinking heart I signed the papers, took his money, shook his hand, and ordered the geldings loaded.

The truck had been backed up against an earthen embankment so the horses could be brought on. One of the policemen lead Pahlwan in first. The big gray had been through too many adventures to pay much attention to one more truck. He climbed in and took his place at the head of the steel box. As soon as Pahlwan's lead rope was tied down, Pajaro went on next. The beautiful bay was as quiet and well mannered as always. He walked in beside his companion and began nibbling at the straw piled around his feet.

I would not let anyone else lead Pasha on.

Taking his lead rope, I lead him to the foot of the truck. He hesitated for an instant, looking into the steel box, unsure what I was asking of him. I clicked my tongue and gently pulled on his rope. The big dun followed my last command and walked into the truck that was to separate us forever. I tied his lead rope securely, checked the other two ropes as well, then walked out and went straight to Ishaq.

"I was taught that every grain of barley given to a horse is inscribed by Allah in the ledger of good works. Let it be with you and these horses or I shall hear of it," I warned the fat man.

If Ishaq wanted to answer he never got the chance. He was interrupted by Raja. The young Pathan came running into the police compound, looking frantically in every direction. The moment Raja saw me, he ran to my side.

"Ali Muhammad has gone to Bajaur with Shaheen," he gasped.

"What? When?" I asked, unwilling to believe so bizarre a tale of even my impetuous friend.

"Just a little while ago. A man came to the door who claimed to be her brother. Within a few moments Shaheen and the man had both come inside the house. They convinced Ali to go with them into tribal territory, saying he could marry Shaheen there."

Ishaq wasn't interested in the details of our troubles, and he also recognized nothing else was stopping him from leaving. He ordered the back of the truck closed off.

At first Pasha laid his head over on Pajaro's shoulder so that he could keep me in sight. When the truck was closed Pasha lost sight of me. He immediately started neighing frantically, sensing that this was our final separation. Ishaq ordered his men into the truck, then climbed into the Mercedes and drove off. The truck followed within seconds.

I heard Pasha screaming and kicking the steel walls of the truck, watched the strength and wisdom that was the best horse I ever knew dwindle into a speck of loneliness on the Grand Trunk road, felt the tender thread of fate that had tied us together snap.

When there was no longer any sight of them I turned to Raja.

"Why didn't you try and stop Ali?" I asked.

"I did. I told him, 'If you go with her to Bajaur you have a better chance of getting buried than married.'"

"An evil day," I said and shook my head sadly. "All I do goes amiss."

Then I turned aside from my grief at losing Pasha and went to find my friend.

We hurried to Hasht Nagari, running through streets that resembled narrow gorges, flew by houses steeped in shadow, traveled through lanes so constricted two people could barely pass one another, until we at last came to Gari Syeddan and the home of Ali Muhammad.

The house was empty, my horses were gone, and so was all trace of Ali Muhammad.

45
Uninvited Guests

There had been no omen in Ali Muhammad's soul the fateful morning Shaheen appeared, no premonition from Allah hinting that the course of his life was to be forever altered, no signpost warning that his heart's desire was finally to be fulfilled, no subtle indication that the emotional toll on the road up ahead would cost him everything he knew and once was.

My friend had seen me come, and then reluctantly leave without him. He had shaken off the suggestion to accompany me to the stables. Plenty of time for that final heartache, he reasoned to himself. He did not want to linger saying goodbye to Pahlwan, in fact he wanted to remember the big gray as he had been on the parri, the steadfast companion who had carried him to the limited safety of Shaheen's arms.

But the woman was gone and Ali Muhammad knew that with the horse's departure he now faced the loss of yet another remnant of his time with her. Ali's soul had grown weary since learning of her escape. He felt old and withered inside. The taste of ashes and defeat lay strong in his mouth. He had no patience for the clamoring of the outside world.

After my departure Ali Muhammad sat cross-legged in the main room of his house. He heard Raja quietly rustling about in the kitchen. When the Afridi boy appeared with a tray bearing two cups of chai, Ali smiled weakly, grateful but by no means hungry. The Pathan placed a cup in front of him, then took a seat nearby, leaning up against the pillows that lined the walls and keeping his own cup of chai close at hand.

It was a large luxurious room, as befitted a Peshawari man of taste and elegance. It was painted in a soft off-white to keep down the heat. An expensive scarlet red Turkoman carpet covered the brick floor from wall to wall. Various photographs hung in matching silver frames on the walls. They showed Ali Muhammad playing instruments with musicians from around the world, some of which impressed Raja, like the one showing Farzana the Pushtu nightingale smiling at his friend. Others, like the one of Jimi Hendrix and a younger Beau Fontaine playing electric guitars in a London jam session, meant nothing to the boy.

A serviceable *punkha* (fan) whirled softly overhead. Two walls were lined with the large *mutakas* (pillows) that served as furniture. A built-in bookcase held the gaudy trinkets that had caught Ali Muhammad's eye in the bazaar over the years. Ancient leather-bound Qu'rans shared shelves with silver nomad jewelry. Chunks of lapis lazuli were tossed on top of imported volumes of sheet music. Costly, hand-embroidered tapestries covered the old walls. Once commonplace, the war in Afghanistan had brought their production to a halt. The shimmering silks could have graced a museum so fine was their intricate geometric construction. Yet in this room full of Oriental splendor they were but a single element of the whole of Ali Muhammad's world, a place of rich color now devoid of its heart and purpose.

An array of various musical instruments hung on pegs or leaned against the walls of this sanctuary, including a beautiful sitar from old Delhi, a battered but serviceable dutar from the bazaars of Herat, a cherry-red Gibson electric guitar, and two tablas from the nearby Dobghari bazaar, home of Peshawar's musicians. The musical cornucopia reflected Ali's wide travels, his eclectic musical tastes, and his many harmonic talents.

With the chai steaming before him the American reached over and picked up his favorite instrument, the rebob. Ali's rebob was a beautiful hand-crafted piece of workmanship. Two feet long, it was a graceful wooden instrument shaped like a deep hulled boat joined to the short tapering neck of a guitar. It had been lovingly carved from a mulberry trunk, before its hollowed heart was covered by a taut sheepskin. Beaded tassels hung from the ornately carved head, and mother-of-pearl inlay graced its bosom. Silver-topped tuning pegs adorned the 21 gut and steel strings that never failed to rouse a tribesman's heart. In a city famous for its musical performers, Ali Muhammad's expertise with this Stradivarius of the Orient was legendary. The other musicians had often jokingly referred to it as his "wife," so sweetly did he make her sing her invisible mosaics.

That day she did not lift her voice in a melody of happiness.

Raja watched while his friend silently went about plucking and tuning the strings. Ali Muhammad held the rebob in his lap, at first touching the strings lightly, tuning and twisting its pegs in a mysterious manner, searching for a pitch beyond the understanding of a non-musician. Then he tore into a song Raja had never heard him play before. At first the music was hot and erotic. Ali savaged the rebob, making her scream of hunger and desire, of secret fleeting pleasures, great beauty and uncontrollable compulsions.

Ali Muhammad's upper body swayed with the music as his hands flew across the strings in remembrance. His eyes were closed. He did not appear to be breathing. His soul was gone on the wind of the music. Then his mouth compressed. His lips became a thin line separating his internal pain from the outside world.

The rebob pulled Raja into a melody of tenderness and the sound of gentle rain, of shadowy lanes and the warmth of an anxious heart on a chilly Lahore night. It sang of despair, of hopelessness and torment that knew no end. It drove out Raja's former interpretation of music and replaced it with the sounds defining the loneliness of a foreign man in a foreign land.

And then Ali Muhammad began to sing, softly unreeling the secret melody that twisted inside his heart.

"Kusa dei larrey, kor nesdee dei, ro keda qadamuna layla Shaheena," (the road is long, the house is close, take slow steps Shaheen my darling.)

My friend played as the tender voiced rebob sang an aria of pain.

"I was born that night you kissed me. I died that day you left me. I lived the few weeks that you loved me Shaheen."

The song evoked a wound in even Raja's strong Pathan heart.

The two friends sat enveloped in the invisible gossamer of the troubadour's making, until a knock on the front door brought them out of their reverie. Ali continued to play softly to himself, aware of the interruption, but giving it neither thought nor consideration. Raja went to the door as Ali Muhammad knew he would.

A few moments later the American looked up from his music when he saw Raja re-enter the room.

"Is Asadullah back so soon?" Ali asked.

"No, there is a bearded man at the door wanting to see you. He would not tell me who he is, but he is wearing a pistol."

The information describing a bearded pistolero could have fitted a third of the men in Peshawar. Ali Muhammad was reluctant to leave his self-imposed isolation for an unknown stranger.

"Tell him to go away."

"I already did," Raja quickly replied.

With a sigh of exasperation Ali Muhammad laid aside the rebob and walked down the hall to the front door.

Raja had been correct. The handsome young man standing before him did have a black, spade-shaped beard, as well as deep-set eyes that gave him an altogether untrustworthy appearance. He wore no hat nor turban atop his coal-colored hair. His shalwar kameez was old but serviceable. The bullets lying across his chest, however, were shiny. They were slipped into the bandoleer that held a leather shoulder holster under the man's left arm. The oiled butt of the .32 caliber semi-automatic pistol peeking out of its holster told Ali Muhammad that the gun, and not the man's poor clothes, were his priority. Though Ali could not place the man's face, he seemed vaguely familiar.

Before Ali Muhammad could say "Assalaam aleikum" the mysterious caller asked him a question.

"Who is your best friend in Pakistan?"

Ali felt a cold shiver run down his spine. He knew this was no ordinary beggar come looking for a handout from a kind-hearted foreigner. He hesitated for a moment, then answered truthfully.

"I had only one best friend, but she is gone."

"No, she has come to Peshawar to find you," the man said softly, and before Ali Muhammad had time to digest this news, the stranger turned and beckoned to a woman who stood further down Gari Syeddan hidden under the folds of a royal blue burkha.

Ali Muhammad stood frozen in place. In his heart he knew who was walking rapidly towards him.

"In the name of Allah the woman and I risk our lives standing here. Let us in," the man at the door urged Ali.

The American barely had time to move aside before the stranger crowded through, so anxious was he to vacate the doorway. Raja was standing close behind Ali Muhammad. He gave the stranger a hard look, but said nothing when the other man entered.

The woman in the burkha hurried towards the door, trying not to trip as she made her way across the cobble stoned street. Her careful steps denounced her as an amateur in finding her way with only the narrow mesh net of the burkha as her guide. Yet she navigated her way across the lane, through the door, and into the hallway wordlessly before stopping.

"Is there anyone else here?" the stranger asked Ali nervously.

"No, we are alone," Ali Muhammad confided, as he closed and locked the big door behind them.

He motioned the two uninvited callers to follow him into his main room. The *punkha* still whirled softly overhead. The rebob lay leaning against the wall, her musical prayers about to be answered. When all four people were standing in the room, the woman slowly pulled the burkha from over her head. Ali Muhammad stood looking at the blaze of Shaheen's revealed beauty.

"Did you forget me Ali Muhammad?" she asked and smiled mischievously.

"I've forgotten a lot of things, Shaheen, but you'll never be one of them," he replied honestly.

She stood there exposed for what she was, wife, mistress, whore. The bold smile on her face told all three men that this was a woman who made no apologies for using the only tools Allah had granted her, a raw sexuality and mystifying beauty. Her white satin shalwar kameez looked travel-stained and dusty. More importantly Ali recognized it as the first thing he had ever seen her in, back on the fateful evening they first met in Lahore.

Since then Shaheen's delicate cheek bones had grown more pronounced. Her brilliant black eyes seemed unnaturally bright. Her face radiated a magnetic intensity. She glanced quickly around the room like a hunted animal. Feeling safe, she then brought her gaze back upon her American lover. At the sight of Ali's hungry devotion she laughed that warm, comfortable laugh that told him to be at ease, then gave him one of her saucy reassuring smiles, before gliding towards him.

Gone was the smell of jasmine blossoms entwined in her long wet black ringlets from that night so long ago. Now she smelled of dust, diesel fumes, sweat and fear. Her wheat colored skin had taken on a uncharacteristic pale pallor. Close up he could see that her smile was a lie. She did not look confident, only weary. But regardless of her faults Shaheen understood Ali Muhammad. She put her arms around his neck, the smile on her face reassuring him that she still remembered the urgent and painful secret her presence brought about. For on the instant the warmth of her full ripe breasts pressed up against him, Ali felt his manhood rise as it always did in her presence, and he knew if she had bidden him he would have sacrificed anything to sample her sweets.

Raja gave her a poisonous look, and felt his heart die when he saw the love Ali Muhammad held in his eyes for the whore. The two lovers stood locked together in obvious need of privacy. Without a word the young Afridi turned and left the room. However he went only so far as the hallway, carefully leaving the door ajar in order that he could eavesdrop.

Shaheen had not risked her life in order to pleasure an ardent lover. The moment the embarrassed Raja left the room her immediate purpose was complete. She took her arms from around Ali's neck and turned her gaze on the other man in the room.

"This is my brother Pervez," she explained in way of a brief introduction, and then without prompting turned and took a seat against the pillows lining the wall.

The two men followed Shaheen's cue, sitting down on either side of her.

"Maroof told me he was going to cheat you, to take your money and then turn you into the police. When I said I wouldn't help him, he beat me very badly. Pervez came to visit but took me away in order to protect me," Shaheen told Ali Muhammad. "I came away so I could be with you," she added.

If the American heard a false note he gave no indication. He was content to rest his eyes on her beauty, to feel the warmth radiating off the curves of her body, once again to be within her presence though they might be sharing a cell in Hell itself.

"Shaheen is afraid that *dahloose* (king of the pimps) will seek revenge and kill her. Our mother sent word from Swat that Maroof has already been there. That's why I brought her to our uncle's house in Bajaur," Pervez told the American.

"Don't let anyone know I am here or Maroof will slay me," Shaheen pleaded.

Ali Muhammad nodded in agreement. An assassination was a cheap commodity in a country full of armed and dangerous men. Five thousand rupees would see a bothersome individual done in quietly. As in all instances, women came cheaper.

"I thought I had lost you," Ali Muhammad told Shaheen, heedless of the man sharing the room with them. "I went to Lahore when I finished my horse trip and found you gone."

Shaheen smiled tenderly.

"Do you still want to marry me Ali Muhammad?"

"You know I do."

"When I told Pervez about you he said he would never marry me to a Angrez, but I told him you were a good Muslim."

The brother gave a weak smile in way of agreement.

The American offered no sign that he did not believe her so Shaheen continued.

"I love you and want to marry you," she said, then asked him the question that had been burning a hole in her mind. "What about the money? Do you have it here?"

"Five hundred thousand rupees is a lot of money," he told her.

"Is it?" she asked and smiled. "Do you have it here?" she repeated insistently.

Khyber Knights

Ali felt an involuntary shiver run down his back. Suddenly he remembered that Maroof had told him Shaheen had run away with a lover from Bajaur. He wondered how much truth was in her story, or Maroof's tale. Pervez looked enough like her to be a brother, but Ali Muhammad knew that could be a mere coincidence. He suddenly began to wonder how they had located his house, and if love was the real reason she had risked her life to see him.

At first Shaheen soothed away his anxieties. He had forgotten, she said, that he had told her where he lived in Peshawar. As he kept up his questioning her smiling answers turned into impatient shrugs. Finally she lost her temper, turning the white hot rage he had seen her unleash on the Punjabi pimps in his direction.

"Stop the questions. Just get the money and pay my brother. Then we can be together," she snapped.

He did not answer. But she was quickly all smiles again when he stood up and left the room purposefully.

When Ali Muhammad came into the hallway he saw Raja lingering outside the doorway, defiant and making no pretense at hiding. Ali noticed, but walked by quickly without a word. The Afridi deliberately maintained his post and watched as Ali Muhammad went up the stairs leading to his bedroom. Raja could hear Pervez and Shaheen whispering conspiratorially in the other room, but could make out nothing except the feeling that neither of them meant his friend any good.

Within a few minutes Ali Muhammad returned to the main room. In his hand he carried a small brown paper bag. After sitting down next to Shaheen, Ali handed it to her. She quickly tore it open, her sigh of satisfaction an audible compliment at the sight that greeted her. Lying there in her hands were six matching gold bangles. They were an extravagant, kingly gift delicately wrought from soft 22 karat gold. Shaheen was clearly delighted. When she slipped them over her small wrist, their filigree gleamed in the morning sunlight.

"See," she told Pervez defiantly, "I told you he loved me."

Ali Muhammad was glad to see Shaheen so pleased.

"I carried them in my pocket to Lahore. Then when I found you gone, I brought them home again. Their beauty matches your own."

He watched the delight shining in her eyes and knew true joy for a brief moment. Then he turned to her brother.

"I can get the money but it will take a little time to raise it," Shaheen's suitor explained.

The visitors exchanged a look as if they had foreseen this possibility.

"We can't stay in Peshawar. It is too dangerous. Are you sure you want to marry me?" she said.

He looked at the expensive bangles and then back at her face.

"How can you ask me that."

"Good, then come with us to my uncle's house in Bajaur."

"When?"

"Now. We can get married there."

Even so deep a love as Ali's had perimeters. His initial enthusiasm was replaced by a sense of unease at the unreasonable suggestion.

Ali Muhammad tried stalling Shaheen, pleading at first that he was needed at the stables to help load the departing horses and asking them to wait until later in the day. The prostitute was contemptuous of such a paltry delay, wondering out loud why she had risked her life for a man who valued a horse more than her love. Finally Ali broached the subject which he had been avoiding. He said Shaheen should be willing to put her thumb print on an *e jaza nama*, a document stating she was neither married nor engaged to anyone else.

But to all his requests she had an excuse or a prohibition.

"Maroof was never my husband. We can be married secretly. No court. No judges. A tribal affair," she urged him.

"If I am to be married my friends should come," he said.

Yet even this slim thread was denied him.

"No, we must go back now and alone. After I'm your wife we can come back to Peshawar quietly. You can tell your friends then, before you take me away to some place safe. Now come, before they find and kill us," she told him and seeing his hesitation, she laid her hand on his own to emphasize the physical bond that lay between them like an open secret.

My friend sat there undecided. He knew I was expecting him, but reasoned the trip was finished and his obligations to the horses were at an end. Finally he admitted to himself that he was not hesitating because of Pahlwan's departure. Ali Muhammad knew in his heart he did not fully trust Shaheen, realized she wanted to lead him down the rest of an unknown road with no protection except the love that he bore her.

"I am leaving. Come with me," she pleaded.

He heard a note of finality in Shaheen's voice and knew he was going to lose her forever if he did not immediately follow her into the void. Suddenly he was no longer torn. He suspected she was a liar, a rogue, and he put his life in her hands anyway.

"This thing I do for myself alone," he thought, "by myself alone."

"Yes, I will come with you," he said and stood as though he were ready to depart. "Let me get my pistol and papers."

"No need," Pervez said, "you will be our guest and safe in tribal territory."

Ali Muhammad looked at Shaheen for confirmation. She said nothing, only smiled. He studied her beauty and knew if she were standing in front of a pit of fire and held out her arms, he would take a deep breath and step towards his doom.

"Yes I am coming," he heard himself say, as he slipped on a light cotton vest and adjusted his turban.

Shaheen quickly donned the burkha and the three of them were instantly ready to depart. As soon as they entered the hallway Raja began protesting. Pervez and Shaheen did not linger to hear the complaints of the man they deemed the house servant. Ali too ignored Raja's vehement complaints.

"Tell Asadullah I'll be back in a few days with my wife," Ali Muhammad said as he started towards the door.

"You'll be back dead," Raja said and tried to physically restrain his friend from leaving.

The magnetic attraction of Shaheen proved stronger than the young Afridi's grip. Ali Muhammad shook off Raja's hand, refusing to acknowledge his friend's protests. When the water is already over your head the depth makes no difference. Ali Muhammad just walked out of the house as if he was strolling no further than the corner bakery. He had only gone a few steps when he turned as if a last-minute thought had just cropped into mind.

"When you see Asadullah, ask him if he wants to buy my house?" he told the Pathan youth.

Ali Muhammad's eyes were glazed. His mind was already up ahead, fixed on the backs of the two departing strangers. Raja knew he had no pistol, no papers, and no prudence.

My friend never looked back and with a burst of speed soon caught up with Pervez. They made their way side by side through the winding streets of Peshawar. People greeted Ali Muhammad warmly. He was a minor celebrity in the Hasht Nagari neighborhood, well known, well loved, well respected. No one suspected the purpose of the bearded tribesman walking beside the foreign-born Muslim. Ali Muhammad and Pervez exchanged pleasantries, while Shaheen followed slowly in her burkha fifteen feet behind. It would not do to be seen walking next to her. In rumor-happy Peshawar, such an act would cause a tidal wave of gossip that might filter out to Maroof in Lahore. Yet when he glanced back, Ali saw the gold bangles riding on Shaheen's slender wrist. The sight made his heart fly up to meet the hawks soaring over the old city.

They traveled in two different rickshaws to the Charsadda bus stand, with Ali Muhammad going alone. The noise from the nearby road was fierce with assorted brightly-painted buses pulling out for destinations ranging from Quetta to Kohat. Drivers honked horns and shoved their unwieldy mechanized beasts of burden around their competitors. *Kalendars* (conductors) screamed out destinations and tried to grab late-arriving passengers. Cassette tapes blared a Babel of competing musical dissonance. It was just another day at the bus station.

"It's a difficult journey to Bajaur," Pervez told the American as the three of them prepared to board a bus going in their direction.

"Leave him alone. He rode a horse to China," Shaheen hissed from underneath the blue sack hiding her from the rest of the world.

Ali Muhammad knew Shaheen did not know where China was, but at that moment he would have boarded the bus bound for purgatory. He watched the woman he loved take careful mincing steps up the slippery metal stairs leading into the bus, all the while holding the steel hand rail and trying to see through the narrow mesh net of the burkha. When she and Pervez were safely on board, the American followed.

The bus was nearly full. Shaheen sat next to a similarly clad woman in a seat close to the front. Pervez and Ali took up aisle seats opposite each other, a few rows back. They were not long in departing. The bus pulled out with horn blaring and the *kalendar* screaming, "Charsadda, Shabqadar, Gandao - Charsadda, Shabqadar, Gandao," over and over. As they sped north out of Peshawar no one noticed that the old bus was full of Pathan men, women, children, and one very doubtful American.

46
Into the Lawless Land

Pakistan did all she could to set Ali Muhammad's heart at rest.

He watched as the well-known countryside of the Vale of Peshawar unrolled before his eyes. How long ago it seemed since he had wandered down the rim of those mountains separating him from war-torn Kabul. He had thought he would have returned to New Orleans before now. He had not foreseen the Jihad lasting so long, had not counted on becoming so entrenched in the North West Frontier Province, had not believed he could fall so deeply in love.

The summer was well worn. The corn fields were tall. The sugar cane waved in the hot sunlight. When the bus started passing acres and acres of dark green tobacco fields he knew they were nearing Charsadda. The three travelers stayed on the bus while it briefly stopped in the busy market town.

Looking through the open window Ali Muhammad saw the usual shops selling bolts of bright cloth, little boxes of imported medicine, guns and ammunition, or stacks of Pushtu cassette tapes, some of which he realized he had recorded. Further down the street he heard the noise of men beating hammers on metal and knew there was a truck repair shop nearby. Directly out of the window he saw the familiar pink walls of the Venus Hotel. He looked back in his mind and saw three travel-stained equestrian explorers crawling out the hotel window because the front door was still locked. For a moment he remembered the clip clop mantra of big Pahlwan's hoofs as they carried him away from Charsadda on that morning not so long ago, on to Chitral, over the Babusar Pass, home to Peshawar and now full circle onto that crowded bus with Shaheen.

As Ali sat lost in thought, people departed and new arrivals climbed on board, all the while the *kalendar* yelled their intended destinations. Only this time the young man added a sinister name to his litany.

"Shabqadar, Gandao, Bajaur," he yelled out the door.

When Ali Muhammad heard the sound of their final anchorage, he knew he was voluntarily moving away from even the half-wild traces of the world he had normally called home. For with every turn of the bus wheels he was traveling further away from Peshawar and the truth.

Two hours later the now-crowded bus passed beyond an invisible boundary and entered into the shadowy zone known as "tribal territory." The driver halted at the village of Shabqadar, not only to let off passengers, but because a government road-block barred his way.

The last twenty miles had seen the villages becoming not only less frequent but increasingly less prosperous. Shabqadar had little to boast of even in the best of times. Sitting on its southern borders now was an impressive array of federal power. A dozen armored cars, several pieces of heavy artillery, and four tanks dozed in the sun. Both sides of the road boasted machinegun emplacements. Dozens of nearby tents clearly hosted the troops necessary to man all the imported American military equipment.

The musician did not know the reason for the unexpected presence of Pakistani troops. The government in Islamabad had inherited a time-honored system from the British Raj that tolerated an uneasy status quo with the Pathan tribesmen residing along the country's western borders. Something was clearly wrong, though Ali Muhammad knew he did not dare chance asking even Pervez the answer to the puzzle.

A glance out the window did tell the American several things. He immediately noticed that the six soldiers manning the check point had new G-3 assault rifles. They were armed with the high-powered automatic weapons so they could outgun the local Pathans, who carried the smaller caliber AK-47 machine guns.

Plus Ali Muhammad did not need to be told that he risked immediate arrest if he were found so far off the beaten track. If detected, he would be lucky if he was only interrogated as a spy and ejected from the country with a few broken bones. Looking at the royal blue burkha sitting in front of him he knew he could not risk revealing his foreign origins.

He had little time to debate his situation. Any idle chatter among the other passengers ceased the moment a soldier came on board to search for concealed weapons. The Pathan passengers glared sullenly at the dark-skinned, young Punjabi private who represented a despised government. The soldier made his way uneasily down the aisle, pretending to make a cursory check. Everyone on board knew he wouldn't have the nerve to make a fuss unless he tripped over a grenade launcher sticking out from underneath a seat.

Shaheen's foreign lover tried hard to blend in, looking out the window in an effort to appear casual. But the light skinned passenger halfway back had caught the soldier's attention. The private carefully made his way down the aisle towards Ali Muhammad.

When my friend saw the soldier approaching out of the corner of his eye, he did the only thing he could do in the situation. He reacted like a true Pathan. As soon as the soldier drew near, Ali Muhammad snapped his head around and glared up at him.

"What are you staring at blacky?" he shouted at the startled soldier in guttural Pushtu. "Why don't you go back to Lahore where you belong?"

The verbal attack took the entire bus by surprise. Pervez was the only one to react. He reached over with his left foot across the aisle and lightly tapped Ali Muhammad's sandal, as a sign to behave himself.

The American, however, continued his bluff. He looked at Pervez like he was some sort of unwelcome insect, then glanced down at his offending foot.

"You *kumaqual spay zoi* (stupid son of a bitch) that shine is only a week old. Get your damn foot off me," Ali Muhammad shouted in mock anger.

Into the Lawless Land

Despite the passenger's light complexion the Punjabi soldier knew that only a Pathan would react so boldly. He left hurriedly and the bus was immediately waved through. An old tribesman sitting behind Ali reached up and slapped him on the back, congratulating him on his rude behavior. The only thing that mattered to Ali Muhammad was the flash of Shaheen's bright eyes through the net of the burkha, when she briefly turned around.

Soon all questionable traces of Pakistan's official power evaporated. The bus took them over the backbone of grim mountains that marked the borders of their eventual destination. Ali Muhammad knew they had ventured into a portion of Pakistan that relished her isolation, a place where legends said vice and villainy walked at noontime unveiled. Out the window he saw toothy crags snapping at the blue sky. This was the beginning of Bajaur, a place whose stony soil mothered murderers and rogues without number. Old and inhospitable when Alexander the Great forced his way through, the Mohmand tribesmen of that territory were still a fanatically independent people much addicted to intrigue, treachery and murder.

Bajaur existed on the official map as one of seven Federally Administered Tribal Areas, a ten thousand square mile zone of questionable allegiance running down the western side of Pakistan. The FATA ran from Chitral south all the way past Quetta. Dwelling within the different tribal territories were the seven tribes of the Orakzai, Kurram, Khyber, Mohmand, Bajaur, and North and South Waziristan agencies. Back in Islamabad the pencil-pushers maintained a pretense of controlling the tribal belt. In reality the natives paid as little attention to the federal government in Islamabad as seven other tribes, the Apaches, Comanches, Kiowa, Sioux, Blackfoot, Cheyenne and Crows, once had to distant Washington DC.

In those untracked mountains the 20th century ran head-on into the dark ages and lost.

The word "Pakistan" was an imposed foreign concept of no daily importance. In Bajaur anyone not a Pathan was an alien. That all-important classification meant the difference between life and death.

Even other Pathans were not above suspicion.

Traditionally the country of the Pathans had been ruled by the ironclad concept of *nang* (honor). In areas where this all-important axiom held sway there was little social stratification and no central political authority. *Pukhtunwali*, the ancient code of honor, was the final deciding factor in all matters of conflict. Down country, in the Vale of Peshawar, the western concept of *qalang*, or land ownership, had gained precedence over the Pushtu traditions of patriarchal lineage and personal honor. Membership in much of Pathan society had been eroded by outside values stressing power held by the various strata of a domestic and foreign aristocracy. The ancient teachings of the *Pukhtunwali* were held in polite, if quiet, contempt down country.

Nowhere was this combat of philosophies better exemplified than in Bajaur.

Khyber Knights

The Mohmands who occupied those mountains saw the federal government's role as being one of extracting taxes, raising conscripts and eroding their time-honored cultural values. Historically all efforts to encapsulate Mohmand territory into a political system seen as alien had met with bloody conflict. The men of Bajaur had resisted Alexander the Great, the British Raj, and were now prepared to take on General Zia.

Ali Muhammad watched the unknown country rumble by. The green fertility of Peshawar lay far behind him. He knew that even in the best of times the government only claimed to control the main road. Anything falling outside its immediate confines was by definition a local matter.

The old bus dipped up and down the mountains into small, isolated valleys. Here the American began to see the various mud forts that dotted the landscape. Gone were all traces of mere domestic housing. The dry, barren mountains gave the Mohmands the building material needed to construct the brown adobe walls and fortresses they called home. The forts differed in size and complexity, some enclosing vast acreage behind their secretive walls. Others, though smaller, were equally dour. All however boasted at least one high tower. Even from a distance Ali Muhammad could make out the black twinkle of the popular Dashakha anti-aircraft guns sticking out of slits cut in the tower walls. The big shells from the captured Russian .50 caliber machine gun were longer than a man's hand and would have ripped the bus in half.

This was the part of the world where blood feuds and tribal skirmishes were still common. The men Ali Muhammad saw through the windows walked tall. Even the young boys had a martial bearing about them which demanded respect. Unlike the once-proud, but now degenerate, Bedouin tribesmen of Arabia, the Mohmand Pathans remained largely unfettered by the weakening influences of western conformity. Their scattered villages may have been poor and forlorn, but their ancient way of life was still largely intact.

Ali Muhammad gave it all little thought. Looming ever nearer was Afghanistan, now an uncivilized place inhabited by people even more savage than those gathered on the bus around him. The American ventured on heedlessly, his love for Shaheen his sole ideology and defense.

By early afternoon the old bus reached its final destination, the outlaw town of Gandao. Nothing from down country went any further inland than that dusty depot of desperation. The few remaining passengers climbed off, as did Ali Muhammad and his two guides.

Gandao was a tough town even by Pathan standards. Ali Muhammad had often ducked falling bullets while strolling through the armed streets of Darra. Though forbidden by law, he had ventured alone several times into the sunken alleys of Landi Kotal, long reputed to be the smugglers' capital of Pakistan. By nature and inclination an adventurer, his various sojourns had thrown him into more out-of-the-way spots than most other *ferenghis* foreigners) in recent history. Gandao was different. It didn't exist to impress. Its air of common criminality had no hint of the exotic.

Into the Lawless Land

No one outside Bajaur knew or cared about its existence. If another foreigner had ever ventured there, no written record survived.

When he glanced around, Ali Muhammad saw all the signs of Mohmand defiance. In addition to openly selling every type of rifle and handgun available on the North West Frontier, the town's mud huts boasted Russian land mines, Chinese grenades, .50 caliber anti-aircraft guns, and rocket-propelled grenade launchers. There were also ample supplies of hashish, opium and raw heroin on hand. One Mohmand had set up a metal recycling shed where, in addition to the usual rusty truck and bus parts, he sold scraps from the nearby Afghan war. Several smashed Soviet missile launchers, half a T- 64 tank, and parts of a salvaged Hind - 24 attack helicopter attested to the adventurous spirit of the salvaging shopkeeper.

It was a thriving Robbers Roost where anything in Bajaur could be smuggled down country and anything, or anybody, could in turn be kidnapped and held in Gandao for ransom. In Peshawar, Ali Muhammad remembered, they said that all bad things were available in Bajaur, and that all bad things were also condoned there. All the evidence pointed in that direction.

After they climbed off the bus, Pervez pointed out the only building of any real size in the bazaar. It had been a local school constructed at government expense. Ali's guide explained that a large hole in one stone wall was caused when one of the local lads had smuggled a faulty grenade inside. That however was not why school was suspended.

"Some Mohmands have kidnapped a rich miller's son from Peshawar," the Bajauri confided. "The governor of NWFP has given us an ultimatum. We are to release the boy and surrender our heavy weapons, or he will send in the troops we saw back in Shabqadar."

Ali Muhammad stared at the man beside him. The news of an impending government attack was not the kind of political triviality even a Pathan usually glossed over. It seemed no coincidence to Ali Muhammad that this information was withheld from him before their departure.

"Are they going to release their victim?" my friend asked.

Shaheen's brother gave Ali a look as if he was the village idiot. Pervez's attitude was quickly changing from polite future brother-in-law to pushy backwoodsman.

"The school teacher fled because he knew the men of Bajaur will tolerate no threats and that fighting was imminent," Pervez replied sarcastically "You wait over there while I get us a ride to my uncle's home."

A wave of Pervez's hand indicated that Ali Muhammad was to take up a station and wait close to Shaheen. He didn't need to be told to maintain a low profile in Pervez's absence. The woman of Ali's dreams was already squatting nearby in the dust. He saw that she had hunkered down into an unobtrusive bundle, staying as close as possible to an adjacent adobe wall.

It was time for the *Asar* (late afternoon) prayer. Most of the shops were temporarily empty, their goods and guns unattended and in plain sight, their owners' trust placed in Allah even in so desperate a town.

Though the street was nearly deserted, Shaheen had followed custom and turned away from what little traffic plied the dusty, sun-baked road. Even though the burkha's mesh netting gave her next to no vision out onto the world, it was considered promiscuous for a woman to gaze upon men going about their business.

There was no shade to be had for a mile and within minutes Ali Muhammad was parched with thirst. The occasional passing vehicle left a curtain of fine lingering dust that threatened to choke the already dehydrated American. Yet luck was with the journeyer. Spying the stranger, a village boy came up holding a metal bucket full of Ruh Afza. A large chunk of dirty ice floated in the middle of the rosy red syrup drink. One look was enough to convince Ali that the scabby brat had never washed in his life. His tattered shalwar kameez was burdened gray with years of unrepentant grime. Even his hand-me-down skull cap was black with dirt.

"Drink?" the kid asked, and held out a chipped glass smeared with the filth of ages.

Ali Muhammad didn't hesitate. It was hot and he had long ago dismissed any feeble phobias regarding microbes. He told the boy to fill the glass, which the urchin did by dunking it straight into the bucket.

The Ruh Afza was sickly sweet and tasted of pomegranate, but it was deliciously cool. It took two glasses to quench the American's thirst. When Ali was finished, the boy collected his five rupees and walked off with out so much as a glance in Shaheen's direction. Being female she was of no interest to the brat. He recognized her as being nothing, a nonentity who neither bought nor sold in the marketplace of men. Besides, though the boy was illiterate, he knew enough to realize that a woman in Bajaur territory had no right to converse publicly with a stranger, even a lowly juice seller. So the boy ignored the thirsty female, never viewing her as a possible source of revenue. Instead he carried away his polluted but refreshing bucket, all the while Ali Muhammad looked the other way, pretending he was not a part of this thirsty deception. For, like his lover, my friend knew the unwritten rules of the town he and Shaheen both temporarily occupied.

The woman Ali loved gave no sign acknowledging his betrayal of her basic humanity. She sat there alongside the road with her eyes staring down dutifully into the hot dirt before her. Here in plain sight sat the hidden half of Pakistan's version of Islamic apartheid. Shaheen squatted there in the dust, ignored in the suffocating blue burkha that stripped her of both identity and dignity. Thus the wicked town of Gandao taught the once-proud Shaheen that any powers she once held over men were an illusion of the past. In Bajaur territory she was no longer deemed a desirable siren. She was merely a royal blue sack of meat left out in the sun, doomed to wait patiently for her male guardian to return. If she had collapsed in the blistering heat from sunstroke no one from the village

Into the Lawless Land

would have raised a hand to help her. The beautiful courtesan had fallen to the level of a Pathan brood mare, fit only to be tied to an invisible hitching post, and ignored by the cruel, pious men of Gandao who were too busy with their prayers to notice her.

Pervez returned within a few minutes. He was sitting up front in the cab of a small Toyota pickup, next to the hard-eyed, bearded driver. The American was told to climb in back with the two other male passengers. Shaheen was ordered to get up front with her brother. Ali Muhammad was barely seated before the Mohmand driver roared down the dirt road.

At the far end of Gandao the Pathan chauffeur stopped at the town's only gas station. Ali watched as the driver pumped the gas, all the while a cigarette dangled carelessly from his lips. All mini-trucks were called Datsuns on the Frontier, be they Mitsubishis, Toyotas, or coincidentally Datsuns. When the off-white vehicle was filled, the driver wasted no time in leaving.

Every passable track before that town could have been classified as some sort of road. Nothing from there on could have dignified the term correctly.

They roared across the rocky country, heading for a cleft in the mountains. Ali Muhammad overheard the passengers call the it the Nahakki pass, otherwise he would never have known where they had been. The Mohmand driver seemed intent on reaching a new speed record. Even in a country full of maniacal drivers, the Bajauri native set a new definition in contempt for his passengers' safety.

The mechanized fatalist threw his vehicle at the offending mountain, spinning the Toyota's wheels inches away from the unguarded, thousand foot drop as they climbed. A glance down into the nameless canyon showed Ali Muhammad the crushed remains of another truck. The rusted reminder of carelessness or mechanical failure brought no response from the other two men. They sat silently, ignoring the bone-shaking hairpin turns, accepting as normal the gut-swaying switch backs.

Ali Muhammad hung on for dear life, gripping the side rails as the little truck roared up into the mountains. Just before the crest the little Toyota tilted precariously over the edge but at the last minute righted itself and sped forward, pulling them all at last to the crest of the steep pass. Before them lay a lunar landscape, a small isolated valley ringed with jagged mountains. The sheer desolation was a visual reminder of why Muslims believed that Paradise consisted of green grass, running water and cloudy skies. As they clattered down the far side, Ali Muhammad knew that behind him lay every trace of the modern world. He had ventured beyond experience and definition. He knew if he disappeared out there even Allah wouldn't find his bones.

The love-struck American did not have time to worry about such trivialities. He was too busy trying to stay alive. The back of the truck was terrible. The three men sat there with squinting eyes, trying in vain to see through the clouds of dust thrown up by the truck's rear wheels. To make matters worse another "Datsun" came up behind them and what had been a brisk descent became a motorized dual, and a possible plunge to the death for the loser.

Ali Muhammad gripped the side rails of the truck so hard he thought his fingers would snap. After what seemed like an eternity the lunatic up front managed to reach the valley floor. His compatriot was close behind but almost immediately turned off and headed north. Even allowing for the dust, Ali could see nothing remotely inhabitable in that direction.

Their own truck plowed on faster than ever, bearing down on a tiny group of huts. Half way across the valley they gratefully stopped at these rude adobe shacks. The open-fronted shelters were roofed over with canvas scraps salvaged from tents donated by the United Nations to the Afghan refugees. Ali Muhammad saw no one about, yet the other two passengers got off and started walking towards a nearby fort. No one spoke. They simply left without a word.

Immediately the driver headed the truck due west, pointing his vehicle directly towards Afghanistan. The mountains separating the two countries slashed across the skyline. They resembled a row of rotten teeth looming along the horizon like a foreboding promise. As travel-hardened as he was, Ali Muhammad knew he was nearing the limits of his endurance. He hung on grimly as the driver continued to torture and steer his vehicle like an escaped convict. The only moment of relief came when Shaheen glanced back in his direction. Even then he hoped the trip would soon be over.

Finally the track they had been following became so bad that even the Mohmand maniac reluctantly had to slow down. They made their way over the rutted road, skirting a few fields and passing around the outskirts of more adobe forts. When they were within five miles of the oncoming mountains, they pulled up in front of an average-sized mud fort. Even though the dust was still swirling in the air, Ali Muhammad could see that it only had one tower placed in the far corner.

When Shaheen and Pervez climbed out of the cab, Ali Muhammad realized that stopping had not been a mistake. Ali climbed down, stiff and dirty, and looked around while Pervez paid off the driver.

It was the poorest *kor* (household) he had seen so far. A few sickly hens scratched through the dust out in front of the fort. The building's twin metal gates had never been painted. They were the dull brown that only arrives after years of weathered abuse and constant oxidation. Looking up, Ali Muhammad could see gun-ports cut into the fifteen foot high mud walls. The only apparent luxury seemed to be the small sitting area adjacent to the front gate. Four-foot walls gave this area a feeling of limited privacy. The small acacia tree in its center threw a smattering of shade over the two **charpoys** (rope beds) sitting close by.

The driver roared off while Ali Muhammad was looking about.

Within a few moments the little truck had disappeared in a cloud of dust. Pervez headed towards the gate, leaving Ali without a word. The silence was suddenly deafening. Once they were alone Shaheen lifted her burkha. It seemed like years, not mere hours, since he had last seen her face. Ali Muhammad was alone at last with the woman he loved, and

Khyber Knights

"The burkha made the beautiful Shaheen a nonentity, a royal-blue sack of meat stuck out in the sun. The courtesan had fallen to the level of a Pathan brood mare, fit only to be tied to an invisible hitching-post and ignored."

yet he felt his heart beating uneasily, like it did when he first saw the black hole of the Judas gate waiting to suck him into the bowels of Pindi Prison.

Shaheen told him to come and rest in the shade of the tree.

The two *charpoys* (rope beds) placed there were so old they squeaked when the lovers sat down opposite each other. Both travelers were content momentarily to rest in the peace and quiet, letting the polluting noise of the truck drain from their memories. There was no sound to be heard. The land itself seemed to be dozing.

Their short reverie was interrupted when one of the gates screeched on its rusty hinges. A boy emerged holding a battered aluminum pitcher and a matching metal glass. He walked directly towards the tired couple, and handing Ali Muhammad the proffered cup, immediately poured him a glass of clear water.

"I am Wakeel. My father is away fighting the government. Pervez says you are to rest here," the boy informed Ali Muhammad.

The water was surprisingly cool and Ali Muhammad was too tired to want to move. He just nodded in silent agreement and then took the pitcher which the boy held out to him. His own drink finished, the American immediately poured Shaheen a glass of water. She took it gratefully and immediately drained it off. The boy, who looked about twelve, gave Shaheen a disapproving glance, then turned and left. As he walked away he pulled out a homemade slingshot from underneath his shirt.

Wakeel did not go far, walking to the edge of a nearby corn field where he took up a position of silent anticipation. Ali Muhammad and Shaheen took advantage of the time alone to discuss the recent events of their lives. She asked him questions regarding the horse trip, and seemed anxious to hear news of her former home in Lahore. But she volunteered no information as to the details regarding her escape.

Ali Muhammad was too tired to try and pry open her shell of secrecy. He watched as Wakeel shot and killed a crow and two sparrows with uncanny accuracy. The American was surprised to see two smaller boys appear. Shaheen informed him they were neighbors and lived in the closest fort, a larger structure half a mile off. When Wakeel returned with the dead birds, Shaheen immediately got up.

"I will bring you something to eat," she told Ali, then disappeared into the fort.

The boy followed, carrying the dead birds with him.

It seemed like an eternity since Ali Muhammad had been alone. He knew logically that he had been resting at home earlier that same morning. However time itself was fluid out on the Frontier, defying the western definition, and cramming more life into a twenty-four-hour period than back in the western world. His bones ached, and he knew without looking that every pore on his body was caked with the dust of the trip.

The overwhelming silence was a blessing though. He leaned back on the charpoy, resting his elbows on the tired old ropes and wondering what lay in store for him and Shaheen. Nearby the two little boys were peeping over the short wall at him as if he were a man from Mars or at least a child-eating cannibal. Their big-eyed wonder was clear evidence that neither had ever seen such a light-skinned stranger before.

The American's quiet contemplation was broken by a sound up above him on the wall of the fort. When he turned he saw that Wakeel had tied the dead crow to a string and was busy hanging it from a post sticking out of the mud fortification. The small dead body twirled in the slight breeze, its black wings hanging limp, all dignity stripped away by the cold embrace of death. The little boys chattered gaily at the sight of such casual cruelty. Wakeel waved at his two friends before disappearing behind the wall, leaving Ali Muhammad to wonder why he had wandered so far from home.

He had little time for further internal questioning as Pervez reappeared from the fort and immediately sat opposite him on the other charpoy.

"How do you like tribal territory?" Pervez asked, clearly fishing for a compliment.

Perhaps it was due to fatigue but Ali Muhammad was suddenly too weary to maintain any polite pretense. Plus he had noticed that the further they progressed into Bajaur, Pervez's actions had become increasingly rude. Ali was used to more gracious behavior and did not enjoy being left stranded outside a gate.

"I have seen much of Pakistan," he said with a note of noncommittal.

Pervez ignored the tone in Ali Muhammad's voice. He picked up the pitcher and glass off the ground then poured himself a glass of water. He held the metal container in his hand while his gaze wandered out over the nearby cornfield, taking in the sparse, dust-covered crop with a look of true concern.

"If it doesn't rain soon all the crops will burn and die. We do not irrigate here," he said and looking into the pitcher, he studied the cool water lying there.

"All our water comes from wells. Ours is one hundred and twenty feet deep and dug by hand. Theirs is more than 300 feet deep," he continued and pointed in the direction of the neighboring fort.

At that moment Ali Muhammad heard the roll of thunder over the horizon. Turning on the charpoy in the direction of the sound, the American found himself facing the jagged mountains due west of them.

"Well you're in luck. Rain is coming," he told his host.

Pervez only smiled.

"That is not thunder. It is the sound of the mujahadeen fighting the Russians," he said.

A look of incredulity crossed the American's face.

"See that trail," Pervez said and pointed towards a dim white line snaking up the nearest mountain. When Ali Muhammad nodded in agreement, his host continued.

"That leads directly to Afghanistan. We are less than five miles away," the Bajauri said in way of an explanation.

Pervez let the news sink in for a moment, then stood to leave.

Into the Lawless Land

"I will see why your dinner is taking so long," he told Ali.

In the brief time they had spent together Ali Muhammad had studied Pervez's face long and hard. Seeing his host preparing to depart again, Ali asked the question that had come to him during the long truck ride from Gandao. Some nagging feature of Pervez's bearded features had been bothering the American since meeting him earlier that morning.

"You're a Mohmand Pathan aren't you?" he asked Pervez.

"Of course."

"But Shaheen told me her family belonged to the Kaka Khail tribe," Ali Muhammad said.

"On our father's side," Pervez hastily explained.

He immediately turned and walked back into the fort, but not before Ali Muhammad had seen the falsehood written all over his tanned face. The lie was no longer important. While being bounced in the back of the Toyota Ali Muhammad had recalled the photograph Shaheen had once shown him in the Lahore brothel. Standing in the photograph had been a beardless youth several years younger than Shaheen. Ali was sure she had told him that youth was "my only brother."

It was quiet in the desolate Bajaur countryside. Ali Muhammad sat there for a while, thinking in English, muttering in Pushtu, wondering why the woman he loved had lied to him, and wondering who Pervez really was.

The sun was beginning to set before anyone came to see to Ali Muhammad's needs. Wakeel came walking out of the fort with a lota of water in his hand and an old blanket tucked under his arm. Far away in the distance Ali could hear someone calling out the reassuring lullaby of the *azan* (Muslim call to prayer). Its sweet words urged the Muslims of Bajaur to lay aside sin and attend the *Maghrib* (sunset) prayer. The boy had brought the water so the American could wash before making his devotions.

Wakeel laid out the blanket. The *qibla*, direction of prayer, happened to point directly towards Afghanistan. The American Muslim gave it no thought, just went about washing his hands, face, arms and feet in the ritual method proscribed in Islam.

"Your prayers will be na *qabool* (invalid) because you missed the ends of your toes when you performed *wuzu* (ritual ablution)," Wakeel scolded his fellow religionist.

The adopted Peshawari gave no heed to the protestations of this prepubescent rustic. When Ali Muhammad took up a place on the blanket, Wakeel stepped up beside him. They stood shoulder to shoulder, then both lifted their hands to their ears and then quietly said, "*Allah akbar*" (God is great) before praying. Each softly spoke the words of their prayers in Arabic, as taught by the Prophet, though it was not the mother tongue to either of them. Then they began bending when required, prostrating themselves before Allah, asking the Divine ruler to overlook the frailty of their lives and the accumulated sins that blackened both their souls to varying degrees. Like most men, they felt secure in their individual interpretation of religion, believing that Allah gave precedence to the whispers of one over the other. The boy considered the foreigner barely better than an infidel. The man thought the boy little more than a savage. Both sought to gain an advantage in their physical lives by the direct interdiction of the Lord.

It didn't matter which one had washed his toes. All their feeble prayers were doomed to fall on deaf ears.

A few minutes later when both had finished, Ali Muhammad shook out the blanket.

"I went to school," Wakeel proudly announced.

The American nodded politely and swept a few dead leaves off the corner of their impromptu prayer rug with his hand.

"I was in second class. Won, tuo, tree, fuor, rat, bat, cat. Look," the boy said in English and picking up a stick carefully traced out the roman letters that represented his name.

It did not surprise Ali Muhammad that a twelve year old boy had no more education that second grade. Life was hard on the Frontier. Any education was a blessing. He wondered if Wakeel had been the kid who accidentally blew up the grenade in the classroom. Such occurrences back in New Orleans would have been newsworthy. In Bajaur they were viewed as mere boyish pranks. Ali Muhammad didn't mention the grenade, just handed Wakeel the blanket, then glanced at the ground. He took the stick from the boy and corrected his spelling.

Wakeel was a bright boy. He smiled, pleased at the attention and the pin drop of further education.

"Does Pervez live here with you and your father?" Ali Muhammad asked casually.

"No, in Mardan with his wife and children," the boy answered, while trying to study the letters traced in the dirt.

"What's his connection to you?"

"He's my half brother."

"And Shaheen?" Ali said.

But my friend received no answer. Wakeel quickly rubbed out the letters spelling his name and grabbed the blanket. As he walked away he said over his shoulder.

"You wait there."

With nowhere to go, Ali Muhammad did as he was told.

There was little light left in the sky when Shaheen came out bearing a much-dented tray with his dinner. The smile on her face was bigger than the meal she brought him. A battered tin plate held a single fried egg, a spoonful of boiled spinach and a day-old piece of *roti* (bread). Resting on the tray next to the plate was a cleaning rod from an old Enfield rifle. The two tiny sparrows had been cleaned and roasted on the rod.

Shaheen sat the humble meal before him. The last time they had shared any food was in Lahore. Regardless if it was curried buffalo stomach or tiny birds, Ali was sure his future life with this woman was never going to be a bland culinary experience. He wondered what she would do when he showed her the wonders of an American supermarket. When he looked at Shaheen's face he knew she was worried he would

Into the Lawless Land

not approve, knew without words that she had done the best she could with the limited material she had on hand.

It didn't matter to Ali Muhammad what she brought him. He knew that love only devoured the starving, not the other way around. Yet he smiled and made sure to encourage her.

"It is difficult to know what to say about such a meal," he said truthfully and then immediately began eating to prove his devotion.

Ali Muhammad could tell Shaheen was pleased but she remained uncharacteristically quiet.

"Pervez says he is sick and cannot join you," she said, trying to sound casual.

The egg quickly gone, Ali mopped up the rest of the spinach with the last scrap of bread. The birds he had eaten whole, bones and all. The lack of cutlery bothered him not at all. He had long ago adopted the philosophy that food tastes better when eaten with the fingers. Besides he reasoned, unlike a fork, they had not been in anybody else's mouth. The meal was short and already his mind was elsewhere. They both knew that you don't break bread with a man you intend to harm. Ali Muhammad wiped his fingers on the rag she had brought him.

"Pervez doesn't look like your other brother," he said offhandedly.

Shaheen appeared surprised Ali Muhammad had remembered that bit of information.

"No, that brother lives in Swat with my mother," she said in the way of an explanation.

It had become so dark that Ali could barely see her face. He tried finding the truth in her eyes but could see nothing. Wakeel picked that moment to reappear with a lighted kerosene lantern.

"My father is not coming back tonight. We must lock the gate. Go to the toilet," the boy said and pointed at the cornfield.

Ali Muhammad got up, relieved to move around. He walked the short distance over to the corn, went a few steps down one row, then prepared to urinate.

With such baggy clothes the casual operation was always a tricky proposal. The foreigner tucked the end of his shirt up into his mouth. Then he carefully untied the cloth string that held up his voluminous pants. Because the belt ran inside a small enclosed loop running around the perimeter of the pants, it was a disaster if one became hurried and allowed the belt to pull out or slip back inside the wide folds of the pants. Your trousers became an eight foot long length of uncontrollable cloth. In such a case you had to get a "pants tooth," a stick with a string tied through one end. This was passed through the pants until the offending belt reappeared and one's composure was regained.

Ali Muhammad therefore made sure he had the belt in his left hand and the front of his shirt held securely in his mouth before he knelt down. The back of his shirt was getting dirty but that couldn't be helped. It was the urine that concerned him. All Muslims considered bodily fluids a major pollutant. Even the slightest drops on a wearer's clothes would invalidate the person's prayers until they were completely bathed and the clothes washed. Ali tried to make sure to shake off any spare drops of urine, then followed local custom by wiping the end of his penis with a small dirt clod to be sure. When he stood back up, my friend was just as careful about tying up his pants.

When Ali Muhammad walked back it was pitch dark.

Shaheen and the boy were waiting for him. They were talking quietly but stopped when he came close. Ali had thought they were going to ask him to sleep under the tree. The walled-in area was obviously the poor fort's answer to a *hujra* (guest room.) He was surprised when they lead him through the gates.

Though it was difficult to see anything in the darkness, Ali Muhammad could make out doorways built along one wall. They were obviously entrances to the fort's few rooms. A dim light burned in one window. Otherwise there was no visible sign of Pervez's whereabouts.

Wakeel took his guest directly towards the tower. When they reached the door Ali Muhammad could see by the lantern light that it was constructed from thick planks and steel bolts. Wakeel pulled back on a heavy hasp and threw the portal open. He handed Ali the lantern and indicated that he was to enter.

"Don't go outside during the night. The local people will kill any strangers, or their dogs will eat you," the boy warned.

Ali Muhammad nodded to indicate that he understood then walked inside. The lantern showed a beastly den, dark, dirty and depressing. Its sole furniture was a dilapidated *charpoy* shoved against the far wall. It was innocent of mattress or blanket save for a heap of nasty-looking empty grain sacks heaped on one end. Normally such conditions would have disgraced a prison, but the musical wanderer was happy not to have to rest on the hard ground.

When the tired traveler turned he saw the dark shapes of Wakeel and Shaheen framed in the doorway. Their faces were masked by the darkness.

"Be sure you don't put your feet down in the dark or the scorpions will bite you," Wakeel warned.

Then Ali Muhammad saw the boy close the door. The traveler heard the soft click of a lock being snapped through the hasp. He stood there wondering which one of them had locked him in. When he glanced around he saw that the walls were at least eighteen inches thick. There were gun ports far up in the tower but access to them was impossible without a ladder. Even if he could get out, what was the point?

My friend reluctantly sat down on the charpoy and placed the lantern beside his feet. He told himself that he had to believe in Shaheen. But in his heart he worried that she was a smiling villain whose beautiful eyes had heaped betrayal on the burning embers of his sweet love.

He laid down. Far above him he could see two little windows. It was still too early for the stars to come out. When he looked back towards the door he saw that he had overlooked a ragged poster when he walked in. It was tattered and old. The script was in Farci, the national language of Afghanistan. He didn't need to read it to know what it said.

Rows and rows of little black and white portraits were crammed onto the surface of the poster. The Afghan men and boys gathered there had all been staring straight at the camera when their portraits were taken. They differed in ages. Some were old, had beards, and looked like village mullahs. Others were barely in long pants and had tried to appear educated in their imported eyeglasses or second-hand western clothes. They were all there, those faded flowers of Afghan pride, young and old, rich and poor, sons of ignorant farmers and sons of haughty professors, sitting shoulder to shoulder on their dusty poster, sharing a silent secret with their unexpected American guest.

Because regardless of what they had been, or who they might have loved, Ali Muhammad knew they were all dead. The poster was a memorial to a handful of the thousands of freedom fighters who had been slaughtered in the blood bath lurking a few miles away from the tower.

My friend stared at their dead little black and white eyes, saw the look of forced bravery they all sported, then turned over and faced the other wall, trying to ignore the morbid implications of the tower's only decoration. He lay there in a silence so thick it could be felt, grasping at the few frail fragments of truth he knew he shared with Shaheen.

Khyber Knights

47
A Friend Betrayed

He dreamed that night of Shaheen, of walking with her through New Orleans' swirling French Quarter, of seeing her smile as she relished her new-found freedom in the safety of his boyhood home, and in his sleeping heart he knew happiness in the brief moment that he held her warm body in his hungry arms.

The rising sun brought an end to his fleeting mirage. Ali Muhammad awoke and instantly knew where he was. There was little light filtering into the cool gloom of the tower, but far above his head he could see the sky brightening through the tiny windows, so he lay there wanting one thing more than water, more than food, more than life itself. He was desirous of Shaheen's company.

There were no sounds coming from outside his gloomy hostel. Once he thought he heard the sound of the big metal gates being quietly opened, but then silence reigned once again, and he lay there feeling forgotten and lonely. Finally, after what seemed hours since the sun had risen, he heard someone fumbling at the tower door.

As the door slowly opened Ali Muhammad sat up on one elbow in anticipation of seeing the woman he loved. Instead standing before him was a haggard old woman. Her clothes were so ragged and patched they would have been comic if they had not been an open confirmation of her abject poverty. Her face, like her shabby clothing, was covered in dust and soot. She wore no veil nor made any pretense at hiding her face in modesty. Instead her weather-ravaged countenance was framed by lank gray ropes of hair that ran like uncoiled snakes off her head. Every fold of her face and hands were wrinkled and blasted by the constant savage attention of the brutal sun of Bajaur. She looked eighty. Knowing the hardships of tribal life Ali Muhammad suspected she was more likely forty five.

The crone peered into the darkness of the tower, unable to adjust her eyes to the darkness that shielded Ali Muhammad in the back of the tower. Seeing her inconvenience and thinking she had arrived in welcome, Ali sat up on the charpoy.

"*Assalaam alaikum*," he said quietly.

The sound startled his unnamed visitor. She whirled in the direction of his voice and took one timid step into the darkness. When she was near enough to see him she pointed back towards the door.

"*Ooza! Ooza! Oba de tari*! (Get out! Get out! They will tie you!)," she warned him in a hoarse whisper.

Before he could question her a shout came from the direction of the fort's living quarters. A look of abject fear came over her face when the woman glanced back over her shoulder towards the door. In the dim light she seemed to quiver and shake, and thinking she was going to collapse on the spot in fear, Ali Muhammad hastily stood up and moved in her direction, his arms widespread in an effort to save her from falling. His movement did nothing but startle her. Her message delivered she hurried through the doorway, turning back into the bright sunlight awaiting her return.

Ali Muhammad heard the sound of Wakeel's voice raised in anger. The boy screamed obscenities at the old woman and ended by threatening to tell his absent father what she had done. Then Ali Muhammad heard the boy's footsteps running across the courtyard. Within seconds his slender body was framed in the bright doorway. He too peered into the darkness in an effort to locate the American. Ali Muhammad could see that the boy was relieved to find him still inside.

"Come, I have tea for your breakfast," Wakeel exclaimed, trying to sound as if nothing untoward had occurred.

"I want to see Shaheen," Ali Muhammad informed his boyish jailer.

"She has gone with Pervez to inform my father of your arrival. You are to wait. When they return you can discuss everything with him," Wakeel informed him.

Beyond that declaration the boy was unwilling to tell the American any more. He once again led Ali Muhammad outside to the charpoys under the tree. There the suspicious guest was served chai and bread for his morning meal. Ali was told that he could once again visit the nearby corn field to attend to his bodily functions.

When my friend returned to the walled-in guest area, Wakeel pointed to the nearest fields belonging to his neighbors. When Ali Muhammad looked in that direction he saw two men plowing a field. Though they were a half mile away Ali could clearly see one walking behind a bullock. The other seemed to be pacing alongside, peering at the horizon, keeping a watchful eye while his companion tended to the mechanics of agricultural achievement. Both men were clearly wearing rifles on their backs, an unmistakable indicator of the seriousness given to local blood feuds.

"You are a stranger. If you are seen by the other men in this valley you will be shot as an enemy. Stay here where you are safe until my father comes," Wakeel warned and motioned for the American to be patient and make himself comfortable on the dilapidated charpoy placed at his disposal.

"When will Shaheen be back?" Ali Muhammad asked hopefully.

"Allah knows," the boy said, and turning back to the fort, left the American alone.

Ali Muhammad had not worn a watch in years but a glance at the sun told him it was mid-morning. Pakistan had taught him many things, among them patience. He did as he was ordered, waited, wondered and waited yet again.

During the long still hours of that otherwise peaceful day he had time to reconsider the various actions and coincidences that had gathered together out of time and space to place him in such a desolate spot. He watched the Mohmand plowmen taking turns behind their rude wooden implement. Except for not having tried to buy Shaheen at an earlier date from Maroof, Ali Muhammad had no regrets. Overhead he watched crows swirling in to rob the growing corn. He ran the emotional gamut during those long hours, being alternately impatient or listless, but strangely, never afraid.

Once Ali was sure he heard the sound of gunfire coming from the direction of Afghanistan, yet he had long ago learned to distance himself emotionally from any conflict that was not laid directly at his feet. Of more concern were the unresolved issues regarding Shaheen's connection with the Bajauri family. As he waited my friend contented himself with believing he could solve or buy her out of whatever minor allegiance held her to Pervez and his kin.

He knew that Shaheen's idea about having a tribal wedding was only another indication of her innocence of worldly affairs. Though she lived in a universe without written rules, Ali Muhammad understood that he would never be able even to apply for her American visa unless he had a *nikha nama* (marriage certificate) from the proper municipal authorities proving he had married her legally. Shaheen's naivety of the need to create a authorized paper trail was only one of the problems facing the two lovers.

Marriage in the North West Frontier was seen as a means of allying two extended families. The future husband and wife were considered representatives of their respective families in a contractual arrangement that was typically negotiated between the male heads of each household. Personal emotions were rarely allowed to color decisions affecting the good of the family and tribe. The concept of romance between the prospective bride and groom was thus seldom given any consideration in such a tactical union.

A matrimony between families in Pakistan was primarily the process whereby one acquired new relatives or reinforced already existing ties. Ali Muhammad knew from his own lonely experience that in order to participate fully in Pakistani society a person needed to be married. Bachelors, especially foreign-born ones, were viewed with suspicion. Social ties were cemented by giving away daughters and receiving daughter-in-laws in return. The marriage relationship extended beyond the immediate couple, and its importance to both families lasted well past the actual wedding. Because land and property were given away with the bride's dowry, the most desirable marriages were those which involved the union of first cousins. Both families viewed this arrangement sympathetically because it meant that any property exchanged during the ceremony stayed within the confines of the patrilineal line of descent. Yet Ali Muhammad knew that marriages with outsiders did occasionally occur, even within the strict confines of Pathan tribal society.

Regardless of whether she married outside her immediate family or not, a new bride was considered subservient to her mother-in-law. Thus her situation was sometimes made easier if this authority figure was also her aunt. The only sure way for a bride to achieve status and power in her new household was by her providing her husband with sons and heirs. Daughters were viewed as only a liability to be given away in expensive marriages with their virginity intact. Sons were seen as assets and protectors in Frontier society.

Looking into his future, Ali Muhammad did not care if Shaheen bore him sons or daughters, though he knew that if he did not produce a suitable male heir it would be perceived locally as a lack of virility on his part, as well as a weakening of family ties with Shaheen's relatives. He well remembered the Peshawar friend who explained the size of his own family to the American.

"I only have two children (meaning sons) and five daughters," the man had admitted apologetically.

Despite the cultural difficulties that lay ahead, Ali was confident he could grease enough palms to make Shaheen officially his wife in the eyes of the Peshawar court. Then he would use that paperwork to obtain her an American visa. Once she was safely in New Orleans he could stop looking over his shoulder for lethal reminders of her past activities.

Ali Muhammad stayed lost in such reverie for most of the day, content to observe the quiet peacefulness of his rustic abode, thinking of the steps that would be necessary to buy and legalize Shaheen's allegiance to his wayward heart.

Late in the afternoon Wakeel emerged to bring him a scanty lunch of chai, bread and a small plate of boiled okra. The boy stayed nearby, watching Ali eat and occasionally making comments or asking him questions regarding the outside world. The dirty plate was already set aside when Ali Muhammad noticed a stranger coming down the dusty track in their direction.

In the few minutes preceding his arrival, Ali saw that the figure Wakeel was eyeing so warily was only that of an old man. It was relatively cool and shady under the tree but one look at the dust covered wanderer told the American how hot it was out in the sun blasted countryside. As soon as the old man neared the two figures sitting on the charpoys he came to a halt.

He pointed his right index finger up towards the sky, silently reminding the man and boy of the unseen Majesty watching over the movements of all men. The old fellow then began to recite *ayats* (verses) from the holy Qu'ran. It came as no surprise to Ali to see a religious mendicant even in that backwater. Islam was famous for its tolerance of wandering holy men.

What did surprise Ali was to see Wakeel reach down and pick up a stone. The nasty look on the boy's face was a clear indication that he planned on harming and running the old man off. This lack of respect to the less fortunate angered Ali. God's pilgrims were treated with open admiration in Peshawar.

Before Wakeel could raise his hand in anger, the American stood up and walked over to the old fellow. Seeing his approach, the fakir brought his quotation from the Qu'ran to an abrupt end. The look on his face

A Friend Betrayed

clearly told Ali Muhammad that even a man of faith was unsure of the reception he would receive from the hard-hearted denizens of Bajaur.

A look of relief flooded over the old man's face when he saw Ali reach into his vest pocket and remove his wallet. His look of eagerness was replaced by one of amazement when Ali Muhammad peeled off a five rupee note and handed it to the harmless beggar.

"Pray for me *chacha* (uncle)," my friend asked sincerely

The old man held the note in awe. The look on his face revealed that it had been a long time since he held so much money. Ali doubted if there was any place closer than the outlaw village of Gandao where the beggar could buy anything, much less cash the note. Ignoring Wakeel, the old man smiled at the generous stranger. Reaching across he took Ali Muhammad's right hand in both of his own and told him what a good Muslim he was, before departing. The American watched the fakir make his way across the bleak valley, wondering where he was headed, and who among such a flint-hearted populace would shelter him. Suddenly his patience had eroded. He was tired of waiting in the sun with no answers and no Shaheen. Before he could turn and ask Wakeel how much longer they had to endure, he heard the boy say, "Look."

The youth was pointing at a dust cloud that was obviously heading their way.

"That will be my father. Wait here until I return," the boy told Ali, then turned and made his way hastily through the gates of the fort.

Ali Muhammad stood watching the oncoming dust storm, knowing in his heart that the cumulus cloud roaring toward him also had the woman he loved hidden within its brown interior. His emotions were suddenly a jumble.

It was late afternoon. The sun was beginning to set behind Ali Muhammad's back, the orb reluctantly disappearing below the mountains of Afghanistan. The last of that bright light was pouring directly into the eyes of the truck and its passengers. The American watched as the oncoming vehicle grew in size and distinction. He was still standing expectantly when the battered Datsun stopped near the fort's gate.

Dust swirled in the stillness of the quiet afternoon air, boiling up in a cloud of gritty dragon-smoke as three passengers disembarked. Ali Muhammad saw Pervez climb down from the rear of the truck, carefully stepping over the feet and legs of five other Mohmand men similarly crammed into the back. More important to Ali was the sight of a royal blue burkha that got out of the cab. Only this time the woman inside did not make her way confidently toward the charpoys, nor even move towards the privacy of the fort. Shaheen stood like a dog on a chain, waiting in silent obedience for the man in the front seat to disembark.

Ali Muhammad never forgot his first sight of Maqbool Khan. The Mohmand warrior climbed out of the truck carefully, placing his feet down with the deliberation of a cardinal alighting on holy ground. When the man stood up Ali saw that he was tall even by Frontier standards. The gaunt giant reached six foot eight in his rugged brown sandals. Cradled in his arms was a gun which he clearly handled with great care. While

Khyber Knights

Shaheen and Pervez hung back in respectful silence, their fellow passenger threw a few rupees into the cab of the truck.

The driver began to argue voraciously, shouting that the scanty amount was far less than he had been promised.

"A donkey can mount your mother for all I care. Take it and get out," the former passenger said, and pointed the gun barrel in the direction of the driver's head to seal their argument. Ali watched as the driver grabbed the money, cursed all Mohmands for cheats, then slammed the truck door and sped away.

The armed passenger turned and caught sight of Ali Muhammad. The two men stood and stared at each other across the dusty distance. Then the Mohmand began walking in Ali Muhammad's direction, while Shaheen and Pervez followed silently behind.

To an eye trained to the nuances of the Frontier, a quick glance told Ali Muhammad a great deal about Maqbool Khan. Even in the harsh terrain of Bajaur, Ali instantly knew the man was obviously a living anachronism of a more violent age.

The tall man walking towards Ali was in his early fifties. He carried himself completely erect, shoulders thrown back, his demeanor exuding an air of enormous dignity. His eyes prowled restlessly as he strode towards his house guest. The man's thick crinkly beard was as black as a crow's wing. Only a few white hairs growing timidly near his chin dared to remind him of his advancing age. High, thick cheekbones stood out from dusky skin. The wide nose perched above his thick mustache only heightened the message that this man was a natural predator. Lying deep beneath two thick black eyebrows were unforgettable eyes. His right eye boasted a black pupil and an iris yellowed by years of recurrent malaria. The left orb was milky white, his resultant partial blindness a result of trachoma, a common Frontier ailment.

If his face and bearing were a warning of his emotional nature, the man's clothing only confirmed his lack of civilization. Maqbool's shalwar kameez were a deep iron gray. His shirt was encrusted with sweat, the large salty rings under both armpits evidence that the man gave little thought to either physical comfort or western notions of personal hygiene. His pants too were obviously homemade, the trouser legs intentionally left high above his thick ankles. In Peshawar such pants instantly branded the wearer an ignorant rustic. A contempt for fashion was what it stated in Bajaur. Taken together Maqbool's simple clothes were not only durable, they were perfect camouflage against the stony gray landscape.

It was Maqbool's *puggaree* (old-fashioned turban) that warned Ali Muhammad of the man's strict adherence to traditional Pathan values. Turbans were as common on the Frontier as cowboy hats in Dallas. Yet even such pervasive hear-gear was subject to shifts in fashion. Maqbool's style of turban had not been seen in Peshawar in fifty years. Yet the man's boldly-wrapped *puggaree* looked like it just came off the shelf. An antiquated Pathan fashion, the mushroom shaped cap sat above the wearer's eyes. It base was then wrapped with a length of blue

A Friend Betrayed

and white silk, the end of which was left to flare out dramatically. Once a common fashion among the isolated Pathans of the North West Frontier, the old style *puggaree* had long ago disappeared off the heads of all but a few respected elders in Peshawar.

Giving Ali Muhammad even more cause for concern was the armament draped like tribal jewelry around the oncoming man. Green canvas suspenders held up a webbed belt encircling the Mohmand's narrow waist. Hanging in front of Maqbool's stomach from the belt were three long canvas pouches. Ali knew they each held an additional clip for the Kalishnakov AK-47 automatic rifle Maqbool carried. Augmenting the man's armament were six Chinese grenades. Three of the lumpy green pineapples hung down the front of each suspender, swinging merrily on their master's chest.

Cradled in the Mohmand's arms like a slumbering baby was his AK-47. In addition to the magazine resting inside the receiver, it had a second clip taped upside down next to its companion. This allowed the gunner to quickly snap out one clip and with a flip of the wrist, ram home its 48-shot brother in under five seconds. Though Ali Muhammad had seen and fired a few of the famous assault rifles, this was the first one he had seen boasting a BG-15 grenade-launcher under its ugly little black muzzle. From the side the black six-inch cylinder looked a fat flashlight resting innocently under the barrel. Its gaping mouth promised short-distance destruction to anyone naive enough to mistake its intentions.

Ali Muhammad took in all the obvious clues defining the man known as Maqbool Khan. A young Russian conscript drafted to fight in Afghanistan would have quailed at meeting the Mohmand tribesman. The American watched the hardened killer approach, weighed him carefully, steeled himself to do some hard bargaining with such a tough customer, and still underestimated his opponent.

The American knew not to extend his right hand in the customary western greeting. When he neared his guest, Maqbool handed his rifle back towards Pervez, knowing without having to look that his son was in close attendance. With his hands now free Maqbool immediately began to hug Ali Muhammad as if he were a long-lost relative, each man repeating the time honored phrases meant to denote respect and good wishes among the free men of tribal territory.

Only when such linguistic formalities had been set aside did Maqbool finally take Ali Muhammad's right hand in both of his own large, work-roughened paws.

"Welcome, a thousand times welcome," Maqbool told his guest, all the while studying the stranger like a snake about to swallow a rabbit.

Up close Ali Muhammad could see that his host's face was as hard and lean as his body. His eyes were at best cold and calculating, at worst cruel and indifferent to the pain of others. On the Mohmand's face were stamped the effects of his ruling passions, greed, cruelty, treachery and lust.

"I am Maqbool Khan," the older man proclaimed as if the mere mention of his name should have brought a jolt of recognition to his guest.

Wanting to be polite and searching for a neutral topic, Ali Muhammad made the mistake of remarking on Maqbool's absence. Though he had good reason to believe the man had only just returned from some nefarious activity, Shaheen's lover believed it best to act diplomatic.

"Have you been visiting in Peshawar?" Ali asked naively.

The mere mention of the bright city offended Maqbool's concepts of dignity and propriety. He hastily withdrew his hands and stepped back from Ali. His visage was stern and unforgiving.

"I don't ever go there. Pakistan is my enemy. Look at my bombs," he exclaimed and looking down on the American, patted the grenades on his chest to emphasize his open hostility.

Ali Muhammad's silence only further provoked Maqbool.

"I am leading the men of Bajaur in our Jihad against General Zia, that *Punjabi da khanzir bachey* (the son of a Punjabi pig)," Maqbool declared and spat to show his contempt for the military dictator.

He motioned for the American to sit down on one of the adjacent *charpoys*. Before taking a seat himself, Maqbool stretched out an impatient hand towards Pervez. It was only when the younger man had handed back the AK-47 that the bearded patriarch seemed to relax slightly. The Mohmand then sat down on the edge of the *charpoy* opposite his guest, but not before carefully leaning the treasured rifle next to his end of the rope bed.

Pervez sat down next to Ali Muhammad. He seemed oddly silent and withdrawn in his father's stern presence. Shaheen had followed both men, only withdrawing the burden of her burkha when the truck was far away. She stood nearby, nervously kneading the empty burkha, clearly an uneasy witness to the preliminary negotiations affecting her future. After greeting Maqbool, Ali tried to catch the eye of his beloved, only to observe her studiously keeping her own gaze downcast, thereby avoiding any chance of exchanging even an informal greeting or a smile with the man who loved her.

When Maqbool was seated, his back was turned towards the woman. Shaheen took that opportunity to start to walk quietly towards the fort. She had only gone a few steps when the Mohmand snapped his head her way.

The old man gave her a withering look and ordered Shaheen to sit down next to him. Ali Muhammad was startled to see her instantly obey like a frightened animal that had been repeatedly beaten.

It was an uneasy gathering with invisible currents of tension rippling under the surface. Everyone seemed relieved when Wakeel emerged from the nearby fortress bearing a large hookah (water pipe). Maqbool did not thank his son, only took the proffered pipe and laid a blazing match to the bowl. The rough cut local tobacco was old and dry. It blazed up instantly, sending a billow of gray smoke curling skywards as Maqbool Khan sucked the flame in with his hearty lungs.

A Friend Betrayed

For the next few moments no one spoke. The gurgling of the hookah was the only noise disturbing the little *jirga* (tribal gathering). After smoking for several moments Maqbool offered the wooden stem of the water pipe to his American visitor. As the water in the bottom of the big ceramic bowl bubbled, Ali's host explained his recent absence.

The Bajauri native made no attempt at disguising his heartfelt political beliefs. He proudly admitted he had been preparing to fight the soldiers sent by the national government in Islamabad.

Like his forefathers, it was the tribe, not the country, that was everything to Maqbool Khan. It defined his personal identity and just as importantly offered him collective security against the outside world. This ancient web of tribal kinship delighted in rejecting the dual concepts of national allegiances and international boundaries. The Durand Line which separated Bajaur from neighboring Afghanistan was a good example. Drawn up in 1893 by a British commission, it was viewed with disdain by the Mohmand tribesmen who lived on both sides of the imaginary barrier. They traveled across its invisible boundaries with defiant impunity, fighting against either Kabul or Islamabad as it pleased them, knowing they could seek sanctuary on either side of the invisible line conveniently dividing their land.

Maqbool and his Mohmand neighbors viewed their host nation of Pakistan with an equally jaundiced eye, ignoring the government's repeated attempts to subdue, civilize, or in anyway bring them into the fold of national conformity. While in theory the nearby international boundary divided the Mohmand tribe between two nations, in reality it was used to further their already legendary smuggling pursuits. Stolen goods were brought into Pakistan, thereby denying the struggling country legitimate tax revenue. In addition, the sophisticated armament of the nearby Afghan conflict was being funneled into neighboring Pakistan via Bajaur as fast as disgruntled domestic buyers could be found.

Maqbool Khan looked up to Allah, eye to eye with other Mohmands, and down on everyone else. Though Bajaur was a poor area, and he was impoverished even by local standards, Maqbool held no beggarly resentment or envy of Ali Muhammad's American status. What little he knew of the United States caused the Bajaur native to hold that mighty nation only in contempt. Instead, because the Mohmands had never been enslaved, Ali's host believed he was innately superior to his more educated guest. Poverty was a state of mind Maqbool was not willing to accept. The Mohmand believed he was destined to be king of all that he could seize.

Ali Muhammad's host saw life in brutal terms. Strife was a mere fluctuation in the market place, human suffering offered a time to strike, and weakness was something to be exploited. Maqbool made no attempt to hide his involvement in the recent kidnapping of the rich miller's son from Peshawar. He had been at the hideout where the unfortunate little boy was being held when Pervez had tracked him down. When Ali Muhammad mentioned the heavy armament they had viewed on the way in, and mentioned the governor's threat to retaliate if the child was not returned, Maqbool just scoffed.

Hadn't the Pathans fought the British to a standstill he boasted What could even an army of Punjabis do against the might of the Mohmands Maqbool bragged with homicidal eloquence.

Ali Muhammad had no answers to such ancient questions and poisonous prejudices.

As the hookah passed among the three men, Maqbool began questioning Ali Muhammad on his own background, asking how long he had been a Muslim, and why he chose to live in Pakistan. Ali weighed each answer carefully. Despite the smile on his host's bearded face, the American could sense that only Maqbool's lips were talking. His villainous soul stood detached in the distance, watching, weighing, and undecided about Shaheen's and Ali's fate. Maqbool lead the conversation around to Ali's recording business and to the size of his home in Peshawar. Then, before my friend realized it, the innocent small talk had been slyly twisted onto the subject of money.

"Did you bring any of the money to buy the woman?" Maqbool asked.

"No, you know I didn't. I told Pervez it would take a few days to raise it," Ali answered.

The look on the host's face implied he did not believe the American could not immediately lay his hands on the funds.

"Do you keep it buried it in the walls of your house like the Hindus do?" the Mohmand queried.

Ali Muhammad assured Maqbool that his banking methods were not so traditional, then emphasized again that he had already explained the situation to his son.

"I can get some of it immediately but I will have to sell my house to raise the rest. Maroof knew that," Ali Muhammad said, not bothering to hide his rising irritation.

At the sound of the pimp's name, Maqbool looked across to his son for tactical support.

"Who is Maroof?" he asked Pervez, clearly puzzled.

"You remember, that is the man who kept her," the son hastily added.

Ali Muhammad shot Shaheen a glance, hoping to see on her face what he already knew in his heart, that Maqbool was not her uncle and some evil was afoot in this pretense of a negotiation. The courtesan refused to so much as look in his direction, staring at the ground in embarrassed silence, tearing at the burkha in nervous desperation.

When the American turned his gaze back toward Maqbool Khan he saw a man trying to maintain an already-dissolving pretense. The big Pathan nodded in Shaheen's direction, then spoke to Ali.

"She is a good girl and comes from a good family," Maqbool told his skeptical guest.

The air was starting to cool as the sun sank lower into the west, but that was not why Ali Muhammad felt a chill run down his back. It was the sound of Maqbool's words. He knew if the man was truly Shaheen's uncle then he would realize the depth of her physical involvement in the

Khyber Knights

"Maqbool Khan looked up to Allah, eye to eye with other Pathan tribesmen, and down on everyone else."

A Friend Betrayed

brothel's business. No one could argue over her beauty but to classify her as a "good girl" wasn't just idealistic, it exposed her "uncle's" lack of knowledge. Besides that Shaheen's mother, who was supposedly Maqbool's sister, had been a whore as well. Such women did not come from "good" Pathan families. At that moment the American knew conclusively that all three of them were deceiving him. Only the why of it eluded him.

"You're a liar," Ali Muhammad told Maqbool quietly.

The air went suddenly still but the American didn't stop there.

"I don't know why Shaheen is here, but you're not her uncle," he said defiantly.

The big Mohmand measured him like a hound that required the whip, then lashed him with the truth.

"This fool brought the woman to Bajaur," he said and jutted his chin in Pervez's direction with contempt. "I was going to waste a bullet on her but it was the whore's idea to bring you here. When she told me you had promised to pay her husband five lakh rupees for her, I thought better me than some Lahore pimp."

Then Maqbool Khan confessed his own plans for rebellion. The thought of seizing Ali's money intoxicated him. He planned on using the booty to further his fight against the Pakistani government. He was already in contact with the communist government in Kabul. They were sending in arms to his fellow tribesmen to stir up trouble. Ali's host picked up the elite rifle next to him, tendering it with more sign of obvious affection than he ever displayed to either of his natural offspring. The sophisticated black metal killer was concrete proof of his communist connections,

It was clear the bearded Mohmand was untroubled by any pangs of conscience. He defiantly believed he lay beyond the reach of time and the modern world, his existence a confirmation of his own tiny but evil orbit. Ali Muhammad listened and realized he was not dealing with the head of a rebel government. Maqbool was even worse. He was the leader of localized pirates.

The Mohmand finished by denouncing his elder son, saying he was weak for journeying beyond Bajaur and wasting his money and time in a Lahore whorehouse. Such an unworthy son was a wart on a father's face, to leave it a blemish, to slice it off a pain. Maqbool called Pervez a wastrel and proclaimed the younger son his true heir and hope for the future. Wakeel stood close by, proud of the compliment. Pervez sat alongside Ali, sullen and defiant.

"He thought he could hide his play pretty with me here in Bajaur," Maqbool said, and looked at Pervez with disgust. "Lucky for this slut the honey pot between her legs drew you into the trap."

My friend sat there, momentarily too stunned to respond.

He realized that this was no accidental evil he had wandered into by mistake. He looked at the four people waiting for his reaction to this horrid revelation. When Ali Muhammad studied each of their countenances the American traveler saw them for what they were, thieves, liars, kidnappers, rebels and whores.

Sitting there in stunned silence Ali Muhammad wondered that no comet blazed across the darkening sky to announce the death of his love. For he believed that this was the most unkind cut of all, that Shaheen had martyred his affections to her own greed. He looked in her direction for confirmation but she continued to avoid his eyes, the look of shame voiding any possibility of her innocence.

In his heart Ali wept a silent stream of grief. Too late he recalled her husband Maroof's bitter words denouncing her avarice and cunning, words her lover had failed to believe. He felt his body stiffen in an effort to hide the shame and betrayal he felt when he realized his love had been plundered by the knavish whore.

When he looked at Shaheen he once again saw the raven black hair and beautiful body that had blinded him to all life's warnings. Only now for the first time he observed the treason in her eyes and recalled the words she used to lure him into Bajaur, the same words that now defiled his ears, betrayed the blessings of her womb, and desecrated the constancy of his affection. Ali Muhammad realized Shaheen could no more read the words of love engraved for her on his heart than she could understand the mysterious movements of the hands moving around the clock.

My friend stood rooted in the realization that he was standing at the edge of a precipice he had almost willingly jumped over. Until a few minutes ago, Shaheen's smile would have caused him to cast himself into the fires of Hell if it had pleased her. Suddenly he saw that revealed before him was not the beauty of Shaheen, here was the golden calf of mankind's making. Here was the false idol. Here was the siren who had said, "Worship me," and Ali Muhammad had, running to embrace Shaheen's false promise of reciprocated love.

Islam taught Muslims not to worship false gods. This meant more than graven images. It incorporated any misplaced devotion such as an overriding love of ancestors, money, power, politics, material objects, nationalism or the love of a woman. Ali started to become white hot in his growing hatred and anger. His love had blinded him to all these facts. His soul's warning had fallen on deaf ears. Yet when he reached up and broke off the cruel iron yoke of his own emotional slavery, that burden he had willingly chained around his own neck, the knowledge threatened to slay him.

Ali Muhammad had sought for the truth and now he would have given his soul to look away from what lay revealed. Having been blinded by the excessive glory of his love, Shaheen had at last opened his eyes to the realities of the world he had formerly traveled through like a naive and trusting child. His teacher and her mischief stood revealed as waves of anguish threatened to consume him. Here was love without redemption, beauty without meaning, chaos enshrined in the myth of romance.

Shaheen had ignored every clue of love he had brought her, and had now in turn brought them both into God-forsaken Bajaur. Ali realized that

A Friend Betrayed

in her ignorance Shaheen had only dimly perceived the truth he held out to her, the offers of a new life, a new name, a new country. Shaheen had chosen Pervez, Ali believed, because she had let tradition, ignorance, sin, avarice and fear overrule the goodness and light reflected in his actions. In contrast, Ali's love was an frightening, foreign concept that threatened to tear down the values her life had been built upon.

When he looked at her stunning beauty, Ali Muhammad knew that no matter how hard he tried he was still a *ferenghi* (foreigner) from "Ah-mare-ee-kah," a convert, an unknown quantity, a non-Pathan, a racial oddity who had brought her presents and impressed her fellow whores with his puppy-like devotion. He believed that out of habit Shaheen had embraced the wickedness that had polluted her blood for generations, squandering her chance to escape because she was afraid to depart with him into the unknown.

The traveler sat there looking across at her from the other side of an invisible chasm of unbridgeable cultural differences, as the foundations of his half-tangible fulfillment dissolved, and the treasured mirage of inner joy her beauty had always brought him withered and burned like a scrap of Paradise.

It was in that instant in his existence that the full blaze of knowledge illuminated his mind. He knew Shaheen had inadvertently exposed the lie that until then had guided his life, revealing by accident the sham of his Lawrence of Arabia lifestyle. She had shown him that no amount of play-acting, no preening through the streets of Peshawar with his foreign clothes just right, no Richard Burton linguistic feats with his skilled Pushtu, no perfect Arabic prayers nor Islamic ritual, none of that mattered. It was all window-dressing, hiding the shameful truth that he was a self-deluded westerner who thought he could be accepted if he but outwardly conformed. Ali knew at that moment that he was no different than the water boilers he despised. He was only a more penitent one, rejoicing in eating and drinking all the filth of his adopted city.

My friend hung his head in his hands, feeling a fool. His cheeks burned with the shame of realizing what role he played in Shaheen's life, knowing he was lower than the evil Maroof, who was at least a cuckolded husband. Even worse, Ali knew he was only a deceived lover. He believed in his broken heart that Shaheen had never seen him as a possible husband, only a rich Angrez fit only to be exploited. He believed she had never viewed him as Ali Muhammad the man who loved her, and ultimately, that is what hurt him the most.

When he lifted his head his countenance had changed. His heart had waxed hot and shame burned his features in the gathering darkness. Bitterness filled the sacred spot where love once lingered, sending it skyward in clouds of steam as the fires of rage melted the cool disbelief that had recently ruled his impetuous heart. To his credit Ali Muhammad bade his face, that most expressive part of man's essence of being, to be steady, giving no hint of the hurt and pain that filled the gaping void where his devotion had but a moment ago resided.

He took a deep breath and stood up. He did not look at Shaheen, only announced his intentions to his Mohmand host.

"There will be no wedding. I am leaving," he said, though in the back of his mind he doubted the truthfulness of his latter statement.

Maqbool Khan followed the American's lead, only when he stood he brought the scarred and wicked gun that never left his side along with him. The favorite son of Bajaur towered over the smaller Ali Muhammad. He grinned with delight at the emotional agony he had caused my friend, then snatched control of the situation by shoving the muzzle of the AK-47 hard into Ali's stomach.

"You're not going any further than my tower. I'll decide what to do with you later."

"If I don't return my friends will send the authorities to find me," Ali countered, knowing it was an empty threat.

The Mohmand native laughed, showing his utter contempt for the accident of birth that granted Ali Muhammad his privileged, unearned position in the modern world. Maqbool sneered at the thought of the American being rescued.

"Let them come. My fort can withstand anyone," the brigand said defiantly.

Ali Muhammad looked up into the milky white eye peering down at him.

Here stood the Pathan invincible.

Maqbool Khan was not like his tame cousins further down country, who by accidents of geography or politics had been encircled and subdued. He was a Mohmand first and a Muslim second, fearing nothing, not man, not guns, not God, and certainly not death.

The big man jammed the rifle even harder into Ali's stomach, then with a flick of his big right thumb, flipped off the safety switch. Maqbool's index finger was poised on the trigger. The decision to advance and die, or retreat and live, was clearly up to Ali Muhammad.

The two men stood staring at each other. At that range Ali knew the bullets would splash his guts all over the landscape like overripe grapes. He hesitated for one long breath, then turned and began the long walk toward the confines of the tower.

48
Shaheen's Heart

Bajaur was a state of mind induced as much by geography as eons of evil, the land itself giving off a sense of dark energy.

Ali Muhammad sat alone, locked in the fastness of both that province and the Mohmand tower. His sole companion was the feeble flicker of a kerosene lantern. Long hours had passed since Maqbool Khan had shoved him into the mud-walled room. At first Ali paced the floor, angrily denouncing Shaheen's treachery. Then as the gravity of his situation ebbed in, his censures died away and he found himself sitting on the edge of the charpoy, caught in a nightmare of utter impotence.

Anyone spying on the American from then on would have quickly turned away, relieved to discover Ali locked in the same pose hour after hour. The stars and moon rose without his notice, for he sat secluded in the silence of that great beyond known as Bajaur, where the only noise was the tumbling in of his razor sharp memories.

The slow rise and fall of his chest became his only concession to life. In his mind he was no longer a prisoner in the tower, only of the love that had dominated his life since meeting Shaheen. His mind had whisked him away, back to Lahore, to that night when she drifted towards him as she dried her wet hair, to the first sight of her naked body, of the feel of her nails digging into his back, of the smell of jasmine and the taste of forbidden love on his tongue.

If he thought to relieve the passionate pleasures of his past, he learned their eventual rediscovery only returned him back to the painful present. Ali shook his head at the anguish the memories brought him. He consoled himself by recalling that even men who never trusted a brother often trusted a woman.

"Ah," but he told himself, "she was different. Surely there was some spark of goodness that I sensed through the depths of her deception."

He knew though that such evidence had eluded even his extraordinarily patient search. Ali reviewed the facts, then reluctantly concluded he had been nothing more that a fool who allowed his heart's thirst to ruin his life.

In such a manner did the jilted lover pass the early part of that night. In his preoccupation he never gave any thought to the dinner he was missing. He was a graduate of Pindi Prison's deprivations. Plus the horse trip had long ago inured him to hunger. Even though most of his meals of late had been insufficient, Ali Muhammad was fit and healthy. Lost in his memories, his body grumbled while his mind wheeled on.

Eventually he lay down in defeat, wounded and vindictive. Through the little windows overhead he caught glimpses of a sky as black as the color of his sorrows. The traveler knew it was going to be easier to go to bed than to succumb to sleep. He told himself to believe that the night had at last grown a few shades cooler than that burning day. The silence of the tomblike tower was suffocating and life for Ali Muhammad during that long night became a burden and a curse. He was unutterably weary but even worse, unspeakably lonely. In such dire contemplation did he dwell, giving no thought to the passing of the night. How long he had lain there he later never knew.

It was the soft rattle of the lock and chain on the outside of the tower door that roused him. He instantly recognized its sound as preceding the opening of his mud-walled cage. Instead of waiting to be gloated over by his Pathan captors, Ali Muhammad rose silently and quickly ran behind the door. He had no definite plan, only an intense desire not to miss any opportunity to escape.

The American heard the outside chain drop softly, then saw the thick door open gradually. Ali stood pressed against the wall, suddenly ready to pounce on Maqbool Khan or his sons even if they were armed. His breathing was rapid and shallow, his body tense with anticipation, when he saw Shaheen step carefully and quietly past the opened door.

She was barely inside before she began peering into the shadows obscuring the charpoy. Not seeing her lover, the courtesan softly whispered his name.

"Ali ..... Ali."

The man she sought stood close beside her in the dark, alternately watching and hating her. Before making good his escape, he considered reaching out and choking her to death in payment for her treachery. Then he saw the undisguised fear written plainly on her face and he hesitated.

Instead of harming Shaheen, Ali Muhammad pushed the door shut behind her, fully exposing himself. The sudden action scared the young woman so badly she jumped away from the movement behind her in the dark. When she saw him, Shaheen began to cry and ran to his side.

"I'm sorry. I'm sorry," was all that she said between the kisses she rained upon her former lover.

He stood unmoved, too shocked at seeing her to respond immediately. Yet she interpreted his silence for disapproval and even worse, dismissal. She choked off her cries and pulled back, prepared it seemed to depart with the message of his undisguised rejection. It was only in that moment when her face was truly unguarded that Ali Muhammad saw a different woman than the one who had lured him into Bajaur.

Vanished now was the supreme charm he had hitherto seen in her every movement, gone now her fragile web of accompanying lies. Looking at her fadeless beauty still threatened to rip away the groundwork of his soul. Her soft wheat-colored skin was warm to the touch. Her black eyes still captivated his heart. She remained without physical blemish, only now one new overriding emotion dominated her features, fear of the injurious monster ruling her life.

"Help me," she pleaded and placed her hands on his chest in lieu of support.

When she did, Ali Muhammad reached down and placed his own hands around her wrists.

"Where are your gold bangles?" he asked, though he felt he knew who had taken the expensive gold baubles.

"Maqbool took them," Shaheen confessed.

Even in the dim, flickering light the woman appeared pitiful. Ali Muhammad however stood there unconvinced, fearing another snare, worried she was too deeply dyed in sin to tell him the truth even now. He held the power of her beauty at bay while his heart weighed its misgivings. Standing before him was no longer the radiance he had worshipped, but the doubts and suspicion of fraud that had so recently brought such disquiet to his grieving soul. Shaheen said nothing, a helpless witness at her mute trial.

My friend hesitated but knew in the back of his mind that what we perceive in this world is only a small portion of what truly exists. How he wished there had never been any lies between them. Ali Muhammad believed that true love from Shaheen could only come with a total change of heart, and yet, and yet. Even though evil existed in the world, and at that moment was sleeping close by, this was no reason to lose all faith. Ali knew he ought to be filled with apprehension, anxiety, and trouble, but he could not deny Shaheen the opportunity at least to tell her side of what had happened.

The hard look in his eyes weakened, then disappeared altogether. He took one of her proffered hands and whispered for her to follow him. Leading her to the nearby *charpoy* Ali asked her all the questions that had been burning holes in his mind since Maqbool locked him in the tower. Why didn't she wait for him to return to Lahore? Why had she betrayed him to this outlaw?

If Ali Muhammad had expected a reasonable list of logical excuses he had forgotten where he lived. Shaheen told him a tale of sordid dealings that always came back to one unforgiving fact, she had been born into a family that prostituted its own women. Shaheen grew up watching her own mother flick the curtain, and then hand the profits of her sin to the girl's father. In hurried whispers she admitted Maroof had been both her first cousin and her husband.

Shaheen said part of what she told Ali Muhammad in Peshawar had been true. The incestuous husband who sold her soft body had been planning on betraying Ali, first by taking his money, and then by turning him into the authorities as a violator of the *zina* ordinance. Maroof paid bribes to the police in Hira Mandi to stay in business. She believed the same corrupt cops would assist her husband for a cut of the embezzled dowry.

Ali Muhammad listened in silence, nodding his head in agreement at the idea of Pakistani cops being crooked. Nor did he comment when he learned Maroof had beaten her for refusing to betray the wealthy American.

"Why didn't you wait for me to return?" he wanted to know.

She had no answer. Perhaps she thought the promises he whispered over her naked body would not bind him, that like so many other men she had seen walk into her crib this foreigner would never return. If that is what Shaheen thought of Ali Muhammad she had the wisdom to hide that misbelief from him.

Men had always used her. That was the way of her world. In Pakistan a woman was lucky if she learned her ABCs, a few verses from the Qu'ran, and simple housekeeping. Shaheen had never even been tossed those crumbs. She had been taught to say "*Bismillah*" (In the name of God) before letting her husband crawl on top of her belly.

When life had become so untenable at the brothel that she decided to escape, her chances of success were infinitesimal. She had never seen a map, had no comprehension of compass points, provincial boundaries, or even the concept of distance and direction. The sun rose and set. Why, she never knew? Shaheen was a medieval woman whose life had always been dictated by outside forces and corrupt men.

Yet if it was true the courtesan was abysmally ignorant of scholastic matters, she had a rare cunning. She realized none of her regular customers could help her, even if they had been willing to risk their lives to do so. They were all either from her own city of Lahore or some portion of the surrounding Punjab province. In either instance eventual detection so close to home was almost a foregone and deadly conclusion. Though illiterate, Shaheen knew she needed someone from "away."

Ali Muhammad realized the woman did not know the legalities nor the punishments proscribed by her country's military dictator for the action she planned. All Shaheen understood was that the outraged pimp who called himself her husband would slay her the moment he discovered her hiding place.

Or worse.

Pervez had seemed to be the answer to her prayers. The Pathan had been to the brothel on three occasions, each time bragging about his wealthy family and his politically powerful father. When she carefully hinted at her unhappiness, the Bajauri braggart quickly grabbed his chance to aid in her abdication.

The Mohmand was handsome and apparently rich. More importantly he promised Shaheen to make her his second wife and secret her away in his home in distant Mardan. Not only did it sound safe, Pervez was a fellow tribesman who spoke her language and understood her culture, not a foreigner from another Pakistani province.

Shaheen spent the next few days holding back as much of the money from her work as she dared. The night she fled for her life she had the clothes she stood up in, a blue burkha, and three hundred and fifty rupees, roughly twenty American dollars. She had earned about a dollar a year for prostituting her body.

The lantern gave off its dim glow and Ali Muhammad had to lean forward to hear the rest of her story for her voice continued to drop as she shared her tale.

Pervez took her money as soon as they were safely out of Lahore. She said nothing, content to be free from Maroof. They went by bus to Mardan, all the time her rescuer grew increasingly nervous as he brooded over the consequences of his rash act. Shaheen's protector did bring her to the discreet hideaway that he had promised. Pervez's wife screamed in fury when her husband brought another woman home unannounced.

In theory the husband needed to acquire the permission of the first wife before marrying again. Ali knew that in the modern age plural marriages were a Muslim right rarely practiced or asked for by Pakistani husbands. Fearing disclosure, Shaheen had not objected when Pervez rushed her out of the house, promising to take her to the isolated safety of his father's home in tribal territory. It sounded ideal.

Journeying through the desolation known as Bajaur, Shaheen had peered through the mesh net of her burkha with a sinking heart. She knew very little of the world. Her travels had only shown her brief glimpses of Peshawar, Rawalpindi and sections of Lahore. But she knew they were like the stars above compared to the hellish country she saw there below. She sweltered in the burkha, sitting alongside another woman on the bus taking them into Mohmand territory. In the back of her mind she wanted to go home, to gladly face another beating if Maroof would only let her wash her body and change her clothes.

That was not to be.

Even if she had known how to get back to Lahore she knew Pervez would stop her from returning. His cowardly life was forfeit the moment Maroof tortured Pervez's name out of her. With a sinking heart Shaheen ventured further and further not only from her former home but the limited luxuries of her previous life.

When she met Maqbool Khan at that ill-omened fort Shaheen knew she had arrived in the annex of Hell.

She and Pervez had gone into the main room of the fort. There they found Maqbool and his younger son Wakeel. They were being served food by an old woman who she later learned was Pervez's mother. Shaheen had taken a seat next to the wall, trying to appear small. The older woman scuttled away the moment the dishes were sat on the ground before the men. Pervez lost no time in trying to explain his and Shaheen's unexpected presence.

The son had tried to bluster, telling the patriarch he wanted to leave Shaheen in Bajaur temporarily, hinting at important business deals down country, and promising to return shortly to take her back with him to Mardan. Maqbool Khan was a caliph of corruption. He knew Pervez was a liar and wasted no time allowing the pretense to continue.

When he wasn't shoving food into his maw, Pervez's father began abusing his son and the whore, showering verbal filth on both their heads. Maqbool didn't need to be told the woman defiling his front room was a slut. If she had come to Bajaur with Pervez there could be no other explanation for her presence. Pervez's father concluded by saying his eldest son was as worthless as the mother who bore him.

Shaheen told Ali Muhammad she had sat silently as Maqbool Khan slandered his heir. She had known hundreds, many thousands of men, some big, some small, some good, but none as bad as that man.

By the next day Shaheen realized Maqbool was thinking of killing her.

All her life Shaheen had been accounted beautiful. If her life in the brothel had been degrading, it had also indirectly fed her ego. At an early age she had learned to use her bewitching power to bend men to her will. Without realizing it she grew used to exercising a great deal of authority over the other prostitutes working for Maroof, as well as the customers who paid for her services.

In Bajaur she made a frightening discovery. Her beauty was meaningless. For the first time in her life she was no longer the quintessence of sexual desire or a paragon of forbidden love. In Maqbool's fort she was merely a strumpet, a jade, and a drabbing. Though she was accustomed to men paying for her pleasures, Shaheen recognized a woman-hater like Maqbool. She had on rare occasions met such unnatural creatures. The brutality and violence they nurtured in their hearts became a taste, then a lust, and finally an obsession.

Soon after arriving she overheard father and sons discussing what should be done with her. The little sadist Wakeel voted for killing her immediately. Pervez believed she could be quietly sold over the border to the Afghans. The father leaned towards that idea. However Maqbool did not believe Shaheen should escape without first being marked as a Pathan whore.

A look of intense horror passed over her lovely face at that remembered thought. Such was her state that even if Ali Muhammad had not known and loved the woman huddled in front of him he would have wanted to console her. Sitting there in that dusty sepulcher, Shaheen told Ali Muhammad the secret nightmare that had hung over her existence since she was a girl. Though she had no knowledge of Zia's courts, the prostitute knew full well what Maqbool Khan was referring to when he threatened to brand her Pathan style.

"I remembered when I was small girl still living in Swat. My mother, her sister and many other women were gathered in the back room of a house. A woman came in to visit. Her husband was out front with my father. When she took off her burkha I saw that the front of her face was gone," Shaheen reported.

"Because her husband thought she slept with another man, he cut off her nose and upper lip. Later he discovered he was wrong. The day I saw her they were on their way to Peshawar to see a Nazarene (Christian) doctor. He could supposedly remove a portion of her forehead and sew it over the hole where her nose had been."

Later Shaheen heard the older women whispering that the unfortunate woman's forehead had proved too short for the operation and that for thirty rupees the husband had bought her a metal nose in the Peshawar bazaar.

"My own mother said that was a good bargain because the woman had only cost her husband eighty rupees new," she told the shocked American.

The day she overheard Maqbool was when Shaheen realized she had stuck her head into a noose of lies. Even Maroof had been better than where she now found herself. The cold hand of fear clutching at her heart convinced her that even if Maqbool left her leave alive, he would mutilate her first. Shaheen realized that the limited power of her former degrading life was now utterly stripped away. In Bajaur she was merely a puppet in the hand of a creature to whom true goodness was nothing but a name.

That was the point in their hurried conversation when she admitted to Ali Muhammad it was her own desperate idea to draw him back into her life. She could not read books, but she could read men. So Shaheen appealed to Maqbool's only weakness, greed, telling him about the rich foreigner who would buy her, if she was sold unmarked and unharmed. In a shallow whisper she told the American she had not even been sure if he had enough money to buy her freedom. But more importantly Shaheen had believed Ali Muhammad would help her if she could only get word to him of her plight. She had been literally confined under a gun since the moment they met again in Peshawar.

All these whispered secrets had taken but a few minutes to recount. In point of fact the lovers were rapidly losing awareness of their wretched surroundings. If times had been different Ali Muhammad would have laid down on the charpoy, content to once again feel her body next to his. Shaheen saw the old look in the American's eyes and realized she had bet on the right man.

From that point on they spoke rapidly of many things, not forgetting to mention escape and love, and though each lover recited from the heart neither heard the other, for their words came from two different streams of humanity, hers the ancient world undisturbed by any political, religious or social creed, his the entrancing newness of modern aspirations that thought to explain the ages of the moon and to count the beams of the sun.

Ali Muhammad's love for Shaheen was a western idea, a cultural extravagance she neither believed in nor understood. While he tried to prove the sincerity of his romance, she was pleading for rescue and offering her only treasure, her own lovely body as surety in exchange for her life. She was a volatile mixture of many things, a serving of wildness blended with an impetuous tenderness. As he spoke she tried to overcome her vague misgivings at his foreign origin. Shaheen did not truly understand him emotionally but she knew two important things about Ali Muhammad. He cared for her, and more importantly, he would not mutilate or kill her because of her past.

So in those brief minutes they shared a reunion in that wretched mud tower. All their plans had gone astray. They were both carried far, far away from their original designs, having now neither internal peace nor external gain, the hope of a happy future having proved to have offered everything, yet delivered nothing but the empty promise.

Despite those odds Ali Muhammad grabbed at the chimerical hope sitting before him. He took Shaheen's hands in his own and whispered timid tenderness to this woman who he loved more than his faith and his life. In her presence he once again felt the need to exercise all five senses in order to appreciate the joy her presence demanded of him.

Their brief peace was over the moment the door flew open. The sound brought them back to the present as they scrambled to their feet. Ali Muhammad immediately moved in front of Shaheen but his effort was of little use. A furious Maqbool Khan stepped inside, followed by his two sons. The murderous little black eye of the AK-47 was once again peeking at the American.

Ali could barely see the tall Mohmand's face in the murky light. He didn't have to be any closer to know Maqbool was a breath away from killing him and Shaheen.

"Let her go and I'll give you the money," Ali Muhammad told his captor.

Even Satan admired Maqbool Khan's sense of cruelty.

"*Chup shah, khor ghod* (Shut up, sister fucker)!" the Mohmand kidnapper shouted with open contempt, then snapped the machine gun to his shoulder, pointing it at Shaheen's face. The terrified girl shrank behind her lover.

It was a relief to see Pervez step away from his father and approach them. He carried a length of chain and two padlocks in his right hand. No one spoke as the older son knelt down and reached under the charpoy. In a few seconds Ali Muhammad heard the chain being run through a previously-unnoticed iron staple set in the mud wall under the charpoy. He heard a padlock snap one end of the chain in place. A moment later Ali Muhammad felt Pervez grabbing his left ankle. When the American acted as if he was going to resist, a guttural animal noise escaped from Maqbool's throat. When my friend looked back he knew if he moved so much as a hair he would die.

The moment Ali Muhammad stopped resisting, Pervez wrapped the open end of the chain tightly around his ankle, then snapped the second padlock in place. As soon as his oldest son was back on his feet, Maqbool moved towards the lovers. He aimed the gun at Ali, then reaching down, Maqbool grabbed Shaheen by the hair and threw her across the room in the direction of the door.

"You bastard," Ali shouted, not realizing that in his anger he was resorting to his native tongue.

Maqbool Khan paid no attention, just backed carefully out the door. Pervez grabbed Shaheen and propelled her outside. Wakeel waited till the others were gone before picking up the lantern. He sneered at Ali, then turning, left the American standing in complete darkness. The moment they all exited Ali Muhammad heard the door slam shut and the

Shaheen's Heart

chain being locked in place. Even through the thick walls of the tower my friend heard the sound of blows, followed by Shaheen crying.

Ali Muhammad became white with wrath. He reached down and tore at the chain like he had never done in Pindi Prison, shaking and screaming in indignant rage. The merciless links held. They cut into his flesh but did not hurt him as much as that invisible chain reaching out through the dark to the woman he loved. In desperation he screamed Shaheen's name. But if anyone in Bajaur heard him they gave no clue, nor ever came.

The padlock on his ankle and the padlock on his heart both held. Finally in utter desperation he collapsed on the charpoy. His steel leash was so short he was forced to leave his left foot sitting on the floor. As the silence of Bajaur once again settled over the tower, Ali Muhammad heard the scorpions scuttling across the floor in the dark. Though he was only wearing sandals, he made no attempt to lift his foot.

Man's entire life is involved in the struggle between right and wrong, between distinguishing clarity and confusion. That night Ali Muhammad lay there chained and prayed in desperation.

"Deliver me by thy mercy from those who reject thee," he began to recite from the Quran.

Then Ali Muhammad's breath came in great sobs as his prayer faltered, then faded away. His heart tore in grief as he begged Allah not for his own safety but that of Shaheen's, asking God to protect the girl from the villains who ruled her life. Lying there in the velvet darkness he got no answers. His only solace was the small view he got of the sky's unnumbered sparks twinkling through the gun-port far above his head.

The silence of the grave hung over the fort the rest of that weary night.

When dawn found Ali Muhammad he was lying there thinking. As compensation for a smaller share of caution, Allah had given him a larger measure of cleverness. The long hours had allowed him to see he had but one weapon at his disposal. Maqbool Khan had no respect for Ali's knowledge of Pathan ways. Plus the kidnapper slandered the foreign Muslim's long experience in Pakistan, as well as underestimating the wisdom he had gathered in the North West Frontier.

During the night Ali realized Shaheen had been right about one critical point. She understood Maqbool's itching palm was the way to his undoing. The armed bully's avarice might blind his eyes to Ali Muhammad's skills.

Lying there waiting for dawn, my friend tried to possess his soul in patience. He remembered in Peshawar they said, "Pity the man who must beg of a beggar." In his mind he feared his was a reckless plan born out of such beggarly desperation. Regardless of what happened to him, Ali Muhammad met the new day knowing that to rescue Shaheen he must send Maqbool Khan to the fiery pit, a place the tribesman so justly deserved for his part in this reeking betrayal.

In Bajaur no man knowingly insulted another unless he knew the injured party was powerless to retaliate. That school of tribal savagery taught that only bribery or fear could cause such dangerous men to conduct themselves decently.

When the door opened in the morning, young Wakeel made no pretense at hospitality. He believed the prisoner helpless and therefore worthy only of contempt. Ali Muhammad had been waiting, hoping the younger brother would come to check on him. The arrival of the boy brought a slight smile to Ali's dry, parched lips. Already well awake, as soon as Ali saw Wakeel he stood up and verbally assaulted him.

"Where is that *kafir* (unbeliever) you call your father?" Ali Muhammad bawled at the startled boy. He gave Wakeel no time to think or answer, only continued his unexpected attack.

"Maqbool Khan calls himself a Muslim and a Pathan. What kind of Muslim treats his guests like this?" the American shouted at the boy.

"My father is a good Muslim, a strong Muslim," Wakeel replied unsteadily in his father's defense.

"You're a liar. Your father's a coward. Take me to him so I can prove it. Take me to see that coward, that *kafir*, that whore's son."

The boy stood frozen, unsure what to say or do with this suddenly insane foreigner. Then Ali Muhammad shook the chain and glared at the boy.

"What's wrong, are you afraid like your coward father? Here," Ali said, and held his hands up away from his chest. "Keep the chain on me and you can walk me to where Maqbool is hiding. Come on you little *kuni* (faggot) take me to him now."

Surprisingly the youth did what he was told. At first Wakeel advanced cautiously, then as his anger rose, he became eager to march the suicidal American into the presence of a man who would kill him before breakfast. Wakeel ordered Ali Muhammad to move as far away from the charpoy as the chain would allow. When the captive crossed his arms over his chest in contempt and looked away, the boy quickly reached under the rope bed and unlocked the padlock holding Ali Muhammad to the wall.

It took but a minute for Wakeel to lead Shaheen's resourceful lover across the courtyard of the mud fort and up to one of the doors opening into the living quarters. The boy motioned for his prisoner to wait. Wakeel then tapped on the door before cautiously peering in. Suddenly he wondered if his father would be glad to see the American?

The moment Wakeel opened the door, Ali had a partial view of the room inside. Looking over the head of the twelve year old, Ali Muhammad could see the commonplace objects that made up a Pathan household. A few bolsters lined up against the wall passed as furniture. A piece of plastic served as the table cloth for the crude morning meal spread on the floor for Maqbool and Pervez Khan.

As soon as Ali Muhammad saw his captor eating breakfast he made his move. Without waiting for Wakeel to get permission, Ali shoved the boy aside and opened the door. He could feel his heart beating up in his throat in fear when he walked boldly into the room. Maqbool was so shocked at the appearance of his prisoner, he failed to pick up the gun sitting next to him and shoot the bold American.

Ali Muhammad did not hesitate. He held up his empty hands as a sign he was unarmed, walked straight through the door, dragging a surprised Wakeel in tow on the other end of the chain, and promptly sat down on the opposite side of the table cloth from Maqbool. Before the amazed Mohmand could determine Ali's plan, my friend reached out and tore off a huge chunk of the bread lying before him on a plate.

He immediately began to shove it into his mouth. Before even half of it was chewed, Ali Muhammad looked at Maqbool and said," I demand my right to *nanawatai* (the right to seek asylum)."

The American kept chewing, grabbing a second chunk of bread before the first one was even eaten.

"The Prophet Mohammad ordered all Muslims to treat a guest with reverent care and respect. Is this how you define *Pukhtunwali*? Is this how you treat your guests, to bring him here with lies and then chain him?" Ali Muhammad asked Maqbool, all the while chewing furiously.

The American swallowed the bread and looked at the Mohmand expectantly.

In theory the bond of bread and salt was now good for the next twenty four hours, or until the guest's body had voided the food that placed him under his host's protection. Ali Muhammad was banking on the fact that this Pathan tribesman who did not respect any man made laws would not violate the sacred tenets of his own tribal code of honor. The wayfarer held his breath, waiting to discover if the *Pukhtunwali's* belief in hospitality was practiced in Bajaur.

Maqbool Khan sat there, a bronzed, forbidding, grimly taciturn statue struck dumb by the cool daring of a foreigner who had the courage to taunt and insult him with his own moral code. His cold white eye looked off into space, while its yellowed companion stared at Ali Muhammad like a feral beast, glaring and full of hate.

My friend ordered his face to be constant, lest his own eyes betray the rage he felt when he looked at the indescribable pollution who had abused the woman he loved. Ali Muhammad swallowed his poisonous spleen, painting a reconciliatory smile on his face and pretending not to notice the powder-keg whose fuse he had lit.

"Tell your sons, are you a Pathan chief who offers me hospitality, or a *kafir* who will keep me a prisoner?" Ali asked and waited for Maqbool to kill him in swift retaliation for such effrontery.

The two men stared at each other, the good and evil of their respective souls poles apart. Maqbool's face contorted in a fierce frown, yet Ali's coolness was slowly eroding the brigand's supremacy. Faced with dishonoring his tribal code of honor, Maqbool Khan started to sheepishly make excuses. The big man began by feigning loyalty and affection.

"We only chained you for your own safety, to keep you from wandering into danger during the night. If you had left the fort you would have been killed as a stranger," he assured Ali Muhammad. "Besides I trust you."

"Is this how you trust me, with ten feet of trust?" was Ali Muhammad's explosive reply, as he snatched the offending chain out of Wakeel's hands.

Now the shame began to mount up on Maqbool's bearded face. He ordered his younger son to unlock the American, then, placing a tea cup before Ali, invited him to drink.

"Never. I'm a prisoner not a guest."

"No. No. You're our guest. Besides you're mistaken. We've already fed and honored you on the night you arrived," the host emphasized.

Remembering the two tiny sparrows he had received for his only meal, Ali Muhammad said, "Yes, I got two chickens as big as your heart."

Maqbool did not understand the remark and thought Ali was complimenting him.

"Come, you can have the woman. Let's discuss the payment," the Bajauri urged his guest, and while Wakeel grudgingly unlocked Ali Muhammad, the father pressed food and drink on the American.

So both men temporarily laid aside their open hostility for each other and began a new game. This time it was decreed that according to the ancient code of *Pukhtunwali* Maqbool must offer hospitality to his guest and using the same rules, Ali Muhammad silently vowed to return revenge for the insults heaped on him.

They sat there, these smooth-talking enemies, negotiating and dancing about on the end of a needle, smiling like old friends as they discussed the subject of a woman's freedom and a man's life. Maqbool tried to act as sharp as a knife when it came to striking a bargain. He swore he had always intended to let Ali Muhammad marry Shaheen. Neither man had the bad taste to mention the fact that the brigand had no right to hold the woman, much less sell her. They both silently understood that physical possession equated law in Bajaur.

The Mohmand's main priority was to establish how much money Ali Muhammad could immediately raise to purchase Shaheen's release. Quickly figuring up his finances, Ali Muhammad held his breath and offered a paltry sum compared to Maroof's exorbitant asking price. Still hoping to enrich himself beyond the dreams of his shameful avarice, Maqbool Khan accepted the offer with alacrity. Ali Muhammad maintained a tone of terrible self-repression. Maqbool's quick acceptance convinced Ali the brigand would never allow him or Shaheen to either live or leave. Ali understood the moment Maqbool had the American's money he would slay the lovers.

Once the amount had been settled they began trying to agree on how the money would be handed over. Maqbool did not trust Ali Muhammad to return to Peshawar, obtain the money, and then journey back into Bajaur. He wanted Ali to send word and have the ransom cum dowry handed over to his older son Pervez.

"I will send Wakeel to a nearby fort. They have a tape recorder. You can use it to make a tape in Pushtu telling your friends in Peshawar to

Shaheen's Heart

give my son the money. When it arrives you and the woman can leave," Maqbool said confidently.

Ali Muhammad understood such an arrangement disguised his kidnapper's real reasoning. Ali did not have to be told the Pathan insisted on a tape instead of a written note because Maqbool was illiterate. Plus Ali realized Maqbool wanted him to speak in Pushtu so he could monitor the contents, making sure the American did not slip in an English plea for help. However Ali carefully hid these perceptions and countered with the only plan that offered either him or Shaheen any trace of hope.

"That will never work. The bank will only deliver my money to me and not my friends. If you want it I will have to go there myself."

"No! You can send a message," Maqbool countered, worried about losing his grip on his Angrez pigeon.

"And who will deliver such a message? You are afraid of going there and no one will give money to this," Ali Muhammad said and pointed with undisguised contempt at Pervez.

The insult on his courage caused Maqbool to rage. If he was not wanted by the government, he screamed, he would deliver the message personally.

For several minutes silence reigned as the Bajauri tried to come up with a counter argument. Having tried brute force and failed, he realized he was temporarily stalemated by the wily foreigner. This made little difference to Maqbool, for in Bajaur treachery looked upon verbal argument merely as an amusement. Its chief weapon was still physical force. The brigand contented himself with the evidence proving the American truly was mad for the worthless woman and would therefore be foolish enough to return. Maqbool Khan had good reason to believe the implied threat of violence to Shaheen could control Ali Muhammad.

A smile that held no trace of grace played across the Mohmand's face.

"I think you are too good a Muslim to contrive treason against me," Maqbool said, his one good eye looking sly and malignant.

When Ali Muhammad agreed, his captor leered in satisfaction. Maqbool ordered Wakeel to fetch a copy of the Quran. Placing it under Ali's right hand, the kidnapper said he would allow the American to go to Peshawar in the company of his oldest son to retrieve the money, only so long as Ali vowed he would not instead escape to America. Holding Ali's hand over the holy book, Maqbool did not understand that neither his implied threats nor his AK-47 could extinguish so great a love as Ali Muhammad felt for Shaheen. The American was not cowed by the gnarled hand holding his own over the Quran. Maqbool's victim had every intention of returning

Yet Ali's silence was an eloquent answer to such a request. If my friend had previously lacked substantial evidence, this latest action convinced him he was in a den of thieves. His blue eyes regarded Maqbool with great disgust. The commonly-accepted oath taken over the Bible in the western world had a long tradition whereby the speaker's words were believed to be free of perjury. In Islam however an equally ancient tradition held forth that men who swore oaths over the holy book were often themselves unrepentant liars.

In 656 AD, a little more than twenty years after the death of the Prophet Mohammad (PBUH), his wife Ayesha was herself a witness to the first mass swearing to such a blasphemous lie. Before his death, the Prophet had warned his wife she would one day find herself fighting on the wrong side in a place known as Hawab, where the dogs would bark at her. Many years later, while leading her army against the Prophet's son-in-law, Imam Ali, Ayesha heard dogs barking as she passed through a small village. Remembering the Prophet's admonition, she asked the name of the place, only to be told it was known as Hawab. However some of her companions quickly brought forth forty men who swore falsely over the Qu'ran that the village was not so named. Ayesha and her army marched on to disastrous results.

Through it been centuries since the dogs barked in Hawab, much of mankind had never changed. The dogs were dead but evil still walked the world in disguise. Nowhere was that more apparent than in Bajaur, where many men were all too eager to use the holy Quran to mask their unholy deeds. These sons of Satan took the name of Allah lightly. They delighting in using an oath as an excuse for not doing what was right. If pressure was brought to bear on them, urging them to renounce injustice, or not commit some injurious act, they pleaded that it was a holy oath that bound them to their tortured path. Thus they doubly dishonored the holy words that crossed their polluted lips.

Ali Muhammad knew it would be easier to get justice from a crew of pirates than to pry the truth from the incarnation of scheming, pitiless evil sitting before him. However he held his hand over the Qu'ran and vowed to return to Bajaur before he journeyed to the United States.

"I swear by the resurrection day and the self-reproaching spirit that I shall come back to Bajaur, back to this house, and back for the woman," Shaheen's rescuer said, and meant every word.

A smile crossed Maqbool's face.

If the vow was meaningless to the Pathan kidnapper, it did matter to Ali Muhammad. My friend knew Maqbool Khan couldn't be trusted, remembering the old saying that you could coax a Bajauri into Hell but couldn't force him into Heaven. Regardless, Ali Muhammad demanded Maqbool give him a vow in return, wanting to hear the faithless words if only to ease his own heart.

"You in turn must swear that no harm will come to the woman in my absence," Ali Muhammad made Maqbool promise.

The bearded man gladly gave Ali a worthless oath.

"I swear by what you see, and what you see not, that I will not hurt the woman during your absence," the big man said with his lips, all the while the glaring white eye reassured the American of the worthlessness of the soiled words tumbling past Maqbool Khan's stained teeth.

With the vows said, the shamed Qu'ran was once again put away. Only the Divine Author of that great and holy book knew the secrets lurking in both men's souls.

Shaheen's Heart

With the matter agreed upon, Ali Muhammad was suddenly afflicted with impatience. He sat there studying Maqbool Khan, disguising the hate he felt for this foul human disease whose soul was so full of discord and disharmony. Regardless of the danger, Ali knew he was going to return, but with guns not money.

During the course of these negotiations there had been no sign of Shaheen, Maqbool counting her opinion of no more importance than that of the other livestock. Ali Muhammad insisted he be allowed to see her alone before he and Pervez departed for Peshawar. Maqbool ordered his younger son to escort Ali back to the tower, where the woman would be delivered.

As they walked side by side the boy took the opportunity to chide the American for his lack of faith.

"I told you my father was a good Muslim," Wakeel countered.

All Ali said was, "Yes, depending on your definition."

The boy left him inside the now familiar tower. Ali Muhammad waited only a few minutes before Shaheen walked through the open door. In the clear morning light he saw her face was thin with worry, pinched with hunger, and bruised from beating. Yet she remained permanently and profoundly beautiful. That was the first time my friend saw not just Shaheen's external beauty, which could be perceived by the eyes in his head, but her internal beauty, which had been waiting to be discovered with the eyes of his heart. That emotional divulgence had been left lying under a covering of dust until the traveler stumbled upon the truth lying hidden in his path.

At first he stood there mired in inarticulate inadequacy, unsure of what to say, or how much to divulge. She stood there revealed, a deceiver, a professional counterfeit of passion, a squanderer of that sweet love he had brought into the desert. For a moment he once again mistrusted her, the old poison in his veins threatening to overturn his remembered passion.

"Beggar that I am, I am yours," Shaheen told him quietly.

When Ali Muhammad heard her words his heart bent like a great tree in the wind, groaning under the silent strain of loving her. From that moment Ali swore to forever ignore Shaheen's shameful past, trusting instead in her inner goodness. He stood there with misery in his heart and nothing to offer her in his hand. All he knew was that no impediment save death could stop him from returning for her.

"40,000 Bajauris could not equal my love for you," he told her, then pulled her towards him and kissed her goodbye, knowing he was bidding farewell to that time in his life when loving her had seemed simple by comparison to the rocky path standing before them. He felt the warmth of her breasts, the starved outline of her ribs under his hands, smelled the last traces of jasmine in her hair, saw the silent need in her eyes.

"I will come back for you though Hell itself should bar my way," Ali Muhammad said softly, trying to press into a few words the message that love was all he had to offer, that it would have to be enough to save them both.

Khyber Knights

If Shaheen sensed the misery written large on his face she said nothing. When two lovers part it is the one going on the journey who suffers the least. The inevitable diversions of travel and change help drug the pain of departure. The woman understood she would have no such mental or bodily distractions. Her bleeding heart could not take refuge under the cloak of action. Yet she hid the bitterness that lay in her cup, taking Ali Muhammad's hand instead and leading him outside to the gate of the fort where their captors impatiently awaited them. She ignored Maqbool and looked up into Ali's warm, tender eyes.

"Let nothing come between us," she cautioned him, then stepped back to let him go.

He wanted to reach out and pull her back but resisted the temptation.

"*Au revoir*. It means until we meet again," he explained.

The foreign words only heightened her own uncertainty in this strange man who had entered into her life. Shaheen managed to give him a weak smile in return.

"*Pa makha de kha*, (May the path you face be bright)," she replied, telling him the traditional Pathan farewell.

"*Amin sara*, (yours also)," Ali Muhammad said, then turned to face her captor.

Maqbool had no single redeeming virtue except his courage, yet Ali Muhammad thanked him for his hospitality and gave the Pathan his word he would return. Then the American walked through the gate, not waiting to see if Pervez was following. Ali heard Maqbool yelling hastily at his eldest son to keep track of the captive. This announcement was followed by the sound of running steps. The Mohmand minder caught up with the American before he could outdistance him.

The two men had not gone very far, when Ali turned to look back over his shoulder. His eyes, which had witnessed much injustice during his years on the Frontier, saw Shaheen still standing at the gate, smaller than he remembered, a tiny, lonely atom of human dust. He lengthened his stride, more determined than ever to put his plan into motion and return for her.

More than an hour later the two men still marched on, avoiding other forts, their mouths parched, their bodies roasting in that oven known as Bajaur. When a small Toyota truck coming from the direction of Afghanistan slowed down they bargained for a lift as far as Gandao. Neither of them asked where the driver and passengers were coming from. No one knew or cared about their fellow passengers.

During the course of that long day Ali Muhammad found himself unwillingly yoked to Pervez. Though the son was an man of little merit, he was only the ass bearing the father's villainous load. His role was to groan and sweat as he helped further the ambitions of Maqbool Khan, that master of mischief. Yet father and son shared one common trait. Both their souls were slaves to evil.

While the American and his captor sat stranded, waiting for a ride out of the outlaw village of Gandao, Pervez gave broad hints he had repeatedly raped Shaheen during her captivity. When a mini-bus finally arrived bound for Shabqadar, Ali Muhammad sat locked in stony silence as Pervez spent the time trying to pry information about America out of the foreigner. Like a naive child wanting to see Toyland, the Mohmand pestered Ali Muhammad about the chances of getting him a visa so he could visit and work in the United States.

My friend paid no attention to the man who had led Shaheen into such treacherous surroundings. Ali Muhammad sat beside Pervez lost in long thoughts. The American understood he was a slave to Shaheen's memory and the love he bore her. It gave him no comfort to realize the beauty that should have been her blessing had been transformed into an ugliness used to serve men's basest lusts. As Pervez and the bus rattled on towards the borders of Bajaur, for the first time in his life Ali Muhammad felt remorse and shame in being male, knowing that it was his sex that had twisted Shaheen's beauty into a poisoned fruit, that it was men who had taken the delicate sculpture Allah had crafted and turned it into a whore full of false fire, that it was his Muslim brothers who had killed the date palm and brought up a crop of thorns.

If Maqbool and his son, Pervez Khan, had a weakness, it was that they felt safe in their sins and smug in their arrogance. When the bus reached the large village of Shabqadar, the streets were full of people and soldiers. There was much turmoil and confusion. Not being handcuffed or in any way physically attached to his haphazard captor, it was not difficult for Ali Muhammad to slip away in the crowd from Maqbool's son. While Pervez was still searching for him in Shabqadar, Ali Muhammad used his knowledge of the countryside to jump quickly on a bus bound north for Timagura. He stayed on that vehicle only long enough to reach the village of Charsadda. There it was easy enough to climb on yet another bus and double back in the direction of Peshawar.

"Allah be my guide," was painted over that derelict's windshield, but the saying held true. Ali Muhammad returned late that evening, arriving at his house empty and fragile, his grief and love demanding atonement.

Khyber Knights

49
The Death of Beau Fontaine

"*Shukrallah*, (Thanks be to God)," Raja said when he opened up the door and saw Ali Muhammad standing there.

The weary American said nothing to the Pathan, just walked inside the house that no longer had any meaning. Ali did not look right or left. He made his way silently to the large sitting room on the main floor. When he opened the door he did not see the collected treasures, the costly tapestries, nor the finely-crafted musical instruments. His eyes saw only the place where Shaheen had stood when she lifted off her blue burkha. When he moved his eyes towards the wall he saw the pillow she had leaned against. It was to that lodestone of his heart's desire that he made his way.

He was unaware of how he looked. He was unaware of how his glazed and rigid stare frightened Raja. As he walked across the plush carpets of the hushed room Ali Muhammad only knew that this particular spot was where Shaheen had sat and spoke to him a lifetime ago.

The tired traveler did not follow custom and kick off his sandals at the doorway. Instead he made his way directly to that place where he and Shaheen had discussed their forthcoming marriage. Ali dropped wearily, leaned back against the bolster and tried to summon up the essence of the woman who ruled his heart. He closed his eyes and opened his nostrils, hoping to catch a faint trace of jasmine. When he smelled nothing the delayed effects of the past few days began to wash over him in waves. Suddenly he was overcome with fatigue and gloom. He felt his eyes misting over underneath his closed lids. He did not need to open them to know that the faithful Raja was standing in the doorway. Ali Muhammad knew he needed privacy to grieve and to plan.

"Would you boil me some water so I can take a bath," he asked Raja, without opening the eyes that would betray him.

"Of course. Can I do anything else?" the Afridi asked, eager to please.

"Later I could eat," Ali told him. "The chickens are very small in Bajaur."

He opened his tear-filled eyes as he said this, giving Raja a glimpse inside the windows of pain that covered his heart. The boy nodded, pulled the door quietly closed but made sure he peeked back inside the moment he thought Ali Muhammad wouldn't notice. Shaheen's lover had leaned his head back. His arms were thrown out on both sides of the pillows that lined the wall. He looked crucified from the effort of coming home.

Raja Bahadur Khan was born clever. He went to the nearby kitchen where he made a great deal of noise lighting the little gas stove and sitting a large pot of water on to boil. Believing he had made enough commotion to convince Ali he was busy in the kitchen, Raja instantly slipped away.

As he made his way through the twisting streets, our old cell-mate realized even the commonplace events pointed to something being extremely wrong.

The Pathan knew that normally the master of the house would have strolled down to Hasht Nagari and taken a bath in the neighborhood *hammam* (bath house). Being a man who took great pride in his appearance, Ali Muhammad was fond of the careful shave and the perfumed tinctures of the barber shop. Yet such a common-day occurrence would cost privacy as well as fifteen rupees. The prying, curious neighbors would undoubtedly quiz Ali Muhammad on where he had been and what business took him away.

My Afridi companion found me at home in the Amin Hotel. Even without the latest information, I would have come running. The water had barely come to a boil before Raja and I slipped quietly back into Ali Muhammad's house. While the Afridi made his way back into the kitchen, I in turn went to the door of the *hujra* (guest room) where Ali was sitting. Something made me knock before I dared venture inside. There was no answer, so I knocked again. The silence did nothing but alarm me further. I opened the door carefully and peeked my head inside.

Ali Muhammad was sitting across the room, still leaning up against the pillows. At the sight of movement in the doorway he looked my way.

He had aged ten years.

Never during the worst days of the horse trip, nor even when we had shared a prison cell, had I seen my old friend look that bad. His normally elegant clothes were not just dirty or travel-worn, they were filthy. Even from where I stood I could see that every inch of him, from the turban on his head to the sandals still on his feet, was covered in either dust, dirt, or mud. Where his clothes had become creased from travel or sleeping, the cloth spoke through in darker colors. Otherwise the once-proud shalwar kameez looked like it had stood still and given no resistance when a bucketful of muck was thrown in its direction.

His normally polished sandals had lost their usual high gloss black shine. They too were caked with what looked like a mixture of mud and cow dung. It had been days since Ali shaved. The whiskers disgracing his fine features only heightened the unmistakable sharpness of the cheek-bones protruding from his sunken cheeks. Yet it was his eyes that frightened me. They glowed like hot coals, their bloodshot message telling me their owner was bordering on being half mad.

I stood there transfixed, too shocked at his degraded appearance to enter, too frightened to leave him to his fate. Our hearts beat a slow cadence in silent recognition of each other, but otherwise he offered me no greeting, said no word, just turned and faced away from me in mute warning and rebuke.

It was only then that I dared enter to what had once been a room as much like my home as his. I slipped off the riding boots I still wore, left

The Death of Beau Fontaine

them at the door and walked across the *hujra*. When I sat down next to Ali I smelled him before I heard him. He had grown rank with the sweat of effort and fear. No sooner had I become seated than he turned and faced me. For all the years that I had known him, Ali Muhammad had been afflicted with that particular restlessness that so often accompanies the artistic life. I had seen him highly strung, often bored, occasionally lethargic, but never completely exhausted. Clearly he had seen so much, suffered so much, that he was left barren of everything except love and anger.

As a journalist I had long ago learned that sometimes the best way to get a difficult story out of an unwilling person is to let silence bear down. Regardless of the country, or the language, most people cannot stand to have someone sit and stare at them. Usually the human clam opens up angrily within the first sixty seconds. The resultant interview often starts out tense and bumpy but at least you're on your way to getting the facts.

Ali Muhammad was no exception.

I was waiting in patient silence when Raja entered the room.

"Your water is ready," he said, then placed himself down next to me, clearly anticipating Ali Muhammad to relate what had happened.

Like many Orientals, Pakistanis have little regard for privacy. Where as I may have been content to let Ali Muhammad eventually open up to me after a few embarrassing moments of silence, Raja had no patience for such American idiocies. He bluntly demanded to know what had transpired. Ali Muhammad might have turned on me in anger at such a request, but he still held a soft spot for that faithful youth. Raja and I sat there and listened as our friend related the events of the last three days. Being at heart a polite Occidental, I said nothing, weighing the evidence, looking for clues, doubting the intentions and honesty of everyone involved except Ali Muhammad.

Raja was a brash blue jay to my silent Cock Robin. He clucked. He sighed. He cursed. He grumbled. Whereas I never moved, listening and learning for the first time of the activities of Maqbool and his nasty clan, Raja alternately pounded his fist into his hand in fury, or scrunched up his face in grim anticipation of the tale's ending.

When Ali finished speaking I urged him to use caution in regards to all the players, especially Shaheen. The woman had given nothing in return for his love except a worthless promise, I argued. Now was not the time to stock up on more trouble. To risk his life the first time by venturing into Bajaur had been romantically foolhardy. In my opinion to voluntarily go back was nothing short of suicidal.

In Peshawar they say that love never sleeps in a safe corner.

Ali Muhammad proved the truth of that old statement the moment I closed my mouth.

I had inadvertently roused his anger. For a brief second I thought he might reach out and grab me in explosive ill humor. His eyes blazed but their fire was kept under control by those accumulated years of long friendship. He gave a sigh of frustration and then tried to explain the reasoning behind both his past and proposed actions.

"All my life I've been in search of someone I couldn't find. Now I know who it is and the misery of it is I can't reach out and touch her. I've already lost my dignity and my pride. My money will go next and I don't care about losing that either. All I know is I will love Shaheen the rest of my life. It is laid upon me to go back for her," Ali Muhammad told me, not caring if I agreed or not.

If I had thought to find an ally in Raja I had neglected to remember the hot Pathan blood that coursed through his own veins. There was never any love lost between the Afridi and Mohmand tribes, but in our young friend's eyes Maqbool Khan's actions were tantamount to Frontier treason. A *jirga* (tribal council) might have debated the idea of assisting Ali Muhammad in his search for revenge, but there was no hesitation with Raja Bahadur Khan. The Afridi Pathan had always been true to his salt. Raja threw prudence to the wind and sided with Ali.

"What is written is written. We will go back with you," Raja said without bothering to ask my opinion, his own views reflecting the note of fatality I had already detected in Ali Muhammad.

I looked at the two madmen sitting on either side of me. Raja was a Pathan so I expected him to act insanely when it came to matters of love and honor. Ali Muhammad, I reluctantly admitted to myself, had always followed his own inclinations, regardless of the personal costs. Reason, I knew, could not prevail over blind passion. It is vain to hope to persuade a man if his mad desires lie unconquered. No one could undertake to lead or guide or teach my friend, for Ali Muhammad obeyed no law now save that of his heart's desire. I knew he longed to return to the slavery of Shaheen's love.

I decided there was no point in playing devil's advocate any longer.

"I don't know why I'm bothering to argue with you," I told Ali, "you never listen to me anyway."

Though I had agreed to join them I would not budge on the idea of rushing off without plan nor ploy. Ali Muhammad's idea to arm himself and hurry back to somehow rescue Shaheen was romantically improbable. He agreed to rest the night and wait to leave until the next morning, by which time I hoped to arrange private transportation to take us in, and more importantly out, of Bajaur. Even Raja concurred with this argument, assuring Ali Muhammad that even if they succeeded in beheading Maqbool Khan, it would still be a long walk home with Shaheen.

When Ali realized he was going to receive no more arguments he agreed to rest the night in Peshawar. He bathed, fed and finally slept, trying to take refuge at last in that passive oblivion. Yet lucky is the traveler who can close his eyes and expect the vain spectacle of life to pass softly by. While Raja and I quietly planned we heard Ali Muhammad mumbling and crying in his sleep as grief poisoned his dreams. Even there in his own home his sick soul found no harbor from Maqbool's dull revenge. Maybe he learned in his dreams that beauty falsely worshipped was but a fleeting bridge to temporary treasures. If in truth he worshipped her physical beauty alone then he was caught in a web of

The Death of Beau Fontaine

disguised self-indulgence. Only if he loved the eternal beauty of Shaheen's soul was he going to find happiness, for the difference between the two was as gold and dross.

If Raja was brave he was also too superstitious to go check on our friend. When I quietly looked into Ali Muhammad's room, even in the dark I could see that the mercy of deep sleep was denied him. Watching his restless slumber I knew he was consumed with passion for this questionable woman, yet I did not hold him out into the wind of blame. If there is special providence in the fall of a sparrow then what could be accounted for the death of so great a love as his. For even in my ignorance I knew that not even the weight of an atom in faraway Heaven was hidden from Allah. So surely He knew of Ali Muhammad's pain for He saw all things both open and secret.

"My father told me there is no greater torment than to be separated from your beloved," Raja whispered from behind me. "But to worship a woman so deeply is both foolish and futile."

I had no answers for either Raja or Ali. I closed the door quietly, knowing in my heart that such questions would linger on until all human vanities passed away on the torrents of time. The date palm, the corn and the grape were all fed by the same stream of water but how different the harvests which they yielded. So it was with we three friends. I bid my dear friend Ali Muhammad a silent good night, wishing him sweet dreams, but knowing he was more likely to cry out in longing for Shaheen's corrupted flesh, though she stood waving from beside their two graves with a look of doom on her soft face.

The uneasy night proved but a preparation for that woeful dawn, for when the sun arose it brought with it no signs of enlightenment to the house in Hasht Nagari.

It came as no surprise to discover Ali Muhammad had been awake before sunrise. Even though I had come over early I discovered him impatient to leave. If I hoped to discover that sleep had unblocked his channel of reasoning, I was sorely disappointed. Shaheen's memory was still green, and he lay grappled to the memory of her sweet breasts with invisible hooks of steel.

A sleepy-eyed Raja came into the *hujra* in time to hear Ali Muhammad cursing Maqbool Khan, swearing to confine that leprous distilment to an early grave. Ali's rage provoked him to make vile oaths of desperation. There in that once-happy house, now grown silent with sorrow, Raja and I watched the sun rise on a day that promised a series of dire events. Outside were the reassuring noises of the aged city coming out of her slumber. Children chattered. Peddlers yelled. But behind the walls where I stood, Ali Muhammad swore he would pay his kidnapper back, but with vengeance not wealth. I watched my friend bubbling over with a serpent's mixture of bile and revenge. The beloved musician of Hasht Nagari, once so full of humor and sweet spirit, was gone, replaced in the night by a man who had no dread of death. Standing there impatient to rush to his paramour and his doom was a creature who was no lover of old age.

Khyber Knights

What could Raja and I say once we learned Ali Muhammad had no desire to repent, was determined instead to fly back towards the bright flame of Shaheen's love with its promise of certain immolation? There were only three diseases on the North West Frontier that affected men like us, malaria, hepatitis and cowardice, the latter alone being held incurable. We understood the ancient Pathan adage, "Me against my brother. Me and my brother against my cousin. Me, my brother and my cousin against the world," or in this case Bajaur.

We set about to help Ali Muhammad.

For a few brief moments it felt like we were back on the horse trip, each of us quickly and easily agreeing to take on a certain task before riding on from yet another village. That fleeting mirage of happier times lasted only long enough for us to bid each other goodbye. Raja stayed behind, intent on his own duties. Ali Muhammad and I parted outside in the street. I left to find the Afghan truck-driver I knew.

Meanwhile Ali Muhammad made his way across Peshawar towards Chowk Yadgar, the money changers' bazaar. Though he had no intention of paying a ransom to his enemy Maqbool Khan, Ali Muhammad believed hard cash might come in handy as either a bribe or a bluff for any soldiers or police we encountered. Though it was still early the little shops that served the monetary needs of Peshawar's citizens were already awake. Boys were running in with tea trays. Phones could be heard ringing. Customers sat huddled in secretive conferences with currency peddlers, for in Chowk Yadgar it made no difference what country a man hailed from. In those cubbyholes every man spoke the same language, "money."

Shiraz Gul was like all the money changers, untrustworthy. The only difference was that Ali Muhammad and I had been doing business with him for years.

More importantly he had two wives.

In his late thirties, Shiraz might be going bald but was already fat. His corpulent face with its weedy black mustache boasted two restless eyes that sought for any advantage against his customers. Yet we considered him no more of a crook than some of his competitors. What endeared him to us was that after the haggling over the rate of exchange was concluded, Shiraz could be counted on to lapse into his latest installment of domestic hell. While an assistant opened the small safe and counted out the currency, the money changer would regale us with a new story about his battling wives.

Having become rich by cheating his fellow citizens, Shiraz had purchased a younger, second wife over the objections of his primary spouse. Over the years everyone in Chowk Yadgar came to learn of how Shiraz Gul had been forced to buy a second home in order to separate these battling shrews. Despite his wealth Shiraz was an unhappy man. The Quran admonished a husband not to incline towards one wife lest on the Day of Judgment he be paralyzed on one side. Everyone in Chowk Yadgar knew Shiraz Gul already had a glimpse of Hell. He spent alternating nights between the two wives, neither of which trusted him, and both of which lashed him with their tongues.

It was Shiraz who had told us with great conviction that the punishment for having two wives, was two wives. There is an old Pushu saying, usually uttered when friends meet, "*Singa Ae* (how are you)?" to which the answer is, "*Dwou khazo khwand na kha aem* (I am better than the husband of two wives)."

That particular morning Ali Muhammad had no interest in either Shiraz Gul or his loving family. He laid out his wallet, an embroidered affair from Afghanistan. From its inner recesses he brought forth the battered American currency he had been hoarding. He kept back several of the hundred dollar notes, then shoved the rest in the direction of Shiraz Gul. If the money-changer noted any difference in Ali Muhammad's demeanor he was wise enough not to comment. Outside the streets were starting to become packed with citizens and animals. No one gave any notice to the goings-on inside the money-changers' shops. Every one understood that these were the "people's banks" and that this time-honored custom, known as *hundi*, was a necessary fact of life.

Hundi was a unique system of banking and currency exchange as old as Islam. It relied on family ties and the honesty bred within the strict confines of the religion. In the days before electronic currency exchange and telegraphs, *hundi* was the method invented whereby currency could be safely transferred.

An agent in one city would take a client's money. He would then authorize his associate in another city, usually a trusted relative or lifelong friend, to release the money to a recipient designated by the client. The result was a discreet method of transferring funds to friends and family across great and dangerous distances. For hundreds of years *hundi* had been the only way to get money throughout greater India and much of the Islamic world.

Shiraz Gul and his fellow agents in Chowk Yadgar raked in a ten percent commission on any transaction. They also made loans and exchanged foreign currency for Pakistani rupees. It was an easy, profitable business with only one drawback. If the money did not arrive on the other end of a transfer the *hundi* agent usually ended up dead.

Since the 1970s Chowk Yadgar's hundi agents had branched out. The exodus of Pakistani men going to high-paying jobs in the oil-rich Middle East gave a strong international push to Peshawar's currency market. Customers still sat on the floor as they had for centuries, but now the shops of Shiraz Gul and his competitors were equipped with telephones and fax machines. The bulging money-changer reclining in front of Ali Muhammad shuffled currency across borders with no questions asked. There were no laws regulating the trade. No currency-reporting requirements or tax collectors dared interfere in the time-honored tradition that moved a physical truck load of money in and out of Peshawar every day. For with the war in nearby Afghanistan had come thousands of refugees with bundles of near-worthless communist currency. These desperate refugees would place stacks of "Afghanis" in

Khyber Knights

front of Shiraz Gul and be glad to depart with a pocketful of Pakistani rupees.

Ali Muhammad was no exception.

In silence he drank the traditional cup of tea offered to customers, thanked the unhappily married man, and left Chowk Yadgar with 50,000 rupees in red 100 rupee and purple 500 rupee notes.

My own errand took me far longer than those of my two companions.

Men like Ekram Shinwari and Chopendoz aren't found easily.

The one was a driver, the other a killer.

I needed them both.

From the first cool gleam of dawn the skies over Peshawar had been covered with white clouds. A false sense of tranquillity floated over the vast vale that I called home. When I left Ali Muhammad I caught a rickshaw on the Grand Trunk road and ordered the driver to point his noisy three wheeled vehicle in the direction of Nasir Bagh, the sprawling Afghan refugee camp lying a few miles outside Peshawar. The morning came on rapidly. As I drove away from the great city I could see the sky had taken on that soft opal glow that occurred before a rain storm lashed the North West Frontier Province. I watched as the silky outline of the clouds was broken, leaving troughs in the sky. Delicate blue contrasted up there with curious reflections of light. When I lowered my eyes I saw that such majestic beauty was in hushed contrast to the dark brooding mountains of Bajaur that clouded the rim of such a soft horizon.

I hated the refugee camps, even the one I sought.

Though the Afghans made every attempt at keeping them clean, the great mass of tented human poverty stank of despair, anger, fear and revenge.

I had come to the right place.

The only consolation I felt as I walked down the dusty lanes running between the tents was that my turban and knee high buz khazi boots didn't stand out. Even my freckled skin and red hair were explainable in Nasir Bagh. There were light-skinned, red-haired Turkoman refugees from the north of Afghanistan living in the camp who could have passed for my brothers. It was only among the darker-haired Pakistanis that my foreign roots were immediately noticeable. I passed a large open-walled tent where small boys were being taught verses from the Quran. The weather was good so their older brothers were off fighting in the Jihad with uncles and fathers. There was one tent I avoided. A line of Afghan women clad in burkhas squatted in the dust waiting to see the foreign woman doctor inside. The Afghan women had few legitimate chances to escape the drudgery of their wretched existence. They lined up at the doctor's every day to gossip quietly before going back to their tents with another handful of tranquilizers. I cut right, kept my eyes discreetly to the ground and found the tent I was looking for.

Luck was with me. Ekram Shinwari was at home.

He was a smiling devil, short, pudgy, with a firm handshake and an enviable reputation. He was a Shinwari Pathan and a member of the Jamiat Islami mujahadeen group. More importantly, he knew every goat

The Death of Beau Fontaine

track from Kohat to Chitral. His exploits behind the wheel were legendary. He made his living running the Soviet blockade between Pakistan and Afghanistan in small four-wheel-drive Toyota pickups. Ekram ran clandestine loads of gas and ammunition into Afghanistan for the resistance fighters, then brought refugees and wounded out on the return trip. It was an enterprise not without some small risk.

Hundreds of drivers had been killed in Soviet-planned ambushes. The Russians weren't kidding when they wrote warnings on the rocks that said, "If we catch you we will strip off your skin." In the years since we first met, Ekram had lost three vehicles. Which was not surprising when one considered he was often chased by helicopters during the day and by tanks at night. He was a blockade-runner in the traditional sense. Nothing could stop him, until he recently caught a slug in his right arm.

The Shinwari came right to the point.

"Let me guess, you're in trouble?"

"Everybody in Pakistan's in trouble," I cautioned him.

He only grinned then quoted me a price.

I had come to him because of his ability to get my friends and me into Bajaur undetected. The idea of meeting the members of the various police checkpoints between Peshawar and Maqbool's fort held no interest to me. Ekram may have been the expensive alternative, but I had long ago learned that economy in travel is the most costly economy of all. As soon as we agreed upon the money, he assured me he would drive me to Hell's front door if that's where I wanted to go.

It took but a few seconds for Ekram to pack. He tossed a light *patou* (blanket) over his left shoulder and announced he was ready. His stubby little legs had trouble matching my longer stride as we made our way across dusty Nasir Bagh camp. Despite my various visits there it was Ekram who knew where to find Chopendoz. On the outskirts of the refugee encampment the little driver took me into a ramshackle chaikhana. The place was as slovenly as the owner. A few rickety tables hosted some creaking wooden chairs. The place was too poor to boast even a single overhead fan. The big man sitting in the back looked like the most solid object in the dump.

Ekram and I sat down opposite Chopendoz. His face displayed no trace of emotion at my arrival. That came as no surprise. He wasn't known for being polite, just for killing people. His name wasn't really Chopendoz but that didn't matter either. Before the Jihad he had played *buz khazi* in the north of Afghanistan. Like the majority of *"chopendoz"* (riders) who participated in that berserk game, the hawk-faced man sitting across from me had huge hands. I had seen him lean out of his saddle in the middle of a *buz khazi* game, sweep up a 90-pound dead calf from beneath the stomping feet of his opponent's raging horses, then dash away. His was a dark tale long known to me. Outside the saddle, his special talent was that he spoke Russian. Chopendoz was fond of luring naive young Soviet soldiers into dark corners with promises of cheap hashish, then cutting their throats.

He owed me.

Khyber Knights

I explained the situation with Maqbool Khan as Chopendoz swigged his tea. He didn't care if it was Bajauri brigands or Saudi smugglers. He preferred killing pagan Russians but a Mohmand kidnapper would do if it evened our score. It may have been stupid but I felt I needed to warn him of the dangers.

"You may have to risk your life," I said.

He snorted with contempt, drained his tea cup, then stood up ready to leave.

"What does my life matter? I don't have anything else to do. I'll kill this overlooked dog of God for you," he told me with great finality.

Within the hour I was sitting in the front seat of Ekram's four-wheel-drive Toyota Hi-lux pickup. Originally dark blue, it had been scraped down both sides to bare metal. Cracks ran through the windshield, and the passenger side door was tied shut with a piece of rope. It was the string of bullet holes along the driver's side that concerned me. Despite the host of stickers pleading in Arabic for Allah to protect the vehicle, its driver, and passengers, I felt less than content. Chopendoz sat in the bed of the truck. An AK-47 lay next to him wrapped in his *patou*. His infamous killing knife rested in its hiding place under his long shirt.

The journey back to Peshawar was only a matter of negotiating the traffic on the Grand Trunk road, but by the time I reached Hasht Nagari it was already mid-morning. Ekram parked the truck around the corner from the Kabuli teahouse. The sight of two Afghans having a cup of tea in that well-known establishment would raise no eyebrows. Further back on Gari Syeddan street where Ali Muhammad lived, the lane was not only too narrow to accommodate the truck, the presence of two Afghans would immediately arouse suspicion. I bid them wait, and went in search of Raja and Ali Muhammad.

When I went back into that familiar house my news brought mixed results. Raja looked relieved to have the help. Ali Muhammad appeared non-committal. We three friends wasted no further time in discussion.

Raja, once beardless, had now traveled a long way down the highway of manhood. He looked like a grown man, not the hungry boy I had met in prison. His rough shalwar kameez suited him. Already sinewy, he had waxed stronger during the horse trip. His hands were rough, his eyes stern. He had turned into a man to be reckoned with. In my absence he had cleaned, oiled and loaded our weapons. The sawed-off shotgun and carbine were little enough but better than nothing. Raja tossed me my pistol. I slipped the well-oiled brute into its holster, then buckled it and my sword around my waist.

Ali Muhammad was completely silent, unless you counted the sound of him slapping a clip-full of ammunition into the bottom of his big pistol. He said nothing to me, just jacked a round into the deadly mechanical cobra he held in his hand. The look on his face told me everything I needed to know.

That was the morning Ali Muhammad forbade weakness to enter his heart in case it might enfeeble and westernize him again. Watching him load that gun I knew he would never again be Beau Fontaine. He had let

Khyber Knights

"Chopendoz's special talent was that he spoke Russian. He was fond of luring naïve young Soviet soldiers into dark corners with promises of cheap hashish, then slitting their throats."

The Death of Beau Fontaine

go of his conflicted past, putting behind him the sentimental deceptions he had carried like invisible icons for so long. Shaheen had shown him the true light of understanding. Everything he had once believed in had been burned away by his brutal and beautiful teacher. She had taught him it wasn't what you wore, but what you believed that made you a Pathan. To be a man of the Frontier was to think and react like one. So as he slid the pistol into its holster, I could see that he had learned the lessons she had taught him, the lesson from the Pukhtunwali code of honor that said faithlessness deserved death.

Ali Muhammad had graduated. He had turned his back forever on New Orleans, discarding his native country with its customs and costumes. He now knew what he believed. At last he understood Shaheen and the land that bore her, and in exchange for that knowledge he stood ready to rescue her if she loved him, or kill her if she betrayed him.

Raja and I waited silently, ready to help him teach his kidnappers manners with gun and blade, determined to assist Ali Muhammad solve the bloody riddle set by that shrewd contriver Maqbool Khan.

"*Zai chay zoo*, (lets go)," the former American said.

Without a word, we picked up our *patous* and followed him into the street.

Khyber Knights

50
Maqbool's Revenge

We three were only a tiny *lashkar* (tribal raiding party) but that did not matter. Each of us knew that on the Frontier bad blood did not sleep. I gave us little chance of either escape or survival, yet better the crow than the carrion. When Ali Muhammad locked the door to his house on Gari Syeddon street, we turned our backs and made our way down the twisting lane, walking towards the heart of Hasht Nagari with no visible sense of regret. All around me the city I had come to know and love went about her daily routine, for sweet Peshawar was unaware of my fool's errand. Only the reassuring slap of my sword's cheek against my thigh brought me any comfort. The old blade whispered that no matter the cost at least Maqbool Khan, that vile apostle of *Shaitan* (Satan), would suffer and die.

Ekram saw us coming. He and Chopendoz had taken up positions at one of the four wooden tables outside the chikhana. From there they could easily watch the truck, the police station across the street, and pedestrians passing in all directions. I saw him throw a few rupees on the table top before drifting towards his Toyota. Neither he nor Chopendoz acted in haste. Even at the Kabuli restaurant, a well known rendezvous for mujahadeen, it did not pay to draw attention to yourself.

By the time we reached the vehicle Chopendoz had climbed in the truck bed. The big man deposited his burly body securely up against the back of the cab, making sure it seemed to be able to grab a hold of the truck bed in both directions. I gave his choice of seating little thought. It was going to be just as cramped in one direction as the other I reasoned.

The Toyota was a visual nightmare no matter where you sat. Where it wasn't rusted, scraped, dented, rolled, kicked, or punched, it was violated by bullet holes. Ali Muhammad climbed up front by agreement in order, we thought, to be able to direct Ekram to where we were going. He placed the rifle and shotgun, wrapped in his blanket, on the floorboard underneath his feet. Raja and I climbed into the truck bed, crossed our legs and faced each other. Because we had chosen the short side of the truck we were unable to stretch our legs out in any one direction. Our choice of seats, and the idea of Ali being in charge of the directions, was a reflection of how naive the three of us were.

The chunky driver started the truck and drove quietly out of Hasht Nagari. At the end of our neighborhood he brought the truck to a halt in front of that river of traffic known as the Grand Trunk Road. Two great streams of movement confronted us. Every kind of vehicle known to God and Pakistan was traveling as fast as possible in both directions down that wide ribbon of blacktop. Lumbering water buffalo pulled carts and demanded space alongside speeding Bedford trucks. Bicyclists darted in and out like locusts. There was of course no stop light, and we needed to get clear across to the far side to be pointing in the direction of Bajaur.

Maybe Ekram had driven Chopendoz on some other occasion. Perhaps the Afghan killer just knew the nature of the beast behind the wheel. Regardless, for that brief second we were at a standstill I saw our fellow passenger put his hands together, palms upward in supplication, and offer a silent *dua* (prayer) to Allah.

If I had known what was coming I would have prayed out loud, then crawled out the back.

Before the words were off Chopendoz's bearded lips the blue wreck shot out into the busy road. Ekram launched, not drove, the Toyota straight across the bow of the oncoming traffic. I felt him punch the accelerator and start shifting gears. As my body lurched eastward I saw a blur of outraged faces pointed my way. Big Bedford trucks swerved. Huge Flying Coach passenger buses came blaring directly at us. A tonga horse reared, and oncoming cars screamed their horns in protest. My eyes had barely witnessed this metal horror show before Ekram swerved the truck sharply to the left, going now in the opposite direction. Immediately the sounds of people about to crash into us was now directly behind me. The look on Raja's face convinced me not to turn around.

I suddenly understood why the Russians had never caught the mad Shinwari driver.

Once we were safely on the road I settled back to enjoy the ride. True, we were cramped and the bottom of the truck bed was ridged, thereby making it even more uncomfortable. I gave it little thought, having no comprehension nor apprehension about the conditions that lay ahead.

It was loud in the back of the Toyota and the wind whistled around my turban. I had ridden on top of too many funky buses not to have expected that common complaint. Before leaving Hasht Nagari, Raja and I had both wrapped our headgear extra tight. Even with a strong buffeting from the wind a well-wrapped turban could be taken off and on intact for a couple of days if handled with care. The alternative was to have to flip laboriously the thirty-foot long length of silk around your head repeatedly. It was an involved process, not like tossing on a cowboy hat, though the resultant headgear said just as much about a man's personality.

At first we headed northwest across the Vale of Peshawar. The fields and villages were well known to both Raja and me, so we were content to sit quietly in the truck, watching the country roll by and hoarding our memories. We had left Charsadda behind before my companion ventured into conversation. I saw him studying Ali Muhammad through the rear window.

I too could see the expatriate's face. A fire still flickered over the ashes of Ali's icy fury. One look and I knew there was no turning back for him or us. Even in the rear of that windswept truck it was plain to me that the misfortune of Ali Muhammad's nature was that he worshipped love above all else. Without this ruling passion his life was a dreary void. No

Maqbool's Revenge

other earthly blessing could compensate its loss. He sought its elixir like the air he breathed. Having now cast the dice, he was betting his life without regret, hoping that Shaheen would return such an alien devotion.

Raja must have seen me studying our friend and guessed my doubts.

"My father told me a man can get a glimpse of Paradise and thereby ease his heart from sorrow in only three ways, in the study of God's word, on the back of a beautiful horse and between the breasts of a beautiful woman," Raja said over the sound of the roaring Toyota.

Did this apply to Shaheen I wondered, a woman who had trodden on the naked hearts of so many men, including Ali Muhammad's? In ancient Greece such women were known as *hetaera*, beautiful courtesans who used their charms to gain wealth and social prestige. Was that who we were rushing to rescue? To such ruthless women sex was a tool and love a trade. The heat of such a deed deprived a man of his reason and the amorous act was reduced to trivial insignificance. What could have been a uniting of two hearts became a mere mercenary coupling. Such a woman wasn't a lover, she was a warm corpse.

Those thoughts blew away on the wind when Ekram left the main road, turning off into a dirt track that ran through a sugar cane field. Immediately Raja and I were whipped by the green leaves towering above us. Seeing Chopendoz sheltered behind the cab I began to understand why he had chosen his position. Like Raja, all I could do was lean in away from the offending leaves. I thought this was a temporary inconvenience. I was very wrong.

We no longer traveled in a straight line. We twisted and turned, traveling two miles for every hundred yards in the right direction. Ekram kept off the paved roads controlled by the government, thereby avoiding police checkpoints. What had started out as a rescue turned into a endless, dreary weariness of unnamed and unremembered tracks that would have baffled a donkey. As the day wore on the farmlands fell behind us. Now we found ourselves drowned in dust. Even Chopendoz pulled the end of his old turban across his face, his slanted Turkoman eyes staring like two cruel almonds back towards Peshawar.

For a long while the summer sun beat down on us unmercifully and I believed that things could not get much worse.

Then the Toyota began snaking its way up a serpentine track that wound up into the beginnings of the mountains. With gears grinding Ekram drove over a rock-strewn course with such force we three passengers hung on for dear life. Despite our grip on the side of the truck, we floundered and knocked into each other as the little truck rose and fell with such violent motion it threatened to hurl us over the sides. We could do nothing but hang on in helpless despair. Our only comfort came when we shifted our weight slightly, thereby letting the rigid truck bed bruise us in a new location. By early afternoon we had managed to avoid the military checkpoints Ali Muhammad had seen at the town of Shabqadar. However the cost of this success was the feeling that Ekram had dislocated several of my bones in the effort.

Khyber Knights

We were well into Bajaur before the blockade-runner turned the truck back onto what could be even loosely defined as a road. Sitting there in the back of that bouncing Japanese steel box my legs had become stiff and my temper frayed. Yet the Shinwari driver had successfully penetrated tribal territory, that secret and jealously-guarded land where men recognized no law other than their own illegal desires. All around us lay a country that was increasingly stark and mournful.

"The only reason more people don't come to see beautiful Bajaur is because the road is so bad," Raja shouted at me, smiling in jest.

Chopendoz gave him a hard look.

"This is the custom on such journeys, little one. Be quiet and submit. It will only get worse," the older man told the younger tribesman.

Despite our fellow passenger's gloomy assessment we began to see alarming signs he was right. I was beginning to think we would never find a spot level enough to stop for a break. Suddenly we saw the first signs revealing the terrible price the Mohmands had paid for their false pride. For centuries this tribe of Pathans had swept down from their rocky fortresses like wolf packs to rob the villages in the Vale of Peshawar. In their arrogance they had thought they could continue their age-old offensive habits, defying even the iron fist of General Zia. As we passed through the first war-torn village we learned how wrong they had been. The federal forces had rolled over the Mohmand rebels. They had used tanks to knock down shops, destroy homes, and blow apart mud-walled forts. It was the terrible reality of 20th century warfare being played out against medieval warriors. Refugees passed us on the dirt road, making their way towards Peshawar, and the safety of the civilized cousins they normally despised. As the Toyota took us closer towards Maqbool Khan we encountered only ruins and destruction.

If the sun had been out I would have judged it to be late afternoon, but that shining orb had taken refuge behind the clouds that threatened us earlier. I saw Ali pointing up ahead and Ekram nodding in agreement. The little Shinwari never slowed down, only yelled back that there was no way around the outlaw village of Gandao. Apparently he and Ali Muhammad believed Zia's wrath had not reached so deep into Bajaur. None of us in the back of the truck had the strength to argue. I was so dusty, grimy, bruised, and hungry that I welcomed a gunfight more than another shared mile with that little mechanical sadist Ekram Shinwari.

They had forgotten to roll out the red carpet for us in Gandao.

We hit the outskirts of the little town within the hour. Even if I was expecting nothing better than sheep fat and gritty water I would have been disappointed. The bazaar was destroyed, bulldozed to the ground. Only the government school and the mosque were still standing. Otherwise all trace of the Mohmand Robber's Roost was gone.

For once Ekram slowed the truck. The sight of such brutal devastation was commonplace in his native Afghanistan, but this was supposedly civilized Pakistan. The hardship of living in the wretched place before it was destroyed could only have been imagined. Now there was nothing left except the ruins of miserable huts. On all sides was a waste of stone and dust that couldn't help but reflect the hard hearts of the Mohmand men who had once called that place home. General Zia had left them nothing soft or kind enough to grow a single seed.

We drove down the silent street. On both sides of us were heaps of rubble. The only clue to what happened were the hundreds of empty machine-gun cartridges littering the ground. Raja didn't say a word, too surprised like me at the savagery to comment. Chopendoz appeared bored. I was still trying to take it all in when Ekram turned the corner and drove us straight into an army checkpoint.

The first clue I had that something was wrong was when the blockade runner jammed on the brakes, throwing Raja and me onto Chopendoz. Being an optimistic but hungry idiot I thought Ekram had found a restaurant. When I managed to sit up and look ahead I learned the only meal being offered was lead. Three soldiers stood pointing G-3 machine guns at Ekram's chest. The Shinwari driver didn't argue when one of them shouted at him to shut off the truck. The moment the engine stopped I was aware of the deep silence lying over the destroyed town. It was so palpable the soldiers must have heard us coming for miles.

I was wondering why they hadn't bothered to open fire when I saw Chopendoz slide his hand under his patou. I could see his big fingers locking on the AK-47 at the same time one of the soldiers broke away and approached Ali Muhammad's side of the truck. I tried to catch Chopendoz's attention, but he was too busy looking over his right shoulder at the oncoming soldier.

The military man was in his early thirties and despite the harsh terrain looked starched and professional. Three large red sergeant stripes were pinned to his left sleeve. A thin David Niven style mustache graced his lip. He lowered his rifle and took a hard look at Ali Muhammad.

"*Assalaam alaikum*," he said, making no point in hiding his obvious suspicion.

My friend gave a curt nod and replied with the traditional "*Walaikum assalaam*."

"I've seen you," the soldier said and studied Ali's face intently.

At that point I saw Chopendoz carefully reach over and place his other hand on the thin blanket, obviously preparing to yank it off in a hurry.

"I don't think so," Ali Muhammad told the soldier.

"Maybe not in Bajaur," the sergeant said thoughtfully.

Then the image he was searching for came to him.

"Now I remember. It was in Peshawar. I saw you about a year ago in Sherbaz Music Studio. You're a friend of Master Ali Haider aren't you?" the sergeant asked, his voice and Chopendoz's hand both relaxing.

"Yes the Master and I are old friends. He often plays music at my house."

"You were recording Farzana when I visited the studio. Do you know her?" he asked with anxious expectation.

Farzana was the reigning diva of Peshawari Pushtu music, and one of the many local musical stars Ali Muhammad knew. By American standards the Nightingale of the Frontier was no beauty. Yet every man from Quetta to Passu nearly swooned when they heard her entrancing voice. As soon as this information was confirmed the sergeant turned and repeated it to his soldiers, who immediately lowered their rifles. They looked relieved they didn't have to kill us. I mutely seconded the motion.

With the tension broken the sergeant leaned onto the side of the truck and began to gossip about recent events. After the expiration of the federal deadline the governor ordered the entire district isolated. In an effort to surprise the rebellious Pathan tribesmen, the troops deployed at Shabqadar launched their attack at midnight.

Though taken by surprise, the Mohmands fought back fiercely. By sunrise Bajaur was a battle zone.

"The Mohmands counter-attacked. It was a very beautiful fight with much firing," the sergeant said and looked to his fellow soldiers for confirmation, their agreeable nods ratifying that fact. "They shot two of my men when we tried to take Gandao."

Despite his heavy weapons, the Pakistani commander called in air strikes and deployed his tanks against the armed insurgents. Beside leveling Gandao, more than fifty forts were destroyed in the immediate area. A powerful explosion occurred when one fort was hit and a hidden arms depot exploded, killing eleven civilian defenders and wounding dozens of soldiers. A rain of rockets stored in the fort showered the adjoining vicinity. Most of the fighting was over by ten that morning, just as we were unknowingly preparing to leave Peshawar. The government had arrested a score of outlaws and rounded up truck-loads of weapons, including mortars, rocket-launchers, and cases of land mines and hand grenades.

In response to a question from Ali Muhammad, the sergeant informed him that no one had found any sign of the kidnapped boy from Peshawar.

"This caused a great resentment with our commander, who says the guilty rebels will rot in prison for ten years. He ordered all the homes and shops in Bajaur destroyed in order to punish the enemies of the government."

To this day I'm still not sure if it was luck, or Farzana the nightingale, that made them let us go?

The sergeant glanced in the bed of the truck to make sure we weren't carrying any heavy weapons, then waved us through. Ekram didn't linger. Suddenly a sense of increasing unease had descended upon us. Instead of dreading our arrival at Maqbool's fort, I was suddenly anxious to reach there. The same anxieties had obviously crossed Ali Muhammad's mind. The Toyota had barely left Gandao in the distance before we saw our friend urging Ekram to even greater speed.

We barreled across an increasingly dead landscape. The only relief came from the occasional rain drops that began to spit down on us. When I looked up I saw no trace of golden forgiveness in that darkening sky.

Maqbool's Revenge

I never want to remember the journey over the Nahakki Pass. Ali Muhammad was urging Ekram to hurry, though the portly Shinwari already had the Toyota screaming for mercy. Nothing in my life, and no previous journey in Pakistan, could have prepared me for that ride from hell. The little truck spun around the corners of the narrow track, climbing, grabbing, dragging our battered bodies up the last mountainous barrier standing between us and Shaheen.

We were close to the top of the pass when our driver took a turn too fast. The rear tires spun out over the cliff. The tail end started to fishtail. Ekram slammed on the brakes but we slid towards the doom that awaited us. I saw Raja's side of the truck tilt up in the air at a 45 degree angle and understood we were about to flip off the road. At that instant Chopendoz and I both threw out bodies up against Raja's side of the truck. Our combined weight was enough to throw the airborne tires back onto the ground. Ekram punched the accelerator. The tires grabbed. The truck righted itself and we pressed on as though nothing had happened.

I needed no further evidence to convince me of Ekram Shinwari's cheerful disregard for our lives. Chopendoz looked pale. Raja had been too scared to scream. Ali Muhammad never even bothered to look back to see if we were still alive. His eyes were glued to the distance and the valley that lay exposed before us.

The sun was sinking when I first saw that wild place never belittled by fences. Ekram held the truck flat out as we sped across the valley towards our confrontation with Maqbool Khan. Even though the landscape was a blur it looked devoid of life. The empty white dirt road threw clouds of dust up behind us. Otherwise there was no movement. Her legendary isolation pierced at last, Bajaur's heart had grown sullen in defeat.

If Raja and I had been hoping to sneak up on Maqbool Khan we were fated to be disappointed. Ekram brought the truck to a screeching halt where the fort should have been.

There was only a smoldering ruin.

Tank tracks were everywhere.

The twin gates lay crushed and twisted like discarded toys.

Ali Muhammad threw open the truck door and ran towards the collapsed mud walls that had so recently held him captive. Ekram shut off the truck, as my fellow passengers and I climbed down stiff and sore.

"Shaheen! Shaheen! Where are you?" Ali Muhammad screamed.

There was no sign of life anywhere. The only remnant of the woman's presence was a sense of loneliness that had no equal. Chopendoz grabbed his rifle out of the back. Raja and I armed ourselves with the shotgun and rifle, but there was no need. In all directions there was nothing but further destruction and an added sense of desolation.

We four men gathered at what had been the front gate of the fort and watched Ali's frantic search through the rubble. Raja looked in all directions and just shook his head.

"This was the place that Allah created at the end of time," he said in a voice just above a whisper.

Khyber Knights

"A dog wouldn't stop to piss on the dump," Chopendoz threw in, then walked in to investigate what had once been the fort.

I watched as Ali Muhammad made another hopeless sweep of the ruins. Chopendoz kicked around the edge of the living quarters looking for plunder, but soon returned, convinced there wasn't anything fit to steal.

"We're even," he grunted to me, then strode away and took up a position as sentry, too old a warrior to let his guard down even then.

Raja, Ekram and I watched as Ali kept calling Shaheen's name to no avail. A look of sadness crossed the little drivers face.

"*Kala kala dasay keygee*, (sometimes these things happen)," Ekram said, then walked back towards his truck, content to go back, or go forward, as the situation demanded.

I made no effort to enter the ruins that had served as a paradise for Pathan plotters. Standing at a distance I could sense that the place was still haunted by the ill deeds done there, for one of the consequences of evil is that it loves to nest where it occurred. These cheerful thoughts were running through my head when I heard a commotion behind me. Turning quickly I saw Chopendoz charge into a small patch of corn the tank had neglected to trample. Within seconds we saw the big mujahadeen struggling with someone. Then there was a loud rustle as he threw an old man from his hiding place in the corn out onto the dirt road.

"*Chacha* (uncle)," Ali Muhammad yelled, and went running towards the elderly beggar before the Afghan assassin could shoot him.

Raja and I reached the old man seconds after Ali did. My friend had already knelt down in the dirt and helped the old man to rise up on one elbow. At first my friend's attempts to help were shaken off, as the frightened old fellow clearly expected to be injured or slain. He avoided looking at his captors, only squirmed and then managed to sit up.

"I didn't do anything. I didn't do anything," he kept repeating.

"*Chacha*," Ali Muhammad shouted and shook the old man until he looked up into his eyes.

The sight of the familiar face brought a smile to the elderly beggar.

"Oh," he said in recognition. "It's you. Why have you come back?"

None of us needed to be told the old man had lost what little bit of sanity he once possessed.

"Look," the beggar whispered, and reaching into the pocket of his dirt-encrusted shirt he withdrew the five rupee note my friend had given to him. He held it up towards Ali Muhammad.

"Do you want it back? Is that why you returned?"

"No, *chacha*," Ali Muhammad told him and helped him rise to his feet.

Raja and I rushed to assist, but the old man shrank back against Ali Muhammad in search of protection and support. Chopendoz had also moved closer as if to help but the sight of the bearded, armed man clearly frightened the oldster.

"Put down that gun," Ali Muhammad screamed at Chopendoz.

It was the look of borderline insanity, not the pistol on Ali's hip, that convinced the bigger man to comply. He grunted in disgust and walked over to wait with Ekram by the truck. As soon as Chopendoz walked away Ali Muhammad turned his attentions back to the local resident.

"*Chacha* where is Maqbool Khan?" he asked gently, while holding the old man's shoulders.

"All gone. All gone. They got word the soldiers were coming. Then all the people left. You could walk through the valley at noon and not see another person, or you could knock at one door, and then at another door, and find no one to answer you."

"Where did they go, *chacha*? Where did Maqbool go?"

"All the people were traveling south to Peshawar from the terror that was on them. There was fear and dread on every person I saw."

"Did Maqbool Khan go to Peshawar?" Ali Muhammad asked hopefully.

The old man stared up at my friend, a look of wonder on his white bearded, dirty face.

"No, no, the *malik* (tribal leader) fled across the mountains to Afghanistan. Maqbool is very brave but even he could not face the tanks," he said and pointed towards the grim mountains looming over our heads to emphasize the destination.

The news that the kidnapper had fled caused Ali Muhammad to let go of the old man. He stood there staring at the ground, momentarily speechless. The beggar looked at me, confident now that Raja and I meant him no harm. His rheumy old eyes were yellow with malaria. When he spoke I could see he was nearly toothless.

"Allah's favors are showered on the just and the unjust," he told me and a chill ran down my back, for the old man's voice had changed, indeed it had deepened, but his face looked altogether blank. Maqbool, who once elated in his arrogance, was gone but his sins stood unforgiven. Then just as suddenly the old man seemed to walk back into his decrepit body. He noticed Ali Muhammad standing there.

"Do you want the money back friend?" he said and offered the five rupee note back to Ali. "When the soldiers came I hid away. I wouldn't give it to them, but you can have it if you need it."

Ali Muhammad chose that instant to look up. He seemed not to have heard his benefactor and did not take the proffered crinkled bank note.

"And the woman, did Maqbool Khan take the woman?" he asked merely to confirm his worst fears.

The old man answered without hesitation.

"Oh no. The woman died. I buried her," he said and pointing at the small tree where the charpoys had sat, we all noticed for the first time a patch of freshly turned earth.

That man once known as Beau Fontaine blanched. I rushed to his side and grabbed him, thinking he would fall from the shock of the news. As I held him up I saw that even though his face was disfigured by grief, the relief of tears was denied him. I held him erect as some essential element of his soul collapsed inside his body. I said nothing, just held him at arm's length until he could regain his composure.

They were all gone I thought.

A wind came charging across the ravaged valley, scattering Shaheen's memory like the dust rising off the rubble of the fort. The light was failing and suddenly it felt like we were standing in a graveyard at dusk.

Raja came and put his hand on Ali's shoulder.

"Come, let us go home. There is nothing you can do here," he told Ali Muhammad softly.

I let my hands drop off Ali's shoulders. A blank look of shock rested on his face and he shivered in the wind that blew ever stronger. What little sun was left to us was almost gone. The mountains rearing over our heads seemed intent on hiding the last of that light, as well as Maqbool Khan.

"Give thanks for the memory of the love you bore her. You should be glad she died before she dwindled and lost her beauty. Now come," Raja urged him again, "Allah does not want us to waste time on fruitless regret. Let us go back to Peshawar and speak of other things."

I stood there, naught but a witness, with no words of easy wisdom running off my tongue. Maybe Raja was right? Perhaps Shaheen was better off dead? I didn't pretend to know. I knew more about horses than love, knew that mighty chargers preferred to fall in combat rather than pass away forgotten by their riders, dreading to die by slow degrees of uselessness in lush but lethal pastures. I kept such limited wisdom to myself, watching Ali Muhammad bow his head under the weight of a sadness without limit. For a brief time Allah had given him a joy so strong he believed his love for Shaheen would have reached the North Star. Now he stood torn and bleeding inside, his heart's desire overridden by the curse of his late arrival.

At last he started to move away from us, taking a small step towards the truck and recovery. Then he turned and looked one last time at the elderly bearer of such terrible news.

"How did she die?" he asked.

The rain picked that moment to reappear, dropping in scattered drops before the old man could answer. The sky seemed to be growing as bleak as Ali Muhammad's despair.

"How did she die?" Ali repeated.

"She refused to go with her husband and when the tanks came the walls collapsed on her," the old man said, delivering the news that was to change our lives forever.

Suddenly the truth soaked in like the wind-swept rain. The elderly beggar was speaking of the old woman, Maqbool's wife, not Shaheen. Ali Muhammad rushed back and grabbed the pauper by his arms, shouting over the sound of the elements, "The young woman, was she still alive?"

The old man shrank in fear, turning his head slightly and trying to pull free. Ali Muhammad began shaking him.

Maqbool's Revenge

"Where is the girl?" he screamed.

"Maqbool took her when he fled with his sons."

At the news Ali Muhammad released the messenger.

"All the people have gone away, gone away," the old fellow said softly and sensing his release, he turned and began walking away from us on a road that lead nowhere.

A strange tranquillity came over Ali Muhammad's face. He turned and faced the mountains behind us. I could sense his soul struggling with the news. For a second he seemed to be unaware of all perception, blind to the sky, unaware of the lashing rain, a lost and weary bird wondering if it had the strength to fly over those sullen mountains. The wind moaned and blew the rain into our faces. The earth itself seemed disturbed by the revelation of Shaheen's continued existence. When the first low rumble of thunder rolled across the sky I saw Raja look anxiously at the truck.

Ekram and Chopendoz had taken shelter in the front of the Toyota. Suddenly even a scrap of food, a sliver of soap, and a dirty towel seemed like heaven. My meager desires were never expressed. The longing for Shaheen had closed in on Ali Muhammad from all sides like a restricting garment.

"She burned too bright for this world," Ali said, his voice sounding detached and distant. Then his face was once again consumed with anger as he said, "Don't cut the grave too narrow Maqbool, I'll be along shortly."

I had no way of knowing if the old man was lying about the prostitute being alive or not. All I knew was that the old codger was certifiably crazy and we were all getting drenched. I sympathized with my friend's strange circumstances, but there were limits to what a man could do. I didn't know if Allah had commuted Shaheen's sentence and allowed her to continue living. Ali Muhammad didn't know either, but when I looked at him I could sense the constriction of his heart and see the pain of his futile quest. His soul must have told him she was alive and still suffering the injustice of her fate.

Suddenly Ali Muhammad turned and faced Raja and me. Rain was dripping down the high cheekbones of his face, but his eyes looked bright and determined.

"I'm not going to let her journey to Hell alone and unaccompanied," he told us.

Who except Allah can say whether a man is right or foolish if he follows the call of his conscience? Only the Almighty could have seen through the rain and the curtain of time to solve that riddle for Ali Muhammad. Yet as if in answer the wind picked up and began to blow stronger, trying to scatter the ashes of his love and dispel the limited blessings of his devotion. What had been a gentle shower now threw aside all such polite pretense. Heavy night smells began to seep out of the deserted earth. Darkness lay all around us except ahead to the west. There a red light lingered beneath the storm clouds hanging over the sullen skies of Afghanistan.

Khyber Knights

Suddenly I felt a clutching desperation and a need to run away from the wretched ruined fort. I understood that for Ali Muhammad his love had become his daily bread. What if his heartache could not be confined to one season of his life? He loved the whore, not I. I thought to grab him, reason with him, use Raja's help to force him to leave with us.

One look at his rain-swept face and I knew there was no was no use talking to Ali Mohammad. All trace of reason and Beau Fontaine were gone. This new man stood there groping in his memory for the dream that was Shaheen's face. I watched him travel through bliss and then saw the approach of desolation and horror when he realized his vision was fleeing, leaving no trace, as it sought to find Shaheen on the other side of those forbidding mountains. In that instant I knew my friend was determined to follow Shaheen regardless of what it cost him. The realization brought with it immense distress as I stood there wondering how long he had left to experience the wonder and beauty of the world.

"I'm going after her," Ali Muhammad said again, giving voice to my prophetic intuition.

The wind howled before I could speak, baying like a hound from hell, trying to blow away my arguments as well as the patterns of time and eternity. I thought I heard the land groan beneath my feet. How futile seemed all human longing in a place as accursed as Bajaur. All passion, all love, were forfeit in that terrible bleakness. No man should ask another to bear his burden, yet I could feel the vicarious burden of guilt trying to shove itself down onto my shoulders.

"If we go in there we should carry our shrouds under our arms," Raja said over the sound of the rain.

I snapped my head in the direction of this fellow fool. I knew he was right. Anyone stupid enough to venture into Afghanistan in search of a woman could expect to find neither hope nor pity from Kabul to the sea. The country had become as guarded and unknowable as the grave. The old Buddhist manuscripts in the Peshawar museum did not lie when they called it "Ambulima," the "geography of demons." I had been through perils enough to slay nations, and yet how I dreaded the thought of re-entering that cauldron of madness and menace. Death was as frequent there as a hot day. Every man was a solider. Every child had a knife. Things happened behind those mountains which humanity hid away. Cruel things man was ashamed to name lay naked there without fear or regret.

In my heart I wondered if I still had the cold iron courage to venture back into that corner of Hell? Was it worth risking my life on the ghost of a chance of finding a woman I had never met? That seemed too thin an excuse.

The rain stood like smoke around us, drowning my meager hope of turning Ali Muhammad aside from his suicidal mission. I did not believe he could ever find Shaheen. Even if she lived, Maqbool Khan would have tortured or sold her off at the first opportunity. I was sorry that this journey's end had brought them no lover's meeting. But how can human understanding comprehend the will of Allah when such sad events are allowed to gladden Satan's heart. Some things were meant to stay a mystery I wanted to shout, for even God has his terrible whimsy.

Looking at the two men standing there before me I knew they were not going to turn back. Not even that black rain was going to extinguish the fire in Ali Muhammad's heart.

There is always something about the turning of a road in one's life.

Before us lay the mountains which marked the beginning of the true heart of Asia. I thought of the *buz khazi* horses I had not seen in years. Like Shaheen they lay past the faint trail winding up into those bleak and terrible mountains. Each soul bears but its own responsibility I told myself one last time, trying to deny the unifying factors that bound me to my two friends.

When they saw me looking up at the mountains, Raja and Ali Muhammad also turned and stared. As we stood there I was sure I felt the earth shift all three of us away from what we had known and been.

What we once were........

What we once rode.......

What we once loved.......... were all gone.

I stood there, a man in conflict with his destiny, knowing in my heart what I must say and do.

But that, as they say in Peshawar, is another story.

Khyber Knights

Epilogue

Epilogue

Military dictator General Mohammad Zia ul-Haq ruled Pakistan for eleven cruel years. The people of his country whispered that the powerful and victorious man sought to pacify Allah for Prime Minister Bhutto's death by zealously waging war against sinners. Though Zia had succeeded in every political enterprise, they said he was plagued by an incessant fear and lived in daily dread of the wrath of God.

On a hot August day in 1988 Zia and a plane-load of VIPs were scheduled to return to the nation's capital of Islamabad, after viewing a demonstration of a lone American made Abrams tank in the Pakistani desert. Aboard Pak One were the Chief Marshal Law Administrator, as well as ten of his trusted Pakistani generals, the current American ambassador, an American general heading the military aid mission, and various Pakistani staff officers.

Moments after take off from the military air base outside Bahawalpur, villagers reported seeing the C-130 Hercules aircraft lurching up and down in the sky. It then plummeted to the ground, where it exploded into a ball of fire. All thirty-one passengers were killed. The large bomb used to destroy the aircraft had apparently been smuggled aboard inside a crate of mangos, Zia's favorite fruit.

Though several eyewitnesses were later discovered murdered, a hasty investigation revealed the aircraft's crew had been incapacitated by a rare nerve gas. Zia was so widely hated, both at home and abroad, the wide list of possible assassins resembled "Murder on the Orient Express." However no official report was ever released by either the Pakistani or American governments, and the United States State Department blocked the FBI from pursuing an investigation.

In Pakistan there were no cries for vengeance. When it was reported that no trace of the once-powerful tyrant could be found, many Pakistanis whispered that Allah's divine intervention had wiped out all trace of the man who had exploited the name of Islam.

Benazir Bhutto, the daughter of the executed Prime Minister Zulfiqar Ali Bhutto, and herself once a prisoner of General Zia, was soon after elected to lead Pakistan, the first time in Islamic history a woman had been so honored. The end of the Cold War marked the end of Pakistan's political importance to the United States. Newly-elected President George Bush forgot his previous pledge of lifelong support to Pakistan. No longer considered a valuable pawn, the United States terminated its self-interested friendship, ending all financial and military support to its former ally.

Khyber Knights

The Soviet Union ended up fighting the Afghans longer than they did the Nazis in World War Two. At the conclusion of the Afghan Jihad at least 10,000 foreign Muslim fighters were left unemployed, including a wealthy Saudi Arabian expatriate named Osama bin Laden. The Pakistani Narcotic's Control Board was discovered to be so riddled with corruption the majority of its officers were fired. The influence of the heroin Mafia at that time supposedly reached into the Pakistani government at the federal level.

After General Zia's assassination and incineration, Pindi Prison was utterly destroyed by the new civilian government. Godwin Mujumba, my Tanzanian cell mate, was never seen or heard from again. His disappearance remains, to my eternal regret, a mystery to this day. This book serves as a memorial to Godwin and the unremembered souls who suffered and died inside those accursed walls.

Glossary

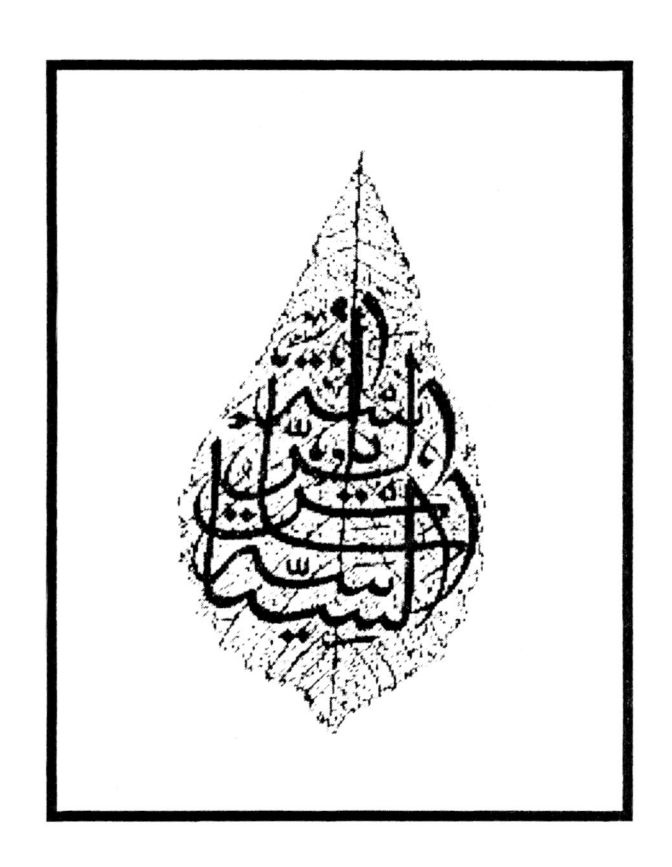

Glossary

Aid wallah - Wallah is an old British Raj term used to designate a common laborer. Its Arabic root means "boy."

AK-47 - The term AK-47 stands for A-automatic K-carbine designed in 1947. One of the most famous killing machines ever invented, the AK-47 was devised by a self-taught Russian engineer, Mikhail Kalishnakov in 1947. At the onset of World War Two the Soviet Union, like the majority of other European powers, was still relying on the outdated technology and expectations of World War One trench warfare. Russian soldiers initially carried heavy rifles with five-shot clips armed with high powered ammunition. These same rifles had once been effective at the long ranges required from soldiers firing at ease from inside protected trenches. This previous armament mythology was shattered by the rapid-firing Nazi blitzkreig. Having served as a tank commander in the early days of World War Two, the diminutive Kalishnakov knew from experience how deadly the machine guns used by Hitler's Wehrmacht could be. The Nazi tactics rewrote the armament history books, proving to generals and solders alike that warfare now demanded a fast-firing, lightweight, durable assault weapon. The AK-47 with its distinctive short stubby profile and 30-round clip was the Russian answer. A masterpiece of engineering simplicity, the AK-47 is able to withstand almost any abuse. Nearly indestructible, it shrugs off mud, water, sand and rust. It has become the most widely accepted gun in history. There are an estimated 50 million AK-47's in existence today. They can be found in almost any country and often cost as little as $50.00 to purchase. The AK-47, and its successor the AK-74, were critically important in the Afghan jihad. Initially the mujahadeen were only equipped with outdated, single-shot British Enfield rifles. The Soviet invaders made short work of anyone foolish enough to match the two weapons. It wasn't until the resistance started capturing their own AK-47's that the gap in firepower closed. In the later portion of the jihad as the Soviet small arms armament advantage started to evaporate, Mikhail Kalishnakov introduced the AK-74 into Afghan combat. It was designed to fire a bullet that caused extreme trauma to human tissue. Ruthlessly effective, most mujahadeen wounded by the AK-74 never survived their battlefield injuries. Though the AK-47 has been used in conflicts around the world, it proved to be the pivotal weapon, not just of the Afghan jihad, but of the 20th century.

Angrez - Common slang term for "English" or any other light skinned foreigners.

Assalaam alaikum - "Peace be upon you." Standard greeting used among Muslims.

Badal - Revenge. See pukhtunwali for details.

Bamboo Bar - In the summer of 1987 two West German hippies who were partying at the Bamboo Bar repeatedly tried to talk a young Swiss girl into taking heroin with them. After her refusal, they injected her in the buttocks while her back was turned. Her death from the resultant heroin overdose was used as an excuse to close down the infamous speakeasy.

Banchowd - An extremely vile epithet often used in Pakistan to designate a man who enjoys illicit sexual relations with his sister. The use of this sort of cursing, known as *kunzil*, is quite common on the Indian sub-continent. Muslims believe that the pronunciation of such language is a deprivation of Allah's grace and mercy, as well as a pollution on the tongue.

Bhang - Marijuana. Commonly found growing throughout the North West Frontier Province as an insignificant roadside weed, marijuana thickets sometime include plants in excess of eight feet tall. Unlike Americans, Pakistanis never smoke the leaves of this wild weed, preferring to turn the plant into the far more powerful hashish.

Buk shah - A homosexual slang term literally interpreted to mean, "assume the position of a goat." This degrading reference is used in the same context as its English brother, "bend over and get the soap."

Burkha - An all-encompassing silk garment designed to cover extremely modest Muslim women from prying male eyes. Designed basically like a sack, the burkha fits over the woman's head and reaches to her toes. The crown of the restrictive garment fits on the woman's head by use of a cap size section. The sleeves are designed to reach the fingertips. The wearer's only window to the outside world is through an embroidered screen which measures roughly two inches wide by six inches across. The overall effect can only be compared to that of small children dressed in bed sheets at Halloween. Despite the country's soaring temperatures, the garment is commonly used in Afghanistan. It is seldom seen in Pakistan, except for portions of the North West Frontier Province which have a large population of Pathans. Many Afghans believe the burkha is an ancient symbol of female chastity handed down from the pious founders of Islam. In fact sources point out that this claustrophobic article of clothing was first seen in Afghanistan in the mid-nineteenth century. Upon his arrival at the royal court in Kabul, the wives of the ambassador from Turkey were wearing the burkha. Fearing the reputation of the Afghans, the wily Turk bade his wives hide their beauty in a garment designed to thwart the salacious Kabulis. Considering the reputation for homosexuality among the 19th century Kabulis, the Turk's precautions were unnecessary and the adoption of the tent only a cruel twist of nature. Ironically, according to legend, the Turks themselves adopted the burkha from the Byzantium Christian emperors. The rulers of Constantinople used it in their harems. Not suspecting its origins, the Afghan men viewed the burkha as a grand idea, as well the height of

Glossary

sophisticated Turkish fashion. Today most Afghans believe the vaunted burkha is as old as Adam and as chaste as Eve, little suspecting they are in fact aping an early Christian habit.

Buz-khazi - Meaning "goat grab." Buz khazi dates back to Afghanistan's infancy and is an Afghan equestrian free-for-all that combines elements of rugby, tug-of-war and rodeo. The *chopendoz* (riders) who participate ride their horses like lunatics, fighting furiously over the decapitated body of the animal. The game is traditionally played on the plains of northern Afghanistan in the cool weather of early fall. On the day before the game starts, a goat or calf is first ritually slaughtered, beheaded, gutted filled with sand, sewn up and soaked overnight in cold water to increase its density and weight, which totals close to one hundred pounds. Its feet are also cut off, in order to make it more difficult to grasp. The following day, the carcass is laid inside a circle marked on the ground by a line of white chalk. The *chopendoz*, whose numbers are unlimited but never less than ten, immediately begin to fight each other for possession of the dead animal. They reach down from the saddle, keeping their left knee hooked around their saddle's high pommel, and all the while their stallions are trying to maim the other riders and horses. When some lucky fellow manages to secure the goat, he places it under his right leg for protection, then sets out hell-bent-for-leather towards a distant point designated as the goal. A vigorous chase ensues as the other *chopendoz* chase the rider holding the dead "football." The goal may be many miles away, depending on the strength of the horses and the abilities of the riders. During the ensuing chase *chopendoz* use any tactic short of murder to control possession of the dead animal. In the early 20th century the Amir of Afghanistan outlawed the use of knives due to multiple deaths. Otherwise few rules are observed from start to finish. Riders may use any type of cunning or sheer brute strength in order to deprive, steal or retain possession of the goat. They may not tie the carcass to their saddle, but a few brutal *chopendoz* have even conspired to drown their opponents. It is common for *chopendoz* to continue riding with broken limbs and various head-injuries. Even the stallions used in the game are taught to show no mercy to either man nor beast. The horses tear, bite and stomp their human and equine opponents at every opportunity. From the moment of their birth, these magnificent horses are never allowed to fall, for it is believed that this would "break their wings." For the first five years they are allowed complete freedom. Then they are trained for the game that will dominate their life. Once a *chopendoz* rounds the goal marker, the race is on to return the goat to the white circle, known as the *hallal* or circle of justice, where the game originated. Spectators are especially susceptible during this stage of the game as it is common practice to race the horses through the crowd in an effort to throw off one's pursuers. Being stomped into the mud on the sidelines is a definite possibility and adds to the excitement.

Cavan - That portion of northern Ireland traditionally associated with the ancient kingdom of the O'Reilly clan. Located north-west of present-day Dublin, this large tract of land was known as the kingdom of Breifne, before it was conquered by Oliver Cromwell and his Puritans in the late 17th century.

Chador - A long loose cloth worn by Pakistani women, much like a lightweight cloak. The chador is worn over the woman's head and then loosely draped around her body. It may also be lifted to cover the bottom of her face if she wishes to hide her features from men. The use is based on the Islamic injunction for women to cover their hair before praying. It is a symbolic act meant to show that though the world may judge her by her looks, Allah only considers her heart and actions.

Chai - Black tea brewed with milk and sugar. First introduced into the North West Frontier in the early 20th century, it was originally denounced by Afghans and Pathans as another subtle effort by the British to influence their respective cultures. It has long ceased to have any political implications and is now the oil on which roll the wheels of conversation from Herat to Lahore.

Chaikhana - A tea house, chai-khana. Traditionally they served as crude hostels for weary travelers and their animals throughout Persia, Afghanistan and Pakistan.

Chapplis – Open-toed sandals worn throughout Pakistan.

Charpoy - Four-legs, char-poy, the term used to describe a rustic native bed. It is a horizontal frame resting on four wooden legs. Instead of a mattress, coarse manila rope is criss-crossed back and forth to create a strong webbing which serves to support the sleeper. Used as a bed at night, it is common practice to drag the charpoy into use during the daytime as a crude sofa. Surprisingly comfortable, they tend to squeak in hot weather and often serve as host to legions of fleas.

Chowk - An open area formed at the junction of several streets. The term is loosely used and can apply to nothing more grand than the space between buildings, or a formal public area reserved for political meetings.

Chowkidar - Night watchman who patrols the street with a lantern and a lathi.

Dardistan - Land of the Dards. The term Dardistan was coined by an English professor who lumped all the different Muslim peoples in a vast mountainous area into one group, in an effort to ease efforts to categorize the local populace. This vast 40,000-mile area, in what is today northern Pakistan, lies sandwiched between Tibet and Afghanistan. Unlike the passive Buddhists of neighboring Ladakh, the fiercely independent Muslims who resided in these gigantic mountains resented any intrusions by snooping Europeans from either Czarist Russia or British-controlled India.

Farsi - The national language of Iran and parts of Afghanistan, its sweet, melodic sounds trace their roots back to ancient Persia. A

Glossary

common saying in Peshawar was that Arabic was the language of God, Farsi was the language of kings, and Pushtu was the language of Hell.

Ghazi - The English occupation army stationed in Peshawar misused this term to denote any murderous native madman intent on killing foreigners. However the Arabic term is properly only used to define a mujahideen who kills an enemy of Islam during a condoned war against non-believers, i.e. "*kafirs*." The slaying of such an enemy allows the bearer to be known as a ghazi.

Ghee - Clarified butter commonly used in the Indian subcontinent for every day cooking.

Ghurra-burra - A loud commotion, donny brook, or pandemonium.

G.T. Road - The common abbreviation used for the "Grand Trunk" road. Built by one of the Mughal emperors of India, the original road ran from the Khyber Pass to the city of Delhi. Now the main artery serving east-west traffic in Pakistan, it runs east from the Khyber Pass, past Peshawar, on through Rawalpindi, ending at Lahore. Now asphalted and in theory reserved for motor traffic, every traveler knows one is just as likely to run up behind a buffalo cart laden with bricks as an overcrowded bus full of weary locals. It is an anything-goes road with few rules, no speed limit and plenty of unmarked graves going in both directions.

Gup shup - Peshawari slang expression for gossip among friends.

Hajii - A Muslim man or woman who has made the *Haj*, a journey to Mecca, Saudi Arabia, the spiritual center of the Islamic world. All Muslims are enjoined to make this journey at least once during their life. Upon completion of this pilgrimage the term Hajii is affixed as an honorary prefix to the male traveler's name. Women are thereafter called *Hajjah*. The term carries with it great spiritual honor and immense social prestige in the Islamic world. No single religious rite has done more to unite the world's Muslims than this pilgrimage. Each year millions of pilgrims meet and worship together in complete equality, demonstrating the fraternalism of Islam.

Hasht Nagari - A blue-collar neighborhood in Peshawar, Pakistan. The name is said to refer to the fact that the city's *hasht*-eighth *nagari*-gate was located there. Other residents prefer to tell the traveler it means there were eight villages located outside this section of the city walls.

Hindko - A regional language spoken in the city of Peshawar by families who originally immigrated there generations ago from India proper. It has many linguistic roots in Hindi, the national language of India.

Hindu Kush - The mountain range that has traditionally served for centuries as both a geographical and cultural boundary between the Hindu and Afghan peoples. The words mean "killers of Hindus" and represents the brutal reality of the mountains and the world that lies hidden behind them.

Hookah - Water pipe. Unlike Turkish hookahs, Pakistani water pipes do not use tubes coming off the water pipe, relying instead on a long bamboo stem. These metal hookahs are most often topped with very large ceramic bowls which not only hold enough tobacco to satisfy several men, but are broad enough to leave coals resting on top if so desired.

Jihad - An Islamic concept often misunderstood in the western world, jihad is an Arabic word meaning "struggle" or "striving." It is seldom reported that there are two types of jihad, "striving within oneself" being the greater *jihad*, and "striving against political oppression" being the lesser. The inner *jihad* is personal and is carried out by word and deed. Political *jihad*, and its accompanying use of military force, may only be entered into if the Muslims being attacked have first resorted to all other methods, including the use of "pen and tongue," before entering a state of warfare. Thus Muslims are allowed to take up arms solely as a last resort. Even then the term *jihad* would not apply unless the Muslims were fighting *"kafirs,"* people who had no belief in God. The atheist Soviet Union's invasion of Muslim Afghanistan certainly qualified in this regard.

Juma - Friday afternoon congregational prayers.

Kabuli - A slang term used by the more sophisticated Pakistanis to describe Afghans, whom they considered uncouth hillbillies.

Kabuli Jon - A friend of Kabul. This was an ironic name for this particular Hasht Nagari restaurant because it was owned by a pleasant, overweight Peshawari who had never visited either Kabul or Afghanistan. Yet the wily restaurateur employed countless Afghans who cooked and served *pilau* and chai to the many mujahadeen who frequented this friendly establishment.

Kafir - Pagan. Unlike Jews and Christians, who are respected by Muslims as being fellow "peoples of the book," referring to the Old and New Testaments, *kafirs*-pagans are viewed with extreme intolerance by Muslims in Pakistan. The Kalash *kafirs* for example are under constant pressure to conform religiously by converting to Islam. The Kalash tribe's history and cultural heritage are seen by many Pakistanis as being indicative of licentiousness and moral decay.

Kafiristan - Land of the pagans.

Kaka Khail - A Pathan tribe located around the Swat valley.

Kameez - The shalwar and kameez combination of baggy trousers and long loose fitting shirt is worn by both men and women in Afghanistan and Pakistan. The styles for this shalwar/shirt differ depending on which portion of the Indian sub-continent one visits. The basic design is an extremely loose fitting shirt that is intentionally designed to allow air in to cool the wearer. It reaches to the knees and is never tucked in. Afghan men traditionally preferred not to have collars on their kameez, insisting instead on having the fronts of their shirts covered with intricate embroidery work that took female family members months to complete.

Glossary

After the Jihad started in 1979 this famous needlework disappeared entirely. Mujahadeen started wearing kameez with a military flair, sporting not only collars but epaulets and various pockets designed to hold pistols and magazines of ammunition. Unlike Afghans, who usually had a tailor prepare their clothes, most Pakistanis preferred buying matching shalwar and kameez ready made. The inhabitants of Pakistan could be seen sporting pastel colors, while Afghans preferred more traditional earth tones.

KHAD - *Khadamate Ettelaate Dowlati* - The dreaded and pervasive Afghan communist secret police, its system of informers and operatives extended into virtually every aspect of Afghan life. Generously funded by the KGB, KHAD's mission was multifaceted, including the gathering of intelligence and the suppression of anti-regime elements both inside Afghanistan and abroad. East German intelligence specialists trained the KHAD operatives, who ran eight detention and torture centers in Kabul alone. KHAD was responsible for recruiting pro-regime mullahs to spy on their worshippers, sending Afghan orphans to the Soviet Union for indoctrination, torturing thousands of political prisoners, and running press gangs that forced Afghan men to fight for the Russians. Its cadres were credited with multiple foreign assassinations and had even sent informers on a government-sponsored trip to the holy Muslim city of Mecca on the annual *Haj* pilgrimage.

Khuda hafez - The peace of God go with you.

Khutba - The sermon delivered to the Muslim congregation on Friday, as part of the congregational prayer.

Kohistan - Land of mountains. Stretching from the Chitral road on the west to the Indus river in the east, Kohistan is the least known, most dangerous portion of Pakistan. Comprising more than 3,000 square miles full of sky-scraping mountains and secret valleys, Kohistan lies in the middle of Pakistan like an unknown piece of the geographic puzzle. Most maps still show large white spaces designating their ignorance of this outlaw state. No outsiders, including other Pakistanis, are welcome. Its mountainous depths have never been violated by a westerner, even during the height of British military power in the 19th century Raj. Kohistan's highly armed citizens enjoy a well-deserved reputation for complete lawlessness. They loot civilian buses plying the nearby Karakorum Highway with great frequency, then flee back into a trackless wilderness that brags of no road wider than a cow track. Western tourists foolish enough to skirt police checkpoints and slip inside have been sodomized, robbed and killed. Having successfully resisted all attempts at integration into Pakistan, Kohistan sits in smug isolated contentment, relishing her nickname, Yaghistan the land of murder.

Lal bazaar - The *lal* (red light) bazaar was an important part of the Raj army of occupation. British military authorities considered their English

Khyber Knights

soldiers to be full of "beer, beef and lust" and believed it was dangerous to deny them sexual outlets. Due to the severe lack of suitable English female companionship available to the BORs, British Other Ranks, enlisted men were encouraged by their officers to make use of the abundantly-available native whore-houses. The military brothel in Agra, for example, was located less than a mile from the soldiers' barracks. It housed nearly forty prostitutes who ranged in age from twelve to thirty years old. This handful of women was considered adequate for the one thousand five hundred British troops garrisoned nearby. These army approved brothels, known as "rags," restricted native men from sharing women reserved for British soldiers. The sex was remarkably cheap. A sliding scale started at one rupee for a sergeant and went as low as four annas, (less than a nickel) for a private. If overworked, these women were by no means ugly. The Quartermaster General of the British army had studied the question of how to make native brothels appealing to English troops. He advised his garrison commanders to "take care that they (the prostitutes) are sufficiently attractive." British army medical personnel tried to register and maintain health records on the prostitutes with varied success. Venereal disease was often endemic among British soldiers stationed in India. During the year 1895, there were 536 venereal reports per thousand British troops in the subcontinent.

Lathi - A stout pole, made of bamboo or hardwood, the lathi is usually at least five feet long. The handle tapers to a wider end and is often weighted with metal. Wielded properly it can split a man's skull like a ripe melon. It is used by police as a stave to strike everyone from protesting university students to rioting prisoners.

Levy - A national guardsman recruited to patrol roads, protect travelers from bandits, and maintain law and order in otherwise uncivilized areas of the tribal areas of Pakistan.

Lota - Small metal jug kept next to the toilet. It contains the water used to wash oneself after defecation.

Malik - A tribal leader or man of prestige.

Marvasi - An elderly man who rapes, fondles or engages in homosexual behavior with young boys.

Melmastia - Pathan tradition of offering hospitality without obligation. This classic custom includes giving sanctuary even to enemies or criminals fleeing the law. The offer, once accepted, is inviolate. Pathans believe such hospitality invalidates blood feuds for twenty four hours.

Mujahid - Singular for mujahadeen.

Mujahideen - A collective term for Muslims who believe they will attain Paradise if they die in battle. Mujahideen fight in the name of God for a sacred cause.

Nan - A delicious unleavened bread. Only one of several types favored by Pakistanis.

Glossary

Naswar - A violently strong snuff, made from tobacco and quicklime, used in both Pakistan and Afghanistan. Its effect on the first-time user can only be described as like having a hot bomb go off in your mouth. Your mouth salivates copiously, causing you to spit continually, the resultant projectile being the same bright green color as the naswar. During the Jihad a English journalist wanted to blend in with his Afghan hosts. After dinner was over the naswar can was passed to him. He watched as his hosts placed a large pinch of the green snuff under their tongues. Not speaking the language, the Englishman placed the naswar in his mouth, not understanding it was a tobacco product and not an after-dinner aperitif. The immediate effect so startled him, he panicked. Not wanting to offend his hosts, the Englishman swallowed the naswar. He later told me that though he did not die, he certainly wanted to.

Nawab - King. One of the terms used to describe the rulers of several small principalities now lying in Pakistan. The fiefs of the Nawab of Dir and his fellow aristocratic rulers, such as the Wali of Swat, the Mir of Hunza and the Mehtar of Chitral, were all seized by the federal government of Pakistan. These lands became known as the "merged areas." While the other placid former rulers were allowed to retire quietly on government pensions, the former Nawab of Dir was viewed in Islamabad as a serious political threat. He was kidnapped from his palace by army commandos, exiled down country to the Punjab province, and never allowed to return to his homeland. His son, who died in a plane crash soon after his father's loss of power, was a political disappointment to the old man. The articulate grandson of the former Nawab, educated like his wife in the United States, has returned to Dir and is making every effort to modernize this once-barbaric corner of the old world.

Nazarene - An insulting term used by Muslims to denote Christians, it refers to Nazareth, the birthplace of Jesus Christ. This disparaging term was a playback of the Christian slur commonly used when they referred to Muslims as "Mohammadans." This term implied a personality cult worshipping the Prophet of Islam, PBUH, a teaching expressly forbidden by both the Prophet and the teachings of Islam. Muslims are taught by the Qu'ran to respect "the peoples of the book," referring to both Jews and Christians. The Prophet of Islam taught that Allah had revealed that both the Old and New Testaments were to be respected as predecessors of the perfect message later revealed in the Qu'ran. Jews and Christians were seen as people who refused to acknowledge the existence of God's new Prophet and the perfect message he taught. In addition Muslims believe and respect Jesus Christ as a prophet of Allah. Yet centuries of antagonism, coupled with European colonialism, had dangerously eroded the Prophet's message of religious tolerance and racial restraint. By the early 20th century many well-meaning mullahs confused political murder with religious aspirations.

NWFP - North West Frontier Province, one of the four provinces of Pakistan.

Pakul - A flat-topped wool cap with a rolled-up brim. It resembles the cap often seen in paintings done of the English King Henry the Eighth. The pakul is to the mountaineers of northern Pakistan what the turban is to the Afghans. The warm cap can be unrolled during harsh weather to cover the owner's head and ears. It comes in two colors, a natural brown or a snow white.

Pathan - The largest tribal society in the world, made up of various tribes including the Afridis, Mahsuds, Mohmands, Yusufzai, etc. They have an estimated population of fifteen million, of whom ten million reside in Pakistan and the remainder in southern Afghanistan. Traditionally they have shown no respect for the invisible line dividing the two countries, preferring to come and go as they please. Their ethnic origins are lost in the dim recesses of history. While many Pathans prefer to adhere to the legend that they are one of the lost tribes of Israel, anthropologists have discovered no evidence supporting this claim. Historically the Pathans have a well-earned reputation for murder, savage border warfare, kidnapping and xenophobia. The fearsome warriors helped one Afghan king sack Delhi, India. They fought the British Raj with understandable intensity. Proud, dangerous, and extremely cruel in warfare, they pride themselves on their observance of pukhtunwali, a strict code of honor centering around the concepts of revenge - *badal*, hospitality - *melmastia*, and refuge - *nanwata*.

Paunch - A silky material imported from Japan especially for turbans. The material is favored by many Afghans from the southwest of that country. Like the cowboy hat of the Old West, the turban of Afghanistan often reveals a man's geographic origins. The way it is wrapped, the length and type of material used, the color chosen, etc., are all silent signals revealing more about a man in an instant than anything else he wears.

Peace Be Upon Him - Muslims without exception follow the name of the Prophet of Islam with the traditional epithet, "*sala Allah alayhi wa salaam* (God's blessings and peace be upon him)." In addition the name of Allah is followed by "*subanna wata* Allah (Glory be upon Him)." To expedite the flow of my native language these and other similar phases have been largely omitted. Muslims are invited to add them as they read the text.

Pilau - A savory dish much favored in both Afghanistan and Pakistan, it consists of steamed rice laced with raisins. It is often served with chunks of roast chicken or tender lamb.

Pukhtun - The name favored among members of the extended tribal society often called "Pathans" to describe themselves. The more commonly used term "Pathan" was a Hindustani word originating in India.

Glossary

Pukhtunistan - Land of the Pukhtuns or Pathans. A political concept formulated in the 1940s to describe a proposed independent homeland for all the Pathan people living in both Afghanistan and Pakistan. This idea took root in 1946 when Pathans, like hundreds of thousands of other Indians, were pushing for independence from the British Raj. Some Pathans, lead by the fiery patriot Khan Abdul Ghaffar Khan, called for a separate homeland for the Pathan people, seven million of which lived inside British controlled India. Ghaffar's Red Shirt political party allied itself with Mahatma Gandhi, Pandit Nehru and the Hindus of the Congress Party. When Pakistan became a political reality, offering all Muslims on the Indian sub-continent a homeland, the issue of Pukhtunistan died on the table. In the late 1940s the Afghan Prime Minister Mohammad Daud revived the idea, hoping to split off part of a newly-formed and weakened Pakistan. He gave refuge to Pathan insurgents, broadcast inflammatory radio messages to the citizens of the North West Frontier Province, and made every attempt to weaken the new country from within. Though sharing cultural and historical links running back centuries, Daud insisted in 1947 that Afghanistan go on the record as being the only country to vote against Pakistan's entrance into the United Nations. The issue of Pukhtunistan finally reached a crisis point in the early 1960s. The two neighbors narrowly averted a catastrophic war, though embassies were burned in both nations. Daud, the supreme political opportunist, later seized the throne from his first cousin, the Afghan King Zahir Shah, who was on a state visit to Italy. Having turned Afghanistan into his private fief, the perfidious Daud was captured and executed in his Kabul palace during the 1978 communist coup. Today the issue of Pukhtunistan lies dormant. The majority of Pathans refer to Pukhtunistan as more of a spiritual homeland that runs across artificial boundaries, the idea of a Pathan reservation having long been laid to rest.

Pukhtunwali - The code of honor whereby Pathan men measure their actions and the actions of others. This unwritten tribal law, ruthlessly enforced, is based on three principles: revenge-badal, hospitality-melmastia, and refuge-*nanwata*. The usual violations of the code result from cases centering around gold-*zar*, women-*zan*, and land-*zamin*. The resulting blood feuds between Pathans often involve large groups of combatants and may rage on for years, with all parties intent on attaining revenge. Pukhtunwali also encourages the concepts of steadfast loyalty to friends, gracious hospitality to travelers, bravery to the point of suicide, sincere devotion to Islam, pride in Pathan heritage and self, and the pursuit of romantic interests regardless of any danger. The result is often comparable to the caballeros of early California who likewise took the pursuit of honor and love to a cultural extreme. The Pathan poet Khusal

Khan Khattak summarized *pukhtunwali* when he wrote, "I despise the man who does not guide his life by honor, that very word drives me mad."

Punjab - One of the four provinces of Pakistan, it is known as the "Land of the five rivers." The other major states are Baluchistan, Sind and the North West Frontier Province. Pakistan is also home to *Azad* (Free) Kashmir, a political protectorate.

Punjabi - A language spoken in the eastern portion of Pakistan, especially around Lahore.

Purdah - The practice of excluding women from public sight. This practice is debated among Muslims worldwide. The Qu'ran instructs women to cover their hair and maintain their modesty. The role of women in the Muslim world is a highly-charged issue and differs in interpretation from country to country. While Pakistan elected Benazir Bhutto the first prime minister of a Muslim country, in neighboring Afghanistan a woman could be beaten and imprisoned by Muslim extremists for going shopping without a male family member in attendance. The Pathans have long favored the latter conservative view point. A well-known expression among these men is "A woman's place is in the home or in the grave."

Pushtu - The language of the Pathans. It is primarily found in the North West Frontier Province of Pakistan and south east Afghanistan. It is often described as a harsh, guttural language. One legend says Pushtu is the language spoken in Hell.

Qissa Khani - Designated the "Street of Story Tellers," Qissa Khani is the legendary boulevard, close by the old Kabuli Gate, where in days of old caravans would rest and gather the news, i.e. "stories" from local residents and other travelers. It is now a busy street with various shops. Because of its wide avenue many foreign dignitaries use it as a stopover on whirl wind tours. They are hustled in by Pakistani handlers driving foreign, air-conditioned cars, who show them enough of the picturesque "old city" to ensure a few good photographs, before rushing them back to the relative gastronomic safety of the Intercontinental Hotel. Princess Anne of England made one such brief, albeit highly publicized, appearance.

Quad-I-Azam - Meaning "The great leader," the term used to refer to Muhammad Ali Jinnah, the father of Pakistani independence. Jinnah struggled for years against incredible odds to ensure the birth of a homeland for the Muslims of the Indian sub-continent. Unfortunately he died of tuberculosis soon after Pakistan was created in 1947. The resultant power-vacuum was exploited by both India, Pakistan's deadly enemy, and various shady Muslim politicians and military dictators bent on lining their own pockets. Jinnah's death is widely viewed as a pivotal political event, after which the country slowly swung into warfare with India, lost half of its original geographic mandate, and descended into dictatorship and ethnic rebellion.

Glossary

Qu'ran - Though commonly written "Koran" in English, throughout the Muslim world the more widely accepted translation of the word is "Qu'ran." The Arabic term means "Reading," and refers to the divinely-revealed instruction book Muslims use to elevate their minds and hearts to a higher level. Islam teaches that the Qu'ran is Allah's final message to the world. It was revealed between the years 610 and 632 to an Arab named Muhammad (PBUH). As a young man, Muhammad enjoyed a reputation as being a trustworthy, albeit illiterate and simple man. He made his living as a caravan trader and called the dusty town of Mecca, Arabia his home. In addition, he was also devoutly religious, and often voluntarily withdrew to a cave close to his home where he would fast and pray. One night he was awakened in the cave from a sound sleep. The angel Jibar'il (Gabriel) appeared before the frightened man and commanded him to, "*Iqra* (read)!" Muhammad protested that he was illiterate, at which Jibar'il grabbed him, squeezed him so hard he could not breathe, and again commanded the terrified man to "Read." The angel then began to recite, "Read in the name of your Lord Who created humans from a hanging embryo. Read for your Generous Lord, the One Who taught people with the pen, taught humans things they didn't know before." When the angel released him, Muhammad ran from the cave, only to again see the angel, whose vision now filled the entire horizon. Rushing home, the frightened man confided to his beloved wife, Khadija, the vision he had encountered. Knowing her husband to be a man of integrity, she comforted him by saying that Allah would never let anything evil befall him. After some time, Jibra'il again appeared. This time Muhammad was prepared for the otherworldly experience. When the angel finished speaking, Muhammad memorized the revelation from God. The entire Qu'ran was written down in the lifetime of the Prophet Muhammad, and personally arranged by him. Copies of these earliest Qu'rans are still in existence. Though the Qu'ran has been translated into various languages, the original Arabic version remains the standard throughout the Muslim world. It has thereafter survived unchanged for 1500 years. Written in *Fus-ha* (pure Arabic), it is divided into chapters (*Sura*) and verses (*ayat*). *Hafiz* is a proud title claimed by any Muslim who has memorized the entire Qu'ran, a task often completed by children as young as twelve years old. Because Muslims believe the Qu'ran was directly revealed from God, they treat any copy of the Qu'ran with the utmost respect. Recognizing that they hold Allah's words in their hands, they make sure that they are symbolically clean before even touching the sacred volume. Desecration of the Qu'ran is considered an unspeakable offense against God. One of the defining moments in the Afghan jihad occurred when photographs began circulating of Qu'rans which had been burned and desecrated by invading Russian troops. The sense of moral outrage that swept across the country helped solidify resistance to the communists.

Raka'at - The Muslim prayer unit made up primarily of standing, bowing, prostrating and sitting.

Rickshaw - The term "rickshaw" is a misleading one in Pakistan. It seems to imply the classic example of one man pulling another. This is not the case as, unlike the Chinese, Muslims believe it is degrading for one person to pull another in any sort of taxied vehicle. A rickshaw in Pakistan refers to a small three- wheeled motorcycle, equipped with a tiny two-stroke engine. It is fitted with a single seat in the front for the driver and a small bench seat in the rear for the passengers. The passenger section is enclosed in a hood of bright blue plastic. Doors are hung during inclement weather to shield the passengers from being splashed with mud. Though designed for two passengers, the tiny machines are often seen with three or more riders. The driver carries no meter and charges whatever he believes he can squeeze out of his riders. As a result arguments, and even deaths, between both parties are not infrequent. Because Pakistan has no air-quality control or emissions standards, rickshaws are among the major contributors of smog. Most lack any sort of muffler. Their old, inefficient engines run a mixture of thick oil and cheap gas, a noxious combination which spews smoke everywhere.

Rupee - The monetary unit used in Pakistan. In 1984 the exchange rate was 17 rupees to the US dollar.

Sadhu - Hindu holy man and mystic.

Salat - One of the five obligatory daily prayers to be performed by Muslims at stated times, after ablution is made.

Sarhad - Frontier. Referring to the North West Frontier Province of which Peshawar is the capital.

Shalwar- Because of the extremely hot temperatures encountered in the Indian sub-continent, these baggy, voluminous trousers have been favored for centuries. They are gathered at the waist by a string belt and once untied, for example to visit the toilet, must be handled with care. If the string gets loose the wearer is suddenly holding yards of loose material. The string runs inside a small loop running around the top of the pants. The tool used to thread the string through the trousers is known as the "pant's tooth."

Sherob - Slang for whiskey or any forbidden alcoholic drink.

Shia - Doctrine which holds that Ali ibn Abi Talib, the fourth of the Orthodox Muslim Caliphs, was the true spiritual and political heir of the Prophet Mohammad (PBUH). Less than ten per cent of the Muslim world are Shiites who adhere to his doctrine and belief. Shias are geographically strongest in Iran. Because of the intense persecution they experienced over the ages, Shias adhere to the doctrine of *taqiya*, the necessity of hiding one's true religious beliefs when among non-Shias. They also retain the peculiar custom of allowing legal temporary marriage between a man and woman for the sake of mutual pleasure.

Glossary

Sikunder Pura - The street of Alexander the Great. Revered across the Indian sub-continent, Sikunder-Alexander is remembered as a warrior prince, part Solomon the wise, part Rambo the terrible.

Somasa - Small fried pastry filled with either ground meat or vegetables.

Sunni - One who follows the Sunnah, the traditions and practices of the Prophet Mohammad (PBUH). The majority of the world's Muslims are Sunnis.

Tanzim - A political organization comprised of Afghan men who were dedicated to the struggle to free Afghanistan from Soviet occupation and communist influence. Peshawar was originally home to seven major resistance groups including the National Islamic Front of Afghanistan, Hezb-I-Islami, the Afghan Liberation Front and Jamiat Islami. By the late 1980s any thought of political unity among the resistance leaders had been shattered by the corrupting influences of wealth, intrigue, and assassination. One leader, Professor Sighattula Mojadeddi, confided to me how he was sure a ruthless rival, Gulbuddin Hekmatyar, was trying to have him killed. His suspicions were well founded. Sources in Peshawar said Hekmatyar had just authorized the murder of an outspoken critic, a Kabul University professor who had documented proof of organized crime in the refugee camps. Of course during the interview with Mojadeddi, I watched as various Afghan mujahadeen, rugged mountain men used to killing Russians with both hands, groveled in front of the resistance leader, kissing his soft hand and begging for cash assistance, arms and ammunition.

Tonga - A classic form of horse transportation in use for centuries in the Indian sub-continent. The tonga consists of a two-wheeled cart equipped with two seats facing front and back. The wheels stand nearly six feet high. A single horse working between a set of shafts pulls the light-weight wagon and three or four people quite easily. Passengers enter the tonga by a small metal step, placed fore and aft. Equipped with metal springs, the ride is surprisingly comfortable. The tonga reached the level of an art form in pre-Jihad Afghanistan. Ornately painted, and festooned with red pompoms, the gaily-decorated carts could be seen running squads of school children to and from school, or citizens about their daily chores. Unlike Pakistan, whose uncouth drivers rely on the whip to urge on their horses, Afghan tonga drivers pressed their foot on a lever which in turn rang a loud bell. The more urgent the ringing the faster the horse's gait. Tonga travel, while still widely in use throughout both countries, has been severely depleted by the incursions of motor rickshaws. The best Pakistani tongas are always pulled by snow-white horses, whose dashing drivers have painted them with black designs signifying good luck, protection from the evil eye, and speed.

Turkoman - An ethnic group of people with Oriental features, today they can be found inhabiting the newly formed country of Turkmenistan - Land of the Turkomans. They were once a ferociously independent people. Mounted on a breed of swift horses bearing the same name, for centuries the Turkomans raided deep into Persia for slaves and loot. In the nineteenth century Russian troops under the Czar invaded and conquered the ancient country of these nomadic horsemen. Many Turkomans fled across the Oxus river, seeking safety under the protection of the Muslim Amir of Afghanistan. They lived there in peace until the Russians, this time under the direction of the Soviet Union, once again disrupted their pastoral lifestyle in 1979.

Urdu - National language of Pakistan. It was originally chosen by a Mogul emperor as a linguistic bond to unify his multi-national army. No language united Pakistan when it was created. Choosing one of the many indigenous languages as the national language would have further exacerbated existing regional differences. Urdu, already seen as the language of Muslim nationalism, was chosen much like Gaelic in Ireland as a linguistic effort to unify a diverse people. Though Pakistan still remains linguistically diverse, hosting dozens of languages and dialects, Urdu is spoken by all educated Pakistanis. It is not only used in all official government documents and daily newspapers, but additionally it is a soft-sounding language which lends itself to beautiful poetry.

Walaikum assalaam - "And upon you be peace." Standard response to a greeting between Muslims.

Water boilers - A disparaging term invented by a Swedish veteran of the French Foreign Legion to define those westerners who lived in hotels or other safe accommodations in Peshawar. In an effort to maintain the delicate safety of their stomachs, they insisted their servants only serve them boiled water.

Wuzu - Before Muslims pray they must be physically clean. The idea behind this act is more than simply washing one's dirty hands. It is an effort to bring about a unity between the body and spirit before entering into prayer before Allah. The actual act consists of washing the hands, forearms, face, and feet, as well as rinsing one's mouth with clean water.

Yaghistan - Land of Murder. See Kohistan.

Yusufzai - Probably the oldest, largest, and most sophisticated of the Pathan tribes, they inhabit the mountains from Malakand to Dir.

Zina - Any illicit sexual intercourse, including adultery or premarital sex.

About the Author: **Asadullah Khan a.k.a. CuChullaine O'Reilly** has been described as "an exile and traveler who is no longer entirely American." After extensive travels in Afghanistan, CuChullaine converted to Islam and journeyed to the Muslim holy city of Mecca. He taught journalism for Boston University to Afghan guerrilla fighters resisting Soviet invaders and was marked for assassination by KHAD, Afghan communist secret police, for his work with the mujahadeen resistance groups. CuChullaine has spent more than twenty years studying equestrian travel techniques on four continents. He made lengthy trips by horseback across Afghanistan and Pakistan before leading the Karakorum Equestrian Expedition through five mountain ranges, including the Himalayas, and traversing the Diamer Desert, thereby setting the record for the longest recorded horseback ride in Pakistan's history. He is one of the Founding Members of The Long Riders' Guild, the world's first international association of equestrian explorers. CuChullaine is the author of "The Long Riders," an exciting equestrian travel anthology, and is currently at work on "Saddle Up - The Equestrian Explorers' Handbook." He is married to Basha Cornwall-Legh, the Anglo-Swiss equestrian explorer.

Some of the other titles in the Equestrian Travel Classic series published by
The Long Riders' Guild Press. We are constantly adding to our collection, so for an up-to-date list please visit our website:
www.thelongridersguild.com

Title	Author
Tschiffely's Ride	Aime Tschiffely
The Tale of Two Horses	Aime Tschiffely
Bridle Paths	Aime Tschiffely
This Way Southward	Aime Tschiffely
Bohemia Junction	Aime Tschiffely
Through Persia on a Sidesaddle	Ella C. Sykes
Through Russia on a Mustang	Thomas Stevens
Riding Across Patagonia	Lady Florence Dixie
A Ride to Khiva	Frederick Burnaby
Ocean to Ocean on Horseback	Williard Glazier
Rural Rides – Volume One	William Cobbett
Rural Rides – Volume Two	William Cobbett
Adventures in Mexico	George F. Ruxton
Travels with A Donkey in the Cevennes	Robert Louis Stevenson
Winter Sketches from the Saddle	John Codman
Following the Frontier	Roger Pocock
On Horseback in Virginia	Charles Dudley Warner
California Coast Trails	J. Smeaton Chase
My Kingdom for a Horse	Margaret Leigh
The Journeys of Celia Fiennes	Celia Fiennes
On Horseback through Asia Minor	Fred Burnaby
The Abode of Snow	Andrew Wilson
A Lady's Life in the Rocky Mountains	Isabella Bird
Travels in Afghanistan	Ernest F. Fox
Through Mexico on Horseback	Joseph Carl Goodwin
Caucasian Journey	Negley Farson
Turkestan Solo	Ella K. Maillart
Through the Highlands of Shropshire	Magdalene M. Weale
Wartime Ride	J. W. Day
Across the Roof of the World	Wilfred Skrede
The Courage to Ride	Ana Beker
Saddles East	John W. Beard
Last of the Saddle Tramps	Messanie Wilkins
Ride a White Horse	William Holt
Manual of Pack Transportation	H. W. Daly
Horses, Saddles and Bridles	W. H. Carter
Notes on Elementary Equitation	Carleton S. Cooke
Cavalry Drill Regulations	United States Army
Horse Packing	Charles Johnson Post
Mongolian Adventure	Henning Haslund
The Art of Travel	Francis Galton
Shanghai à Moscou	Madame de Bourboulon
Saddlebags for Suitcases	Mary Bosanquet
The Road to the Grey Pamir	Ana Louise Strong
Boots and Saddles in Africa	Thomas Lambie
To the Foot of the Rainbow	Clyde Kluckhohn
Through Five Republics on Horseback	George Ray
Journey from the Arctic	Donald Brown
Saddle and Canoe	Theodore Winthrop
The Prairie Traveler	Randolph Marcy
Reiter, Pferd und Fahrer – Volume One	Dr. C. Geuer
Reiter, Pferd und Fahrer – Volume Two	Dr. C. Geuer

The Long Riders' Guild
The world's leading source of information regarding equestrian exploration!
www.thelongridersguild.com

Printed in the United States
2359